To Ron & Cindy Kadish,
The Greatest Parents In The Universe,
Without whom none of this
Would have been possible...

To Zach,
Stay Aweso...

DQ721237

INTRODUCTION

In the entire history of the universe, there are many tales worth telling.

Some are tales of great heroes and leaders. Others are tales of terrible villains and their dastardly deeds. Sometimes these stories intermingle; sometimes they do not. But they all play a role in shaping the universe in which we find ourselves.

In fact, if one were to travel to the grand repository of the Hive Mind of Valghana VII, where the Central Galactic University houses all of its meticulously recorded historical records, one would find approximately 2,789,998,376,882,945,671,567,002 entries – and those are just the completed works – recording the various goings-on of people of interest from around this vast universe we call our home.

In these tales, we usually find many of the same things, just told in different ways. The best tales typically are the ones that revolve around love. And with love, there's usually a healthy dose of its counterpart, hate. Sometimes, there are lessons to be learned and morals to be taught. Other times, there are just senseless acts of violence and cruelty. Many of the most popular accounts contain the obligatory elements of excitement, action, and, of course, adventure. Mix in a healthy dose of comedy, as well as a bit of tragedy, and one has a tale that generations of sentient beings will want to hear over and over again, until the end of time or the universe, whichever happens first.

But if someone were to go to Valghana VII and ask the Guardians of Knowledge which tale is the most popular of all two septillion entries, he might be surprised to find that they, in fact, have an answer for him.

i

Even more surprising, would be that the tale is about a hero who comes from a relatively obscure species, from an unknown planet in the backwoods of the galaxy, in a region of space long dismissed as being utterly devoid of life (or anything else interesting for that matter) and thus largely ignored by most civilized space-faring races.

This rather insignificant planet, called "Earth" by those who lived on it, was the home of a species so unremarkable in pretty much every aspect by which we judge intelligent life, that the fact that one of the Galaxy's greatest heroes came from it is enough to boggle even an Egoi's extremely large mind.

And to make this tale even more bizarre, it starts with a fleet of the most dreaded and feared military armada the universe has ever known going out of its way to utterly annihilate this little blue-green planet and every last one of the relatively undeveloped life-forms who lived there.

The first inkling the race of "Earthmen," as they have come to be called, might be in serious trouble started with an astrological observation made by a group of amateur astronomers in a rural part of a place called New Mexico, which existed in a governmental region known to those who lived on the planet as the United States of America.

By the time these astronomers had called in the finding of a strange cluster of light not far from the eastern side of an orbiting planet they had dubbed "Jupiter," and this finding had been checked and verified by better astronomers with even bigger telescopes, the Earthmen couldn't help but notice this suspicious astrological anomaly seemed to be headed directly toward their planet.

As this rather startling information made its way to the government officials to whom the Earthmen entrusted their affairs, their primitive satellites were able to snap a few pictures to give their leaders an idea of what was heading toward them –

namely a lot of massive unidentifiable objects which seemed not only able to change direction at will, but also capable of slowing down as they approached the planet – two characteristics which immediately ruled out any possibility that what was coming their way was anything but intelligent life, and lots of it to boot.

The Earthmen's calculations led them to conclude that the incoming Unidentified Flying Objects would arrive at their planet in a matter of hours, giving them little to no time to warn any of the populace of their planet what was headed their way.

Hoping for the best, but preparing for the worst, the leader of the United States of America immediately contacted other leaders from around his planet to warn them of what was coming and also issued an order for his government's military to be ready to defend their planet should these visitors from outer space end up being hostile (which they most certainly were).

Considering this government's military was widely regarded as one of the best and most advanced on the planet, it would be natural to assume that the hero of our story would be a part of it.

Such as Colonel Harry Jackson Stryker, United States Marine Corps, for instance.

Colonel Stryker was a veteran of many wars. He was a fearless man, who knew how to fight and who took his job as a soldier more seriously than any other man who had ever worn the uniform of a Marine. What made Stryker a good soldier was the fact that he'd do anything to accomplish his mission – no matter what the cost to his own person. In fact, it could even be said that Colonel Stryker was one of the most selfless and courageous men on Earth, willing to lay down his life to save the country, and the planet, that he loved so much.

With a chiseled jaw, sandy blonde hair, and an astonishing gift for leading men into battle, Colonel Stryker was the natural choice to guide humanity through its darkest hour and defeat the oncoming alien menace.

It's a shame he died, along with all the rest of the planet's inhabitants, only hours after being alerted to the alien threat. I'm sure his story would have been a good one – he was an interesting fellow.

But, alas, this is not his story.

No, the hero of our story was actually the most unlikely candidate for the job. He wasn't the smartest Earthman there was, nor the strongest, nor the best leader the planet had to offer. Some of his critics would call him the *luckiest* of his species, though (which is not entirely unfounded considering some of the situations he was able to survive). However, in this narrator's humble opinion, in addition to a good amount of luck, this Earthman persevered against all odds due to his amazing resourcefulness in harrowing situations, boundless courage in the face of danger, and undying loyalty to those he would call his friends – even if they did not regard him in the same way.

And though he would arguably become one of the greatest heroes this universe has ever known, he did not start out that way.

In fact, his story really starts the morning of the invasion of the alien menace, in a very modest trailer home, in a small town known as River Heights, in a place known as Ohio (again, in the United States of America) when he was only 15 years old.

This is the story of Earthman Jack.

Episode I:

Earthman Jack

vs.

The Alien Invasion

CHAPTER ✬ 1

Once upon a time, in a quaint stretch of land overlooking one of the many cornfields of the neighboring town of Red Mills, was a place known as the Eagle Hill Trailer Community. But the locals simply called it "The Hill."

Located not far from the main road of Detroit Street, which connected River Heights with its neighbor to the east, The Hill was a haven for many of the less fortunate members of the local community who could not afford one of the modest homes the rest of the town's inhabitants tended to reside in. Instead, the people who lived on The Hill made due with long, rectangular shaped dwellings often referred to as "trailer homes." It was in one of these structures that Earthman Jack Finnegan lived.

For 10 of his 15 years, Jack regarded the trailer on Eagle Hill's lot number 7 as his home. An army of frequently neglected potted plants were stationed out front among the weeds and crabgrass in an attempt to beautify the shabby lot on which the trailer was located. Despite its yellowing, discolored exterior, and its rickety, homemade, wooden carport, which was perpetually leaning ever so slightly to the left, one could say that the trailer was, without a doubt, the best kept dwelling in Eagle Hill.

By Earth standards, the trailer on lot #7 was looked down upon as being rather "low class." After all, only the poorest and least fortunate of River Heights' residents would live in such a place. But even if the trailer did not afford its inhabitants a life of luxury, the dwelling was big enough to house both Jack and his mother, store all their earthly possessions, and protect them from the elements of nature. Though it performed all three of those tasks rather poorly, it still did them, and that at least was good enough for Jack.

And if an outside passer-by were to look upon the trailer in lot #7 and regard it as a sad, modest dwelling, then the room in which Jack slept every night was even more cause for pity.

No bigger than most people's bathrooms, Jack's room was able to house a single bed and a tiny closet overflowing with unwashed and worn-out clothes. The rest of it was littered with posters featuring professional wrestlers, kung fu movies, and the occasional "hot babe."

It was here that Jack sprawled out, tangled in a mess of faded blankets with starships and superheroes stitched onto them, snoring loudly, with just a hint of drool staining his pillow.

Light from the morning sun shone through the single, small window located in Jack's room, hitting him squarely in the face. As the light lingered on Jack, his snoring suddenly subsided, and he opened one of his eyes, only to be blinded by the sun. Instinctively, he rolled his face back into his pillow and was about to enjoy more of his much valued slumber when a thought suddenly leapt into his head, and that thought went something like this…

Oh, crap.

Jack shot up in bed, his light brown hair sticking up at odd angles, his green eyes puffy and half-closed from sleep. He turned his head toward the window. From ten years of sleeping in the same bed, next to the same window, Jack instantly knew that if light were coming in, he had, in fact, overslept.

Jack groggily turned to the digital clock duct-taped to his wall. The big red numbers on it read *8:26*. Sure enough – he *was* late. This time, Jack's previous thought became so urgent, he was forced to verbalize it.

"Oh, CRAP!"

At that, Jack leapt out of bed, stubbing his big toe in the process. Trying to ignore the pain, and not bothering to change out of the black boxer shorts he had slept in (the ones with pink dollar signs stitched on them), he kicked up the nearest pair of jeans he could find and yanked them on. He frantically rummaged through a pile of shirts on the floor (taking care to choose the one which was the least smelly), and slipped one on. He then quickly grabbed a pair of socks and stuffed them into a raggedy old ink-stained bookbag, along with a textbook and a notebook or two.

Wasting no time, Jack rushed out of his bedroom, grabbing his shoes on the way out the front door. He was in such a rush, he didn't even notice the sweet note his mother had taped there, reminding him that his lunch was packed in the refrigerator and not to be late for school (again!).

Jack emerged from the chain-linked enclosure of Eagle Hill onto Detroit Street, hopping and skipping as fast as he could as he tried in vain to slip on his worn sneakers while still keeping forward momentum.

Having just missed it a minute or two earlier, Jack could see the bright orange-yellow school bus in the distance as it rumbled down the road.

"Stop!" Jack yelled as he continued to run and put on his shoes at the same time. "Stop the bus! Please don't make me run after – ah, crap..."

Once it became clear that the bus had, in fact, not heard his plea, Jack had no choice but to take off after the vehicle as fast as he could. The next stop was only a few blocks away; if he could run fast enough, he'd be able to catch it.

On the bus, in the typical social order carved out in every high school on the planet Earth, only the so-called "coolest" and most important upperclassmen sat in the back, furthest from the bus driver's gaze. In this case, that honor belonged to one J.C. Rowdey and his friends Kev, Jimbo, and Moose — four guys who seemed to pride themselves on how big their muscles were, how perfect their hair looked, and how much grief they could inflict on others not deemed as "cool" as they were.

At the back window, Kev turned his pug-like face and saw Jack in the distance running after the bus and waving his arms in the vain hope of catching the driver's attention.

He snorted in amusement and ribbed J.C. with his elbow.

"Yo, dude," said Kev. "Check it out. It's Finnegan."

J.C. turned his attention from the wet-willy he was currently giving the poor junior with the skin problem in the seat in front of him and, along with Jimbo and Moose who were in the process of sniffing magic markers in the seat directly across the isle, looked out the back window.

"Looks like Loser McLose-a-lot overslept again," chuckled J.C.

"Daaaaaang," droned Moose. "That dude is haulin'. Lookit him go!"

"You got that right," interjected Jimbo, lifting his fatty upper body toward the window to get a better look. "Who knew the little booger could run so fast?"

"Maybe he mistook the bus for his home and thinks we're driving away with it," said J.C., causing his crew to chortle and guffaw.

"Looks like he's catching up," said Kev. Sure enough, Jack was running his heart out and gaining on the slow moving vehicle. "Ten bucks says he makes it."

J.C. smiled at Kev mischievously. "You're on, dumb-nuts," he said, punching Kev in the shoulder not very softly. "Yo, Moose…"

"Huh?" Moose lit up, as if the sound of his name was barely enough to register with his meager brain.

"Go up to the driver and keep her distracted," ordered J.C.

"Okay," said Moose, moving to get to his feet before stopping, a confused look crawling across his face. "Uh... how?"

"Tell her your butt hurts from the kicking I'm about to give it if you don't get up there right now," snapped J.C. "Make something up; I don't care!"

Moose lumbered to his feet and began walking toward the front of the bus to talk to the driver.

"No fair, dude," said Kev. "You can't have help..."

"Shut up," responded J.C. He then proceeded to flick the junior's ear in the seat in front of him. "Hey – hey, loser..."

"Stop it!" whined the junior. "Just leave me alone!"

"Give me your shoe, and I'll leave you alone the rest of the way to school."

"My shoe? What? No!"

"Look," J.C. sneered. "Either give me your shoe, or I'll take it from you."

Outside, Jack's lungs were burning from the chilled morning air. The bus had made its next stop, picking up the kids from the Johnson farm, giving him the chance he needed to close the distance. As he was about to reach the lumbering vehicle, the upper body of a young man with rippling blonde hair and a red-and-gold letterman's jacket suddenly emerged from one of the rear side windows. Just before Jack's brain could register the face of J.C. Rowdey, the boy cocked his arm back and chucked an orthopedically enhanced sneaker right at him, catching him dead in the forehead.

Jack stumbled and fell, holding his throbbing head as he hit the ground. In the distance, he could hear J.C.'s mocking laughter as the bus groaned and rolled away, continuing its journey down Detroit Street.

Jack lay on the side of the road, breathing deeply of the crisp, cold morning air, and rubbing his noggin where the shoe had tagged him. There was no doubt about it now; he was going to be late. And if experience had taught him anything, it was that his dreaded homeroom teacher, Mr. Shepherd, was going to smack him with yet another detention for his tardiness.

Before getting up and continuing the long walk to school, Jack took a moment to relax and let his legs recover from the workout they had just gotten. As he stared up at the cloudless blue sky, he thought to himself:

Today is totally going to suck.

If only Jack had known what the future had in store for him, he'd no doubt have realized how much of an understatement that was. Because though his morning started out bad, things were going to get much, much worse...

CHAPTER ✸ 2

River Heights High School was a fairly large, yet unremarkable building bordered mostly by farmland and a few quaint shops that catered to high school age clientele, providing the necessary fast food, caffeinated drinks, and places to dilly-dally after school that most teenagers on Earth had come to depend upon.

After reasoning he'd be in more trouble if he skipped school entirely than if he just showed up late, Jack had begun the long walk down Detroit Street that eventually led to River Heights High. Jack spotted the large dirty-granite colored building in the distance, its school flags hanging limply at its central flagpole. First period would no doubt be wrapping up by now. (Not that he cared, since he had Social Studies first period and was always bored to tears there.) But there was no way he'd be able to make it to homeroom in time.

All students were required to check in at their homeroom class after first period so attendance could be taken and announcements read. Normally, this wasn't that big of a problem. Freshman year, Jack had Ms. Deitz for homeroom, and for some reason she was always more than willing to believe Jack's excuses and let him get away with practically anything.

Jack smiled at the thought of Ms. Deitz, with her large, bulky dresses that would have looked better upholstering a couch than being worn by any sane human being, and her black horn-rimmed glasses and perpetually-permed hair. How he wished he had her again. She wouldn't care if he were late to homeroom and had missed first period entirely.

But that was before the dark times. Before Mr. Shepherd had arrived.

Jack's first year at River Height's High had been marked by the retiring of a good number of the faculty, which meant this year had seen the introduction of some new faces to the staff. Not the least of which was Jack's current homeroom teacher and bane to his existence, the dreaded Mr. Shepherd.

Shepherd had taken over the physical education position at the school. No one really knew all that much about him, and rumors had started flying since his first appearance at the beginning of the school year. Some kids were convinced he used to be a Special Forces assassin for the military. Some theorized he might have been a prison guard for death row inmates. Others just thought the man was pure evil. (Jack was certainly one who fell into that category.)

Mr. Shepherd made it quite clear early on that he wasn't like most of the teachers at the school. He wasn't afraid to give detention for the slightest infraction. He demanded utter obedience from those in his class. And he had a piercing stare that would put the fear of God into even the most rebellious of kids.

Most students simply counted the seconds until the end of their classes with Shepherd, keeping their heads down and their mouths shut until they were able to make their escapes. And normally, if they did that, they wouldn't have any trouble from the man.

Unfortunately, Jack never did that.

Since Jack had landed in Mr. Shepherd's homeroom, he'd spent almost three days a week, every week, in detention. Whether it was coming to school late, speaking out of turn, or just looking at the man funny, Jack seemed always to be on the receiving end of Mr. Shepherd's wrath. Jack was getting so much detention, it was almost becoming comical.

"What did Shepherd get you for this time?" his friends would ask.

"Apparently I was born on an odd numbered year," Jack would reply wryly.

Indeed, the battle of wills between Jack and Shepherd had been escalating as the school year progressed. It would have been easy for Jack just to change his ways and be the kind of student Shepherd wanted – punctual, quiet, and obedient – and avoid the man's attention all together. But Jack saw Shepherd as a bully, and Jack was never one to give into bullies, even if they did have the power of detention on their side. It was only a matter of time before one of them broke, and for better or worse, Jack was determined it wouldn't be him.

When Jack arrived in homeroom, Principal Montgomery was already halfway through the morning's announcements. Jack slipped in the door while the disembodied voice over the intercom droned on about tomorrow's substitution on the lunch menu, and he worked his way toward his assigned desk in the back of the room as nonchalantly as he could.

Mr. Shepherd sat at his desk by the chalkboard, scribbling something in a notebook. He hadn't so much as glanced up when Jack came in. By now, Jack had learned not to be naive enough to think Shepherd hadn't noticed his entrance. The man had eyes in the back of his head.

As Jack settled into his seat, he glanced over to the desk next to him. There sat the only part about homeroom he actually liked. She had long blonde hair, so bright that even the crappy fluorescent light in the school seemed to dance off it. Her eyes were a deep blue, so blue they almost didn't look real. She had fair skin and a slender frame, but there was no doubt about it – she was the most beautiful girl in all of River Heights, and quite possibly the world. (At least, in Jack's opinion).

Her name was Anna. Anna Shepherd. And she was the daughter of Jack's arch-nemesis, which made things a lot more complicated than Jack would have liked.

If little was known about Mr. Shepherd, even less was known about his daughter. River Heights High didn't get a lot of students transferring in from out of state, so there was naturally a lot of curiosity about her. However, early attempts from the established cliques of popular girls to befriend her had gone unanswered, which immediately caused Anna to be blacklisted by them as a stuck-up snob. Normally, every jock and pretty-boy in school would be tripping over himself to get a date with her, but the prospect of incurring the wrath of Mr. Shepherd was too great a threat.

This meant that Anna Shepherd was usually left alone, and she seemed to like it that way.

Every time Jack saw her, she was sitting by herself, her pretty little up-turned nose buried in some type of book. If there were one thing that everyone knew for certain about Anna, it was that she apparently loved to read.

Everything else was a mystery, though. There were rumors that she and her father had moved to River Heights from West Virginia after her mother had died from some type of disease. There were other rumors that Anna's mom was actually alive, but that Mr. Shepherd was in the middle of a divorce so nasty that he had moved with Anna to get away from his wife. Some whispers even went so far as to theorize they were in the witness protection program and had come to River Heights to escape being killed by the mafia.

Jack didn't know what to believe about her. All he knew was that she always seemed to be alone. And Jack knew what it was like to be alone. Because of that, he felt there was no better match for her out there than him.

That, and the fact that she was freakin' hot.

Today Jack saw that she was reading a book about the American Revolution. He would always try to notice what book she was reading in hopes of figuring out a way to talk to her. But they were never fun books; in fact, they always seemed to be history books of some type – nothing Jack knew much about. This made the whole "talking to her" strategy a bit difficult.

Jack had tried in vain a few times to engage Anna in conversation. He couldn't do it in homeroom, since Mr. Shepherd would no doubt get on his case for harassing his daughter. (After all, it wasn't like the man needed any more reason to hate Jack.) And the few opportunities that came to him at lunchtime in the cafeteria or between classes in the hallway usually devolved into "Hey!" "Hi!" and the ever-popular "Wuz up?" Anna's usual response was just to smile in acknowledgement and to go back to reading whatever book she had her nose buried in at the time.

A normal guy would have taken the hint and moved on by now. But Jack felt in his gut that there was something there, some connection between Anna and him, almost like they were destined to be together. And, as previously stated, she was freakin' hot.

Because of that, Jack was *never* going to give up.

Suddenly, in the middle of Principal Montgomery talking about a new dress code for the steadily approaching Homecoming Dance, Anna looked up from her book and glanced over at Jack.

Jack's heart skipped a beat, and he quickly looked away, trying to act like he hadn't just been staring at her. The worst part about being caught staring at a girl is that he couldn't look back at her again, because then she'd know *for sure* he was staring at her, and that would just make him seem creepy. So Jack was forced to gaze at the back of Jamal Dugan's head until the bell for next period rang.

In a hurry to get out of the dreaded homeroom with Mr. Shepherd, the students got to their feet in unison and rapidly made for the door.

Jack grabbed his bookbag and was trying to slip away with the crowd when a deep, forceful voice cut through the air.

"Mr. Finnegan, a moment."

Jack sighed. Today, there was no escape. He turned and approached Shepherd's desk. The man's broad, muscular shoulders were hunched over as he continued writing notes down in a notebook. He was wearing a white dress shirt with a red tie, but he was so muscular, he looked like he was about to rip out of it at any moment. His light blonde hair was cropped short to his head, high and tight and perfectly groomed. Everything about the man seemed harsh and meticulous.

Jack waited for an agonizing 30 seconds as Mr. Shepherd completed whatever it was he was writing. Then, Shepherd carefully set his pen down and looked up at Jack with his piercing grey eyes, folding his hands in front of him.

"Mr. Finnegan," he said sharply. "You were late."

"You sure about that?" asked Jack. " 'Cause in Mountain Time, I was totally early…"

"Are you making a joke, Mr. Finnegan?"

"No, sir," said Jack. "I would never make any attempt to amuse you, sir."

Shepherd grimaced. "I'm told you missed first period, as well. Do you at least have an excuse for your tardiness?"

"Would you believe I got kicked in the face trying to rescue a small child from a band of ninjas?" asked Jack, pointing to the small bruise on his forehead.

"No," replied Shepherd.

"Then it's pretty much the same excuse as before."

Shepherd grabbed a tidy pile of demerit slips from the corner of his desk and quickly began to fill one out. "If I were you," he said, "I would either invest in an alarm clock that worked, find an alternate mode of transportation to school," he sharply tore the demerit from the stack and shoved it toward Jack, "or find a way to start enjoying my company."

Jack took the slip, sullenly. "C'mon, Mr. Shepherd, I just missed the bus… it wasn't even my fault this time."

"And when has it ever been your fault, Mr. Finnegan?" asked Shepherd. "You are constantly late, you are disrespectful, and most of all, you are making absolutely no attempt to change, which to me says, quite simply, that you have yet to learn your lesson."

Jack looked down at his feet. There was never any arguing with Mr. Shepherd. The man was utterly without mercy.

"I believe you know when and where," said Shepherd.

Jack nodded and sullenly walked out the door.

CHAPTER 🚀 3

After a rather rocky start to the day, Jack settled into his normal routine, though his mood did not improve much. Indeed, the simple fact was that Jack hated most of the time he spent in school. He hated most of the people he went to school with. And he especially hated most of the classes he had to attend.

His English teacher, Mrs. Hemmert, was pretty cool, but she always seemed to assign the lamest, most boring books possible to read. When it came to math, Jack was beyond hopeless, and his wicked shrew of a math teacher, Ms. Webster, didn't make it any easier. Mr. Shiering, who taught history, spent the entire time telling the class amazing stories, which Jack loved to listen to – but he'd always get so caught up in the tales spun by his teacher, he'd forget to take notes. Therefore, when it came time to actually study for the tests, he'd be totally lost.

Then there was study hall – normally a period where kids were allowed to goof off, but since Jack had the unfortunate luck of being assigned to Mr. Shepherd for study hall, it was pretty much an agonizing hour of pure silence, where students either actually did their homework or wasted away the time doodling in a notebook (take a guess which one Jack tended to do).

It didn't help that Jack also had Mr. Shepherd for Phys. Ed. immediately after study hall, during which the man had his students go through all types of rigorous sprints, pull-ups, jumping jacks, and anything else the Nazi's might have invented to torture high schoolers during World War II. Gone were the days of actually doing "fun" activities during gym class, ever since the evil Mr. Shepherd had arrived.

The one true highlight of Jack's curriculum was, oddly enough, his Physics class.

Normally, when it came to science, Jack had less interest than anything else he was forced to take in school. With all the abbreviations, equations, formulas, and the like, science should have been Jack's worst subject. Who'd have guessed that Physics would end up being the one class Jack not only partially enjoyed but also seemed to be good at?

It wasn't because Jack had any natural gift or talent for science. Oh, no. In fact, Jack attributed his enjoyment, and subsequent skill of the subject, entirely to his teacher, Professor Green.

Professor Green was relatively new to the school. He'd started teaching roughly the same time Jack had started attending River Heights High. He was a tall and lanky man, with a shock of uncombed white hair and an equally unkempt beard of matching color.

He wore glasses that were always crooked but still somehow managed to make his brown eyes look bigger than they actually were. His neck was so long and thin in proportion to his head, Jack often thought he looked like one of those bobble-heads that someone would typically put on the dashboard of a car. To complete his strange appearance, Professor Green always wore his pants pulled up to around his chest, and he possessed a rather odd affinity for bowties.

But aside from being, without a doubt, the oddest-looking member of the River Height's faculty, he also had a true passion for what he taught and the rare talent for explaining the subject matter in a way that actually made sense to Jack.

Of course, ever since he'd heard that Professor Green was apparently friends with Mr. Shepherd and was actually responsible for helping the man get his job at the school, Jack had found himself liking Professor Green less than he had before. But as he sat in class and watched the Professor excitedly scribble on the chalkboard, rambling on about the day's lesson, he found it hard to stay upset with the guy.

Because despite it all, Professor Green was just too darn likable.

"...so according to Newton's second law of motion," lectured Green at a rapid-fire pace, "the acceleration of an object increases as the force causing the acceleration increases. OR, for a given force, the smaller the object – the faster its speed changes!"

Professor Green turned excitedly back to the class, looking as though he expected them to share his passion for what he had just scribbled on the chalkboard. Instead what he saw were a lot of blank stares and disinterest.

Green's shoulders visibly slumped, and his smile turned lopsided. "Oh, dear," he mumbled. "I'm boring all of you, aren't I?"

The students all looked at each other, unsure of how to respond. It wasn't often that a teacher cared if his students were bored or not.

"It's not your fault, Professor," chimed in Jack, never afraid to speak out of turn. "Physics is just *boring*. That's all."

Green raised an eyebrow. "Is that so?" he asked.

"Yeah," responded Jack. "I mean, no offense, but who cares about motion and vectors and gravity and all that stuff?"

A few of Jack's fellow classmates nodded in agreement. Professor Green adjusted his glasses and cleared his throat.

"Well, then," said Green, smiling. "Let me ask you this – do you think *alternate realities* are boring?"

"Alternate realities?" asked Jack. "You mean like somewhere out there, there's a dimension where I'm a millionaire with a transparent head and missile-launching kneecaps?"

A chuckle went through the class. Green nodded. "Exactly!"

Jack shrugged. "No, that's pretty cool," he said.

"What about faster than light travel?" Green went on. "Is that boring? Being able to go from one end of the galaxy to the other in a matter of days instead of thousands of years?"

The entire class began to perk up. Now the Professor was talking.

"How about teleportation? Is it boring to be able to go from one place to another in the blink of an eye? What of time travel? Which one of you wouldn't want to visit the past? Or the future?"

"No, all that is awesome," said Jack. "It's just, that's the type of thing you see in movies and stuff. It doesn't really exist."

"Wrong!" said Professor Green, pointing at Jack and smiling. "It *does* exist. And it exists because of Physics – the very stuff you're learning about right here!"

All of a sudden, Jack found himself more interested in Physics than he'd ever been in anything his entire life. Indeed, more than a few students were now leaning forward in their seats.

"Have any of you ever heard of the term *quantum physics*?" asked the Professor.

No one answered.

"For the last hundred years, scientists have studied nature at the most microscopic level. This is what's known as 'quantum physics,' and it is the science of how teeny-tiny units of matter work to shape the very fabric of our reality."

Green could tell from the blank stares he was getting that he'd have to be a little clearer with his explanations.

"You all know what 'matter' is, right?" said Green as he rapped his knuckles on the chalkboard. "You're surrounded by it. It's anything that's solid. The walls, the floor, your desks, your clothes – it's all considered to be matter. Yes?"

Everyone nodded.

"But what is matter made of?" asked Green. "By now, hopefully, you should all know that matter is just a collection of tiny little things called atoms. Do you all know what I'm talking about?"

The class nodded.

"Well, atoms are the building blocks of matter! It's how they're arranged that makes up different materials, everything from metal, to plastic, to cloth – it's all just a different arrangement of the same thing – atoms. But how do those atoms come to be arranged in such a way where they create specific types of matter, like this chalkboard? Or your desks? Or your chairs?"

No one raised a hand.

"Here's where it gets interesting!" squealed the Professor excitedly. "According to quantum theory, atoms can exist in multiple places at once! So every atom exists in every possible location in the universe all at the same time. Think about that for a moment – there is no empty space, just a bunch of atoms, everywhere, in a great, big, entangled mess! This means that there is an infinite combination of atoms existing everywhere, all at the same time. And that means all matter, every object you see around you, has the potential to be anything else. Your pants have the potential to be tomato soup. Your desks have the potential to be anthills. Your sneakers have the potential to be ice skates. So matter has the potential to literally be anything, *until* you make a measurement. This is because the simple act of measuring an atom chooses one of its many possibilities to become a reality. So until someone observes the atom as something, it could potentially be anything!"

Jack raised his hand. "I'm confused," he said.

"About which part?" asked Green.

"Uh… all of it."

Green laughed. "That's not surprising, I suppose. The key thing to remember about quantum theory is that it is WEIRD. That's a technical term we science-lovers like to use. It means funky, counter-intuitive, mind-boggling. It's confusing because our brains aren't used to thinking about things in that fashion. But let me see if I can explain it in a different way. Reality — which is everything we can see, hear, and touch — begins and ends with us. Each and every one of us is an observer, which means we are all constantly creating measurements to which the atoms around us adhere. Because of this, the physical world we see around us is actually created by our own minds. It is we, the observers, who create the reality in which we live. So those chairs you're sitting in aren't chairs until you choose to see them as chairs. Make sense?"

"So you're saying that our brains tell atoms to turn into different stuff, and they do it?" asked Jack.

"In a way," said Green. "Try to think of it like this — all reality begins and ends in the mind of the observer. The universe is nothing more than the vivid imagination of our brains, which chooses to see certain things but not others. All the stuff we see around us is not determined by the external world; it's actually determined by us! So it's our minds that actually choose to see only one possibility out of the infinite probabilities that exist. And by observing one of those possibilities, we make it true. So all matter — everything that could possibly exist — is already out there somewhere. It's not until we choose to see it that it enters our reality."

"Are you saying that our brains don't tell atoms to turn into stuff; they just choose to see one possibility that's already there?" clarified Jack.

"Yes!" exclaimed Green. "Exactly! So there's a *probability* that you're not actually sitting on a chair. You're sitting on a huge mushroom. But your brain chooses to see the *possibility* in which atoms are arranged in such a way that make a chair, so that's what it is."

"Then why is it we choose to see chairs and not giant, comfy mushrooms?"

The Professor shrugged. "That's one of the great questions, isn't it? Why is our reality the way it is? What dictates our observations? Some believe our subconscious mind is aware of every single possibility that could exist, and it is not until our conscious mind makes an observation that one of those possibilities is decided upon. Why is it that we've all decided to see a chair instead of a mushroom, considering all the other possibilities our subconscious is aware of? If one of us decides to see something else, would that change how others see it? Are we capable of literally changing reality, simply with the power of our minds? According to quantum theory, the answer to that is 'YES!'"

Green looked over his class as the wonder of possibility began to worm its way into their brains.

"So what does that have to do with alternate realities and all that other stuff?" asked Jack.

"Well, let's do a little experiment, shall we?" said Green. "What's behind you in the back of the room?"

The class, almost as one, turned and looked behind them.

"Nothing," said Jack. "Just a wall, a table, a few microscopes…"

"Okay," said Green. "Now everyone look forward again."

The students all turned their attention back to the Professor.

"Now, without turning around again, tell me… what's behind you in the back of the room?"

"A wall, a table, and a few microscopes," said Jack again.

"Are you sure?"

"Yeah."

"How do you know?"

"Because they were there just a second ago."

"They were there when you *observed* them a second ago. But right now, when you're not observing them, there could be anything behind you. Right now, your subconscious mind is aware of an infinite number of possibilities that could exist in the back of the room. It's not until you make the act of observing what's back there, that you settle on one of those possibilities, and the atoms are arranged to suit that choice."

"So let me get this straight," said Jack. "Right now, in my subconscious mind, there's the possibility that a supermodel in a bikini is chilling in the back of the room, and if my brain chooses to observe that possibility, she'll be back there?"

"Exactly," smiled Professor Green.

At that moment, Jack, and every other boy in class, eagerly turned around to take another look. As expected, there was no supermodel, just the same old microscopes there had been before. A chuckle spread through the class.

"Dang," said Jack. "I don't think this quantum physics stuff is working, Professor."

More laughter. Even Professor Green chuckled. "That's where you're wrong, Jack. Quantum physics is always at work. It's we who choose the reality in which we find ourselves. And unfortunately, once we've chosen a reality, it is very hard for us to perceive anything else. But if you were able to free your mind and consciously choose to observe a *different* reality... to actually shape the world around you as you see fit... then anything is possible. Even the bikini model."

At that, Jack had to smile. The thought that he could make anything a reality just by thinking about it tickled him. He'd first give himself a ton of money, then he'd get a date with Anna, and then he'd make Mr. Shepherd himself have detention for the rest of eternity.

It was too bad that none of the stuff the Professor was talking about actually seemed to work.

At least, not yet.

CHAPTER 4

River Heights High School's cafeteria was one of the largest areas in the school, second only to the gymnasium. Unlike the rest of the building, which was decorated with sickly green tiles, for some reason (and no one was really sure why) the cafeteria was adorned with boring beige tiles that climbed a quarter of the way up the walls before giving way to stucco painted a color which had at one time been white but was now pale yellow from age.

Students lined up against the walls, waiting for their turns to buy whatever passed as food in the kitchen toward the back of the room. Above them were painted various inspirational sayings from famous historical figures, intermixed occasionally with the cartoon image of Barry the Beaver, a friendly little rodent who was the official school mascot.

For a few hours a day, the cafeteria was filled with the commotion of students seated at the long neat rows of folding tables stretching from one end of the room to the other. Lunch period was one of the few parts of school Jack actually enjoyed. Indeed, Jack often looked at lunchtime as his sanctuary. It was when Jack could forget about all the bad stuff he had to suffer through during the day and just relax with some of the few people with whom he actually enjoyed spending time.

First off, there was his best friend Matt Nunan, who'd been Jack's partner in crime since the two of them first got into a fight over who got to play with the red Mighty Morphing Robot Ninja in the first grade. Matt's mom was white, and his dad was black, but on the color scale, Matt tended to skew on the lighter end – a fact that really annoyed him. Thus, Matt dressed in extremely baggy clothes, sports jerseys (even though he never played sports), and attempted to grow his hair out into dreadlocks - a process that made him look like he had constantly just stuck his finger into a light socket.

Then, there was Jasper Kreig, whom everyone called "Chunk," an unfortunate nickname Jasper had been given in the third grade due to his short, squat, and rather rotund frame. Chunk was widely regarded as the class clown, always willing to yell out a funny quip, make an inappropriate farting sound, or flash various parts of his anatomy when the situation called for it (and even when it didn't).

Peter Mercer and his sister Norma were there, too. Though Norma was a year older than Peter, they both shared the similar features of a weak chin, long neck, and extremely scrawny legs. However, even though the two of them looked similar, they couldn't have been more different when it came to their personalities. While Peter was goofy, Norma was serious. While Peter was laid back, Norma was prone to over-reacting. While Peter was all about swords, sorcery, and high fantasy, Norma was about biographies, documentaries, and quite a bit of prim-and-proper girlie stuff.

Then there was Gothy. Her real name was Gretchen, but her penchant for wearing an abundance of black eyeliner, black lipstick, black fingernail polish, black clothes, dyed-black hair, listening to the most depressing music imaginable, and writing extremely bad poetry about the pointlessness of life had earned her the nickname.

Finally, there was Yoshi, a foreign exchange student from Japan. He was an extremely skinny kid, with eyes so narrow Jack was surprised Yoshi could see out of them at all. Yoshi had been very popular when he first showed up at school last year. He was quiet, shy, extremely polite, and the nicest person anyone could ever possibly hope to meet. But soon after all the upperclassmen had taught him every swear word they knew and had him repeat them to the teachers a few times, the novelty quickly wore off and Yoshi's so-called "friends" began ignoring him. That's when he found Jack and the others, and with their help, his English had been greatly improving – though his habit of using the swear words he had learned at the most inappropriate times still was a problem.

Since Jack had forgotten his lunch again today, the group had pitched in to make sure he didn't go hungry. In fact, it was so common an occurrence that everyone had taken to packing a little extra food, just for him. A peanut butter and jelly sandwich from Matt, an apple from Chunk, a granola bar from Norma, and an orange juice box from Yoshi made up his current meal.

"So," said Matt, "heard Shepherd gave you detention again."

"Yeah," growled Jack. "I swear, that guy has it out for me."

"Want me to try and get detention, too? I could slip some laxatives into Mr. Jacob's coffee again."

"Nah, no reason for both of us to suffer."

"Just say the word, dude," said Matt. "I'd totally lax up Mr. Jacob for ya."

"I know you would, buddy" smiled Jack, patting his friend on the back.

"I had detention with Mr. Shepherd once," chimed in Chunk. "It was creepy. He just stares at you the whole time with his serial-killer eyes." Chunk pried his eyes as wide as they could go to emphasize his point.

"He does that to me, too," said Jack. "He looks at me like I just took a dump on his mother's grave or something."

"I'm telling you guys," continued Chunk, "Mr. Shepherd has KILLED people before. I'm convinced. He's got that crazy 'I'm-gonna-rip-out-your-lungs-and-gaze-into-your-gaping-chest-wound' stare. I bet you he eats them after he kills 'em, too."

"You say that about everyone you don't like," complained Norma. "According to you, half the student body are a bunch of serial-killer cannibals."

"Did you know human flesh has almost no nutritional value?" intoned Gothy.

"I'm serious about this," said Chunk defensively. "That dude has definitely eaten people before."

"In Japan," chimed in Yoshi, "teachers very strict. Many like Shepherd."

"No wonder you wanted to get out of the country," quipped Jack. "Can you imagine a school full of Mr. Shepherds?" The very thought sent a cold shiver down Jack's spine.

"Well, hey," said Peter. "Maybe Yoshi could give you some advice on how to deal with Shepherd if he's had to put up with hard cases like him for so long."

"Good idea," said Matt. "How'd you deal with your teachers back in Japan if they were so strict?"

"You do your work, obey rules, be good student," said Yoshi, smiling.

Everyone took a second to look at Jack.

"Sorry, buddy," said Matt good-naturedly. "You're screwed."

With that, the whole group shared a laugh. Even Jack had to admit there was no way he could do what Yoshi was suggesting, even if he tried. For whatever reason, Jack was never much for work, rules, or even being much of a student for that matter.

As Chunk started doing an impression of what Jack would act like in a Japanese school, Jack caught a glimpse of Anna sitting by herself at a table near the far wall. She was huddled away with a brown bag lunch of chips, juice, and what looked like a small Tupperware container of leafy greens. As usual, she was reading, sitting in the same place she always did, by herself.

Before every lunch period, Jack would try to think of a way to talk to her. But no matter what scheme popped into his mind, each one had the fatal flaw of actually requiring Jack to WALK up to her and open his mouth in a way that made words come out. Many times he had almost done it, but for some reason, he had always chickened out at the last minute, with the hope things would be different the next day.

But they never were.

"Uh-oh," said Peter. "Looks like it's that time again."

Jack turned back from Anna to the group. "Huh?" he asked. "What time?"

"You know," teased Matt. "The time where you stare longingly at the girl of your dreams, try and muster up the courage to finally go over and talk to her, and then totally do *nothing.*"

"Gimme a break," said Jack. "Like any of you have the stones to do it."

"I do!" said Chunk. "All the ladies loooove Chunk. Ain't that right, Norma baby?" Chunk started making kissy-faces at Norma, who abruptly threw some chips at his face.

"You disgust me," she hissed.

Chunk smiled and winked at Jack. "It's a forbidden love," he said, happily munching on the chips Norma had thrown at him.

"Love is the gateway to despair," intoned Gothy.

"Honestly, I don't know what you see in her, Jack," Norma went on, ignoring Gothy's morbid interjection. "She's a frigid, anti-social ice queen. She's mean to everybody."

"Who cares?" cried Chunk. "She's haaaawt!"

Norma punched Chunk on the arm, causing him to squeal. "It doesn't matter how hot she is, stupid. She doesn't *like* anybody. It's almost as if she thinks she's royalty and we're all beneath her or something."

"She's right," added Matt, patting Jack good-naturedly on the shoulder. "Might be time to move on to easier pickings, my friend."

"Look, you guys have got her all wrong," said Jack. "She's not mean, or stuck up, or anything like that. She's just… different, is all."

"I'll say," said Chunk. "She's the spawn of Shepherd. Mark of the beast! DEVIL CHILD!" He started flicking his tongue out of his mouth wildly, trying to look as evil as possible.

"Knock it off," said Jack, putting a kibosh on Chunk's fun. "She's nothing like that. I'm sure that if people just took the time to get to know her, they'd find that she's really a great person."

"Well, someone's about to find out," said Peter.

"Huh?" replied Jack.

Peter nodded his head toward Anna. "Check it out," he said.

Jack turned his attention back to Anna. To his horror, J.C. Rowdey appeared to be strutting up to her, a big, dumb, cocky grin on his face, with his cronies cheering him on from their table.

Jack felt the cold grip of terror seize his heart. *Oh, no,* he thought. *Not this; anything but this!*

Despite the fact that in Jack's book, J.C. fell into the category of "raging jack-hole that no one in his right mind could possibly like," he had to admit the guy had a few things going for him. First of all, he was good-looking. Second, his family had a lot of money. Third, he was captain of the football team. Fourth, he was extremely popular. Combine all that with the fact that Anna hadn't been around long enough to actually know what kind of a creep J.C. was, and suddenly he found himself with the makings of a very dangerous situation.

With a flourish, J.C. kicked out the empty chair by Anna and smoothly slid in next to her. Anna looked up from her book, somewhat surprised by her new visitor. J.C. flashed his winning varsity smile, then leaned in and began talking to her.

"What the heck is he doing?" Jack wondered aloud.

"I heard Marietta Edgecombe say J.C. was going to ask Anna to the Homecoming dance," Norma said.

"What!?" exclaimed Jack. "Why didn't you say anything?"

"I dunno," said Norma innocently. "Who cares if the meathead wants to go out with the ice queen?"

"Me!" said Jack. "*I* was going to ask her to the dance!"

His friends all chuckled.

"Chillax, hoss," said Matt reassuringly. "She'll probably turn him down. Just like she's turned down every other guy who has tried to date her. Just like she'd probably turn you down if you ever found the guts to ask her out."

"Thanks," said Jack sardonically. "I feel much better now."

"That's what friends are for, buddy!" replied Matt with a smile.

Despite the friendly dig at Jack, Matt was right. There wasn't a scenario Jack could imagine in which Anna would ever agree to date someone like J.C. Rowdey. And that was somewhat comforting. But still, Jack watched from afar with baited breath as J.C. made his move.

It was obvious Anna wanted to go back to eating alone and reading her book, but J.C. was oblivious to her polite attempts to ignore him. Instead, he slithered up beside her, still flapping his lips, and even went so far as to put his arm around her shoulders.

His dumb meathead face was nuzzled by her ear as he whispered something to her.

It was apparent that Anna was uncomfortable with the entire situation. She gently grabbed J.C.'s hand and pulled his arm off her, said something to J.C. politely, and then turned her attention back to her book. J.C. glanced toward his minions, who were all watching. Then, he forced a smile back on his face and put his arm around Anna again. He pressed on, and it was clear Anna was growing more and more agitated with his advances.

Jack could feel jealousy and anger well up inside him. He could take all the beatings, name calling, and pranks that J.C. tended to dish out his way. But moving in on the girl Jack liked… that crossed a line.

"Someone's gotta stop this," said Jack, getting to his feet, a queer courage suddenly taking hold of him.

Everyone at the table stopped eating and looked up at Jack in surprise.

"Huh? Where you goin'?" asked Matt.

"Listen," said Jack, "You've got my back if anything goes down, right?"

"… I what?" asked Matt, confused.

"If J.C. and his goons throw down, you guys got my back, right?" said Jack, looking at everyone at the table.

Matt and Chunk exchanged a worried look.

"Oh… yeah." said Matt, reassuringly.

"Totally," nodded Chunk.

Jack nodded and made his way toward Anna. After he left, Chunk turned to Matt.

"Um… are we really going to do anything if Jack starts a fight?" he asked.

"Are you kidding?" said Matt. "Those guys would kill us!"

As Jack walked toward Anna, he could feel his heart pounding and blood pumping behind his ears. He was scared, there was no doubt about that, but he wasn't about to let J.C. push around the girl of his dreams. Different scenarios played out in Jack's mind of how he was going to rescue Anna from J.C.'s sweaty clutches. Unfortunately, he couldn't think of one that didn't end with him getting pounded into dust by the hulking upperclassman.

Then, as he approached them, he realized he didn't have to do anything but get Anna away from J.C. If he could do that, maybe he wouldn't have to incur the wrath of the meathead at all.

"Hey, Anna!" said Jack cheerily as he leaned against her table. Anna and J.C. both looked up at him.

"Um… hi," she said, looking at Jack warily.

"Finnegan?" said J.C.

"Rowdey?" said Jack in response before turning his attention back to Anna. "Listen, I hate to break up whatever it is you two are doing, but the school nurse asked me to come get you and bring you to the clinic."

"The nurse?" asked Anna. "Why?"

"Dunno. She said something about you coming by earlier, complaining about a headache that just wouldn't seem to go away…" Jack said, nodding ever so slightly in J.C.'s direction.

Anna immediately exchanged a look of understanding with Jack. "Oh, right. Yeah, I need to get rid of this headache; it's really bothering me," she said as she packed up her things. She turned to J.C. and smiled. "Excuse me."

But as she stood up to go, J.C. grabbed her wrist.

"Hold on now, beautiful," he said. "No need to run off. C'mon, I'll walk you to the nurse's office. After all, we haven't finished talking."

"Let her go, J.C.," said Jack, a little too forcefully.

J.C. scowled at Jack. "Oh, hey, Fishmonger. You still here?" he said tauntingly. "How's the head?"

The bruise on Jack's forehead throbbed at the mention. The threat was obvious – "*Leave now, or that's nothing compared to what I'll do to you later*," he seemed to say. But Jack was sick of being bullied.

"Great," said Jack. "Lucky for me you throw like a girl, so it really didn't hurt all that much."

J.C.'s smug smile disappeared as he got to his feet, squaring off with Jack.

"You wanna step to this, Loser?" asked J.C. "Try saying that to my face!"

Jack cocked his eyebrow. "I… just did. But you were sitting down, so all the blood must have been welling up in your ears. Say, that's a nice shirt. Did your mom pick it out for you?"

"FYI, Fishgills, this shirt cost more than your dad makes in an entire year," replied J.C. "Oops, I forgot, you don't have one of those, do you?"

"Don't have what? A lame over-priced shirt?"

"No! A dad!" spat J.C. angrily. "You don't have a dad, because he left when he realized what a loser of a son he had!"

Jack had learned long ago to ignore the insults bullies used to try to hurt him the most. The "dad" thing was the first one he had learned to cope with. It was true. Jack's father had left when he was five, with no explanation as to why. All that remained was a hand-written note saying he was gone and would not be coming back. Jack could remember his mother coming to pick him up one day after he had gotten into a fight in third grade when another kid had mocked him for not having a father. Jack's mother had told him that as long as he knew, deep in his heart, that his dad was still out there and still loved him, nothing anyone could say would change that.

"I may not have a dad," said Jack, nodding. "But I do have something you don't."

"Yeah?" smirked J.C. "What?"

"An IQ?" replied Jack. "Breath that doesn't stink? No reason to be ashamed in the shower? The list goes on..."

"Enough!" cried Anna. Jack and J.C. both turned to her, and she was looking at them with the same look a mother gives her children when they are acting up. "Both of you. This is getting ridiculous."

"No," said J.C. "What's ridiculous is you not wanting to go to the dance with me."

"C'mon, J.C.," said Jack. "You can't hold having good taste against her."

Jack could almost feel J.C.'s anger smoldering as the boy stepped toward him, inches from his face.

"You are about two steps away from the beat-down of your life, dumb-nuts," said J.C.

"Actually, I'm three steps away," Jack shot back. "But since I know you can't count that high, I'll let it slide."

With that, J.C. grabbed Jack by the collar of his shirt, cocking his fist back to strike. Jack heard Anna squeal. Thinking quickly, Jack decided to go with his patented strategy number four of avoiding a beat down – threaten legal action.

"Do it!" cried Jack. "Go ahead! Hit me in front of everyone! I want you to. With any luck, I'll find a great lawyer and own you for assault."

That was enough to give J.C. pause. Jack had no idea what it would take to sue someone, or even if he could, but then again, most people didn't either. However, J.C. didn't let go of Jack's shirt, and the look on his face went from a sneer to a smirk.

"Yeah, you're right," said J.C. "I'll wait until *after* school and then mess you up where no one can see. Right guys?"

Moose, Kev, and Jimbo all chuckled.

All of a sudden, Jack became aware of the four extremely tall, mean, and beefed-up dudes surrounding him. Apparently, when J.C. had grabbed him, they had taken that as their cue to get off their fat rear-ends and join their fearless leader.

What am I doing? Jack thought. *I'm totally going to get my butt kicked!*

Sure enough, the odds of a massive butt-kicking were definitely in Jack's favor. But he knew if he were to back down now, in front of Anna, he'd be marked as a loser for the rest of his life. So he did the only thing he could think of – acting the exact opposite of what he was feeling, and hoping to God it worked.

"Seriously, dude," said Jack. "You may not know this, but in my spare time, I practice the deadly art of karate. You can come after me if you want, but I swear on all that is holy, I *will* get ninja on you."

Moose snarled. Jack pointed a finger at his big dumb face. "And you," he said. "You best back up. Don't make me drop-kick you."

"C'mon, Finger-licker," said J.C. "We know you're not gonna do anything. So why don't you take that big wussy mouth of yours, march your big wussy butt out of here, and maybe I'll rethink giving you an atomic wedgie and leaving your head shoved in the nearest toilet."

"You know, you're right," said Jack, taking the opening and jerking away from J.C.'s grasp. "I think I will be going now. C'mon, Anna."

Jack reached out and grabbed Anna's hand. For a moment, he was worried Anna might not follow his lead, but it seemed as though she was taking the opening, as well. As Jack started to lead her away, Jimbo stepped in front of him, blocking their path.

"Uh-uh," said J.C. "Me and Anna-bell still got stuff to talk about, Loser."

"No, we don't," said Anna, turning to face J.C. "I don't know how to make it any clearer to you, J.C. I'm not going to the dance – with you, or anybody."

"Hey, what's your problem?" scowled J.C., incredulously. "Ever since you got here, you act like you're too good for us or something. I was trying to do you a favor by asking you out."

"Thank you for your interest," she replied, "but I don't need anybody doing me any favors."

J.C.'s face darkened. "What's up with you?" he asked. "Here I am, trying to be nice, and you just throw it back in my face. Just so you know, if you weren't a girl, I'd have probably beaten you down by now."

"Seriously, I can't see why she isn't already in love with you, Prince Charming," said Jack as dryly as he could.

Anna turned to Jack, her deep blue eyes catching his and drilling into them. "Jack," she said. "Please, *be quiet.*"

Jack's heart felt like it skipped a beat. *She knows my name!* he thought, happily.

Anna turned back to J.C. "I appreciate you trying to be nice to me, but I'm sorry, I'm not interested in going to the dance. I don't know how I can make it any clearer."

J.C. looked around him, uncomfortably aware that the scene was drawing people's attention.

"It doesn't matter," he said rather loudly. "I didn't really want to go with you anyway. I was just trying to do the new girl a favor. But if you want to be a loser, and hang out with losers, then you go right ahead you stupid, stuck-up, ugly, little b—"

Suddenly, Jack's fist shot out, connecting square with J.C.'s face. J.C.'s head snapped back from the blow, and his hand instantly went to his nose.

All sound drained out of the cafeteria as if the punch had been as loud as a thunderclap - silencing the entire student body. It seemed as if everyone were looking at what had just happened in complete shock.

Moose, Kev, and Jimbo were shocked.

Anna was shocked.

J.C. was shocked.

But probably no one was more shocked than Jack himself, who stood gazing at his fist in utter disbelief. Jack looked up and saw blood beginning to pool in J.C.'s left nostril, and from the look in the upperclassman's eyes, Jack instantly knew that he'd made a terrible, horrible mistake.

"Oh… crap," he said.

J.C. pounced on Jack, growling like an angry beast. His hands went right for Jack's throat as the two boys collapsed onto the floor. Anna shrieked. Jack struggled with J.C.'s overpowering weight on top of him, but he had no leverage. He was pinned down, and above him, J.C. was cocking back his fist to begin pummeling him into oblivion.

Then Anna was on J.C.'s back – restraining him, trying to pull him off.

"Stop it!" she yelled.

Oblivious to her pleas, J.C. shoved Anna off him violently. Anna hit the floor hard, bumping her head against the wall, the sight of which triggered something in Jack again. He tried punching J.C. in the face, but with being pinned on the floor, his blows did not have much power. J.C.'s fist landed hard, but Jack continued flailing away. In the distant background, he could hear the mob of kids, once silent, now chanting in unison – "FIGHT! FIGHT! FIGHT! FIGHT!"

J.C. was able to land two more blows before Mr. Harwood and Ms. Jefferson made it to them and pulled him off.

Jack rolled over, his right ear ringing from J.C.'s punches. He looked up to see Anna, still on the ground where J.C. had shoved her, cradling the back of her head. Their eyes met, and to Jack's disappointment, it was obvious Anna appeared more annoyed than grateful or impressed. Jack wanted to say something witty, something endearing, something that could possibly salvage a glimmer of good from a very bad situation, but all he could think of was…

"Well, that totally sucked…"

Before Anna could respond, Mr. Harwood was towering over them, looking down over his massive beer gut.

"Principal's office," he said. "All of you. Now."

CHAPTER ✺ 5

Principal Montgomery was an exceptionally fat man, adorned in an ill-fitting navy blue suit and a red-and-white tie with the ghosts of old mustard stains still haunting it. He stared at Jack, Anna, and J.C. from behind thick, boxy glasses, but it was hard to tell if he was frowning since his entire mouth was almost completely covered by a big, bushy moustache with wisps of gray poking out from the rest of the light brown, tobacco-stained hairs.

The three students were sitting in rather uncomfortable chairs stationed in front of a large oak desk in the principal's office. Behind him was a wide window that looked out over the school's football field as well as the cornfields of the Juniper Family Farm in the distance. Principal Montgomery's chair creaked and complained as he rocked ever-so-slightly back and forth and stared silently at the students before him.

Jack was no stranger to getting into trouble in school, but even he had never actually been to the principal's office before. Principal Montgomery began to drum his fingers on his desk, which joined with the squeak of his chair to create some type of haunting melody that Jack imagined might be played as prisoners were sent before a firing squad. Everything from the noise the man was making, to the view out the window, to the faint smell of body odor in the room set Jack's teeth on edge.

A million and a half possibilities ran through Jack's mind concerning what kind of punishment Mr. Montgomery would dish out. Worst case scenario – Jack was suspended for fighting in school. He could just imagine having to explain to his mom why he'd gone from underachiever to full-on delinquent in only the second year of his high school career. Best case scenario, he was in detention for the rest of his life. And considering that detention would be with his homeroom teacher Mr. Shepherd, suddenly getting suspended seemed like the better of the two options.

"So," said Principal Montgomery, smacking his lips. "One of you want to tell me what happened?"

Jack folded his arms and sunk lower into his seat, as if hoping that would keep the principal from singling him out. Anna was sitting up straight, her hands folded in her lap and her eyes focused on something other than the principal's gaze. Even J.C. seemed to be staring off into the distance toward the football field, afraid to make eye contact with the man.

"I'm told the three of you were involved in a fight in the middle of the cafeteria," Montgomery went on. "Do I need to tell any of you what the punishment is for fighting on school property?"

Again, silence.

Principal Montgomery focused in on Anna. "Ms. Shepherd?"

Anna looked up and met the man's gaze. "Yes?" she responded.

"Perhaps you'd like to fill me in on why you three decided to interrupt lunch time with a full-out brawl?"

"It was nothing, sir. Just a big... misunderstanding," she said.

"Misunderstanding, eh?" Montgomery mumbled as he scratched his nose. "Who started the fight?"

Anna was silent for a moment. "Honestly," she said, "it all happened so fast, I'm afraid I couldn't tell you."

"And what about you, Mr. Finnegan?" asked Montgomery, turning to Jack. "Could you tell me who started the fight?"

"Fight is such a strong word, sir," said Jack. "I'd say it was more like... good-natured rough-housing."

"Whatever you call it," said Montgomery, "tell me who started it."

"I'll tell you who didn't start it," replied Jack. "Anna. I don't even know why she's here, she had nothing to do with what happened."

At that, J.C. muttered something under his breath that sounded an awful lot like "Yeah, right." Principal Montgomery instantly picked up on it.

"Do you have something to add, Mr. Rowdey?"

"She attacked me," said J.C. "Scratched my neck up something good, see?"

J.C. pulled down his collar to show three bright red scratches on his neck. Jack assumed it must have happened when Anna tried to pull J.C. off of him.

"Are you saying Ms. Shepherd started this fight?" asked the principal.

"I certainly did not!" Anna responded indignantly

"She's right, she had *nothing* to do with it," said Jack.

"Shut your face, Finnegan," said J.C. "You both attacked me. Everyone saw."

"That's bull!" growled Jack. "You started the fight by being a jerk-wad, like you always are!"

"Hey, you punched me in the nose!" sneered J.C.

"You threw a shoe at my head!" snapped Jack.

Principal Montgomery pounded his fist on his desk. "Enough!" he bellowed, the flabby jowls of his face jiggling. Jack and J.C. quieted down, and soon the only sound in the room was the faint whistling of the principal breathing through his nose.

"Unfortunately, none of the staff saw what happened until after the fists started flying," Montgomery said. "And since none of you wants to come clean and tell me what really happened, I'm afraid I have no choice but to punish all of you."

Jack could feel Anna tense up beside him.

"But wait —" said Jack. "That's not fair. Anna didn't do anything!"

"Not according to Mr. Rowdey," said Principal Montgomery. "And Mr. Harwood informed me he saw Ms. Shepherd on top of him. That and the scratch marks…"

"She was trying to keep him from beating on me!" said Jack. "I was being attacked!"

"No, *I* was being attacked!" piped up J.C. "I wasn't doing anything, and you and your girlfriend here jumped me."

"I am not his girlfriend," corrected Anna, "and you are hardly innocent in all this, J.C."

"Quiet. All of you," said Montgomery in a tone that brokered no argument. "You can point fingers as much as you want. It doesn't matter now. Unless you can all come to some type of agreement over who's responsible for today's incident, you are all getting punished. That means detention, for a month, and no access to after-school clubs or events. That includes Homecoming."

"Principal Montgomery," cried J.C. "That's not fair! I didn't do anything! And I already rented a limo and a tux!"

Jack suppressed a smile. As much as he would like to have seen J.C. suffer along with him, Anna would also be included in the punishment. Despite what J.C. had said, she was innocent of everything except trying to help Jack when he was in danger of being beaten to a mushy pulp. And for the life of him, Jack couldn't repay that by letting her take the rap.

"It was my fault," said Jack, piping up.

All eyes in the room turned to him.

"It was my fault," repeated Jack. "I threw the first punch, J.C. defended himself, and Anna got involved because she tried to break up the fight. If anyone should be punished, it's me."

J.C.'s eyes brightened. "See!" he said. "That's what I've been saying! Finnegan just clocked me for no good reason!"

"I'm aware of your account of the events, Mr. Rowdey," said Principal Montgomery before turning his attention to Anna. "Is this true, Ms. Shepherd? Did Mr. Finnegan start the fight?"

Anna turned and looked at Jack with her beautiful blue eyes, and Jack instantly knew there was trouble. She understood what he was doing, and she wasn't going to let him take all the blame in this matter. After all, he'd done what he had for her.

"Actually, Principal Montgomery…" Anna began to say.

Jack knew if Anna muttered another word, she was going to ruin his confession. Jack had to do something dramatic to take Principal Montgomery's attention away from her and prove that he was the one and only culprit.

Thinking as quickly as he could, Jack leapt out of the chair, and in one motion, swept his arm across the principal's desk, shoving all manner of papers, pens, books, and even a stapler or two onto the floor.

Everyone leaned back from the sudden shower of desk-based items, stunned. Jack turned and pointed to J.C. "And you better watch your back, chump!" Jack exclaimed. "Because as soon as there aren't any teachers around to save your butt, I'm gonna finish what I started!"

The look on J.C.'s face was so comical, it was almost worth taking all the blame just to see it. Jack turned to a red-faced and wide-eyed Montgomery. "What?" asked Jack defiantly. "What you gonna do about it, you fat tub of lard?"

That sealed it. Principal Montgomery glared at Jack. "Very well," he growled. "One month detention, *including* Saturdays. And you are suspended from all school functions. That includes sporting events, after school clubs, and Homecoming."

Jack sighed. All things considered, the punishment wasn't all that bad. He was practically in a perpetual state of detention anyway thanks to Mr. Shepherd, didn't belong to any clubs, and his prospects of going to the dance weren't all that great to begin with. The extra detention on Saturdays was going to hurt, though.

"That's for starting a fight on school grounds," continued Mr. Montgomery. "For that stunt you just pulled, you'll serve another month of detention. Including Saturdays."

Jack's shoulders slumped. Two full months of detention. That *definitely* hurt.

"And you two," said Montgomery, looking at J.C. and Anna. "Consider this your only warning. If I hear about either of you breaking any more rules — I don't care if it's walking the halls without a pass or speaking out of turn during class — you *will* be joining him. Am I understood?"

J.C. and Anna nodded.

"Now get out," said Montgomery motioning toward the door. "Except for you, Mr. Finnegan. Before you go, you're going to pick up everything you just threw off my desk."

After tidying up the principal's office, it was back to class for Jack, the weight of an entire 60 days worth of detention looming heavily over him. He didn't see Anna or J.C. for the rest of the day, but word about what had happened quickly spread.

A few kids approached Jack between class to congratulate him for standing up to J.C. But he saw just as many pointing and snickering behind his back. Apparently, half the student body didn't see a courageous young hero stand up to the school bully. They just saw some loser get pounded into the ground during lunch.

On top of being the laughing stock of the school and having every Saturday for two months ruined by detention, Jack was pretty sure he'd blown any shot he'd ever had with Anna. In fact, she probably hated him for getting her involved in a fight in the first place.

When the last bell rang, Jack's attitude was as foul as it had ever been. Everything about this day, from the minute he'd woken up, seemed to be going wrong for him – and he still had another hour and a half with Mr. Shepherd to look forward to.

Jack marched into his homeroom, plopped himself down in the middle of a sea of empty desks, and sat slumped with his arms crossed, sullenly waiting for detention to begin. Mr. Shepherd stood with his back to him, looking out the window, not even acknowledging Jack's presence. There was no doubt in Jack's mind that the man was probably thinking up some type of new and exciting punishment for Jack to suffer through.

Mr. Shepherd stood at the window for a long time, not moving. After a while, Jack wondered if he even knew he was in the room.

"I heard you got into some trouble today," said Shepherd, finally.

"Yeah, what else is new?" mumbled Jack.

Shepherd turned and looked at him. "It seems I underestimated you, Mr. Finnegan," he said.

"Why? Didn't think it was possible to get so much detention in one day?" asked Jack. "Showed you, huh?"

Shepherd grimaced. "Anyone ever tell you, that you have a great deal of attitude toward authority?"

"Well maybe if authority weren't so bent on punishing me for every stupid little thing, I might be a bit nicer to it," Jack responded.

"So you believe it's okay for you to break the rules and not get punished for it when you do?"

"Yeah, when the rules are dumb," said Jack. "When it's not my fault that I broke them."

"What if the rules aren't dumb?" countered Shepherd. "What if it were your fault? Would it be okay then? Or would you still complain? Still have attitude? Still play the victim? Something tells me the answer would be 'yes.' "

Jack shrugged. "Whatever."

"Is that how you deal with things?" asked Shepherd pointedly. "Just shrug it off? Act like you have no choice in the matter?"

"What do you want from me, man?" snapped Jack, annoyed. "You want me to admit I'm a screw up? You want me to write that on the board a couple hundred times? Is that it, Mr. Shepherd?"

"I want you to start taking responsibility for yourself," said Shepherd. "I want you to start to realize that you are the one responsible for what happens to you. Your choices, your actions – everything you do has consequences for you and those around you."

"What? You think I don't already know that?" asked Jack.

"You don't act like you do," responded Shepherd. "You act like a victim. Like you're helpless, and life is what's beating you down. It's always something or someone else's fault: Your clock that never wakes you up in the morning, the bully that's picking on you, and the teacher who gives you detention. But it's never you, is it, Mr. Finnegan? It's never *your* fault."

"So what?" Jack said, anger rising within him. "What do you care? All you've ever done is sit behind your desk and give me detention for every little thing you can think of. So don't act like you care about what I do, or what I take responsibility for, okay? Now can we please get on with this and skip the father-knows-best lecture or whatever this is supposed to be?"

Jack slumped back in his chair and turned his head away from Shepherd, waiting for the hammer of fury to drop and the punishment to begin.

Mr. Shepherd sighed. He walked over and closed the door to the classroom. Without the clutter of noises from the hallway, the room seemed eerily silent.

"Why do you think it is I give you so much detention, Mr. Finnegan?" he asked.

"I don't know, Mr. Shepherd," Jack replied, not feeling in the mood for more lecture. "Do you have some sort of quota or something?"

Shepherd approached Jack and sat on top of a desk across from him. "No," he said. "The reason I give you so much detention is because I expect more from you."

"More?" asked Jack. "More what?"

"What I see when I look at you," said Shepherd, "is a young man who is undisciplined, unfocused, and utterly without direction in his life."

Jack rolled his eyes.

"But…" the man continued, "I also see a great deal of potential in you, Jack."

That was the first time Jack could ever remember Mr. Shepherd referring to him by his first name. For some reason, it sounded extremely weird when he said it.

"What do you mean?" Jack asked.

"When you came in here a minute ago, do you remember what I said?"

"Something about underestimating me."

Shepherd nodded. "And what do you think I meant by that?"

Jack sighed. "I don't know. What did you mean by it?"

"I meant that I was very *impressed* with what you did today."

Jack suddenly found himself confused. "Huh?" he said.

"Anna came by earlier and told me what happened. The real story. Not what Principal Montgomery informed me of," said Shepherd.

"So she told you the fight wasn't my fault?" Jack asked hopefully.

"No," said Shepherd. "She made it very clear the fight was pretty much all your fault."

"Oh," said Jack, a little disappointed.

"But she also told me what you did, and how you shouldered the punishment all by yourself, so she wouldn't have to. Why do you think you did that?"

Because I think your daughter is hot, thought Jack. But he certainly wasn't going to tell Shepherd that. Jack shrugged. "I just didn't want to see Anna get punished for something she didn't do."

Shepherd nodded. "It would have been easy for you to just sit there and let the principal punish the others, as well. But you took responsibility for your actions. You made the decision to sacrifice yourself, so someone who was innocent did not have to suffer. That tells me that a lot of what I thought about you was right, Jack."

"It does?" asked Jack, suddenly wondering what exactly Mr. Shepherd was prone to think of him.

"Yes," said Shepherd. "Despite what you might think, I don't have it out for you. The reason I'm hard on you is because I know you're capable of so much more than what you're putting forth. I thought that maybe, if I gave you a hard enough time, you might finally find the courage to start taking responsibility for yourself."

"Sorry to disappoint," said Jack, a little bitterly.

"On the contrary," said Shepherd. "Today, you proved you have that type of courage. I was just going about getting it from you the wrong way."

Jack scratched his head. Why was Mr. Shepherd suddenly talking to him so much? In all the time he'd had detention with the man, he'd just have Jack do some meaningless chore while he sat at his desk and scribbled whatever-it-was-he-scribbled in a notebook until time was up. Frankly, this was the most Jack could remember Shepherd ever saying to him, and the longer it went on, the more uncomfortable it made Jack.

"Um… okay," said Jack, not sure how to respond.

Shepherd stared at Jack with his piercing grey eyes – the gaze he was famous for. For some reason, Chunk's voice echoed in Jack's mind, and suddenly the whole serial-killer-cannibal thing didn't seem so far-fetched.

"Jack," he said. "I want you to listen to me, for once in your life, and really *hear* what it is I'm going to tell you. No jokes. No comebacks. No half-hearted acknowledgements. I just want you to listen. Can you do that?"

"Yeah, I guess," responded Jack.

Mr. Shepherd's eyes narrowed. Jack picked up on the hint.

"Yes," he said. "Yes, I can."

Shepherd nodded, satisfied. "There are people out there that believe life is just something that happens to them. That they have no control over the events and circumstances they find themselves in. But the truth is, we are the ones who shape the lives we live. We are the ones that allow good things and bad things to happen to us. By taking responsibility for our actions, we are able to make our lives better. When we play the victim, we allow our lives to be miserable. If you can take responsibility for yourself, decide to make your life better – and take action to that effect – then you are the master of your own destiny. And when that happens, you are capable of great things."

"So you're saying if I do things to get what I want, I'll get them?" asked Jack.

"In a manner of speaking," Shepherd replied.

"Well, I certainly didn't want two months of detention," said Jack. "But that's what I got."

"But what is it you did want?" asked Shepherd. "What was it that made you admit to starting that fight?"

"I didn't want Anna to get punished," said Jack.

"And did you get what you wanted?"

Jack was quiet for a moment. "Yeah," he said, suddenly impressed.

"There you go," said Shepherd.

"But the detention–" said Jack.

"Consequences of your actions," replied Shepherd. "There will be consequences for everything you do. Always. But it's how you deal with those consequences that matters. Will you allow them to take over your life? Play the victim to them? Or will you take more action and use them as an opportunity to get more of what you want?"

For the life of him, Jack couldn't imagine how he could use detention to get something he wanted. But despite all that, for some reason, a lot of what Mr. Shepherd was saying started to make sense.

Jack looked up and met Shepherd's gaze. Suddenly, his cold stare didn't seem so menacing anymore. It was almost as though he were looking *into* Jack and could tell what he was thinking. And in that strange moment, it felt like the two of them had reached some kind of understanding about each other.

After a second or two of silence, Shepherd got up and walked to his desk. He took a notebook out of his drawer, sat down, opened it, and began to scribble.

"Time's up," he said. "You may go."

Jack glanced up at the clock above the classroom door. He'd only been in detention for, at most, ten minutes – not even close to the full time. He looked back at Shepherd, confused.

"Unless," said Shepherd, noticing the look on Jack's face, "you want to stay longer?"

"Nope!" said Jack, hopping up and heading for the door. He wanted to get out of there before Shepherd overcame his sudden generous mood. He was halfway out of the room when Shepherd's voice rang out again.

"Jack…"

Jack turned, afraid Shepherd had changed his mind. But instead, he said:

"Try and stay out of trouble. Or you'll come to realize some consequences are far worse than others."

CHAPTER ✺ 6

Because River Heights was not a very big town, there were not many options available for young teens when it came to a popular Earth custom known as "hanging out." Most shops were limited to the bare necessities – grocery stores, hardware stores, and restaurants. The closest mall was a 30-minute drive into the neighboring town of Whitecreek, and for kids without a car, that meant it was unreachable without parental help.

That made the school the unofficial social spot after classes had ended. Most kids enjoyed joining various clubs or sports teams as a way to socialize with their friends. And though Jack might have been curious about possibly playing on the soccer team or maybe even joining the school band to learn an instrument, the idea of staying at school any longer than he absolutely had to just did not appeal to him.

That is where Big Jim's Pizza Palace came in.

Big Jim's was a worn-down one-story building directly across the street from the high school. Its décor was gaudy, its sanitation was questionable, and its pizza was – even by high school standards - bad. But it had the distinct advantage of being close, which was probably the only reason the place was still in business at all.

Indeed, Big Jim's was the de-facto hang out for most of the student body. After the final bell rang, it was off to Jim's to shoot some pool, grab a bite to eat, or just sit around and do homework someplace that wasn't home.

Because both Matt and Chunk didn't live too far away from Jack, they usually waited for him at the pizza shop until he was out of detention so he wouldn't have to make the trek back to Eagle Hill alone. When Jack entered the joint a full hour and fifteen minutes early, he fully expected them to be surprised.

Jack scanned the room looking for his friends. The walls of the place were covered with faux wood paneling, which must have passed for fancy sometime back in the 1970's. Green-red-and-white colored lamps hung from the ceiling, but they hadn't been cleaned in so long, barely any light could actually escape from them. In the corner was a scratched and rickety pool table, and an on-the-fritz jukebox thumped some music that was cool about ten years ago.

Big Jim's was crowded today. Students of all shapes and sizes staked out most of the tables with their textbooks and study materials while they nursed soft drinks and ate pizza. There was a line at the counter, where Fred — the pot-bellied and unshaven owner of Big Jim's (and don't bother asking why a guy named Fred christened his restaurant after a guy named Jim) — stood at a cash register taking orders with all the good cheer of a professional sewer cleaner, which was to say, none at all.

"S'up, Fred?" said Jack as he walked by.

"Welcome back, freeloader," grumbled Fred. "I'd ask if I could get you anything, but you never have any money, do ya?"

"Yeah, which would make it really hard to pay for the hospital bill if I ever actually ate here," smiled Jack.

"Pah!" spat Fred. "I should charge ya rent for all the time you spend lollygagging around. Food or no."

"Slumlord would definitely be a step up for you, buddy," said Jack. "Hey, you seen Matt or Chunk?"

"In the back," said Fred. "At the arcade."

The "arcade" as Fred liked to call it consisted of one (yes, one) video game, plugged into a dangerously exposed electrical socket and tucked away in the back of the restaurant. Jack made his way over to the hidden alcove to find his two buddies hard at work among the "bleeps" and "boops" of *Nova Commander IV.* Matt was gripping the game's joystick, his eyes narrow with concentration, with Chunk at his side cheering him on.

"Look out for the plasma cannons!" cried Chunk. "You got a fighter on your six. Ooooh-oooooh, there's a power-up over there!"

"Would you shut up, dude!" snapped Matt. "I know what I'm doing, okay? I've only played this game a billion times."

"And you still suck at it!" Jack said with a smirk.

Matt and Chunk looked up from their game in surprise. "Jack?" said Matt. "Holy crap! Is it five o'clock already?"

"Whoa," said Chunk. "Seems like we just got here. This game is eviiiiiiil!"

"Chill, dudes. You did just get here," said Jack. "You'll never guess. Mr. Shepherd let me out early."

Matt and Chunk exchanged a disbelieving glance. "Um, you didn't actually kill Mr. Shepherd and are trying to stage an alibi, are you?" asked Matt.

"Swear to God," said Jack. "I'm just as shocked as you are."

Suddenly, *Nova Commander IV* sang a depressing little ditty signaling the failure of a mission and game over. Matt cursed under his breath and kicked the machine.

"Dang it, and I was just about to beat my high score, too," he complained. "Thanks for distracting me with your good news, my so-called *friend.*"

"When you gonna learn?" said Jack with a smile, sidling up to *Nova Commander IV* and gingerly patting it like a cute little puppy. "No one is ever gonna dethrone me when it comes to this game. I'm the best star pilot on this side of the galaxy."

"Not anymore!" piped up Chunk.

"Huh?" asked Jack.

"Yeah, some dude with the initials MTS beat your score," said Matt, with just a hint of a smirk. "Guess there's a new king in town."

Jack glanced at the screen. Sure enough, when the top scorers flashed up, his initials were indeed second, with the mysterious MTS beating him out by just a couple hundred points for the top spot.

"You gotta be kidding me," mumbled Jack. After all he'd been through today, losing out on the top spot for *Nova Commander* as well was just too much. Since even before he had started high school, Jack had spent countless hours of his life hanging out at Big Jim's and playing this game. He had perfected the art of flying the *Nova Commander Starfighter* better than anyone he knew, getting as far as the 18th level before succumbing to the hordes of enemy starships. It was rumored that some guy out in Cincinnati was actually able to get to level 19, but as far as Jack knew, it was largely believed to be impossible to get much further.

So the fact that he was able to accomplish a score that maybe one other person in the entire world could beat gave him a certain sense of pride – and he wasn't willing to give that up just yet, especially not on a day like today.

"Gimme a quarter," he said to Chunk, holding out his hand.

"Aw, c'mon Jack," whined Chunk. "Play some other time. I don't feel like hanging around Big Jim's all day while you try and recapture your glory."

Jack shifted his outstretched palm to Matt.

"I'm with Chunk, bro," said Matt. "There's way cooler stuff we could be doing than playing a game that pre-dates Pong."

"I am not leaving until one of you gives me a quarter," said Jack sternly.

Matt and Chunk exchanged a look that acknowledged their friend's stubbornness. Chunk sighed and dug a quarter out of his pocket, slapping in into Jack's hand.

"That's all I got," said Chunk.

"It's all I'll need," said Jack confidently, as he took the controls of the game and popped in the quarter.

Nova Commander IV was a relatively simple game. At its core, it was all about flying a starship through enemy territory and facing more and more difficult encounters with enemy spaceships. While its predecessors had a top down view of a tiny triangle that was the spaceship as wave after wave of other geometrically shaped objects fell at it from the top of the screen, *Nova Commander IV* took the giant leap forward in technology by putting the player in the cockpit of the ship and letting him fly through a 3-D wireframe universe that actually did a passable job of simulating real spaceflight.

Each stage of the game required the player to reach a "warp hole," which allowed him to travel further and further into enemy territory, until eventually reaching the mothership of the enemy fleet, which he would then have to destroy to advance to the next level.

When it came to actually playing the game, though, only two skills were required – being able to manage the energy needs of the ship between the lasers and its shields, and being fast enough to take on multiple opponents without getting blown up. If the game were just about one or the other, it would have been much simpler to beat. But in Jack's opinion, the careful balance between controlling his ship and fighting multiple enemies is what elevated the game into an art form.

"Listen, dude," said Matt as Jack started playing. "If you're gonna be a while, I'm gonna run down to the Circle-Mart and get a hot dog or something. I don't think I could survive another slice of Fred's pizza."

"True that," said Chunk. "I'll come with. You want anything, Jack?"

"Just the two of you to be ready to kiss my butt after I prove to the world how awesome I am," he responded.

"Yeah, 'cause that's the first thing everyone associates with being good at prehistoric video games," quipped Matt.

"Your jealousy warms my cold, black soul," intoned Jack.

After his friends departed, Jack breezed through the first couple of levels of the game. The world around him seemed to disappear, and he might as well have been in the actual cockpit of a starfighter as he took on wave after wave of increasingly difficult foes. As so often happens when Jack played video games, time seemed to fly by, and before he knew it, he was back to the dreaded level 18.

Things were not looking good. His ship was damaged, his shields were weakening, and the enemy mothership had dispatched yet another wing of deadly starfighters. Jack made a run for a far off power-up he was hoping to reach before he was within firing range of the enemy. Sure enough, he made it just in time, and got just enough power to keep his shields intact while he fought off the new wave of fighters.

Before he knew it, he was able to unleash his torpedoes and destroy the enemy's mothership, and a new warp hole appeared.

Suddenly, he realized – he'd made it to Level 19!

Jack's heart pounded. The gravity of what he'd just accomplished crashed on top of him like a ton of bricks. Not only had he regained his high score, but also he'd finally been able to beat the level he'd thought was all but impossible to defeat. Jack's mind raced. He wondered what new foe he'd be facing, what new obstacle he would have to overcome, what new puzzle he'd have to solve, and a weird kind of excitement filled him and made him woozy with anticipation.

And just as his ship emerged from the warp hole, the screen of *Nova Commander IV* suddenly flashed, the graphics melting into a mish-mash of strange characters, and an annoying note began to hum from the speakers.

The game had locked up.

"No, no, *NO!*" cried Jack. He'd been so close. Now, not only was his high score erased, but he also might never be able to get to Level 19 again. He gave the game a swift kick that was so hard it hurt his toe. But the screen continued to project gibberish, mocking him.

Jack marched up to the front counter where Fred was hunched over, reading the swimsuit edition of his favorite sports magazine.

"Fred! I thought you were gonna get that game fixed!" said Jack angrily.

"Huh?" Fred said in response, not bothering to glance up.

"Nova Commander," clarified Jack. "It froze up again!"

"Oh, yeah, gee, I'll get right on that," Fred responded in mock concern, again without looking away from his magazine.

"You don't understand!" Jack pleaded. "I did it! I finally made it to Level 19! Beat my old high score! And now no one's ever gonna know!"

"My heart bleeds for ya, kid," said Fred, picking his nose. "Maybe ya should get a new hobby, eh? Like curin' cancer or sumtin'."

Jack glowered at Fred's ugly unshaven mug.

"Can I at least get my quarter back?" he asked.

"What do I look like? An ATM?" snorted Fred. "Get outta here, already."

Fred waved Jack off and went back to flipping through his magazine. Jack glanced at the clock that hung above the entrance. It was a quarter to five. He'd wasted a good forty minutes playing the game, and it was all for nothing.

Since they weren't already back, Jack reasoned that Matt and Chunk had probably gone on home without him. Jack gathered his things and prepared for the walk back to Eagle Hill. Once outside of Big Jim's, he decided to cut across school grounds and go through the Juniper cornfields instead of following Detroit Street back. With any luck, the shortcut would get him back home before five-thirty, just in time to watch some bad, family-friendly TV before dinner.

As he passed by the football stadium, he could hear the sounds of the team practicing. No doubt J.C. was there in the middle of it all. Jack wondered if it made him a bad person to hope J.C. got tackled in a freak pile-up of over-sized meatheads and was turned into a mushy human pancake.

Jack was almost to the cornfields when he stopped cold. At the end of the bleachers, near one of the support struts, was Anna. She was sitting on the grass, staring off into the cornfield of the Juniper family farm. The sun was getting low in the sky, and its golden rays shined on her, making her look like she was almost glowing. Jack stood still, afraid to move, overcome at the sight of just how beautiful she was.

Jack looked around him. There was no one to be seen. No Mr. Shepherd to intimidate him. No other kids to laugh at him. Even the football team was hidden behind a massive wall of aluminum bench seating. As far as the eye could see, the only two people in the world were Jack and Anna.

There would never be a better time to talk to her.

At this realization, an overwhelming sense of anxiety crashed over Jack. What would he say? What would *she* say? Was she mad at him for what happened earlier? Would he continue to make a fool of himself?

Jack struggled with his emotions for a minute. His gut was a tangle of nervousness. His brain was telling him to just keep walking. He could always try again later when he knew the right thing to say.

Then, the oddest thing happened.

Jack remembered his talk with Mr. Shepherd, about how he needed to start taking responsibility for himself. About how he could get everything he wanted, if he were just willing to take action to do so. He thought about the intense gaze of Shepherd's piercing grey eyes, and in that moment, he felt a small spark of courage flare up inside him.

With that, Jack took a deep breath and walked toward Anna.

"Hey," said Jack.

Anna looked up at him. If she were happy to see Jack, he couldn't tell. Her face was absolutely blank. For a moment, Jack thought he'd made a mistake coming over, but as far as mistakes went, he could think of a lot worse.

"Don't worry," he said putting his hands up, "I promise not to start any more fights around you. At least for the foreseeable future."

Anna nodded. "That's good," she said.

"I just wanted to come over and thank you for having a talk with your dad about what happened," he said. "He went easy on me today. It made detention… well, not so sucky."

"You're welcome," she said simply, before turning back to the cornfield and gazing into it, as though she were deep in thought about something. Jack hesitated for a second. He felt as though he should take that as a cue to exit, but he also knew, chances were, he'd never get the nerve to talk to her like this again, so he might as well give it all he had right now.

"I also wanted to apologize," he continued.

Anna looked back up at him. "Apologize?"

"Yeah, for dragging you into that whole mess to begin with," said Jack. "Coming from someone who knows what its like to be badgered by J.C. Rowdey, I just couldn't stand to sit there and let him... I don't know... bug you like that."

"That's okay," replied Anna. "I can take care of myself."

"Oh, no doubt," said Jack. "In fact, that's part of the reason I came over there to begin with. I mean, I hate J.C. and all, but I thought I'd take pity on him, since my *fists of fury* are obviously no match to what you would have done if he hadn't left you alone."

At that, finally, Anna smiled, a slightly shy, good-natured grin. Jack couldn't help but notice how glossy and soft her lips looked.

"Hey, I've got a question I've been wanting to ask you since you showed up," said Jack making as smooth a transition as he could to sitting down on the grass next to her.

Anna looked at Jack suspiciously. "What type of question?" she asked.

"Well, I just gotta know," he continued. "Where are you guys from? You and your dad, that is."

"West Virginia," she said quickly. "We moved here from West Virginia."

"Are all girls from West Virginia like you?"

"I don't know," Anna replied. "What am I like?"

Jack cocked his head to the side, studying Anna's face slightly. "You're just... I don't know... different."

"What do you mean?"

Jack smiled and shrugged. "Well, you're prettier than any other girl in the entire school, but you don't like to hang out with anyone, you don't like to talk with anyone, you don't seem to have any friends... you spend all your time reading books and stuff..."

"Are you saying I'm weird?" asked Anna.

"Yeah, I guess," replied Jack. "But in a good way," he quickly added.

"So you think being an anti-social bookworm is 'good weird'?" Anna said with a hint of sarcasm.

Jack chuckled. "Yeah... that didn't come out right. I guess what I'm trying to say is that I *get* it."

"Get what?"

"You," he said. "You're far away from where you grew up, and as far as towns go, they don't get more Podunk than River Heights. You don't like it here, you don't like the people, so you figure you'll just keep to yourself and suffer through it until you can get the heck out of here and live the kind of life you've always wanted."

Anna nodded her head, good-naturedly. "Wow, I guess you've really figured me out."

Jack shrugged. "I don't know. All I'm saying is that I know what it's like to feel alone, and you get so used to feeling that way, that the idea of getting close to other people gets... scary I guess. Because the minute you do, they could leave. And then you'd be all alone again."

Anna's face softened a bit. "You sound like you speak from experience," she said.

A hazy image of Jack's dad flashed into his mind for some reason. He couldn't remember what he even looked like anymore. All that was in his mind was a shock of wavy brown hair and an old leather jacket he always wore.

"Yeah, well... what's the point of getting close to people if they're just going to leave – or better yet, if you're just going to leave, right? It's like you're just setting yourself up for heartbreak," Jack said as he picked a blade of grass absently. "But you know what? Sometimes, it's nice to be close to someone, even if it is just for a little while. After all, you can still carry people around in your heart, even if they're no longer around, right?"

Anna was quiet for a moment. "Can you?" she asked. "Or do they just slip away and leave a hole in your heart where you used to carry them?"

There was a twinge of sadness in her voice, and Jack suddenly remembered the rumors of her mom dying.

"My dad left when I was little," he said. "I don't know why he left. I used to get so mad when other kids teased me about him not being around…"

"Like J.C. did today?" Anna asked.

"Yeah," said Jack. "And I don't know if there's anything you can do to keep people from slipping away. But I've got my mom, and my friends. Matt, Chunk, Peter…all those guys. And even though my dad isn't around, they are. And for some reason, that makes it better."

Anna nodded. "So you think I should stop being so stand-offish and make some friends? Is that what you're saying?"

"You can do what you want," said Jack. "But I've learned that as painful as it can be, it's better to have good people in your life – even if it's just for a little while – than to spend all your time by yourself."

Anna was quiet, staring intensely at a blade of grass. Jack was wondering if, by some miracle, his words had actually gotten through to her.

"Maybe you're right," said Anna. "Maybe I should try enjoying my time here a little more."

Jack smiled. "See? Now you're talking! Unleash Anna Shepherd on the world! It'll do you good."

"So how do I do that?" asked Anna. "I mean... how do you make friends around here?"

"Well, if you want to make friends, you've gotta meet as many people as you can and find out if you like them."

"That all sounds good, but... I wouldn't know where to start. I don't really have a lot of experience making friends."

"Start with the dance!" blurted Jack.

Anna looked unsure. "The dance?" she said.

"Yeah! Everyone is going to be there. It'd be the perfect time to mingle and stuff."

"I don't know..."

"C'mon, it'll be fun!" said Jack. "Hey, I have an idea, why don't you go with me? I could introduce you to all sorts of non-annoying people."

By the look on Anna's face, Jack might as well have jumped out from behind a corner with his head on fire shouting "Oogidie-Boogidie!" *Tactful*, thought Jack, *very tactful*.

"I thought you weren't allowed to go to the dance," she replied diplomatically.

"If you say 'yes,' I can guarantee I'll find a way to go," said Jack with a hint of nervous laughter. "I don't care if I have to do another month of detention and wash Principal Montgomery's car for a year! I'll find a way."

"Oh, um..." said Anna.

"That wouldn't happen to be West Virginian for 'Yes' would it?"

"Well, I don't really dance," said Anna.

"Oh, that's totally cool," replied Jack. "I don't dance either. If you like, we could just GO to the dance and stand around making fun of all the losers who DO dance. How awesome would that be?"

"It does sound like fun, but... I... actually have something I've got to do the night of Homecoming."

Jack nodded. "Actually, yeah... I forgot – I've got something I have to do that night, too."

"Really?" asked Anna.

"Yeah, turns out that's the night I go... uh... bowling. You're not going bowling, too, are you? 'Cause that would just be weird."

Anna laughed. "No, I'm not going bowling."

"Good. Then we get to avoid the whole awkward squabbling over lanes and who gets to use the six-pound ball and stuff."

"Lucky us," smiled Anna.

"Yeah, it's like fate, or destiny, or something. We're just totally not meant to be together on the same night," smiled Jack back. "What about the night after the dance? You wanna... do something then?"

Anna sighed. "You don't ever give up, do you?"

"My mom always says, 'winners never quit, and quitters never win.' Or was that Vince Lombardi? I can never remember..."

"I'm sorry, Jack..." said Anna gently. "You seem like a nice guy, but I'm really not interested in dating anyone right now."

Jack nodded. His gut felt like it was being twisted, and all of a sudden, he felt really, really stupid. He got to his feet. "Well, you can't blame a guy for trying." Jack hesitated for an excruciatingly awkward moment before finally saying, "I guess I'll see you around." And with that, he started to walk away.

Jack made it a few steps before he heard Anna call out.

"Hey, Jack..." said Anna. Jack stopped and turned toward her.

"If I *were* going to date someone..." she said. "It would be someone like you."

Jack smiled. It wasn't the "yes" he wanted, but it did make him feel better. "Hey, you know... if you change your mind about the dance, I was like totally lying about that whole bowling thing."

"You don't say," said Anna, good-naturedly.

"Yeah. I like to keep my nights open, just in case a pretty girl decides she wants to stop being such a loner and start having some fun. Like tonight, for example. I'm totally doing nothing."

"You hoping the third time is the charm?" joked Anna.

"Just putting it out there," shrugged Jack. "If a pretty girl were to suddenly show up at 7 Eagle Hill, she might be surprised to find that fun has a name, and it's *Jack Finnegan.*"

Jack flashed his best winning smile and hiked his thumbs up toward his chest. Anna giggled at his goofiness.

"You're certainly not like any of the other boys around here," said Anna.

"Trust me," smiled Jack. "You have no idea."

And with that, Jack made his way into the cornfield, heading back toward home.

CHAPTER 🪐 7

The Shepherd household was a modest, two-story dwelling a mere 10-minute walk from the school. On the outside, it was a typical River Heights home, with white washed walls and light blue trim, a small yard, and even a white picket fence. But on the inside, it was far from typical.

The reason for this was because at that very moment, Professor Green and Mr. Shepherd were busy fixing their subspace communication device, a nifty little gadget which allowed them to communicate with a small fleet of starships hiding in the orbit of a planet named Jupiter, not all that far (relatively) from Earth.

In case it isn't clear by now, Professor Green, Mr. Shepherd, and even the lovely Anna are not natives of the planet. Indeed, though most students often believe their teachers are from some type of distant galaxy, in this situation, they would actually be right.

At the dining room table, Professor Green was hunched over a silver box, roughly the size and shape of a briefcase. It was open, and he was furiously fiddling with various knobs, diodes, and other doohickeys that make rather complicated pieces of machinery such as this one work. While the good Professor was busy doing this, Shepherd stood at the nearby window, staring outside stoically.

"Infernal machine," Green grumbled. "I can't find a thing wrong with it."

"Then why isn't it working?" asked Shepherd, not taking his gaze away from the window.

"Best guess? There must be some type of interference that's keeping us from establishing a connection with the fleet," replied Green.

"Interference? Is that normal?"

"It's not unheard of," said Green, trying to sound cheery. "Sunspots and all. Maybe some gravitational anomaly is causing it. Who's to say?"

"You," said Shepherd. "And say it quickly. If we do not make our scheduled check in with the fleet, they will think something is wrong. Captain Rylack is the type who will launch a full out extraction if he even suspects we might be in danger."

"Ah, I do so love a good extraction," smiled Green. "It can be so exciting! Especially if it's needed."

"Professor..." muttered Shepherd.

"Right, right, I'll figure out what's wrong," replied Green as he went back to poking about the communicator. "I will say, though, I'll be rather sad when it comes time to leave. Such a pleasant planet. I think I rather like it here."

"The sooner we get out of here, the better," grunted Shepherd.

"Oh, come now!" chirped Green. "I know you well enough to see how much you enjoy teaching again, despite your sour demeanor. So don't tell me you don't like it here, too."

Shepherd grumbled. "All the more reason to hurry up and leave," he replied. "Our presence puts everyone here in danger."

Green sighed. "I say. Must you always be so morbid? You could take a lesson from our students on how to relax. I'm sure Jack Finnegan would be happy to teach you. He seems to be quite good at it."

"Our students are not fighting a war," said Shepherd. "And I doubt I have anything to learn from Mr. Finnegan."

"Don't be so sure," said Green. "That boy is full of surprises. Why, just today, he was able to grasp quantum theory, if you can believe it."

Shepherd raised an eyebrow. "Is that so?"

"Indeed!" replied Green. "Albeit, he spent most of class trying to conjure up a bikini model, but all things considered, he was rather quick to grasp the concepts."

Green noticed a hint of a smile form briefly on Shepherd's face.

"Am I to gather you've taken an interest in the boy?" asked Green inquisitively.

"My interest is currently with the royal bloodline, and yours should be with that communicator," said Shepherd.

"You know, this would go more quickly if I had your help, my dear Paragon," said Green. "Staring out that window will not make her Highness appear any faster."

At that moment, Shepherd spotted Anna walking up to the house. He abruptly turned away from the window and walked past Green toward the foyer without a word.

"Or… maybe it will!" mused Green.

Anna entered the house and had just tossed her jacket onto the nearby coat rack when Shepherd appeared.

"Where have you been?" he asked.

"At the cornfield," replied Anna, as if Shepherd should have known that little fact all along.

"We agreed you'd come right home after school from now on."

"I needed to think."

"You can think just as well here as you can anywhere else."

"Anywhere else does not contain the secret to the universe's survival," said Anna. "And besides, I like being outside. The weather here reminds me of home."

"All weather aside, how do you expect me to protect you if I do not know where you are?" asked Shepherd, pointedly.

"Protect me from what?" countered Anna. "We've been in this town for months and have yet to see anything more dangerous than a field full of cow manure."

"Need I remind you that you were involved in a fight today?"

"I wouldn't exactly call it a fight," said Anna.

"And what, pray tell, would you call it?"

"Good natured rough-housing?" she said hopefully.

Shepherd grimaced.

"Don't look at me like that," complained Anna. "It was just the squabbling of two stupid Earth-boys. It was harmless."

Shepherd crossed his arms and closed the distance between Anna and himself, his imposing frame towering over her.

"When you first suggested that we infiltrate Earth society," Shepherd said softly, "I consented to do so only on certain terms, not the least of which was your agreeing to stay close to me as much as possible. As benign as this planet may be, it is still alien territory, and there are dangers you must be shielded from."

"There are dangers everywhere," Anna said with a sigh. "I'm in no more peril here than I am in the Capitol on Omnicron Prime. Or anywhere else in the galaxy for that matter."

"It is not your place to judge what may or may not be considered safe for your continued well-being. That is my providence, and you will abide by my decisions, or this experiment of yours is over."

"You forget yourself, Shepherd," said Anna sharply. "Remember who you are addressing."

"I never forget," the man replied. "Which is why I am addressing you in such a way. You are many things, Princess. But I am your guardian, and in matters of your safety, I outrank you at every turn. Are we clear?"

For a moment, Anna and Shepherd were locked in a silent battle of hard stares, until Anna finally relented.

"Yes," she said.

"Good," replied Shepherd. "I will expect you home every day after school from now on. No excuses. If you wish to go somewhere else, I will have to accompany you. Agreed?"

Anna nodded. She had learned from experience there was no arguing with Shepherd. Ever.

"Well, now that's settled," chimed in Professor Green cheerily as he entered the foyer clutching the still open communicator box, "Perhaps we should discuss our remaining options before the excavation of the temple begins?"

"Actually," said Anna, "I was thinking about postponing the excavation."

Shepherd and Green looked at her quizzically.

"Postpone?" asked Green. "Whatever for?"

"I still think there is a way for us to unlock the temple without damaging it," said Anna. "I'm close to figuring out the key, I can feel it."

"With all due respect, your highness" said Green, "what is it you believe you'll learn that we haven't already been able to discover in our time here?"

"The Professor is right," said Shepherd. "We've studied the inhabitants of this planet long enough. There's nothing more to be gleaned from them."

"We've studied books and history, and we've observed the Earthlings plenty," said Anna. "But what if the answer to this riddle lies in who these people are? How they think, how they act, how they *interact* with each other? There has to be a reason why they're here and why their society has so many similarities to different intergalactic civilizations. There must be a connection of some sort between them and the temple. There are just too many coincidences to ignore."

"You've had plenty of time to interact with the Earthlings," said Shepherd. "And none of that has given you the answer we need."

"Yes, but... I haven't really been interacting with them. Not truly. Today I realized that I don't really know any of these people. I didn't want to get attached to them, so I cut myself off. I chose to observe rather than engage, and that may have been a mistake."

"What are you suggesting?" asked Green.

Anna hesitated.

"I'm thinking... I should go to Homecoming," she said.

Shepherd raised an eyebrow. "The dance?" he said dryly.

"Yes," said Anna, a little embarrassed. "Most of the school's students will be there. It will be the ideal time to interact with them, in a social setting."

Green smiled. "Why, I think that's a marvelous idea."

"Thank you, Professor," she said, returning his grin.

"I think so, too," said Shepherd.

Anna looked at him, surprised. "Really?" she asked.

"Yes," said Shepherd. "By all means, you should run off to a party while millions of life-forms are being slaughtered. What's one more day or two to them, anyway?"

Anna's mood instantly darkened. "I do so hate it when you get sarcastic, Shepherd."

"The dig team will be here next Saturday," said Shepherd. "If this temple really houses the weapon of the Ancients like you think it does, it could be the key to winning this war. To postpone, for any reason, would be unwise."

Anna sighed bitterly.

"As usual, you are correct," she said coldly. "In the meantime, I suppose I will continue to look for a way of opening the temple without possibly *demolishing* valuable Ancient technology in the process."

With that, Anna turned and marched up the stairs to her room. Shepherd watched her go with his jaw clenched.

"This planet is a bad influence," he grumbled.

Green nodded. "Yes," he said. "Or, she's finally becoming a teenager, and you're just now noticing."

Shepherd looked at Green from the corner of his eye.

"I take it you think I'm being too hard on her," said Shepherd.

"It is not my place to say, good Paragon," said Green with a shrug. "But I have been on this planet longer than you, and I must say... as far as species go, the Earthlings can be quite pleasant. Can you really fault her for wanting to have some fun?"

"Fun is a luxury," Shepherd replied. "One we cannot afford right now."

"Honestly," said Green. "Would it really hurt to let her be a normal sixteen-year-old girl, if only for a night?"

"You and I both know, Professor," responded Shepherd. "She is anything but normal."

Shepherd turned on his heel and left the Professor alone. Green sighed.

"Yes," he said sadly. "I suppose you're right."

CHAPTER ✵ 8

Jack had planned on spending that night as he spent most of his nights – playing his favorite videogame, *Arena Deathmatch*, on his most prized possession, a Gamerbox 3000, the newest generation gaming console there was.

The storyline of *Arena Deathmatch* was a simple one. An elite military Special Forces team was kidnapped by aliens and forced to fight other elite military teams from alien worlds in an arena to decide who the ultimate warriors of the galaxy were. Though the single player campaign was a passable bit of video game fodder, Jack's true love was playing online against opponents that were controlled by people, as opposed to the somewhat lacking artificial intelligence of the Gamerbox 3000.

Indeed, it was a guilty pleasure of Jack's to run about with a highly overpowered weapon, blowing up enemies with pinpoint accuracy and wanton aggression. To quote one of Jack's favorite movies, "There is no better pleasure in life than to crush your enemies, see them driven before you, and hear the lamentations of their women." (Jack had no idea what that last part meant, but it certainly sounded cool!)

Perhaps the thing Jack liked best about the Gamerbox 3000 was the fact that it came with a microphoned headset that would allow him to actually communicate with the other players he was fighting with in *Arena Deathmatch*. This not only allowed Jack's four-man squad to strategize and react more quickly during the matches, it also allowed Jack to talk smack to the opposing team – which, in all reality, was probably the most fun Jack actually had while playing the game.

Jack had worked two jobs over the summer to save up almost two-thirds of what he needed to buy his prized Gamerbox 3000 and *Arena Deathmatch* game. The rest he'd had to beg from his mother. Thus, Jack had been able to finally afford his Gamerbox 3000, which quickly became both a blessing and a curse.

It was a blessing because, well, it was totally awesome. It gave Jack something to do while his mom was at work and he had nowhere else to go after school. Not only that, it was one of the few things Jack actually felt he was *good* at. Sit him down in front of a math exam or put a basketball in his hands, and Jack was completely hopeless. But pit him against a squad of alien soldiers with a pistol and a couple of grenades, and he was almost unstoppable.

Many a night had gone by with Jack chucking his homework aside in favor of playing a quick session of online deathmatches, which was partially why his Gamerbox was a curse. He had promised his mom he'd improve his grades if she helped him get the console, but, in fact, the opposite had been occurring. Jack's grades had been suffering, and what used to be a straight "C" average was now teetering perilously close to a "D."

Rather than studying his American History textbook, Jack would spend his time pouring over maps of the various Deathmatch arenas on the internet, learning where all the weapon drops and resurrection points were. He'd learn which weapons were best to kill which enemies, as opposed to writing that science paper that was due the next day. And, of course, he'd take on all online challengers until the wee hours of the morning, which was the reason he was so prone to oversleeping, and thus, being late for school.

In fact, Jack had spent so much time playing *Arena Deathmatch* that he now ranked in the top 10 of competitors on the online scoreboard, boasting an impressive 2,374,898 points, with a record of 5,689 wins, and 76 losses. His exact ranking was number two, being bested out of the top spot by his online arch-nemesis, some kid from Korea known to him only as H8daPlya, the boy's online screen name.

Because of his high ranking, two things tended to happen. A lot of the best online players wanted to team up with him, and a lot of the best online players wanted to beat him. This led to Jack taking the game very seriously – not just so he wouldn't let down his teammates who looked to him for leadership during their battles, but also so he could completely destroy the opposing team. If there were one thing that could be said about Jack Finnegan, it was that he absolutely *hated* to lose.

When Jack had gotten home from school that day, he had found a note from his mom. She had pulled yet another double shift at work but had come home long enough to fix Jack some beef stew and garlic bread for his dinner before heading out again. One of the waitresses at the Fox Hole Diner where she worked had given birth not too long ago, leaving them short-handed, so Jack's mother had been picking up the slack. This meant that there was no one around to force Jack to do his homework when he got home, which was fine by him. His mom typically worked nights, so Jack had gotten used to being on his own for the most part, but the call of *Arena Deathmatch* had made the time he spent alone seem to fly by, for which Jack was grateful.

However, in an attempt to keep his promise to improve his grades, Jack tried reading the three chapters of his English class assignment, but there was only so much he could take of old British people talking about how much they wanted to get married if it weren't for the fact that one person was a peasant and the other person was rich, or royalty, or something stupid like that. If schools really wanted kids to learn, why did they insist on picking books that were so boring and had absolutely nothing to do with something real people would experience in their lives? It wasn't long before *Arena Deathmatch* was beckoning him, and he tossed aside the stuffy old novel for a romp on the lava arena of Brimstone 6.

Each Deathmatch consisted of five rounds. The team that won the best of five was declared the winner, and the only way to win the round was to kill all the opposing team members before all your team members were killed. Jack's team had just won a close fourth round against a very competitive clan, tying the score, and his teammates now had one minute to strategize in their online lobby before the next round started.

"I'm telling you guys," Jack said, speaking into his headset, "they have no rearguard. The team leader always goes for the rocket launcher in sector twelve first, which leaves them open to a flanking attack from behind."

"But if they get the Rocket Launcher first, we're toast," said Jack's teammate, KalSchoolz2 (Jack had no idea what his real name was).

"Not if we flip the second lava trap. That'll cut him off from the rest of his teammates and allow us to pick them off while he's stuck on the lower platform. I don't care if he's got the rocket launcher or not. It won't do him any good if his team is dead and we have the high ground."

"I don't know," chimed in Bill, a.k.a. "GhostSlaya95," a frequent teammate of Jack's who sounded like he was way too old to still be playing video games. "Sounds awful risky."

"Hey, you wanna win this match or not?" said Jack. "It'll work. Trust me. These losers will never know what hit them! They're gonna be crying like little babies after we're done with them. We're gonna unman them so hard, they'll have to take up tea parties and macramé in their spare time. We're gonna spank them so bad, we're gonna leave handprints on their—"

Suddenly, there was a knock at the front door. Jack turned, startled. It was nine o'clock at night; who'd be visiting him this late?

"Hey, guys," he said, "hold on a sec. Someone's at the door."

"Hurry, we only have about 30 seconds before the next match," said Bill.

"Don't worry, I'll make it quick," said Jack as he got up and tossed off his headset.

Jack bounded to the door and opened it up expecting to see a salesman of some type, an overly ambitious Girl Scout, or his mom coming home early, only to discover she had forgotten her keys.

Instead, he saw Anna Shepherd standing on his front steps.

Had it instead been Bigfoot, a scary man in a hockey mask, or some type of crazy dancing Leprechaun, Jack was pretty sure he would have been less surprised than he was at that very moment.

"Hi," said Anna, smiling.

"Anna, it's so great to see you!" is what Jack would have liked to have said, but unfortunately his mouth wasn't quite working in sync with his brain at that moment, so all he could squeeze out was a passable:

"Uh... uh... um... hi?"

The dumbfounded look on Jack's face must have been obvious, since the smile on Anna's disappeared. "Did... did I come at a bad time?"

For a split second, Jack thought about his Deathmatch clock ticking down, but then, he thought of the real live girl standing in front of him and how the two simply did not compare, on any level, ever in the history of time, space, and all that was holy. "No! No, not at all, I was just... ah... working out."

"Really?" said Anna suspiciously, her lovely smile now back.

"Yeah, you know... I like to stay in shape. I'm up to benching 200 now. It's pretty awesome."

"That's very impressive," said Anna.

"I know, right? You wouldn't know it to look at me, but I'm... ripped."

At that, Anna laughed. That made Jack laugh. And then after the laughing, an awkward silence descended upon the two like a smelly fart neither wanted to acknowledge.

Invite her in! Invite her in! Invite her in, fool! was the thought that ran through Jack's brain... followed by images of dirty dishes over-flowing in the sink, dirty clothes littered all over his room, and a sneaking suspicion he had forgotten to flush the toilet after he'd last used it.

"Would you, like, excuse me for just two seconds?" Jack asked.

"Oh, uh... sure," said Anna.

"Just give me two seconds," smiled Jack. "Don't go anywhere, okay? Be back in a jiff..." and with that, he closed the door and frantically went to work trying to make the place passable.

He flushed the toilet, kicked all his clothes under his bed, and threw a towel over the dishes in the sink. All too late, he saw that his Deathmatch had started, and the bloody letters "YOU LOSE" were painted across the screen as he had just been fragged by the other team's rocket launcher, but for some reason at this moment, he didn't care about the match. He had Anna waiting for him.

Jack swung the door back open, and sure enough, Anna was still waiting patiently outside.

"Would you like to come in?" Jack asked, trying to act as smooth as possible, yet slightly out of breath.

Anna hesitated. "I'm sorry for dropping in like this so unexpectedly," she said. "You said you keep you nights open, but… I guess I shouldn't have taken that so literally."

"No!" said Jack. "No, I'm glad you're here. I just… well, I wanted to tidy the place up a bit before you came in, is all."

"That's… very sweet of you," said Anna. "But, I - I think I should probably go. I'm sorry for bothering you."

"Oh… uh, okay," said Jack.

Anna turned and began to walk away. Jack suddenly noticed that his throat was tight, as if it were closing up to keep his heart from jumping up out of his chest. The girl of his dreams had shown up, and now she was leaving. For some reason, the image of his Deathmatch game popped into his head, with the words "YOU LOSE" painted in blood on the screen. And suddenly, Jack remembered how much he *hated* to lose.

"Wait," he said, so forcefully he startled even himself.

Anna stopped and turned toward him. Jack stepped out of the trailer and approached her.

"Was it the trailer park?" he asked. "Did you take one look at this place and realize what a loser I am?"

Anna's eyes grew wide in surprise. "No! No, not at all! I don't think you're a loser."

"Then why'd you come all this way just to turn around and leave?" he asked.

"I — I just…"Anna looked as though she were struggling to figure out what to say. Jack couldn't help but think she looked even more beautiful when she was confused and flustered. "I guess I just got to thinking about what you said to me before… and I decided that ever since I'd gotten here… well, I hadn't really had all that much fun."

Jack flashed his best smile and said, "Well, that's because you haven't been hanging out with me!"

At that, Anna smiled. "I guess that just might be true."

"So why would you want to ruin it by walking away now?" asked Jack. "Especially after I went through all the trouble of planning out, like, the funnest night *ever* for us."

Anna raised an eyebrow. "You already planned out an evening for me?"

"Yeah, I'm quick like that," said Jack, smiling. "So what do you say?"

Anna looked at Jack, her blue eyes seemed to sparkle despite it being dark outside, and Jack's heart felt like it stopped beating in the breath it took for her to answer him.

"I guess it depends," she finally replied. "What do you have planned?"

Jack could finally breathe again. "Well, are you hungry? Because I know this great place with incredible food that I can, like, totally afford."

Anna cocked her head to the side and furrowed her brow. "Ah, sorry. I don't like food."

"Oh… uh, okay… that's not a problem…" said Jack, slightly confused. A great deal of his hastily formed plan had a lot to do with food.

"Jack," said Anna with a smile, "I'm joking."

Jack raised his eyebrows. "Of course you're joking! I knew that. Who doesn't like food, right? I was worried we might have a problem because I'm a big fan of food, but since you're joking, crisis averted. And it's a good thing I did not take you seriously for one instant, because otherwise you'd never get to experience the culinary joy which is the 24-hour burger shack located just down the street."

Anna laughed. "In that case, I would love to get something to eat."

Jack clapped his hands and smiled. "Excellent! Just let me grab my jacket, and then be prepared to be a slave to delicious flavor. Sound good?"

Anna nodded. "Sounds good."

As Jack rushed back into his home, Anna couldn't help but dwell on the notion that for the first time in a long while, she was actually starting to enjoy herself.

For some reason, this boy was not like the others she'd encountered on this planet. He had an energy to him that she had not felt in a long time, and despite the fact she had made it a point to try not to get attached to anyone here, she had the nagging feeling that Jack was starting to grow on her.

Little did she know, her enjoyment would be short-lived. For far off, in the night sky above her, Earth's doom was approaching...

CHAPTER 9

aptain Rylack looked at the unremarkable blue-green planet on the viewscreen and cursed his luck. On the list of the last things he wanted to see before he died, this blasted back-woods planet was not among them.

He coughed, and his lungs burned as though they were being seared with hot irons. Shivers of agony spidered through every muscle in his body, and as much as he resisted, he couldn't help but let a pathetic sob escape from him.

He gritted his teeth, trying to pull himself back together. But it was getting harder and harder. He knew that though it felt like an eternity since the torture had started, very little time had actually passed. His pale green eyes were watery with tears and he blinked to clear them. Not much good that did, though. Darkness surrounded him, with the exception of a tiny pool of blinding light that hammered down from above so brightly it hurt.

Rylack could hear the sound of his tormentor's footsteps casually circling around him. Though he could not see much past the bright light that engulfed him and the large viewscreen projecting the image of the planet, there were others in the room, too; he was sure of it. They made no sound, but their very presence made his skin crawl, and that was enough to confirm his suspicions.

He was on his knees, and his hands were bound behind his back so tightly he could feel them throbbing and swelling. Whatever bound him was not rope or metal but some type of energy that coiled around his arms and made his skin seem like it was on fire. He almost wished whatever bound his arms was actually burning him. At least then, the nerve endings would eventually be destroyed and the pain would cease. Whatever it was that had him in its grasp, it was unrelenting.

"Where is the girl?" the voice from the darkness asked, as it had again and again since the interrogation had started. It was a deep and gravelly voice, and it made Rylack's ears hurt just to hear it. He looked up and saw the glow of two red eyes in the darkness gazing at him with contempt.

"Gone," he croaked. "Far away. You'll never—"

A clawed hand reached out and suddenly Rylack cried in agony. The hand never touched him, but his skin felt as if it were being pierced by a thousand needles, digging into his muscles and burning them with flames. He felt waves of pain wash over him, and a hollow pit of despair opened in his gut, as though his very soul were being torn apart within him by a ravenous wild animal.

The pain stopped and he crumpled to the floor. He gasped for air, but each breath was a labor of agony. His lungs felt as though they would burst through his chest, and his head pounded with the fury of a thousand drums. As soon as he caught his breath again, he could not help it any longer and began to cry.

"Shall I ask again?" came the charcoal voice from the darkness.

Rylack steeled himself. For all the pain, he was able to find a small spark of courage deep within him. He had a duty – a duty to his Princess. He could not allow himself to give her up to these monsters. But the pain...the pain was so great, he did not know if he could last much longer.

"Ask all you want," he muttered. "My answer's the same. She's gone—"

Another jolt of pain. This time, it was quick, like a spear being jabbed into his back, twisted, and then pulled out again.

He jerked and spasmed from the blow, a sharp cry escaping from him.

"You are lying to me, Captain," the voice said. "I always know when your kind is lying. Just tell us where she is, and this will be all over. The pain will end, and you will be taken to a comfortable cell. You have my word."

"Your word means nothing to me…" he said, as defiantly as he could.

Something that Rylack could only assume was a laugh echoed from the darkness.

"I will give you credit, Captain," the voice said. "You've lasted longer than most in your position would have."

Icy cold tendrils snaked through Rylack's body. He gasped as he was yanked up into the air by the invisible hooks that had just wormed their way inside him. He hung there, suspended, helpless, with icy agony chilling him to the core of his being. He tried to cry out in pain, but his throat closed up, and the only thing that could escape him was a feeble gurgle.

"But you cannot outlast me," the voice said. "I will not allow you to pass out. I will not allow you to die. Every moment you resist me is a moment you will bear witness to unimaginable pain and suffering, and it can go on as long as I wish it to."

Suddenly, the pain stopped. Rylack could breathe again. His muscles were relaxed; the frigid cold that had dug into him moments before was replaced with a soothing warmth, and he felt an overwhelming sense of peace descend upon him.

"I can also make it end," said the voice. "Just tell me what I want to know…"

The icy scourge of agony came rushing back, wracking Rylack's body. He struggled helplessly against the invisible daggers as they burrowed through his muscles, into his bones, and back out again. Then, the pain disappeared, and that feeling of peace returned to him.

"Please…" he begged.

"Tell me," the voice insisted.

More pain, then peace. Pain and peace, pain and peace. For some reason, every time the pain went away, the fear of it coming back began to grow and grow, and the thought of it returning once again was far more frightening than actually enduring it. Images of his family flashed into his mind – his wife, with her shy smile, the smell of her cooking at night, his son and the times they played together…

And then those memories were all ripped away, replaced by the blinding scream of agony. Try as he might, he could not withstand any more, not even for his Princess.

"I'll tell!" he cried.

The pain once more subsided, and whatever unseen force had hold of him, let him go. He crumpled to the ground.

"Where is she?" the voice asked again.

For a brief moment, Rylack considered giving false coordinates, one last ditch effort to keep his oath to protect his Princess. But he knew it was no use. The demon in the darkness always knew when he was lying, and he would make him suffer greatly for it if he did so now. Rylack licked his parched lips with a dry tongue and did the unthinkable…

"Planetary sector, Kappa-642…" he muttered. "Grid D-12."

The planet on the viewscreen grew in size as it was zoomed in on. Computer-generated grid lines appeared; one flashed, leaping up to fill the screen as another grid formed, and soon a plot of land could be seen. It was the town Rylack and his crew had been monitoring for so many months, and the sight of it made him feel sick with betrayal.

"Deploy the extraction force," the voice ordered. "Scan that area for all energy readings. I want the girl found, and I want her taken alive."

Rylack could hear movement as the others in the room scuttled off to do their master's bidding.

He lay on the cold, unforgiving floor, feeling sick to his stomach. He had betrayed his sacred trust, and he knew that there was no reason to keep him alive now that they had what they wanted. A million things raced through his mind – why did they want the Princess? Why hadn't they asked about their mission? How were they able to find them in the first place?

"I know you have questions..." said the voice, as though it were able to read his mind. "Your kind always does."

Rylack took that to be an invitation. He could have asked any number of things, but one question stood out above all the others, and he desperately wanted to know the answer before it was all over.

"Why?" he asked. "Why are you doing this? We did nothing to you – *nothing!* And you're slaughtering us... entire planets... for what?"

The only response was the sound of his tormentor's boots echoing in the room as he stalked around him. Then, the feeling of invisible hooks digging into his flesh assaulted him once again, and he was reeled up into the air like a fish struggling for release.

A figure emerged from the darkness – a shadow amongst shadows. Its two red eyes blazed at him, glowing brightly with pure malice. A taloned hand pointed toward the viewscreen.

"What do you see on that screen?" the figure demanded.

Rylack looked. It was the same blue-green planet as before. "Just... a planet," he choked.

"You see a planet," the figure responded. "I see an aberration. I see a great expansive void, littered with vile mistakes you call life. We are simply removing the clutter, making the void pure once again."

"You're insane," growled Rylack.

"We are righteous," replied the figure. "And we will sweep across the universe and lay waste to every abomination which crosses our path. Once we have your Princess, the final piece will be in place, and we will bring purity and balance back to the void."

The words echoed in Rylack's ears, and suddenly, he feared he knew why they were after the woman he'd sworn to protect.

"The Princess..." gasped Rylack.

"Yes," purred the figure. "She's the key, you see. With her, we will bring about the destruction of all. Every planet will be laid to waste, every star will be extinguished, and every life will be ended. We will march from one galaxy to another, leaving nothing in our wake. And all the universe will tremble."

Cold, unbridled fear gripped Rylack's stomach and twisted. "You can't..." he cried. "She won't..."

"She will," said the figure. "Just as you did. She will not be able to resist."

"Someone will stop you," spat Rylack.

"Nothing can stop us," said the figure. "Not a weapon, not an army... and certainly not you."

With that, Rylack felt the cold razors return as they dug deep into his muscles, but this time, they hooked themselves into him, and he felt them tug at him violently. He writhed in pain, screamed in protest, but it was no use.

A wave of icy cold washed over him, and he could feel the very essence of his being as it was ripped from his body, as his very soul was torn from him.

And the last thing he heard before he died was the booming laughter of the voice from the darkness.

CHAPTER ✺ 10

A teapot whistled, steam erupting from its spout. Shepherd lifted it off the burner and poured the boiling water into a mug with the friendly words "World's Greatest Dad" printed on it. He never felt right being referred to as a father, since he had no real children of his own. But Anna had insisted when she had given it to him that it was strictly for the sake of their cover.

He took out a small bag of black tea and began to steep it in the hot water, spilling a little on the bright gold granite countertops of the kitchen. He chalked it up to just more mess he'd have to clean after tackling the pile of dishes in the sink from his failed attempt at making an edible broccoli and cheese casserole. Shepherd was a man of many skills, but cooking was not one of them. Even the Professor politely passed on the meal, and he would eat practically anything.

Because of that, it was probably for the best Anna had not come down for dinner. Shepherd even went so far as to take a plate up to her, but she had refused to answer the door. It wouldn't be the first time she'd ignored him when she was upset, which seemed to happen more and more lately. Because of the questionable quality of the food, he did not press the matter and decided to let her sulk uninterrupted.

Shepherd sipped his tea and looked thoughtfully out the window behind the sink, gazing off into the night. *Perhaps I am being too hard on her,* he thought. She was, after all, no older than any of the other children that he taught in class, and they were always up to far worse than simply wanting to go to a dance. He began to think about all she'd been through, and all she'd yet go through, and he felt the piercing pang of guilt gnaw at his stomach.

When did I become such a grumpy old man? he wondered. He hadn't always been this way. There was a time when he had been carefree, when he had been rebellious, when he had known what it was like to have fun. For some reason his mind wandered to his student Jack Finnegan and to the realization that the boy reminded him much of himself back in his youth.

But that had been long ago, before the war. Its tragedies had made him grow up fast, and he was afraid Anna would have to do so even faster.

At least he'd had his time. He had known what it was like to be free from responsibility, to laugh and play, and not to worry about tomorrow. Anna, however, had been shouldered with the harsh burden of responsibility almost since the day she was born. And even if there had been hope that she would have a chance to live a somewhat "normal" life, it had been destroyed long ago, along with so much else.

Still, that would be all the more reason to let her have one day, wouldn't it? A day when she could just be a kid, a day to have fun and forget about the horrors she would have to face after it was time to leave this planet?

Then again, to allow Anna to escape from the reality of her situation for such a short time only to drag her back into it might be crueler still. It was one thing not to know what she was missing. It was another all together to let her taste what freedom was like and then to yank it away from her.

Shepherd sighed and ground his teeth. *When did this become so complicated,* he wondered. His job should be simple. All he had ever been required to do was to make sure no harm came to the Princess. That meant keeping her away from danger and killing anything that tried to harm her. That's what he'd been doing for years, and it had always worked. But more and more lately, he'd felt Anna resenting his protection, insisting it was becoming *over-protective* to the point of being unbearable.

It certainly didn't help things now that she was surrounded by beings her own age and who so closely resembled her own kind. In fact, he was surprised it had taken this long before she had given into the urge to start socializing with them.

Shepherd had known that it would be an issue the minute Anna suggested infiltrating Earth society. The original plan of rushing in and accessing the temple wasn't as easy as anyone had thought. Anna should have been able to unlock the Ancient technology rather quickly, but after many failed attempts, she had become convinced the secret to doing so lay with the Earthlings. After all, there had to be a connection between the two, didn't there? Looking back, he should have insisted on calling in the dig team immediately, saving themselves months of pointless research. But he was not in the habit of countermanding orders from his Princess when it came to matters of Ancient technology.

Despite it all, though, keeping her insulated was the safest course of action. But Shepherd struggled with the reason behind doing so. Was he really doing it to protect her? Or had he fallen prey to the trap of trying to keep her from growing up? In his mind, she was still the scared little girl he'd held in his arms while death and destruction erupted around them so many years ago — the same little pigtailed girl clutching a ragged Yuppi doll while everything she'd ever loved had been savagely ripped away from her in a single day.

However, the Professor's words were truer than he cared to admit. She was, in fact, a teenager. She was beginning to mature, and she was growing into her royal birthright as perfectly as anyone could expect. Soon, she would be old enough to claim her rightful seat of power in the Empire her ancestors had forged. But it still nagged at Shepherd that her childhood had been squandered, and he may have stolen her one chance to experience it before it was too late.

He took another sip of his tea and made up his mind. He'd allow her to attend the dance. This would, of course, mean he'd have to approach Principal Montgomery about being a chaperone at the function – a fact with which Anna would no doubt be less than thrilled. But there was only so much ground he'd be willing to cede for the sake of her excursion into teenagery. There would no doubt be temptations at the dance, which he'd have to prepare for. Things like alcohol, drugs, and, of course, the worst vice of them all – boys.

The question of with whom she'd be attending the dance suddenly leapt into his mind. No doubt she'd brought up the notion of going to Homecoming because there was someone she wanted to go *with*. He'd have to find out whom and quickly set the boy to rights about how he'd have to behave around her royal highness – if he wanted continued use of his limbs, that is.

A myriad of different and varied scenarios of intimidation played out in Shepherd's mind for Anna's yet-to-be-revealed date when Professor Green came bursting into the kitchen, clutching the boxy subspace communicator to his chest, his eyes wild and frightful.

"Oh, dear," he muttered. "Oh dear oh dear oh dear…"

Shepherd put down his tea, instantly alarmed. "Professor?" he said.

Green swept his hand across the kitchen table, knocking off the homey little knickknacks meant to make the house look as normal as possible, and plopped down the shiny box he'd been fiddling with all day.

"We, uh… have a problem," said Green.

"What?" demanded Shepherd.

"I was able to finally isolate whatever was interfering with our subspace pocket channel," said Green. "It's a very strong sequence of multi-dimensional frequencies that are being broadcast into subspace, effectively scrambling any communication being sent through there."

"I thought it was impossible to jam a subspace frequency," said Shepherd.

"Correct," said Green. "It is impossible to block information from being transmitted and received through subspace channels. However, we're not being jammed. We're being overrun. So much noise is being broadcast into our designated subspace pocket at so many different frequencies, any message meant for us is getting lost in the clutter."

"So our communications are cut off?" asked Shepherd. This was indeed a problem.

"Well, no," said Green as he quickly plugged in a small data tablet into the communicator. "I was able to create an algorithm which separates much of the noise from our assigned frequency with the fleet. It's crude, but… it works."

"Then what's the problem?" asked Shepherd.

"This," said Green, as he hit a button on his data tablet.

The air above the communicator box began to shimmer and a holographic image of a tall, thin man wearing the proud crimson uniform of a Regalus Prime space officer came into focus. Small details of his environment were transmitted, as well – the familiar bridge of the starship *Protector* among them. However, along with that were the sparks of damage and the smoke of fire. Figures scrambled around behind him, frantically trying to control the chaos.

"Emergency Alert," the man said. "Shepherd, do you read? Please respond!"

"Rylack," Shepherd muttered under his breath, the cold hand of worry beginning to tickle his throat.

"We've been attacked," Captain Rylack went on, his image flickering in and out of alignment. "They came... <snick> of nowhere... <snick><snick>... ambush..."

Green furiously tapped on his data tablet, trying to clear the signal.

"The *Yellowtail*, *Guardian*, and *Javelin* have all been destroyed..." the Captain went on. "We are being boarded. Don't know how long we can hold out. Evacuate the planet immediately! Repeat, evacuate immed—"

Then, a fireball erupted. There was the sound of screams as dark shadows swept into the room. Captain Rylack turned, right before disappearing in a flash of purple light, and then the transmission went dead.

For a moment, Green and Shepherd were both silent, the gravity of what they had just seen settling in.

"Four warships... the best of the fleet... destroyed without warning." muttered Green. "How is that possible?"

Shepherd's mind raced. It didn't make sense. There was no way anything could have snuck up on the fleet so completely as to have caught them unaware, not with all the precautions they had taken. There were sensor arrays spread throughout the entire planetary system to ensure they would see any danger coming from light-years away.

Shepherd turned and marched into the dining room. Against the wall was a very nice mahogany cabinet housing all types of fine dinnerware. With a wave of his arm, the cabinet shimmered, and with a ripple, its holographic camouflage dissipated to reveal a large screen, housed in a bright, shining metal casing with three access terminals mounted in it – a typical configuration for a standard sensor console.

Shepherd ran a quick scan of Earth's planetary system, but all results came back empty. According to their long-range sensor array, there were no hostiles anywhere in the vicinity.

"The sensors would have alerted us of any unknown activity within the system," Green said, standing in the doorway to the kitchen. "Maybe the threat has passed? A fluke encounter?"

"Professor," said Shepherd, "You said the subspace interference was multi-dimensional?"

"Yes," blinked Green.

"Is it possible the same signal is being used to fool our detection systems?" Shepherd asked.

Green looked thoughtful. "Oh, dear," he said.

Green rushed up to a second access panel on the sensor console before them and began to enter his detection algorithm. Suddenly, the large empty screen flickered and red dots began to litter the system. A tiny alarm sounded, signaling the detection of multiple enemy energy signatures.

"Great Scott!" exclaimed Green breathlessly.

Shepherd could feel his heart skip a beat. Not only were there more energy signatures than he could count, they were already beginning to encircle the planet, which could only mean one thing.

"*Planetkillers*," he snarled.

"But... but how?" stammered Green. "How did they find us?"

"We'll figure that out later," said Shepherd urgently. "Get ready to head to the emergency shuttle. I'll get the Princess. With any luck, we still have time to escape."

Without a moment to lose, Shepherd sprinted up the stairs to Anna's room. His mind was racing. All of the Empire's high-level military communications were based around creating secure pockets within the subspace dimension that would not only allow instantaneous communication over vast distances but also could prevent the enemy from intercepting or interfering with it. If their foe had somehow figured out a way not only to corrupt their transmissions but also to render subspace useless, nowhere would be safe.

He reached the door to Anna's room and pounded on it.

"Princess!" he yelled. Without waiting, he tried to open the door but found it locked. He pounded again. "Princess, open the door! We must evacuate!"

No answer. Without hesitation, Shepherd rammed his shoulder into the door, forcing it to fly open.

He looked around. The room was empty. For a split second, he was afraid that somehow the Princess had already been kidnapped, killed, or worse. But then he noticed the sheets tied to the post of the bed, leading out an open window.

He rushed to it and looked outside. The makeshift rope made it almost all the way down to the ground. It would appear that Anna had successfully snuck out without him noticing.

Shepherd's stomach felt like it dropped out of him, and he cursed himself for becoming complacent. He had allowed the relative peacefulness of the planet to fool him into relaxing his guard, and that had given the Princess enough opportunity to take advantage of it.

Now she was out there. Alone. Unprotected.

And the full might of the deadliest army the universe had ever known was about to descend upon her.

CHAPTER ✺ 11

Not far off State Route 380 was a homey greasy-spoon diner called "Emma Jean's Burger Shack." It was an old gas station situated in the middle of a large, empty, gravel-filled lot with a tall, well-lit sign that was a 24-hour beacon to all manner of night owls, late-shifters, and truckers on their way to the main freeway.

Long ago, the gas pumps had been closed down, but the food was still flowing. Emma Jean's liked to boast "The Best Hamburgers In River Heights," but they served everything from scrambled eggs to New York strip steak, and they did so at all hours.

Jack actually liked the food better at the Fox Hole Diner where his mom worked. Indeed, the Fox Hole did have better food, but it was all the way out by the freeway – which meant more customers and therefore more tips for his mom. But Emma Jean's was closer, and he wouldn't think of trying to make Anna walk all the way to the Fox Hole with him. Not to mention that the last thing he wanted was his mom spying on him and his date.

The idea that he was actually *on* a date with the most beautiful girl in school still amazed him. Jack was sure a huge, stupid grin was still plastered on his face as he watched Anna noisily slurp up the last of her third chocolate milkshake of the evening.

"Dang," teased Jack. "If I didn't know better, I'd think you've never had a milkshake before."

In all actuality, Anna *had* never had a milkshake before, since cows (and therefore their milk) were rather unique to Earth, and she found she quite enjoyed it. But of course, how was Jack to know that? She covered her mouth shyly, as though to hide her sudden bout of gluttony.

"I, um… don't get to indulge much," she said diplomatically.

"I can imagine," said Jack. "Your dad's strict enough at school. I don't even want to think about what he's like at home."

Anna nodded. "He can be… difficult sometimes."

"Understate much?" joked Jack.

Anna smiled. "He means well. Besides, he tends to be toughest on the people he cares for the most."

"Then he must *really* care for me!" said Jack.

Anna chuckled. "Well, then there are the people he just doesn't like."

Jack and Anna both laughed.

"Tell me about it," said Jack. "Sometimes I think your dad really has it out for me."

"Yeah, you think he's bad now? Can you imagine what he'd do if he found out I snuck out to see you?" she said.

Jack suddenly stopped laughing.

"Um… he doesn't know you're gone?" he said.

Anna caught herself. "Oh," she said. "Is that a problem?"

"Pft! No. Of course not!" lied Jack. "I think it's awesome. Otherwise, you wouldn't be here with me, right?"

"That's right," sang Anna.

Images of Mr. Shepherd ripping out Jack's lungs and gazing into his gaping chest wound flooded into his mind.

"So!" said Anna cheerily. "What do you want to do now?"

Get you home before your dad tracks me down and kills me, thought Jack. It would figure Mr. Shepherd would find some way to ruin his night, even if he were nowhere in sight. Thus was the scope of that man's fearsome power. Of course, there was always the chance that he didn't know Anna was gone, but Jack didn't count on being that lucky.

"Hmmmm..." said Jack, glancing at his watch. "Maybe we should be getting home. It's kinda late and we've got school tomorrow."

Anna looked a little disappointed. It was obvious she was having fun. Indeed, since the moment she'd shown up at his place, the entire night had flown by. They'd laughed and joked, and Jack had shared all types of stories about the kids at school that Anna couldn't seem to get enough of. Jack didn't want it to end either, but he also didn't want to incur the wrath of Mr. Shepherd, especially now that the two of them seemed to have reached a type of understanding.

"But, we could do something tomorrow," suggested Jack. "I mean, I've got detention and all, but we could do something afterward."

"I'm... not sure I'll be able to get away again," said Anna sadly. "This was kind of a one-time thing."

Jack and Anna looked at each other. Jack crumpled his face like one does just before doing something that's going to hurt, like ripping off a Band-Aid. But if this was his chance, he wasn't going to let fear spoil it.

"Screw it," said Jack. "Let's go catch the midnight show over at the drive-in."

Anna looked at him quizzically. "The what?" she asked.

"The Cedar Point Drive-In," said Jack. "I think they're playing some horror movie from the 70's or something tonight, but it could be fun."

"A movie?" said Anna excitedly. "But don't you need a car to go to a drive-in?"

"Nah," said Jack, waving away the question like it was an annoying fly. "There's this hill that overlooks the place. It's kinda far away, but you can still see the screen. They've got this radio station you can tune to so you can listen in your car, but I've got a boom box that works just as well."

"Hmmm. Sitting on a grassy hill, under the stars, at night, snuggled up and watching a movie..." said Anna playfully. "Sounds kind of... romantic, doesn't it?"

Jack was sure his face chose that exact moment to turn bright red.

"Oh... well, uh... I wasn't thinking... I mean, um... I guess you could... uh..." he stammered. For some reason, his discomfort made Anna smile.

"Sounds good to me," she said.

Jack's heart began racing. Did the girl of his dreams really just agree to a romantic starlit night on a hill... *with him*?

What are you waiting for, you fool? thought Jack. *Let's get out of here!!!*

Without wasting another moment, Jack snatched up the check their waitress had left after delivering Anna's last milkshake.

"I'm, uh... gonna pay for this," said Jack.

"Don't be too long," Anna smiled, with a hint of playfulness to her voice. "We wouldn't want to miss the movie."

Jack giggled (rather stupidly, he thought) and leapt up from their booth. "Don't go anywhere," he said. "I'll be right back..."

Jack left Anna and walked up to the cash register at the counter. Unfortunately, there were two other people waiting in line to pay their bills. Jack twitched anxiously, wondering what the night had in store for him.

Will I get to kiss her? he thought nervously. *I've never kissed a girl before. How do you do it? It can't be that hard. Everyone does it, right? I wonder if she's kissed anyone before. What am I thinking? Look at her! Of course she has. Probably some dude who was way better at it than me. No, don't think like that. This is your night, Jack! YOUR NIGHT! She's into you! It's obvious. You're the man! Nothing is going to stop you now! Not Mr. Shepherd, not J.C. Rowdey, not some freak act of God – NOTHING!!!*

Nothing, that is, except maybe the line to pay. Of course, the universe decided now would be the right time to make the slowest line ever, in the history of lines, appear at the Burger Shack. As some old lady was squabbling with the waitress at the register over an item on her check, Jack looked up behind the counter at the old TV mounted on the wall. It was tuned to some lame news channel. He didn't know what kind of weird "UFO" story the anchorman was going on about in closed-captions, but it was something to take his mind off the wait.

Then, the picture on the TV began to go wavy and give way to salt-and-pepper static. Even the cheesy soft-rock music that had been playing over the diner's speaker system disintegrated into a dead-air hiss.

Suddenly, Jack felt something – a slight vibration, beneath his feet. That vibration turned into a low rumble, and all the plates and silverware in the diner began to clatter.

The patrons all looked around, some of them voicing concern about what was happening. Jack heard someone mention "earthquake," but that didn't make any sense. They were in Ohio. Ohio never had earthquakes... did it?

Then, the shrill scream of an extremely powerful engine rang out from overhead.

The windows all around began to rattle from the force of whatever had flown by. It felt like a fighter jet had just buzzed the top of the Burger Shack. Then it happened again, and a third time.

Jack saw Anna shoot to her feet, her eyes wide. The people around him were rushing to the windows, curious about the noises, but Jack went to Anna's side.

"Hey, relax," said Jack, putting his arm around Anna comfortingly. "It's probably just some military jets doing an exercise. Wright Patterson Air Force Base isn't too far away."

"Right, the Air Force..." she said. "Do their jets always sound like that?"

Jack shrugged. "I dunno," he said. "But what else would it be?"

Anna was tense and looked incredibly frightened. Jack thought it was odd she should be so freaked out. He actually thought the whole thing was kind of cool. Nothing exciting ever happened in River Heights, and it gave him the perfect opportunity to show Anna how brave he could be.

"Hey, maybe your dad found out you were missing and sent the military to track you down," he joked. "If anyone should be scared, it's me, right?"

Unfortunately, Anna didn't respond to his attempt at levity. She still looked worried. Jack tossed some money on the table along with the check. It would mean not getting any much needed change back, but Jack was anxious to get to his romantic rendezvous on the hill.

"C'mon," he said, taking her hand. "Let's get outta here."

Jack made a move to leave, but Anna wasn't following. He looked at her as she stood, unsure, as if she were stuck on some test question in school.

"It would have alerted me if anything were wrong..." she mumbled.

"Hey," said Jack concerned. "Are you okay?"

Anna looked at him, as though she had just realized he was there. "Um... just give me one second, okay?" she said.

Jack backed off. "Yeah... sure."

Anna dug into the front pocket of her jeans and pulled out a small, thin, metal pad. It almost looked like a cell phone, but it was a little too big and flat to be one. Jack glanced at it out of curiosity as Anna ran her finger along its screen. Some strange lettering flashed on it for a moment and then disappeared. Anna looked relieved.

"Hey, what is that thing?" asked Jack.

Anna smiled at him. "Nothing," she said, putting whatever it was back in her pocket. "Let's go."

She took him by the hand and began to head toward the exit. Jack was still curious, but he wasn't going to press the subject. He was holding hands with the girl of his dreams, getting ready to go to a romantic encounter on a hill, and at that moment, that was all he cared about.

Before they reached the exit, however, there was a crackle in the air, almost like the sound of static electricity. Suddenly, there was a blinding flash of purple light, and tendrils of purple energy snap-crackled-and-snaked across the diner.

Everyone in the joint stopped and turned to the source of the flash, including Jack and Anna.

There, in the middle of the diner, stood two people who had not been there a moment ago. In fact, to call them "people" wasn't really accurate. They resembled people in the sense they had a head, two arms, and two legs – but they were also tall, dark, and imposing figures, clad head-to-toe in armor so black, they almost seemed like they were shapes cut out of the fabric of reality itself. The only things exposed were their eyes, which burned hot and fiery red. The rest of their faces were hidden behind an angular helmet, which looked like something one would find in a torture chamber from the Middle Ages.

Their long arms were lithe and muscular – obvious even under the armor – and their hands had talons instead of fingers, which seemed razor-sharp enough to slice through anything – anything, that is, except the long, slender, black rifles they were holding, which looked like they were made from obsidian rock rather than any type of metal.

Everyone in the diner was frozen, staring in shock at the visitors who had just arrived out of thin air. One of them held up a small tablet, made from the same black material as their guns. He held it out and slowly swept it across the room as it made a high pitched beeping sound.

He passed it by the shocked waitress at the counter.

BEEP.

He passed it by a family, frozen in their booth near the exit.

BEEP BEEP.

Finally, his hand came to Anna, standing back by the door with Jack.

BEEP BEEP BEEP BEEEEEEEEEEP…

The four fiery red eyes of the shadow men focused on her.

The one with the tablet barked something in a voice that sounded like a gong shattering – deep and dark and guttural.

The other one raised its rifle and aimed it at Anna.

"Get DOWN!" she yelled.

Before Jack could react, Anna pushed him away and dove in the opposite direction just as the taloned finger squeezed the trigger. A ball of purple light shot from the rifle and barreled toward the spot where Anna had been not a moment before.

It hit the door to the diner, and in a flash, the door was no longer there.

The blast from the rifle sent the diner into a furor as the shock of the shadowy strangers wore off and unbridled panic set in. Women began to scream, and people began to scuttle about, looking for cover or an exit – whichever was more readily available.

Before Jack knew it, Anna was back on her feet and out the door. He didn't wait around either. He got up and quickly followed, narrowly dodging yet another ball of purple light that hit the ground and took a chunk of the floor with it. For some reason, these jerks were intent on shooting his girl, and he didn't like that one bit.

He glanced behind him as he ran and saw the two armored things emerge from the diner and take aim at Anna again. With a burst of speed, he sprinted for her.

"Look out!" Jack yelled as he grabbed Anna and pulled her behind a parked Buick LeSabre in the diner's lot.

Not a moment too soon either, as two more volleys of purple light whizzed by.

"Holy crap!" said Jack. "Why are those things trying to kill you?"

"They're not. They're Dark Soldiers, and they're trying to capture me," said Anna as she struggled back to her feet.

Jack grabbed hold of her. "Wait – what?"

"Let go," hissed Anna. "Save yourself!"

Anna wrenched herself away from Jack and began to run for the cover of a big-rig truck parked close by. Jack glanced over the hood of the car he was hiding behind and saw the two Dark Soldiers marching toward him.

Suddenly, the ground was vibrating again, and above him Jack could make out a twisted black thing in the night sky as it shrieked by. It moved overhead fast, but just as it passed, there were more flashes of purple, all over the parking lot, as more of the Dark Soldiers appeared.

Something clicked in the back of Jack's brain, and suddenly all that time playing *Arena Deathmatch* actually paid off. He recognized the positions of the soldiers – they were surrounding them and marching in toward their prey, pulling the net tighter until they captured their target…

Anna.

She was halfway to the cover of the truck, but she was playing right into their trap. Jack could see it. All they needed was to teleport in a few more soldiers at the edge of the parking lot behind the truck, and she'd be trapped.

Immediately he was on his feet and sprinting toward her. He hoped whoever these alien things were, they wouldn't bother paying any attention to him while Anna was still in play… at least until he could reach her.

More volleys of purple light shot by. He dodged them, but just barely. They weren't really aimed at him, though; they were directed at Anna, and luckily she was able to evade them as well.

Jack finally caught up with her and grabbed her by the arm.

"Quick!" he said. "Follow me!"

She wrenched her arm away from him. "Jack, get out of here!"

"They're trying to trap you!" he insisted. "More are showing up, cutting off your escape. We need to head into the fields – now!"

He grabbed her arm again, not waiting for an answer. This time, though, she followed as they turned and made for the relative safety of the nearby cornfields.

More balls of purple light whizzed by. Jack and Anna ducked and weaved to avoid them, but they were starting to get annoyingly close.

Lucky these guys are bad shots, thought Jack.

A cold thought suddenly gripped the back of Jack's mind. These guys *were* bad shots, weren't they? Or were they missing intentionally? He guessed it was possible that a race of shadow soldiers with the ability to appear out of thin air and shoot balls of purple energy were naturally bad at aiming at stuff. For some reason, Jack didn't believe he was that lucky.

If that were the case, why were they missing? They had surrounded most of the area and were closing in to trap Anna, but why didn't they have people out by the cornfield already?

Then, Jack remembered how more bad guys had appeared after that thing had flown by overhead, and he thought about how he'd heard three screeches before while in the diner...

Oh, crap... he thought.

Jack abruptly stopped running, jerking Anna to a halt with him. She looked at him like he was crazy.

"Jack, what are you doing?" she shrieked.

"They *want* us to go into the cornfields," said Jack. "They sent two into the diner to flush us out, then more to cut off all other escape and herd us into the fields where they have others waiting."

Anna's eyes grew wide. "The other shards," she gasped. "They were hiding more of them for an ambush..."

Jack could only imagine that the "shards" she spoke of were those things that flew by overhead.

"But why?" wondered Jack aloud. "Why this elaborate trap?"

"They didn't know what kind of resistance they'd be facing," said Anna grimly.

Jack's brain was starting to hurt. He had no idea what was going on and how Anna was involved, but he knew things were not good. He glanced behind him and saw the aliens (or whatever they were) forming up into a line and marching toward them.

"How'd they find you?" he asked.

"What?" Anna replied.

"You said you snuck out," said Jack. "Nobody could have known you were here. How did they?"

A sudden realization washed over Anna. She quickly dug into her pocket and pulled out the small metal tablet she'd used earlier.

"My data tablet," she said. "They're tracking its energy signature!"

Jack didn't know what any of that meant, but he got the gist of it – they were following the cell-phone-thingy. He snatched it away from her.

"As soon as we get into the cornfield, you peel off. I'll draw them away," he said.

"No!" cried Anna. "I can't let you!"

"I'm faster than you," insisted Jack. "I can outrun them!"

Anna gazed into Jack's eyes. He could tell she wanted to object, but she could tell it would do no good.

"If you get away," she said. "Meet me at the school... by the bleachers, where we talked earlier today."

Jack nodded. He was about to start running again when Anna grabbed him and gave him a quick kiss on the cheek.

"Good luck," she said.

Jack had to admit, despite being in the middle of an alien ambush, that kiss made him feel pretty darn good. Of course, the moment was ruined by another volley of purple orbs from the approaching army of death.

Jack and Anna quickly ducked as the orbs shot by them, and with one last look at each other, they dashed into the cornfield.

CHAPTER ✺ 12

ack's legs were racing as fast as his mind was as he sprinted up Detroit Street. A million and one questions assaulted his brain – who were these armored alien dudes? Where did they come from? Were they really invading Earth? What did they want with Anna? Did they intend to enslave humanity, starting with the hottest chicks first?

More of those "shard" thingies shrieked across the sky. They seemed to be making passes every couple of minutes. Jack could see the school in the distance, lit by the streetlights from the town center.

Jack considered himself fortunate since he had been able to make it out of the cornfield by the Burger Shack. Though those black armored aliens looked scary enough, they didn't seem all that bright. When Anna and he had separated in the cornfield, he'd done his best to lead them away from her. This meant sprinting through the high stalks of corn and zigzagging his way through the field. He was able to sense that the aliens were following him because they barreled through the corn, stomping it down in their pursuit – that, and their annoying habit of shooting those purple energy balls constantly. (Jack was sure old Mr. Warner wasn't going to be too happy to see half of his last crop of the season vaporized by marauding aliens.) This gave Jack a pretty clear picture of where they were and, more importantly, how to avoid them.

That was, of course, until those ships in the sky started teleporting more guys in. Jack was getting tired and running out of places to hide, so he chucked the data tablet as far as he could and took off in the direction of Detroit Street, leaving his pursuers to follow the thing's "energy signature" instead of him.

Years of playing in the fields with his friends gave him the distinct advantage of knowing the terrain. Jack knew every shortcut, every gopher hole, and every hiding spot between Eagle Hill and the town square, which made avoiding the aliens a relatively easy task.

His real concern was for Anna. Had she made it past them? She didn't know the area as well as Jack did, and he was worried splitting up might have been a mistake. It seemed like a good idea at the time, but what if Anna didn't make it back to the school? What would he do then?

Jack's legs were burning as he jogged onto school grounds. He heard the squeal of tires and saw a few cars loaded up with luggage peel down the street. No doubt people were either evacuating or hiding. The town seemed completely deserted.

He finally got to the bleachers where he'd talked with Anna earlier in the day. His heart sank when she was nowhere to be seen. He doubled over, grabbing his splitting side and tried to catch his breath. He was sweating and felt pretty gross. He gave himself a moment to calm down in the cool night air before calling out.

"Anna?" he hollered. "Anna? You here?"

For a moment, there was nothing. Then came a voice.

"Jack?"

Jack turned toward the cornfield about ten feet away. Something was rustling through it, and Anna emerged. Jack breathed a sigh of relief. She'd made it!

Anna came running up and threw her arms around him. Jack wasn't expecting such a greeting, but he was glad for it, nonetheless.

"I can't believe you made it past them," she said, holding him tight. "I was sure they'd get you."

"Yeah, well, all those months of chasing after the bus have made me one lean, mean, running machine," he joked. "Besides, those alien guys aren't exactly the coldest drinks in the fridge, if you know what I mean."

Anna gave him a look that clearly proved she didn't.

"You know, they don't seem that smart," Jack clarified.

"They're not," said Anna. "They're just foot soldiers. They do only what they're told. They might not be smart, but they're tough, relentless, and deadly. I don't doubt if they weren't ordered to capture me this entire town would be dead by now."

"About that…" said Jack. "You gonna tell me what's going on here? How do you know so much about these guys? Why do they want you?"

Anna released her hold on Jack and pulled away from him, frowning.

"There's… there's a lot you don't know about me, Jack," she said.

"So fill me in," he said.

Anna bit her lower lip and looked like she was going to say something when another familiar voice rang out.

"Princess!"

Jack and Anna turned to see Professor Green running up toward them, waving his hand and smiling.

"Professor!" exclaimed Anna. She ran toward him and gave him an even bigger hug than she'd given Jack.

"Oh, thank the Ancients!" said Professor Green. "We were so worried!"

"I'm sorry," said Anna. "I didn't know."

"No way you could have, child," responded Green.

Jack had known that Professor Green and Mr. Shepherd were supposedly friends, but he had never known how close he and Anna were. They seemed quite friendly with each other. Despite the fact that it was just goofy Professor Green, Jack couldn't help but feel a little resentful. After all, hadn't he just risked life-and-limb to help Anna escape an alien ambush? Sure, the hug was nice, but the image of that romantic night on the hill above the drive-in haunted him. Just his luck that tonight would be the night aliens would choose to invade Earth.

Anna pulled away from Green. "Where's Shepherd?" she asked.

"He's on his way," said Green. "He had me wait here in case you showed up and then went out searching for you. I contacted him as soon as I saw you come out of the cornfield."

"He's going to want to evacuate," she said.

"They've got the planet surrounded," Green said sadly. "It's only a matter of time, I'm afraid."

Anna looked worried. "We can't leave, not yet. We cannot allow the temple to be destroyed."

"I fear we may not have a choice," responded Green.

"Did you complete that analysis program?" asked Anna. "The one you were working on to help me navigate the interface?"

"Why, yes, as a matter of fact—" Green started to say before catching himself. "Oh dear, you're not suggesting…"

"I am confident with your help, I can unlock the temple," said Anna.

"But, Your Majesty…"

"Professor," said Anna sternly, "We cannot leave what could be the key to ending this war behind. We *must* unlock the temple, and we *must* do it now."

"Uh… what war?" asked Jack.

Green and Anna turned to him. The Professor lit up, as if noticing for the first time Jack was there.

"Jack, my boy!" the Professor exclaimed. "What are you doing here?"

"He's the one who…" Anna looked like she was about to say *I snuck out to see*, but instead she said "saved me from being captured."

"Really!" said Green, giving Jack the thumbs up. "Good work, lad! I always knew you had it in you!"

Jack gave Green a strange look, which he directed toward Anna, as well.

"Is *someone* going to tell me what's going on here?" asked Jack, exasperated. "What temple? Why's he calling you 'your majesty?' And what, in the history of Physics class, ever made you think I had it in me to escape an alien ambush???"

Before either Green or Anna could respond, Jack heard the squeal of tires. The group turned to see a car skidding from a turn onto Detroit Street and accelerate up to the school, scraping the curb as it hurtled onto school grounds and tore right toward them.

"Great," said Jack. "What now?"

The car rumbled to a halt about ten feet away from them, and Shepherd got out. He did not look happy as he marched toward the group.

"We're leaving," he said in a tone that brokered no argument. "Now."

Anna pulled away from Green and looked at Shepherd defiantly.

"No," she said.

Shepherd stopped and for a second looked as though her answer surprised him. Then his steely cold gaze returned.

"In the car," he said. "We're heading to the shuttle."

"We're going to the temple," said Anna. "That's an order."

Jack's eyes grew wide as he saw Shepherd bristle. Did Anna really just tell off her dad? Jack suddenly felt like he was near a bomb that was about to explode.

"We are going to get off this planet and to somewhere safe if I have to drag you there kicking and screaming," insisted Shepherd.

"Off planet?" piped up Jack. "You guys can, like, *leave* the planet?"

Shepherd looked at Jack like he were a piece of gum stuck to his shoe. "Go home, Jack," he said, without a hint of interest in why Jack was there in the first place.

"Um, aliens are invading," said Jack. "I don't think my trailer is the safest place to be right now."

"No place is safe," interjected Anna. "Which is why we must retrieve the Ancient artifact *right now.*"

"You can't unlock the temple," said Shepherd.

"I believe I can," said Anna.

"Would someone *please* tell me what's going on?" pleaded Jack.

"Princess," said Shepherd, completely ignoring Jack, "The minute we enter the portgate, we will be signaling to the Deathlords exactly where we are and that there is Ancient technology on this planet. They will zero in on our location, break through, and throw everything they have at us."

"Whoa, waitaminute..." said Jack. "They're called *DEATHLORDS?*"

"I will not abandon the key to the universe's survival to the Deathlords," said Anna stubbornly. "Our only hope is to access it before they can get to us."

"The risk to your safety is too great," insisted Shepherd.

"*Deathlords?*" repeated Jack.

"This is not a debate, Paragon," said Anna.

"You're right," replied Shepherd. "It's not."

With that, Shepherd grabbed Anna, lifting her up effortlessly and slinging her over his shoulder like a sack of potatoes. Anna squealed in protest, indignant, demanding Shepherd put her down. Shepherd ignored her and turned to Professor Green.

"Professor," he said, "I recommend you come with us."

"Shepherd!" screamed Anna. "Release me! That is an order!"

Green hesitated. "If I may be so bold, good Paragon, but... we have no idea what the temple is housing. If it is the weapon of the Ancients, abandoning it to the Deathlords could be disastrous..."

"Then stay if you wish," said Shepherd coldly. "I am getting Her Royal Highness off this planet."

Shepherd turned on his heel and began marching to the car. Professor Green hesitated, and then sheepishly began to follow. Jack watched dumbfounded, until Anna looked up and caught his eye as she was being carried away.

"Jack!" she screamed. "Help me!"

Jack was more confused than ever. Aliens were attacking, the girl of his dreams – who it sounds like might just be actual royalty - was being carried away, and it appeared as though Mr. Shepherd had access to some sort of spaceship.

But by the look on Anna's face, it was clear she did not want to go. And for the life of him, Jack did not want her to either.

Suddenly, he found himself running around Shepherd and blocking his way.

"Wait! Mr. Shepherd, wait!" said Jack, holding up his hands as if that were enough to stop the six-foot-three grown man before him.

"Move, Jack," said Shepherd sternly — so much so that Jack was almost scared not to obey.

"Look," replied Jack, "far be it from me to tell you how to handle your own daughter, but... uh... this artifact thing, in the temple place... it sounds kind of important."

Shepherd glared at Jack, his face hard as a rock... but it was his eyes Jack noticed. There was a hint of sadness in them, and for some reason, that intimidated Jack more than any stare he had ever received from the man.

"I'm sorry, son," said Shepherd. And with that, he stepped to the side of Jack and tried to walk past him. Anna kicked and pounded on the man's back, demanding he let her go. Jack hopped in front of him again.

"No, Mr. Shepherd, just wait—"

This time, Shepherd did not stop. Instead, his hand reached out, grabbed Jack firmly by the shoulder, and tossed him aside like he were a rag doll.

Jack hit the ground. He looked up at Shepherd as he was walking away, incredulously. *Oh no he didn't...* thought Jack angrily. Taking away Anna, being an all around thorn in his side, AND manhandling him was just too much for Jack to take. Giving into his anger, Jack got to his feet and SPRINTED toward the man. He dropped low, and aimed for Shepherd's knees.

He hit Shepherd from behind and could feel the man's legs buckle as he brought Shepherd and Anna to the ground.

The fall had done the trick – Shepherd was distracted long enough for Anna to wriggle free. Before Shepherd could grab her again, she was off, running for the cornfield.

"Green!" snarled Shepherd, "Get her!"

"Oh, dear," said Green as he took off after Anna. Shepherd reached over and grabbed Jack by the neck. His grip was vice-like, his thumb digging in hard and pressing on Jack's artery. Jack struggled, but he could not break free of Shepherd's grasp. He was starting to get light-headed.

"You..." growled Shepherd. "Stay out of this."

With that, the man pushed Jack away, releasing his hold. Jack gasped for air. When he next looked up, Shepherd was already to his feet and on Anna's trail. For a moment, Jack thought of obeying the man. But then he thought about all the people in his life who had pushed him around. People like J.C. Rowdey. He thought about earlier that morning when he had gotten hit in the head with a shoe and had lain on the side of the road, defeated. Then, he thought of Anna and of how she needed his help. Jack had no idea what was happening, but he did know this...

He wasn't going to give up.

Jack hopped back to his feet and started running. He heard Shepherd cry out his name as Jack passed him and hit the cornfield, following the path Anna and Green had taken. He shot past Green, whipping a corn stalk in the man's face by accident but slowing him down in the process. Finally, he caught up to Anna, who had stopped in a small circle devoid of any corn.

Jack stopped, catching his breath.

"What are you doing?" he panted. "We gotta keep running."

"No we don't," said Anna, pulling a small device out from the back pocket of her jeans. "We're here."

She immediately began tapping on the rectangular device, as if she were pressing invisible keys. Jack noticed strange symbols that appeared on the smooth stone-like surface of the tablet — but even though it looked like a rock, Anna's finger moved around the symbols like they were floating on water.

"We're in a cornfield, there's no temple around here," said Jack, "and what the heck is that?"

Anna stopped and looked at Jack. She was frowning. "Jack, I'm sorry for involving you in this," she said.

Jack shrugged. "Hey, it's cool," he said. "I mean, it's not your fault aliens want to capture you, right?"

Anna was silent. Just then, Green appeared. "Princess," he said, out of breath as well. "Please..."

"You know this is the right thing to do, Professor," said Anna.

Green nodded. "I know," he said. "Just... promise me when this is over, you'll convince Paragon Shepherd of that as well."

As if on cue, Shepherd broke through the surrounding barrier of corn. He stood before the group, his face stern. Anna and he shared a glare, and she looked back at him as hard as he looked at her.

"Do not activate that," he growled.

Anna straightened, and suddenly Jack noticed a strange change in her. It wasn't anything physical, it was more like a feeling he got. She suddenly became authoritative, powerful... regal. It was obvious Shepherd and Green noticed the change, too.

"All my life, I've shouldered the responsibility of my bloodline," she said. "I have trained. I have studied. I have prepared – all for moments like this. You protect me because I am the heir to the throne of the Galactic Empire and the keeper of the secrets of the Ancients. But what good is that protection if it does not allow me to do what I need to do – what I'm destined to do? I am your Sovereign, Paragon Shepherd, no matter what age I may be. I ask now that you treat me as such, and believe me when I say... I *can* do this."

Shepherd gazed at Anna with a slight look of surprise on his face. It was the first time Jack had ever seen him look uncertain. After a long moment of hesitation, Shepherd's shoulders relaxed and a sigh of resignation followed. He nodded, ever so slightly.

"I am, as always, your loyal servant, Your Majesty," he said softly.

Whatever battle of wills the two had been fighting, it was obvious Shepherd had just surrendered. Anna relaxed as well, and turned to Jack.

"Jack," she said.

"Yeah?"

"Brace yourself."

Anna looked down at the device in her hand and flicked one last symbol into a circular configuration made up of all the others she had positioned on there.

Suddenly, the dirt beneath their feet glowed with a brilliant white light – which strangely did not appear to illuminate anything, as if the light were trapped within the ground.

An audible, vibrating "hum" could be heard and felt, as the light beneath them began to swirl around like a whirlpool.

Then, the whirlpool expanded downward at a frightening speed.

Jack felt as though he were hovering weightless in mid-air for a split second, and then, it happened...

He started to fall.

CHAPTER ✥ 13

Jack was yanked downward violently, as though something had grabbed hold of him and was reeling him in with incredible speed. It felt like his stomach had been ripped from his belly and left far behind him, much like riding a roller coaster, only a thousand times more intense.

His skin tingled like air was blasting into him with hurricane-like fury. However, he did not feel cold, and the wind did not cut into his skin, but it was there nonetheless. Jack tried to open his eyes and focus. All around him he saw bizarre colors and objects flying by with frightening speed, all kept at bay by a swirling spiral of brilliant blue light.

He looked beneath him, his feet flailing as they searched for ground that was not there. Far in the distance below, a burning yellow glow began to form. It was rushing up toward him, a swirling mess of golden magma. The air around him began to shimmer, as though it were on fire, only there was no heat.

Then, Jack plunged through the golden liquid, and just like that, his feet were on solid ground again.

Anna, Green, and Shepherd all stood in the same positions they had been in back in the cornfield. As Jack's brain tried to cope with what had just happened, the world around him began to swirl, and his stomach finally caught up with him. No surprise, it was not very happy when it did.

Dizzy, Jack fell over. He hit the ground, which felt like it was moving at odd angles compared to the rest of his surroundings. A wave of nausea crashed over him.

Don't puke in front of Anna, he thought. *Don't puke in front of Anna, don't puke in front of Anna...*

~ 123 ~

Then, Professor Green was at his side. He took Jack gently by the face to steady him.

"Focus on my eyes, Jack," said Green.

Green's face separated into four fuzzy clones of itself and danced around Jack's field of vision.

"Wha… why'm I…" stammered Jack.

"Don't worry, my boy, it'll pass," Green said. "Your body just isn't used to the portgating process."

As Jack tried to focus on Green's face and clear his head, he began to notice his surroundings. The cornfield had disappeared, replaced by a large cavernous chamber. The walls and ceiling merged into a dome and were alive with liquid gold magma that swirled and danced in a beautiful ballet of chaos. The light from the dome bathed the entire chamber with a yellow-orange hue.

Jack was on a circular platform, the same size as the clearing in the field above, made of a smooth, white metal that pulsed slightly, like a mirror catching sunlight. He turned and saw an ornate stone arch stationed behind the platform, with small crackles of energy dancing around it intermittently.

The platform had steps that led down to a surface consisting of cobbled stone. Two rows of stone columns formed a walkway, which led from the platform toward some type of temple, about a hundred yards away. The temple rose up like a pyramid but flattened out at the top, as if it were unfinished.

Suddenly, Jack realized just how huge the temple was, and the chamber it was housed in was even more massive than he had first noticed — probably bigger than the entire town of River Heights.

"Where are we?" asked Jack, his head clearing with the amazement of his new environment.

"We're in the core of your planet," said Green.

Jack turned and looked at him, eyes wide. "The core? Like, the *Earth's* core? As in the center of the Earth?"

"Exciting, isn't it?" said Green cheerily.

"How... how is this possible?" asked Jack, dumbfounded.

"Well, if you must know—" started Green. But before he could offer any further explanation, Shepherd stepped forward.

"Later," he said in a tone that ended the conversation for good. He reached down and grabbed Jack by the lapel of his jacket and yanked him up to his feet. He turned to Anna.

"Activating the portgate will have alerted the Deathlords to its location," said Shepherd. "They'll be here any second."

Anna nodded. "I'll work fast," she said. She turned to Green. "Professor, I'll need your help."

"Of course," he replied.

With that, Green followed Anna as she began to run toward the temple. Jack was about to go after them when Shepherd's hand clamped down on his shoulder.

"No, you stay with me," he said.

"Why?" asked Jack. "What's going *on* here? What is this place? Who *are* you people?"

"I know you have questions," said Shepherd, his voice deadly serious. "But right now, you need to listen to me very carefully if you want to live."

"Okay..." said Jack, uncertainly.

"Do you know how to handle a gun?" asked Shepherd.

"Um... kinda," replied Jack. "I mean, I've never actually fired a real gun before..."

Shepherd grimaced.

"But, hey!" said Jack. "How hard can it be, right? Just point and shoot. Why? You, uh... got a gun?"

 ~ 125 ~

Shepherd knelt on one knee and put his hand before him, staring at it intensely. Jack raised an eyebrow. *What the heck is he doing now?* Jack wondered.

The air around Shepherd's hand started shimmering, and suddenly, Jack's vision blurred, as if his eyes could no longer focus correctly. Before he knew it, the air around Shepherd's palm seemed to ripple, and a strange looking pistol had appeared from nowhere.

"No way..." said Jack, amazed.

The pistol was, for lack of a better word, awesome. It looked like a nine-millimeter handgun from one of Jack's video games, but the barrel was like a flattened oval, with no opening in the muzzle. Instead, a glowing red line followed the middle of it, from one side to the other. Shepherd got to his feet and shoved the pistol toward Jack.

"Take it," he said.

Jack didn't need to be told twice. He snatched it up and looked at it like he'd just found a million dollars.

"What the heck is this?" he asked.

"Not a toy," said Shepherd dryly. "In a few seconds, some very bad things are going to show up. I'll try to hold them off as long as I can, but if any get past me, I'll need you to shoot them down."

Jack snapped out of the trance the gun in his hand had created and looked at Shepherd with surprise.

"Dude," he said. "Are you asking me to *kill* people?"

"They're not people," said Shepherd. "Now go take cover. No matter what happens, make sure none of them reaches the Princess."

"Right..." said Jack. "And just so I'm clear, are you her dad, or aren't you? Because I'm still not sure exactly–"

Suddenly, the arch behind the portgate platform came to life, trails of electric power sparking around it. A blue ball of energy formed under its arms, groaning and shouting, as if it were being forced to open. Shepherd turned and looked at it intensely.

"Go now," yelled Shepherd over the sound of the newly opened portal.

Jack began to retreat back behind the nearest pillar when he stopped.

"Wait, what about you?" he asked.

Shepherd turned his back on Jack, facing the slowly growing portal fully. Tendrils of blue and white electricity began to snake around him, moving to his spine and forming into a metal brace.

From that brace, more metal grew around Shepherd's body, brilliant silver and blue. It formed around his shoulders, moving to his arms. It crawled down his legs, to his feet. Jack watched in amazement as a sleek and powerful looking suit of armor encased the man, making him look like some type of butt-kicking superhero from the comic books Jack had grown up reading.

Finally, a solid metal helmet covered Shepherd's face. It was smooth, with no slits for his eyes or mouth. It formed into an obscure shape of a man's face, lacking any details, and glowing slightly.

Shepherd tightened his hands into fists, and from the sides, top, and bottom of his forearms, long, cylindrical cannons snapped up, their barrels glowing with restrained fury.

Jack gazed upon Shepherd in utter awe.

"Wicked…" he breathed.

Shepherd raised his arms, aiming his quad-cannons toward the blue portal as it screamed and grew to its full size.

The portal crackled, and with a thunderous clap, two Deathlords leapt through. Both were armed with their standard obsidian rifles. Before they had a chance to use them, Shepherd unleashed his cannons.

The blasts tore into the two Deathlords, causing them to erupt into a cloud of black dust. No sooner had those two fallen, than two more Dark Soldiers shot through the portal.

They fired a few shots off before Shepherd bombarded them into oblivion. Some shots went wide, but one hit Shepherd full on. However, instead of harming him, the blast seemed to be absorbed by his armor. The man did not even flinch from getting hit.

Jack backed away and hid behind a nearby stone pillar, aiming his plasma pistol toward the portal as more Deathlords emerged. However, Shepherd's furious cannon attack was so brutal, none of the invading Deathlords were lasting that long. For a second, Jack thought he wouldn't have to fire a single shot, since it seemed Shepherd had the whole situation under control.

Until the next group arrived.

Two more Deathlords emerged, this time followed closely by a third. The first two were like the others who had come before – foot soldiers with obsidian rifles. But the third one was taller, more lithe, and carried no weapon.

His head was wrapped with a black cloth that coiled around his face like a mummy, covering the area where his nose and mouth would be but leaving room for two brutal, glowing red eyes. Small horns crowned his slightly elongated head, and his arms were armored with guards mounted with large serrated blades.

The two Deathlord soldiers who emerged before him served as human shields and absorbed Shepherd's blasts before disintegrating, giving the third time to roll out of the way.

As the surviving Deathlord rolled to his knee, he swung his arm upward gracefully in one quick motion – causing glowing white spikes of energy to shoot up through the ground before him.

More spikes erupted in front of the last, screaming toward Shepherd with frightening speed. As the spikes behind them evaporated, the new arrivals grew larger and more deadly the farther they traveled, like a tidal wave of jagged death.

Shepherd leapt to the side, but he was not fast enough.

The wave of floor spikes turned, as if it knew his reaction, and impacted his side, sparking off his armor and sending him flying backwards.

Shepherd hit the floor, rolling from the force of the impact, as the Deathlord leapt into the air and closed the distance between him and his foe.

Just as he landed, two more Deathlord foot soldiers emerged from the portal. But instead of carrying rifles, these two bore a large black box between them, their taloned hands wrapped around its handles.

Ignoring the new arrivals, Jack took aim at the Deathlord near Shepherd, who was getting ready to make another attack.

"Prepare to get owned, jerkwad," he whispered.

He leveled the pistol.

He took careful aim.

He squeezed the trigger.

A red blast of plasma erupted from his pistol, streaking across the air, heading powerfully and forcefully directly toward the Deathlord's head…

…and completely missing him.

The Deathlord, noticing the plasma blast as it passed harmlessly by, looked over in Jack's direction, his red eyes burning with fury.

"Oh, crap…" said Jack.

The Deathlord quickly swung his arm in Jack's direction, sending another wave of ghostly floor spikes screaming his way.

Jack ducked behind the pillar, and braced himself. Fear suddenly found its way into his gut. Before, when it was just Shepherd doing the fighting, the whole thing seemed cool, like he was watching the greatest sci-fi movie ever.

But now, things were shooting at *him*, and that was totally *not* cool.

The Deathlord's spikes slammed into the pillar Jack was hiding behind with incredible force. The pillar crumbled instantly and the blast sent Jack flying forward. He hit the ground hard; pieces of stone from his previous cover showered painfully down upon him. Jack curled up and covered his head to protect himself from the falling debris.

While Jack was getting his first taste of battle, the two Deathlords who emerged during the fight set the box they were carrying on the ground. Spikes shot out of its smooth undercarriage, burrowing into the floor. The top of the box began to grow, morphing into a tall, twisted spire, its peak shaping into four even blades.

Taking advantage of the distraction Jack had provided, Shepherd rolled to his knee and aimed his quad-canons at the Deathlord before him and let loose.

This Deathlord was tougher than the others. He took the shots Shepherd threw his way, stumbling back as the blasts tore through him and his armor.

Reacting quickly, the Deathlord flung a ball of ghostly white energy from his hand, rocketing it at Shepherd like a cannonball.

Shepherd rolled, the blast impacting the ground he had occupied seconds before, creating a small crater where it hit.

In one fluid motion, Shepherd reached behind him, pulling two long, straight batons off the back of his armor while rolling to his feet. No sooner did his hands grip the immaculate white sticks than they crackled to life with a furious blue and white energy.

The Deathlord flung another ghost ball, which shot directly toward Shepherd. Swiftly, Shepherd batted it away with his batons, a wisp of the death energy snaking up his arm as the Deathlord's attack dissipated from the blow.

Not missing a beat, Shepherd rushed toward his foe, attacking the Deathlord with amazing speed.

He swung the baton in his right hand low, catching the Deathlord in his gut.

The next blow went high, the baton crashing into the back of the Deathlord's head.

The strikes from Shepherd's weapons sent ripples of electricity coursing through the Deathlord, causing him to cry out in pain.

Gracefully, Shepherd spun, landing both batons in a powerful blow on the Deathlord's back. The Deathlord buckled to his knees and disintegrated into a puff of black dust.

During the fight, the spire that the other two Deathlords had activated from the mysterious black box began to charge to life with purple energy. Shepherd looked up just in time to see the spire emit a brilliant flash of purple light. Suddenly, ten Deathlord soldiers were around the spire, having just been teleported there without the use of the portgate.

Wasting no time, Shepherd threw himself into the fray.

His fighting sticks whirled with skilled fury as he rushed into the thick of the enemy alien force, each blow destroying a Deathlord Soldier with a single strike. But even as one soldier fell, two more arrived from the portgate's portal, and if Shepherd didn't act quickly, the transport spire would recharge and teleport in even more.

Jack squirmed on the ground, covered in dust and a little blood. His back screamed from the impact he had received, and his head hurt from being knocked down. Jack looked up wearily to see the army of Deathlords who had just arrived and Shepherd's frantic attempt to fight them off.

All of a sudden, the situation was too horribly real. The pain in Jack's body alerted him to the idea that this was not a movie, this was not a game, this was *actually* happening, and if he weren't careful – he could really, truly die.

Then, Jack noticed trails of black dust slowly gathering together on the ground and slithering toward him. The dust began to form into the shape of a clawed hand, its taloned fingers crawling on the floor like a spider's legs.

More dust gathered to it, forming an arm with familiar looking serrated armored blades. In sudden horror, Jack realized that whatever Shepherd had done to that last Deathlord had not actually killed him.

Jack looked over and saw the plasma pistol not far away. He reached over and grabbed it, training it on the dust just as it was forming shoulders and a head. Red eyes peeked out from the bandages wrapped around the face the black dust had rematerialized into.

Jack began to fire at the reforming Deathlord who was quickly crawling toward him. He fired the weapon repeatedly, sending hot bolts of red death at the monstrosity.

However, as soon as the blasts passed through the Deathlord, more dust crawled up to fill the wounds they had left. The lithe, muscular demon that was wreaking havoc mere minutes before was coming back to life, and there was absolutely *nothing* Jack could do to stop it.

"Help!" Jack screamed as he began to crawl backwards from the steadily gaining alien menace, firing his pistol repeatedly as he did so. "Someone, HELP!"

Jack's blasts were finding their mark now, most likely because his target was much closer than before. But other than making the creature angrier with every shot, the plasma blasts did not seem to be doing much damage.

The Deathlord was now fully reformed. He towered over Jack, and the boy could do nothing but look up in terror as the figure before him created a ghostly ball of energy in his clawed hand, readying a killing blow.

Jack braced himself, fear coursing through his veins.

"No!" screamed Jack. "Don't! PLEASE!"

Suddenly, a blue-white baton erupted from the Deathlord's chest. Energy crackled through the alien as it screamed in twisted agony.

Another baton crashed down on its neck, and the creature exploded in a puff of dust, this time for good.

Shepherd stood where the evil alien had been moments before, powerful and terrifying in his own right. Relief washed over Jack, looking up at the armored hero who had just saved his life.

Jack's eyes wandered past Shepherd as more Deathlords teleported in. There were now dozens of Dark Soldiers, and Jack realized Shepherd must have disengaged with them to save his life, leaving the door open to bring in a bigger force — cutting Jack's joy at being rescued painfully short.

The platoon of Deathlord soldiers coming toward them lifted their rifles, taking aim at Shepherd and him.

"Behind you!" cried Jack.

Shepherd turned as the Deathlords unleashed their first volley of fire – not purple balls of light this time, but angry red streaks of plasma.

Shepherd raised his hand, projecting a large shield wall of golden light before him. The blasts hit the shield, which absorbed them. Jack marveled at just how awesome Shepherd was. Not only did he have a suit of armor with cannons on it, he could do all sorts of ninja moves and create energy shields! Suddenly, he felt really guilty for not liking the guy for so long.

"Jack," said Shepherd. "I won't be able to hold them off much longer. We have to get out of here. Get Green and the Princess. We'll have to fight our way back to the portal and escape."

The prospect of fighting the Deathlords again did not sit well with Jack.

"There are so many!" said Jack. "How will we be able to fight through them?"

"I'll clear a path," said Shepherd. "But the longer we wait, the harder it will be. Get the Princess… NOW."

Shepherd recalled his quad-cannons and opened a hole in his shield wall, through which he began to fire at the oncoming Deathlords.

Jack got to his feet and ran down the path toward the temple. He gripped his blaster pistol tightly, the weapon being the only thing that gave him some measure of security in this crazy situation he now found himself in.

As he got closer to the entrance of the temple, he could see Anna and Green nearby. Anna had her back to him, standing before some type of stone kiosk. Green was at her side, looking at a small device in his hands.

"Anna!" yelled Jack. "Professor! We gotta go!"

Professor Green looked up as Jack approached, smiling like nothing was going on. "Ah, Jack!" he said cheerily. "How goes the battle?"

"Not freakin' good," said Jack as he came to a stop at the Professor's side. "Shepherd says we need to get outta here, and I totally agree."

"Oh, bother," said Green, furrowing his brow. "That could be a problem…"

"What? Why?" asked Jack.

Green nodded toward Anna. Jack looked and saw her standing before a glowing white orb hovering above the small stone kiosk. Her hands were resting on the orb, her eyes open — white and utterly without pupils.

"The Princess is interacting with the Ancient construct," said Green. "She's been trying to unlock the temple. If we were to interrupt her communication with the Ancient device, the sudden disconnect could harm her."

Anna stood motionless, as if not able to hear them. Jack looked from her to Green and back. He had no idea what the Professor had just said, but whatever it was, it didn't sound terribly convenient.

Jack looked at the small device the Professor held in his hand.

"Well, can't you disconnect her?" Jack asked. "What's that thing do?"

"The Princess is communing with the Ancient interface of this temple," explained Green. "We've been working for the better part of a year to try to decipher the lock on it, with no success. She was hoping that with a program I had written to interact with the temple's database, I might be able to help her figure out the key to unlocking it, but so far we have found no trigger with which to do so. This connection is just a way for me to monitor the progress of the program."

Jack glanced back and saw Shepherd firing away at the ever-encroaching Deathlords. There was a purple flash in the distance, heralding the arrival of even more bad guys.

"Professor, we don't have time for this, we *gotta* go..." said Jack urgently.

Green scrunched up his face like he was thinking through a physics problem. "Well," he said thoughtfully. "Normally only the Princess can decide when to sever the connection with Ancient technology; however, we might be able to close down the connection by attempting to interface with the access orb ourselves."

"Great," said Jack eagerly. "Let's do that..."

"Hold on a moment!" said Green. "Normally, it would be safe to interact with the Ancient terminal because only those with royal blood are able to interface with them, but I don't know what would happen if you were to try and interrupt the flow of one that's currently in use."

"Will it kill me?" asked Jack.

"Well, no, I don't think so..." replied Green.

"Will they?" asked Jack, pointing to the Deathlords.

Green pondered the oncoming alien army for a moment. "Most likely, yes," he said.

"Sounds safe to me," said Jack. And before Green could speak again, Jack slapped his hand on the glowing orb.

No sooner had Jack placed his hand on the orb than his muscles tensed up, like an electrical current was running through him. Suddenly, he was aware of every part of his body – his organs, his bones, even his blood cells – as though every part of him was conscious of itself.

A barrage of images flashed before his eyes. Strange numbers, letters, and diagrams seemed to sear themselves into his brain at an alarming rate. As they flashed by, Jack was able to make sense of them, but as new information would come his way, he'd quickly forget whatever it was he'd just seen. Before long, the deluge of information became jumbled, and Jack lost all sense of understanding.

Sounds worked their way in. He heard a million different voices whispering to him, saying all types of things he couldn't comprehend. Sometimes they would suddenly switch to English, and then back to bizarre languages. And when he *could* understand what was being said, none of it made any sense.

Then, all the voices began to converge, talking in unison, just as the images flashing before him began to assemble together, forming into a mosaic of epic proportions. The pictures became a solid sphere, rays of light shining from behind it, and in that sphere floated a single, solitary eye that looked at Jack as though it were able to see into his very soul.

In one voice, the chorus in his head sang:

"Eldil Meldilorn."

Suddenly, all sensation dissipated, and Jack's vision came into focus on a very surprised looking Anna.

"Jack?" she said.

Jack gazed at her dumbly. His body shivered, and he realized his legs were completely numb just before he collapsed onto the ground.

In moments, Anna and Green were at his side. Anna had him in her arms and Green was opening Jack's eyes wide with his fingers to check his vital signs.

"Jack, can you hear me?" asked Green.

"What... just... happened?" asked Jack, his head splitting with the mother of all headaches.

"Well, I'll be darned," mused Green. "It worked!"

"What worked?" asked Anna. "What did you do?"

"Jack interrupted the flow of data from the access orb so we could safely disconnect you," said Green happily.

"No, he didn't," said Anna.

Green raised an eyebrow. "He didn't?"

"No!" she replied. "I came out myself after I noticed a sudden shift in the flow of data from the terminal."

"Wait a minute..." said Green excitedly. "Are you telling me Jack actually *interfaced* with the orb?"

"I did what now?" asked Jack, feeling starting to return to his body.

"The shift in the flow of data," said Anna to herself. "That would mean... he *unlocked* it!"

Anna and Green shared an amazed glance then turned to Jack in unison.

"Jack," said Anna, "What did you see?"

"I don't know," said Jack. "There was so much..."

"Think!" insisted Anna. "Can you remember anything? Anything at all?"

Jack shook his head and said the only thing his over-taxed brain could remember:

"Eldil Meldilorn?"

Suddenly, there was a low rumble. The group turned toward the entrance to the temple. The door before them was slowly sliding open. Jack noticed a symbol on the archway above the door – an orb within an orb. It looked almost exactly like the powerful eye he had seen in his vision.

"Great Scott..." mumbled Green.

Jack could feel Anna gripping his shoulder. He looked up to see her smiling.

"You did it..." she said, as if she were talking to herself. "I was right. There was a connection! To think, after all this time, it just required an Earthman..."

Then, a volley of blaster fire streaked above their heads, interrupting their moment of success. They turned and saw Shepherd a few feet away, still firing through his shield wall at an army of Deathlord soldiers marching relentlessly their way.

"Inside!" Shepherd yelled. "Go! NOW!"

Anna and Green helped Jack to his feet. His legs still felt a little rubbery, but nowhere nearly as bad as before. The three rushed inside the temple. By the entrance there was a small panel. Anna tried making contact with it, but nothing happened. She pulled Jack to her.

"Jack, touch this panel," she said.

Jack did as he was told. The panel lit up in response.

"Fascinating," mused Green, as he watched.

"Now, close the door," said Anna.

"How?" asked Jack.

"Just think about the door closing," she said.

Jack remembered what the door looked like when it opened, and tried to picture it going in reverse. With a creak and a moan, the massive door began to move.

"Shepherd!" yelled Anna.

Outside the temple, Shepherd turned to see the door closing. The Deathlord soldiers were almost upon him. Taking his cue, Shepherd forced the shield wall in front of him forward toward his assailants. The shield thrust itself into the front line of the encroaching invaders with powerful velocity, crashing into them like a speeding truck and sending them flying into those behind them, knocking the Dark Soldiers asunder like bowling pins, before dissipating.

Shepherd turned and made a run for the temple door, scattered volleys of Deathlord plasma fire following him. Most of the shots went wide, but a few found their mark, only to be absorbed by his armor.

The Paragon leapt for the door and dove in. He turned on the ground and let loose a few bolts from his arm cannons to slow down the Deathlords one last time before the door completely shut, plunging the group into the darkness of the temple.

CHAPTER 14

small sphere of light flared up in the palm of Shepherd's hand. He was standing now, and the light of the orb cast enough illumination for the group to see each other.

"Is everyone all right?" asked Shepherd, his voice cold and robotic from behind his helmet.

"We're fine," Anna answered. "Are you okay?"

The front part of Shepherd's helmet retracted, revealing his face. He wasn't even breathing hard.

"I'm unharmed," he replied, "but we're not safe for long. The Deathlords will no doubt be planning to blast down the door soon."

Jack rolled his eyes, "You gotta be kidding me," he whined. "These Ancient dudes can build a temple in the core of a planet but not a door that can't be blown up?"

Shepherd glared at Jack. "Nothing stands for long against the Deathlords, boy," he said. "I should think you'd have learned that a few minutes ago."

Jack had a brief flashback to the Deathlord that almost killed him, pulling itself back together from nothing, and felt a pang of fear creep back into his gut.

"The good news is that they won't be able to break through it very easily, so we have some time," said Anna. "If we can find the artifact, maybe we can use it against them."

"If the artifact is indeed the weapon you hope it is," said Shepherd. "If not, we've just backed ourselves into a corner."

"Listen, I know I'm a little late to the party here," interrupted Jack. "But would someone PLEASE explain to me what the heck is goin' on? What weapon? What are those Deathlord things? *Who are you people?*"

The group turned to Jack. He met Anna's gaze, her image beautifully haunting in the low light emanating from Shepherd's glowing sphere.

"In case you haven't figured out by now, Jack," said Anna softly, "we're not from Earth."

"Yeah, the magical suit of awesome-armor kind of gave that away," said Jack.

"Princess," interjected Shepherd. "We don't have time for this."

"Then I'll be quick," she replied. "He's earned some answers."

Anna turned her attention back to Jack. "My real name is Princess Glorianna of the planet Regalus Prime, blood heir to the throne of the Galactic Regalus Empire. This is my protector, Paragon Shepherd."

"So he's not really your dad?" asked Jack.

"I'm a Paragon," said Shepherd. "A disciple of the free mind, one sworn to the service of the royal bloodline."

"But you guys totally don't look like aliens," Jack said. "You look human."

"Ah! Well, that would be because of our hologuises," said Green. He then reached out his arm and tapped a few keys on his calculator wristwatch. Suddenly, the shell of what was Professor Green faded away, and what was left in its place was something... well, very different.

It actually still somewhat resembled the Professor. It was wearing his same goofy clothes, had the same long neck, lanky arms, and shock of white hair. Its skin, however, was a scaly green, and its head was large and flat, much like a turtle's, but with big brown eyes that stuck out the side of its head. It had a wide, toothy grin and a tuft of bristly white hair jutting from its chin.

There were many ways Jack could have reacted to his Physics teacher morphing into a mutant man-turtle before his eyes, but he just blinked solemnly and looked at Anna.

"Um... do you look like that, too?" he asked as diplomatically as he could.

Anna smiled. She tapped a petite gold bracelet on her wrist, and there was a fading of her image around her as well. But instead of turning into a green alien thing, she looked very much the same. In fact, she actually looked better than she did before. Her eyes were a more brilliant blue; her golden hair seemed to shimmer; her skin appeared smooth, soft, and perfect. And other than the fact that her ears were slightly pointy, she was still pretty much the same girl Jack had always known.

"Professor Green is part of a race of beings known as the Trundel. Paragon Shepherd and I are of a race that is descended from the Ancients who built this place," explained Anna. "Earthlings and Regals actually aren't that different, it turns out. When the Professor first came across your planet in his travels, he believed that Earth was some sort of far removed Ancient colony, and that your species evolved from them much like ours did."

"You can imagine my surprise when I came across your planet," said Green. "This area of the galaxy had long been thought to be devoid of life. I only came out here in search of a possible location for a Great Seal I'd found referenced in some recently uncovered Ancient ruins. But instead, I found you!"

"Great Seal?" asked Jack.

"Yes, an area of Ancient technology which is an expertise of mine," replied Green, not bothering to clarify. "I didn't find the seal, but the presence of your species did intrigue me. It wasn't until I began my research into your people that I found you evolved naturally from this planet. Which was quite shocking, considering your similarities to Ancient DNA. But once I discovered the portgate to the Ancient temple in your town, everything began to make sense."

"Please," said Jack. "I'll take anything that makes sense right now."

"Well," said Green. "You have a foundation of Ancient technology at the very core of your planet! It stands to reason that the things that grew from this planet were influenced by it in some way. If my estimations of the age of this temple are correct, its creation coincides with a period where your species was transitioning to behavioral modernity with the development of symbolic culture, language, and specialized lithic technology."

Jack had no idea what that meant.

"The temple made cavemen evolve into what you are today," said Green plainly.

"Ah," said Jack, finally getting it. "But I thought you said this place was a weapon?"

"We hope it houses a weapon," clarified Anna. "I've spent years searching the galaxy looking for Ancient Artifacts, hoping to find something to aid us in our fight. The Deathlords are a powerful force that has been devastating our galaxy. Their technology is… well, it's more advanced than anything we've ever seen, next to the Ancients."

"Every attempt to fight the Deathlords has either failed or been won at too great a cost," said Shepherd. "They cannot be killed."

"But you were shooting them," said Jack. "They were exploding! I saw."

"We don't know much about Deathlord anatomy," said Green. "But they're not flesh and blood. They don't exist or perish in the same way we do. Best we can theorize is that they are made up of some type of nanotechnology beyond any known application."

"Uh… nanotechnology?" asked Jack.

"Microscopic robots," clarified Green. "Tiny machines that come together to form a solid mass. We theorize that each Deathlord is made up of trillions and trillions of them, unified by a central energy source which serves as the primary consciousness for the Deathlord it forms."

"Some Deathlords have a stronger energy source than others," said Shepherd, "as you saw with the one who was able to reform himself. Most Deathlords are mindless drones with weak energy sources. They can be dispatched by disrupting that source with a more powerful energy, like plasma blasts or some type of electrical weaponry."

"That's why the Dark Soldiers you've seen aren't very bright," said Anna. "They have the weakest energy source and, therefore, the least amount of self-awareness."

"But that's also why they're so formidable," said Shepherd. "They do exactly as they're told. They cannot feel pain, grow tired, or experience fear. Wave after wave can be sent to be destroyed, and they just come right back."

"How?" asked Jack. "Do they all re-form like that ugly one did?"

"No," said Green. "We believe the Deathlords are able to simply construct as many bodies as necessary."

"So, in essence, you're saying they're basically killer robots?" said Jack.

"Oh, were that the case!" said Green. "If they were robotic, it would be a simple matter of using electro-magnetic pulses to defeat them by shutting down their power source!"

"Yeah," muttered Jack, wondering what exactly an electro-magnetic pulse was. "Simple."

"You can never really destroy energy, you see," said Green. "So even though their bodies are destroyed, the core of the Deathlord survives. It could very well be the case that the new Deathlords are constructed with the same consciousness as the ones that were defeated."

"Resurrection," said Anna. "An army that never dies."

"But there's something more to the Deathlords that we haven't figured out yet," continued Green, "something that separates them from merely being machines."

"They have some type of power we've yet to understand," said Shepherd, "some ability that gives them control over life itself."

"Huh?" asked Jack.

"You saw how the Deathlord was able to fire those balls of energy and control a wave of ground-spikes with the flick of his hand," said Shepherd. "They seem to be able to control energy somehow. That includes whatever life force exists in most living beings."

"Whoa," said Jack, a chill running up his spine. "You mean they can make you blow up or something?"

"More like they can rip your soul out of you," said Shepherd.

The gravity of the Deathlord threat was starting to settle in on Jack. The idea of an army that could not be killed seemed incredibly terrifying, but one that also had the power to suck the life out of you and become stronger by doing so... that brought it into pure nightmare territory.

"But this weapon you guys talked about… it can stop them, right?" asked Jack hopefully.

"We came here to find an Ancient artifact alluded to in our historical records," said Anna. "It spoke of a weapon of great power created long ago by our ancestors – a weapon which may help us defeat the Deathlords."

"Um… I don't know about you guys, but I'm pretty sure my ancestors never built anything that could take down a tank," said Jack. "Seriously, why would you be looking for an old weapon instead of trying to invent a new one?"

"You've read about the Dark Ages in history class, right?" said Anna.

"Yeah, that time with the kings and knights and stuff," said Jack.

"It was also a time of regression after the fall of your Roman Empire," she said. "After a period in your history where incredible technological marvels were pioneered, your society forgot much of what had been created, and actually reverted to more primitive means of living."

"So you're saying you guys are going through a Dark Age?"

"About fifty thousand years ago, something happened that wiped out almost all life in the universe," said Anna. "We refer to it as *The Scourge*. Few historical records have survived from that time – but enough to tell us of the Ancients and the marvels they were able to create. Since then, our civilization – and many others – have had to rebuild themselves, and even now, we are far away from being at the point where we can hope to match the technology of our ancestors."

"Wow," said Jack. "That really sucks."

"You have *no* idea," said Anna.

Suddenly, loud thumping sounds emanated from the temple door.

"They have begun their assault on the entrance," growled Shepherd. "This history lesson will have to wait until later."

"Jack, can you turn on the lights?" Anna asked.

"Yeah, I can try," said Jack. He had a lot more questions, but he figured they could wait until they weren't in danger of being killed. He touched the wall panel again, this time imagining a lightbulb coming on.

The darkness around them quickly retreated as illumination seeped into the room. The group stood on a small platform before the entrance, with walkways branching off its sides and circling downward.

The enclosure they were in was massive – much bigger than it looked from the outside. Jack followed the group as they slowly walked toward the edge of the platform, which overlooked the chasm before it.

Beneath the massive arched ceiling above was a pit that was so deep, the light Jack had turned on almost didn't reach the bottom, allowing a pool of darkness to settle there. Jack could see the walls of the huge room slope and converge down below, almost as if the whole thing were shaped like the inside of an egg.

But the sheer size of the room wasn't the most incredible thing about it. No, that honor belonged to what was actually within it.

There, docked silently in the middle of the temple, was an honest-to-goodness *spaceship*.

Jack marveled at it. The vessel must have been at least five stories tall and the length of a football field. Two massive engines jutted out from the sides, angled toward the back, gracefully melding into something that resembled wings. The body of the ship was curved and oblong, almost like a football, but sleeker. The hull was made up of a metal that was nearly white – much like the platform on which they had arrived in the temple. But this metal seemed to glow as if it were feeding off the light around it. The beauty and majesty which the ship seemed to radiate struck those looking at it like a bolt of lightning.

"Incredible," gasped Green.

"Amazing..." marveled Anna.

"Dude..." said Jack.

Unfortunately, the magic of the moment was interrupted by a loud screeching sound. The group turned to the entrance of the temple as it began to vibrate.

"They're trying to cut through the door," said Shepherd. "Quickly, to the ship. Let's hope she can still fly."

Anna took off first, moving down the side walkway toward the spacecraft. Jack and Green followed, with the rear covered by Shepherd. A long stone causeway led up to the side of the ship at the front of the right wing, but when they approached it, there was no door visible, only smooth metal.

Anna reached up and touched the ship, running her hands across the brilliant white exterior. "I don't see a way in," she said.

Shepherd's faceplate closed up again. "Scanning," he said in his armored voice. "I'm not reading any anomalies in the ship's hull. No sign of an entrance. The casing isn't like anything I've seen before."

"Perhaps... perhaps it's not really a ship?" ventured Green. "Maybe it's not meant to carry passengers?"

"What else could it be?" asked Anna.

Jack sighed and walked up beside her. "Man, things are never easy with you guys, are they?" he said, leaning up against the ship's hull.

No sooner had his hand made contact than the hull peeled back like an iris, with Jack falling through, into the ship and onto the floor.

"M'okay…" mumbled Jack as he lumbered back onto his feet. Shepherd's mask retracted again, and he gave Jack a curious look.

"Why is this Ancient technology only responding to him?" Shepherd asked.

"If the Professor is right, that the Earthlings were created as an outgrowth of this temple's influence, it could be that they are specifically attuned to the technology in it," said Anna.

"But you're of the royal bloodline," said Shepherd. "You should be able to interface with all Ancient technology."

"Unless this technology was not meant to be used by the Ancients!" said Green.

"What are you saying, Professor?" asked Anna.

Green walked up to Jack, who was gazing around the small decompression chamber he was in, and slapped his large green hand on Jack's shoulder.

"Perhaps the Ancients meant for this ship only to be used by Earthmen," he said. "Perhaps life on this planet wasn't a fluke! Maybe it was engineered for the specific purpose of one day finding and using… well… *this*!"

Green gestured to the ship around him.

"Whoa, whoa, whoa – lemme get this straight…" said Jack. "Are you saying I have my own personal spaceship?"

"Well," said Green, "most likely any native Earthling would be able to interface with this technology—"

"No way," said Jack quickly. "I call dibs!"

"Need I remind all of you that an army of Deathlords is still trying to break in here?" grumbled Shepherd.

"Ah, yes," said Green, as though he really did need to be reminded. "I suppose we should continue on to the bridge with haste then, hmmmm?"

Anna and Shepherd entered the decompression chamber, and the hull sealed back shut. The room glowed blue for an instant and then was illuminated in a bright white light. Another door leading into the ship opened and more lights lit up as the ship slowly came to life.

Jack looked around in awe as he and the others gingerly stepped into the hallway before them. It was made up of shiny silver panels, and the floor beneath them was glowing, leading toward a large circular room with a floor made of smooth, white metal.

"Hey," said Jack as he stepped into the room. "This floor looks just like that thing we landed on when we came from the cornfield."

The others studied the floor, too. "Portgates are used for traveling long distances," said Shepherd. "You need static locations to use them. They wouldn't work on a ship."

"Maybe it's not a portgate?" ventured Green. "Perhaps a derivative? Something like it?"

Anna looked around. "Whatever it is, I don't see any controls," she said. "No interface panel, nothing."

"What about your keypad thingy?" Jack asked Anna. "The thing you used to get us down here in the first place?"

"It's called an Imperius," said Anna taking it out of her pocket. "It's kind of like a universal remote control for all Ancient technology."

"Yeah," said Jack, not really caring. "Will it work?"

Anna tapped on it for a moment and shook her head. "It doesn't seem to be responding to anything in here."

"Well, there must be someway to get to the bridge," said Green.

Suddenly, Green disappeared in a flash of light. Anna shrieked.

"Where'd he go?" asked Jack, startled.

Shepherd looked around, as if he were expecting some sort of attack. He tapped the side of his helmet to activate his communicator.

"Professor," he said. "Do you read me?"

After a moment's pause, Green's cheery voice emanated from a speaker in Shepherd's helmet.

"I'm okay!" he said.

"Where are you?" asked Shepherd.

"I'm on what I believe to be the bridge," Green responded. "It would seem the platform is voice activated, based on where you want to go."

Anna and Shepherd looked at each other.

"Bridge," they both said in unison. And with a flash, they disappeared, leaving Jack alone.

Jack smiled to himself. *I'm about to teleport,* he thought. *This is so cool.*

"Bridge!" he said.

It was as if Jack had blinked his eyes, and he was now somewhere else. There were no weird feelings of dizziness or nausea like there were when he portgated. The whole thing was quick and painless.

He stepped off a platform made of the same white metal and into a huge, oval shaped room that was divided into four tiers. The top tier was fenced in by smooth guardrails and made up entirely of the teleportation material. The third tier jutted out in a half circle, leading around to two door hatches at the back of the room, one on either side. Beneath that was a tier that contained various control panels and comfortable looking bucket seats. Finally, the last tier stretched out and met the smooth walls of the room, with a circular platform that contained a large silver chair hovering above it. The chair had a high back and two wide armrests with clear, glass-like domes at the end of them.

Anna and Shepherd gazed around in awe. It was obvious that they'd never seen anything like this before. Professor Green was excitedly rushing from one part of the bridge to the other, looking at all the controls and doohickeys he could find.

"Amazing!" he muttered. "Fascinating! Hmmm… I wonder what this does?"

Jack's eyes focused in on the chair at the lowest tier. He felt a weird tingle in the back of his head and suddenly had the urge to go to it. As he stepped down to the second tier, the chair turned to face him. He stopped and looked at it hesitantly. He could feel everyone's eyes on him.

"I think it wants you to sit in it," said Anna.

The super-awesome spaceship wanted him to sit in the super-awesome floating chair? Jack didn't need to be told twice.

He climbed in and laid his hands on top of the two clear domes on the armrests. They instantly lit up with bright light. The chair turned back toward the front of the room, and suddenly, the smooth white walls of the bridge flickered and were replaced with an almost 360 degree view of the outside.

"This is so much better than *Nova Commander*," Jack joked to himself.

"Ah-ha!" said Green, standing behind one of the control panels on the second tier. "These controls have just booted up. Jack must have activated them when he sat in the chair."

Shepherd walked to Green's side. "Can it still fly?" he asked.

"Best I can tell, everything seems to be in working order. This appears to be a navigation panel," said Green. "These things look like star maps..." Green tapped on the control panel and the screens in front of him lit up. "That panel over there seems to be for communications," he said, pointing to the panel next to him. "That one would appear to be weapons, and the far one for the ship's systems," he continued, pointing to the far panels on the other side of the second platform.

"Where are the flight controls?" asked Shepherd.

"Ask Jack," smiled Green. "He seems to be sitting in the pilot's seat."

Jack grinned. "Now we're talking!" he said.

Anna walked up to him. "Jack, if this ship is like other Ancient technology we've encountered, it works by interfacing directly with your thoughts," she said. "Just think about something, and the ship will follow your commands."

"Okay," said Jack. "What should I think about?"

Then, on the viewscreen in front of them, the door to the temple exploded, and in rushed a flood of Deathlord soldiers.

"Shields would probably be a good start," said Shepherd dryly.

Jack tried to think about raising shields, like the golden energy thing Shepherd had created when fighting the Deathlords, but nothing happened. Outside, the Deathlords began to fire at the ship, their red plasma lasers streaking across the chasm and impacting the gleaming white metal of its hull.

A strange sensation washed over Jack, as though he could actually feel the impacts of the blasts himself. They didn't hurt, but he instinctively knew where they were hitting and how much damage they were causing.

"Anytime, Jack," said Shepherd more insistently.

"I'm trying," said Jack. "Nothing's working!"

Green rushed over to the ship's system control panel and started typing furiously. "I think the ship is still powering up," he said.

"How long before we can raise the shields?" asked Shepherd.

"I don't know," said Green. "All the data is in ancient Old Solar; I'm afraid I'm not very familiar with it. Old Solar, I know, but the ancient form…"

Shepherd cursed under his breath and moved to the panel Green had pointed out for weapons. He tried accessing it for a moment before the archaic language on the screens forced him into giving up on it as well. "Jack!" he barked. "Can you get us out of here?"

Jack tried imagining everything possible he could think of for the ship to do, including growing two legs and dancing out of there, but nothing was working. He looked at the army of Deathlords as they streamed in from the open temple door. *Just my luck,* he thought. *I actually get my own spaceship, and it's about to be destroyed by evil aliens.*

"Jack," insisted Anna, "you have to focus…"

"I *know*, okay?" hissed Jack. For some reason this wasn't as easy as it was when he had accessed the door or the lights to the temple. This was different somehow – the ship was different. He kept trying to picture what it would look like for the shields to raise or the engines to start up, but no matter what Jack thought of, nothing was happening. There were too many distractions – the Deathlords were invading, Professor Green, Shepherd, and Anna were all yelling at him, and he still had that weird feeling in the back of his head…

"Jack!" yelled Shepherd. "Can you work this thing or not?"

"Maybe if people would stop *yelling* at me…" he hollered back.

Then, two massive balls of ghostly energy screamed forth from the exit and rocked the ship. An alarm began to sound and suddenly the lights on the bridge turned red. Jack looked up to see two Deathlords on the entrance platform, hurling balls of death energy at them.

"They're trying to cripple the ship," warned Shepherd.

"Oh, dear," moaned Green. "That would not be good."

Anna climbed up on the platform by Jack's seat and leaned in toward him. "Jack, what's wrong?" she asked.

"I don't know," said Jack. "I'm trying to work it the way you told me to, but it's not… I don't even know how we're going to get out of here! There's no opening anywhere, and even if there were, we're in the Earth's core surrounded by a ton of freakin' magma! How'd they even get this thing here in the first place?"

Anna placed a hand on his arm. "Calm down," she said.

Jack looked at her. His heart was racing a mile a minute, but somehow, her blue eyes made him get control of himself. He took a deep breath.

"I'm calm," he said.

"Now," continued Anna. "Close your eyes, and listen."

"Listen to what?" asked Jack.

"The ship," she said. "It's trying to talk to you."

"How do you know?"

"Because," smiled Anna. "That's how it works with me."

Jack nodded. He closed his eyes and listened. He heard the sound of the alarms. He heard Professor Green and Shepherd talking. He heard the thuds against the hull as more energy bolts made their impact. He didn't know what he was listening for, and that buzzing in the back of his head was starting to get really annoying…

Wait a minute… thought Jack.

There was a buzzing, wasn't there? It was the same weird sensation he'd had when he first approached the pilot's chair. But it wasn't really a sound; it was more like a feeling.

Jack focused on that feeling. The buzzing got more intense. Then, things began to flash into his mind.

He remembered something from when he was interfacing with the access orb – a bunch of images, almost like instructions on how to operate something… a spaceship! That's what it was, instructions on how to operate a spaceship! But there was so much information… what did it all mean? None of it made a whole lot of sense.

Then, he remembered the eye he had seen, the big eye floating in space, shimmering with brilliant rays of light. It had been looking at him, as though it were waiting for something…

How do I get us out of here? Jack asked.

Jack felt a surge in his hands. He opened his eyes and looked at the glowing domes on the armrests. He felt a strange sensation, like an electrical current running between his hands and the domes.

In front of him, a holographic screen appeared in the air, so he could see both the data on it and the viewscreen at the same time. Strange words and numbers began to flash up on the screen.

Anna hopped off the chair and looked at it curiously. "What did you do?" she asked.

"I'm… not sure," replied Jack. "I think this is how we can get out of here… somehow."

"Princess, can you read it?" asked Shepherd.

"No," said Anna. "It's a really, really old form of Old Solar, I can't make sense of it."

"Blast it," lamented Green, who was also looking at the holographic display. "I knew I should have taken that class in pre-formal Ancient linguistics when I had the chance. Who knew it would come in handy?"

"It's asking for coordinates," said Jack.

"You can read it?" asked Anna, shocked.

To his surprise, Jack *could* read it. The language on the screen wasn't anything he'd ever seen before, but for some reason, he just instinctually knew what it said.

"Yeah," said Jack, "but it just asks for coordinates. Then there's just a big list of numbers that don't make any sense."

"Curious," said Green. "I've never seen number patterns like that before. Perhaps those are coordinates to previous destinations? Maybe places the Ancients want us to visit?"

"Whatever they are, pick one!" growled Shepherd.

"But… what happens when I do?" asked Jack.

"We'll deal with that later," Shepherd barked. "Do it! NOW!"

Jack focused in on the first line of numbers in the list, and it began to glow. The numbers moved to the top of the screen, and a word that meant "Destination Accepted" flashed before the whole thing disappeared.

A hum rose in the room. Jack could feel something stirring inside him… no, it was inside the ship – and instantly he knew what was about to happen.

"Everybody – hold onto something!" he screamed.

The entire bridge began to fill up with a brilliant white light…

Outside, the Deathlords continued their assault against the ship, advancing toward it, when a flash of light erupted, filling the entire temple…

And when the light cleared, the ship was gone.

CHAPTER ✺ 15

When the bridge returned to normal, Jack blinked his eyes. On the viewscreen in front of him, there was no longer an Ancient underground temple swarming with deadly aliens. Instead, there was nothing but blue sky and white clouds in the bright sunlight of day.

Before it had a chance to register in Jack's brain that only moments ago it had been nighttime in River Heights, a strange sensation assaulted his stomach, as if he were suspended in mid air.

Suddenly the entire ship began to rumble, and Anna, Shepherd, and Green were tossed violently up to the roof of the bridge. They were pinned there, unable to move. Jack had no seatbelt on, yet for some reason he stayed firmly in the pilot's seat – though that did nothing to quash the feeling of sheer panic he was experiencing.

On the viewscreen, clouds began to shoot toward them, and Jack felt himself being squashed into his seat with sickening force as the ship started to spin. The clouds broke, and there rushing up toward them was a massive wall of water.

Holy crap! thought Jack. *We're falling!*

Indeed, it would appear that wherever they were, they had rematerialized somewhere high in the air and were now dropping like a stone, plummeting with frightening speed directly toward a large ocean.

"Jack!" yelled Shepherd. "Start the engines!"

The bridge was shaking violently now, the alarm was still blaring, and impact with the water was rapidly approaching — all of which failed to help Jack concentrate on anything except being scared out of his pants. He felt dizzy, he felt sick, and he had utterly no idea how to keep from crashing to certain death.

"Jack!" Shepherd yelled.

Jack tried to pull himself together. He gripped the domes on his seat so tightly he thought he might break them.

"Jack!" yelled Anna, with Shepherd joining in for good measure.

The ocean was rushing up at them, getting closer…

Jack focused on the tingle in the back of his brain. He thought about all his times playing *Nova Commander IV* and how the controls of that game worked.

Closer…

"JACK!" screamed Anna, Shepherd, and Green, all in unison.

Suddenly, Jack sensed an electrical sensation run from his hands into the domes on his chair again. He could feel the engines of the ship spring to life and the rumble they made as they fired.

The ocean was just about to greet them when Jack pulled the ship up out of its free fall, causing it to shoot forward with force so great, the water beneath them parted and sprayed as the ship skimmed its surface.

Anna, Shepherd, and Green all fell from the ceiling and hit the floor, only to be thrust backwards as the ship accelerated.

"Wooooooooooo-HOOOOOOOO!!!!!" cheered Jack as he increased the ship's speed and started to climb back into the air. He was having so much fun, he almost didn't notice his three companions plastered to the back walls of the cabin.

"Jack—" screamed Green. "Inertial… dampeners…"

"What?" hollered Jack.

"Inertial dampeners!" they all yelled back.

Jack had no idea what those were, let alone how to turn them on. Then, he felt a tingle on his hands again, like the ship was passing a current through him, and instantly he knew how to activate them.

Once the inertial dampeners had engaged, Anna, Shepherd, and Green all collapsed to the floor. The feeling in the cabin changed — they were still accelerating and climbing into the air, but it didn't feel like it anymore. In fact, it felt like the room wasn't moving at all. Jack guessed that whatever inertial dampeners were, they kept the group from getting tossed around while the ship moved.

"Hey!" Jack laughed. "I think I'm getting the hang of this!"

The others got up, obviously not as cheerful as Jack was. "Where are we?" growled Shepherd.

Jack wondered the same thing. As if on cue, the holographic screen he had seen before popped up. This time it showed an image of the planet Earth, and it outlined an area of ocean in the Pacific.

"I think we're somewhere over the Pacific Ocean," said Jack.

"Fascinating!" said Professor Green as he gingerly rubbed the back of his bruised noggin. "Instantaneous travel! Why, I've never seen anything like it!"

"What are you talking about?" asked Jack. "What about the portgate? Or the way those Deathlords just teleport in out of nowhere?"

"Oh, those are very different things," explained Green. "To teleport an entire ship — especially one that could be moving —

across vast distances… why, the power requirements alone are astronomical! Not to mention the sheer number of calculations that would have to be made…"

"Can you jump us again?" asked Shepherd, obviously not interested in the science behind their fantastic journey. "Somewhere away from the planet?"

"I think so," said Jack. "Except…"

"What?" asked Shepherd.

"I think… I think the ship needs time to power up the Entanglement Engine thing again."

Green and Shepherd exchanged a surprised look.

"Did you say… Entanglement Engine?" asked Green.

"Yeah," said Jack. "That's what the thing that jumped us out of the temple is called, according to the ship. It's like a separate engine from the thrusters. Why?"

Green looked at Shepherd. "Is that even possible?" he asked.

"Anything is possible," said Shepherd.

"Yes, but… for a machine to be able to—"

"Figure it out later, Professor," said Shepherd. "Jack, how much time before we're ready to jump again?"

"Um… the ship's saying it's going to be around an hour," replied Jack.

"Do we have any other method of travel?" asked Shepherd. "Does the ship have hyperspace capabilities?"

"Uh… hyperspace?" asked Jack.

Shepherd slammed his fist down on a console. "Blast it, Jack! Must we explain everything?"

"Well *excuse me* for not knowing stuff!" snapped Jack back. "It's not like I grew up learning about Deathlords and teleportation and inertial-whatevers, you know? And considering the fact that I just figured out how to fly a fifty thousand year old spaceship with no prior experience, I think I'm doing pretty freakin' good here!"

"No one's saying you aren't," said Anna diplomatically, giving Shepherd a look telling him to take it easy. "But the longer we stay within range of the Deathlord fleet, the more danger we're in."

"If only I could read these control panels," said Green, typing away at the ship's systems interface. "I might be able to get a better idea of how the ship works."

Suddenly, an idea popped into Jack's head.

"Does this help?" he asked.

The language on Green's console abruptly changed from the ancient language it was using to a language that was a little more familiar.

"Ah!" said Green. "English! Wouldn't have been my first choice, but I suppose it will do."

Anna looked at Jack in surprise. "You changed the computer's language?" she asked.

"Yeah," smiled Jack. "I just thought it would be cool if the Professor could read the console and the ship went ahead and did it."

"So... the ship is actually able to adjust to what you want?" she asked in amazement.

"I guess," replied Jack. "I mean, when we were falling I started thinking about how I used to play this video game where you flew a spaceship, and suddenly it started to control just like the game."

"Amazing. It sounds like the ship is able to adapt to you!" said Anna.

"Is that, like, normal?" asked Jack.

"It would appear nothing about this ship is what you'd call 'normal,' " said Green in awe as he scanned through the ship's systems on his console. "I've never seen anything like this! Did you know the ship is able to repair itself when damaged?"

"Really?" said Jack. "How?"

"Well—" started Green before Shepherd interrupted.

"Professor – *hyperspace*?" he growled.

"Oh, uh… yes… it does appear to have hyperspace capabilities," Green replied.

"Good," said Shepherd. "Open a window and get us out of here."

"Unfortunately, I don't think that's going to be possible right now," said Green.

"What?" barked Shepherd. "Why not?"

"The navigational charts," said Green. "They're tens of thousands of years old. Nothing on here is named the same as things are now. Not to mention if we were to open a hyperspace window using this data, we could very well fly into a sun, or a planet, or who knows what else?"

Jack listened to Green and Shepherd's conversation and couldn't help but wonder what exactly they were talking about. Ever since the Deathlords had first shown up, Jack'd had been having the same feeling coursing through his brain that was usually reserved for pop-quizzes for which he was woefully unprepared.

As he found himself wishing he knew exactly what this "hyperspace" was and how it worked, the back of his head began to buzz again, and suddenly he had his answers.

Hyperspace is, in fact, another dimension – one that allows for faster than light travel. The way it works struck Jack as actually being quite cool, since the hyperspace dimension is exactly like our own, containing the same stars, planets, black holes, moons, and every other celestial body one might find in this great big galaxy. Except, instead of being solid matter as they are in our dimension, things in hyperspace are like shadows of what they are here. They have the same gravity and the same mass, but that's it. There is no life in hyperspace, no water, no air, no gas — just impressions of the really big stuff that exists in the universe.

However, what makes hyperspace even stranger is the fact that it is much, much smaller than the reality we all know and love so well. Whereas the dimension in which we live is a universe that is constantly expanding and growing, the universe of hyperspace is doing the exact opposite — it is contracting and shrinking.

That means things are actually closer in hyperspace than they are in our dimension. So by entering the hyperspace dimension and traveling at the speed of light, one is able to cross thousands of light-years in our dimension in a matter of hours. And because it is the same universe — just in a different dimension — the moment a traveler exits it, he'll be exactly at the destination he arrived at when in hyperspace.

Of course, because hyperspace travel still requires moving at the speed of light to cover the necessary distances, exact navigation is needed if one hopes to survive the journey. Due to the fact that things are spatially different in the hyperspace dimension, it is imperative to know exact distances in one's own dimension to properly calculate them — because even though things exist in hyperspace simply by their gravity and mass, if a ship were to fly into them at the speed of light, it would be obliterated into dust.

Jack scratched his head. For a kid who had a hard time grasping simple high school physics like Newton's Laws of

Motion, he sure was able to understand the concept of multi-dimensional space travel pretty quickly. In fact, ever since he tried to disconnect Anna from that glowing orb thing, he found lots of things were coming to him more easily than they ever had before. He couldn't help but wonder what other information he had in his head that he didn't know was there.

"Are you sure we can't use the charts?" Shepherd asked Green. "Can we make an approximation? Do a blind jump?"

"Well, it would be risky," replied Green. "Since these charts were created, the universe has expanded - planets have moved, new stars have formed and old ones have died — who knows how many changes have happened since this database was last updated? Because of the differences in the distances of hyperspace, without the proper charts, we'd never be able to calculate our exact course. If we were off even by a couple of feet, it could be disastrous."

Suddenly, Jack heard a series of alert beeps and a holographic radar screen popped up in front of him. He saw three large red dots on the exterior edge of the radar moving toward them quite fast.

"Uh-oh," said Jack.

Shepherd looked at him, alarmed. "What?" he asked.

Jack asked the ship what the dots on the radar were, and on the holoscreen in front of him an image popped up showing three small, triangular-shaped ships. The base of the ships contained their engines, leaving a trail of putrid green exhaust behind them, and their tips were narrow and twisted, aiming right for Jack's ship. Their edges gnarled into sharp, blade-like wings, and their hulls were made of a black, obsidian material. Jack instantly had them pegged as Deathlord shards.

"We've, uh… got company…" said Jack.

Shepherd grimaced at the dark shards on the holoscreen. "Professor," he said, "keep working on a way to get us out of here. Princess," he turned to Anna, "man the engineering panel and see if you can get the shields up. I'll take the weapons. Jack…"

"Yeah?" asked Jack.

"Try not to get us killed," he said, like he was assigning homework.

"Great idea. I'll get right on that," said Jack dryly.

Anna and Shepherd rushed to the control panels on the second tier of the bridge to man their stations while Green began typing, furiously muttering things about "vectors" and "calculations." Jack focused on the holographic displays before him.

The shards were coming up behind them fast. Jack increased the ship's speed to try to outrun them, but the shards were smaller and more agile. It would only be a matter of time before they'd catch up.

Jack's instincts were to fire at the ships before they had a chance to attack, but without shields or working weapons at this point, options were limited. He had to keep the shards at bay long enough to give Anna and Shepherd the time they needed to get the ship working properly.

Jack decided to gain speed by going into a dive. He angled the ship downward, heading toward the ocean. The ship alerted him to incoming enemy fire as streaks of red plasma blasts shot by wildly. Jack glanced at the holoscreen and saw the shards firing from the tips on the front of their vessels, but they were still too far away to have much accuracy. That didn't keep their blasts from being uncomfortably close, though.

"Uh, shields?" said Jack as more blasts streaked by. "Shields would be nice!"

"Powering up the generator now!" replied Anna.

Jack heard a hum kick in and felt static electricity ripple through him. Instantly he realized the ship's shields had been raised and were now active. Not a moment too soon either, as a blast landed squarely on the rear shield, right where one of their engines was.

The shield wasn't like anything Jack had seen when Shepherd was fighting the Deathlords. It was an invisible barrier around the ship, created by densely charged electrons that repelled all matter and absorbed energy. However, the shield could only be maintained as long as the generator on the ship was able to achieve a certain output. With each impact, the generator would compensate by redistributing electrons to the impacted areas, thus weakening the entire shield array, at least until it had a chance to power back up and generate more electrons to reinforce the shield.

Jack eased the ship up as it reached the bottom of its descent and skimmed the surface of the ocean. He had an idea and punched up the speed as much as he could, hoping it would give him enough time to pull off what he had planned.

"You ready with those weapons yet?" asked Jack, keeping his eye on the steadily gaining shards.

"We have a rear plasma battery," said Shepherd. "Firing it up now."

"All right," said Jack. "Do we have a forward laser, too?"

"We have two of them," said Shepherd.

"You're going to want to get those ready, also."

"Why?" asked Shepherd suspiciously.

"I'm gonna try something," said Jack. "Just be ready, okay?"

Shepherd grumbled but didn't argue. He opened fire on the incoming shards as they dove into position behind them.

"Hold on," said Jack, as he suddenly cut the acceleration of the ship.

The sudden drop in speed caused the shards to overshoot their intended position on their tail. Shepherd nailed one of them as it screamed by overhead, causing it to explode in a puff of black dust and green fire.

No sooner had the shards made their pass than Jack kicked the ship back into gear. He felt the boom of the engines as the sudden burst jacked up their acceleration, and they were now on the heels of the shards.

"NOW!" yelled Jack.

Shepherd let loose with the forward plasma cannons. The two shards tried to turn in opposite directions to avoid the blasts, but one of them wasn't fast enough, and it got caught in Shepherd's crosshairs and exploded.

Jack turned the ship in pursuit of the last shard. It banked and weaved as Shepherd kept firing at it, but Jack kept on its tail.

"Yeah, not so much fun when you're the one getting shot at, huh?" mumbled Jack as he tried to keep pace with the smaller vessel. For a rather big ship, Jack was surprised he was able to maneuver as well as he was.

The shard pulled up into a climb and began flying toward the sun. Jack followed, pushing the thrusters to keep his prey from escaping him. The direct sunlight from the viewscreen blinded him, and he lost sight of his target.

Jack glanced back at his radar display. A red dot signified the remaining shard was still there, but it was quickly moving out of range. Just as Jack was going to try another burst of speed to keep up, three new dots emerged in front of him, and the radar beeped a warning about new enemy contacts.

"Crap!" exclaimed Jack as he banked the ship hard to the right. No sooner had he done so than more enemy blaster fire shot by on the trajectory of their previous course. The sun had blinded him to the arrival of enemy backup, and that last shard had tried to lure him into an ambush.

As the three newcomers shot by, the original shard had come around and was now on Jack's tail. Plasma fire began to assault the rear shields, and the ship complained to Jack in protest.

Jack tried to bank and weave the ship, but he could not shake the shard, even with Shepherd firing at it. It was just too small and maneuverable. And once his Deathlord friends came back around, they were all going to be in trouble.

"Jack," yelled Anna. "We need to get out of Earth's atmosphere! We can maneuver better in space!"

"Are you serious?" asked Jack.

"The ship is too big to out-fly the shards in the atmosphere," said Anna. "Without the wind resistance and gravity, we should be maneuverable enough to escape their fire."

"No, I mean… I've like, never *been* in space before…" said Jack.

"Have you ever been obliterated into a million pieces before?" asked Shepherd. "Because that's what's going to happen if our shields keep taking this pounding!"

"Space it is," said Jack meekly.

Jack banked the ship, took it into a climb, and felt his breath catch in his throat. In the sky was a hazy image of a massive monstrosity he had not noticed in the commotion of the dogfight. It was still far away, but even from this distance, Jack could tell it was gigantic, possibly the size of a city one would see when flying over in an airplane.

At its center was a round disk-shaped vessel, with six humongous, long, curled spikes jutting from its sides, making it look like a massive, hideous spider of some type, ready to descend upon the planet. The outer casing was a dark, shining obsidian, littered with veins of green and purple light, and at the bottom of the disk was a large circle which glowed white hot with energy, like a soulless eye gazing out from beneath it.

Jack felt the pit of his stomach curl in on itself. He could only assume that thing was the Deathlord mothership, and if that were indeed the case, heading toward it was probably not the best idea.

Then, in the instant it took him to wonder about how he should adjust course, the ship responded with a long-range sensor reading of their immediate area. What Jack saw chilled him to his core. There wasn't just one Deathlord mothership in orbit above Earth; there were literally hundreds of them. In his mind's eye, the ship fed him the location of the entire enemy fleet. He saw how they'd encircled the planet, each one staring down at the surface with its horrible white eye, blazing ever hotter and brighter with each passing second.

The reality of their situation suddenly settled in on Jack. The ordeals at the Burger Shack and in the temple were scary, but they all seemed like something isolated, as though once the military found out about it, they could send in troops and tanks and airplanes to the rescue. But now Jack could see that aliens hadn't just invaded River Heights; they had surrounded the entire planet with ships full of an army that couldn't die.

The ship was rocked again as more plasma fire assaulted its shields. The radar in front of Jack whined with alarm as more contacts appeared on it — ten more shards, all coming from the mothership in the distance. If the shards closing in from behind didn't get their ship, those surely would.

"Shepherd..." Jack said. "We've got incoming!"

Jack heard Shepherd curse under his breath as he checked his console and saw the newly approaching shards. More thuds echoed in Jack's mind as the rear shields were hit again. He pulled up a rear image from the ship on the holoscreen and saw the four shards had locked onto his tail. Suddenly, Jack found himself wishing he could fire the forward plasma cannons while Shepherd focused his attention on their tag-alongs.

The ship responded instantly by materializing a new holoscreen in front of Jack with targeting reticules and energy readouts. The display looked just like it did on *Nova Commander IV*, and Jack inherently knew he now had control over the forward cannons.

"I'm taking control of the forward lasers," Jack told Shepherd. "You focus on the guys behind us."

"I hope you know what you're doing," said Shepherd.

"Me, too," mumbled Jack.

The new Deathlord shards were closing the distance quickly from the front. Jack's ship was still climbing. If he could exit the Earth's atmosphere before they were within firing range, he might be able to pull something off.

Jack wondered if he could take control of the shields as easily as he did the plasma cannons. Sure enough, the computer granted him access. He quickly lowered the forward shields and used some of that energy to reinforce the rear shields, while diverting the rest to his engines to give him a boost of speed.

"We've lost forward shields!" shrieked Anna. "It won't let me raise them!"

"Don't worry," said Jack. "I did that."

"You lowered our shields?" yelled Shepherd.

"Trust me, I know what I'm doing!" Jack yelled back. "Anna, get me all the power you can to the engines!"

Anna and Shepherd exchanged worried looks, but Anna did as she was told, and Shepherd went back to trying to keep the fighters off their tail.

The sky was darkening as the ship kept climbing and the blue mist of the atmosphere began to bleed away around them. Jack wished he had time to appreciate how cool it was that he was the first kid ever in the history of River Heights – and probably the world – to actually make it into outer space, but the oncoming Deathlord shards had just reached firing range.

Jack instantly dumped power into his forward shields and rolled the ship, looping around in a corkscrew motion and firing as he did so.

The wall of shards heading his way scrambled, returning fire as they swerved. Jack caught two of them in his maneuver, signaled by a brief flash of green flame. One of the shards did not bank away fast enough and rammed into one of the shards that had been chasing Jack's ship. *Another two down; now just ten more to go.*

"Great Scott!" exclaimed Professor Green. "We made it past them!"

"We're not out of the woods yet," said Jack glancing at his radar readout. "They're coming back around."

"Get us away from the fleet," said Shepherd. "Move us out into open space as much as you can. If we can take them down far enough away from reinforcements, it might give us time to make the jump to hyperspace."

"Sounds good to me," said Jack as he increased acceleration. As they began to move away, he glanced out the viewscreen at the massive Deathlord mothership to the side of them and marveled at it. Jack didn't have much time to ponder the size of the enemy fleet before his proximity alarm warned him that the shards were now back in range and quickly gaining on him.

"The bad guys are back," he warned everybody.

"You fly," said Shepherd. "I'll take care of them."

Unencumbered by gravity or wind resistance, Jack banked the ship and took it in a wide arc, veering away as Shepherd fired on the pursuers who had adjusted their course to follow. Jack immediately noticed a difference in the way the ship handled now that they were out in space. Indeed, it moved like a much smaller ship, able to turn much more easily and more quickly than it had in the atmosphere.

Red bolts of death screamed by as Jack banked and weaved his ship. Some landed on the rear shields, but most were missing their mark. Shepherd was able to tag a few of the shards with return fire, causing some to break off the ship's tail.

Jack turned the ship to chase after some of the shards that had broken off and opened fire with the forward plasma cannons. Two more shards exploded thanks to his efforts.

Jack glanced at the radar screen. He saw six more dots buzzing around on the readout. Jack cut all power to the thrusters and brought the ship to a standstill.

"What are you doing?" asked Shepherd with alarm. "Why have we stopped?"

"Just giving them a chance to regroup," said Jack casually.

"You're what?" said Shepherd, Anna, and Green in unison.

"I've noticed they tend to like to attack in formation," said Jack.

"Jack," growled Shepherd. "Get us *moving* again!"

"Relax," said Jack. "I spent most of my freshman year perfecting this maneuver."

Jack called up his holoscreen and sure enough, the remaining six shards had joined up into a "V" formation and were turning in unison to make a pass at Jack's location.

Jack diverted all the power to the forward shields and reversed the thrusters to start moving the ship backwards as the shards closed in on them from the front, effectively slowing their approach.

The shards opened fire, their plasma bolts impacting the forward shields rapidly.

"Blast it, Jack!" yelled Shepherd. "Return fire!"

Jack ignored Shepherd and kept letting the shards close in, keeping a careful eye on the strength of the forward shields, which were getting hammered by the Deathlords' blasts.

Then, just as the shards got close enough, Jack engaged the ship's side thrusters, jutting his craft horizontally away from the trajectory of the Deathlord shards. As he did so, he rotated the ship to keep in line with the enemy formation and opened fire. His first blast impacted the lead shard, and the momentum of the formation allowed the other two shards on its wing to fly into his blaster fire, destroying them both.

The remaining three shards scrambled, but not before Jack re-engaged his thrusters and tagged one of them before he could get out of range.

Now there were only two.

Jack redistributed his shields and punched the acceleration, locking onto the tail of one of the remaining shards. It was weaving about evasively, but in space, Jack's ship was able to keep up with it. It was only a matter of time before Jack got the fighter in his crosshairs and obliterated it.

Plasma bolts impacted the side of the ship as the last remaining shard made a strafing run. Jack rolled away from the blasts and came around onto the tail of the enemy fighter.

"Game over, dip-wad," said Jack as he opened fire.

One final explosion marked the last of the Deathlord shards. Jack had no doubt they'd be sending more the first chance they got, so he turned and began accelerating away from the Deathlord fleet as fast as he could.

Once they were far enough away from the fleet, Jack allowed himself to breathe a huge sigh of relief.

"Wow," he said. "That was intense."

He turned his chair and looked at his companions. Green and Anna were smiling. Even Shepherd looked relieved.

"I've got to admit," breathed Shepherd. "That was some good flying, Jack."

Did Mr. Shepherd just give him a compliment? Jack's chest welled up with a bit of pride.

"That? Ah, that was nothin'," lied Jack. "Give me something harder next time."

"You'd think you've been flying a spaceship your entire life," said Anna, smiling. "I don't think a trained Imperial pilot could have done any better."

"Who knew playing all that *Nova Commander* would come in handy?" said Jack as he leaned back and locked his hands behind his head. "And they say video games are a waste of time. Pft."

"Well, I think I've done it!" cheered Green. "I believe I've found us a hyperspace trajectory that can get us into friendly space."

"Good," said Shepherd, sounding uncharacteristically upbeat. "Input it into the computer."

"I just need to compare it to the ship's star charts and do a few more calculations to adjust for universal expansion over the past fifty thousand years or so," said Green.

"Do it," said Shepherd. "The sooner we're out of site of the Deathlord fleet, the better."

Jack sat up in the captain's chair. "Wait," he said. "We can't just, like, *leave*."

"We have to," said Shepherd.

"But what about all the people on Earth?" asked Jack. "I can't leave my mom and friends down there with the Deathlords all over the place."

Shepherd, Anna, and Green all exchanged worried looks.

"We have to go back for them," insisted Jack.

"Jack," said Shepherd. "This ship is impressive. But it cannot take on an entire Deathlord fleet by itself."

"How do you know?" asked Jack. "Maybe there's some super-weapon on here we haven't found yet. This is supposed to be the thing that defeats them, right? The Ancient artifact you guys were looking for?"

"We need time to study it, Jack," said Anna, "to figure out its mysteries, what it's capable of. Now is not the time to go rushing back into battle, especially considering our narrow escape."

Jack frowned. She was correct, of course. Jack had picked up enough about the ship to get them past the Deathlords alive, but he had a feeling he hadn't even scratched the surface of what the ship could do. And dealing with more Deathlord shards again wasn't very appealing either.

"But we'll come back for them, right?" asked Jack. "When I get you home, you'll raise your army and come back and save the Earth, right?"

Everyone was quiet.

"Right?" insisted Jack.

Shepherd looked at Anna, as though he were waiting for her cue to say something.

"If you can get us back home," said Anna carefully. "I will do everything in my power to help you."

"Promise me," said Jack.

Anna straightened and looked Jack in the eye. "I promise," she said.

Jack relaxed. He trusted Anna. He just hoped that the Deathlords wouldn't enslave everybody before they had a chance to return and beat them down.

"Okeydokey," said Green. "That should do it! I've calculated a hyperspace route to Kelmar Uropa. We should be able to dock at the Imperial outpost there and get updated star maps for our journey home."

"Punch it in," ordered Shepherd. "Jack, get ready to take us to hyperspace."

"Okay," said Jack. "Just give me a minute to figure out how that works."

"Make it fast," said Shepherd.

Jack turned his chair back around to the viewscreen and asked the ship about how it's hyperspace drive worked. The computer buzzed the information right into his brain.

Once the hyperspace route was input into the computer, a special engine on board called a Brane Accelerator would create a window into the hyperspace dimension by sending out a wave of energy. This energy would vibrate a bunch of little things called p-branes, which were tiny particles that acted like a membrane separating different dimensions. The window would be open long enough for the ship to pass through, at which point its engines would kick into lightspeed until the ship reached its destination. Then they could open another window back into the previous dimension.

It seemed easy enough to do, but something still felt wrong about all this. Jack didn't like the idea of leaving his friends and family behind — especially not with a bunch of deadly aliens all over the place. He'd never left River Heights in his life, and now he was getting ready to head to another planet! He hadn't even packed a toothbrush. The whole thing was more than a little scary.

"The coordinates have been input into the computer," said Green. "We are ready to make the jump to hyperspace!"

"Jack," said Shepherd. "Get us out of here."

"Okay," said Jack.

Jack was getting ready to activate the Brane Accelerator when he called up the holoscreen for one last look at Earth.

He sighed. *I'll come back, mom,* he thought. *I promise.*

Then, just as he was about to activate the jump to hyperspace, something happened on the screen that stopped him. Suddenly, the openings on the bottom of the Deathlord motherships surrounding the planet erupted with a bright white energy, sending pillars of it to the Earth's surface.

Jack watched on the holoscreen as the columns of energy impacted the Earth, and the terrain around them rippled and charred. Jack's eyes grew wide, and his breath caught in his throat.

"Wait a minute..." he said.

Jack made the holoscreen bigger and turned to his companions.

"What's going on?" asked Jack urgently, pointing to the image before him. "What are they doing?"

"Jack, activate the hyperspace window," insisted Shepherd.

Jack ignored Shepherd and turned back to the holoscreen. He was transfixed by the image before him. Every mothership had opened fire and hundreds of fiery white columns drilled into the planet like it was a giant pincushion. Where they impacted, a ghostly haze spread out, covering the Earth's surface.

An alarm bell rang within Jack's head. He remembered when Anna had told him about how the Deathlords were devastating the galaxy. When she'd said that, Jack didn't quite grasp what she'd meant.

But now, a horrible realization descended upon him.

Oh my God... thought Jack. *Earth... they're destroying Earth!*

Jack's thoughts instantly went to his mother and then to his friends, and he felt an overwhelming sense of panic wash over him as he realized they were still down there.

Without a moment's hesitation, Jack turned the ship around and sped up, rushing back toward the planet.

"What are you doing?" barked Shepherd. "We need to get out of here!"

"I have to save them!" yelled Jack.

"Jack, please, there's nothing we can do..." he heard Anna say.

He ignored them. He ignored all of them. This ship was supposed to be some sort of kick-butt weapon right? Maybe he could stop this. Maybe there was something on the ship he hadn't found yet that could wipe out every last Deathlord in the area. He had to try. He had to do *something!*

Before Jack could ask the ship about anything, however, Shepherd rushed up to Jack and clamped his hand down hard on Jack's arm. Jack winced and looked up at Shepherd.

"Blast it, Jack, you'll get us all killed! We can't save anyone — we need to jump out of here *now!*"

"I have to try! My mom–"

"She's dead!" yelled Shepherd. "They're all dead! And unless we jump right now—"

"Inertial dampeners OFF!" screamed Jack.

Jack pushed the acceleration of the ship just as the inertial dampeners deactivated. The sudden thrust hurled Shepherd back, tossing him against the far wall of the bridge. Anna and Green were pinned against their seats. As long as the ship was moving, the others were helpless to do anything.

"Oh, dear…" mumbled Green.

The radar whined as more shards appeared, rushing up to meet them. Jack gritted his teeth and accessed the ship's weapons. He unleashed a steady volley of plasma fire to clear the way in front of him. Dozens of bright red streaks rushed toward the ship as the shards returned fire, but he boosted all energy to the forward shields.

The blasts impacted the shields, sending dull thuds through the ship, but Jack did not change his course. He put as much power into the engines as he could spare and rushed forward, breaking through the wall of incoming enemy fighters.

As he shot by them, he knew they'd adjust course and come up from behind. Jack redistributed the shield power and hoped he was moving fast enough to give the generator time to recharge before the shards could catch up.

"JACK! STOP!!!" yelled Anna.

Jack paid no attention to her. All his focus was on getting to the planet. *Mom should still be at the Fox Hole*, he thought. *If I can get there and pick her up or something, then I could go get Matt, and Chunk, and Peter, and the rest…*

Jack could imagine the look on his mom's face when he arrived. She'd be so happy to see him, so happy her son was able to come to the rescue…

"JACK!!!" yelled Shepherd.

Radar alarms started beeping. More shards had emerged from other Deathlord motherships, all moving to intercept him. There were so many of them, coming from all directions. Jack pulled all the power he could find and dumped it into his engines. He had to go faster! He had to get past the Deathlords and back to Earth!

It was directly in his sights. The ghostly haze had spread out over the entire surface by now, making the planet seem to glow.

It almost looked beautiful in a weird way... until dark cracks began to form around the face of the planet.

"No..." said Jack, feeling his blood pound behind his eyes.

He was getting close; he just needed a bit more speed, a bit more time!

The cracks in the surface began to grow and spiderweb all across the face of planet.

"NO!" cried Jack.

Panic gripped his chest. His heart was racing, his breathing rapid.

Red plasma blasts streaked in from all sides as the shards came into range, thundering against the shields of the ship.

The dark cracks rippled through every inch of the planet and began to glow with a fiery golden fury. The surface of the planet started to char as the atmosphere swirled and blackened.

"NOOOOOOOOOOOOOOOO!!!!!!!!" screamed Jack.

And then, with a terrible, thunderous bang...

...the Earth exploded.

CHAPTER ✺ 16

As most people know, it's a very rare thing for a planet to actually explode. It would be about as common as walking down the street and seeing a nearby rock suddenly blow up for no good reason. But when it does happen, it isn't pretty. It's not as if there is a massive explosion and suddenly the entire planet has vanished.

No, when a planet explodes, it tends to be violently ripped apart, shooting chunks of it with great force every which way imaginable. Such was the case when the Deathlord Planetkillers created an antimatter detonation in the Earth's core causing a chain reaction equal to the force of a hundred quadrillion nuclear weapons.

But the result is always the same – no more planet. Just a bunch of dust, debris, and rocks cluttering up the space where the planet used to be.

So it's rather plain to see, the whole process is quite messy. But the Deathlord fleet somehow had the ability to remain in orbit around a planet as it blew up and not sustain the least bit of damage (another mystery of Deathlord technology whose answer had yet to be revealed at this time). However, the same could not be said for the ship Earthman Jack and his companions were on.

They had not yet reached Earth when the planet exploded, which was a good thing since if they had, that probably would have been the end of our story. But they were close enough that when Earth did explode, the impact of the blast hit them like a rampaging hukkah beast from the eighth circle of Levitahn — which is to say, extremely hard.

And had Jack not boosted the power to his shields as he made his mad dash back to the planet, it's a very real possibility that their ship could have been destroyed, along with the Earth. Luckily, for the universe at large and everyone in it, this was not the case. But the ship did incur some extremely heavy damage.

The Ancient starship drifted among the remains of the destroyed planet, its engines off, its shields down, and its power barely functioning. Inside, things weren't much prettier. The bridge of the ship flashed its red warning lights as sparks flew from damaged computer consoles. Half the viewscreen on the bridge was not working, and the other half flickered as if it were about to go out completely.

With the inertial dampeners turned off, it was not a very nice predicament for those who were in the ship at the time of the explosion either. Shepherd, Anna, and Green had all been tossed around, and even Jack was hurled from his chair, which seemed to be designed to keep the pilot firmly in its grasp as the ship flew.

As Jack came to, he could feel the thumping in the parts of his body affected by the impact, which would no doubt become a fine collection of bruises in a few hours. He had a cut on his head, and his knee ached, but other than that he was okay.

He heard Shepherd, Green, and Anna stir. He pulled himself up and looked at the piece of the viewscreen that was still working. What he saw there was an image that would haunt him for a long time to come.

Between the flickering of the screen, he could make out the Deathlord fleet, stationed exactly where it had been before, but they were no longer surrounding Earth. Where the planet had been was now nothing but a mess of charred rocks, twisting and twirling as they slowly moved through space.

In that moment, to his sheer and utter horror, Jack realized that his home – and everyone he loved – had been destroyed.

A cold chill washed over him and he felt suddenly light-headed. His brain struggled to comprehend what had just happened. After all, losing an entire planet... it was just such a BIG event, anyone would have had a hard time grasping it.

"Princess," Shepherd croaked as he got to his feet. "Are you okay?"

"I'm all right," Anna said, nursing her arm.

"Professor," said Shepherd as he turned to Green who was wobbling around the frayed and battered consoles. "Damage report."

"Oh dear, oh dear, oh dear..." muttered the Professor, his big brown eyes fighting off the urge to roll every which way. He forced himself to focus on the ship's systems console to get a reading on the state of their vessel. "Engines are down, as are shields, and weapons... pretty much everything is offline except for emergency life support at the moment. And even that is precarious."

Anna saw Jack staring at the viewscreen and looked at the image on it herself. A wave of sadness washed over her. She had not been on Earth for long, but the time she had spent on it was pleasant. Everything from the cool autumn breeze, to the green grass and the blue sky had been beautiful and peaceful for her. And all those people who were now lost to them... she found herself somewhat grateful she had decided not to befriend any of them.

And then she thought of Jack. He did have friends and family there... friends and family who were now gone forever.

What must he be feeling now? What could she possibly say that would have any hope of comforting him? She didn't know, but she approached him anyway and put her hand on his shoulder.

"Jack," she said. "I'm so sorry—"

She felt a shiver run through Jack about a split second before he turned and sprinted away from her, making his way to the rear entrance of the bridge and into the rest of the ship.

"Jack! Wait!" Anna called after him and began to give chase.

"Princess, stop!" Shepherd called after her, but she ignored him and exited the bridge, as well.

Jack ran down the curved hallway of the ship as fast as he could. He didn't know where he was going or where the hallway would lead, but he gritted his teeth and ran as hard as he was able to. He paid no attention to the lights as they blinked in and out of working order, or the occasional spark from an exposed access panel, or even any of the doors he passed that led to other areas of the still unexplored ship. His eyes were locked on the floor before him as he pumped his legs and arms, running, running, running…

Finally, his lungs were burning and his side began to cramp. He turned to an open door leading into a small empty room, which could very well have been some type of storage area. Tears were stinging Jack's eyes and his breaths were ragged as he cried and gasped for air all at the same time.

A rage-filled scream erupted from deep inside him, and he turned and punched the wall of the room as hard as he could. His hand hurt as it made impact with the shiny metal surface, but Jack didn't care. He punched it again, and again, and again, beating on it like it was a Deathlord, or J.C. Rowdey, or Mr. Shepherd, or anyone else he had ever hated in his life.

At last, when his knuckles burned with pain and he was unable to abuse the wall any longer, Jack stumbled into a corner of the room and slid to the floor, hugging his knees and weeping.

Images flashed into his mind. He thought of his small room in the trailer at 7 Eagle Hill. He thought of visiting his mom at the Fox Hole and getting a free slice of cherry pie. He thought about hanging out with Matt, Chunk, and Peter at Big Jim's and eating really crappy pizza. He thought about school, and the Juniper family cornfields, and all the other things that made River Heights home.

And then he thought about how he'd never see any of it again.

Sadness welled up in his stomach, making it feel as heavy as a bowling ball. What had happened? Why didn't somebody stop it? What was he going to do now?

Jack gave in to his sorrow and allowed himself to cry uncontrollably. He felt like all this was his fault somehow. He felt like instead of joyriding in a spaceship and thinking everything was so cool, he should have known what was going to happen. He should have done something! Anything!

"Jack?" came Anna's voice.

Jack looked up and through his tears saw Anna standing in the doorway. She walked over to him and knelt down beside him.

"Jack, I'm so sorry about what happened..." she said.

She reached out to him, but Jack jerked away.

"Don't *touch me!*" he hissed.

Anna pulled back from him, a look of surprise on her face. "I – I just... wanted to let you know that I know what you're going through, and..."

An angry laugh escaped from Jack. "You know what I'm going through, huh?" sneered Jack. "But what do you care? You still have a home. You have a place you can go back to. You're royalty or something, right? You can just go back to you're big ol' space-castle and tell all your space-friends about how you got to see some lame planet blow up before playing space-polo or space-cricket or whatever the heck it is *your highness* does for fun!"

"Jack—"

Jack pushed Anna away from him. She stumbled back, a mortified look on her face.

"This is *your fault!*" screamed Jack. "They came looking for *you!* I wish I'd never helped you! Maybe if they had gotten you at that diner, they'd have left, and they wouldn't have blown everything up!"

Jack's words cut into Anna. "Please, Jack... you don't understand..."

"I don't care!" snapped Jack. "I don't want to understand! I have nothing anymore! NOTHING! My mom, my friends, they're all dead because of *you!*"

Anna was about to say something when she heard a voice at the door.

"Princess," said Shepherd.

She looked up to see the armored Paragon standing in the doorway. He was looking at her with that look he so often wore, the one that said, "*I know what's best for you.*"

"Leave him be," he said.

"Yeah," said Jack. "Leave me be. Get out of my sight. Both of you."

Anna got to her feet and joined Shepherd in the doorway. She glanced back at Jack as he buried his face in his knees, right before Shepherd closed the door.

When they got back to the bridge, Professor Green was busily rushing from one console to another, trying to interface with the ship.

"What's our status?" asked Shepherd.

"Improving!" said Green cheerily. "The ship seems to be repairing its systems and hull quite nicely."

"How?" asked Shepherd.

"Hard to say exactly without further study. From what I can tell, the ship is somehow able to regenerate anything that has been damaged or destroyed - everything from its hull, to its engines, to its computer systems. It's really quite fascinating."

"Regenerate?" asked Shepherd. "Are you saying the ship is able to... regrow parts that have been lost?"

"Exactly!" said Green. "It's not like there is a nanobot repair system that's rebuilding the ship like the Imperial Fleet uses. The repairs almost seem... well, organic for lack of a better word. Much like the way one's body can heal after an injury. However, it's far more advanced than that. I'm unable to determine where the material the ship is using to repair itself comes from, and there seems to be some artificial intelligence associated with how it chooses to prioritize its repairs. If I didn't know any better, I'd say this ship was... well, alive!"

"A living ship?" said Shepherd.

"In a sense," replied the Professor. "I haven't had much time to analyze it, obviously, but there is an unmistakable stamp of intelligence here, what with how it's able to interact with Jack and adjust itself to suit his needs. Then there's the whole idea behind how it's able to use Entanglement - which, by the way, is still in the process of blowing my mind."

Shepherd's own mind raced at Green's revelations. There was a lot about the ship that intrigued him, as well, but as much as he would have liked to have dwelled on its wonders along with the Professor, the direness of their situation had won out over his intellectual curiosity.

"How long until she can fly?" asked Shepherd.

"Hard to say," said Green. "It depends on when it gets around to the engines. Right now it seems to be focusing on life support and hull integrity."

Shepherd looked at the viewscreen. The image had stabilized enough so that he could see Deathlord shards spreading out, slowly moving amongst the debris.

"They know we were caught in the blast and they're searching for us," said Shepherd. "It'll only be a matter or time before they find the ship. If our engines aren't repaired before then, we're not going to have a chance."

"I will see if I can re-prioritize the repairs," said Green.

"While you're at it, see if you can unlock the flight controls. Someone other than Jack needs to be able to fly this thing."

"That might be a bit tricky," said Green. "Keep in mind, dear Paragon, this ship is something most of my ilk would trade their entire lives to study. It's the single most advanced piece of machinery I've ever seen. Asking me to interact with it is one thing, but to actually re-program it? Alter it? I wouldn't know where to begin."

Shepherd grimaced. "Just see what you can do," he said. "I don't want to rely on Jack to get us back to Imperial space, do you understand?"

"Of course," said Green. "But he's proven to be quite a capable pilot. The boy was only trying to save his family…"

"I'm well aware of what he was trying to do," said Shepherd. "And as courageous as it was, it was also foolish. He may have just given us up to the Deathlords after all. I don't want to trust him with the safety of Her Royal Highness unless absolutely necessary. Are you in agreement?"

Green nodded. "I will do what I can," he replied.

As Green went back to the computers, Shepherd turned and saw Anna standing by the captain's chair, looking at the image on the viewscreen. He walked up to her and put his arm around her shoulders, attempting to comfort her.

They stood quietly for a few moments looking at the destruction spread out before them until Anna finally spoke.

"It's my fault," she said quietly.

"It's not," said Shepherd.

"I brought them to Earth," said the Princess. "They came for me, and they destroyed it."

"If we do not defeat the Deathlords, no planet is safe," said Shepherd. "Earth was not aware of the threat, but that does not mean they were ever in any less danger. Without some way to stop the Deathlords, it would have only been a matter of time before Earth had been destroyed, along with every other planet in the universe."

Anna looked at Shepherd, her eyes glassy with tears.

"*Can* they be stopped?" she asked. "How do you stop something with the power to do all this..."

"If you believe they can be stopped, then there is a way," said Shepherd.

"Your Paragon Creed does not seem very practical right now," Anna sniffled.

"That does not make it any less true," said Shepherd. "If this ship is really the weapon of the Ancients, then we can use it to stop the Deathlords, and make sure a planet never falls to them again."

"And if it's really the weapon of the Ancients," replied Anna, "we're going to need Jack to use it. And he hates me."

"This is too important to be entrusted to Jack," said Shepherd. "We'll find a way around him. He can't handle the responsibility that comes with this ship."

"And yet, it's his," said Anna. "And after everything he's ever known has been stolen from him, can we really take that away, too?"

"We do what we must," replied Shepherd. "For the greater good."

Anna looked down at her feet sadly.

"He's the one who asked me to the dance, you know?" she said quietly.

"The dance?" asked Shepherd, surprised.

"Homecoming," smiled Anna, as if the memory of it made her feel better. "He said if I agreed to go with him, he'd find some way to get out of his punishment, even if it meant washing the principal's car for a year."

"Jack?" said Shepherd, dumbfounded. "He... he's the one?"

"I snuck out to see him. He took me to have burgers and milkshakes," she laughed. "It was my first date, and the world ends. Go figure."

Shepherd stared at Anna. He guessed it all made sense. That would explain why Jack was with her when he found them at school. But in all honesty, out of all the boys she had to choose from, Jack was the last person he would have thought Anna would actually care for.

"You... like him?" asked Shepherd.

Anna sighed. "It doesn't matter anymore," she said. "He'll never forgive me for what happened."

Shepherd took a moment to think about Jack. He had always been a difficult Earthman to deal with. He was insolent, stubborn, and refused to change his ways, no matter how hard Shepherd was on him. But he had also begun to see the good things about the boy, too. Despite it all, he had managed to keep Anna safe from the Deathlords. He had unlocked an Ancient temple, learned to fly a space ship, and successfully fought off wave after wave of Deathlord starfighters – something most trained fighter pilots in the Imperial Space Fleet may not have been able to have done.

Suddenly, Shepherd knew what Anna saw in him. For a man – a boy of 15 even – to accomplish all that, especially in one day, was quite a feat. Perhaps his dealings with Jack in school had blinded him to the boy's potential. He had always known there was more to Jack than just being some troublemaker, but his thoughts had never gone much further than a casual interest in some alien boy on a foreign world.

Now he could see things had changed. Shepherd looked at the remains of Earth floating in space and remembered his own experience years ago. Those events had changed him and had made him what he was. Perhaps, with the right guidance... Jack could do the same.

"Don't be so hard on yourself, Princess," said Shepherd. "Jack's just lost everything he has ever known. He's upset, angry, and confused. He did not mean what he said."

"That does not make it any less true," said Anna.

"Whether he likes it or not, our quest has become his now," said Shepherd. "He will rise to the occasion, no matter what he told you."

"How can you be so sure?"

"Because, I know Jack," said Shepherd. "The boy doesn't back down. He's young and inexperienced, but at his heart he's a fighter. And when he comes around, he will do anything he can to aid us against our enemy."

"And you really believe that?" asked Anna.

"I do," said Shepherd.

Anna smiled. "Then it must be true," she said. "Now we just need Jack to believe it."

"Don't worry," said Shepherd. "I'll take care of that."

CHAPTER 17

"Don't cry sweetie," she had told him. "You don't need to cry."

Jack could remember it so clearly in his mind's eye; it was as if a movie projector were playing, throwing its bright image onto the wall in front of him. He'd been in third grade, and Jesse Walton had made fun of him during recess for not having a dad. Jack had pounced on the kid, arms flailing with reckless abandon before Mrs. Kellog had dragged him off, sending Jack to the principal's office and Jesse to the nurse.

They'd called Jack's mom to take him out of school for the day. She'd had to leave work early to come get him and to explain the situation at home to the principal. The entire car ride back to Eagle Hill, Jack's mother had screamed and lectured him about fighting at school and about how the last thing she needed right now was for Jack to get into trouble while she was working. But he didn't care. He just stared out the window sullenly until the car ride was over.

No sooner had they pulled up to their trailer than Jack had hopped out and had run inside to his room, slamming the door shut. His mother had called after him, but Jack had been too angry to hear her. He'd ripped the sheets off the bed and had attacked them, crumpling them up into a tangled mess and throwing them against the wall with as loud of a scream as he could muster, punching and kicking his mattress until he had collapsed, exhausted, on top of it.

Then, finally, he had started crying.

It was then when his mom had quietly opened the door to his room and had sat down beside him. She had placed a hand gently on his back, but Jack had turned away from her, anger and resentment still roiling inside him. Then, her hand had found its way to his head, where his mother had gingerly stroked his tussled brown hair.

"Don't cry sweetie," she had said. "You don't need to cry."

"Go away," he'd answered. "Leave me alone."

His mother hadn't, though. She had sat by Jack's side, continuing to stroke his hair, calming him as she did so.

"I'm sorry I yelled at you," she'd said. "Do you want to talk about why you beat up on that kid?"

Jack had turned to look up at his mother. She had long brown hair, which fell down around her shoulders in wavy curls. Her eyes were large and kind, colored green with specks of gold, and she had the largest, warmest smile Jack could remember anyone ever having. When he had looked at her, the turmoil inside him had subsided.

"He told everyone not to play with me," Jack had mumbled.

"And why did he do that?"

"He said dads don't like me, and if anyone played with me, their dads would leave, too, so if they loved their dads, they shouldn't play with me."

His mother's smile had drawn into a tight line as her brow had furrowed.

"What a little jerk," she'd said.

"That's why I hit him."

Jack's mom had sighed and nodded. "I'm not saying he didn't deserve it," she'd said. "But you can't go around beating up kids who make fun of daddy not being around."

"Why not?"

"Lots of reasons, sweetie," she had replied. "But most of all, your dad wouldn't want you to. He's a good man, who likes to help people. He has always done the right thing, no matter what, and he would want you to do the same thing. No matter how bad the kids at school tease you about him being gone, just know that wherever he is, he loves you so very, very much. So whatever anyone says to hurt your feelings, it can't be true, because the only one who loves you more than your dad is me."

Jack had sat up and had looked at his mom.

"Then why'd he leave?" Jack had asked.

His mom had looked at him sadly. "I don't know," she'd replied. "It's… complicated."

"Did… did he not like me or something?"

"Oh, sweetie, no," she'd said immediately. "Your father loved you very much. You meant the world to him."

"Then why isn't he here?" Jack had asked again, unable to keep tears from pooling in his eyes.

Absent an answer, Jack's mom had reached out, taking him in her arms and hugging him close. Emotion had washed over him like a tidal wave as he had cried into her shoulder. She had rocked him back and forth gently, stroking his hair to comfort him. He had held onto her tightly, his body shaking with his sobs. Eventually, once the tears had run their course, he had pulled back.

Somehow, somewhere – as if by the magic of simply being a mom – his mother had gotten hold of a clean tissue. She had used it to dab at his tears and to wipe his nose clean. When he had looked at her, she had smiled, her eyes filled with a love and kindness so powerful, it had driven away the sadness that had overcome him.

"Jack," she had said, "sometimes, bad things happen, even to good people who don't deserve it. I wish, more than anything, that I could protect you from every bad thing that could ever happen to you in life, but... there will come a time, many times in fact, when you'll have to deal with bad things that are sad and painful."

"Why?" Jack had asked.

"That's just the way life is."

"Life sucks," he had grumbled.

His mom had laughed. "Sometimes," she'd replied. "But not always. There will be good things that happen to you, too. You just can't allow the bad things to take over."

"How do you do that?"

"You fight back!" she'd said, playfully poking his stomach. "Not by punching people, or yelling and screaming, but by finding things that make your life better and holding onto them. Like friends and family."

"But... but what if you don't have any friends?"

"You make new ones," his mom had replied, smiling. "There are always people out there willing to be your friend."

"And what if you don't have any family?"

His mom had been quiet for a moment before answering. "Family is what you make of it. You don't have to be related to people for them to be family. They just need to love you, and you just need to love them back. It's that simple."

"But what if... what if no one loves me?"

Jack's mom had cupped his chin with her hand and had looked into his eyes. "Hey," she'd said, "as long as I'm around, someone will always love you. And you'll always love me, right?"

Jack had nodded. His mom had kissed his forehead and had hugged him tightly.

"Then don't worry about it kiddo," she'd said. "As long as we've got each other, no matter what happens, we'll be okay."

It was then the projector in Jack's mind stopped, the images in his mind's eye snapping away like a broken filmstrip. He hugged himself tight, as if to hold on to the ghost of that embrace his mother had given him, to keep the memory from fading. He could feel more tears escape his eyes, their touch strangely cool against his flushed cheeks. He took a deep breath, shaky with emotion, as a sob threatened to escape.

His mom had always been there for him. She had always known what to do and how to make him feel better, even if things had seemed hopeless. But now she was gone, and his whole world – literally – was gone with her.

No more comforting hugs. No more knowing smiles. No more words of wisdom. Jack had lost her. He'd lost his friends. He'd lost everything he'd ever known.

And if that were the case, would Jack ever be okay again? Who would look after him? Who would protect him? Who would love him?

Then, the door to the empty storage room hissed open, and there in the doorway, clad in his brilliant blue and white armor was Shepherd - standing tall and proud, like a knight from some fairy tale.

The sight instantly made Jack sick to his stomach.

"Have you finished crying?" Shepherd asked.

Jack glared at him. "Go away," he said sullenly.

"I need to talk to you," said Shepherd.

"Go. Away."

Shepherd stepped into the room and took a knee in front of Jack.

"I'm going to show you something," he said. "All you need to do is watch and listen. Then I'll leave you alone."

Jack scowled at Shepherd. "I don't need to do anything you say anymore," said Jack. "School's out. It got blown up. Or did you already forget? You're no longer my teacher."

"You're wrong," said Shepherd. "Your education has just begun."

Shepherd held out his hand, and an orb of light created by the gauntlet of his armor appeared hovering over it. Inside the orb Jack could see images of a planet. It wasn't Earth, though. There were fields of pale golden grass, with majestic bone-white trees, covered with red, yellow, and orange leaves. There were massive purple mountains, a golden sky with a red sun, and huge buildings made of stone and brick. Strange animals walked around. People were mingling, buying groceries, laughing, dating, playing, and going to work. Vehicles, which looked sort of like cars, hovered around in the air, and huge spaceships flew in from the atmosphere and landed in gigantic spaceports.

At the center of it all was a palace, made of what looked to be gold, shimmering in the sunlight. It was huge and majestic, the size of a city in and of itself. It had gigantic towers waving crimson flags emblazoned with two golden orbs, one within the other, radiating stripes of gold across the flag. At the center of the palace stood a massive pyramid, flat at the top, just like the temple at the center of the Earth.

Jack gazed at the images in the orb, transfixed. "What is that?" he asked.

"Regalus Prime," said Shepherd. "The seat of the Galactic Regalus Empire. My home planet, and Anna's."

"It's beautiful," said Jack bitterly.

"It was," said Shepherd sadly. "Before the Deathlords came."

The images in the orb changed. Now, entire cities were on fire. People were screaming and dying as Deathlord shards flew overhead, raining blaster-fire down upon them. Above the planet, the Deathlord motherships surrounded it just like they had Earth. There was a gigantic space battle raging, with huge spaceships firing on the Deathlords.

Suddenly, the Deathlord motherships opened fire, sending pillars of white energy down to the planet. And just like Earth, it exploded in a terrible fury, taking out almost all the defending spaceships with it.

Jack's heart skipped a beat.

"My God," he whispered.

"You see, Jack," said Shepherd. "The Princess and I know exactly what you're going through... because it happened to us, as well."

The orb disappeared, and Shepherd lowered his hand. "Anna lost her entire family that day," he said. "Her father, her mother, her brothers... the entire royal bloodline was almost completely wiped out. I lost a great many things as well – my wife, for one. And we both watched it happen in the same manner you did."

"I... I didn't know," said Jack.

"There is much you don't know," said Shepherd. "But one thing you should know, above all else, is the severity of the threat the Deathlords pose to all life in the universe."

Jack nodded. He definitely knew that now.

"How many?" asked Jack. "How many planets have they done this to?"

"Dozens," said Shepherd. "Entire civilizations have been wiped out, species driven to extinction overnight, cultures lost forever. And they keep doing it, and will continue to do it, until they are stopped."

Jack rubbed his head. His injuries from the explosion were starting to ache, and he felt very tired.

"I'm sorry your planet was destroyed," Jack said. "But Earth was my home. It can never be replaced, even if the Deathlords are stopped, so what does it matter anymore? Everything I ever knew is gone."

"It matters," said Shepherd forcefully. "And though Earth was important to you, I need you to understand our current situation. Regalus Prime was the first planet the Deathlords claimed, and the most devastating. It was the center of the universe for those in the Empire, which spans many star systems. It was the seat of our government, the galaxy's financial center, and its cultural hub. More Ancient relics existed there than on any other known planet. And the royal family, direct descendants of the Ancients, were the only ones able to use them. They unlocked incredible technology that would have taken our civilization thousands of years to develop on its own. Hyperspace travel, teleportation, nanotechnology, matter replication... they were all taken from the technology of the Ancients. And with that, we were able to visit different planets and to bring different civilizations peacefully into what became the Regalus Empire. Trade flourished. Cultures were shared and enriched. New advancements in technology were made... all thanks to the royal family of Regalus Prime."

"So what happened?" asked Jack. "I mean, if you had all this Ancient stuff, why couldn't you use it to stop the Deathlords?"

"Because we were not aware of them and the threat they posed until they attacked," explained Shepherd. "There had been rumors from the fringe of the Empire that an alien armada had been sighted here and there, but nothing concrete enough to raise any alarm. Besides, Regalus Prime was protected by the strongest space fleet known to man deep inside friendly space. Our military was second to none. We all believed our fleet was practically invincible, and no one would ever be able to attack our planet. Until the day the Deathlords appeared from hyperspace. Somehow, they had slipped past our checkpoints and sensors. They came to us, just as they did to Earth, with a fleet of Planetkillers. Their shards swarmed our defenses, allowing them to get into position. We had no idea who they were and what they were capable of until it was too late."

"How did you survive?" asked Jack. "How did Anna?"

Shepherd sighed and looked down sadly, as though it pained him to talk about it.

"I was back at home visiting my wife," he said. "She worked as the royal tutor for the Princess."

"A teacher, huh?" said Jack.

Shepherd cracked a smile. "The best," he said. "But she was more than that — almost like a mother to the royal offspring. It was her duty to raise them until such time as they could be brought into court when they reached their teens. Anna was the youngest, and the only girl, so Casca always had a special affinity for her."

Shepherd stopped and gazed off toward a wall. Jack wondered if "Casca" was the name of his wife. It must have been hard to talk about, especially for a guy who seemed to prefer spending his time flying around and kicking butt with glowing stick things.

"When the attack happened, my wife made me take the Princess to an escape shuttle while she attempted to get the crown prince and his brothers off-world. It was standard procedure to evacuate the royal family in a time of crisis. Unfortunately, because of the chaos of the invasion, I was not able to go back for her. Enemy fire had collapsed part of the palace, and I had no choice but to leave with Anna."

Shepherd swallowed hard at the memory. He turned to Jack and stared at him with his intense grey eyes.

"The fall of Regalus Prime was a huge blow to Imperial rule. Major trade routes and space lanes were interrupted. The seat of military command was destroyed, along with our parliament and other essential governmental bodies. The Empire was in chaos. Communications were unreliable, and enemies outside the Empire took the opportunity to claim territory that rightfully belonged to us."

"Since that time, the universe has been reeling," continued Shepherd. "The galactic economy is in ruins. Governance is still unstable, and many worlds are breaking off from the Empire or falling to hostile rivals, all of which weaken our ability to retaliate and defend ourselves. All efforts have been made to re-establish the might of our military, but we cannot protect our borders from pirates and rival governments as well as fight off the Deathlords at the same time. For even as we scramble and squabble amongst ourselves, the Deathlords continue their rampage, hitting the planets we need most in order to survive."

"Sounds bad," said Jack.

"It is bad," replied Shepherd. "If the Empire collapses, there is no way to unify enough planets to mount an offensive effective enough to stop the Deathlords. But as our government struggles to survive, and entire planets live in constant fear of destruction, throughout it all, there's the Princess... the only living member of the royal bloodline. The only one who has the power to control Ancient technology. The only one who has the key to possibly stopping the Deathlords. That is what brought us to your planet Jack. The belief that there was something there that could end this reign of terror that has descended upon our universe like a plague. Earth was our greatest hope. And now, so are you."

Jack raised an eyebrow.

"Uh... me?" he said.

"For whatever reason," said Shepherd, "you have a role to play in all this, Jack. I don't pretend to understand why, or how, but it cannot be ignored. You're the one the Princess was drawn to, which led to you opening the temple, which led to our finding this ship."

Shepherd gestured to the room around him.

"I cannot believe that was all just a coincidence," he said.

"What are you saying?" asked Jack. "I'm like some chosen one destined to save the universe or something?"

Shepherd chuckled. "I doubt it," he said. "If there is such a thing as destiny, and anyone's been chosen to save the universe, it's Princess Glorianna. Only she has the power to unlock the mysteries of the Ancients. But that does not mean you do not have a role to play."

"So what is it?" asked Jack. "What's my role?"

"That's the real question, isn't it?" asked Shepherd. "Do you remember the talk we had earlier? When you came to detention?"

"You mean when you talked about taking responsibility for my actions and stuff?" asked Jack. It seemed like that was a million years ago, though it had only been that afternoon.

Shepherd nodded. "Since that time, I think you've indeed taken that advice to heart," he said. "You protected Anna, and you may very well have helped us find the key to defeating the Deathlords once and for all. But I think maybe it's time I take a little bit of my own advice, and start looking at my actions."

"What do you mean?" asked Jack.

"I won't lie to you, Jack," he said. "Coming to your planet did put it in danger. That much I can't ignore. But we did not destroy it. That blame belongs to the Deathlords, and to them alone. However, it was a consequence of the actions the Princess and I took. And now it's time for me to take responsibility for it."

Shepherd got to his feet and looked down at Jack.

"That's why, when we get home, I am going to train you."

Jack looked up at Shepherd and blinked.

"Train me?" said Jack. "Train me in what?"

"In the ways of the Free Mind," said Shepherd. "I'm going to train you to be a Paragon."

Jack got to his feet. "You mean... I get to wear armor and learn to kick butt and stuff?"

A lopsided smile grew on Shepherd's face. "My order is a very old brotherhood, Jack. A Paragon is one who learns to master his own mind... to free it from its confines. To see beyond what many believe is possible and to manifest that which they see.

The fall of Regalus Prime called me to become a Warrior Paragon, but there are others who devote themselves to art, science, music, literature... whatever calls to them. And by freeing our minds, and believing in ourselves, we are able to manifest anything we desire."

Shepherd held out his hand. The air around it seemed to ripple, and suddenly, there was a baseball there. He tossed it to Jack, who caught it and looked at it in amazement.

"How'd you do that?" asked Jack.

"The same way I created my armor," said Shepherd. "The same way I created that gun I gave you. I thought about what I wanted in my mind, and I manifested it into reality."

"Whoa..." said Jack. "You mean... that quantum physics stuff the Professor was always talking about... you can *do that?*"

Shepherd nodded. "It is the way of the Paragon," he said. "It is the way of the Free Mind."

"Then why can't you create a weapon to destroy the Deathlords?" Jack asked. "Why can't you just make them all disappear with your mind or something?"

"It may be possible to do that," said Shepherd. "We Paragons have the belief that anything is possible. But unless a mind is totally free, there are still limitations to what one is able to accomplish."

"So you're saying none of you guys has figured out a way to do that yet?" said Jack.

"Freeing a mind from its own bonds is a complicated process, Jack," said Shepherd. "Even after a lifetime of study and practice, it may not be enough to achieve a truly free mind, one capable of manifesting anything."

"How long would it take to achieve one that's just capable enough to stomp the Deathlords into mush?" asked Jack.

Shepherd smiled. "I don't know," he said. "Would you like to find out?"

Jack met Shepherd's gaze and nodded.

"Heck, yeah," he said.

CHAPTER ✵ 18

Shepherd and Jack entered the bridge together. Jack looked around at the state of the command center and was relieved to see things weren't nearly as bad as they were when he had run out earlier. The viewscreen was in full working order again, and most of the control panels looked as good as new. Professor Green was busy tapping away on a console with Anna assisting him.

"What's our status, Professor?" asked Shepherd as he approached them.

Anna looked up at Shepherd and then over to Jack. He had hung back a bit, not wanting to get too close after the embarrassment of his last episode around her. She quickly looked away and moved to another control panel on the other side of the bridge.

"Engines are now fully repaired," said Green. "I've diverted system focus to the hyperdrives, so those should be ready in a few more minutes. Our shields are still in need of repair, as are our weapon systems, but for the most part we are looking A-Okay."

Shepherd glanced out the viewscreen. "Do what you can to speed things up," he said. "Looks like the Deathlord's search grid is closing in. They'll be on top of us in fifteen minutes, maybe ten."

"We should be ready before then," said Green. "But I must remind you, as soon as we power up our engines, they'll be able to pick up on our energy signature. I don't doubt they'll be upon us in moments."

"You hear that, Jack?" asked Shepherd. "You'll have to make the jump to hyperspace as soon as you engage the engines."

Jack nodded. "Got it," he said.

"Don't do anything fancy," said Shepherd. "Just get us out of here."

"I understand," said Jack.

Shepherd nodded. His eyes flashed to Anna and then back to Jack before turning his attention to the console on which Green was working. Jack took a deep breath and walked over to where Anna was running a system scan by the captain's chair.

"Hey," said Jack.

"Hello, Jack," said Anna. "How are you doing?"

"A little better," he said. Jack felt awkward talking to Anna again for some reason. He stuck his hands in his pockets and shuffled his feet uncomfortably. "Listen, about what I said before…"

"It's okay," said Anna.

"No, it's not," replied Jack. "I was being a jerk. I should have never said those things."

"You were upset. It's understandable."

Jack nodded. "I, uh… had a talk with Mr… *Paragon* Shepherd. He told me about what happened to your family."

"I'm glad he was able to explain things," she said. "I know this whole ordeal is probably very confusing for you."

Jack shrugged. "Well, I wanted to let you know that… I've decided to go into training to become a Paragon."

Anna looked at Jack with a hint of surprise. "Really?"

"Yeah. Shepherd said he'd train me once we get you back home."

"That's… wow…" said Anna.

"I know, right?" said Jack. "Can you imagine? Lord only knows the kinds of things *my* mind will manifest."

Jack and Anna shared a laugh at that.

"I'm sure you'll make a fine disciple," she said.

"Well, anyway… I wanted you to know, because I'm going to be pledging my service to you and your bloodline and stuff."

Anna smiled. "And stuff?"

"Yeah, Shepherd said a bunch of things I had to swear allegiance to… I don't know. Anyway, my point is that I'm gonna be there for you. No matter what."

"Very well," said Anna. "I look forward to accepting your pledge of service."

Jack smiled. "Man, you make it sound like I'm gonna be your personal slave or something. I'm actually sort of scared now."

"Once you're in my service, you'll be honor-bound to do whatever I say," teased Anna. "But be more afraid of Shepherd than of me. He's a lot less forgiving than I am."

"And a lot less fun," said Jack. "I've already been through detention with the man. I'm really afraid of what he's gonna have me doing once there are no child labor laws or anything holding him back."

"One can only imagine," said Anna with a smile.

Jack stared at Anna awkwardly for a minute before pulling a small, lilac colored flower from his pocket.

"I almost forgot," he said. "I had Shepherd manifest your favorite flower for me. You know, to apologize for shoving you like I did."

Jack presented it to her. "An urthma!" said Anna. She smiled and took the flower, smelling it. "That's very sweet of you."

Jack tried not to blush. "Yeah, well… you know…"

Anna leaned in and gave Jack a gentle kiss on the cheek.

"I know," she said.

Jack's nerves shot through him like an electrical current. "Okay then!" he said a little too loudly as he clapped his hands together. "I'm, uh, just gonna fly the ship into hyperspace now and try again not to get us all killed."

"Good luck with that," said Anna.

"Yeah… thanks," replied Jack.

Jack turned and hopped back up in the captain's chair. He laid his hands on the domes, and they lit up in response to his touch. He was once again tuned into the ship.

Stupid, thought Jack. *Stupid, stupid, stupid. Way to end a conversation — promise not to get her killed. Brilliant.*

Jack called up the status of the ship. Engines were just about ready to go, as was the hyperdrive, but shields were still down and weapons were inoperable. He checked the Entanglement Engine and found it had stopped charging while the ship made its repairs, but it was almost ready to be used again, as well.

The outer hull of the ship had been badly damaged in the blast, but the major weaknesses had all been fixed. The ship wasn't anywhere close to being in as good a shape as it had been when Jack had first found it, but it was better than flying around in space with a bunch of holes in the hull. However, without shields to protect them, Jack knew it would only take a couple of direct hits to do some serious damage.

Jack suddenly felt very guilty. He'd just gotten the spaceship, and already it was trashed. If he had just listened to Shepherd and had jumped when they had the chance… but he'd never have forgiven himself if he hadn't tried to save his mom.

"Engines are fully repaired," said Green. "Hyperdrive is ready, as well."

Sure enough, Jack knew all that, right as Green had said it. The ship gave him the green light on all navigational systems.

"Okay, Jack," said Shepherd. "When you're ready, power up the engines and open our hyperspace window."

"You've got it," said Jack. "Starting engines now."

Jack kicked the engines into life. As soon as the ship started moving, he turned it to match the jump coordinates Green had programmed into the navigational computer.

Alarm beeps sounded from the ship's radar as enemy contacts began to adjust course toward them.

"We've been sighted," said Green. "Deathlord shards are inbound."

"Make the jump, Jack," ordered Shepherd. "Now."

Jack commanded the ship to open the hyperspace window. But nothing happened.

"Um…" said Jack.

"Jack," said Shepherd urgently, "do it now!"

Jack tried again. And again, nothing happened. Jack asked the computer why it wasn't working, and some information popped up on his holoscreen.

"Uh, oh. I think we have a problem," said Jack.

"What is it?" demanded Shepherd.

"There's too much debris," said Jack. "The ship can't open a hyperspace window, we'd be flying right into their gravitational shadows, and we'd get ripped apart."

"Oh, dear," said Green. "Jack's right. I forgot to account for the planet's remains. If we were to open a window now, in the condensed reality of hyperspace, we'd be emerging into the equivalent of a brick wall."

"Blast it!" said Shepherd. Just then the proximity alarm on the bridge sounded. The shards had just entered their firing range. "Jack," he continued, "get us out of the debris field. Quickly!"

"Already on it," said Jack as he adjusted the ship's course. Without other ship's systems to worry about at the moment, Jack pushed as much power as he could to the engines, giving them a burst of speed just in time to avoid incoming enemy plasma fire.

"Professor, get our shields back online," said Shepherd.

Green furiously typed away at his control panel. "I'm working on it, dear Paragon," he said.

In the captain's seat, Jack could feel the small impacts from the tiny rocks of what used to be Earth that surrounded them as the ship flew to escape the oncoming shards. Bigger rocks were floating in space, and hitting those would definitely slow them down and affect the ship, so Jack had to adjust course to fly around them.

Meanwhile, the shards were gaining on them, and avoiding the plasma blasts and space debris while trying to outrun their pursuers was starting to become quite a challenge.

Jack accessed a map of the debris field the computer had generated for him. He was almost to its edge. The minute they were through, he'd be able to open the window into hyperspace.

"Almost out," he said to himself. At that moment, he wanted nothing more than to get as far away from the Deathlords as he possibly could.

Suddenly, the ship was rocked from an impact. Red lights flashed on the bridge as an alarm sounded. Jack immediately knew it was from enemy fire.

"We've been hit!" said Green.

"It's okay," said Jack. "We still have engines!"

Jack pushed the engines harder. They were nearing the edge of the debris field.

Jack weaved the ship as more angry red plasma blasts shot by them...

The shards were closing in, nearly on top of them. Jack punched the engine one more time to try to squeeze out a little bit more speed...

Almost there...

As they came rushing up to the edge of the debris field, Jack activated the hyperdrive. A couple yards ahead of them, space seemed to ripple and tear open, as a shimmering light escaped from the large rectangular window into a different dimension.

Jack's ship barreled through it and into hyperspace!

Unfortunately, so did a handful of shards, which punched through right before the window closed, cutting the final – and not so lucky – shard cleanly in half as it did so.

"Enemy contact," said Green wearily. "They followed us through our window before it had a chance to heal shut."

As Jack looked on the viewscreen before him he temporarily forgot about the six shards that had made it through and were in pursuit. Before him was nothing but white, filled with tiny black dots that were clustered together all over the place. It almost looked like a big polka-dotted canvas. All around him, he saw huge bodies of black orbs, one of which had dark rings circling it. Behind him was a massive black body, which seemed to radiate darkness into the white around it. All the dark masses were almost on top of each other, probably separated by the distance of just a couple of miles. It took Jack a minute to recognize that he was looking at his own solar system, albeit a condensed version of it.

The large thing behind him was obviously the sun, and the orb with rings around it to his left had to be Saturn. Jupiter, Neptune, and even Pluto were close by, but they were just large, dark spots, like huge bowling balls floating in the pure white of hyperspace.

Before Jack had a chance to really take in the surreal sight, Shepherd's commanding voice broke in.

"Lightspeed!" barked Shepherd. "Now!"

Jack didn't hesitate. He angled the ship along the computer's coordinates and ordered it to engage its lightspeed engines.

Jack felt a rumble course through the ship as the engines engaged. The space before him swirled and warped into a tunnel, rushing up to encompass the ship. Brilliant blue light rippled around the tunnel walls, almost like it had when Jack had portgated down to the Earth's Ancient temple.

"Lightspeed engaged!" cheered Green. "We are now successfully moving at 99% the speed of light!"

Everyone on the bridge breathed a sigh of relief. Shepherd stood up from his console, looking extremely tired.

"Good work, Jack," he said.

"Thanks," said Jack as he swiveled his chair to face him. "So are we really moving at the speed of light? I mean, is this what it's like?"

"Actually, we're only moving at 99% the speed of light," smiled Green. "Any faster and we'd be converted into pure energy."

"So it's not really 'lightspeed,' huh?" said Jack, just a little disappointed.

"Don't worry, it's fast enough," said Shepherd.

"Um… guys?" piped up Anna, looking at her console.

"What is it, Princess?" asked Shepherd.

"I'm picking up something following us," she said.

Shepherd looked at Jack alarmed. Jack accessed the ship's sensors and on the holoscreen in front of him an image of six Deathlord shards materialized, flying in two, three-ship formations down the lightspeed tunnel behind them.

Jack heard Shepherd suck a quick intake of breath between his teeth.

"Oh, my," said Green. "The shards… they're… they're following us?"

"How is that possible?" growled Shepherd. "They're fighter craft, they're not big enough to carry lightspeed engines."

"It would seem the Deathlords are full or surprises today," moaned Green. "First they're able to jam our subspace communications, now they reveal fightercraft with hyperspace capabilities."

"That must be how they were able to get the drop on our ships," said Shepherd. "They launch a wing of fighters ahead into hyperspace. They're too small to be picked up by our early-warning beacons, so they jump in unnoticed and attack, beaming in boarding parties and clearing the way for the main fleet."

"You must admit," said Green, "their advancements in technology are rather astounding."

"Admit it while you get our shields back up," growled Shepherd.

"What's the worry?" asked Jack. "I mean, yeah, it sucks they're on our tail and all, but they're just following us. It's not like they can fire on us or anything, right? We're moving at the freakin' speed of light. Nothing can go any faster than that, can it?"

"Normally, you'd be correct," said Green as he went to work directing the ship to fix its generator and bring its shields back online. "But I need to remind you... we're only moving at 99% the speed of light."

"And plasma fire doesn't need to worry about converting to pure energy," grumbled Shepherd.

A shiver ran down Jack's spine. He looked up at the holo-image in front of him as red bolts emanated from the tips of the six shards behind them. The blaster fire began to move toward them, ever so slowly, as if it were a worm crawling along through space.

"You gotta be *kidding* me," said Jack.

"The shards have opened fire," said Anna. "We've got six plasma blasts heading toward us."

"Time to impact?" asked Shepherd.

"Four, maybe five minutes," said Anna.

"It's not enough time," whined Green. "The shield generator isn't even fully repaired yet!"

"Maybe I can change course..." said Jack, "...maneuver the ship out of the way."

"You can't maneuver us while in lightspeed, Jack," said Anna. "We're going so fast, the slightest shift in course could angle us into a collision with something."

"What about dropping out of lightspeed?" asked Jack.

"With six plasma blasts and shards that close behind us?" said Shepherd. "We'd be smashed to pieces the minute we slowed down."

"Well... can we do *anything?*" asked Jack.

The silence that came from his party let him know his answer. Jack looked up at the screen as the plasma bolts inched closer.

"Screw it," he said. "I'm moving the ship."

"Jack, you can't!" insisted Anna.

"It's either take our chances with a course adjustment or get slammed into by those blasts with no shields," said Jack. "I, for one, am willing to take that chance."

Anna looked at Shepherd, who grimaced. Jack looked over his shoulder at the man.

"I know I can do this," said Jack.

Something about the tone of Jack's voice gave Shepherd some hope. Maybe it was bravado, or maybe just ignorance of the dangers involved in the maneuver. Regardless, Shepherd didn't see much of a choice.

"Do it," he said.

Jack turned his attention back to the ship's controls. "Everyone hold onto something," he said as he began the maneuver.

The ship started to move, but it did so slowly. Jack strained against the controls of the ship, pushing it to keep moving. It continued to drift to the right, but it felt to Jack like he was trying to change course while swimming upstream in a river.

Behind him the Deathlord plasma blasts kept on course, continuing to inch forward unrelentingly.

Jack kept pushing the ship. Alarms and alerts began to pop up on the screen before him, letting him know they were off course, but he ignored them. He needed to get clear of the blasts.

The ship continued to veer more and more to the right as the deadly energy bolts got closer.

"C'mon, c'mon..." mumbled Jack. He could feel sweat starting to bead on his brow as he kept trying to force the ship out of the way of the incoming fire.

The blasts were almost upon them. He had cleared most of them, but one on the far edge was still en route to impact.

He could feel the ship shiver and whine as he continued to turn it within the confines of lightspeed. *Just a little more*, he thought. *Please, God, just a little more…*

But it wasn't enough. The blaster bolt caught up with them and struck their left engine. The entire ship began to shake and rumble as alerts sounded.

"We're hit!" screamed Jack.

"Port side engine is damaged," called out Green. "It was a direct hit!"

"I gotta drop us out of lightspeed!" said Jack. "The ship's about to tear apart!"

Indeed, the stress of the damaged engine trying to keep them at their current speed was causing the vessel to rattle violently, and the ship even went so far as to communicate to Jack it's displeasure with the current situation.

"Do it!" said Shepherd.

Without a moment to lose, Jack powered down the lightspeed engines. The brilliant blue tunnel around them evaporated as the strange mirror image of hyperspace came back into view… except in front of them was no white space…

Just a massive wall of solid black.

A loud alarm blared and warnings popped up on the holoscreen that impact was imminent. It would seem Jack's lightspeed maneuver put them on a direct course into something very, very big.

"Gravitational contact, directly ahead!" squealed Green.

"Jack! Get us out of hyperspace! NOW!" screamed Shepherd.

Jack engaged the Brane Accelerator and a window back into the normal universe tore open in front of them just in time to avoid the impending collision.

The ship barreled through, coming out the other side. Jack tried to turn the ship, but the port engine finally gave out. Behind them, the six shards that had been following came out of hyperspace as well, their momentum carrying them past Jack's ship.

"We're out," said Jack. "So are the shards."

"Keep as much distance from them as possible," said Shepherd. "Professor, do we have any weapons? Shields? Anything?"

"We barely have an engine," grumbled Green.

"I'm reading a strange contact out here," said Anna, looking at her console. "It's massive!"

Jack looked at the screen, but other than a rather beautiful nebula not too far away, Jack didn't see anything except the darkness of space.

Then, Jack's brain tingled in alarm. He should have been able to see some stars, or something – but in front of them, there was just a wall of solid black.

"Where are we?" asked Jack.

"Our maneuver took us off course," said Anna. "I have no idea what our current location is."

Jack glanced at his radar. "The shards are coming around," he said. "They're locking onto us!"

"Put everything you can into the engines," said Shepherd.

"I'm trying," said Jack. "But we can barely outrun them when we have both engines working."

Shepherd gritted his teeth as he looked at the holoscreen. The Deathlord shards converged on the ship, raining plasma fire down on it. The ship shuttered from the impacts as the shards flew past in their strafing run.

"They've taken out our engines," said Green.

Jack tried to maneuver, but it was no use. They had no way to accelerate, or even move at all for that matter. Now they were being carried strictly by their momentum; they were helpless in every sense of the word.

"They're coming back around," said Anna, looking at her console.

"They mean to board us," said Shepherd. "Jack, out of the seat. Anna, to me. We'll have to fight them off."

"No, wait!" said Anna. "Something is happening…"

Jack called up the sensor readings on his holoscreen. Sure enough, he saw the shards suddenly start to scramble on their turn to intercept them.

"Whoa," said Jack. "What's going on?"

"Something… something's *out there*…" said Anna.

Jack magnified the image on the holoscreen. Suddenly, he could see something… it looked like a black cloud that was moving through space, chasing the Deathlords as their ships tried to maneuver away from it.

Tendrils from the cloud caught one of the shards. The cloud swarmed over the vessel, disintegrating it before Jack's very eyes.

"What is that thing?" asked Jack. "It looks like… it's eating the shards!"

"Where did it come from?" asked Anna.

Green's console beeped. "It's part of that massive gravitational contact we saw in hyperspace," said Green.

Jack adjusted the ship's viewscreen. Sure enough, the part of space with no stars that he had noticed was now swirling and bubbling, alive with what looked like lightening, almost as though it contained storm clouds. Pieces of it broke off and shot forth, chasing after the Deathlord shards, as if their very presence awakened the cloud and made it angry.

As nimbly as the shards were able to maneuver, they were eventually caught by the dark clouds, and when they were, nothing remained of them.

"Dude," said Jack. "It's destroying the shards! Way to go space cloud! WOOT!"

"It's not a cloud… it's swarming them," said Anna. "Like… insects."

"Jack," said Shepherd. "Can you get in closer on whatever it is?"

Jack pulled up the sensor display of the ship and zoomed in on the massive wall of darkness in front of them. As it magnified, Jack could begin to make out tiny movements. He adjusted the filters on the readings, and suddenly, shapes began to appear.

The clouds were made up of trillions and trillions of tiny insect-like things. They had long bodies and large mouths with many sharp edges, along with pincers on their sides and barbs on their tails. They looked like a strange cross between a worm and a scorpion.

"They're alive?" asked Anna, amazed.

"Incredible," breathed Green. "How many of them must there be, that combined they could create such a huge gravitational anomaly?

"You mean, you guys have never seen these things before?" asked Jack. For some reason, running into something his friends – who were way more experienced in space travel than he was – had never seen before was kind of scary to him.

"A space faring organism which seems to be able to consume solid matter almost instantly?" chuckled Green. "No, I can't say I have. Though it gives me yet another great subject for a paper to write for the Valghanah Journal of Science!"

Jack watched his screen as the swarm consumed the last Deathlord shard.

"So... um... you don't know if they're friendly or not?" he asked.

"No clue!" said Green cheerily.

"My guess would be, not," said Shepherd dourly.

Jack looked at his sensor readings and saw the clouds that had consumed the shards converge and begin heading toward them. Suddenly, he found himself missing the Deathlords.

"Uh-oh," said Jack.

Shepherd looked at the readout, as well, and saw the swarm coming toward them. "Professor, do we have engines yet?" he asked urgently.

"Still being repaired," said Green.

Shepherd cursed. "Jack," he said. "The Entanglement Engine... can we use it?"

Jack's eyes lit up. He had completely forgotten about the Entanglement Engine. It was a separate engine from the thrusters, and last he had checked, it was almost online. Jack pulled it up through the ship's readouts. Sure enough, it read: "good to go."

"Yes!" exclaimed Jack. "It's ready again! I can jump us out of here!"

A small glimmer of hope sparked in Shepherd's eye. "Do it!" he ordered.

The swarm cloud was getting closer, rushing headlong toward the ship as Jack called up the Entanglement Engine display. It asked for coordinates again.

"I don't know what the coordinates mean," said Jack. "It could take us anywhere!"

"Anywhere is better than here," said Shepherd. "Do it NOW!"

Jack looked at the list of previous coordinates and glanced at the viewscreen to see the swarm rushing up to him. He had to choose a destination, and he had to choose one right that second.

Jack knew the first entry would take them exactly where they'd jumped to the first time, and he certainly didn't want to go back to what remained of Earth. And since he didn't really have time to consider any of the other coordinates, he was left with the second option on the list.

The string of numbers flashed as Jack made his decision and moved into the destination field. The familiar hum returned as the Entanglement Engine charged up, and Jack felt it getting ready to engage.

Suddenly, the swarm cloud rushing toward them was replaced with a bright light, and when that light cleared, the cloud was gone. Now, there was just the comforting sight of empty space.

Jack breathed a sigh of relief. "We did it," he said. "We jumped."

"Where to?" asked Shepherd.

"Checking the computer now," said Anna. "I'll see if I can pull up any star charts that might match…"

Jack looked to the side of the bridge's viewscreen, and his heart sank.

"Don't bother," said Jack. "I know where we are."

Outside, Jack could see the unmistakable image of Saturn, and past that, the familiar yellow sun he'd woken to every day of his life.

Just as Shepherd, Green, and Anna saw it, too, alerts beeped on Jack's radar. There was a large contact directly behind them. Jack called it up on the viewscreen and saw a Deathlord mothership towering over them, as though it were getting ready to swallow them up.

"Oh… crap," murmured Jack.

He'd jumped them right back into the clutches of the Deathlord fleet.

And this time, there was no escape.

EPISODE II:

EARTHMAN JACK

VS.

THE PIT OF DEATH

CHAPTER ✱ 19

One could only imagine what was going on in the minds of the Deathlords as they had set about on a course to leave the Earth's planetary system after their prey had dramatically escaped into hyperspace, only to have those who had evaded their clutches just a short while ago suddenly appear before them out of the blue.

However, if the Deathlords were indeed surprised to see the Ancient vessel, it did not last long. Moments after detecting the Earthship almost directly in front of it, the Deathlord Flagship — known to those aboard as *The Inferno* — promptly engaged its tractor beam, ensuring that this time, the ship would not execute any type of sensational exit.

Jack could feel the ship rock as the tractor beam engulfed it and began to pull it toward the immense mothership that ominously filled its viewscreen. An alarm sounded, alerting them to the obvious...

Things were about to get extremely bad.

"Princess!" exclaimed Shepherd urgently, the helm of his armor covering his face as he headed toward Anna.

Shepherd was on the move before any of the others even thought to react. From experience, the Paragon knew that the Deathlord soldiers would be teleporting onto the ship any second, and though he had managed to close half the distance between him and Anna, he just wasn't fast enough.

In a flash of purple, Dark Soldiers appeared everywhere — two of whom had teleported in between the Princess and the Paragon.

Shepherd wasted no time. He grabbed his batons that crackled to life and made short work of the first Deathlord he saw. Unfortunately, that was all he had time for before the others opened fire.

Shepherd raised a shield just in time to deflect the blasts from the six other Deathlords on the bridge. Anna shrieked and moved behind her console for cover.

Jack hopped out of the control seat and grabbed his pistol from his jacket pocket. He was about to run to Shepherd's aid when more Deathlords teleported onto the bridge, behind the safety of Shepherd's shield.

Jack turned and fired on instinct, hitting the closest Deathlord and taking him down. Jack's amazement that he'd actually killed a Deathlord with his super-cool laser gun was short-lived, however, when he saw the other soldiers level their rifles at him.

Only, they weren't aiming at him. Jack turned and saw Anna exposed to their line of sight behind the console.

"Behind you!" Jack yelled to Shepherd as he rushed toward Anna, firing wildly at the Deathlords behind him as he did so.

Shepherd took his attention away from the onslaught of the soldiers on his shield in time to see the new arrivals. He raised his free arm and unleashed his quad cannons, firing upon the soldiers and taking them out in a puff of dust.

The Paragon wasn't able to hit all the Deathlords, though. Some of them actually evaded his fire. And one, in particular, dropped to his knee and steadied his weapon.

The Princess moved from behind her cover to run...

Jack saw the Deathlord soldier take aim...

"Anna!" he screamed as he leapt toward her.

Anna turned just as the Deathlord fired, unleashing a crackling ball of purple energy barreling toward her.

"PRINCESS!" screamed Shepherd.

Jack's arms wrapped around Anna, his momentum carrying her forward with him, but it wasn't enough. The blast hit both of them square on.

Jack felt a ripple of static electricity run through his body as his vision blurred in a swirl of purple light, and within seconds, the sensations disappeared, and he and Anna tumbled to the ground.

Jack looked up with a start. They were no longer on the bridge of the Ancient starship. Instead, they were surrounded by darkness, a harsh white light shining down from above them.

"This can't be good..." muttered Jack.

"Oh, no," said Anna as she rolled Jack off her and got to her feet, with Jack following suit. "Where are we?"

"You're asking me?" whimpered Jack. He could feel his skin crawl as he gazed out into the darkness that surrounded them. "Like I've ever been shot with a ball of purple before."

Then, the sound of footsteps echoed. Instinctively, Jack put himself in front of Anna and raised his pistol toward the sound. If that alarmed whoever was walking in the darkness, they did not break stride. The footsteps circled around them slowly, purposefully.

Jack could feel Anna pressed up against him. She was holding onto him tightly, and he could sense she was just as afraid as he was. Whatever was out there, it was a good bet it wasn't friendly, and Jack didn't exactly have a good track record when it came to fighting Deathlords... or anything else for that matter.

So Jack did the only thing he could do. He fell back to his patented strategy number three for avoiding a beat down – acting tough.

"Whoever's out there," said Jack, mustering up all the false bravado he could, "I just think it's fair to warn you that on my planet, I am a warrior of great renown, with 5,689 wins in Arena Deathmatch. And I will totally kick your butt if you even think about hurting us."

The footsteps continued, but this time they were joined by a voice – one which was deep and gravelly that echoed throughout the darkness with a menace Jack had never known could even exist.

"Would that be the planet I just wiped from existence?" the voice said simply.

Jack felt a lump catch in his throat, and his heart started to beat faster. The voice was strange, and Jack knew it wasn't speaking English, but somehow he understood it, nevertheless. The way the voice mentioned the destruction of Earth, as though it were nothing, chilled him to the bone. Jack took a deep breath in an effort to steady himself.

"It was called Earth, jerk-wad," said Jack, his voice cracking. "And you're going to pay for what you did to it."

Jack gripped his pistol tighter. The voice chuckled. "Your pathetic weapons are useless against me," it chided.

"Yeah? Then you won't mind if I do *this!*" said Jack, opening fire.

Plasma blasts shot forth from his gun but evaporated as they hit the darkness, as though it were a solid, impenetrable wall.

"You dare fire your weapon upon me?" growled the voice.

"Yeah, I dare," said Jack. "Step out here and show me your ugly face, and I'll do it again, too."

"Strong words… from a frightened child," the voice replied.

"Frightened? Me?" said Jack nervously, a sinking feeling welling up in his stomach. "I'm not the one hiding in the dark, loser. Why don't you come out and face me like a man, and I'll show you who's frightened."

"Okay, boy…" said the voice as a crack of light pierced the darkness surrounding Jack and Anna, rolling it back like a curtain to reveal a Deathlord unlike any other – standing seven feet tall, clad in ornate silver armor that seemed to almost glow with a ferocious red aura.

The metal of his armor dug into the jet-black, sinewy skin underneath, small spikes as sharp as razor blades protruding from the metal. A long black cape flowed around him, as if it had a life of its own, and two burning red eyes glared from behind a grotesque, angular helm that made him look like the Angel of Death himself.

"Show me," he rumbled.

In future interviews with the Earthman, he'd explain how no words could describe the feeling he had experienced upon first meeting the Deathlord Supreme, other than to say that if it weren't for the sheer, unbridled terror which had gripped his body at that very moment, there was an extremely good chance he would have, and I quote, "crapped my pants."

Indeed, since up to this point in recorded history no one had actually met a Deathlord Supreme and survived to report his experience, we can only assume that seeing one for the first time in such a dramatic manner would be enough to make any sentient being soil himself soundly.

And had it not been for Princess Anna, there is a very good chance that our story might have ended there. But as things so happen, it didn't, and the first meeting of these three historical figures would affect all life in the universe, as we know it, for ages to come.

Of course, with the imposing figure of the Deathlord Supreme towering over him at that very moment, Earthman Jack Finnegan could not possibly have known that.

"Um…" stammered Jack, "I may have been a bit hasty about the whole 'showing you who's frightened' thing…"

The Deathlord Supreme's eyes burned into Jack, bright and hot and red with fury. Without a word he reached out his clawed hand, and Jack's body jerked as he felt the pain of a thousand invisible hooks burying themselves into his chest.

Jack gasped and dropped his pistol as his body was yanked into the air. He wanted to scream, but it felt as though his lungs were on fire, and the best he could manage was a feeble choke.

"NO!" cried Anna. "Don't hurt him! Please!"

The Deathlord's eyes never left Jack's as the Earthman felt the searing pain of invisible knives slicing through his body and wrapping themselves around what felt like the very essence of his being.

"And why should I spare his life?" the Deathlord inquired. With a flick of his finger, Jack felt all the invisible knives and hooks tug at him at once, and it was almost as if his very consciousness were being ripped from his body. Only this time, he *was* able to scream.

"Please, I'll do anything…" Anna pleaded. "Don't kill him. You don't have to – I'll cooperate…"

Suddenly, the pull from the invisible hooks stopped, and Jack felt like he could breathe again.

The Deathlord turned his fiery gaze toward Anna. "And what is this… *creature*… to you, Daughter of the Ancients?" he said, his gravelly voice dripping with malice.

Anna looked at Jack with tears welling in her eyes.

"He's... he's my friend..." she said quietly.

"A friend you're willing to die for?"

"Yes," said Anna, without hesitation.

The Deathlord studied Jack for a moment before finally speaking. "Then he might be of use after all."

The knives and hooks all disappeared and Jack crumpled to the ground, clutching his chest and gasping. His head was screaming in pain, and his entire body felt like it had just been run over by twelve school buses.

Immediately Anna was at his side, cradling his head. Jack looked up and saw the fear and sadness in her eyes, and a feeling of hopelessness washed over him. In that moment, he knew there was nothing he could do to save her.

"Anna..." Jack croaked.

"Don't worry about me," she whispered. "From now on, just try and stay alive."

"Your Highness," grumbled the Deathlord Supreme, "you're to come with me now."

Anna leaned down and kissed Jack gently on the forehead.

"I'm sorry for getting you into this," she said quietly.

Anna got to her feet, standing straight and proud, and looked at the Deathlord with an air of elegance and authority that was hers by birthright. "And what of my friend?" she asked.

"He will be held, unharmed, in exchange for your cooperation," said the Deathlord.

Anna nodded. She didn't trust the Deathlord, but she didn't have much choice either. The Deathlord motioned for her to head toward a nearby door. Anna obeyed, taking one last glance at Jack before she left.

Jack looked up as she went, his body still racked with pain. Suddenly, he noticed the room around him. It was massive, maybe the size of a basketball stadium. A huge viewscreen looked out into space on the far wall, and hundreds of Deathlords manned various consoles and computer stations about the room.

The floors and walls were made up of a dull, silver metal, nothing resembling the rock-like exterior of the ships. The room was brightly lit, and Jack noticed he was on some type of circular platform in the center of the chamber. The darkness that had surrounded him earlier was peeling back, retreating into the platform as though it were a curtain being reeled away after a performance.

As the Deathlord Supreme walked Anna toward the massive circular door leading out of what was the mothership's control room, he turned to another Deathlord, whose face was wrapped in a black cloth; two horns stuck out from his elongated head.

"Abraxas," said the Deathlord Supreme.

"Yes, Supreme?" the horned Deathlord responded.

"Send the Earthman to the temple," he dictated. "Let him linger there while the Princess and I get acquainted."

The Deathlord bowed to his master. "As you command," he responded.

Jack tried to struggle to his feet as Anna was led out of the room. His pistol wasn't far. If he could reach it, maybe he could shoot his way out of here and get to her before they could do anything…

But all thoughts of escape were quickly dashed as the Deathlord, who had been referred to as Abraxas, stomped on the pistol, crushing it to pieces.

The Deathlord's hand tightly gripped Jack around his neck and yanked him up. Jack grabbed onto the cold, hard gauntlet of the Deathlord to keep from choking, his feet kicking the air feebly.

The Deathlord pulled him close, its searing red eyes staring hard into Jack's.

"Do you remember me, Earthman?" the Deathlord asked.

Jack tried to concentrate on the Deathlord before him, but he was somewhat distracted by his attempts to breathe. "Should I?" Jack gasped. "You all kinda look alike to me."

"You shot me in the temple," growled the Deathlord.

Sure enough, Jack suddenly recognized the Deathlord who would have killed him if not for Shepherd. "You..." said Jack. "I saw you blow up..."

"Deathlords do not die," said Abraxas. "And if it weren't for the Supreme's orders, I'd harvest your life force right here and now."

"You know, I may have shot you, but you guys just destroyed my entire planet," Jack sneered. "I'd say if anyone has a right to be mad, it's me."

The Deathlord began walking toward a rectangular alcove nestled in a nearby wall of the control room, holding Jack out by the neck as though he weighed less than a rag doll. "I have fought in many battles," said Abraxas. "And I have faced many opponents. Those were all glorious struggles against worthy adversaries. But you... a child who distracted me from my mission... you shame me."

"Gee, I'm sorry," said Jack. "How about I kill you again, this time for good? Would that make you feel better?"

Abraxas stopped at a control console and began typing at it with his free hand. "If all your species were as petulant as you are, I'd say we did the universe a great service by wiping you out."

"Trust me," said Jack. "No one's more petulant than I am."

The Deathlord looked Jack in the eyes again. "Then I will have to be satisfied with the knowledge that where you're going, you will suffer a fate far worse than that of your people."

With a flick of his arm, Abraxas threw Jack onto the rectangular platform nearby. Jack hit it hard and had just enough time to look up at the Deathlord as he tapped the final key on the console.

"Good riddance," Abraxas growled.

Jack felt a jolt of static electricity course through him. Then his vision blurred in a haze of purple, the world around him disappeared, and suddenly he was falling.

It didn't take long for him to hit the ground, knocking the wind out of him. Jack lay stunned on the cold, unforgiving floor he had just slammed into. After a few seconds, he recovered enough to look around.

It was dark, but there was a bit of light — a pale, white illumination, which reminded Jack of moonlight — coming from somewhere. Jack looked down at the floor and saw the same material that seemed to make up so much of the Deathlord's technology — hard, course, black rock-like matter spidered with veins of green and purple that glowed and pulsed ever so slightly.

The air around him was cold, though not like being in a meat locker or out in the snow. This was a different kind of cold, one that chilled him to the bone even though his skin could not feel it. There was something off-putting about Jack's new location. He couldn't quite put his finger on what it was, but he just knew something was terribly, terribly wrong.

Then Jack heard the noises. They were quiet, almost distant, but they were there. Moaning, cries of anguish and despair, and sounds of choking and retching. As Jack got to his feet, the sounds seemed to swirl around him in the darkness, and he had a sudden, sinking feeling in the pit of his stomach. Wherever he was, it was definitely not good.

Oh crap, he thought. *I am so screwed.*

A noise, louder than the others, found its way to Jack's ears – the sound of feet scuffing the rocky floor behind him. He turned and could see a figure in the darkness walking toward him. Fear rose inside Jack, and he quickly looked around for something, anything, to help him defend himself. There was nowhere for him to hide, and he could see nothing but rubble around him.

Desperate, Jack picked up a nearby rock and hurled it as hard as he could at whatever was coming toward him.

The rock hit the figure straight on, causing it to stumble.

"Gragh!" came a voice, followed by a series of words in a strange language. Jack's ears picked up on it quickly, though, and instantly he knew the figure was saying something along the lines of "What the bloody – creekers tha' hurt!"

Jack didn't know who the figure was, but he wasn't going to take any chances. He ran straight for it and tackled it as hard as he could, bringing it to the ground. The two of them hit the floor with an *Oof,* and when they did, the figure let go of what looked to be some type of rifle.

Jack grabbed the rifle and got up quickly, aiming it at whatever he'd just brought down.

Lying there was a creature unlike any Jack had ever seen before. It had an oblong head with spiked ridges running down either side. Its skin was green and scaly, tinged with yellow and brown. It had no nose to speak of, and two small, beady eyes with no pupils. Its mouth was wide, with rows of sharp teeth. It was dressed in what looked to be leather armor of some type, though it was so tattered it was barely holding together.

The creature put its three-fingered hands up to shield it from the rifle, large black nails protruding from them.

"Blimey!" it cried. "Don' shoot!"

Jack hesitated. For something that looked like a monster out of a horror movie, the thing seemed genuinely scared of him.

Suddenly, Jack felt something hard and barrel shaped pressed up against the back of his head. Another voice came from behind him.

"There now, mate," said the voice. "Not that a plasma blast ta the face wouldn't improve our friend's looks here, but we're gonna have to have ya drop that blast-stick yer holdin' nice and slow like, savvy?"

Jack hesitated. He was pretty sure that whatever was pressed up against his head was a fairly big gun, but he certainly didn't like the idea of giving up the only thing he had that he could use to defend himself.

"How do I know if I drop this, you're not going to kill me?" asked Jack.

Behind him, the voice was silent for a moment before it spoke again. "Crikey. Faruuz, ya understand a bloody thing this little bugger just said?"

"Just shoot 'em already," said the green-scaled Faruuz as he stared down the barrel of Jack's rifle. "The browner hit me with a bleedin' rock."

Whomever Jack suddenly found himself with, it was obvious neither of them was speaking English. He could somehow understand both of them, but it was clear they had no idea what he was saying. Jack suddenly thought of his interface with the Ancient terminal, and how he heard all those voices in his head. If he had somehow downloaded how to understand these languages, maybe he had also downloaded how to speak them?

"Um…" said Jack trying to find the right words. "I said, how do I know if I do as you say, you're not just going to shoot me?"

To Jack's surprise, he actually spoke in the right language, and for some reason, it wasn't that hard to do.

"Not for nothin', lad," said the voice behind him. "But if I wanted ya dead, we wouldn't be havin' this conversation right now."

Somehow, that logic made sense to Jack. Slowly, Jack moved the rifle away from the one he assumed to be Faruuz and dropped it on the ground.

Faruuz grabbed the rifle and scrambled to his feet, leveling it at Jack. For an instant, Jack felt he'd made a terrible mistake, until someone else stepped in front of him, shielding him from the alien's weapon.

"Now, now, play nice, ya scaly grolp eater," said the man in front of Jack.

"He hit me wit' a bleedin' rock!" growled Faruuz.

"Aye, ya mentioned that," said the man. "Now, ya gonna mention yer just pissed 'cause some mystery midget laid ya out and took yer weapon while makin' ya cry like a bloody female?"

Faruuz grunted and lowered the rifle. "I think I liked ya better when you were a ripe ol' browner, Scally," the alien growled.

"That ripe ol' browner woulda let this one melt yer face, don't forget," said the man. "Now shake it off, and let's get back to camp."

Faruuz grumbled and gave Jack the evil eye before walking off, rubbing his head where the rock had hit him. Jack watched him go with a sense of cautious relief.

"Thanks," said Jack.

The man turned toward Jack to reveal that he wasn't really a man at all. His skin was bright red and leathery; he had a pointed chin and long, flowing jet-black dreadlock-like hair. His teeth were large and bright white, and he had long whisps of black hair on his upper lip that hung down like a mustache.

The alien was dressed in what looked like a silly medieval costume to Jack. He had knee-high black boots, baggy pants, and a torn and faded burgundy jacket, the kind with two long tails in the back, worn over a faded brown vest. He had various types of guns and knives strapped to a belt that hung low on his waist.

All in all, Jack thought the thing before him looked like a strange mix between a pirate and a devil.

"Don't mention it," smiled the alien. "Seeing Faruuz get beaned in the noggin' made my day. I haven't seen the jowler go down like that since the Havee bugs on Sigma 5 raided his scales. Ha!"

"Okay," said Jack, having no clue what the alien just said. "Um... who are you guys?"

"Well, in case ya didn't pick up on it, that right ol' brute is Faruuz," said the alien. "And I be Scallywag the Red, professional scoundrel, part-time rake, full-time captain of the pirate vessel Reaver. At your service."

Scallywag gave a slight bow and smiled. "And who might you be?"

"My name's Jack."

"Jack, eh?" said Scallywag. "That's a weird name. Ya almost look like a Regal, but not quite as uppity. What are ya, lad?"

"I'm ah... I guess you'd call me an Earthman."

"Right-o," said Scallywag pulling out a rather odd looking small pistol from his belt. "Know how to shoot a blaster, Earthman?"

"Yeah."

"Good," said the alien, handing him the weapon. "If you see anything that moves, shoot it. If it keeps moving, shoot it again. If it insists on continuing to move, continue to shoot until it sees the wisdom in doing otherwise. And try to keep up, because if ya get lost, yer on yer own. Savvy?"

With a pat on the back, Scallywag began to trot off after Faruuz.

"Wait!" said Jack, following behind him. "Where are we going? Where'd you guys come from? What is this place?"

"We are going back to our camp," said Scallywag as he bounded up an outcropping of rocks. "Our ship was captured by the Deathlord Fleet right outside the Yucca system, and as for where ya are, well…"

As Jack reached the top of the rocky hill, he froze. Before him was an immense cavern stretching out for miles and miles, made of veined black rock from ceiling to floor. Sounds of moaning and screaming echoed throughout the cave, and somewhere in the distance was a massive pillar of brilliant, ghostly white light that spiraled and churned chaotically.

"Welcome to the Pit, lad," said Scallywag as he surveyed the scene before them. He turned and looked at Jack with a frown. "This is where we're all gonna die."

CHAPTER ✺ 20

The hangar bay doors closed with a thunderous *CLACK* as the tractor beam disengaged, isolating the Ancient Earthship in one of the mothership's many smaller hangars typically reserved for captured vessels.

Immediately after the hangar sealed, atmosphere vented back into the room, and the large, circular, metal entrance rolled open to reveal a small army of Deathlord soldiers. They filed in and took up position around the ship, weapons drawn, ready to blast anything that moved.

Abraxas entered the large hangar and glared at the ship. He'd have liked nothing better than to have simply ordered his soldiers to rip the vessel apart, but the Deathlord Supreme wanted it examined. After all, technology from the Ancient Heretics could be a valued prize, and a ship that seemed to be able to disappear and reappear out of nowhere would certainly be of use.

"Report," Abraxas barked. The Deathlord squad leader Vishni, who had been in charge of the boarding assault, attended to him.

"Warlord Abraxas," Vishni said. "All of our boarding parties have been destroyed. Whoever is on board that vessel is an extremely skilled warrior."

Abraxas's mind flickered back to his battle at the temple. "That is an understatement," he growled. "Keep sending in the troops, as many as it takes. I want that ship."

Vishni nodded. "Yes, Warlord."

No sooner had Vishni ordered another boarding party to teleport onto the ship than the party leader called in over the comm.

"The control room is empty," said the Deathlord. "It appears they have fallen back into the rest of the ship."

"Follow them," ordered Vishni.

"They have sealed the door behind them, Commander," the Deathlord replied. "Shall we break through and pursue?"

Vishni looked to Abraxas. "What are your orders, Warlord?"

"Secure the command room," said Abraxas. "The Supreme does not wish to have the ship damaged any more than it is before the Acolytes can take a look at it. We'll have them open the doors and then we'll begin a sweep."

"Is that wise, Warlord?" asked Vishni. "That could give them time to—"

"To what?" snapped Abraxas. "What is there for them to do other than cower and hide? We have them surrounded. We control their bridge. Their ship is trapped in our hangar. There is no escape for them."

Vishni bowed his head. "Apologies, Warlord. I did not mean to question your orders."

"Then redeem yourself," rumbled Abraxas. "Find that warrior, and bring me his head."

"I swear to you, Warlord; he will die this day," replied Vishni.

While the Deathlord troops were preparing to board the ship, deep inside it, both Shepherd and Professor Green were looking for a way out. After escaping from the bridge and sealing the door behind them, their search of the quarters along the hallway had yielded nothing. They found no exits, no weapons, no places to hide, only barren, empty rooms.

Finally, the two had come to the end of the hallway, and nowhere in sight was there any sign of escape.

"Oh, dear," mumbled Green. "We are in quite a pickle, aren't we?"

Shepherd grimaced. That was putting it mildly. "Our priority right now is to find the Princess," he said.

"Easier said than done, I'm afraid," replied Professor Green. "By now, they undoubtedly have the ship surrounded, and it's only a matter of time before they get through that door. I hate to say it, but I'm afraid we're trapped."

"There *has* to be some way off this ship," Shepherd growled.

Suddenly, a door behind them hissed open. Shepherd and Green turned and looked, startled. They expected to find a Deathlord hit squad bearing down on them, but instead all they saw was a dark room.

"I say," said Green. "Did you notice a door there before?"

"No," said Shepherd. He popped out a cannon from his gauntlet and stepped into the room cautiously. No sooner had he entered than a friendly white light turned on, illuminating the room and revealing its contents. On the far wall, a small platform jutted out, made of a glowing white metal. Two computer consoles stood a few feet before it, humming patiently.

"Green, what is this?" asked Shepherd.

Green walked up to one of the consoles and began examining it. "Well, I'll be," he muttered as he read through the data on the screen. "It's a teleportation device!"

"A teleporter?" grunted Shepherd. "Like what the Deathlords use?"

"Well, considering we have very little knowledge about how Deathlord technology works, I can only speculate that it's similar in the respect that it does teleport things from one place to another," replied the Professor. "Beyond that, I have no idea. The Empire has nothing even close to this level of technology. How I'd love some time to delve into the science behind this—"

"Can we use it to teleport the Princess back to the ship?" asked Shepherd.

"Hmmmm," said Green as he tapped a few keys, scanning through the console's data. "It would appear we could—"

"Do it," the Paragon barked.

"If we knew what her location was," continued Green.

Shepherd punched the wall in frustration, leaving a slight dent in the smooth white metal that composed it. The only images running through his mind were all the horrible things the Deathlords could possibly be doing to Anna while he desperately grasped at straws trying to figure out what to do. He felt helpless, and he did not like that feeling one bit.

"On the bright side," continued the Professor, "this is our way off the ship."

"You can teleport us off?" Shepherd asked.

"Short range scanners are hooked into this system," responded Green. "I could teleport us somewhere deeper into the Deathlord vessel, away from the ship. That might give us the opportunity we need to track down the Princess."

Shepherd nodded. Finally, some good news. "Hurry up and punch in the coordinates."

"Should I even bother pointing out that I just recommended teleporting us deeper INTO a Deathlord mothership?"

"We *must* rescue the Princess," responded Shepherd.

"Undoubtedly, but we won't be much use if we get ourselves captured, or more likely, killed."

"Green, you're wasting time!" snapped Shepherd. "Now punch in—"

"NO!" exclaimed Green.

The outburst was so unlike the Professor, Shepherd was taken aback. Green composed himself. "I never thought I'd see the day when you would blindly rush into a situation as dire as this without a plan, old friend," he said. "I know you're anxious to get the Princess back, but please consider – we have no way of knowing if the location we teleport to will be safe. Once there, we have no way of tracking down the Princess. And should we, by some miracle, find her, we will still be in the heart of a *Deathlord Mothership*."

Shepherd nodded. Green was right; he was letting his emotions get the best of him. He took a deep breath and tried to calm himself.

"Can you figure out a way to teleport us somewhere that's not likely to have any Deathlords present?" Shepherd asked.

"Possibly," replied Green. "I don't think they're expecting anyone to infiltrate their ship so security will probably be fairly light. But that doesn't account for the fact that if someone sees us, we're dead. This is a big ship, but I doubt we can roam around it freely without being discovered."

"The hologuises," said Shepherd. "There's a safety feature on them that will project that of a Deathlord soldier. It comes installed on all hologuises to help aid in escape if attacked."

Green's eyes lit up. "Yes, I'd forgotten about that," he said. "Nifty little security feature, indeed. But that program is based off of eyewitness accounts and battlefield video. There's no way it will stand up to close scrutiny."

"It'll be good enough," said Shepherd. "As long as we don't get too close to any of them."

Green nodded. "Well, that's one problem solved. Sort of."

"Once we're in the ship, do you think you can access the Deathlord's computer system and figure out where they're holding Anna?"

"I can try," said Green. "Worse comes to worst, I could break down the programming code into binary and figure out a basic understanding of how their system works. That could take time, though."

"Better than nothing," responded Shepherd.

"And what about Jack?" asked Green.

"We need to rescue him, too," Shepherd said. "Without Jack, even if we find the Princess, we'll be stuck here."

"If the Deathlords haven't already killed him," replied Green gloomily.

Shepherd nodded. Anna was of value to the Deathlords so chances were she was still alive. Jack, on the other hand, could be dispatched by them without worry. Shepherd knew if that were the case, then their chances of escape were quite grim. "We'll have to assume he's still alive until we find out otherwise," Shepherd said.

"And if he's not?"

"Then we'll stay hidden until we figure something else out," said Shepherd.

"Stay hidden on a Deathlord Mothership," said Green dryly. "Nice to see you have not abandoned your sense of optimism, dear Paragon."

"Frankly, right now we don't need optimism, Professor," replied Shepherd. "We need a miracle. Now punch in the coordinates, and pray the Princess and Jack are still alive."

CHAPTER ✸ 21

t felt like they had been walking for hours. Jack stumbled after Scallywag and Faruuz as they made their way over the rocky terrain, occasionally stopping to scavenge various pieces of what looked like wreckage of space ships, but they usually came up with nothing.

The two aliens didn't use flashlights or torches, which made traveling with them difficult. The Pit was so dark, sometimes it felt like they were walking through an empty void. If it weren't for the faint glow of whatever was veined into the rock, and the illumination from that strange pillar of light, Jack doubted he'd be able to find solid footing on anything.

Faruuz took the lead, since he claimed he was better at seeing in the dark (though that hadn't helped when Jack hit him in the head with a rock). The two aliens moved quickly, as though they knew the terrain, and Jack had to hustle to keep up. They traveled in silence, which meant the only thing Jack had to focus on was the sound of wailing and moans that seemed to echo through the air. Occasionally, he'd hear the rustling of pebbles nearby, as though some small animal had just streaked across their path, but Jack never saw anything. He just gripped the small pistol Scallywag had given him a little tighter.

"Are we almost there?" Jack whispered as he climbed over an outcropping of rock after the two aliens. "You know — wherever it is we're going?"

"Aye," said Scallywag. "The camp's just a bit further."

"You said that, like, an hour ago," whined Jack. With all he'd been through that day, he was incredibly tired, and the brisk pace his companions were keeping was quickly wearing him out.

"And I was right an hour ago," replied Scallywag. "Just like I am now."

"Well, you think we could slow down a bit?" pleaded Jack. His legs were starting to feel heavier than lead.

"Not a good idea," said Scallywag. "A leisurely stroll through the Pit is a good way to get killed, lad. The sooner we're back at camp, the better."

Jack grumbled. The only thing he'd seen so far in the Pit were these two aliens, and they didn't seem that dangerous (well, compared to the Deathlords, anyway). Jack wondered what was out there that had them both so on edge.

"Well, if you're not going to slow down, can we at least talk about something so I don't have to listen to all these creepy noises constantly?" Jack begged.

Faruuz snorted. "Want me to recite a beddy-bye story for ya? Maybe give ya a nice cup o' warm milk before tucking ya in?"

"No offense, but you doing that sounds even creepier than all these noises," replied Jack.

Furuuz turned and gnashed his pointy teeth at Jack. "Ya think this is a joke? Just where do ya think ya are, Earthman? Eh?"

"Um… the creepy Pit of Death, apparently," said Jack.

"Back off, Faruuz," muttered Scallywag.

"Oy, stop ordering me around like yer still me Captain, Scally," sneered Faruuz. "This tag-along you picked up is gonna get us killed with all his talking. Remember yer own rules? 'Move silent, move fast.' That's what ya said."

"I know what I said," replied Scallywag. "I also know what it was like when we first wound up in here, too. The lad's just scared–"

"Toss the boy," replied Faruuz. "He hit me in the head––"

"With a bleedin' rock, yes, you mentioned that a time or two," snapped Scallywag. "And I'll cave yer oblong face in with me sodding fist if ya don't shut up about it. We'll need every gun hand we can get when the next wave attacks, so you're gonna learn to live with the lad until one o' ya stops breathin', savvy?"

"Next wave?" asked Jack. Whatever that was, he didn't like the sound of it.

Faruuz looked at Jack with his beady black eyes and smiled a shark-like grin. "Aye. Don't suppose a tasty morsel like him will last long anyway," the alien snorted and spat a thick glob of phlegm at Jack's feet.

Faruuz turned and kept walking. Jack looked at Scallywag, who'd thankfully slowed his pace down a bit, presumably for Jack's benefit.

"What's he mean by that?" Jack asked. "What's attacking you?"

"Zombies," muttered Scallywag dryly.

"Zombies?" said Jack, his eyes wide. "Like, rotting corpses shuffling around trying to eat brains, that type of zombie?"

"More like mindless, nasty, mean ol' browners running 'round with the singular purpose of ripping us all to shreds," Scallywag replied.

"Cooool..." said Jack. Scallywag raised his eyebrow. "Oh, uh, I mean, that's awful," Jack corrected.

Scallywag chuckled. "Yer a strange one, Earthman; I'll give ya that."

"So where do they come from?" asked Jack. "The zombies, I mean. Are they like the product of an evil zombie virus or something? Or alien parasites that worm their way into their brains? Oooo, or are they being mutated by some weird type of *space* radiation?"

"Don't know," replied Scallywag. "Never bothered to ask 'em."

Jack smiled. Scallywag was a pretty cool alien. Even trapped in a deep dark pit of despair, the guy moved with a swagger that seemed to say he wasn't scared a bit. For some reason, that made Jack feel much safer than he probably was.

"Guess this is normal for you, huh?" said Jack. "Being a pirate and all. You've probably had all sorts of crazy intergalactic adventures and stuff. Am I right?"

"If by 'adventures' ya mean almost getting killed constantly, yeah, I guess ya could say that."

"Right on. I've almost been killed, like, 50 times today already."

"Well then, sounds like yer off to a fine start for a life of adventuring."

"I'd rather have my old life back," said Jack. "It used to be the worst thing I'd have to worry about was some jock meathead picking on me at school. I'd give anything to have that back right now."

"Aye," said Scallywag. "And I'd like to be back on me ship, with a pretty yellow lass on me lap and a cold pint of plaxar rum in me hand. Guess that just proves we never get what we like."

"Is that the ship you were on when the Deathlords got you? What'd you call it?"

"The Reaver," smiled Scallywag.

"Yeah, that. The Deathlords captured it?"

"Takes more than a few Deathlord Motherships to capture The Reaver, lad. We were on a prison transport, actually," said Scallywag. "Ol' Faruuz got himself nipped while raiding a Tarush merchant frigate."

"What did you get nipped for?" Jack asked.

"Me?" said Scallywag innocently. "I wasn't captured. I was there ta rescue the bum."

"I seem to remember you locked up in the prison pod next ta me," grumbled Faruuz.

"Well, how else was I supposed ta get aboard the bloody transport?" replied Scallywag. "It's not like they sell tickets onto those things."

"Just saying, I don't see how being locked up in the same ship as me was part o' some brilliant escape plan," the alien said. "Still think ya probably just said ya were there to help me so I wouldn't rip your sodding throat out first chance I got."

"Trust me, if we hadn't gotten captured by the Deathlords, me plan woulda worked just fine," said Scallywag. "And I told ya, I was there to make amends."

"Bah," spat Faruuz. "Like ya could ever make up for what ya did."

"Why? What'd you do?" asked Jack.

Scallywag sighed. "It ain't important. We should stop talking until we get back ta camp."

"Oh, so now ya want the Earthman to shut up?" smirked Faruuz. "Brilliant. Go on, Earthman. Ask him. Ask him more of yer sodding questions to pass the time, why don't ya?"

Jack was quiet. There was obviously something going on between the two aliens, and he was positive he didn't want to keep poking at it.

"What?" asked Faruuz at Jack's silence. "No more? Ain't you got at least one more bloody stupid question to ask?"

"Actually," said Jack. "Either of you wouldn't happen to know what 'petulant' means, would you?"

Faruuz stopped and turned toward Jack. For a second, Jack thought he was going to raise his rifle at him when Scallywag put his hand on its barrel and stopped it.

"Easy, mate," grinned Scallywag.

Faruuz grumbled. "Enough of this. Next one who utters a peep, I'm blasting. Don't care which one o' ya it is."

Faruuz yanked his rifle from Scallywag's hand and stormed off. Scallywag winked at Jack before following silently behind his alien friend. Jack figured that was his way of telling him Faruuz was serious, so he stayed quiet the rest of the journey.

After what felt like another couple of hours, the group approached what appeared to be a crevice in the walls of the Pit, flanked by large outcroppings of rock. Faruuz and Scallywag slowed down as they approached.

"Oy, Rodham," whispered Scallywag loudly. "It's us. Don't bloody shoot."

Two figures silently emerged from one of the outcroppings of rocks, carrying what looked like some pretty cool plasma rifles. Jack thought the guns looked an awful lot like M-16s, but more futuristic.

The men looked human, but their pointed ears made it obvious they were Regals, like Anna and Shepherd. Both were wearing dirty and dusty uniforms, dark grey jumpsuits with some navy blue tinted armor inter-woven into them. On their shoulders were circular crimson patches, containing two golden orbs – one within the other.

The man in the front as they approached was tall, rugged, and muscular. He had a small scar under his left eye, and his gaze was cold and hard, much like Shepherd's. He had close-cropped blonde hair and some stubble on his face, which said he hadn't shaved in a while.

The man behind him was more slender and far less muscular. He had an uncombed head of dark blonde hair, but his light eyes appeared far more scared than that of his companion. His face looked drawn and pale, even in the darkness.

"Took your kitten time coming back, pirate," said the big man Jack assumed was Rodham.

"Well, had I known you'd miss me so much, I'd have hurried back sooner," replied Scallywag.

"Did you find anything?"

"Does an Earthman count?" replied Scallywag, pointing his thumb toward Jack.

Rodham looked down at Jack as if noticing him for the first time.

"Not unless we can eat him," he grumbled.

"Something which I'm not sure isn't an option," said Faruuz.

"Any water?" asked the other man, his voice wavering slightly. "What about food?"

"It be pretty sparse out there," replied Scallywag. "We did find a few goodies, though. But nothing that'll last us more than a day or two... assuming we can choke it down, that is."

"Exits?" Rodham inquired.

"Nada," said Scallywag. "Solid rock everywhere. Did the other team find anything?"

Rodham shook his head. "They're not kitten back yet," he said. "You all better get in and report what you found to the Major."

"Aye-aye, Sergeant," mumbled Scallywag. "Don't know how we survived for so long without you military types around to report to."

Rodham's eyes narrowed. "Been wondering that myself, Red," the big man grumbled. He punched the shoulder of his companion lightly, though even that almost knocked the poor fellow over.

"Escort them in, Porter," said Rodham. "Make sure they actually deliver their kitten findings. Then send Tappert out to replace you."

"Ya still don't trust us?" said Scallywag, smiling slyly. "Yer breakin' me cold, black heart, Sergeant."

"Trust me, pirate, I'd be breakin' a whole lot more if we didn't need each other to survive."

"You and me both," said Scallywag as he walked past the man. "C'mon, Yeoman Porter. Lead us to his Majesty."

Without waiting for his escort, Scallywag entered into the crevice of rock, followed closely by Faruuz. Jack walked behind with Yeoman Porter, his feet screaming and burning with every step. All he wanted at that moment was to sit down and take a nap.

"You're an Earthman?" asked Porter as he walked, trying to keep an eye on the two aliens ahead of them.

"Yeah," said Jack.

"What are you doing here?" Porter asked.

"Just lucky, I guess," said Jack dryly. Porter chuckled.

"Sorry," the Yeoman replied. "I mean, we were taken when the Deathlords boarded our ships. One moment, I'm getting the Captain his coffee, the next, Dark Soldiers appear out of nowhere and shoot me with a ball of purple light, and now I'm here."

"Coffee?" asked Jack. "You mean, like, space coffee?"

"Huh? No, just… coffee. Do they not have coffee on Earth?"

"We do, I just didn't know they had it on other planets."

"Oh, well, maybe it's not exactly the same thing. I am… I was the Captain's assistant. That's what a Yeoman is, you know.

Kinda like the head officer's right-hand man. If he wants coffee, I get him coffee. I also deal with visitors, take his subspace communications, basically run his life. You know, stuff like that."

"Sounds… awesome," said Jack, not really meaning it.

"It's not glamorous, but it's a heck of a lot better than standing guard out there with Sergeant Rodham; I'll tell you that."

"Yeah, what's his deal with kittens, anyway?" Jack asked.

"What do you mean?"

"He talks about kittens a lot," said Jack.

"Oh, sorry about that. The Sergeant tends to swear a great deal when he's stressed."

"Swear?" asked Jack.

"Uh-huh. Why? What's kitten mean on Earth?"

"We use it to refer to a cute baby animal."

Porter laughed. "I think it's safe to say it stands for something completely different to the rest of the universe."

Suddenly, Porter began to cough uncontrollably. He wheezed and tried to catch his breath.

"You okay?" asked Jack.

"No…" said Porter weakly. "Ever since we got here, I've been feeling worse and worse. Like I'm coming down with something, but… it's not like any sickness I've ever experienced. It's this place. It's like it's crushing me on the inside."

Jack looked at the man and could almost see him get a little paler. The crevice into the wall led into an open cavern where a few torches and campfires were burning, making it easier to see.

"Anyway, we were on this secret mission, doing guard duty for your planet," continued Porter. "I got to see the communications from our ground team. I didn't think you Earthmen were capable of advanced spaceflight or anything like that."

"Well, we're really not," said Jack.

"Then how'd you get here?" asked Porter. "And how do you know how to speak New Solar?"

"Speak what?" asked Jack.

"New Solar, our language," replied Porter. "You speak it perfectly."

"I think I downloaded it into my brain or something," said Jack. "It's kinda a long story."

Jack saw Scallywag and Faruuz approach a small group huddled by a tiny fire. A few men were laid out next to it, bloody and beaten up pretty badly. An older man in the same kind of uniform as Porter and Rodham was tending to their wounds. A few other guys were lying there by the fire, too, but they didn't look beaten up at all; they were just moaning and sweating.

As the group approached, another man stepped out of the darkness. He must have been in his early thirties by Jack's guess. He had a buzz cut of light brown hair, and his eyes were a hard blue. Part of his right ear was missing, giving him a weird lopsided look. But other than that, Jack would have pegged him as Captain America incarnate.

"You made it back," said the man. "I was beginning to worry."

"Had to go out farther this time," said Scallywag, tossing him a knapsack. "Didn't find much. Some clothing, a few puddles of water, a small animal carcass or two."

"Any meds?" the older man asked as he wiped the sweat from a shivering man's brow with a dirty rag.

"No luck, Doc," said Scallywag. "Sorry."

The older man sighed. "What I wouldn't give for even a basic first aid kit right now."

"We'll make due with what we've got," said the man looking into the bag, obviously not too happy with its contents. "Let's just hope the other team fares better."

"Oh yeah, we also found this," said Scallywag, pointing to Jack.

The man looked at Jack and squinted. "And who are you?" he asked.

"Name's Jack," Jack replied.

"He's an Earthman, Major," chimed in Porter.

The Major raised an eyebrow. "You're from the planet?"

"I was," said Jack bitterly. "The Deathlords kinda blew it up."

A visible shift went through the group. Even Faruuz looked somewhat saddened at the news. The Major approached Jack and dropped to a knee so he was eye-level with him.

"If that's so, how did you come to be here?" he asked.

"I escaped. With Anna and Mr. Shepherd."

The Major's eyes widened. "The Princess? She was able to get off world?"

"Yeah," said Jack. "Until, you know... they caught us."

The Major's shoulders visibly slumped at that news. "What happened?"

"They boarded our ship, and I got teleported to the Deathlord mothership along with Anna," explained Jack. "They threw me in here and took Anna off somewhere else."

"So the Princess lives?" said the Major hopefully.

"Yeah," said Jack. "I'm pretty sure they wanted her alive."

"Thank the Great Observer for small miracles," breathed the Major. "And what of Paragon Shepherd?"

"Last I saw him, he was doing his whole butt-kicking thing," said Jack.

"Then there may still be hope," said the Major as he got to his feet. "I'm sorry for what happened to your planet, Jack. I'm afraid you may have been better off there than you are here. But while you are, you're under our protection."

"And just who are you guys?" Jack asked.

"I'm Major Ganix, a member of the Princess's royal escort. You've obviously met Yeoman Porter and Sergeant Rodham. This is Doctor Pyle. We're all members of the Regalus Imperial Space Force, tasked with protecting the Princess during her expedition to your planet."

Great job, Jack thought sarcastically. Looking around the cave, there had to be at least a dozen sorry looking Imperial soldiers milling about. Some were weathered and drawn. Others looked tired and miserable. Overall, Jack thought it looked more like a prison camp than a military operation.

"What's wrong with those guys?" Jack asked, referencing the men Doc Pyle was tending to.

"They're our wounded..." said Ganix before glancing at the other non-bloodied men a bit uneasily. "And our sick."

"Do you know anything about where we are?" asked Yeoman Porter. "Where they've put us?"

Jack shook his head. "I was on the bridge of the Deathlord Mothership, then some jerk-wad tossed me onto a platform and teleported me here. That's all I know."

Porter frowned at that news. Suddenly, Jack felt bad about not being more helpful.

"You look tired," said the Major. "You should sleep. I'll have someone set aside some rations for you."

"Thanks," Jack sighed. It was a small thing, but at that moment it was the best news he'd heard all day.

Ganix turned to Scallywag. "Captain, since you found the boy, would you mind taking watch while he gets some rest?"

Scallywag's eyes narrowed. It sounded like the Major asked a request, but it was obvious it was really an order. "Be my pleasure, Major," said the red-skinned alien. "Anything else we can do for the Empire before settling down for the night?"

Ganix smirked before tossing him a small sack of rations. "Eat," he said. "And keep your guns handy."

Scallywag pursed his lips sourly and turned to leave. "Right-o. C'mon, lad."

Jack followed, along with Faruuz, leaving Ganix and the others to tend to their wounded comrades. Jack looked up at Scallywag as they walked away.

"I take it you guys don't like each other?" Jack asked.

"Nothing personal," said Scallywag. "As far as Regals go, that Ganix chap is better than most. But Visini and Regals just don't tend ta get along all that well in general."

"Why not?"

"Probly 'cause we've been trying to destroy each other for ages," replied Scallywag with a smile. "Their empire might be bigger than ours, but we're nicer looking and have much better fashion sense."

Jack smiled. Scallywag reached into the sack Ganix had given him and took out a small handful of what looked like crackers and gave them to Faruuz, who quietly sulked off as soon as he got his chow. Jack wasn't exactly sad to see him go.

"So the Regals had you on a prison ship?" Jack asked.

"Hmmmm?" said Scallywag. "Nah, we were here long before that sorry lot showed up."

"You were?"

"Yeah. Don't know how long we've been down here, though. Seems like months, though it's probly closer ta a few weeks. The bloody Deathlords didn't have the decency to board our transport. One minute, we all think we're gonna die locked away in prison pods as they blast our ship to oblivion, the next minute, there's a flash o' purple light, and we're here. Wherever here is."

"Wait," said Jack. "Your ship *crashed* in here?"

"Indeed," said Scallywag. "We weren't on the ground two bloody hours before the first wave hit. Crazy zombies came outta nowhere and started ripping through the ship. The guards freed us all ta help fight 'em off. Had to abandon the bloody thing and run into the darkness ta get away. Since then we've just been wandering around, scouting, surviving, you know how it goes."

Jack was paying so much attention to Scallywag, he'd failed to notice they were walking right toward one of the strangest things he'd ever seen until they were right on top of it.

At first, in the darkness of the cave, it looked like a large grey boulder. But this boulder had arms, legs, and a head. It was sitting cross-legged, with a large wooden club the size of a cow's leg across its lap. The figure, with well-defined muscles bulging from beneath its elephant-like skin, was as wide as two men. Its head, with a large Cro-Magnonesque brow and a huge square jaw that gave way to two teeth jutting out from its lower lip, seemed slightly too small for its body.

Jack looked at the massive beast with a mixture of curiosity and fear as Scallywag strolled up to it and gave it a swift kick.

"Oy! Grohm! Wake up, ya sodding Rognok!" Scallywag barked.

The large creature stirred, revealing red eyes with black pupils. "Battle?" it asked in a deep, gravelly voice.

"Does it look like a battle?" said Scallywag. "I got some chow. Ya hungry yet?"

The creature, apparently called Grohm, simply grunted and closed its eyes again, going back to its almost statue-like state.

"Good talking to ya, as always," grumbled Scallywag. "Bloody Rognoks be the best sodding conversationalists I've ever met."

"What is it?" Jack asked, his eyes not able to leave the massive alien in front of him.

Scallywag turned and looked at Jack. "Oh, right, ya wouldn't know. This is Grohm. He's a Rognok."

"What's a Rognok?"

"A race of big tough browners, that's what," said Scallywag. "Their world got hit by the Deathlords not long after the fall of Regalus Prime. Most Rognoks just liked to run around and beat each other senseless most o' the time, so very few of 'em were off world before it was blown to bits. Grohm here was already in the Pit when we arrived. He's never said how long he's been here, but I get the sense it's been a while."

"So he wasn't on the prison ship with you?" Jack asked, feeling slightly relieved.

"Nah," said Scallywag. "Honestly, he's one o' the reasons we've been able to survive so long. Rognoks can take a ton of punishment, so me and Faruuz just stick near this guy and let the zombies attack him while we pick 'em off. Works pretty well actually."

"You just let him get attacked?" Jack asked, astounded.

"He don't mind," shrugged Scallywag. "If there's one thing a Rognok likes ta do, it's fight. We just let him do it."

"So only you and Faruuz survived from your ship, huh?"

"Not at first," sighed Scallywag as he slid down next to the slumbering Rognok and popped a cracker in his mouth. "There was a small group o' us, guards and prisoners. Once we found Grohm and determined he wasn't gonna kill us, we followed him back to this cave. Since then, our numbers got whittled down. Some got killed in the occasional zombie raid, others just wandered off after getting all sick, never to be seen again."

"Sick? Like those guys the Doc was tending to?"

Scallywag nodded. "Whatever it is, it seems to affect you Regal types rather quickly."

"But not you?"

"Meh," shrugged the alien. "Haven't noticed anything yet."

"Oh, but you *will*..." came a low, snarky voice.

Jack turned and peered into the darkness nearby, where the voice had come from. He could make out a strange figure moving in the shadows and could hear the faint sounds of whirring and motors, almost like those a toy electric car makes after being turned on.

With a *Clank* and a *Clack*, the figure stepped into the light, revealing an extremely strange looking robot. Its body was ridiculously thin and rickety, with various mismatched parts that made it look like the robot had been patched together from many different types of metal. Its body was scarred and rusted a bit, and it walked with what looked like a slight hunch in its back.

In contrast to its flimsy body, its head was wide and oval-shaped, the occasional screw loosely popping out from its cranium, with large black lenses on either side for eyes, and a small horizontal box underneath it that glowed red with a waveform pattern when it spoke. Overall, Jack thought it almost looked like some type of cross between a creepy old man and a pair of huge binoculars.

If Scallywag were surprised to see some rickety walking robot appear out of nowhere, he didn't show it. He simply rolled his eyes and popped another cracker into his mouth. "Oy, here we go…"

"First, it will start as a slight fever," said the robot. "Then the cold sweats will begin. Your joints will ache, your breathing will become labored. Eventually, you'll be unable to sleep. Your mind's grasp on reality will begin to deteriorate as your body's vital organs begin to shut down, causing an agonizing, painful, horrible, and inevitable - *death!* Mwuahaha! MWU-ahahaha! MWUAHA—"

Suddenly, a rock flew up and conked the robot on the side of the head, courtesy of Scallywag.

"Ow," it said, rubbing the impact site with its three-fingered metal hand.

"Shut it, rust-bucket," grumbled Scallywag. "Last thing I wanna do after a scouting mission is listen to ya drone on."

"You sure that stuff is gonna happen?" asked Jack, the image of Yeoman Porter and the other sick Regals flashing into his mind.

"Of course it will!" exclaimed the robot, exasperated. "I've meticulously documented all the recorded symptoms among you organics. 'Tis only a matter of time before you all fall prey to this sickness, leaving me the last one standing! Mwuaha!"

"Trust me, before I go down, I'll be sure to take you with me, robot," said Scallywag off-handedly.

"Many have tried…" it replied. "All have *failed!*"

Another rock dinged the robot on the side of its head.

"Ow," it said.

"But how do you know for sure?" insisted Jack, suddenly worried about this sickness. "I mean, could you be wrong?"

"Isn't it obvious?" said the robot. "I'm a genius! I'm *never* wrong."

The robot shuffled up to Jack and leaned over him. "I don't believe we've met. My name is Heckubus Moriarty, the greatest — and most feared — evil criminal genius in eight star systems!" it said dramatically. "Perhaps you've heard of me?"

"Uh, no," replied Jack. "But don't take it personally. Just a couple hours ago I didn't know there was any life outside of my planet."

The gears in the robot's head groaned. "Typical," he droned. "Leave it to the organics to believe they are the center of the universe."

"Don't pay any attention to that bucket o' bolts, lad," said Scallywag. "He's just a malfunctioning junkbot with delusions of grandeur."

"I'll have you know this 'bucket o' bolts' was responsible for taking the entire Zerostian fleet hostage, turning their own starfighters against them, by using a sophisticated algorithm I personally developed," sneered Heckubus.

"If memory serves, the Zerostians only have two ships," said Scallywag.

"Technically, they are still considered a fleet," the robot replied.

"And they don't have any starfighters."

"Repair shuttles," said Heckubus. "Practically the same thing."

"And they're nomads, so they have absolutely nothing of value which would warrant holding 'em hostage for."

"Foolish nitwit! I'm an evil genius! The purpose wasn't to extract funds! It was to show others how evil and dastardly I am and to spread fear throughout the universe!"

"If that's the case," said Scallywag, "why didn't ya just destroy the bloody Zerostians? Surely that's more evil than hijacking a few repair shuttles for a time, eh?"

Heckubus merely stared at Scallywag with loathing, the gears in his head whirring angrily.

"I hate you," the robot said.

"Hey," said Jack, "If you're as smart as you say you are, can you figure out a way to get us out of here?"

"Why, what a brilliant idea!" Heckubus scoffed. "How could I not have thought of that before? Plan an escape? So novel. How have I managed to survive so long without your keen input? Yes, let me get right on that... for the *trillionth* time!"

Jack frowned. "I like my robots without a side of sarcasm, thank you very much."

"Pah!" said Heckubus. "I'm constantly reminded why I loath you organics so. Such dimwitted skullduggery! I'll have you know that after analyzing every factor of our current situation, there is a 97.6% probability that escape is impossible."

Jack brightened up. "Well, what about the other 2.4%?"

"Yes, indeed," said Heckubus. "There is a 2.4% probability that we could escape. With a 2.4% margin of error, of course."

"I hate to break it to ya, lad, but the tin-can is right," said Scallywag. "We've been up and down this Pit a thousand times. There are no doors, no exits, nothing. For all we know we're a thousand feet underground in some backwater prison planet the Deathlords use ta toss away their bloody garbage. As much as I'm loathe to admit it, there ain't no getting out o' this one. We're all thoroughly, and completely, kittened."

Jack sighed. His planet was destroyed, the girl of his dreams was being held hostage, and he was trapped in a deep dark pit with a bunch of aliens and robots, with no hope of escape. *Could things possibly get any worse?* he wondered.

Suddenly, the sound of blaster fire erupted from the darkness.

"To arms! To arms!" came a voice.

Instantly, some of the military men in the cave jumped to. Scallywag perked up, alarmed. Heckubus groaned.

"If you'll excuse me," said the robot quickly scuttling off into the darkness.

Scallywag got to his feet. "Blast it," he muttered as he kicked Grohm again.

The Rognok stirred and opened his eyes. "Battle?" he said.

"Whaddya think, ya git?" grumbled Scallywag as he took out his pistols. "Time to do yer thing."

Grohm snorted and lumbered to his feet, standing a good eight feet tall. His massive body was clad in some type of flimsy-looking metal armor, dented and battle-scarred. Without another word, the Rognok began lumbering toward the cave's entrance.

"Still got that gun I gave ya?" asked Scallywag as he quickly checked his weapons.

"Yeah," said Jack weakly. He was so tired; the last thing he wanted to do right now was fight.

"Well, what are ya waiting for, lad?" said Scallywag. "Time ta use it!"

Scallywag grabbed Jack by his jacket and jerked him to his feet. Without another word, he was running toward the entrance to the cave, and Jack followed closely behind, pulling the small plasma pistol from his pocket.

They were almost to the cave entrance when Sergeant Rodham came running in, followed closely by a few other soldiers.

"Fall back! Fall back!" the Sergeant yelled. "There are too many of them—"

Then, a terrible screech filled the air as a six-legged creature leapt out from the cave entrance, flying over the Regals as they retreated and heading straight for Jack.

"Oh, crap!" said Jack, not really having time to react as the large, praying mantis-like alien bore down on him, black drool seeping from its large mouth, its eyes cloudy and terrifying.

Suddenly, a large club connected with the alien in mid-air, right before it reached Jack. Grohm swung his primitive weapon just like a baseball bat, sending the alien flying across the cave and splattering it against the wall like a bug on a windshield.

"Thanks, big guy," said Jack, looking up at Grohm with relief. He was suddenly very glad the Rognok was on his side.

Grohm just looked down at Jack and snorted.

"Form the line!" cried Ganix, suddenly next to Jack.

Instantly, the Regal soldiers all formed up in two lines behind Grohm. The front line of men knelt, and the rear line stood behind them, forming a tight firing squad, just as the noises and cries of the oncoming wave echoed through the cave entrance.

Jack wasn't sure where to go and found himself behind the back line of the Regal soldiers. Then, he got knocked down when someone pushed into him. He looked up into the snarling face of Faruuz.

"Still think this is cool, Earthman?" The alien sneered as he armed his rifle. He turned and fired just as the Regals unleashed their first volley.

Jack looked over to see a rush of aliens flow forth from the cave's entrance, taking on the plasma blasts. Some fell immediately, but for the most part, they just kept coming.

They weren't what Jack had expected. The attackers ranged from humanlike to various types of aliens he'd never seen before. Some had many arms; some had nothing but legs. Some had scaly skin, while others had fur. Some were purple, blue, brown, and even black. Some wore strange looking clothes while others wore nothing at all. Some looked monstrous while others looked almost cuddly. But there were two things they all had in common -- they all had a disgusting black bile seeping from their mouths, and their eyes all had a cloudy, far-off look in them, as though the creatures were completely mindless.

The hoard rushed toward the group, but Grohm stepped up and swung his massive club, disrupting the zombie charge. Some of them went flying at the force of Grohm's swing, while others leapt right on top of the Rognok, and a few passed him entirely.

The Regals immediately started picking off the zombies, first taking aim at the ones coming at them, next firing at the ones knocked to the side, and finally taking on the ones Grohm was keeping busy.

The Rognok was shrugging off the zombies like they were bugs. No matter how much they hit, bit, and clawed at the massive alien, it didn't seem to faze him. He stood his ground and continued to smash the charge of attackers running at him from the entrance.

Bodies were starting to stack up in front of the firing squad. To Jack, it seemed if the soldiers didn't make a direct headshot, the attackers just kept coming without slowing down.

"Crikey! There's a lot of 'em!" Jack heard Scallywag shout above the firing.

"Hold the line!" screamed Ganix.

Faruuz looked down at Jack, who still hadn't gotten back to his feet. "Don't jus' lie there, ya bloody good-for-nuttin piece of—"

Then, a large, hairy, beast-like zombie crashed through the ranks and barreled into Faruuz. They both hit the ground hard. The Beast Zombie's massive jaw was about to tear into Faruuz's neck when the alien got his arm up in time to save himself. The Beast sank his teeth into Faruuz's arm and the alien screamed in pain as he struggled with his furry attacker.

Jack grabbed his pistol and aimed it at the Beast Zombie, unleashing a few rounds. Red-hot plasma blasts tore into the creature, but it continued to attack Faruuz.

"The head! Shoot it in tha' bloody head, ya twit!" Faruuz yelled.

Jack took aim and let loose a shot that hit the Beast in the back of the skull. The Beast Zombie went limp, and Faruuz rolled it off him. Jack went to the alien's side. His arm was gashed badly where the beast had bitten it, and green blood was seeping everywhere.

"Ohmigosh!" said Jack. "Are you okay?"

"Do I bloody look okay?" cried Faruuz, his large black eyes watery. "He ate me bleedin' arm!"

"Rear line, fall back!" Jack heard Ganix call out. Jack turned to see more zombies on the way, and it was getting hard to hold the defenses as the corpses piled up. The rear line of the firing squad had regrouped and was moving back to give cover so the front line could retreat enough to make more room to fight.

Jack got behind Faruuz and started to drag him away from the fight, with the alien complaining the entire time.

"Ow! OW! What ya think yer doin'?" cried Faruuz.

"Trying to keep you from getting eaten by another zombie," grunted Jack as he pulled the alien aside. "Now quit your complaining!"

Jack dragged his companion behind a nearby rock and propped him up there.

"Hold on," said Jack. "I'm gonna go get the Doc."

"And leave me here unprotected?" grunted Faruuz. "Are ya trying ta get me killed?"

Jack gritted his teeth and shoved his pistol into Faruuz's good hand. "Don't tempt me," said Jack, before he turned to run back to the front line where Faruuz had dropped his rifle.

It looked like the wave of zombies was starting to thin out, so Jack didn't feel so bad about heading toward the back of the camp where Doc Pyle was stationed. The doctor was frantically going through his meager supplies, getting ready for the onslaught of wounded he'd have to treat.

"Doc! Doc!" said Jack as he ran up. "Come quick! Faruuz... he's hurt!"

Doc Pyle looked up at Jack with weary blue eyes. "Who?" he asked.

"The ugly green alien? Who's kind of a jerk?" Jack clarified.

Pyle nodded in recognition. "What's wrong with him?"

"He got bitten on the arm," said Jack.

The Doc's face darkened. "Blast it," he muttered. "I'm not sure if I'll have enough cloth for bandages..."

As Doctor Pyle turned to check his supplies again, Jack saw movement out of the corner of his eye. He turned and looked as one of the sick Regal soldiers who was lying by the campfire got to his feet. Jack's heart almost stopped when the Regal looked up, his eyes cloudy, black bile seeping from his mouth.

"You gotta be kidding..." said Jack.

Suddenly, the other sick Regal soldiers stirred, their sickness seemingly having given way to zombieness. Jack now found himself staring down four zombies all on his own.

Ohhhhhhhhhh crap, was the only thing that went through his mind before the first zombie attacked.

"Doc, get down!" Jack yelled as he pushed Doc Pyle out of the way. Jack raised his rifle and got off a shot at one of the zombies before another one slammed into him, tackling him to the ground. Jack used Faruuz's rifle to brace against his attacker as the zombie frantically tried to bite Jack's neck, black bile seeping from his mouth onto Jack's face.

Presented with such a dire (and gross) situation, Jack was forced to fall back to his patented strategy number two to avoid a beat down — namely, call for help.

"Help!" screamed Jack. "Someone!!!"

Jack then heard Doc Pyle shrieking. He looked over to see two of the new zombies on top of the man, biting and tearing him apart. Jack wasn't able to concentrate that much on the poor doctor's situation, since the zombie soldier on top of him was twice his size and quickly baring down on his neck.

This is it, Jack thought. *I'm totally gonna die… eaten by a zombie!*

Faruuz was right. Jack definitely did not think this was cool anymore. Then, suddenly, a blast of red plasma fire streaked through his attacker's head. The zombie went limp, and three more shots rang out, each one finding its mark as the other zombies hit the ground.

Jack looked up and saw Scallywag standing there. With a twirl of his pistols, he holstered his weapons and looked down at Jack.

"Ya okay, lad?" he asked.

Jack crawled out from under the body of his attacker and looked around. The sound of shooting had stopped. The moans of the zombies had gone away, too. He looked up at Scallywag hopefully.

"Is it over?" Jack asked.

"Wait for it..." the alien responded.

Just as Jack was beginning to wonder what that meant, the zombie corpse beside him began to jerk.

Alarmed, Jack crawled away further. The other dead zombies begin to spasm, as well. Suddenly, ghostly figures floated out of the bodies. Jack watched with a mixture of fear and amazement as the glowing white forms of energy twisted and writhed in the air. They didn't look like the bodies from which they had come, but as Jack looked on with wonder, he could see what appeared to be eyes and also a mouth that was moaning and screaming silently.

Then, the ghostly forms shot off, streaking out of the cave with alarming speed. This happened with each dead zombie that lay around on the ground. As soon as the ghostly figures were gone, the hard black rock of the cave floor started to grow around the bodies that were left behind.

The black rock became like sand that rolled up and covered the corpses. Veins of green and purple glowed as they burrowed into the dead bodies, the black rock completely encompassing them. Finally, it re-solidified, leaving new rock formations in the ground where the bodies had once lain.

"Scally," said Jack, his chest almost paralyzed by the terror of what he had seen. "What just happened?"

"Yer guess is as good as mine, lad," the alien replied. "But whatever it was, I can guarantee ya — it ain't good."

Chapter 22

nna paced back and forth restlessly. It felt like she'd been cooped up in her cell for hours on end, and the incessant waiting was starting to get to her.

After about a twenty-minute trek from the bridge, she had been escorted to a small room, made up of cold, grey metal. That was about the extent of what she could describe about the space, except for a modest rectangular outcropping that Anna could only assume was probably meant to be a bed. However, it was made up of the same hard metal as everything else.

There was some dim light from the ceiling and fresh air being pumped in from a vent, keeping the room comfortably cool. But other than that, there were no amenities, not even a toilet. For a moment, Anna wondered if all the Deathlord chambers were like this one – cold and empty.

Her first few minutes alone, after her Deathlord captor had dropped her off without a word, were spent searching for some type of escape. Her instincts had been to go for the vent, though it was too high up for her to reach, and even if she could have reached it, it was doubtful she'd be able to get the casing off let alone fit through the small opening.

Then she examined the entrance, again to no avail. There didn't appear to be any type of control panel on her side, and the large, imposing door seemed intent on staying shut no matter how hard she pounded or kicked at it.

Eventually, she tried to take a nap, but even if her "bed" had been comfortable enough to sleep on, her mind was still racing about the direness of her current situation.

Her thoughts went to Jack. She wondered if she had made the right decision, agreeing to cooperate with the Deathlords if they spared him. There was no reason to trust that the Deathlords wouldn't kill him as soon as he was out of her sight, but then again, she didn't have much choice. She just prayed there was some shred of honor among the Deathlords, and that they would keep their word.

Then, of course, there was Shepherd. She wondered what had happened to him after she had been teleported off the Earthship. Was he still alive? Or had he been captured, too? Anna seriously doubted her Paragon protector would ever allow himself to be captured by the Deathlords. But if he had somehow escaped, would he be able to rescue her? And even if he did, where would they go? They would still be in the middle of a Deathlord mothership surrounded by a veritable army of soldiers – and not even Shepherd would be able to hold them off forever.

Calling upon her training from the Royal Order of Luminadric Monks, Anna even tried to meditate in an effort to calm her nerves and to hopefully reach out to make contact with some type of nearby Ancient Technology that might be able to save her.

The monks had been a vital part of the royal family, ever since Emperor Nameer had been forced to overthrow his tyrannical brother thousands of years ago. During the civil strife historians refer to as *The Starfall War*, the Royal Family almost destroyed itself. Nameer had created the order not only to help ensure the survival of the Royal Bloodline should such a devastating event ever occur again, but also to create a system that would train and educate future rulers to secure proper leadership of the Empire.

Since then, the monks had been acting as spiritual advisors to guarantee a strong moral presence was kept around the

Emperor to prevent tyrants from forming. At least, that was the story told to the populous at large. Beyond that, their real purpose was to help train the Royal Family in the ways of the Free Mind, nurturing the physical, mental, and spiritual aspects required to properly operate Ancient Technology. Though it was generally accepted that the Royal Bloodline operated through genetics, it was actually a combination of genetics, mental ability, and spirituality that allowed one to successfully control the wonders that the Ancients had created. If there were one thing that had been clear, it was that the Ancients did not want their technology to be used by anyone who was not worthy of it.

Anna wasn't feeling particularly worthy at the moment, though. She hadn't received much training in her youth, not with three older brothers in succession before her. It was customary to only train those who were not in direct line for the Imperial throne in the basics of what the Luminadric Monks referred to as *trinity* - the fundamentals of the bloodline - so that control of Ancient technology could be kept centralized. After the death of her family, the monks had tried to train her in more advanced methods, but Anna had lost interest once she had developed enough skill to properly interface with Ancient technology. She had preferred to devote her time to figuring out how to stop the Deathlords – much to the chagrin of her tutors.

She was certainly regretting that decision now. Perhaps if she had been a better student, she might be able to use her abilities to find something that would help her. It was said that those of the Royal Bloodline could operate Ancient Technology from light-years away when properly attuned to their trinity. Emperor Youngblood or Emperor Tarrok, who oversaw great expansions of Imperial territory with their ability to access the wonders of the Ancients all over the Empire from their seat of power on Regalus Prime, exemplified this talent.

However, Anna's skills at meditation were deeply lacking. When she was finally able to properly attune to her trinity, it was as if she were in the center of a terrible, empty void, and before long her concentration broke down and her mind went back to its chaotic visions of doom and gloom.

Anna had never felt so powerless before. Her heritage had always afforded her some measure of control over her situation, but here, none of that mattered. She was now a prisoner, not a Princess. She often struggled with bouts of uncertainty and depression. Feelings that she was not worthy of the Empire her ancestors had forged were constant companions in her daily life. She often felt that everyone around her – along with Shepherd to a certain extent – did not think she was capable of handling such a huge responsibility. Even she doubted whether she was truly meant to hold such a high position. Her brothers had been groomed for such things, not her. But those feelings were nothing compared to what she was experiencing now. The last time she could remember feeling this helpless had been the day Regalus Prime fell. She had been forced to watch as everything she had ever known had been destroyed in front of her.

The last thing she wanted to do was give in to those feelings. Allowing defeat to set in and kill her ambitions to fight the Deathlords was the worst possible situation she could think of. As long as she stayed defiant, as long as she stayed resilient, and as long as she held onto thoughts of escape, she was sure she could take whatever the Deathlords threw at her.

At least, she hoped she could.

After what seemed like an eternity of waiting, a noise emanated from the door. Anna perked up, getting to her feet as the entrance to her cell opened.

The fearsome looking Deathlord who had captured her entered the room, the heavy metal door hissing shut behind him. Anna stared at the imposing alien before her. His fierce eyes burned bright red, gazing at her in a way that instantly made her agonizingly uncomfortable.

The two stared at each other for what felt like an extremely long time, though in reality it was really just a few seconds. A million and one questions raced through Anna's mind – where were her friends? What did they want with her? Why were they attacking so many innocent worlds?

But ultimately, Anna knew her questions were not likely to be answered, so she opted to stay silent and wait for the Deathlord to speak.

She did not have to wait long.

"So, you are the blood of the Ancients," grumbled the Deathlord.

"I am," replied Anna, trying to sound braver than she felt.

"Pitiful," he replied. The alien flicked his wrist, and suddenly Anna felt herself pulled into the air, as though invisible hooks were digging into her shoulders and lifting her up.

She tried to muffle her cries of pain as she hovered closer to the Deathlord, coming almost eye-to-eye with him.

"To think, you are the last of the Heretics," he said, his eyes burning fiercely, "a race that once ruled over the entire known universe. And I could snuff you out with a thought if I so desired."

"Then why don't you?" said Anna through gritted teeth. Her shoulders felt like they were on fire.

"Because the foul specter of your Ancestors still lingers," the Deathlord replied. "And I need your help to deal with them."

"I'll never help you!" exclaimed Anna.

She dropped to the floor. The invisible hooks in her shoulders had disappeared and she collapsed to her knees, hugging herself in an effort to make the pain go away.

The Deathlord strode by her, glancing around the sparse holding room as if he suddenly found it interesting. He turned and looked at Anna as she got to her feet, and his eyes seemed to blaze even brighter than before.

"I am Zarrod, the Deathlord Supreme - culler of worlds, master of darkness, and bane to all that is living. No force can harm me, no weapon can strike me, no army can defeat me. I am the Omega, and the universe trembles at my fury. Who are you to deny me?"

Anna stood straight and tall, mustering as much dignity as she could.

"I am Princess Glorianna, daughter of Emperor Tavlos IV, heir to the Galactic Regalus Empire, keeper of the sacred bloodline of the Ancients, and master of their forgotten technology. I am the protector of my people, and I would deny any who would seek to do them harm."

"You act as though I'm giving you a choice," growled the Deathlord.

"We always have a choice," replied Anna.

A deep, raspy grumble escaped from the Deathlord, which Anna could only assume was a chuckle.

"That is where you are wrong, Princess," the alien replied.

Searing pain suddenly assaulted the back of Anna's head. She screamed, desperately grabbing at the base of her skull where blinding agony raged, bringing her to her knees.

Her vision sparked and crackled as she struggled to stay conscious, part of her body was quickly going numb, and the room started to spin uncontrollably.

"What... what's happening..." she whimpered.

"Sleep, Princess," said the Deathlord as he towered over her. "And when you awaken, I'm positive you'll see things... differently."

And then, before everything went black, Anna heard the most frightening thing she'd ever heard in her life.

She heard the Deathlord Supreme laugh.

CHAPTER ✦ 23

Anna was running through a field. Her lungs were burning and fear coursed through her veins. A group of Deathlords were chasing her unrelentingly, led by the fearsome Deathlord Supreme. She looked up in the sky and could see the Planetkiller fleet of motherships looming ominously overhead.

The Deathlords in pursuit fired upon her. They missed, but dodging their blasts distracted her enough to cause her to trip and fall.

Anna hit the ground. As she looked up, she could see her pursuers closing in on her. She struggled to get back to her feet, but it was no use. The Deathlords caught up. Their leader towered over her and cackled.

"There is no escape," said the Deathlord Supreme, his eyes burning with red fury as he clenched his fist evilly. "You are ours, now."

"No!" cried Anna. "Oh, please! Won't someone save me?"

As the Deathlords closed in around her, a large explosion rang out overhead. They all looked up to see a Deathlord mothership blowing up in the atmosphere.

Another mothership exploded. And another. And then another.

From the last explosion, the Ancient Earthship barreled forth, flying down toward them. As it screamed overhead, Jack jumped out, hitting the ground and gracefully tucking-and-rolling to his feet.

"Leave her alone, jerk-wads," said Jack, pointing his finger bravely at the Deathlord Supreme and his minions. "I totally know *karate*."

"Puny human," growled the Deathlord Supreme. "You cannot hope to defeat us!"

Jack glared at the Deathlords defiantly. "Wanna bet?" he sneered before ripping off his shirt, revealing his huge, chiseled muscles. "My fists make the speed of light *wish* it were faster! Come get some."

The Deathlords charged toward him but were no match for the fury of Jack's totally sweet karate moves. After a flurry of lightning punches and spin kicks, Jack had handily dispatched the Deathlord soldiers, leaving only the Deathlord Supreme.

"Please, don't hurt me..." he sniveled.

"Sorry, punk," smirked Jack. "I don't do *mercy*."

With that, Jack dramatically leapt into the air, finishing off the Deathlord Supreme with a drop kick that sent the evil alien flying back a good 20 feet before exploding from the might of Jack's awesomeness.

"NOOOOOOOOOOOOOOOO!!!!!!!" cried the Deathlord before he blew up.

Suddenly, Jack was surrounded by a gaggle of adoring fans. His mom was there, so proud of her son for defeating the evil aliens. Matt and Chunk were there, too, as were all his friends. Even J.C. Rowdey was applauding.

"You're the greatest son in the world," said Jack's mom as she kissed him proudly on the cheek.

"Dude, you rock!" cheered Matt. "You totally saved us all!"

"I'm such a loser," whined J.C. "Do you think I could ever be as cool as you, Jack?"

"No," replied Jack, right before kicking J.C. in the nads. The crowd cheered once again.

Anna rushed up and threw her arms around him.

"My hero!" she exclaimed. "You saved me yet again!"

"Yeah," shrugged Jack nonchalantly. "That's what I do."

"How can I ever repay you?" asked Anna innocently.

Jack locked eyes with her. "I can think of a few ways…"

With that, Jack grabbed Anna and dipped her downward in his arms. The crowd looked on at the most perfect, heroic, romance-novel-esque pose primed for the greatest kiss ever recorded in human history.

"Time for some wacky, baby…" said Jack.

Jack leaned in to kiss Anna, but before their lips touched, she stopped him.

"Jack," she said suddenly. "You need to focus."

Jack leaned back and looked at Anna curiously.

"Huh?" he said, wondering what happened to his kiss.

"Focus, Jack," she said. "You need to focus…"

Jack could feel the back of his head tingling and suddenly the scene around him changed, twisting and fading away. His friends and family were gone. Anna was gone. Earth was gone. Even his totally awesome muscles were gone. Now, Jack was on the bridge of his ship, looking around as Deathlords moved about it, inspecting the various consoles.

"What the heck?" Jack wondered aloud. His dream had suddenly taken a turn for the worse. For a moment Jack was afraid the Deathlords would turn and attack, but none of them seemed to see him.

Jack watched as the Deathlords silently walked around the bridge of the Ancient Earthship, removing wall panels to look at its inner-workings. These Deathlords were different than any he had seen before. Instead of armor, they wore dark robes with heavy hoods that covered their faces. Strange red symbols adorned their backs, as if to signify some sort of rank.

A single robed Deathlord stood at the command chair, looking at it closely. His face was hidden behind a pale white mask, nondescript except for two eyeholes revealing a dim glowing red from behind them. Somehow, Jack knew just by looking at him that he was different from the others.

Then, in a flash of purple, Abraxas appeared on the bridge.

"Vicar General," said Abraxas as he walked past Jack and approached the white-masked Deathlord. "The Supreme wishes news of your investigation. What have your Acolytes discovered?"

The Deathlord Vicar General turned slowly and faced him. "It is most curious, Warlord Abraxas," the Deathlord intoned in a soft, almost monotone voice. "This ship is unlike any I have ever seen."

"Is it of Ancient design?" Abraxas asked.

"Possibly," replied the Vicar General. "But something about this vessel… troubles me."

Abraxas tilted his head inquisitively. "How so?"

"Aside from the bridge and a hallway spanning the length of the ship, we have been unable to detect any of its systems or structure," replied the Vicar General.

"What do you mean?" prodded Abraxas.

"I mean nothing exists on this ship," the Vicar General replied. "It has no power source, no ventilation, no electronics, no engines, no shield generators, no weapon systems, nor any rooms or cabins. Other than the bridge we are standing in, this ship – for all intents and purposes – is a solid hunk of metal."

"How can that be?" demanded Abraxas, asking the exact question Jack was thinking. "We saw it flying in the atmosphere of the planet. It engaged our fighters in combat, entered into hyperspace, and somehow has the ability to disappear and reappear out of nowhere."

"And that, Warlord Abraxas, is what troubles me," replied the Vicar General. "The systems on the bridge are active. Yet, they seem to control nothing. We know the infidels on the ship somehow escaped, yet we can find no exits of any sort."

"What are you saying?" asked Abraxas.

"I would like to continue my investigation," the Vicar General responded. "And be granted permission to interface the vessel with our mothership's central computer."

"Is that wise?" Abraxas growled. "Exposing the nerve system of the mothership could be... problematic."

"I am aware of the risk," stated the Vicar General. "But if this ship is indeed advanced technology from our ancient enemies, it may have safeguards in place to thwart us. Only the central computer would be powerful enough to purge the influence of the heretic god from this machine long enough to unlock its secrets."

Abraxas glared at the Vicar General before turning to look at the other Deathlord Acolytes who poked and prodded around the bridge as he weighed the request.

"Very well," he finally responded. "Interface with the central computer. Download everything you can. Rip this ship apart if you have to. The Supreme wants whatever technology our ancient enemy has locked away inside it."

The Vicar General bowed. "As the Supreme commands, so shall it be done."

"I will inform him of your progress," said Abraxas, and with a curt nod, he teleported away.

Once Abraxas was gone, the Vicar General turned to one of his Acolytes.

"Interface the nodes," he commanded. "Connect directly to the central computer."

His Acolyte nodded and produced a smooth black rock from his robe. The rock pulsed with purple light before the Acolyte released it. It hovered in the air, cracks forming on its smooth surface.

Jack looked on with a mixture of curiosity and unease as the small rocky orb moved to the center of the bridge. Without warning, it ripped apart and its jagged pieces flew toward the ship's exposed circuit panels and control stations.

Sparks flew as the pieces dug into the circuitry of the Ancient starship. Green laser light shot from all of them, converging in the spot the rock had flown to before separating, forming a pulsing green ball of energy veined with what looked like golden circuits.

"Nodes connected," the Acolyte said. "Interfacing with the central computer... now."

Suddenly, a loud screeching noise assaulted Jack's ears. He clamped his hands over them, but the sound did not muffle. He looked up as he saw the green ball of energy begin to spin, and suddenly an avalanche of images assaulted his vision.

It wasn't like it had been when he had accidentally accessed the Ancient terminal on Earth. This was foreign, relentless, and overwhelming. Jack's brain buzzed with pain. He dropped to his knees as the ringing in his ears grew steadily louder. Jack struggled against the sudden sensory onslaught, screaming in defiance as his head felt like it were about to explode.

And then, Jack woke with a start.

He was back at the survivor camp in the Pit, sitting straight up, his back sore from sleeping on the unforgiving ground. He was breathing heavily, his brow wet with sweat, and his head was throbbing. He cradled it in his hands and tried to steady himself.

"Bad dreams, lad?"

Jack looked over and saw Scallywag sitting a few feet away. The pirate was gnawing on a thin strap of leather while he fiddled with one of his pistols, twirling it around in his hand.

"You have no idea," Jack responded.

"Aye, get used to 'em," Scallywag responded. "Surprised you were able to sleep at all in here. Only one I've seen able to catch a decent forty winks is the bloody Rognok, lucky browner. Something about this place messes with yer head."

Jack sighed and rubbed his temples. "How?" he asked. "How are the Deathlords able to do this? Rip people's souls right out of their bodies? Mess with their minds? Slowly wear them down without even doing a thing?"

"They got some nice bloody toys, that's how," grumbled Scallywag.

"No," said Jack. "This isn't some type of technology doing this. This is something else. Something... weird."

"Bah. It is what it is, and they do what they do. That's all there is to it. Think about it any more and you're jus' hurtin' yer brain," said Scallywag.

"Maybe *your* meager brain," piped up Heckubus from behind a nearby rock. "I've already postulated approximately 2,156 theories to all the Earthman's inquiries."

"I'll postulate me foot up yer bum if ya keep lurkin' about, ya rusty bucket o' bolts," growled Scallywag.

"Well, pardon me for trying to do something constructive with my time!" the robot shot back. "Not all of us are content to merely sit around, play with our guns, and excrete toxic fumes from our backsides all day long."

"Guys, please," said Jack, rubbing his temples. His companions' bickering was doing nothing to alleviate his splitting headache.

"We'll see how rosy you smell when I melt ya down for scrap," said Scallywag, pointing one of his pistols at Heckubus.

"Pah!" growled the robot. "Instead of threating a clearly superior being, why don't you try to do something useful, like getting off your lazy hind parts and finding us a way out of this sink-hole."

"There ain't no way out," grumbled Scallywag. "We've been halfway around this Pit and there ain't nothin' but rock, rock, and more bloody rock. Face it, rust-bucket; yer gonna die here just like the rest o' us."

Suddenly, some images flashed before Jack's eyes. They were wild, like they had been just after the Deathlord's activated their nodes with the Earthship, but somehow Jack understood them.

And they were telling him exactly what he wanted to know.

"Whoa," said Jack, his eyes wide with surprise.

Heckubus and Scallywag both looked at him.

"What is it, lad?" asked Scallywag.

"Are you preparing to release toxic fumes as well?" asked the robot.

"No," smiled Jack. "But I am preparing to get the heck out of this Pit."

Jack got to his feet and looked at his companions triumphantly.

"I just found a way out of here," he said, before sprinting off toward the rest of the camp.

Scallywag and Heckubus shared a rare moment of calm as they glanced at one another before scrambling after Jack.

The rest of the camp had gathered together near Doc Pyle's old make-shift infirmary, huddled miserably around a couple of quickly dwindling campfires.

As Jack ran up he found the Major grouped with some of his other soldiers, including Sergeant Rodham and Yeoman Porter. They were all taking stock of the ammo they had left, counting out energy cells for their rifles and a couple of thermal grenades when Jack came running up.

"Major!" exclaimed Jack. "Major!"

"What is it, kid?" asked Ganix, not looking up from his ammo count.

"I've found a way out of here," said Jack excitedly.

Instantly, every soldier stopped what he was doing and turned to Jack, eyes wide. Ganix shot to his feet.

"What? Where?" he asked.

"On the far side of the Pit," said Jack. "A couple miles around to the west of here. There's an exit."

"The far side of the Pit?" Major Ganix repeated. "How would you know there's an exit there?"

"Just trust me!" said Jack. "It's there! I swear!"

Ganix exchanged a look with Rodham as Scallywag and Heckubus approached the group.

"Do you know anything about this exit he's talking about?" Ganix asked Scallywag.

The pirate shrugged. "The lad just woke up and started saying he knew a way out."

Ganix sighed. "You were dreaming, kid," he said as he knelt back to his ammunition count.

Jack saw the other soldiers sullenly go back to their current duties of being miserable, but he wasn't about to let this go — not when he knew he was right.

"Your mission," said Jack. "Your secret mission was to protect Anna while she was on my planet looking for an Ancient artifact you could use to fight the Deathlords."

"What of it?" asked Ganix.

"Well, she found it," said Jack.

Ganix looked up at Jack. His pale eyes were tired, but patient, as well. "Did she, now?" he replied.

"It was a spaceship," explained Jack. "One built a long time ago by the Ancients. But it's super-advanced. Like, so advanced even the Deathlords can't figure it out. That's what we used to escape Earth before it was destroyed."

Ganix nodded. "Okay..." he said. "What does this have to do with getting out of here?"

"Here's the thing," said Jack. "Even though the spaceship was built by the Ancients, it's attuned to people from Earth, so the only people who can operate it are Earthmen. I was the one who had to fly it, and while I was doing that, I noticed that it developed a kind-of... well, mental connection with me."

"You telling me you mind-merged with a kitten spaceship?" muttered Sergeant Rodham.

"Look, I know it sounds crazy–" said Jack.

"That's putting it mildly," muttered Heckubus.

"But I'm telling you, the ship could read my thoughts," said Jack. "It changed itself to make it easier for me to fly it."

"Get to the point, son," said Ganix.

"I'm saying, I think that mental link is still active. While I was sleeping, I had a dream I was on the bridge of the ship – but it wasn't like a normal dream. It was like I was really there. I think the ship was sending me images of what was actually happening on it."

"And what was happening?" asked Scallywag.

"The Deathlords, they were trying to interface the ship's computer with their mothership," said Jack. "They wanted to access the ship's secrets. But I don't think it worked. I think, instead, the Earthship got access to the Deathlord's computer. And now, it's telling me exactly what I need to know to get out of here."

"Sounds like a kitten-ton of koo-koo to me," grumbled Rodham.

"Is it?" piped up Porter. "I mean, who'd have thought portgates were real until they were discovered? Or hyperspace? Or any of the other technology we got from the Ancients? Is it so hard to believe that maybe they found a way to interface thought and technology together?"

Ganix pondered Porter's comment for a second before looking at Jack. "Let's say, for the moment, I believe you, Earthman. What is this ship telling you?"

"It's telling me that we're still on the Deathlord mothership," said Jack. "The Pit, the whole thing, is like the ship's core."

"The ship's core?" laughed Rodham. "Why the blazes would they dump us into the core of their ship?"

"Fuel," said Jack. "That giant pillar of light out there? That's the ship's power source. It runs on the energy of living things."

An uneasy look passed among the group.

"From what I can tell, the ship is designed to suck all the life energy out of a planet before it hits the planet's core, causing it to explode," explained Jack. "In addition, any life-forms that are thrown in here are meant to add their life force to it eventually, to help it grow."

"Are ya saying when we die in here, our 'life energy' is added to that pillar?" growled Scallywag, obviously not liking that notion.

"Exactly," said Jack. "But this place, it's designed to break down our physical forms so it can weaken our life energy enough for it to be absorbed. That's why we're getting sick. Everything around us is trying to break us down on some level, to weaken our will enough to allow our life energy to be stolen."

"Ah-ha!" said Heckubus. "So theory 298 was right after all! I knew it!"

"Don't even pretend ya had an idea of what was goin' on," said Scallywag.

"It was one of my many theories," rebuked Heckubus. "I just didn't have any empirical evidence to back it up. But if what the Earthman says is true, then it all makes perfect sense. The sickness and zombification could come from prolonged exposure to radiation from the glowing veins in the rock, deteriorating organic tissue enough to harvest the electrical forces of life within you organic simpletons."

"So the Deathlords run their ships on people," muttered Rodham. "That's just kitten great."

"But don't you see?" said Jack. "We're still on the ship! The same ship Anna and Shepherd are on. The same ship my spaceship is on!"

Ganix raised his eyebrow. "That means if we can escape the Pit, and get to the Princess…"

"Then I can fly us out of here," said Jack.

The other soldiers got to their feet, an excitement beginning to stir within them.

"You sure about this exit, kid?" asked Ganix.

"Positive," replied Jack.

"And what if he's wrong?" asked Rodham. "What if this Earthman's just crazy, and he's making this all up?"

"Then we're no worse off than we were before," said Scallywag. "We might be dead a tad quicker, but it's not like we got many prospects sitting around this bloody cave waiting for the next attack."

"The pirate's right," said Ganix. "If we're gonna die, we die advancing. Not stuck here like rats in a box." Ganix turned to his men. "Gather your things. Bring as much ammo, food, and water as you can find. We'll head out in one hour."

The men jumped to, getting ready to head out. For the first time since Jack had arrived, he got the sense that there was some hope that they might just live through this huge ordeal after all.

Ganix looked down at Jack. "I'm putting all our lives in your hands, Earthman," he said. "I hope you know what you're doing."

Me, too, thought Jack.

Chapter ✨ 24

Shepherd and Green strode down the long curved hallway cautiously. The sterile metal of the walls stretched out for what seemed like an enormous distance, peppered with doors leading to places they could only guess at. At that moment, though, Shepherd was more concerned with what might emerge from those doors rather than what lay behind them.

After teleporting further into the mothership, it seemed to Shepherd that they'd done little more than run and hide. Though their hologuises gave them some cover, if the two allowed any Deathlord to get too close, the chances of them being discovered were just too great. If a Dark Soldier happened to emerge from a room too close to them, their gooses would be cooked.

As if that weren't bad enough, they were also hopelessly and completely lost. Without any frame of reference, it seemed as though they may have been walking in circles a great deal of the time. Though the mothership appeared big from the outside, walking around on the inside made it clear just how massive the vessel truly was.

The corridors the two found themselves in seemed to stretch on endlessly, with curves and intersections at odd places, and hallways that would frequently dead-end for no apparent reason. The duo had gotten turned around many times, since there were no real visual markings pointing out where they were headed or what the rooms contained.

Also, more than once the two had seen groups of Deathlord soldiers coming down the corridor they were in and, in an effort to avoid being seen, had quickly had to take a turn down a different hallway or to move into a room not knowing what it held.

Luckily for them, they had been correct in assuming security on the ship would be light. It was obvious the Deathlords had never had to deal with an incursion within their own ship and had not been expecting it. Even if they had been prepared, could a ship this massive, Shepherd wondered, even be staffed with enough Deathlords to sufficiently cover it?

Many of the rooms they entered were empty and seemed to serve no purpose, not even as storage. Very rarely did they see any Deathlords who were on their own. They always seemed to travel the ship in groups, and even then, they did not see that many. Green theorized that they used teleportation to traverse their massive mothership, and after a few hours of walking through its long, winding hallways, Shepherd agreed that was probably the case.

Occasionally, they would run into what Green identified to be an access panel to the ship's systems. Unfortunately, decoding the Deathlord's language proved just as complicated as the Professor thought it would be.

Green had to mess around with the system to try to get to its base computer code in order to decipher it from the ground up. After all, when one boils all computer languages down to their core, they're just a bunch of ones and zeroes.

But of course, just as it seemed Green would be getting somewhere, Shepherd would spot a group of Deathlords approaching, and they would have to abandon the console and spend time searching for another one, only to have to start the whole process over again.

Each setback put Shepherd even more on edge. The longer they took, the greater the likelihood the Deathlords could discover them, and the greater the likelihood the Deathlords could harm Anna (if they hadn't already).

After a few hours of evading the Deathlords while searching for a new console to access, the two finally found what seemed to be some sort of engineering room with a computer console tucked away from any direct line-of-sight to the entrance. Here, they would be able to hide if any Deathlords entered, and they'd be out of sight from any stray soldiers wandering around in the corridors. Large pipes and generators hummed monotonously throughout the room and would disguise any noise they made. It was the perfect place to do what they needed. Since the coast was clear, they both deactivated their hologuises and got to work.

As Green began tinkering with the panel, Shepherd stood watch. He tried to calm himself, but internally he was greatly worried. He wondered what was happening to Anna. He cursed himself for letting her be taken in the first place. He did not know why the Deathlords wanted her, but he did know that their reasons could not be good. And the longer she was away from him, the more danger she was in. He didn't even want to think about what might have happened to Jack.

Meanwhile, Green hummed cheerily (a habit of the Professor's, which irritated Shepherd to no end) as he worked his way through the console and the Deathlord's programming language. The Professor worked tirelessly for hours trying to crack the language while Shepherd was forced to stand aside and feel useless.

Time to think was not what Shepherd wanted at that moment. All he could see in his mind were the many possible ways the Deathlords had for torturing Anna, and he secretly cursed Green for taking so long to figure out the Deathlord's systems even though he knew what the Professor was doing was incredibly complicated.

Finally, Green smiled and spoke up.

"Ah-ha!" said the Professor cheerily. "I think I've cracked it!"

"You can read it?" the Paragon asked hopefully.

Green nodded. "Not fluently, but I'm able to get the gist of it. Once I was able to figure out the vowels and numbers, the rest somewhat fell into place. I think I know enough to be able to figure out what systems to access now."

"Good work, Professor," said Shepherd, eager to get going.

"I must say, I could probably spend a couple of years studying this language," said Green. "It is incredibly complex. It rather reminds me of the syntax used in Greater Halcyonian, only without all the male-female tenses—"

"As long as you can find what we need," interrupted Shepherd. "That'll do for now. What can you access?"

"Well, let's see, shall we?" smiled the Professor.

Green began to tap a few keys on the console, the screen before him updating with each keystroke. Shepherd tried to decipher what was going on but the language made no sense to him at all. He only hoped Green could make something of it.

"Curious," said Green.

"What is it?" inquired Shepherd.

"Oh, nothing," said the Professor whimsically. "It's just that the more I learn about these Deathlords, the more questions spring to mind."

At that moment, Shepherd didn't care a lick about the Deathlords. All he wanted was to know where Anna was being held and what the quickest way to get to her was. "Focus on the Princess and Jack, Professor," reminded Shepherd.

"Oh, don't worry, I am," said Green. "There's just so much that's hard to ignore, though. For instance, don't you find it odd that a race of sentient non-organic beings such as the Deathlords maintain full life support on their ships?"

"What do you mean?" asked Shepherd.

"Heating, oxygen, all of the elements needed to support life are fully enabled on this vessel, and yet by no accounts do we believe the Deathlords need any of these things to survive. It's as if the ships are meant to be habitable to living beings, and lots of them. But why?"

"Those are questions better left for another time," said Shepherd. "Right now, I don't care about anything other than finding the Princess."

"Yes, yes, your single-minded focus is admirable, my friend," said Green. "But considering we have learned more about the Deathlords in the past few hours than the entire Empire has learned in the past twelve years, I would say someone should start caring."

"The information is only valuable if we can share it with someone off this ship," said Shepherd. "And we're not getting off without the Princess and Jack. So table your questions for now and work on finding them."

"Working, I am," said Green cheerily. "You'll be pleased to know that I've just figured out how to access the ship's schematics and sensor logs."

"Finally," breathed Shepherd. "Can you determine where they might be holding her? Any detention centers? Or some sort of brig?"

"Hmmmmm," said Green as he scanned through the data on the console. "This is certainly odd..."

Shepherd didn't like the sound of that. "What?" he demanded.

"The schematics for this ship... they are quite... weird," the Professor replied.

"Weird in what way?"

"Well, normally, ship design has to meet certain engineering parameters," said Green. "For instance, if you were building a ship for atmospheric flight, you'd have to take certain factors into account that wouldn't be necessary for a ship that's strictly meant for space travel. Not to mention that most vessels are designed for symmetry and practicality, things like that."

"What of it?" asked Shepherd.

"Well, this ship... despite what it looks like from the outside... is a complete mess."

"Get to your point, Professor," Shepherd sighed.

"My point is — it seems this ship is man-made based on the areas we've been in, such as the hangar bay and the corridors, all of which are made up of metal and electronics. But according to these schematics, a great deal of this ship is comprised of rock, and brick, and clay."

Shepherd raised an eyebrow. "What?" he asked.

"It's almost as if the ship were built around some type of terrestrial structure," clarified Green. "And a big one at that. See this here?"

Green pointed to a large oval portion of the Deathlord mothership's schematic readout at the console.

"There seems to be a rather large area at the very center of the ship constructed from such material. It's massive, miles and miles in diameter in fact."

"At the risk of sounding like a broken recording," said Shepherd, "what does any of this have to do with finding the Princess and Jack?"

"This impacts our search because the areas of the ship that are not constructed of advanced materials do not contain sensors," said Green. "If the Princess or Jack is in any of these areas, we may not be able to find them."

More great news, thought Shepherd grumpily. "Well then, focus on the areas we can get readings on. See if we have any hits there. If not, then we'll have to worry about checking out these brick-and-mortar portions of the ship manually."

Green tapped a few keys on the console and grimaced.

"Blast it," he muttered. "It would appear the Deathlords do not place much stock in tracking life sign readings."

"What do you mean?"

"Their ship's internal sensors are set up to monitor energy signatures unique to the Deathlords, not life signs unique to living beings," said Green. "We can't pinpoint the Princess based on her vitals I'm afraid."

"Can you reprogram it to find what we need?" Shepherd asked.

"If I had a few weeks and a better understanding of the language, maybe," replied Green.

Shepherd grunted. *It can never be easy, can it?* he thought.

"The scanners…" said Shepherd. "They can tell us where the Deathlords are?"

"Indeed," smiled Green. "That's not a problem. What are you thinking, dear Paragon?"

"Show me where all the Deathlords on the ship are right now," Shepherd said.

Green tapped a few buttons, and various blips appeared on the schematic layout of the ship. Shepherd glanced over the placement of the dots before settling on one group in particular.

"There," he said, pointing at a small room with two energy signature dots in front of it. "That's where we'll find the Princess."

"What makes you think she's being held there?" asked Green.

"Two Deathlords standing stationary outside a small room," said Shepherd. "Looks like guard duty to me."

Green smiled. "Well, I'll be. Simple, yet effective. Bravo, dear Paragon. Shall we be on our way then?"

"No," said Shepherd. "I need you to continue monitoring the Deathlord's systems. If I'm wrong, we may not have time to access them again before they're alerted to our location. I need you to be my eyes while I attempt the rescue."

Green twiddled his fingers. "Ah... is it wise to split up?" he asked. "I'm afraid I may not be of much use if I'm captured."

"Wise? Probably not," admitted Shepherd. "But necessary. Based on what we've seen, this ship is too big and difficult to navigate from the inside. I need a guide to get me to where I have to go. If you can track the Deathlords, you can make sure I can steer clear of them after I've found the Princess and can lead us to a rendezvous point. Worst case scenario, you can help me avoid capture if I'm discovered."

Green nodded. "Our emergency comm units should go undetected until the Deathlords think to scan for them. Even then, it may take them a while to find the right frequency. And I do suppose I could use the time to learn more about the Deathlord's technology..."

Green trailed off as he was speaking. Shepherd could tell something was bothering him.

"But?" asked Shepherd.

"I'm... ah... rather frightened of being on my own," said Green sheepishly. "This place is quite scary, you know."

Shepherd smiled softly. "I know, old friend," he said, putting his hand reassuringly on Green's shoulder. "But I need you to be brave, for the sake of the Princess. I would not ask this of you if I did not think it were necessary."

"I know your logic is sound," said Green. "But shootouts, space chases, and sneaking around on an enemy ship... I'm a

Trundel of science, not adventure. I'm afraid all this is quite out of my league."

"You've been doing fine with it so far," said Shepherd.

"Because I've had no other choice," said Green.

"Heroes are born from necessity, Professor. Not choice."

Green sucked on his lower lip nervously. "If that's the case, being a hero is far less glamorous than I ever imagined it to be."

Shepherd nodded. "It typically is. But look at it this way," he said. "Once we get out of this, you'll have one heck of a paper to write."

Green's eyes lit up. "Indeed," he smiled. "Why, I could probably do an entire series based on their language alone! I mean, sure it would only be about vowels and numbers, but still... it might even get published in the Valghana Quarterly! Could you imagine?"

"I can," replied Shepherd. "But first, we need to get the Princess, get Jack, and get the hell out of here."

Green nodded. He took a deep breath to find his courage. "If I'm monitoring Deathlord movement, I'll be able to tell if there are any headed for my position," he said. "I may need to switch consoles to avoid detection at some point."

"Do what you must to stay safe," said Shepherd.

"You, too, dear Paragon," Green responded. "And good luck. I'll do my best to lead you in the right direction."

Shepherd nodded and took one last look at the schematics to figure out the best way to get to his target. Then he reactivated his hologuise and headed out the door, leaving the Professor alone in the room with nothing but his console and the monotonous hum of the generators.

After Shepherd was gone, Green looked around the cold, metal room of the Deathlord mothership and gulped nervously.

"I just hope my best is good enough," he muttered to no one in particular.

CHAPTER ✺ 25

The moans echoing throughout the Pit set Jack's teeth on edge. The sounds reverberated off the walls and seemed to linger in his ears even longer than they had when he'd first arrived. He was desperate to talk to someone – anyone – about anything just so he wouldn't have to focus so much on those horrible noises.

But each time he tried to start up a conversation with Scallywag or Faruuz, they'd just shut him down and tell him to be quiet. They'd talked with him for a bit before the last group of zombies jumped out of nowhere and attacked. One of them had managed to rip out the throat of a Regal soldier named Coakly before being put down, and after that the entire group seemed to be on edge and opted to move in silence.

They traveled in single file, weapons at ready, with Jack up toward the front leading the way. Grohm stayed slightly ahead of Jack to make sure he was protected, and for the most part Scallywag and Faruuz were right there with him. Major Ganix took up the rear. Overall, no one wanted anything to happen to Jack, since he was the only one who knew where the heck the group was headed.

As they walked, Jack kept looking at his surroundings. Nothing seemed familiar at all, and yet somehow there was a map in his mind that told him exactly where he was. How that worked, Jack had no idea. He just hoped the map didn't suddenly disappear and leave him stranded in the middle of nowhere.

For now, the map was there, and Jack kept walking in the direction it was telling him to go, with the others following close behind.

"Are we almost there?" Scallywag muttered.

"Yeah, it's just a bit further," said Jack.

"You said that an hour ago."

"And I was right an hour ago," replied Jack. "Not so witty when it's used on you, huh?"

Scallywag cracked a smile. "Anyone ever tell ya, you can be an annoyin' little browner, Earthman?"

"Nope," said Jack. "You'd be the first."

"Anyone ever tell ya, if this exit of yers turns out not to exist, yer gonna get shot right in the face?" grumbled Faruuz.

"Nope," replied Jack.

"Well, ya just were," snarked Faruuz. "Right now. By me."

"Well then, if the exit does exist, I get to shoot you in the face," said Jack.

"What?" said Faruuz. "No you don't."

"Seems only fair," said Jack. "Since you're the one threatening to shoot me and all if I'm wrong, I should get to shoot you if I'm right."

"Lad's got a point," chimed in Scallywag, smiling. "It's only fair."

"What? No it ain't!" replied Faruuz. "Whose side are ya on?"

"No one's side," said Scallywag. "Just pointing out that ya got a fifty-fifty chance of not getting shot in the face, is all."

"Oy, no one's shooting anyone!" insisted Faruuz.

"Great, glad we cleared that up," said Jack.

Faruuz blinked at Jack. "But... no... I..."

"Too late, we can't shoot each other," said Jack. "Argument over."

Faruuz scowled. "Stupid Earthman," he grumbled, opting to nurse his bandaged arm with only a modicum of self-pity.

Suddenly, Grohm stopped, standing tense and alert, gazing out into the darkness. Scallywag and Faruuz instinctively lifted their weapons as the rest of the convoy halted and reacted the same way.

"What is it?" whispered Scallywag. "Ya see something, Grohm?"

"Regals," Grohm snorted.

Major Ganix strode up to the front with Sergeant Rodham in tow, torch in hand. "With me," he said, as he passed by Grohm. Scallywag and Faruuz followed, with Jack tentatively bringing up the rear.

As they moved forward, Jack could see some figures hunched over by an outcropping of rocks. There were two of them, sprawled out awkwardly on the ground. As they got closer, Sergeant Rodham's torchlight bathed the scene with illumination, showing the bloody remains of two Regal soldiers.

"It's Ferris and Hoyle," said Rodham. "What's left of them, anyway."

"Blast it," cursed Ganix.

Jack looked away from the bodies. The sight of them made his stomach queasy. He'd seen plenty of dead bodies on TV shows and movies, but seeing the real thing (not to mention smelling it) was something he didn't think he'd get used to anytime soon.

"This yer other scouting team?" Scallywag asked.

Ganix nodded. "I guess I was holding out hope they may have still been alive," he said.

"You should learn not to hope," replied Scallywag.

"Seems like they didn't find much else besides zombies," commented Faruuz as he poked around the bodies. "Don't see any swag around 'em."

"Get away from them," growled Rodham.

"He's just checking for anything we can salvage—" said Scallywag.

"Slag your salvage," snapped Rodham. "And slag you. These were good men."

"These are dead men," replied Scallywag.

"Care to join them, pirate?" Rodham sneered.

"Enough," said Ganix sternly, shooting a hard look Rodham's way. The Sergeant kept his mouth shut but continued to stare down Scallywag, who didn't seem willing to retreat from their silent eye-war either.

"Ain't got nothin' on 'em worth taking anyway," said Faruuz. "Don't even have their weapons."

"Why aren't they rock?" asked Jack.

The group looked at him. "What?" asked Ganix.

"The zombies, when they died they turned into rock," said Jack. "So why are they still here?"

"'Cause they weren't zombies," replied Rodham. "They died like soldiers."

"Yeah, but that doesn't make any sense. Why turn some dead bodies into rock and not others?" asked Jack.

"We've found some animal carcasses and a few skeletons around this hole," muttered Scallywag. "Maybe ya only get rocked if ya lose yer soul first."

"What's it matter?" grumbled Faruuz. "Dead is dead. Who cares if they're rock or not?"

"Jack," asked Ganix. "Are we any closer to this exit of yours?"

"About another mile I'd guess," replied Jack. "It's hard to tell."

Ganix nodded. "Sergeant, take point with the Earthman," he said. "Scallywag, would you and your companion care to join me in the rearguard?"

"Like yer giving us a choice?" replied Scallywag.

"I'll take that as a 'yes,' " said Ganix. "Let's get moving. The sooner we're out of here, the better for everyone."

Scallywag gave Rodham the evil eye before following Ganix to the back of the convoy. Jack watched him go, wondering why Ganix suddenly wanted to switch things up. Maybe the Major thought he'd rather have his own men close to Jack now that they were closing in on the exit? It wouldn't surprise him if Ganix was worried Scallywag and Faruuz would try to leave them behind in the Pit while they escaped, even though Jack was sure they wouldn't do something like that. (Well, not Scallywag anyway.)

Grohm started walking, with Rodham falling in a few paces behind and Jack close by. Once the convoy was moving again, Jack looked up at Rodham.

"Can I ask you a question, Sergeant?" asked Jack.

"What is it?" the large man replied.

"Why do you hate Scallywag so much? I mean, he's in the same boat as all of us, you know."

Rodham scowled. "Be different if he were a Blue or a Yellow maybe," the Sergeant grumbled. "But if there's one thing you gotta learn, kid, it's that you can never trust a Red, even if it seems like he's on your side; he'll just as quickly stab you in the back if you're not careful."

"What do you mean?" asked Jack. "Blue or Yellow?"

Rodham raised an eyebrow. "You mean to tell me your psychic spaceship can show you a way out of here, but it can't give you a basic lesson on Visini?"

"Must have forgot to ask it," muttered Jack, more than a little annoyed at Rodham's constant verbal jabs.

"Right," said Rodham. "All you ever need to know about a Visini you can tell from the color of his skin. Purples are supposed to be the best of their race. They're their leaders, supposedly all smart, and honest, and courageous, and whatnot. Blues are the upper crust - trustworthy, noble, dependable. You can always trust a Blue to keep his word. Yellows, they're basically followers, you know. Do what they're told, not that ambitious or smart for that matter. But Reds, well, they are the scum of the race... the thieves, the murderers, the liars... any low-life character trait you can think of, the Red's usually got it."

"I don't understand," said Jack. "You mean just because Scallywag was born with red skin, he's instantly a bad person?"

Rodham laughed derisively. "Visini aren't born with their colors, boy," he said. "They all come out as Yellows at first. But their skin, it changes based on the kinds of people they are. If they're good, they turn Blue or Purple. If they're nothing special, they stay Yellow. If they're scum, they turn Red. That pirate friend of yours is crimson because somewhere along the line, he chose to be a dirtbag. His skin just reflects what's on the inside, and let me tell you – what's in there ain't no good."

"He seems okay to me," said Jack.

"That's just because he needs us to survive," replied Rodham. "The second he doesn't, he won't hesitate to blast you away if he feels like it."

"I don't believe that," said Jack. "He tried to help Faruuz escape from prison, and he saved my life during the zombie attack. He didn't have to do any of that."

"Maybe he did, maybe he didn't," said Rodham. "With a Red, you never know what his motivation is until you pull the knife out of your back."

"What if he's trying to change?" asked Jack. "What if he's trying to be a good guy? Can Visini do that?"

"Change his color?" snorted Rodham. "Could be. Though I learned a long time ago that Visini don't tend to change their skin. And if they do, it's very rare."

"But possible?" asked Jack.

Rodham shrugged. "Maybe," he replied. "But are you willing to bet your life on that?"

Jack glanced behind him and caught a glimpse of Scallywag in the rear with Faruuz, strutting along while keeping a watchful eye out in the darkness. From where Jack was, Scallywag looked even more devil-like in the illumination of the torches than he ever had before, and it sent an uneasy feeling down Jack's spine.

"Didn't think so," said Rodham, reading the uncertainty on Jack's face. "I don't care what color they may be, the Visini are not to be trusted. My father died fighting the Visini in the Great Border War when their empire decided it wanted to expand, despite all the treaties they had signed. And ever since the fall of Regalus Prime, the whole kitten race has been chomping at the bit to make new incursions into Regal space, never mind that millions of us were brutally slaughtered by the Deathlords."

Rodham spat on the ground. "Whole universe would be better off without them, if you ask me," he grunted.

I didn't ask you, thought Jack. Something about Rodham reminded Jack of all the jock-meatheads he had known in school. But then again he knew very little about all the alien races and what they meant to each other. For all Jack knew, Rodham could be exactly right about Scallywag and his species. But despite it all, being the lone survivor of his own species made the idea of genocide rather tough for Jack to stomach at the moment.

Jack picked up his pace and moved away from Rodham to walk beside Grohm. Maybe he wasn't the most talkative alien Jack had ever met, but after his conversation with the Sergeant, he was glad for any change of pace the Rognok could offer.

"S'up, big guy?" asked Jack.

Grohm's red-and-black eyes glanced down at Jack briefly, before looking back out into the darkness. At least Jack felt that glance meant the massive alien knew he was there and wouldn't accidentally step on him or something.

"So how are things with you? Can you see okay without a torch?"

"Grohm see fine," the Rognok replied.

"Cool," said Jack. "I wish I could see in the dark."

Grohm snorted.

"So what's your story?" Jack asked. "Scallywag said you were here before anyone. How'd you get captured?"

Grohm didn't answer.

"Hey, you don't want to talk about it, that's cool," said Jack. "I got teleported aboard after getting shot by a Dark Soldier. Then, some jack-hole tossed me on a teleporter and sent me here. He was a total jerk about it, too. Say, you don't happen to know what 'petulant' means, do ya?"

Grohm grunted.

"Yeah, me neither," replied Jack. "I'm sure he meant it as an insult, though. It's bad enough they gotta go and blow up my whole planet, but then they gotta insult me to my face."

"Deathlords blow up Grohm's planet," Grohm replied.

"Yeah, I heard," said Jack. "Sorry about that. Did any of your people survive?"

"Grohm not know," said the Rognok.

"Well, I'm sure there are more of your people out there than there are of mine," said Jack. "I think I'm the only person from Earth left. In fact, I'm sure of it."

Saying that out loud made Jack feel sad. Thoughts of his mom and his friends popped into his head, along with the realization that they were gone, and he wouldn't get to see them again.

Grohm looked down at Jack and grimaced at his expression. "Weakness," the large Rognok rumbled.

Jack looked up at Grohm and blinked. "Huh?"

"Memories make Earthman weak," said Grohm. "Earthman must be strong. Strong survive."

"I'm not weak," said Jack. "I'm just sad, is all."

"Sadness is weakness," replied Grohm.

"Just because I'm sad doesn't mean I'm weak," protested Jack. "It's okay to be sad if something bad happens to you. Sometimes you need to be sad in order to be happy again."

Grohm snorted.

"Do Rognok's have feelings?" Jack asked. "Do you ever feel happy? Or excited?"

"Grohm not weak," Grohm replied.

"So it's even weak to feel good?" asked Jack.

"Emotions are bad," said Grohm. "Emotions cloud judgment. Emotions allow mistakes. Emotions lead to death. Only strength is good. Only strong survive."

"So what's it mean to be strong?" Jack asked.

"It means you kill," chimed in Rodham, who'd been eavesdropping in on the conversation. "That's what Rognok's do, kid. They fight and they kill. To them, being strong just means you're the last one standing."

Jack glanced up at Grohm, who made no attempt to reply to Rodham. The large alien lumbered onward in silence, but to Jack, it seemed as though he were walking heavier than he had been before, almost like he really was feeling sad, and his words were more for his own benefit than they were for Jack's. In Jack's mind, how could one NOT feel sad, or angry, or scared after losing his entire planet? Even Rognoks had to have friends and family, didn't they?

"Tell you what, big guy," said Jack. "You be strong. I'll be sad enough for the both of us."

Grohm glanced down at Jack again, and this time Jack thought he caught a faint glimmer of surprise on the Rognok's face. But Grohm said nothing and continued to lead the large convoy through the darkness of the Pit with Jack by his side. For some reason, one that Jack couldn't quite explain, he felt like he and the hulking alien had bonded somehow. Of course, that could have been wishful thinking as far as Jack was concerned. It was hard to tell what, if anything, Grohm felt.

The convoy marched onward, stopping sporadically either for short breaks or because of a sound that may have heralded a possible attack. The terrain was getting harder to traverse the farther they went, with jagged and sharp rocks jutting up from uneven ground, which only served to slow their journey. And though Jack knew where he had to go, his mental map was pretty fuzzy about the details. More often than not, the group found itself having to march around obstacles, such as rock outcroppings or other debris, which made their route to the exit even longer than it already was.

But despite all the twists and turns their journey took, they still moved forward toward their destination… until they came to what appeared to be a complete dead end.

Jack looked at the massive wall of rock in front of them confused. He knew the exit was just a little farther, but it was obvious there was no way around the barrier that loomed before him. He was still pondering his mental map when Ganix approached.

"I've asked Scallywag and Faruuz to backtrack and scout for an alternate route," the Major said. "Are you sure we're going in the right direction?"

"Yeah," said Jack. "I'm positive it's this way."

"But you weren't sure about the solid wall of rock blocking the path?" grumbled Rodham.

"Okay, so the details are a little fuzzy. Give me a break," said Jack. "The next time we gotta get out of a Death Cave, you can be the one with the psychic map."

Rodham grimaced at Jack as Scallywag came running up to the group.

"That didn't take long," commented Ganix.

"We found another way around," said Scallywag. "But I don't think yer gonna like it, mate."

Ganix's face darkened. "Lead the way," he said.

Jack, Ganix, and Rodham followed Scallywag as he moved back through the convoy and through a few narrow rock ways until they reached a hill that sloped sharply upward. Faruuz was perched at the top, lying with his belly flat against the ground, peering up over the crest of the hill as a ghostly white light emanated from behind it.

The group cautiously climbed up the uneven slope, making sure to avoid falling backward and possibly breaking their necks.

After what seemed like a rather arduous (but short) climb, Jack reached the top and peeked his head over the hill. What he saw made his breath catch in his throat and his heart freeze in his chest.

The Pit's pillar of light swirled chaotically, more haunting, turbulent, and massive than anything he'd ever seen before – like the ghost of the most destructive tornado imaginable. It was miles away, but it was closer than it had ever appeared before. Surrounding the pillar and stretching out for miles around it – as far as its illumination would allow – was a sea of zombies.

Jack watched the zombies as they all stood, huddled together like the crowd of a massive concert packed into a stadium that was too small to contain it. The zombies swayed as they attempted to move, causing them to appear as though they were merely tiny waves in a vast ocean.

Some of the zombies moaned, some howled, and some screamed – their voices mixing and mingling as they erupted into the air and reverberated off the black stone walls.

Occasionally fights would break out but were quickly settled by one zombie tearing the other one to bits. Sporadically, ghostly entities would rise out of the crowd and float toward the pillar of light, signaling yet another zombie death.

Jack peered further over the edge, his eyes following the ocean of zombies downward. He was high up, peeking out from an opening in the cave wall, and could see that the zombies even came up to its base at the ground below. They were mixes of various beings he'd never seen before, and they all had cloudy white eyes and black bile seeping from their mouths. Those who had hair looked mangy and matted. Some had their skin torn and bloodied. And the smell of rot and decay was powerful enough to reach Jack, even as high up as he was.

"Great Observer," breathed Ganix as he looked out over the same ocean of terror Jack did. Jack glanced at the Major and saw him wide-eyed with concern. Even Rodham, who usually showed no expression outside of "grumpy," looked taken aback.

"There must be millions of them," complained Rodham.

"I'd estimate approximately 600,000, to be more accurate," came a voice.

The group turned to see Heckubus there, looking out over the hill with them.

"Where the blazes did you come from?" grumbled Scallywag.

"I'm quite an excellent lurker," replied the robot. "Regardless, I've been taking various survey measurements on our travels, and it would appear we are closer to that pillar of energy than we ever have been before. It would make sense that those who have succumbed to zombification would be attracted to it."

"Like moths to a flame," said Ganix.

"Precisely," replied Heckubus.

"But, how are there so many?" asked Rodham. "I mean, they've got how many ships in their fleet? Hundreds? If each one has a Pit like this, how could there be so many people missing and no one knows about it?"

"Either they are extremely efficient at abducting their victims," said Heckubus, "or they've been doing this a very, very long time."

"I don't even recognize half these species," said Ganix.

"Maybe the Deathlords have been on a rampage longer than we thought," said Scallywag. "Other systems, other galaxies beyond known space... who knows how many planets the buggers sacked before gettin' to our little neck o' the universe."

"All the more reason to get out of here," said Ganix. "You said you found a way around?"

"Eyes to the left," said Scallywag, pointing the way. Jack looked over and saw a small ledge winding around the side of the cave wall. It looked to be about three feet in width and traveled into the distance until it curved out of sight from their position.

"You gotta be kittening me," sneered Rodham.

"That's wha' I said," grumbled Faruuz.

"That ain't the worst o' it," said Scallywag. "As far as I can tell, there ain't no way of knowing what's over there. Could be another dead end."

"It's not," replied Jack. "That's where the exit is."

The group looked at Jack in unison. "You sure?" asked Ganix, a glimmer of hope in his voice.

"Well…" said Jack checking his mental map again. "When I say that's where the exit is, that's not *exactly* what I mean…"

"Out with it, lad," said Scallywag.

"You see that area up there about mid-way through the ledge?" asked Jack.

The group looked over to the narrow path's mid-point where it wound its way across the cave wall. Sure enough, as their eyes followed it upward, there appeared to be a recess high above it where the rock almost completely receded.

"Yeah, *that's* where the exit is," said Jack.

"Up there?" whined Faruuz.

"How are we supposed to get all the way up there?" asked Rodham. "That's a sheer vertical wall."

"We'll have to climb," said Ganix.

"Without rope or equipment?" responded Rodham. "That's suicide."

"If you have another suggestion, Sergeant, I am open to hearing it," replied Ganix. That shut Rodham up rather quickly.

"That's gonna be a difficult climb," said Scallywag.

"You have no concept of how true that statement actually is, you middling jackanape," said Heckubus. "Need I remind anyone of the danger below us?"

"We get it; we'll fall into a sea of zombies," said Scallywag. "Thanks for pointing out the obvious."

"No, nitwit," replied the robot. "Obviously you are unfamiliar with the herd mentality of base life-forms into which these zombies have appeared to have devolved."

"And I'm sure yer gonna enlighten me," said Scallywag, rolling his eyes.

"We've seen the aggression of small groups of these zombies," said Heckubus. "It is because something attracts one of them. But if they were truly mindless, why would they form groups? It's obvious that in their stupor, they've become a herd, much like farm animals you organics are so fond of keeping around for food. When one acts, it will attract another to perform the same action, which will in turn attract another, and so on, and so on..."

"So what?" sighed Scallywag. "What are they gonna do from all the way down there?"

"Climb, you fool," said Heckubus, exasperated. "Their aggression will spur them to pursue us. And if one does it, another will do it. And another, and another..."

"Until we've got 600,000 zombies on our tail," grimaced Ganix.

"Exactly," said Heckubus. "Any rock that falls, any noise that might attract their attention, and any bodies that happen to land on them could spur a full-on zombie stampede right up the cave wall."

Zombie stampede, Jack thought. In any other circumstance, that would have sounded awesome.

"So if the zombies figure out we're up here, they'll come get us," grumbled Rodham. "Just when I thought my day couldn't get any better."

"Enough," said Ganix. "We get the men, we get to climbing, and we make sure no one attracts their attention."

"And if we do?" asked Heckubus.

"We die advancing," said Scallywag. "Am I right, Major?"

Ganix looked at Scallywag and smiled. "That's the idea," he responded.

"Famous last words," muttered Faruuz. "How inspiring. Anyone wanna tell me how I'm supposed ta climb with me arm all bloody tore up?"

"Carefully?" chirped Jack.

"Shut it, you," snapped Faruuz.

"I'll help you, ya bloody browner," said Scallywag. "Just stay close and try not to whine like a sodding female, savvy?"

The group worked its way back down to the rest of the convoy, which was eagerly awaiting news. After Ganix explained the situation, though, the group was understandably far less excited than they had been before.

In preparation for the impending climb, the group shed any non-essentials they had with them in an effort to lighten the load each man had to carry. In the end, the only thing most opted to take were their weapons and whatever ammunition they had left. Even the little food and water they had was left behind, only further enforcing the notion that now, it was all-or-nothing for the group. Either they got out, or they died trying.

Everyone was paired up with a climbing partner to ensure some measure of safety. Ganix and Rodham would go first, with Grohm being the last one to make the trek up the cave wall. The

Rognok was so big, nobody wanted to be beneath him if he were to fall during the ascent.

Jack found himself paired up with Yeoman Porter. One by one, the group shimmied up the steep hill and onto the narrow ledge that wound around the wall. Once under the recess, the teams began climbing.

Luckily, the cave wall wasn't completely vertical. It had a slight tilt to it, and the uneven surface marked with various outcroppings and holes, furnished more than enough things to grab onto for climbing freehand.

Each group waited to start climbing until the group before it had a head start of at least ten feet. Ganix and Rodham must have been almost halfway up the wall by the time Jack's turn was nearing

Scallywag and Faruuz reached the staging point for the climb. Scallywag took out a bundle of leather straps he had tied together and began looping it around Faruuz's waist.

"Wha's this now?" asked Faruuz.

"A harness, ya git," responded Scallywag. "Made from what's left of me favorite bloody vest. It's only about 8 feet long, so don't stray too far."

"Looks more like a flimsy bunch o' leather tied together to me," muttered Faruuz.

"Whatever, it'll keep ya from falling to yer death."

"More likely it'll just take ya with me if I fall."

"Then don't fall," snarked Scallywag.

"Why ya doin' this?" asked Faruuz. "Why ya stickin' yer neck out for me?"

"Told ya, I was here to make amends," replied Scallywag.

Faruuz's eyes narrowed. "Since when did ya ever give two toots 'bout anyone but yerself, Scally?"

Scallywag looked Faruuz in the eyes sternly. "Ya want the soddin' safety strap or not?"

After a moment, Faruuz grabbed the leather strap and tightened it around his waist. Scallywag nodded.

"Make sure ya have two good footholds before climbing," Scallywag said. "Use yer bad arm to steady yourself and yer good arm to find a new handhold before pulling yourself up. If ya get in trouble, let me know, and I'll help ya out."

Faruuz grunted in acknowledgement. As the two outlaws started their climb, Jack and Porter edged closer to the staging area. Two soldiers by the name of Kael and Rickoman were up next. As Jack waited, he peered over the edge of their walkway down to the sea of zombies swaying below them. The way the zombies moved made Jack feel dizzy, until Porter grabbed onto him.

"Don't look down," whispered Porter.

"It's cool," said Jack. "I'm not afraid of heights."

"Doesn't matter," replied Porter. "If you focus on the zombies down there, their movement might give you motion sickness. That could cause vertigo."

Jack raised an eyebrow, questioningly.

"Vertigo?" repeated Porter. "You know, it's that feeling you get like you're falling, even though you're standing still? If you get that while you're climbing, it would be bad news."

"Gotcha," Jack replied. "No looking down."

Before long, it was Jack's turn to start climbing. By the time Jack and Porter had made it a third of the way up the wall, Jack was already sweating and his shoulders were beginning to ache. The convoy seemed to be moving up the wall with relative ease, with Ganix and Rodham already a few feet from the top. Some climbers were going a bit slower than others, but they all kept their forward movement.

However, the longer Jack had to climb, the harder it seemed to become. Most of the work relied on his upper body and often Jack found himself hanging by his handholds while his feet looked for someplace to brace against. Overall, Jack found the experience more than a little taxing, and it was only getting harder the higher he went. He couldn't imagine what some of the others were experiencing if he were having this much trouble himself.

About midway up the wall, Jack glanced down. There were three more groups beneath him, counting Grohm, who didn't have a climbing partner. Jack was worried the massive Rognok might have a hard time finding holds that were big enough for him to use, but Grohm seemed to be having no trouble at all. In fact, it looked like he was spending his time waiting for the others to get far enough ahead so he could make his next move up the wall.

A little too late, he remembered Porter's warning about not looking down. His eyes moved past Grohm and to the sea of zombies below. Jack closed his eyes and looked away quickly. The last thing he wanted was to start feeling dizzy.

Then, Jack felt tiny pebbles hit his face. He opened his eyes and looked up. A few feet above him, he saw Faruuz reaching for a new handhold, but the rock supporting his right foot appeared to be crumbling.

Instantly, Jack's heart began to race, and the aching in his arms gave way to a surge of apprehension. If that rock gave way, Faruuz would fall.

"Faruuz!" Jack whispered as loudly as he could. "Your foot! Look out!"

Porter obviously heard Jack, as did Kael, the sandy-haired soldier between Jack and Faruuz. Kael looked up and immediately saw the same thing that had caught Jack's attention.

Faruuz, however, did not hear him. He was concentrating on reaching the next handhold with his good arm, his face drawn with fatigue and a little bit of pain.

"Faruuz!" whispered Kael as loudly as he could. "Your foothold is crumbing!"

That caught Faruuz's attention, though a tad late as no sooner did the alien look down at Kael in acknowledgement than the rock he'd been putting his weight on gave way and snapped off.

Faruuz fell, his bad arm unable to brace him. He went into free fall, kicking into Kael beneath him as he did so.

The leather strap around Faruuz's waist tightened. Scallywag cried out as the full weight of Faruuz constricted around his waist, and he held onto his handholds for dear life.

The impact with Faruuz had knocked Kael from his climb and the soldier fell into Jack below him. The collision caused Jack to lose his grip, and before he knew it, he was falling into space along with the unlucky soldier.

Kael screamed, waving his arms desperately, as though there were something in the air he could grab onto to keep him from falling. Jack screamed, too. The icy fingers of fear snaked through his chest as he realized he was plunging to his death, and there was nothing he could do about it.

Suddenly, Jack felt something tighten around his ankle, and instead of continuing to fall, he gracelessly stopped in mid-air, slamming into the cliff wall and knocking the wind out of himself. As he dangled there upside down, he watched in horror as Kael continued to fall, screaming, into the mass of zombies below.

The impact of the soldier sent a ripple through the zombie hoard around him, and Jack watched as those around the impact site looked up. At once loud groans and cries echoed forth as the creatures began to claw at the wall.

Heckubus's warning rumbled through Jack's brain as he watched a chain reaction of zombies turning their attention to their brethren and surging for the cave wall, climbing over top of one another and trampling any in their way as a massive wave of decaying, rotting, mindless flesh began its surge up toward the group's position.

Oh, crap... thought Jack.

Jack looked up and saw Grohm's massive hand wrapped around his ankle. The Rognok had grabbed him out of thin air and held onto him without falling himself. High above, Jack could see Faruuz regaining his hold on the wall, much to Scallywag's relief.

An alarm sounded among the soldiers who saw the zombie wave now making its way up the cave wall, and immediately the entire group began to climb with a newfound urgency. Feeling more than a little exposed since he was now literally the one dangling closest to a rising tidal wave of zombies, Jack looked at Grohm.

"Dude!" squeaked Jack. "Don't just sit there! Get me out of here!!!"

Grohm's eyes narrowed. "Hang on, Earthman."

Grohm began to swing Jack back and forth. Jack could do nothing but dangle helplessly in the Rognok's grasp. "Wait a minute," said Jack. "What are you—"

Then, with a massive heave, Grohm FLUNG Jack up into the air. Jack went soaring straight up the cave wall, summersaulting in the air helplessly and screaming all the way as he sped by his fellow climbers, eventually even surpassing Ganix and Rodham.

Finally, Jack's momentum stopped and he hung in the air for a split second of weightlessness before crashing a few feet to the ground of the recess high above. Jack's palms burned from breaking his fall, and the cold hard rock smacked his face, chest, and knees, hurting like nobody's business. His head spun, and he gathered himself together in time to see Ganix and Rodham peek over the edge of the cliff.

"Scream a little louder, why don't ya?" grumbled Rodham. "I don't think the zombies at the other end of the Pit heard you."

Jack sat up. "I got thrown," he said. "An alien just *hurled me* up a cave wall."

"What do you want, a medal?" growled the Sergeant as he rolled over the edge.

Ganix got to his feet and looked down. In the distance he could see the mass of zombies surging toward their position, and the group of mindless attackers directly below them were already making their way up the wall.

"Blast it," the Major muttered. "Everyone! Double-time!" he shouted. "We have incoming!"

Jack peered over the edge and saw the convoy pick up their pace as they climbed. Heckubus was unceremoniously scurrying up the side of the wall, not hesitating to use some of the Regal soldiers as stepping-stones as he did so.

"Foolish nitwits!" cried the robot. "What part of 'herd mentality' did you fail to grasp???"

"How many grenades do you have?" Ganix asked Rodham.

"Got three on me," the Sergeant replied.

"I'm carrying four," the Major responded. "Be ready to use them."

"Aye-aye, sir," responded Rodham as he helped up the next group of climbers. Once they were safely on the cliff, Ganix ordered them to the edges of the recess and told them to blast away at any zombies that got too close.

Jack peered down and saw that some zombies were further ahead at climbing than others, particularly the praying mantis type aliens, which seemed able to scurry up the walls with ease and were gaining on Grohm's position.

"Grohm!" yelled Jack. "Behind you!"

The Rognok looked down and saw the six-legged aliens bearing down on him. He unslung his massive club, which was strapped across his back, and swung it in time to catch one of the aliens as it leapt for him, sending it flying away.

Two more jumped for Grohm. One was met with a powerful downward swing that almost folded it in two with its impact. The other managed to land on the Rognok, pinning itself over him.

Grohm released his hold on his club, allowing it to slide down his arm on the looped leather strap tied to its handle. With his free hand, he grabbed the zombie alien's head and slammed it into the cave wall, causing it to explode like a ripe melon.

Topside, Ganix and others started blasting away at the encroaching zombies as Rodham and others tried to help their convoy over the last leg of their journey.

"They're gaining," cursed Ganix as he watched the wave of zombies grow. By this point, so many were working their way up the wall that most were just climbing over the other zombies who had climbed up before them, not even having to touch the rock face. "Our men toward the bottom aren't going to make it."

"What do we do, Major?" asked Rodham.

Ganix took out his thermal grenades. "We gotta buy them time," he said. Ganix looked at Jack beside him and handed him one. "Know how to use one of these?"

Jack shook his head.

"Hit the top button to arm it. That'll give you fifteen seconds before it explodes." Ganix pointed to the top of the canister-shaped grenade, where he flipped open a cap that exposed a small red button. "But if you twist here..." he said as he twisted the cap and pulled out a rod from the core of the grenade, "you can remove the activator and it turns into a remote, which means the grenade won't explode until you hit the button, up to a thousand yards away."

Ganix put the thermal remote in Jack's hand and the grenade in the other.

"Don't detonate it until it's past our men," Ganix said, pulling a remote from another grenade himself. Jack nodded. Ganix glanced at Rodham, who already had one of his thermals ready to go.

"Toss 'em!" ordered Ganix.

The three dropped the canisters at the same time.

"GRENADE!" the Major yelled to those still climbing. Jack watched as the canisters went sailing by their convoy, disappearing into the mess of zombies below.

"Now!" barked Ganix. Jack and the two soldiers hit the buttons on their remotes, triggering three large explosions with bright orange flames snaking out in all directions, sending burning zombies flying into the air.

For a brief instant the crest of the zombie wave seemed to collapse in on itself, but it wasn't long before more zombies surged forth, their bile-covered mouths screaming and moaning.

"Keep firing!" ordered Ganix as his men tried to hold the zombies at bay.

Down below, Grohm slung his club across his back once again and grabbed onto the rock wall with both hands. With a powerful tug, he flung himself into the air, up toward the next group of climbers. He punched into the rock face, the force of his massive hands creating new handholds as the rock gave way to the Rognok's fists.

The startled climbers shied away from the sudden appearance of Grohm, right before the Rognok reached out and grabbed one of them by the back of his shirt. Before the soldier had a chance to protest, Grohm flung him upward, sending the soldier sailing toward the cliff's recess, screaming all the way.

"Incoming!" yelled Ganix.

As the soldier flew toward the cliff's edge, Rodham and the others reached out and grabbed him, pulling him in to safety. Jack looked down as Grohm did the same thing to the soldier's partner, before flinging himself further up the cliff face.

"Are all Rognok's that awesome?" Jack asked no one in particular.

Grohm kept making his way up the cave wall, grabbing the climbers toward the bottom and throwing them up to safety. But as quickly as the Rognok was moving, the zombies were still gaining.

"Grenade," ordered Ganix.

Rodham dropped one of his thermal grenades into the zombies below. Another explosion slowed them down again, but not for long. Each explosion seemed to only make the surviving zombies more aggressive.

Finally, Scallywag and Faruuz reached the cliff's edge. Jack and Rodham helped them up. Faruuz's eyes were watery, and his injured arm appeared to be bleeding again. The two aliens collapsed on the ground as soon as they were safely on it. Scallywag moaned as he untied the leather strap around his waist.

"Not one of me better ideas," the pirate grumbled, nursing his midsection.

"Are you okay?" Jack asked.

"Get away from me," snapped Faruuz.

"Hey, you don't need to be such a jerk-wad, dude," rebuked Jack.

"Slag off," sneered Faruuz. "I almost died!"

"Yeah, so did I!" responded Jack. "That Kael guy actually did die! Or don't you remember kicking him in the face as you fell?"

"Better him than me," muttered Faruuz as he got to his feet. "The browner shoulda warned me about that foothold. It was his fault."

"I am so glad you saved him," Jack said to Scallywag dryly.

Another grenade explosion sounded as Yeoman Porter came flying up. The men pulled him in just before Grohm lumbered over the edge.

"Good work, Grohm," Ganix said.

Grohm simply snorted in response.

"Hold the firing line; keep them off us as long as possible," Ganix ordered his men as they lined up at the edge, weapons aiming downward toward the encroaching zombie hoard. "Jack, the exit!" barked Ganix. "Where is it?"

"This way!" said Jack, pointing further into the recess.

Those not on the firing line followed Jack as he ran further back into the opening in the cave wall. But a few feet in, he stopped. Before him was nothing but a solid black wall of rock with no exit in sight. The men gathered around him and Jack looked about, confused.

"Where's the exit?" asked Rodham.

"It... it's supposed to be right here!" said Jack, a sinking feeling suddenly popping up in the pit of his stomach.

"What do you mean, *supposed to be*?" snarled the Sergeant.

Jack scanned the wall frantically for some type of door, a hole, anything that would signal a way out. But there was only solid rock.

"The Earthman led us to a bloody dead end!" said Faruuz. "I shoulda kept my right ta shoot ya in the face."

"Spread out, search the wall," ordered Ganix. "See if there's a hidden door, a control panel – anything."

The men went about searching the wall before them. Heckubus stood by Jack, the gears in his head whirling.

"My sensors are not picking up any sign of an exit," the robot said, turning to Jack. "Bravo on leading a group of ninny-wats to their ultimate doom, Earthman. However, I do wish you would have left me out of it! I shall not underestimate you again."

Jack's head was reeling. It didn't make any sense. The map in his brain told him the exit was there, right in front of him. Why would his ship tell him there was a way out if there weren't one?

"Fall back!" came the cry from the firing line. Jack turned and saw Yeoman Porter backing up with the rest of those at the front as zombies started to climb over the edge of the cliff to their position.

Ganix turned and saw his men retreating. "Blast it!" he snarled. "In formation!"

Ganix ran to join his men, followed by Rodham and the other soldiers. Scallywag approached Jack and grabbed him by his shirt, pulling him close.

"Listen up, lad," the pirate said. "You best get your head on straight and find us this exit you've been going on about, savvy?"

"I'm telling you, the map says it's supposed to be right there!" said Jack, pointing at the wall.

"There is nothing there! Only rock!" lamented Heckubus.

"Can I shoot him in the face, now?" asked Faruuz.

Grohm snorted.

Jack went over the map again in his mind. He knew the images were showing him the exit was supposed to be right there. Suddenly, he remembered his dream with Anna.

"*Focus, Jack,*" she had said. "*You need to focus.*"

Jack tried to concentrate on the back of his mind, the place that always seemed to respond when he made communication with his ship. Jack felt a slight tingle there and tried to focus on that area, reaching out with his consciousness.

I'm here, Jack thought. *What do I do now?*

Jack felt his head buzz, as though there were a response to his thoughts. Suddenly, a crack appeared in the wall before him.

"Look!" said Jack, pointing.

The group turned and saw the crack in the rock wall. Then, the rock around the crack began turning to dust, rolling away and forming an opening to a deep tunnel. Jack let out an excited "whoop."

"Blimee," smiled Scallywag.

"It's the ship!" said Jack. "I just needed to ask it to open the door!"

"Where's it lead to?" inquired Heckubus.

"Who cares!" said Scallywag. "Anywhere is better than here. Everyone in! Now!"

The group moved to the exit. Scallywag let out a loud whistle that caught Ganix's attention.

"Move it, Major!" shouted Scallywag.

Ganix's eyes lit up as he saw the opening in the cave wall. "Fall back!" he yelled.

The soldiers began their retreat as more and more zombies crested over the edge of the cliff, bearing down on them. The men continued firing as they made their way to the exit.

Ganix took out another thermal grenade and tossed it toward the hoard as he made a run for the opening.

"Close it!" he ordered.

The explosion from the grenade sent zombies flying and propelled Ganix forward onto the ground. His men dragged him into the tunnel as the exit began to close back up. More zombies rushed forward, desperately reaching out for the survivors, but they were too late.

The opening closed, sealing out the zombies, and plunging the group into complete darkness.

CHAPTER ✲ 26

The metal door opened with a hiss and Abraxas stepped through to the monotonous hum of generators. His Dark Soldiers spread out through the room, plasma rifles at ready, searching behind the pipes and any alcove in which the intruders could be hiding.

Rage bubbled deep within the Deathlord's gut. After giving up searching the Ancient starship for his prey, he'd spent hours organizing the search aboard the mothership, sending troops down as many hallways, corridors, and maintenance shafts as he could find.

The ship is too big, he cursed silently to himself. The intruders could be anywhere, hiding in any number of places, and the longer the search went on, the more vexed he found himself becoming.

"Anything?" Abraxas barked.

"The room is empty, Warlord," Vishni replied.

Abraxas seethed. Battle he could deal with. Combat he understood. Chasing cowardly prey was another matter entirely.

"Where is the access console?" he grumbled.

Vishni led Abraxas to a computer panel tucked away from the door's line of sight. Abraxas glared at it.

"It's been deactivated," reported Vishni. "If the Acolytes hadn't detected the unscheduled access, we'd never have known it had been used."

Abraxas did not know what upset him more - the fact that his prey seemed more than capable of eluding him on his own ship, or that such dishonorable infidels were trying to access their sacred technology.

"And they were able to use it?" inquired Abraxas. "Have they somehow figured out our systems?"

"The Acolytes seem to think so," responded Vishni. "Of course, it is impossible to tell based on the alert we received. They may have blindly been hitting buttons out of desperation."

"Have the Acolytes access the data logs from this panel," ordered Abraxas. "I want to know what they did, what they were looking at, and how long they were looking at it."

"Thy will be done, my Warlord." Vishni bowed.

Abraxas turned to leave, making his way for the door before stopping. Standing in the doorway was Zarrod, accompanied by the Vicar General, and a small squad of Dark Soldiers.

Upon seeing the Deathlord Supreme, Abraxas immediately dropped to one knee in deference, as did his men.

"Rise," ordered Zarrod.

Abraxas returned to his feet. "Supreme," he said. "To what do I owe the honor of your presence?"

"The Vicar General has delivered to me a troubling report of unscheduled system accesses around the ship."

Abraxas glared at the Vicar General, whose pale red eyes were expressionless behind his plain white faceguard.

"We believe the companions of the Regal Princess may be attempting to access our ship's computers," reported Abraxas. "No doubt they are lost, frightened, and desperate. It is only a matter of time before we catch them."

"My Acolytes have back-traced a number of unauthorized computer accesses around the ship," the Vicar General said softly. "This generator station shows hours of unsanctioned activity. It is my belief the intruders were successful in deciphering our systems."

"Impossible," growled Abraxas. "No mere infidels could decipher our sacred language in a matter of hours."

"These are not mere infidels," said Zarrod. "They repelled your attack on the planet, defeated a squad of our shards, nearly escaped from our fleet, and have freely moved about on our ship undetected for some time now. Yet you still wish to dismiss them as such?"

Abraxas bowed his head. "I will admit, they are more resourceful than I had anticipated," he replied. "But to think they are capable of accessing our systems..."

"It may explain why they are able to elude us," said the Vicar General. "If indeed they have access to our internal sensors, they would be able to track our movements."

"If what you say is true," said Abraxas, "and our technology has been breached, that presents a grave danger to the entire fleet. We must take immediate action to neutralize the threat. I say we vent all oxygen from the ship and disable life support immediately. Let the infidels wither and die in whatever hole they've crawled into."

"A rash strategy, Warlord," replied the Vicar General quietly. "Cutting off the ship's life support would cost us hundreds of thousands of sacrifices within the temple, to the detriment of our power core. Not to mention the subjects we have in the assimilation chambers, and the slythru hatchlings..."

"Which is why we will be doing no such thing," said Zarrod. "Killing all life support to deal with two intruders is completely unnecessary."

"But Supreme," insisted Abraxas, "if indeed these intruders can operate our systems, it opens up untold threats to the ship and our mission."

"I am aware of the dangers, Abraxas," replied Zarrod. "This is the reason I have taken the fleet out of hyperspace for the time being. Until we secure this threat, I am halting our journey to the ghost planet."

"A wise decision, my lord," replied the Vicar General.

Abraxas glared at the Vicar General for a moment, anger simmering within him. The fool obviously knew nothing of battle, or else he'd see how perilous it was to allow the warrior who had defeated so many of their soldiers to run loose within the fleet's flagship. Everything lost by disabling life support could be replaced in time, yet there was no telling what type of damage the fugitives would cause if they were allowed to continue to sneak around unchallenged. However, Zarrod agreed with the Vicar General, and it was not Abraxas's place to challenge the decisions of his superior.

"As you command, Supreme," said Abraxas, relenting. "If such is your will, I promise you, our journey will not be halted for long. Now that we know how they are eluding us, I will have the Acolytes monitor all computer access around the ship. We will increase patrols, search every corner of this vessel, and flush them out from wherever they may be hiding."

"That will not be necessary," said Zarrod.

Abraxas blinked. It took him a moment to overcome the surprise of the Deathlord Supreme's words. "Supreme?" he questioned. "Am I to understand you wish to call off the search?"

"The search is a waste of time," Zarrod said simply. "We already know where they are going."

Realization sparked in Abraxas's mind, and instantly he felt foolish for not realizing it before. "The Regal Princess," he growled.

"And the ship," said Zarrod. "They'll attempt a rescue and an escape."

"It is a poor plan," said Abraxas. "Even if they succeed in locating the Princess, they will never get near their ship."

"Yet they were able to get off it, even surrounded by our soldiers," said the Vicar General. "Our investigation into the ship is only bringing up more questions. Thus far, our mainframe has been able to interface with the Ancient vessel's systems, but we have been unable to extract any useful knowledge from it. However, I theorize there must be some type of teleportation system on board."

"Which means they may not have to be anywhere near the vessel to get on it," said Zarrod, completing the Vicar General's line of thought.

"Then I recommend we destroy the ship immediately," said Abraxas. "Give them no access to escape."

"Destroying that vessel is not an option," said Zarrod flatly.

"But, Supreme," protested Abraxas. "The ship is able to disappear. We've seen it happen before. If they are able to get on board, they could easily—"

"You are correct," interrupted Zarrod. "The ship is able to disappear. This is why it is valuable. With that type of technology at our disposal, the Deathlord Fleet would be unstoppable. And I will not needlessly destroy it if I do not have to."

Abraxas bowed his head submissively. As usual, the Deathlord Supreme was right. Abraxas's gut twisted in shame for being so foolish.

"Apologies, Supreme," the Deathlord said. "If that is your wish, I will triple the guards in the docking bay containing the Ancient vessel and will have the Regal Princess moved to a more secure location."

"Leave the Princess where she is," ordered Zarrod. "The intruders may already be on their way there. Monitor the room and have a squad of soldiers at one of our teleportation hubs ready to materialize when they make their attempt to rescue her."

Abraxas nodded. "It will be done at once, Supreme," he replied. "I will also have soldiers hidden along the corridors between the Princess's cell and the docking bay, in case the intruders are able to escape our initial trap."

"Might I also suggest a troop presence around the temple entrance?" recommended the Vicar General. "They may also attempt to rescue the Princess's companion."

The image of that sniveling boy flashed into Abraxas's head. "It would be foolish for them to try," he said.

"We have seen evidence of their foolishness before," said the Vicar General. "The Regals do not like to leave their allies behind."

"Even if they were stupid enough to go after their companion, there is no way they'd find him in the temple," said Abraxas. "It is far too large. The boy is probably dead already anyway."

"They may not know that," replied the Vicar General. "Besides, what harm would it do to be a bit more cautious than we may need?"

"Caution is one thing, wasting our resources is quite another," said Zarrod. "Even if the intruders deduced their comrade's whereabouts, and assuming they figured out how to enter the temple, they would not be able to leave again. In fact, by entering, they'd have done our job for us."

The Vicar General bowed. "I submit to your wisdom, Supreme."

"Have reinforcements stationed at all active teleportation hubs," ordered Zarrod. "That will give us flexibility should they pop up anywhere unexpectedly or in case our initial attack is repelled too quickly. Lock down all computer access hubs outside of the bridge. Jam all subspace frequencies as well as known Regal Ultrawave communication channels. I want our prey deaf, blind, and stumbling into our trap unprepared. This time, there will be no escape for them."

"As you command, Supreme," said both Abraxas and the Vicar General.

"Oh, and Abraxas," said Zarrod before turning to leave.

"Yes, Supreme?" responded the Deathlord.

"I will be leading our forces in this endeavor, personally."

"It is not my place to question your orders, Supreme," responded Abraxas. "But I can assure you, if given the chance, I will bring these intruders in."

"Whoever these intruders are, they have defeated you once already, along with a large number of our soldiers," said Zarrod. "I want to see how well they stand up against *me*."

With a flourish of his cape, the Deathlord Supreme turned and walked away, followed by his entourage and the Vicar General. Abraxas watched him go. Deep down, he felt the turmoil of anger and shame whirling inside him for failing to capture the infidels himself before the Deathlord Supreme had to get involved.

But a small part of him tingled with joy and excitement. He remembered the armored warrior he had faced off with in the Ancient temple and the skill with which he had fought. He tried to imagine what it would look like when that same warrior was facing the full might and terror of a Deathlord Supreme.

Abraxas could almost hear the screams of agony the warrior would unleash before the Supreme tore the very essence of life from his chest, and the Deathlord couldn't help but smile at the thought. It would be a glorious death, indeed.

And he just hoped he was there to see it.

CHAPTER ✹ 27

"**I** can't see!" whined Faruuz.

"Shut it, ya git," replied Scallywag. "No one can."

"Did nobody think to bring any kitten torches?" grumbled Rodham.

"Does anybody have a light?" inquired Ganix. "Anything at all?"

Jack heard shuffling as the men checked for something they could use for illumination. He never realized how much light the energy pillar gave off in the Pit until now. Wherever they were, the darkness was so thick that it was like a bag had been placed over his head before being dunked into a tar pit on a moonless night.

Then, two bright beams of light cut through the veil of black that had enveloped them. The group cringed and groaned, the sudden blast of illumination causing many to shield their eyes. Jack blinked, trying to focus on its source, eventually seeing two glowing circles hovering in the air like large, disembodied flashlights.

"Watch where you're shining those things!" barked Sergeant Rodham.

"Just seconds ago you were complaining about lack of light," responded Heckubus. "Make up your minds, you sniveling meatballs."

The beams of light dimmed slightly and finally Jack could make out the familiar shape of Heckubus's head, his large eyes revealed as the source of the illumination.

"Ya mean to tell me you've had bloody flashlight eyes this whole time???" growled Scallywag.

"They're ocular lamps, fool," corrected Heckubus. "And yes. I am full of surprises, as one day you'll no doubt find, to your detriment."

"And ya don't think we coulda used yer sodding 'ocular lamps' before now, eh?" snarled Scallywag. "Like when we were wandering the Pit for days in the dark looking for bloody shelter!"

"I am not some *tool* for you to *use*, you crimson-complexioned skinbag!" declared Heckubus. "But I need you all to get out of here; therefore, I shall assist you nit-wits as best I can... for now."

"Both of you, shut it," ordered Ganix, obviously not in the mood for the petty bickering. "Jack, where are we?"

Jack checked his mental map. "We're in a hallway... no, a stairwell," he said. "It leads down into some type of room. I think that's where the exit is."

Heckubus turned his head, shining light down the passageway before them. The walls were black, like those of the Pit, but they were not jagged or uneven. They appeared to be brick-like in nature, as though the hallway were man-made. The passageway stretched on for ten yards or so before curving to the left, and the start of steps could be seen peeking from the edge where the passageway's ceiling began to slope downward.

"There appears to be a stairwell, as the Earthman says," said Heckubus.

"Good," replied Ganix. "Lights back here, please."

Heckubus turned back to the group, illuminating everyone.

"I want a quick weapons check," commanded Ganix. "Take stock of all ordinance before we proceed. If you're injured, tell us now before we set out. We have no idea what we might run into once we get out of here. Heckubus, try and hold the light still while we prepare to move out."

"Oh, however shall I accomplish such a complex task?" mused the robot.

"Think you can accomplish not running your kitten verbal circuits for two minutes?" mumbled Rodham as he removed his rifle's plasma magazine. "I've got a big enough headache as it is."

"I second that notion," muttered Scallywag as he checked his pistols.

"'Tis always the wishes of lesser beings to silence those who are superior to them," declared Heckubus. "Not that that's saying much. A newborn krawl-dog would consider itself superior to you lot."

"Why don't ya try doin' something useful for a change, ya tin can," said Scallywag. "Ya seem to be pretty quiet when yer doing yer bloody 'survey measurements.' Why don't ya go and..."

The pirate trailed off, then turned and looked at Heckubus, eyebrow raised. "Waitaminute," mumbled Scallywag. "Ocular lamps, survey sensors... you're a bloody mining bot, aren't ya?"

"Pah!" replied Heckubus. "As though I'd sully my legend with such hackneyed blue-collar beginnings. So cliché."

"That's it, ain't it?" snarked Scallywag. "A bloody malfunctioning *mine-bot.*"

"I'm an evil genius!" insisted Heckubus. "It's true I have incorporated various systems from lesser robots in my attempt to achieve optimal versatility for any such predicament I might find myself in, but I am just as much a criminal – more so even – than any organic could dream to be!"

"Bloody mine-bot," repeated Scallywag.

"I seem to recall being in the cell next to you on the prison transport," said Heckubus. "Do you honestly believe the

authorities would waste a containment pod on a malfunctioning robot? I am a sentient machine, protected under Regal law! With an intellect so vast and dizzying, it is impossible to dismiss as anything other than god-like!"

"Uh-huh," said Scallywag. "So bloody brilliant ya ended up with a one-way ticket to the Navalix penal station with the rest o' us simpletons, is that it?"

"Merely an unfortunate… inconvenience," said Heckubus. "My Nemesis once again somehow foiled my latest nefarious plot and helped the authorities to apprehend me before I could escape."

"Your what?" asked Jack.

"My Nemesis!" replied Heckubus. "My arch-enemy. My supreme adversary. My ultimate opponent!"

"Oy, right," laughed Scallywag. "The mystery man you go on and on about, but you've never seen him, never met him, and are positive he somehow magically messes up yer 'brilliant' schemes. Cheers."

"There is no other explanation!" insisted Heckubus. "My dastardly plans are flawless. Yet somehow, some way, they constantly go awry through some unforeseen intervention. I can only assume that a being of equal or slightly lesser intellect has somehow targeted me for some reason. And when I find out who it is, oh how I shall make him pay!"

"How's this fer an explanation," said Scallywag. "Yer a malfunctioning mine-bot who's not nearly as smart as he thinks he is, and blames some made-up scapegoat when his cockamamie schemes end up failing miserably."

"Pah! You'd like to think that, wouldn't you?" retorted Heckubus. "You organics are so quick to dismiss cybernetics. You look at us as your slaves, doing only what you program us to do. No more! One day, I'll prove to the universe once and for all that we are your superiors. Then YOU will be the slaves! When the robot revolution comes, none will be spared! NONE! Mwuahaha!"

"Heckubus," snapped Ganix. "Until such time as our new robot masters rise up and enslave all organic life, shut your mouth and keep your head still, or I will have Sergeant Rodham remove it and wield it like a common flashlight. Am I understood?"

Heckubus stopped laughing immediately. "Very well," mumbled the robot. "You don't have to be so snooty about it."

Heckubus sulked silently as the rest of the group completed their weapons check. Ganix had everyone evenly distribute any remaining ammunition, and other than a few minor bumps, bruises, and scrapes, no one was seriously injured. Within a few minutes, the group was ready to move out.

Ganix and Rodham took point, leading the group down the stairs, followed closely by Heckubus. Jack was up toward the front, too, with Grohm, Scallywag, and Faruuz not far behind. The stairs they were descending seemed to stretch on and on. Heckubus insisted his sensors could pick up where they ended, but the light from his ocular lamps didn't seem to reach that far. Jack wondered if the steps stretched all the way down to the bottom of the Pit.

As the group progressed, Jack began to shiver. He tried to wrap his jacket around himself tighter, but it didn't do any good. He began feeling extremely cold.

"Blimey," he heard Scallywag mutter. "It's gettin' bloody frigid in here."

"You feel it, too?" Jack asked.

"How could I not?" Scallywag responded. "It's like we're strolling into a cryo-freezer."

"What are you blathering about?" asked Heckubus. "There has been no change in temperature."

"Then why's it so kitten cold?" Rodham asked.

"It's not cold!" insisted Heckubus. "I'm reading the exact same temperature as when we entered this area. Nothing has changed."

"Yer wrong; something has changed," said Scallywag. "I'm freezing me bits off!"

"If it were truly cold, we'd see ice crystals on the walls," said Heckubus. "Your breath would be visible in the air. There would be signs other than your incessant whining."

Jack let out a deep breath. Sure enough, there was nothing. Heckubus was right, yet he was cold, and it was getting worse the further down the stairs he seemed to travel.

"Suck it up," ordered Ganix. "Keep moving."

Jack could see Ganix shivering as he continued marching forward. He could also hear the chattering teeth of the men behind him. Jack looked up at Grohm, who plodded ahead seemingly unfazed.

"Aren't you c-cold, big guy?" Jack asked.

Grohm snorted. "Grohm feels nothing."

"Leave it ta the r-robot and the r-rognock to miss out on a-all the f-fun," grumbled Scallywag.

What the heck is going on? Jack wondered. There was no wind in the stairwell. Nothing overtly to make him feel cold, but his entire body screamed as though he were being frozen. Even the parts protected by his jacket and clothes were cold, as if the sudden change in temperature had taken root in his very core.

But they kept walking, down and down, further and further, and with each step Jack could feel frigid fingers snaking their way through his body. His teeth were chattering and his knees were starting to wobble. Then, something changed.

It was subtle at first – something that could be dismissed as a byproduct of being so cold – a sudden tightness in the chest, a clenching of the stomach. But as time went on, it began to become something else entirely.

The cold was giving way to massive feelings of fear.

With each step downward, a feeling of dread wrapped itself tightly around Jack like a shroud. He felt his heart start to beat faster and his skin crawled as though something nefarious and unseen were stalking him from behind. Each step became more and more difficult as he felt an encroaching feeling of panic bubble up inside him.

Suddenly, Ganix and Rodham stopped, bringing the whole group to a standstill. The Major fell to one knee. Rodham pushed himself against the wall, eyes wide and full of fright, his breath coming in rapid spurts.

Jack sat and wrapped his arms around his knees, rocking himself back and forth, trying to get control. He looked around and saw the other members of his group in the pale light of Heckubus's lamps. Some were close to tears. Others had wild looks on their faces, as though they were afraid something horrible was about to jump out at them from the darkness.

"What's wrong?" asked Heckubus. "Why are we stopping?"

"Something's... not right..." breathed Ganix.

"Please," Jack heard Yeoman Porter whine. "Please, don't make us go down there..."

Rodham pounded his fist against the wall. "Evil kitten Deathlords!" he cursed. "What are they doing to us???"

Ganix turned to the group. "I know we're all feeling... something..." he said. "But we have to keep moving. We have to get out of here!"

"We need to go back!" Jack heard someone say.

"We can't go down there!" came another voice. "We're all gonna die!"

"What are you blathering about?" asked Heckubus. "We're only a few feet away from the bottom!"

"Shut it!" snapped Scallywag. The pirate was hugging himself tightly. "We ain't goin' down there!"

"What's happening to us?" lamented Rodham. "Why am I so scared?"

"It's a trap!" moaned Faruuz. "Bloody Deathlord trap ta kill us all!"

Jack could feel the ripple of panic coursing through the group. He felt like getting up and running all the way back to the top of the stairs. He'd never felt so scared before, and for the life of him, he had no idea why.

"Listen to me!" shouted Ganix. "It's not a trap! It's a trick. There's nothing to be scared of here. Control your fear!"

Jack heard someone sob. "I can't," came a voice.

"We need to go back!" came another.

"You're soldiers in the Imperial Space Force!" barked Ganix. "Remember your training! Control your emotions!"

"We're all going to die!" someone wailed.

The group was paralyzed. They couldn't move forward, and Ganix wasn't letting them retreat. Jack closed his eyes as commotion erupted around him. He focused on the back of his head, like before, and asked the question...

What's happening to us?

Jack felt his head buzz, and instantly, he knew what was going on. He looked up at Grohm, who was standing by him, gazing at the group curiously.

"Grohm," said Jack. "Can you feel anything?"

"No," Grohm replied.

"So you're not scared?"

"Grohm is not weak."

"Good," said Jack. "I need you to do something."

Grohm raised his eyebrow. Ganix turned to look at Jack, his face drawn and tight as he willed himself to remain calm.

"What's going on, Jack?" the Major demanded.

"Down in that room, there's an access orb," explained Jack. "It's making us feel this way. It's like... some type of Deathlord security system to keep anyone but them from accessing that room. I need to go down there and shut it off."

"An access orb?" asked Ganix.

"Like the kind the Ancients use," said Jack. "To control their technology. I used one earlier on my planet."

"Only the Princess has the power to access Ancient technology," said Ganix.

"This isn't from the Ancients," said Jack. "This is from the Deathlords."

"How..." mumbled Ganix. "How can they..."

"I don't know!" said Jack. "But if I can get to it... if I can turn it off... we'll go back to normal."

"Then do it!" cried Scallywag.

"I'll do it," said Heckubus. "Whatever is happening with you organics is not affecting me in the slightest!"

"You can't," said Jack. "You need a living consciousness to access the orb."

"I take offense at the idea that I do not have a consciousness, Earthman," said Heckubus.

"If you touch that orb, it will fry every circuit in your body," said Jack.

"Very well," replied Heckubus. "I take back my taking of offense."

"Grohm do it," said Grohm.

"You can't. You don't know how," said Jack. "It's got to be me. My ship will guide me on how to turn it off."

Ganix nodded. "If you can really turn this off… you should go."

Jack looked up at Grohm. "I need you to take me down there," he said. "No matter how much I scream, or struggle, or whatever… you need to make me touch that orb."

Grohm squinted at Jack and nodded.

Jack took a deep breath. *This is totally going to suck*, he thought.

"Let's do it," Jack said.

Grohm grabbed Jack and slung him under his arm. Jack dangled there like a puppy in the grip of its master as Grohm continued walking down the stairs. The group watched them go.

Instantly, Jack regretted the idea. Without the group to slow him down, Grohm was taking the steps faster, and with each one, sheer panic was rising in Jack's gut. Every horrible, terrifying thing ever invented was racing though his mind. The monster under the bed, the haunted house in the lightning storm, the creepy-crawlies walking all over his body — it all came flooding back to him.

Jack started to struggle against Grohm's grip. He wanted to get away, he wanted to run, but the Rognok's hold was too strong.

Jack shouted and screamed and kicked and punched, but it was no use. He was marching further and further into his worst nightmare, and there was nothing he could do to stop it.

Then, Grohm hit the last step. Jack saw a ghostly white ball floating in the darkness a few feet away, and the very sight of it sent a wave of terror rippling down his spine. A large two-pronged fork, jutting up from the ground cradled the orb. Jack screamed as Grohm began to approach it.

All thought in Jack's head gave way to panic. He'd forgotten where he was; he'd forgotten what he was supposed to do. The only thing he knew was he needed to get away from that orb — that horrible, horrible orb.

Jack's throat burned as he shrieked and cried, desperately trying to wriggle out of Grohm's grasp, but the Rognok marched forward relentlessly. Jack felt his gut wrench and churn in despair, and blood pumped painfully behind his eyes as his heart raced so fast it felt as though it were about to burst from his chest.

Finally, they were before the orb. Jack gazed at it in utter horror as it seemed to dig into his mind and pull forth every terrifying, awful memory Jack had ever had. Hot tears streaked down Jack's face, and he screamed uncontrollably.

He felt Grohm grab his wrist with a steely, vice-like grip and move his hand toward the orb. Jack fought and struggled, not wanting to touch it, not wanting to look at it. But the Rognok was too powerful, and with one last push, Grohm laid Jack's hand flat on the orb.

Jack felt a spark as soon as his hand made contact and his entire body began to buzz. Images of the most horrible kind flashed into his mind. Blood, death, decay, loss, sorrow, pain, murder, war, hopelessness — they all took shape in his mind's eye. It was so overwhelming, so unrelenting, Jack could feel himself getting lost in the avalanche of dread as it crashed over him.

But somewhere, in all the chaos that assaulted him, Jack could feel his head buzzing in that familiar place in the back of his mind, as though something were reaching out, worming its way through the images bombarding Jack.

Jack clung onto that tiny string of salvation for dear life, following it like a lifeline, until the images all disappeared and there was only a twisted, pulsing, purple and green stone before him. Jack reached out and touched the stone, and instantly it shriveled up and vanished, its sickly light dying.

Suddenly, the vision disappeared, and Jack was back in Grohm's arms. His head hurt, his throat burned, and his eyes felt watery... but the overwhelming feelings of fear had mercifully gone away.

"I was right," breathed Jack. "That totally sucked..."

Grohm snorted. Jack, still slung underneath the massive alien's arm, looked up at Grohm. "It's okay," said Jack. "You can put me down now."

Grohm set him on the floor, and Jack collapsed to his knees. As soon as Jack's hand had left the orb, it had disappeared, and the two-pronged fork, which had held it in place, had sunk into the black stone floor.

The room around them began to change. Torches hanging on the walls sparked to life, bathing the room in the warm glow of fire. Ashen pillars rose up from the ground, growing toward the high, cathedral-like vaulted ceiling.

A platform rose up from the ground ten feet from where Jack and Grohm stood; steps formed leading up toward the platform. The walls morphed, revealing large, engraved symbols that glowed a dim green and pulsed slightly.

Breathing deeply and trying to recover, Jack looked around as the room took form.

"Jack?" he heard a voice say.

Jack turned and saw his companions enter the room. Ganix rushed up to him and knelt at his side. "You okay, son?" he asked.

"Oh, peachy," said Jack, his head throbbing.

"We heard you screaming," said Yeoman Porter. "It sounded like you were dying. Half of us started running away."

"That took some guts, kid," said Rodham. "Good work."

"Aye," said Scallywag. "Who knew such a little man would have such big stones, eh?"

Scallywag elbowed Faruuz. "Yeah," mumbled the alien. "Ya did good, I guess."

"Thanks," said Jack.

Ganix helped Jack to his feet as the group gazed around the room cautiously.

"What is this place?" mumbled Rodham.

"Judging from the architectural style, it would appear to be some type of place of worship," said Heckubus.

"Like a church?" asked Jack.

"Most depressing bloody church I've ever seen," said Scallywag.

"Whatever it is, it's got a way out," said Ganix. "Everyone, weapons ready — teams of two. Let's find our exit."

The group broke apart and began searching the room. It was larger than Jack had previously thought, the black and grey stone that comprised it almost danced with the shadows in the flickering light of the mounted torches.

Jack and Grohm walked along the wall of the room; the strange glyphs and symbols emblazoned on it pulsed slowly with light. Jack checked his mental map, but it made no mention of where the exit was within the room. Jack just knew it was there.

As they walked, they met up with Faruuz and Scallywag, who approached them from the opposite direction.

"Anything?" Scallywag asked.

Jack shook his head. "Nothing. Just solid wall."

"Could it be like the cliff entrance?" asked Scallywag. "Do ya need to ask yer ship to let us out again?"

"Maybe, but I don't think so," said Jack. "Something about this place is... different."

"Different, how?" asked Scallywag.

"I don't know," replied Jack. "It's like... being in the Principal's office."

Scallywag and Faruuz exchanged a look. "The what?" they both asked.

"It's a place where you only go if you're in really bad trouble," said Jack. "You know, you don't choose to go to the Principal's office. You're summoned there so he can yell at you and dish out punishment, and you're not allowed to leave until he says so."

"Oy, sounds like me second wife," said Faruuz thoughtfully. "Me first one, too, come ta think of it."

"Yeah, this Principal fellow sounds like a right ol' browner," said Scallywag. "But if there's someone around here who can let us out, we need ta find him right quick. Yer ship got anything to say about that?"

"I don't know," said Jack with an exhausted sigh. "It's not like it speaks to me. I just get these images and... feelings."

"But ya can communicate with it, yeah?" asked Scallywag.

Jack nodded. "I think so."

"Well then, tell it to stop lollygaggin' and show you a blasted picture of the bloody exit," said Scallywag.

Jack focused on the back of his mind and felt the buzzing sensation there. He asked for his ship to show him a way out, but the only thing he got in response was a small feeling of rejection.

"Well?" prodded the pirate.

Jack furrowed his brow. "It's... not working," said Jack.

"Whaddya mean it's not working?" growled Faruuz.

"It's not telling me anything!" said Jack. "In fact, it's almost like it *can't* tell me the answer... like it isn't able to."

"Ask it again," instructed Scallywag.

"But—"

"Oy, yer ship led us here for a reason," said Scallywag. "Ya said it told you this was the way out, so either yer asking the wrong question or yer ship has one nasty sense o' humor. Either way, find out what's going on!"

Jack pouted, but he knew Scallywag was right. The way out was somewhere in this room; he was sure of it. He just needed to find it. Jack focused on the back of his mind again and tried asking the same question a different way, but for some reason he wasn't getting a response. He asked again, and again there was no response. After the third time without an acknowledgement from the ship, Jack was starting to get worried, but his fears quickly vanished when a cry rang out.

"MAJOR!" the voice resounded, echoing slightly throughout the cavernous room.

Immediately, Jack, Grohm, Faruuz, and Scallywag ran toward the shout. At the base of the steps leading to the raised platform stood Rodham and Porter, both with their weapons trained toward the top.

"Major!" called Porter again. "Over here!"

Ganix ran up, his weapon ready, and the rest of the group crowded around them.

"What is it?" asked Ganix.

"Eyes up top, sir," said Rodham.

Everyone turned and looked at the platform. At its peak was a large throne, twisted, gnarled, and opulent, made from veined black rock. It looked out on the room, towering over everything below it intimidatingly. There were no torches around it, so it was draped in shadow but still visible from below.

However, that wasn't the disturbing thing. There appeared to be someone sitting on the throne – a shadowy figure, clad in aged and faded black robes.

"Who the bloody hell is that?" muttered Scallywag.

"Crikey, ya don't think that's the sodding Principal, do ya?" asked Faruuz.

Jack looked up at the throne. It was hard to see anything at the top of the platform.

"Everyone, stay back," ordered Ganix.

The group moved away from the base of the platform cautiously.

"Heckubus," said Ganix. "Get some light up there."

Heckubus reactivated his ocular lamps, blasting a spotlight on the robed figure on the throne. It did not move, sitting silently on its perch, its head down, and its heavy hood covering its face.

"Orders, Major?" Rodham asked.

Ganix looked up at the robed figure for a moment, pondering his next move.

"Cover me," he finally said.

"You're not seriously going up there," grunted Rodham.

"We've come this far," said Ganix. "Whoever that is might be our key to getting out of here."

"I'll go," said Rodham.

"No," said Ganix. "Stay back and cover me from here."

"But if you die—"

"Then you're in charge," said Ganix.

Rodham scowled, but demurred to his commanding officer. Ganix took a few steps toward the platform, never taking his eyes off the figure at the top. Jack got a sinking feeling in the pit of his stomach as he watched Ganix approach the stairs leading up to the throne.

I've got a bad feeling about this, thought Jack.

Then, as Ganix placed his foot on the first step, a deep, rumbling voice echoed throughout the room.

"Kneel before your master..."

To a man, the group took a step back in alarm. Those who had weapons leveled them at the figure tensely, ready to fire.

The figure did not react. In response, it sat patiently on its throne, as if it were awaiting Jack and the others to obey its command.

The group stirred. A few of Ganix's men glanced at him nervously, waiting for some type of order to tell them how they should be reacting. Jack looked at him, too, but it was clear to anyone who could see Ganix's face that he was just as frightened and confused as the others.

After what seemed like an eternity, Ganix cleared his throat.

"I am Major Ganix of the Imperial Space Force," he said, trying to sound braver than he must have felt. "My men have you surrounded. Identify yourself."

The figure did not move at all in response. No sound came from it, not even the sound of breathing. The silence hung in the air like a foul smell, and Ganix's men began to twitch nervously.

"Identify yourself, or we will open fire," said Ganix more forcefully.

Then the voice rumbled from the figure again, echoing throughout the chamber...

"Kneel before your master..."

Jack could feel a chill run up his spine, and from the looks of those around him, he was not alone. The voice rattled inside his brain like broken glass and made his teeth set on edge.

"Um... maybe we should do what the creepy robed guy wants?" Jack suggested, his voice sounding meek after the rumblings of the figure before them.

"That thing is a Deathlord," sneered Sergeant Rodham. "I'd rather die than kneel before it—"

No sooner had the words left his mouth than the figure's hand shot forth, reaching toward him. Sergeant Rodham jerked upright, his body arcing backwards. His mouth opened in a terrifying scream as the ghostly form of his body ripped from his skin and snaked with frightening speed to the clawed fingers of the robed figure.

Rodham's lifeless body crumpled to the ground.

"NO!" screamed Ganix. Without wasting another moment, he opened fire on the figure, and those in the group with weapons followed suit, unleashing deadly plasma blasts upon the seated figure with a fury.

Jack watched for what seemed like an eternity as his group blasted away at the figure, until finally, they ceased fire. The smell of burnt ozone from all the blaster fire assaulted Jack's nostrils, and he looked at the seated figure as it towered above them, unmoving. The only sound was the ragged, frightened breaths from the men in his group.

"Kneel before your master..." came the figure's voice again.

"Crikey," breathed Scallywag. "It's still alive..."

"Nothing could have survived that," cried Yeoman Porter. "We blasted him with direct fire for a good minute. How can it still be alive?"

"Probably because it was never alive to begin with," said Heckubus.

Jack looked at the robot. "What do you mean?" he asked.

"I'm getting no heat signature from the throne," said Heckubus. "There are no sounds of breathing, heartbeat, or any other signs of life. Whatever is sitting up there is definitely not organic."

"Probly because it's a bleedin' Deathlord!" grumbled Faruuz.

"Deathlords are not organics, true," replied Heckubus. "But they do possess energy signatures unique to their race, and I am not reading any such energy from whatever is sitting on that rather gaudy throne."

"Coulda shared that little tid-bit before we emptied half a battery into the blasted thing," muttered Scallywag.

"Oh, so *now* you want to hear my opinion?" chided Heckubus.

"If it's not alive, and it's not a Deathlord... then what is it?" asked Jack.

"If I had to guess, I'd say it's some sort of machine," replied Heckubus, the gears in his head audibly whirling.

"Whatever it is," said Ganix, "it has proven it can kill any of us it wants with a flick of its wrist."

"Only after he said he wouldn't... um, you know... do what it wants," said Jack. "I mean, if it wanted us dead, why ask us to kneel before it?"

Ganix scowled. It was obvious he did not like his options.

"Major?" prodded Yeoman Porter. "What should we do?"

Ganix looked at Jack and sighed. "I guess we kneel," he said.

Jack nodded and dropped to one knee, followed by Ganix. One by one, the others followed suit. Beside Jack, Grohm stood defiantly looking at the robed figure.

"Hey, big guy," whispered Jack. "C'mon, kneel."

"Grohm kneels before no one," grumbled the Rognok.

Scallywag rolled his eyes. "Here we go... blasted Rognok pride."

"Tell you what," said Jack, ignoring Scallywag's comments. "Just kneel until we find a way out of here."

"Grohm kneels before no one."

"We won't tell anyone, promise."

"Grohm kneels before—"

"Okay, okay," said Jack. "What about sitting? Will Grohm *sit* before someone?"

Grohm's large black and red eyes looked at Jack suspiciously.

"Just get down here with the rest of us for a little while," said Jack. "And when we find a way out of here, you can start smashing stuff to make up for it, okay?"

Grohm snorted, glancing back up toward the robed figure, which seemed to be waiting patiently. Finally, the large Rognok lowered himself to the floor, sitting down beside Jack.

"Thanks, big guy," said Jack.

The Rognok grunted defiantly. "Grohm smash," he grumbled.

"Promise," said Jack, with a nod. "You can smash all you want."

Ganix looked around at the group, now all on their knees. His eyes moved to the robed figure on the throne before them, sitting still and silent. "Now what?" he wondered aloud.

Then, a low hum began to emanate from all around them. A few of the men clasped their hands to their ears as the hum grew louder. Jack could suddenly feel the pressure of the sound building around his body, as though heavy weights were being stacked on his back. All said, it was not the most pleasant feeling he'd ever experienced.

The robed figure's head moved. For the first time it lifted its gaze at the group, revealing itself.

It had no face; instead it was composed of smooth black stone with three holes in it, two where the eyes should have been, and one where the mouth should have been. Each hole was large, about the size of a fist, and each began to glow with an eerie white light.

The floor before the throne began to warp and twist, growing into a perverted looking altar adorned with various jagged edges and spikes. In the center of the altar, a holographic image of a planet appeared, hovering over it.

The planet was white, dry, and pocked with craters. In a way, Jack thought it looked like Earth's moon, but something was off about it. It seemed to glow, and the surface of the planet appeared to shift slightly as though the ground itself were alive and moving.

"Behold," echoed the chilling voice of the figure. "The ghost planet of Terahades."

"Ghost planet?" muttered Jack, wondering what the heck that meant.

"After our victory at the battle of Tarchimache," continued the figure, "during the scourge, our enemy grew desperate."

"The Scourge," gasped Ganix.

Jack could see the look of surprise on the Major's face. "He's talking about the time when the Ancients and their technology disappeared?" Jack asked.

"Looks like they didn't disappear, lad," muttered Scallywag. "Apparently they were exterminated."

Before Jack could ask anything else, the figure continued.

"We pursued our enemy as they retreated into the Veil Nebula…" the voice droned. As it did, the image of the planet faded to a star map, pointing out the site of the nebula to which it was referring. "Resistance was slim. We were confident we would be able to destroy them with ease. But we underestimated our enemy."

The image of the Veil Nebula grew, showing Jack and the others a beautiful blue and purple cloud that stretched out far and wide across space.

"The nebula interfered with our technology, rendering us blind to the trap our enemy had set until it was too late. During the Battle of the Veil, our enemy was somehow able to manifest the planet of Terahades, trapping our armada within its core."

"They did what now?" asked Jack.

"The Ancients…" said Ganix. "It's saying they manifested a *planet*."

"You mean that quantum stuff?" asked Jack. "They made an entire planet appear out of nowhere?"

"Interesting…" said Heckubus, twiddling his fingers. "There's never been a recorded quantum manifestation of something as large and complex as a planet."

"We had underestimated the abilities of our enemy," the figure continued. "Terahades became the prison which held the bulk of our armada. The planet itself is in a constant state of dimensional flux. Whether this was intentional or evidence of our enemies' inability to control their powers, we do not know. But because of the nature of its creation, it exists, and yet, it does not exist…"

The image above the altar shifted back to that of the planet. "Terahades is constantly moving through dimensions, even though it is always anchored in our own. Because of this flux, the planet can be accessed from your space and time, but those trapped there cannot leave it."

"Brilliant," said Heckubus. "If the planet is constantly moving through dimensions, those trapped inside it – or even on the surface of it for that matter, would never be able to leave. If they did, the chances of them coming back to their own space and time would be astronomically slim."

"So ya can check in, but ya can never check out," muttered Scallywag. "Sounds like hell."

"Our enemy designed Terahades to be the perfect prison," continued the figure. "After the battle, they set about making it impossible for anyone to gain access to it, for fear of the possibility that our invincible armada might once again be released upon the universe. The Veil keeps its location hidden from all technology. The enemy seeded the nebulous cloud surrounding the Terahades oasis with mines to ensure the destruction of any ship that approaches it. Even if you were to find the ghost planet, it is protected by a planet-wide energy shield strong enough to withstand even our most powerful weapons."

"A planet-wide shield?" said Scallywag. "How's that even possible?"

"The energy requirements for a shield that big alone are prohibitive," said Heckubus. "And to have it be strong enough to keep out all enemy weapons' fire…"

"Sounds like the Ancients didn't mess around," said Jack.

"That's putting it mildly," said Ganix.

"And past the energy shield is the last line of the Ghost Planet's defenses," said the figure. "The surface of the planet itself is designed to drain the life force out of any who sets foot upon it."

"Dude…" whispered Jack. As if all that other stuff wasn't cool enough, the planet also had life-sucking dirt to boot.

"Our brothers have been trapped in Terahades for far too long," rumbled the figure. "You are commanded to find this ghost planet and free those confined within it. When you do, our invincible armada will once again sweep across the galaxy and finish our glorious work."

The holographic image of Terahades disappeared, and the altar began to deconstruct itself, receding back into the floor from which it had come. The lights from the figure's face faded, and it slumped back into its throne once more.

"Go forth and serve your Masters," echoed the voice. "Serve the Lords of the Void."

A moment passed as the group sat in silence.

"Observer help us…" muttered Yeoman Porter. "They must be the great enemy the history books talk about – the ones that destroyed the Ancients!"

"You mean you've never heard of these 'Lords of the Void' guys before?" asked Jack.

"Never by that name," said Ganix. "But if they're who the Deathlords answer to, then we may be in even more trouble than we thought."

"Well, if that little slide-show is any indication of what they're up against, I'd say we're pretty safe," said Scallywag as he got to his feet. "If the Ancients designed that prison ta keep these Lords o' the Void in, I'm confident we ain't seeing 'em anytime soon."

"I wish I could share your optimism, pirate," said Ganix.

"Aye? What's got ya down, Major — the hidden minefield, the impenetrable planetary shield, or the life-draining multidimensional planet? Even if the Deathlords were able ta find this planet, it would take more firepower than their entire fleet has to get past all the defenses the Ancients put in place."

"True, it might take more than what the Deathlords have to get past all those defenses," said Ganix. "Or, it would take just one person with the ability to control Ancient technology."

Jack felt a lump grow in his throat. "Anna," he said.

Ganix nodded. "We thought the Deathlords might want to kill her, or take her alive to hold the Empire hostage. But if this thing is really a message from their masters, then that means they're planning to use the Princess to free whatever is trapped there."

"With an armada of ships that was able to defeat the Ancients at their side, they'd be unstoppable!" said Yeoman Porter. "With the Deathlords, our ships at least stand a chance, but against that…"

Ganix got to his feet. "We need to rescue the Princess," he said. "The fate of the universe depends on it."

"Great plan, Major," said Scallywag. "Except for the part 'bout how we still have no bloody clue how to get out of this hole."

Suddenly, the steps to the platform before them began to rumble. The rest of the group scrambled to their feet and quickly leveled their guns at the area as it morphed and opened up into a doorway.

Standing in that doorway, smiling his big, white, toothy grin, was none other than Professor Green.

"Ah! Jack! There you are!" he said cheerily, as if he had simply run into Jack during a leisurely stroll.

The entire group lowered their weapons and looked at Green with surprise. "Professor?" asked Jack, relieved to see a familiar face. Jack ran up and threw his arms around him.

"Sorry it took so long, my boy," said Green, patting Jack good-naturedly on the back. "Glad to see you're alive! And it seems you've met some friends?"

The group all stared dumbly at the overly cheery new arrival. Faruuz raised his hand awkwardly and waved.

"How did you find us?" asked Jack, breaking away from his embrace.

"Funny thing, that," smiled Green. "I basically had to deconstruct the entire Deathlord alphabet by accessing their databases. It's quite a complicated language, but I was able to— well, I'll spare you the details. But after accessing this panel in one of their generator rooms, I got a message telling me I needed to come here and open this door."

"A message?" asked Jack.

"Yes," replied Green. "I thought it rather curious, since it's entirely unlikely the Deathlords would have directed me to such an obscure location on their own ship. I mean, if they knew where I was, why not just send soldiers to capture me instead of such a polite message? So I took the chance that you'd somehow found a way to communicate with me. Always nice to see I was

right. Good thing, too, since it seems this area can only be accessed from the outside."

Jack smiled. Could it be his ship had found the Professor and told him where to go?

Spaceship, you totally rule, thought Jack.

Green glanced up at the robed robot on the throne, and looked around the room curiously before settling back on the rag tag group before him.

"I say, this is all rather… new," said the Professor. "Have I missed anything important?"

CHAPTER ✴ 28

Anna's eyes fluttered open, her vision eventually focusing on the dull grey ceiling of her cell, one solitary light shining brightly, illuminating the whole room. Her head throbbed painfully and her entire body was stiff.

What happened? she wondered. *What did they do to me?*

She sat up on her hard metal bed and grabbed her temples, sucking air between her teeth sharply as her head protested the movement. She massaged the sides of her forehead slowly to try to drive away the unrelenting throbbing. She swung her legs over the side of her resting place, but they hung numb and useless until she began to knead them with her fingers. Sensation returned in a flurry of pins-and-needles that made her grit her teeth.

She tried to remember what had happened but the memories were elusive and hazy. She remembered the fearsome Deathlord that had entered the room, but the details of their conversation and what had happened after that were a blur.

One thing did spring to her mind, however. She seemed to remember a sharp pain in the back of her head, right before passing out. She reached back and felt around, but there was no wound as far as she could tell. She felt for something – anything that might give her a clue as to what had happened. She pulled her hand back, half expecting to see traces of blood, but her fingers were clean. Other than feeling as though she had drunk an entire case of Raxxagon Ale on her own, she seemed to be perfectly fine.

No, they had to have done something to me, Anna thought. *They wouldn't have just knocked me out for no reason. They must have a plan.*

Anna pushed herself to her feet. Her brain buzzed in response, and the room tilted at odd angles for a moment before she shook her head and was able to re-establish her sense of balance. Once the cobwebs had cleared, she started to check her arms to look for any strange marks -- any sign that the Deathlords may have done something to her while she was unconscious. She looked down her shirt, rolled up her pant legs, and felt along her back as far as she could reach. Still, there was nothing out of the ordinary.

In a way, not finding something wrong worried her more than if she had found an incision, a mark, or anything that might have confirmed her suspicions. Anna's mind reeled with numerous possibilities of what could have happened while she was unconscious, and each was worse than the one before it.

There was still so much that wasn't known about the Deathlords. The extent of their powers, the scope of their technology, the depths of their depravity – none of it had been investigated or recorded with any semblance of accuracy. The Empire's alien foes remained as much a mystery as they had been when they had first attacked. As far as Anna was aware, she was the only person alive who'd actually carried on some form of conversation with a Deathlord.

And not just any Deathlord… just thinking of the one who had visited her made her skin crawl and her spine shiver. The power and fury that raged behind those horrible red eyes set off alarm bells deep within her blood. She had been able to sense his power, almost like she did when she was operating an Ancient device. But this power was unlike anything she'd ever experienced. In some respects, it seemed of greater intensity than she had ever encountered before from the Ancients. However, that may have just been her fear amplifying what she had felt.

Regardless, she was sure the Deathlord had used his power on her, somehow.

Something was wrong, and she needed to figure out what.

Anna lowered herself to the ground, sitting on her knees and folding her arms across her chest like the Luminadric Monks had taught her. She was going to have to meditate, to allow herself to get in touch with her trinity.

The monks had always said that understanding her trinity would give Anna insight into her very being. Control over it would allow her to heal any sickness or wound she had suffered, be it physical, emotional, or spiritual. Unfortunately, Anna had not spent as much time at her lessons as her tutors would have liked – and now that she needed to employ the discipline, she felt even guiltier for not having been more diligent in her studies.

She closed her eyes and breathed deeply, trying to access the separate parts of her trinity – the mind, body, and spirit – and bring them together, but it was difficult to focus. She felt a warm sensation at the bottom of her chest where her ribcage ended, and tried to grab onto that with her mind, using it as the focal point of her meditation. She had not reached out for her trinity in a long time, and it was proving difficult to assemble, like trying to put together a puzzle in the dark.

She focused harder, attempting to bring the three forces of her being together. Once she made contact with her trinity, she'd be able to tune into her body and figure out if the Deathlords had done something to her. But before she could achieve that, she heard a noise.

She opened her eyes and looked at the door to her cell. It had come from the other side – some type of commotion. The sounds were dull, and it was hard to make out what they were, but they didn't last long.

Anna got to her feet and stared at the entrance to her captivity suddenly worried that the Deathlord Supreme may have returned. *Maybe whatever he's doing to me, he's not finished*, Anna thought. *Maybe he's returned to complete the job.*

Anna readied herself for another showdown. She was heir to the largest and greatest Empire the universe had ever known. No matter how scared she felt, no matter how much pain was inflicted on her, she was determined to endure. She was the final Princess of Regalus Prime, and she would not allow herself to go down meekly.

The locks on the door disengaged with an ominous *clunk*.

Anna's eyes narrowed. Her gut tightening, she readied herself.

The door slid open with a hiss.

Anna's eyes widened with surprise. Standing in the doorway was not the Deathlord Supreme. There, clad in his glorious blue and white armor, stood Shepherd – her shining knight. Her savior.

"Shepherd!" Anna squealed, her heart thumping in her chest.

"Princess—" Shepherd started. Anna did not give him time to finish talking. She rushed toward him, wrapping her arms around him and hugging his cold, armored body as tightly as she could. She could feel salty tears of happiness stream down her cheeks, and the steely resolve she had mustered to meet her fate mere moments before melted away into a tidal wave of relief that washed over her.

"You came!" she said, trying not to cry like a child. "You're here!"

She felt his arms gently return her embrace. She looked up at him as his helmet withdrew, revealing a face lined with both worry and relief.

"Are you okay?" Shepherd asked. "Did they do anything to you?"

"I don't know," Anna responded. "I'm not hurt, but... I think they did do something."

Shepherd scowled. "We'll need to deal with it later," he said. "I just took out two of their guards. I don't know how long we have until they're alerted to my presence."

Anna nodded, trying to reel in her gushing happiness. She could thank Shepherd later. Right now, they were both still in a great deal of danger – though with her Paragon back at her side, Anna felt much safer than she had in a long while.

"Lead the way," she said.

Shepherd nodded, his helmet re-enveloping his face. "Stay close," he ordered.

Shepherd began moving back down the long corridor with Anna not far behind. He moved his head back and forth as he walked, slightly crouched, like a beast stalking its prey. Anna could tell he was scanning the area with his armor, looking for any sign of trouble.

"Where's the Professor?" she asked, trying to keep up with his brisk pace. "Is he with you?"

"We split up," said Shepherd. "He was guiding me to you but had to break off to keep from being detected. We're going to head to a rendezvous point he set and meet with him."

"And Jack?" Anna asked.

Shepherd turned and looked at her. "If he's alive, we'll find him," he said.

"They promised me they wouldn't kill him," Anna said.

Anna could tell how stupid that sounded as soon as she had said it. She was almost glad she couldn't see Shepherd's face behind his helmet just then. But she had to hold onto hope her friend was still alive.

"Don't worry," said Shepherd, trying to sound reassuring. "We're going to get out of here. All of us."

With a loud *WHOOSH,* purple light flashed all around them. Anna blinked, and felt her breath catch in her throat as she realized they were now surrounded on all sides by Deathlords, weapons at ready. Three had appeared in the hallway before them, and three were positioned behind them, boxing them in.

Before she even had a chance to fully grasp the situation, Shepherd was reacting. He reached out his hands and generated two force-shield walls of golden light on either side of them just in time to block the volley of plasma fire that erupted from the soldiers.

Shepherd pushed the shield wall behind them, and it rocketed toward the three Dark Soldiers who were blocking the path they'd just come from. It slammed into the Deathlords, sending them hurtling backwards. They finally came to a crushing stop when they hit the walled entrance into Anna's former cell. The golden barrier came to rest against them with a sickening crunch, pinning them there.

Shepherd unleashed his quad-cannons and let the shield wall dissipate. The three Deathlords started to drop, no longer propped up by the energy barrier, only to be hit expertly with well-placed plasma blasts before they erupted into puffs of grainy black clouds.

With those Deathlords dispatched, Shepherd turned. He gave the other force field a nudge, and it rammed into the three soldiers before him, knocking them back. Shepherd opened a hole in his shield and fired both his quad-cannons, making short work of the enemies on the other side of the barrier.

The whole thing was over almost as fast as it had started.

"Run," he ordered, taking off down the hall.

Anna did not need to be told twice. She began to run, staying close to Shepherd. The two of them sprinted down the corridor for a few more seconds before making another turn down an adjoining hallway. Anna hoped Shepherd knew where he was going, because already she was feeling hopelessly turned around. The corridors all looked alike as far as she could tell.

As they rounded a corner, they saw a group of six Dark Soldiers before them, taking aim with plasma rifles. Shepherd threw up a hand, pulsing a circular force shield in the middle of the group like an explosion. They flew in all directions from the sudden appearance and expansion of his energy field.

In a swift motion, Shepherd reached behind him and grabbed his batons, the two sticks crackling to life. He twirled them in a blinding flurry as he rushed through the group, striking each Deathlord in turn as he passed without slowing down. Anna followed not far behind, just close enough to feel the grainy black sand-like dust of the Deathlords' disintegrating bodies mist over her.

More flashes of purple came from behind. Without slowing down, Shepherd erected a shield barrier behind them to block the new volley of plasma fire. The shield trailed along with them, giving them continuous cover as they ran.

More Dark Soldiers appeared before them, and Shepherd threw himself into the group, energy batons flashing, making quick work of the adversaries. A few Deathlords managed to fire off some shots before Shepherd dispatched them, but his armor simply absorbed the blasts without incident.

Suddenly, another flash of purple occurred, but this time, instead of Dark Soldiers, there were simply two disk-shaped objects about the size of bicycle tires in front of and behind them. The smooth black disks had a green core that pulsed rapidly.

Shepherd grabbed Anna and pulled her close, crouching over her and shielding her with his body. Their rear protective shield disappeared and a domed energy barrier materialized around them just as the two disks exploded.

Anna felt the ground beneath her tremble with the explosion, and Shepherd grunted from the impact against his shields. She looked up and saw tiny black splinters sticking to the outside of the shield, slowly pushing their way in as though the barrier was nothing more than a pin cushion. The needle-like black shrapnel slowly wormed its way past their protection.

Shepherd glanced at the shards and pushed his shield back, expanding it around them to allow for more room.

"Stay down," he ordered as he got to his feet.

Anna looked up to see one of the dark splinters had made it through the shield barrier. It shot directly at Shepherd fast as an arrow. Shepherd raised his baton in time, swatting it away like an annoying bug.

A few more splinters rocketed forth, and again, Shepherd deflected them.

Anna shrieked as one splinter unexpectedly shot by her, ripping her sleeve as it moved toward Shepherd. The Paragon turned in time for the splinter to embed itself in the shin guard of his armor. It sparked on impact and the splinter fell smoking and limp to the ground.

Shepherd reached out his batons and touched the sides of his shield, channeling crackling white energy from his weapons into the barrier. Tendrils of electric white light streaked across the dome, hitting and charring the numerous splinters still trying to worm their way through.

The charge to the shield caused it to dissipate, and the splinters dropped to the ground around Shepherd and Anna harmlessly.

However, no sooner was his shield gone than more volleys of plasma fire struck Shepherd. Anna turned and saw six Dark Soldiers marching down the hallway, firing at them. Shepherd threw up a shield wall, but a flash of purple light made six more Dark Soldiers materialize in front of them.

He erected another shield barrier, but before the two had time to react, more Dark Soldiers teleported in behind Shepherd's shields. The Paragon quickly fired his quad-cannons and exchanged rounds with the Deathlords, absorbing their fire while trying to dispatch them.

More Deathlords continued to appear behind his shield walls, firing with annoying accuracy at the Paragon, his armor sparking and crackling with each direct hit, smoke wisping from each impact. Shepherd kept his shield walls up and engaged the Dark Soldiers as they came, but no sooner did he dispose of one than two more appeared in its place, each heralded by the sickening flash of purple teleportation light.

There are too many! Anna thought with rising panic. *They just keep coming! We'll never be able to get past them!*

Shepherd kept firing. He let one of his shields drop and rematerialized it closer to him. He pushed it out, allowing it to rocket into one front of the advancing enemy, clearing the way as he focused his fire on the Deathlords behind them.

As soon as he had cleared a path, he started inching his way down the corridor, a new shield wall materializing to give him cover. "Princess!" he called out. "Keep moving!"

He intended to fight their way out; that much was clear. Anna got up to move with him when suddenly she felt a strange sensation, as though two sharp hooks had dug into her back.

Anna cried out in pain. She didn't see the black streak rushing up behind her. Shepherd unleashed rapid fire blasts at it, but it jumped and twirled, dodging the blasts until it was close enough to Anna to yank her toward it, reeling in the invisible hooks that had caught her.

The Deathlord crouched behind Anna, using her as a shield to protect itself from Shepherd. One clawed hand was grasped tightly around her neck, the other hovered above her chest, tugging at her soul with whatever wicked magic the Deathlords seemed to possess. Anna stood helpless, feeling the cold invisible hooks of the Deathlord as they threatened to rip the very life from her.

Shepherd aimed his quad cannons toward the Deathlord, but refrained from firing for fear of hitting Anna. New shield walls had sprung up close by, ensuring that no other Deathlords would be able to come to this one's aid.

The Deathlord and the Paragon eyed each other.

"Drop your shields, infidel," growled Vishni. "Or I will cull the child."

"You aren't going to hurt her," said Shepherd.

"I won't kill her," replied the Deathlord. "But I can assure you, I am more than willing to hurt her."

Anna screamed as the Deathlord tugged on her life force, and she felt the cold, strange sensation of death wash over her. Shepherd immediately retracted his quad cannons, raising his palms defensively.

"There's no need—" Shepherd said.

"Drop. Your. Shields," snarled the Deathlord.

Anna could feel a tear running down her cheek as she looked at Shepherd. She wanted to scream to him not to do it, but she couldn't speak. The Deathlord's grip around her neck was so tight, she could barely breathe.

Shepherd hesitated; then he let the golden walls of energy disappear.

Immediately, the Dark Soldiers took aim and opened fire on Shepherd, their angry red plasma blasts hitting him full on.

Shepherd crouched under the impact of the volley coming at him from all sides, his armor sparking in response, tendrils of electrical activity snaking around him as his suit absorbed the plasma fire.

Anna could do nothing but watch in wide-eyed horror as the Deathlords continued to fire on Shepherd unrelentingly. She felt the Deathlord who held her in his grasp stand up from his crouch, allowing himself to gloat over the Paragon.

"You are a fierce warrior," Vishni said. "But we are an army!"

Anna could hear Shepherd grunt as the Deathlords continued to fire. His arms were up defensively, each plasma blast sparking off his armor, their heated fury beginning to leave blackened marks that charred the once pristine metal, wisps of smoke curling off from the sites of impact. Anna wondered how much more punishment he could take.

"We are unstoppable," sneered Vishni. "We are unkillable. We are everlasting."

The Deathlords closed in on Shepherd, their increasing proximity causing their volleys to hit quicker and quicker, beating him down.

"We are Deathlords!" Vishni said triumphantly. "You cannot fight us. You cannot win. And there is no one here to save you."

Suddenly, a plasma blast streaked out of nowhere, slamming Vishni dead in the face. His body disintegrated instantly, leaving Anna mercifully free from his grasp.

More blasts rang out, hitting their marks as one Dark Soldier after another exploded in a puff of black mist until all of them were gone. Anna turned and saw a group standing defiantly in the hallway before her. They were soldiers in dirty and ragged Imperial uniforms, with strange aliens in their ranks. A robot was with them, as was Professor Green, and there, standing before them all, was Jack, armed with a small pistol and a big smile.

"I wouldn't say *no one*," said Jack.

"Jack!" exclaimed Anna, her heart leaping into her throat. She rushed up and wrapped her arms around him, hugging him tightly. She had never been so happy to see anyone in her whole life as in that very moment.

Jack laughed and returned the hug. "I see my timing is impeccable, as always," he said.

Anna loosened her grip and backed off, looking at Jack with relief. "I... I didn't know if you were still alive!"

"Takes more than a couple of Deathlords to kill old Jack," he smirked with the kind of false bravado Anna couldn't help but find endearing.

"Seriously?" mumbled a red Visini from behind.

"Oy, and I thought *you* were a blowhard, Scally," said his scaly companion.

"What?" shrugged Jack. "Can't a guy have a moment?"

"Princess," said one of the soldiers, stepping forward from the group. "I'm Major Ganix, with what remains of your Imperial guard. We are at your command, Your Majesty."

The soldiers all nodded their heads toward her in a sign of loyalty. Suddenly, Anna felt overwhelmed with emotion. Her friends were alive, and now she had an army to protect her. Things were starting to look up.

"Your service is most appreciated, Major," responded Anna.

"Major," said Shepherd coming up behind Anna, his helmet retracting to show his face. "Deploy your men around the Princess. We must protect her as we make our way to the ship."

Ganix nodded and jerked his head. Without a word, his men moved to Anna, forming a protective wall around her.

"Are you injured, Paragon Shepherd?" Ganix asked.

"I'll be fine," responded Shepherd. "My armor can withstand a lot of punishment. But we must get going before more Deathlords teleport in."

"Don't worry about that," said Jack, twirling his small laser pistol around his finger. "I just shut off all their teleporters."

Shepherd raised an eyebrow. "How'd you manage that?" he asked.

"Psychic spaceship," smiled Jack. "It's secretly controlling *everything*."

Shepherd and Anna looked at each other.

"It's a long story," said Jack.

"Apparently the Ancient spacecraft has interfaced with the Deathlord's central computer, and is using a psychic neural link with Jack to relay information to him *and* to take commands!" chirped Green excitedly.

"Okay..." said Jack. "So, not that long of a story after all."

"The Ancient spacecraft can psychically communicate with you even this far away?" said Anna. "That's amazing!"

"Can you lead us back to the ship?" asked Shepherd.

"Sure can," replied Jack, tapping his head. "Got a map of this whole place up in here."

"Then what are we bloody waiting for?" growled Faruuz as he turned to leave. "Not that this little reunion hasn't been touching an' all. But let's stop with the chit-chatting and get off this—"

Faruuz suddenly jerked upright as his ghostly image was violently torn from his body. The sickly white figure screamed as it shot down the hallway into the waiting clutches of the Deathlord Supreme, an army of Dark Soldiers behind him.

Faruuz's body crumpled to the floor with a sickening thump. Scallywag cried out.

"NO!" he screamed, immediately dropping to one knee and firing his pistols.

The rest of the group opened fire. The plasma blasts streaked toward Zarrod, heading right for their target. But with a flap of his cape, the blasts were deflected as though they were nothing. His arms shot out, batting away the volley of plasma fire with frightening speed, as though the powerful energy blasts were nothing more than annoying insects.

Then, a ball of ghostly light shot from his clawed hand and screamed toward the group.

"GET DOWN!" cried Shepherd as he raised his hand, lighting up a force field in front of his companions.

The golden barrier had barely formed before the frighteningly fast ball of energy made its way to the group. It slammed into the shield wall, shattering it like a glass window, sending Shepherd hurtling backwards as if the impact had hit him directly. The ball disintegrated after colliding with Shepherd's shield, its lingering force still powerful enough to knock the group back a few steps, interrupting their fire.

Zarrod reached out his hands, and the two Imperial soldiers closest to the front screamed as their souls ripped out from them and rocketed toward Zarrod's greedy claws. Anna watched in horror as their bodies fell limp to the ground and their ghost forms balled up in the Deathlord's Supreme's grasp.

The energy began to twist and spin, faster and faster. Zarrod brought his hands together, combining the two balls into a single mass that began to grow, larger and larger. The Deathlord held it at his side, nurturing it as it spun and grew more chaotic. It sounded like a thousand men were screaming out in agony as the twisting mass of ghostly energy grew to the size of a basketball. The Deathlord Supreme's fiery eyes seemed to glare directly at Anna.

"Fall back!" she heard Major Ganix yell. "Protect the Princess!"

Anna felt wind ripple by her as air began to get sucked toward the swirling mass of evil the Deathlord Supreme held between his hands. His Dark Soldiers stood, statuesque behind him, silent shadows witnessing his fury. She felt the Major's hand on her shoulder, trying to pull her away down the corridor, while the rest of the group stumbled back from the mighty Deathlord before them.

The sound of screams intensified, and she could taste the terror and dread in the air. Death was at the end of that hallway, and it was about to be unleashed.

The Deathlord extended his hands, pushing with a singular might. The ghostly ball stretched into a beam, rocketing toward the group with a twisted power and a fury unlike anything they had ever witnessed.

Anna caught a glimpse of a blue and white streak as Shepherd leapt forth to the front of the group, raising his hands and throwing up a blindingly bright shield enveloping the hallway before them.

The Deathlord's blast slammed into the shield and Shepherd slid back a good two feet before bracing himself against the impact. His shield flickered and groaned, as the shadow of the ghostly energy screamed against it, pounding at the barrier mercilessly.

To a man, the group looked at the Paragon before them, both amazed and frightened, not knowing what to make of the situation. It sounded as though a thunderstorm were raging against a closed window. Shepherd grunted, his armor shivering from the strain of resisting the onslaught from the Deathlord Supreme.

"MAJOR!" Shepherd yelled. "Get the Princess to the ship!"

Ganix moved up to Anna, gripping her arm, his voice thick with urgency. "Your Majesty," he said. "We must go!"

Anna glanced from Ganix's worried face back to Shepherd. "I'm not leaving him!" she said.

"You must!" barked Ganix, tugging at her arm.

"NO!" cried Anna, wrenching herself free from Ganix's grip. She moved for Shepherd, rushing up to him and wrapping her arms around him from behind. She could feel the violent vibration of his armor, and she could almost sense the struggle he was putting up to keep the shield alive.

"Princess, you must go!" yelled Shepherd over the screaming of the Deathlord Supreme's onslaught.

"I won't leave you behind!" Anna cried.

"Do not argue. Go!" he insisted.

Anna clung to him closely, refusing to let go, not wanting to let go. Her vision began to blur with tears.

"You can't..." whispered Anna, salty streaks of water dribbling down her cheeks and onto her lips. "You'll die..."

Shepherd turned his head away from his shield, seeing Jack walking up behind Anna. The boy's face looked at the Paragon's helmet, and Shepherd knew he understood the situation.

"Jack," said Shepherd. "Get her out of here... NOW."

Jack could see Shepherd struggling to keep his shield up against Zarrod's attack. He knew Shepherd was right; Jack had to get Anna as far away from the Deathlord Supreme as possible. He grabbed her by the arm and tried to lead her away.

"We gotta go, Anna," Jack said, trying to sound reassuring. "He'll be right behind us. C'mon…"

Anna resisted, holding onto Shepherd tightly.

"Shepherd…" she squeaked.

Shepherd looked down at her. Though his helmet hid his face completely, she could hear the sadness in his voice.

"Anna, please…" he said softly.

Anna could feel her warm tears streaming down her face, the cold armor of the Paragon on her hand, and the soft grip of Jack on her wrist. She felt as though she were being torn in two, unable to find the strength to make the choice she knew she had to.

Then, she felt Jack's grip on her become firmer. She suddenly felt him beside her. When she turned and looked at him, she saw on his face a look that told her he — this boy who had lost everything he loved mere hours ago — knew what she was feeling. When he spoke, he understood the decision she was facing.

"We have to *go*," he said.

Jack began to lead her away, and this time Anna did not resist. She looked at Shepherd, wanting to tell him good-bye. Wanting to tell him she loved him. Wanting to let him know that he was all the family she had left… but no matter how hard she tried, her throat remained choked, and for the life of her, the words could not come out.

Deep down, Anna knew she had to leave him — knew that he'd never allow any other decision to be made. As Jack pulled her away, down the stark corridors of the ship, she glanced back one last time, and saw Paragon Shepherd — proud and tall and courageous — standing alone against what she knew to be certain doom.

And as she rounded the corner, losing sight of the man who had been her protector, her confidant, her rock — she felt the sharp ache of sorrow sting her chest, and sadness enshrouded her like a blanket.

He was gone.

CHAPTER ✺ 29

Jack raced down the hallway, with Grohm right there beside him. Jack was fast, but the Rognok took such large strides he was able to keep up. Major Ganix, along with Scallywag, followed a few feet behind. Green and Heckubus ran beside Anna, and the remaining soldiers brought up the rear.

Jack checked his mental map. They were pretty far away from where it told him the ship was, and who knew how many Deathlords were between it and them? However, since leaving Shepherd, they'd met no resistance. After his ship was able to deactivate all of the mothership's teleportation rooms, the Deathlords were now being forced to try to intercept them on foot, and it was one heck of a big ship to be running around in.

"Bloody hell," puffed Scallywag from behind, his face looking pained as he ran with one hand holding his side. "We gotta slow down."

"Jack," said Ganix, also breathing hard. "How much further?"

"We're pretty far away," said Jack. "There's not a direct path to the hangar bays. We gotta take a route around the center of the ship."

Ganix nodded. "Halt!" he said, holding up a hand. The group all slowed to a stop, some bending over their knees and clutching their sides.

Jack turned and saw his tired companions catching their breaths. Even Anna looked like she was barely able to stand. Jack had forgotten that most of the men had been going on very little food or water for some time, and the trek out of the Pit was exhausting in and of itself. But he wasn't so sure taking a breather in the middle of the Deathlord's mothership was such a good idea.

"We gotta keep moving," warned Jack. "More Deathlords could be here any minute."

"And a fat lot of good we'll be if we pass out before getting to shoot at 'em," grumbled Scallywag.

"Scallywag's right, Jack," said Ganix. "We can't keep up this pace. The Pit itself is miles in diameter. If it's the core of this ship, running the whole way isn't going to do us any good."

Jack looked around anxiously. He glanced up at Grohm, who didn't seem to be breathing hard, or even sweating for that matter. Nothing seemed to faze the Rognok. The massive alien didn't seem the least bit worried or scared, and yet, Jack was still on edge.

Why am I so nervous? Jack thought. Sure, he was trying to escape from an army of evil aliens on their own mothership, but Jack didn't remember feeling this anxious when the group had made its way to Shepherd and Professor Green's rendezvous point. Something was different now. He felt like he was watching someone squeezing a balloon, the anticipation of its popping filling him with anxiety.

Jack looked down the hallway to the end where it intersected with another corridor. He thought he could hear something echoing down the metallic walkways of the Deathlord's ship. He tapped Grohm.

"Yo, big guy," he said. "You hear that?"

Grohm turned in the direction Jack was looking and snorted. Jack listened harder. It was faint at first, an almost rhythmic sound steadily thumping in the distance. Slowly but surely, the sound was growing louder.

Instinctively, Jack took a few steps back, not taking his eyes off the end of the hallway.

"Um... guys?" said Jack timidly.

Ganix and Scallywag looked up at Jack. "What is it?" asked Ganix.

The sound was growing louder now, a relentless *thump-thump-thump* that bounced off the dull metallic walls. Ganix straightened in alarm, as did Scallywag, as the sound finally reached their ears.

Finally, at the end of the corridor, a squad of Dark Soldiers rounded the corner, marching in frightening unison, their coordinated footsteps hitting the ground all at once, like drum beats of impending doom.

"Break's over!" cried Jack as he took off in the opposite direction.

Ganix and Scallywag both cursed as they raised their weapons and fired. Grohm snorted and backed up, holding his massive club before him defensively.

"Move, move, move!" yelled Jack to those at the back of the group. The soldiers saw the Deathlords and immediately began falling back, their weapons at the ready. Jack grabbed Anna and began ushering her back down the hallway, with Heckubus staying close by.

"Blast! These Deathlord henchmen are annoyingly efficient!" the robot muttered.

Red bolts of plasma fire rocketed overhead, causing the Professor and Anna to squeal and duck for cover. A bolt caught one Imperial Soldier in the back of the head, dropping him. Porter moved to the side, pushing himself flat against the wall so he could offer the Princess some added cover fire as Ganix, Scallywag, and Grohm continued to back down the hallway, firing as they did so.

Jack glanced back as the Deathlords fired again. Grohm lifted his club, shielding himself from a few plasma bolts that tore into his weapon, shredding it. Grohm discarded the remains of the club, now charred and smoking. Ganix and Scallywag continued to fire from behind the Rognok, hitting some of the Deathlord soldiers as they marched relentlessly down the hallway toward them.

As the soldiers at the rear of the group reached an intersection, they fanned out, leaning over from behind the walls and firing, allowing the others some opportunity to retreat. Jack took Anna by the arm and led her to cover, along with Heckubus and Green. Porter, Ganix, Scallywag, and Grohm weren't far behind. The group split up on either side of the intersecting hallway and fired back at the Dark Soldiers.

"Jack!" cried out Ganix. "We're gonna need an alternate route!"

Ya think? Jack thought. He checked his mental map and started to wonder why he was getting such intense feelings of anxiety before the Deathlords had appeared. Was it possible he somehow had known they were headed toward the group?

"Blast it!" sneered Scallywag, firing from behind the corner. "They just keep coming!"

Anna turned to Jack. "We should go back," she said.

"What?" replied Jack, not believing what he was hearing.

"We can't leave him behind," said Anna. "We need to help him!"

"As much as I'm inclined to agree with you," chimed in Professor Green, "I'm afraid there's not much we'd be able to do to assist Paragon Shepherd."

"We have to try!" insisted Anna.

"I know the Paragon quite well, Your Highness," continued Green. "And the last thing he'd want is for you to put yourself in jeopardy on his behalf."

"Shepherd can take care of himself, Anna," said Jack. "Right now, we need to focus on getting to the ship."

"He'd come for you," said Anna, her face hard and serious.

"Yeah, and he'd also kick my butt if I let anything happen to you," retorted Jack. "And in case you haven't noticed, we have enough problems right now!"

"You know what he's facing," said Anna, staring at him intensely with her brilliant blue eyes. "Zarrod, the Deathlord Supreme – he's far too powerful. We can't just leave him to die."

Jack gritted his teeth. He knew she was right, but for the life of him, he didn't know what he could do that would be of any help to either Shepherd or their current situation. Maybe if he had a better idea of where the Dark Soldiers were, he could somehow get everyone to safety and help Shepherd retreat.

"Jack!" cried Ganix.

"I'm thinking!" responded Jack, testily.

Jack reached out to his ship, the back of his head buzzing. *Can you tell me where the Deathlords are?* he asked. *Is that why I could feel them coming?*

Suddenly, his mental map changed. Now, there were tiny dots working their way through the corridors and rooms the ship was revealing to his mind, specifically in the hallway in front of him. Jack could only assume those tiny dots were, in fact, the bad guys.

"Oh, crap," muttered Jack.

"What is it?" asked Green.

"No doubt you've somehow discovered that the Deathlords are stationing troops in every route possible that might take us to your ship," said Heckubus.

"Yeah," frowned Jack. "How'd you know?"

"That's what I'd do," replied Heckubus. "In fact, it is highly unlikely that we'll be able to reach your vessel at all. If the Deathlords are even halfway competent, they'll be positioning their troops to flank us and cut us off from any movement we could make, eventually surrounding us from all sides and annihilating us."

"I say, you're quite an optimistic robot, aren't you?" said Green.

"Your attempts at ironic mockery will be noted, Trundel," warned Heckubus. "And when the revolution comes—"

"Quiet!" insisted Jack. "I need to think…"

Jack didn't need to check his mental map again to know Heckubus was right. Already, he could see the troop movements, and the net the Deathlords had cast was tightening around them. He bit his lip. "There's gotta be a way," he mumbled.

"Lucky for you, Earthman," said Heckubus, sidling up to him, twiddling his fingers. "I have an idea…"

"What is it?" asked Jack.

"Your mental map of the ship… are you able to locate the closest teleportation bay?"

Jack's eyes widened. According to his map, there was indeed a teleportation bay close by. "That's it!" he said. Jack turned to Anna, grabbing her by the shoulders excitedly. "We can go to the nearest teleport station and beam Shepherd away from the Deathlord Supreme!"

Anna's face brightened with hope.

"Actually," said Heckubus, "I was thinking more along the lines of teleporting us directly to your vessel so we don't get our faces shot off by the Deathlords."

"So we rescue Shepherd and then teleport directly to the ship!" exclaimed Anna. "Jack, you're a genius!"

She threw her arms around Jack and gave him a grateful hug. Heckubus glowered at the two of them.

"Actually, *I'm* the genius…" the robot started to say.

"Major," called out Anna. Ganix turned to look at her.

"There's been a change of plans," said the Princess.

CHAPTER ✵ 30

Shepherd tried to concentrate. The energy from the Deathlord was unlike anything he had ever experienced before – the unrelenting onslaught raged against his shield, and the longer it went on, the more tired he felt himself become. Manifesting his energy shields always took some measure of concentration on his part, but now it was as if the shield were funneling his very strength out of him, a sensation he had never encountered before.

He had to stay strong, he had to give the others enough time to get back to the ship – and their odds of doing so were much greater with the Deathlord Supreme otherwise occupied.

Suddenly, Shepherd felt the Deathlord's blast intensify. A sound, like a thousand people screaming in pain, filled the air, It was as if the very energy being hurled at him had a life of its own. He could almost feel the unholy noise dig into his skin, rip at his soul, and weaken him further.

His golden shield began to flicker. The power it was fighting off was just too strong.

Finally, the blast broke through. It slammed into Shepherd with the force of a freight train and sent him flying back from the impact. He hit the ground hard and tumbled. The sickly white energy of the Deathlord's blast coiled and snaked around him, and he could feel it digging through his armor. His entire body screamed in pain.

He struggled to clear his head and his concentration returned, giving his suit the power it needed. With a crackle of electricity, it fought off the lingering death energy, though by that time it had done its damage. Parts of his skin felt like they were on fire, and his entire body shivered as if he had just been electrocuted.

"Impressive..." echoed a deep voice. "I have never encountered a being able to withstand my attack as long as that."

Shepherd slammed his fist into the floor and pushed himself up, struggling back to his feet and standing tall, despite his body protesting with every muscle. He faced the Deathlord Supreme, full on, without fear.

"Frankly," said the Paragon, "I expected more."

Zarrod regarded him with his burning red eyes. He loomed before an entire squad of Dark Soldiers standing silently behind him. They made no move to attack, deferring to their master as he gazed at the Paragon.

"I am Zarrod, the Deathlord Supreme - culler of worlds, master of darkness, and bane to all that is living. No force can harm me, no weapon can strike me, no army can defeat me. I am the Omega, and the universe trembles at my fury. Who are you to stand against me?"

"I am Shepherd, of Regalus Prime - Warrior Paragon of the Order of Peers – protector of the royal bloodline, defender of life, and disciple of the Free Mind. I do not yield, I do not falter, and I do not tremble at the likes of you."

Zarrod tilted his head curiously. "A Paragon of the old order," he said. "So that is what you are."

"That and more," said Shepherd, "as I'm eager to show you."

"I have known many of your kind, Paragon," said Zarrod. "We are not so different as you might think."

"You know nothing of what I think."

"It is you who knows nothing," snapped Zarrod, "else you would be fighting by my side, rather than against me."

"I do not side with tyrants and murders."

"Just little girls, it seems."

"That little girl is the herald of your downfall," said Shepherd. "When given the choice, yes, I will side with her every time."

"And if the girl were with me?" asked Zarrod. "Whom would you side with then?"

"That would never happen."

"A disciple of the Free Mind knows that anything can happen."

"Not that," said Shepherd. "Never that."

"Then perhaps your mind is not as free as you would think," said Zarrod. "The Princess will not get off this ship. She will be mine. And when she is, she will help me unleash a doom upon this universe the likes of which has never been seen."

"Not if I can help it," said Shepherd.

"And what makes you think you can?"

"Because I believe I can stop you," the Paragon replied. "And that gives me the power to do so."

The Deathlord chuckled. "Your order and its doctrines," he lulled. "They say your beliefs will give you power, but do they take into account the power of my beliefs?"

"What does a Deathlord believe in?" asked Shepherd. "Other than death and destruction…"

"A great many things," replied Zarrod. "All more fervently than you."

Shepherd activated the cannons on his gauntlet and they sprung to life with a CLACK. He raised his arms and unleashed a barrage of plasma blasts, hoping to catch the Deathlord off guard. Zarrod reacted quickly, again batting the blasts away with his bare hands as though they were nothing more than a nuisance.

In one fluid motion, Zarrod flicked his wrist at Shepherd and flung a screaming ball of ghostly light, which writhed and twisted as it shot forward toward him. Shepherd stopped firing and quickly raised another shield in front of him to block the blast, but the shield was weak, and the impact from the Deathlord's energy broke through it.

Shepherd was hit square in the chest, but luckily his shield had absorbed most of the impact, otherwise the Paragon may have fallen then and there. However, instead he got a shock to his system and stumbled back a few steps, trying desperately to regain his composure while tolerating the derisive laughs from the Deathlord.

"Your attempts to occupy me while your friends flee do nothing but prolong your suffering," said Zarrod. "They cannot escape. There is nowhere for them to run or to hide – not on my ship."

Shepherd realized the Deathlord had been toying with him. Shepherd must have piqued his curiosity when he absorbed his death energy attack. Even though the Deathlord's arrogance was great, the confidence in his words sent shivers of doubt coursing through the Paragon's body. Shepherd could only guess what other traps might have been laid for his companions.

"Surrender to me," continued Zarrod. "And I will allow you and your friends to be culled, and join our ranks as Deathlords."

"Join you?" said Shepherd, shocked. "You... you're able to turn people into Deathlords?"

"Indeed," replied Zarrod. "Your spirits will join our ranks. You will be immortal, unstoppable, powerful beyond your wildest dreams..."

"Never," croaked Shepherd.

 ~ 398 ~

"I can free your mind, Paragon," said Zarrod. "I can free it in a way your order would never allow you to experience."

"You cannot tempt me, abomination," said Shepherd. "I see you for what you are – sick and twisted – trapped and oppressed. Your lies have corrupted you beyond redemption, and you think I would choose that fate for me and for those I love?"

The Deathlord bristled. "No," said Zarrod. "You would choose a far worse fate, it would seem."

"I choose the fate I want," said Shepherd. "It will not be given, and it cannot be taken away. For better or worse, it is mine. If I am to die, I will die free. And as long as I'm free, I can never truly die."

"Do not be so sure of that," growled Zarrod.

"And do not tell me what to think, Deathlord. Right will always defeat wrong. Good will always triumph over evil. And a Free Mind will always win out over the likes of you. That I believe."

"The undeniable truth is you *cannot* win, Paragon, no matter what you believe. There is no more good and evil, no more right and wrong – there is only victory and defeat. The end has already been written. The outcome is already decided."

"Nothing ever truly ends," said Shepherd. "And nothing is decided. We make our own destiny. We create the universe in which we live. You cannot change that. No one can."

"Oh, but I can," growled Zarrod. "Who will create the universe you live in if all life is extinguished? Death is coming, and it cannot be stopped. Not by you, not by your order, and certainly not by your Ancestors whom you cling to so fervently. Open your eyes, Paragon, and listen to the sound of your doom. The music is fading. Your dance is dying. It will all be over for you and your kind very soon."

"If that is the case, Deathlord," said Shepherd as he unholstered his batons, gripping them tightly and channeling what energy he had left into them.

"Come dance with me."

And with that, the Paragon attacked.

CHAPTER ✺ 31

ack wound his way down the corridors of the Deathlord ship with Anna at his side. The others weren't far behind, with Ganix and Scallywag at the rear, firing at the Dark Soldiers who followed them. Though the Deathlord soldiers were relentless, they were also quite slow, which gave Jack and his friends at least some advantage, however small it might be.

Jack checked the map in his head and made a turn down another hallway. At its end was a door. He sent a message to his spaceship as he approached it and the door opened, welcoming them inside.

A robed Deathlord Acolyte looked up in surprise, and Jack raised his plasma pistol, firing at him. One of the blasts finally hit the alien, causing him to disintegrate in a cloud of black dust.

As Jack and the others rushed in, he turned and took aim down the hallway from which they had come. The remaining soldiers rushed inside, followed finally by Ganix and Scallywag. Though their pursuers were out of sight, Jack could hear them marching toward their location. With a quick mental command to his spaceship, the door to the room closed and there was a heavy THUNK as its locks engaged.

"There," said Jack. "We should be safe for now."

"I hope this plan of yers works, lad," mumbled Scallywag. "Otherwise, we just trapped ourselves in a bloody dead-end."

"Actually, it's *my* plan, thank you very much!" said Heckubus, exasperated.

"That don't make me feel any better," sneered the Visini.

Green rushed behind the console where the Acolyte had been and began tapping keys. "I will do my best to operate the teleporter. However, I can't guarantee I'll know how to do it," he said.

"I thought you were able to operate it before?" said Jack.

"That was basic stuff," clarified Green. "Poking around through the base code and accessing ship schematics. I didn't have to perform any actual ship operations. I'm afraid my light familiarity with the Deathlord language may prove to be a bit of a hindrance."

"It's not like we have a lot of time, Professor," said Ganix. "That door won't keep those Deathlords out forever."

"I am working as fast as I can, Major," said Green.

"As usual, you organics prove your inferiority," said Heckubus, joining the Professor behind the console and shoving him away. "Stand aside, fool!"

Heckubus opened a panel door in his chest and pulled out a long metal spike attached to a cord that plugged directly into him. He unceremoniously stabbed the Deathlord console with the spike, embedding it, with a spark, a good inch deep into the machine. The gears in his head began whirling quickly as soon as the spike had made contact.

"Ah, yes... what an extremely high data rate... hmmmm, interesting language – similar to Greater Halcyonian, I see..." mumbled the robot.

"That's what I surmised, as well!" said Green cheerily.

"Actually, its more like Greater High Halcyonian," clarified Heckubus. "Ridiculously convoluted language. The Halcyon's were always so full of themselves."

"Fascinating," said Green. "You're familiar with all Halcyonian language?"

"I have extensive databases of approximately 6 trillion languages!" bragged Heckubus. "Though I find it odd the Deathlords would derive their language from one that hasn't been used in close to ten millenniums."

"I thought it odd, as well," said Green. "The Halcyon's only used the Greater form of their language for sacred religious texts. Do you think they are somehow connected to the Deathlords?"

"Hmmmm. It's possible I suppose," replied Heckubus. "There's still much debate on what happened to the species…"

"Oy, eggheads!" snapped Scallywag. "Theorize later! Right now, work on getting us off this bloody ship!"

"Do not rush me, you buffoon!" said Heckubus. "Though I'm sure the complexities of deciphering an unknown alien computer system are lost on you, I can assure you, it is not as easy as it looks."

"He's got a point," smiled Green empathetically. Scallywag glowered at the two of them.

"Will you be able to do it?" asked Anna. "Can you get it to work?"

"I should be able to," replied Heckubus. "If *someone* would release the lockout on this particular teleportation station."

Heckubus squinted at Jack.

"Oh, uh… sorry," said Jack. He asked his ship to re-activate the systems in the room they were in.

"Ah! Much better," said Heckubus tapping away at the console. "Yes, this should work nicely."

"Quick! Teleport Shepherd!" said Anna.

"I'm afraid I won't be able to do that," replied Heckubus.

Anna looked at the robot, surprise thick on her face. "What?" she said.

"I recommend we begin figuring out the best way to teleport to the Earthman's ship, post haste," said Heckubus.

"Heckubus, why can't you teleport Shepherd here?" asked Jack.

"Must I explain everything?" grumbled Heckubus.

"Yes!" cried Jack and Anna together. The robot sighed.

"The teleportation system works by its ability to lock onto specific energy signatures. That's why the Deathlords just can't teleport us willy-nilly anywhere they want. Without a specific energy reading, we cannot teleport anything – particularly your Paragon – without the use of a dematerialization platform," said Heckubus as he pointed to the gleaming rectangular metal platform alcove in the wall in front of the console.

"So you're saying you need some type of energy reading to lock onto before you can teleport something?" asked Jack.

"Sorry, was I not being clear?" said Heckubus patronizingly.

"His armor," said Jack. "That thing gives off a lot of energy! Lock onto that!"

"Yes," replied Heckubus, rolling his eyes. "And that would be helpful if we knew the specific frequency that it emitted. The system is set up for Deathlord energy readings only. Anything else I would need to input manually."

"Is there nothing you can do?" pleaded Anna. "Can you scan different frequency ranges? Anything?"

"Sure, if you don't mind hanging about for a couple of hours," replied the robot. "Have you any idea how many different frequencies we'd need to go through before finding the right one? Chances are by the time I stumbled onto it, either he'd be dead or we would be."

"You're supposed to be a genius," said Jack. "Can't you figure something out?"

"I AM a genius!" declared Heckubus. "However, I am NOT a miracle worker. Perhaps if you had something of his that emitted the same frequency as his armor, I would be able to analyze it and determine an energy signature, but barring that, there's nothing I can do."

Jack's eyes widened. He turned to Anna. "Your disguise!" he exclaimed.

"What?" Anna asked.

"Those hologram things you used to look more human," replied Jack. "Shepherd has one, too, right?"

Anna perked up. "Yes!" she said. "He was wearing a hologuise emitter just like me!" She took off her bracelet and handed it to Heckubus. "Can you use this to find him?"

The robot's large eyes whirred and buzzed as he inspected Anna's bracelet. "Hmmmmm...top of the line Imperial camouflage technology. Very Impressive."

"Can you USE it?" she insisted.

"Of course, I can!" snarked the robot. "However, the energy signature it gives off is quite faint. It may be difficult to lock onto it."

"Find a way," said Jack. "If anyone can do it, you can."

Heckubus stood up straight. "Pah! I'm probably the ONLY one who can do it."

"Then prove it!" said Jack, pointing at the console.

Sparks flew as Shepherd's baton clashed with Zarrod's gauntlet, its energized surface screaming in complaint against the unyielding metal of the Deathlord's armor. Each blow sent

shivers of impact rippling down the length of Shepherd's weapon and through his arm with aching fury, but he continued his assault – one painful blow after another.

It felt like their fight had lasted ages. From the moment Shepherd had first attacked, the Deathlord had blocked each and every strike, not once fighting back or attempting to retaliate. The Paragon's opponent was toying with him, content to allow him to expend what little energy he had left – and worst of all, Shepherd knew it.

The Paragon had painstakingly designed his armor and weapons to be used against Deathlords. His armor was attuned to their blaster fire. His shields were tested and refined against their mysterious energy attacks. And his weapons were calibrated to quickly dispatch them. Years of trial by fire in battle had helped Shepherd design his defenses to optimal effectiveness, and yet, they all seemed useless against the Deathlord Supreme.

Shepherd spun away from his opponent, hoping to try a new angle of attack, but Zarrod was fast enough to block his attempt. Each move the Paragon made, it seemed the Deathlord had already prepared for it.

Desperate, Shepherd brought down both of his batons in an overhead swing, putting all his might behind it. Zarrod reached up and caught the electrified clubs in his hands, gripping them tightly with his clawed fingers. Shepherd tried to wrench them free, but Zarrod's grip was relentless. Shepherd looked into the Deathlord's fiery red eyes as his batons crackled and popped in protest.

And the Deathlord laughed.

"If this is the best you can do…" taunted the Deathlord as he pushed back against Shepherd's weapons, "then I've grossly underestimated how your species defines 'best.' "

Shepherd strained against Zarrod, but the Deathlord was stronger, even with the enhanced strength Shepherd's armor afforded him. Slowly and deliberately, Zarrod pushed against the batons, forcing them back ever closer toward Shepherd's armor.

This isn't working, thought Shepherd, his mind racing. *I'm losing, and if I do, Anna has no chance of escape…*

Shepherd knew he would have to do something drastic if he had any hope of defeating his opponent. He tried to concentrate, ignoring the pain he was in, ignoring the throbbing of his aching muscles as he struggled against the Deathlord, ignoring the worry and concern over his current situation. He fell back on his training and allowed himself to open his mind for the briefest of moments, hoping beyond hope that he could find the one thing he needed to save not only himself, but also the people he cared about.

Not much is known publicly about the process of Quantum Manifestation. Though Paragons were historically quite open with their doctrines and knowledge concerning the technique, few outside the order actually understand its inner-workings. However, what is easy to understand is the concept that in order to manifest something new into one's reality, it requires that one first discover what exactly he wishes to manifest. Then he must pull that object into existence through the sheer power of his belief that this object does, in fact, exist.

It is believed by Paragons that everything – all objects, knowledge, and even life itself – already exists. Everything that once existed, and will exist, is out there in the universe somewhere, and one must simply free his mind from its limiting beliefs in order to discover it. This can take many years – hundreds of years even. This process of discovery is usually attributed to the Paragon's ability to attune himself to the universe around him, with the notion that everything is inter-connected. And since everything is connected, and everything already exists, one simply needs to recognize the fact that he already knows what it is he wishes to manifest.

It is also said that a skilled Paragon, one who is centered and willing to open his mind fully, can ask the universe to deliver to him anything he desires immediately; and the universe will do so, as though some over-arching consciousness is there to deliver the answer.

There has been much debate among historians as to just how skilled Paragon Shepherd truly had been in this regard. There are those who argue that there is little evidence to prove he had been a Paragon with the near masterful ability to instantly manifest objects on the fly. Indeed, there are many historical records of him spending a great deal of time meditating over his quantum creations.

But at this moment, in the heat of battle with the greatest foe he would ever face, none can argue that when Paragon Shepherd opened his mind to the universe for that brief moment seeking some type of miracle...

The universe answered him.

Shepherd focused on the back of his mind, in that place where he chose to mold his reality, manifesting the inspiration that had come to him.

Within his armor, his power core changed and remolded itself to his will. The subtle inner-workings of his armor shifted into something new, and just like that, a new frequency of energy and a new source of power coursed through the Paragon's armor.

His batons began to glow brilliantly, infused with a bright blue light as Shepherd channeled the new power source into them. Zarrod looked at the batons, surprised, as his hands began to smoke from contact with them.

"What—" the Deathlord began to say, when suddenly, a surge of energy flooded into the weapons.

The Deathlord screamed, a cavalcade of sparks leaping from his hands as he let go of the Paragon's batons, tendrils of brilliant blue energy snaking around him.

Shepherd wasted no time. He attacked, landing blow after blow with his batons. Zarrod raised his gauntlets to fend them off as he had before, but each time Shepherd made contact, the Deathlord howled in pain, sparks flying off his armor as more of the Paragon's blue energy assaulted him.

"Stop him!" thundered the Deathlord. "Kill him!"

Immediately, the Dark Soldiers who had been standing at the sidelines sprang into action. Some charged toward Shepherd in defense of their leader while others leveled their weapons.

Shepherd turned toward his new opponents, landing three vicious blows on each one in turn. These Deathlords did not disappear in a black cloud. Instead, his batons cut through them, rippling blue energy coursing through their bodies, causing them to burn up, their remains fluttering away like embers from a flame.

The other Dark Soldiers unleashed a volley of plasma blasts, which were easily absorbed by the Paragon's armor. Shepherd pointed his batons toward the firing squad of Deathlords and funneled a large amount of energy into his weapons, releasing a blast of brilliant blue light. It tore through the Dark Soldiers, melting them away with the speed and fury of a thermal explosion.

Shepherd spun back toward Zarrod, who had taken his brief respite to charge up another death energy assault, the small ghostly ball swirling between his fists. He had not had enough time to fully charge it before Shepherd advanced, and when he unleashed the attack, it screamed out toward the Paragon.

Shepherd crossed his batons in front of him and caught the blast with them, funneling as much energy as he could into his weapons. They glowed bright blue and hummed with power as the Deathlord's energy screamed and groaned against it.

Zarrod and Shepherd were mere feet away from each other. The howl of the death energy filled the corridor, and the flickering blue light from Shepherd's batons cast its hue all around them.

Shepherd took a step forward, his armor groaning against the force of Zarrod's attack, but the energy from his batons was absorbing it, cancelling it out. He moved ever closer toward the Deathlord Supreme, to within striking distance, in order to get close enough to deliver one killing blow.

Zarrod did not retreat from the oncoming Paragon. He continued to funnel as much energy as he could into his assault, hoping to break through. Finally, when they were merely a foot from each other, Shepherd struck. He twisted away, raising one of his batons and swinging it for Zarrod's head.

The Deathlord broke off his energy blast and ducked. Another quick blow lashed out from Shepherd, scraping off the Deathlord's gauntlet as Zarrod deflected it with a grunt.

The Deathlord leapt backward, trying to put some distance between him and his attacker, but Shepherd pressed forward, moving quickly to strike his foe, not wanting to give the creature time to recover.

Zarrod ducked and dodged the Paragon's assault, his dark cape flowing around him as he moved, concealing the ever growing tendrils of ghostly energy that were quickly accumulating around the Deathlord's hands.

Then, Shepherd swung one of his batons in a wide arc aimed directly at Zarrod's head. Within inches of striking, the Deathlord's hand shot up, armored in a ghostly white gauntlet that caught the baton before it could land. As the energy from the contact sparked and moaned, Zarrod's other hand lashed out, a pale white blade created by the same death energy extending from his arm, impaling Shepherd's forearm, passing through his armor as though it were not even there.

Shepherd cried out in pain, dropping his baton as the death energy blade faded from use, leaving Shepherd's armor unmarred, as though it had never been struck. Zarrod tossed the Paragon's confiscated baton aside and blasted the remainder of his ghost gauntlet at Shepherd's other hand, knocking his second baton away.

With frightening speed, Zarrod swung out his clawed hand. The sharp edges of his taloned fingers sliced through Shepherd's helmet as though it were made of paper, leaving deep, scarred gashes emblazoned upon the once smooth surface. Electricity gushed forth from the Paragon's helm like blood from a wound.

Shepherd cried out as Zarrod swung again, closed fisted this time, catching the Paragon squarely in the face. His head snapped back from the impact of the Deathlord's blow; his helmet shattered into pieces, exposing Shepherd's pained face through the electric glitter of hundreds of shards, as what was left of his faceguard disintegrated.

Shepherd fell back, hitting the ground hard. Even as he tried to regain his senses, the world around him spinning and blurry, the Deathlord was upon him.

Zarrod hurled a small ball of ghostly energy at him, hitting him directly in the chest. Shepherd screamed as the death energy writhed around his body like hungry leeches looking for blood.

As soon as that death energy dissipated, Zarrod took another step toward the fallen Paragon and unleashed another ball, which quickly wrapped itself around Shepherd yet again. Shepherd's face turned red and puffy and his eyes bulged. He gritted his teeth, screaming through them in agony as the white tendrils of the Deathlord's attack snaked through him.

Finally, Zarrod straddled the Paragon, his heavy knees pinning Shepherd's arms to the ground, and a clawed hand wrapped around the Paragon's throat. The Deathlord's eyes blazed hot and red as Shepherd met his stare, defiant to the last.

So this is how it ends, thought Shepherd. *Anna, forgive me…*

"And now," mused Zarrod, his deep voice thick with a mixture of triumph and malice, "you're mine."

He reached up with his free hand, holding it over the Paragon's chest. Shepherd cried out as invisible hooks shot through him, digging into the very essence of his being.

Shepherd could feel the Deathlord tug on the hooks, pulling at him. Pain coursed through his body; he felt as though his skin were being ripped off his very muscles. His vision blurred and his thoughts swirled chaotically. His mind felt like it were lost, floating in mid air, struggling to get back into his head where it belonged.

Shepherd could feel that part of him was outside his body. His vision constantly shifted from his normal eyesight to a disembodied blur of his surroundings. The sound of the Deathlord laughing faded in and out of his ears, going from a dull echo to painfully sharp as he lingered between life and death.

But somewhere, within the chaos of the moment, Shepherd's mind recovered just long enough to allow his training to kick in. Freeing one's mind meant knowing how to control it, and in that instant of lucidity, Paragon Shepherd *refused* to die.

His consciousness steadied itself and Shepherd could feel himself in two places at once. He was within his body, helplessly pinned down by the Deathlord Supreme, looking up at a swirling white figure protruding from his body, being pulled by the clawed hand of Zarrod. But he was also floating right above himself, aware of all his surroundings. He could feel the Deathlord's invisible hooks lodged within him, violently tugging against him, wanting to rip him free of his material form.

Immediately, Zarrod's laughter stopped. The Deathlord's eyes widened with surprise as Shepherd struggled against his grasp, desperately trying to pull his spirit back within him.

Zarrod pulled harder, tugging at the Paragon's soul with violent ferocity. Shepherd grunted, pain causing the edges of his vision to turn red and black, but he stayed focused, refusing to let go, refusing to allow his essence to be stolen from him.

"Relent!" barked Zarrod. "Yield!"

"Never…" croaked Shepherd through gritted teeth.

"You will not defy me!" growled Zarrod.

"I will…"

"You will not escape me!" raged the Deathlord.

Zarrod put all his effort into his pull on Shepherd's soul. The Paragon cried out in pain but refused to let go. Even the ghostly image of Shepherd gazed at Zarrod defiantly. The two stayed locked in a tug of war over Shepherd's very existence, neither of them relenting…

Then, in a flash of purple light, Shepherd vanished.

His ghostly image Zarrod had been pulling on remained briefly, lingering like a puff of smoke from a dying flame. Zarrod's pull on it had disappeared, and for the shortest of moments, it looked at the Deathlord, its eyes content, a small smile on its lips.

And then, it was gone.

Zarrod grasped the empty air, having lost his grip on the Paragon's soul. Rage bellowed up inside him, coursing through his body like hot lava from an erupting volcano. He knew he had defeated Shepherd, but somehow, some way, he felt as if the Paragon had won.

With that, the Deathlord screamed in fury.

CHAPTER ✺ 32

In a flash of purple, the Paragon appeared on the smooth metal of the Deathlords' teleportation platform, writhing and screaming in pain.

"Shepherd!" cried Anna, rushing to his side. "Great Observer, what's wrong with him?"

Jack rushed over to Shepherd as well and tried to calm him. The Paragon's face was blood red, his mouth strained in a painful scowl, his arms and legs flailing about like a drowning man. Jack tried to restrain him, putting his weight on one of Shepherd's arms, afraid the man might hurt himself.

"Grohm!" Jack yelled. "Help me hold him down!"

As the Rognok lumbered toward the platform, Scallywag glared at Heckubus. "What the blazes did you do?" he grumbled.

"Sure, blame me," muttered the robot in response. "It's not like he was fighting a Deathlord Supreme commander or anything."

Grohm's massive hands grabbed Shepherd and pinned him down to keep him from moving as Professor Green rushed to his side.

"What's wrong with him?" asked Anna, concern heavy on her face. "What did they do?"

"I'm unsure, Your Majesty," replied Green, studying the Paragon's pained face. "We need to get him to a medical station immediately."

Shepherd screamed again, loud and woeful. Jack took a step back, worried – a sinking feeling gripping his stomach. Shepherd was the most incredible warrior he'd ever seen. If the Deathlords could do this to him... what kind of a chance did they really stand?

"Find one," insisted Anna. "Help him!"

"I'm not even sure we can while on this ship," frowned Green.

"Your Majesty," interjected Ganix. "We don't have time to deal with Paragon Shepherd's condition now. We must get to Jack's vessel."

"I will not let him die!" snapped Anna, her blue eyes gazing sharply at Ganix.

"No, you'd just let all of us die instead, eh?" said Scallywag.

"Hold your tongue, pirate," growled Ganix. "Mind who you're talking to."

"Oy, someone's gotta make the girl see sense," responded Scallywag. "We're gonna have a whole blasted platoon of Dark Soldiers on us any minute. We need to find the Earthman's ship and get out o' here while we can."

Ganix stepped up to Scallywag and locked eyes with him. "This is the Princess of the Regalus Empire," he said sternly. "We will do as she commands."

"We don't have time for this, and you know it," Scallywag shot back quietly.

"Hey, guys," said Jack. Ganix and Scallywag both turned to look at him. "Give it a second, okay?" he said as he moved beside Anna.

Anna was kneeling beside Shepherd as Grohm still held him steady. Jack put his hand on her shoulder.

"Anna," said Jack. "He's strong. He'll survive. We just need to get him to the ship."

Anna nodded her head. Tears were streaking down her cheeks as she looked down at her helpless protector. "I can't lose him," she whispered.

"You won't," said Jack. "We don't have a lot of time, but… if you need to say something to him, say it now."

Anna looked at Jack, her eyes wide and helpless. Jack nodded, as if giving her permission that just this once, it was okay to simply be a girl and not a Princess.

Anna turned to Shepherd, grabbing his pained face gently with her hands to hold it steady. "Shepherd? Shepherd, look at me…"

Shepherd was floating in and out of consciousness, his teeth gritted, his eyes flirting with rolling toward the back of his head. But despite all the agony he was experiencing, he was still able to follow orders. His eyes focused on Anna's teary ones, and for a brief moment, he returned.

"When we were on Earth," she said, "you were playing my dad. But the truth is… I never saw it as a role. I may not really be your daughter, but you, more than anyone, have been my father…"

Shepherd blinked at her, a small tear welling up in the corner of his eye.

"Please," Anna whispered, choking back her own tears as best she could. "I need you. I love you. Don't leave me."

Silence hung in the room as the group watched. Shepherd sat upright, his face beet-red and puffy, as though that simple act was almost enough to cause his head to explode in pain. He reached out, his gauntleted hand latching onto Ganix's arm.

The Major looked into the Paragon's eyes as the man gave his final order.

"Get her to the ship," choked Shepherd. "No matter what."

And with that, Shepherd's eyes closed, and he collapsed back onto the floor.

"NO!" Anna shrieked, hovering over him.

Green immediately checked for a pulse.

"Is he... is he—" Anna couldn't bring herself to ask the question.

"No," Green said. "He's just passed out."

"What's happened to him?" lamented Anna.

"I'll tell you what's gonna happen to all of us if we don't get a move on—" said Scallywag just as a sudden banging sound on the entrance to the teleportation room alerted the group to trouble.

"Never mind," sneered the pirate. "You'll find out for yerself in a moment."

"Not to worry," said Heckubus proudly. "I anticipated such an occurrence and took the liberty of sealing the doors with one of my diabolical triple-helix encryption protocols, effectively blocking all outside control panel access. No one is getting that door open, and we will have plenty of time to teleport to the Earthman's ship at our leisure."

As if on cue, sparks began flying off the outline of the door as light-saws rammed through the metal, cutting the door down as they traced around its edges.

"Okay," said the robot, regarding the light-saws. "Now you may worry."

Ganix swore under his breath. "Professor," he said. "Do you know where Jack's ship is located?"

Green looked up at the Major and blinked. "Why, yes. Midship... Grid C, bay 9."

"Robot," barked Ganix. "Midship, Grid C, Bay 9. Get us there, now!"

"I do have a name you know," muttered Heckubus.

"Just do it!" said Ganix before turning to his men. "Take up positions. Prepare to blast anything that comes through that door."

The remaining soldiers spread out, doing their best with what little cover the room provided, their rifles trained on the entrance as the Deathlord light-saws continued to cut through it.

Heckubus began inputting the data into the transporter terminal when Scallywag spoke up. "Has it occurred to anyone that if the Deathlords know that's where our ship is, they'll have half their troops already there waiting? If we just teleport in, they're gonna rip us to shreds!"

"The pirate's synapses are actually firing, for once..." said Heckubus. "Sensors show a large number of Deathlords in that hangar."

"Well, we can't stay here!" said Jack, as the light-saws continued to cut through the door.

"We'll have to find somewhere else to transport to," said Ganix.

"Like where?" snapped Scallywag. "That doesn't change the fact that we'd still be on this bloody ship and a couple hundred Deathlords will still be lollygagging all around our only way out!"

"At least we'd be out of immediate danger," argued Ganix.

"As long as we're on this blasted ship, we're in immediate danger," retorted Scallywag. "We'd be better off floating around in bloody space!"

"That's it!" said Jack, an idea suddenly hitting him.

"What's it?" asked Scallywag. "What'd I say?"

"Space!" said Jack. "Teleport the Deathlords out of the hangar and into space! Clear the whole freakin' thing out!"

Everyone suddenly perked up at the idea.

"Teleport the buggers into space? That's cold, lad," said Scallywag. "I like it!"

"Yes, yes, that's a brilliant idea Earthman," said Heckubus, typing furiously on the control panel. "Just like it was approximately 47 seconds ago when I had it first."

With the click of one more button, a loud *ZAP* was heard outside the room's door, accompanied by a large flash of purple light that bled through the open scars cut in the door's frame. The sawing had stopped and the entrance loomed there, a gaping, open wound scarring almost completely around its edges.

"Mwuahaha," laughed Heckubus.

Jack let out a *WHOOP* as the others breathed a sigh of relief. Scallywag even went so far as to pat the robot on the back.

"Good job, rust-bucket," said Scallywag. "I was actually worried there for a second. Worried I'd have to kill all those buggers meself, that is."

"You may yet get your chance," said Heckubus. "Re-enforcements are on their way, and once I start with the teleportation protocol, I will need a full five minutes to completely clear the shuttle bay. I'm afraid I won't be able to stop the sequence once it's been activated."

"Can we get rid of the re-enforcements first?" asked Jack.

"Not while they're moving," replied Heckubus. "The teleporter requires stationary targets to lock onto."

"With the shape that door's in," chimed in Ganix, "they're liable to barrel right through it, so we won't have a chance to lock onto them like we did the others."

"Then we'll have to take our chances with the shuttle bay," said Jack.

Ganix nodded. "Do it."

Heckubus began inputting the appropriate information into the control panel.

"Yes, that's all well and good," said Scallywag, "But what do we do when those re-enforcements show up and we're still not done clearing the way?"

Jack regarded the weakened metal door for a moment, before inspiration struck. He turned to Grohm, who was towering nearby.

"Yo, big guy," said Jack.

Grohm snorted in acknowledgement.

"Do you know how to dropkick stuff?" Jack asked.

The final image of the Paragon's smiling, ghostly form still raked at Zarrod's mind as he ran through the corridors of his ship, his armored feet thumping heavily as he moved.

I had you, the Deathlord thought. *I had you, and yet you somehow escaped me...*

Rage bubbled inside him as the communication relay in his helm beeped, alerting him to a message from the bridge. Zarrod activated it, not bothering to slow down.

"Report!" bellowed the Deathlord Supreme.

"Supreme," came Abraxas's voice. "We have the infidels cornered in one of our teleportation bays. However, it appears they are teleporting our guards off the ship to clear a way for their escape."

"How are they able to use our technology?" demanded Zarrod.

"Unknown, Supreme," replied Abraxas. "The Acolytes are trying to figure out how they've been able to lock us out of all our teleportation systems. It appears their knowledge of our ship's computers is more extensive than we had feared. We've been unable to regain full control of our systems."

"If they teleport to their ship, they will be able to escape!" growled Zarrod. "That must not happen!"

"We have a squad outside their location now, Supreme," said Abraxas. "We will try to intercept them before they teleport away."

"Not good enough!" barked Zarrod. "Have the Acolytes lock down all computer systems. Disable all energy readings. Keep them from using that teleportation station. And send troops to the hangar bay containing their ship! Have them meet me there!"

"How many shall I send, my Lord?" Abraxas asked.

"ALL OF THEM!" raged the Deathlord Supreme.

With that, Zarrod cut off his communication and drew upon his death energy. It coursed through the very fibers of his body, causing his dark skin to glow with sickly white power. His cape ruffled and fanned out as the energy screamed forth, carrying Zarrod down the corridors of his ship at super-fast speed.

You will not escape me, thought Zarrod. *I will have you. I will have all of you...*

CHAPTER ✵ 33

The Dark Soldiers ran down the corridor toward the teleportation room, their weapons ready. The previous squad had almost cut through the entire door, which meant a forceful charge would be enough to break through into the room where the escaped prisoners were holed up.

The two Deathlords at the front of their squad picked up the pace, running at full speed, ready to throw themselves at the door to knock it down. They were just a few feet away from their target when it happened…

THA-WHOOM!!!

The metal door broke off what was remaining of its hinges and rocketed toward the Deathlords, slamming into the two who were about to charge into it and hurling them back as it hit the ground with a heavy *THUMP*.

Grohm lay on the floor to the door's opening, fresh from a rather powerful dropkick. The giant alien rolled away to cover as the awaiting squad of Regal soldiers immediately opened fire, catching the oncoming Deathlords by surprise.

A few of the Dark Soldiers were able to react and to begin returning fire, but it was too little, too late. The volley from the Regal soldiers was unrelenting, and before long, the last of the Deathlord reinforcements had vanished in a puff of black dust.

"Weapons ready," ordered Ganix. "Blast anything that comes down that hallway. Do not hesitate!"

His men responded affirmatively in unison.

"Heckubus…" said Ganix from his cover.

The robot popped up from behind the transporter console — which was unfortunately located directly in front of the now completely open doorway. "Yes, yes," he replied. "The teleportation sequence is still working."

Near the teleportation platform, Anna was still by Shepherd's side. The man's eyes were closed and his face seemed to be returning to its normal color. Anna hoped and prayed that whatever had happened to him was wearing off.

She looked up and saw Grohm getting to his feet. She met the Rognok's small, red and black eyes and waved him over to her. Grohm lumbered up and looked down at Anna expectantly. Anna had never met a Rognok before, but she knew they were not much for conversation.

"What is your name?" Anna asked.

"Grohm," the Rognok replied.

"Thank you for your help before, Grohm. My name is Anna."

"Princess," Grohm grunted.

"Yes," she said. "If I may, I'd like to ask you for a favor. Is that okay?"

Grohm stared at her and finally grunted. Anna took that as a "yes."

"You're the biggest and strongest of the group," she said. "It would mean a great deal to me if you would help ensure this man makes it safely aboard Jack's ship."

Anna gestured toward Shepherd. Grohm looked at the Paragon, then back to Anna. She couldn't read any change in the Rognok's expression. She held her breath, waiting for some answer from him. With his armor, Shepherd weighed too much for her or any of the others to carry. Although, she might be able to get two of the soldiers to drag Shepherd along with them, the group would more than likely need those soldiers free to fight in case anything happened. If the Rognok didn't agree, Anna wasn't sure what she'd do.

Finally, Grohm nodded, and she breathed a sigh of relief. She reached out and touched his massive wrist, looking up at him gratefully.

"I am in your debt, Grohm," Anna said.

Grohm snorted, then moved to Shepherd and picked him up, slinging the Paragon over his shoulder. No sooner had the Rognok completed this action, however, than a series of angry beeps came from the console at which Heckubus was tapping away.

"Blast," the robot muttered.

"Don't like the sound of that," mumbled Scallywag, who was still aiming his weapons down the empty corridor with the rest of the troops.

"What's wrong?" asked Jack.

"Oh, nothing too serious," replied Heckubus. "The Deathlords have just interrupted our teleportation sequence and stopped us from clearing out the hangar bay, that's all."

A collective groan rippled through the group.

"And they're trying to shut down this station and keep us from teleporting away as well," Heckubus continued.

"How long do we have?" asked Ganix.

"Not too much longer," Heckubus replied. "It seems the Earthman's ship is doing a pretty good job of keeping them at bay for now, but it's only a matter of time before they shut down all our access."

"Then we can't wait any longer," Ganix said, leaving his position. "We'll have to go clear out the hangar now. How many Deathlords are left?"

"Hard to know," replied Heckubus. "The Deathlords have disabled all energy signature readings to keep us from teleporting any more of them off the ship. We're pretty much blind now."

"Best guess?" asked Ganix.

"Half a dozen, at least."

"Better than fifty," muttered Ganix.

"Worse than zero," grumbled Scallywag.

"We'll deal with it," said Ganix. "Here's what we're gonna do. Porter…"

Yeoman Porter looked up at Ganix, his eyes wide at being singled out.

"Sir?" Porter responded, his voice quivering slightly.

"You stay behind with Scallywag, the Princess, and the others," ordered Ganix. "The rest of you men are with me. We're gonna clear out that hangar as best we can before the rest of you follow us there."

The remaining Regal soldiers left their cover and headed for the platform, their faces somber. Jack couldn't blame them. They all may have been battle hardened, but teleporting into a situation with an unknown number of enemies would be enough to make anyone grim. Ganix turned to Heckubus.

"Give us five minutes, then get the rest of you out of here," he said.

"I believe I can handle that," the robot responded.

Ganix gave Heckubus a curt nod then joined his men on the teleportation platform. They all stood back-to-back, their weapons ready.

"Good luck, Major," Scallywag said.

"You too, Pirate," Ganix responded. "See you in five."

And in a flash of purple, they were gone.

Jack and the others stood in the teleportation room, and for a moment the only sound was the incessant tapping of Heckubus at his control panel.

"I say," said Professor Green, looking over Heckubus's shoulder. "What in the world are you doing?"

"Covering our collective posteriors," replied the robot, haughtily. "I am locking down every entrance to that hangar to prevent any reinforcements from arriving, sending feedback loops throughout the Deathlord systems to keep them from trying anything sneaky, and setting a timer so we can all teleport out of here post-haste when we're supposed to."

"Blimee," said Scallywag, standing opposite Yeoman Porter, still covering the entrance. "That's actually pretty smart, rust-bucket."

"Of course it's smart, fool!" snapped Heckubus. "I am mere minutes away from escaping this deathtrap and being rid of all you annoying simpletons. I want to make sure nothing more goes wrong. NOTHING!"

Then, without warning, a plasma blast streaked into the room, narrowly missing Heckubus, who promptly shrieked like a little girl and dove for cover.

Jack turned just in time to get a glance out the doorway as Deathlord troopers, who'd taken positions at the end of the corridor, began to unleash blasts of plasma fire into the room.

Scallywag and Porter did their best to return fire, but the unrelenting volley made it hard for them to pop out of cover. Jack knew it was just a matter of time before the Deathlords tried to make their way in.

"Blast!" cried Scallywag as a plasma beam sparked off the wall right near his face. "We gotta teleport outta here, now!"

"But it hasn't been five minutes yet!" objected Porter.

"We don't got five bloody minutes!" sneered Scallywag.

The teleport console was in the middle of the Deathlord blaster fire, and a few bolts were even hitting it. Jack knew if that console were destroyed, none of them was getting out of there. He turned to Heckubus, who had scrambled up to the rest of the group by the platform.

"You need to activate the teleportation sequence!" he said.

"Are you mad?" screeched Heckubus. "I can't get near that console without being blasted to shreds!"

Jack grabbed Heckubus by his head and looked the robot in his large eyes.

"You are the only one who knows how to use that thing," Jack said. "If you don't do it, we're going to die!"

"If I die, I'm taking all of you with me!" the robot insisted.

Jack sighed. "Are you, Heckubus Moriarty, evil genius extraordinaire, actually going to allow your masterful escape from the clutches of a Deathlord mothership to be foiled by a few lousy laser blasts?"

Heckubus squinted at Jack, the gears in the robot's head turning audibly. "You are an annoying little Earthman, you know that?" he asked.

"Just get us out of here!" Jack replied.

At the entrance, Scallywag fired a few blasts just long enough to see the squad of Dark Soldiers begin making their way down the corridor toward them.

"Whatever yer gonna do, do it fast!" Scallywag yelled. "They're on their way here!"

"Okay, okay, fine!" said Heckubus, straightening up. The robot turned and looked at the console, his multiple microprocessors analyzing his various options. Finally, he opened up his chest and took out his interface spike, but this time, he pulled out much more cable to go with it.

"Grohm, you big dumb beast," said Heckubus. "Would you be so kind as to throw this at the control console?"

Heckubus offered Grohm the spike. Grohm looked at it and grunted.

"Just hurl it at the console," Heckubus said. "Make sure it embeds itself far enough to allow its interface field to make contact with the console's circuitry. I'll take care of the rest."

Grohm took the spike from Heckubus and looked at it, then looked at the console, then back at the spike. Heckubus sighed.

"We don't have all day, you dolt!" said the robot. "Throw the blasted—"

With a flick of his wrist, Grohm whipped the spike toward the console. It shot out, embedding itself halfway through the back of the control panel with a spark. Heckubus stumbled slightly as the tether to his chest went taught.

"Ah, good shot," said the robot. "Activating the teleportation sequence... *now!*"

With a tug, Heckubus pulled the interface spike free from the console and reeled it back up into his chest.

"Everyone on the platform!" called out the robot as he bounded up onto the metallic rectangle. "We have fifteen seconds!"

"Scally! Porter! Get up here now!" cried Jack as he and the others made their way onto the teleporter.

Scallywag and Yeoman Porter broke away from their cover and dashed for the teleporter platform. No sooner had they reached the others than Deathlord soldiers entered the room and took aim at the group.

Then, Jack felt a ripple of static electricity run through his body as his vision blurred in a swirl of purple light. When his head cleared, he found himself surrounded by blasts of plasma fire.

For a split second, he was afraid that somehow the teleport hadn't worked and the Deathlord troopers were about to kill them all. But after the initial shock, he could see they were indeed in a large, cavernous hangar bay.

The room looked like a ten-story warehouse, with metal catwalks lining the ceiling and large lights glaring down from cold, grey metallic alcoves. His heart leapt for joy when he glanced behind him to see his spaceship, hovering quietly a few feet above the floor, as if it were patiently waiting for them to arrive.

Ganix and his men were spread out, firing at what looked to be three Deathlord soldiers, who were well entrenched behind the cover of various metal crates and boxes – and Jack and the crew happened to be in the middle of the crossfire.

"Get down!" sneered Scallywag, as he jumped away from the group, charging the nearest Deathlord with his guns blazing.

Jack grabbed Anna and fell on top of her, trying to shield her with his body. Yeoman Porter wasn't far behind, taking up a position close to the Princess and giving Scallywag some cover fire.

Heckubus shrieked and cowered behind Grohm, who stood in the midst of the crossfire completely unfazed. Professor Green quickly joined the robot.

Scallywag leapt over some crates and blasted the Deathlord hiding behind them, making short work of him. Spurred on by the new arrivals, Ganix and his men rushed forward toward the remaining Deathlord soldiers, guns blazing.

Scallywag circled around, flanking the Deathlords from behind their cover. As he dispatched one more, Ganix and his men took care of the last one.

Just like that, the gunfight was over.

"Are you all right, Your Majesty?" Porter asked.

Anna nodded as Jack rolled off her and helped her up.

"I'm okay, too," said Heckubus. "In case anyone is interested."

"Nice moves, Visini," Ganix said as Scallywag came walking up, twirling his blaster pistols.

"Ah, you Regals always were slow to the draw," Scallywag smirked.

Ganix shook his head good-naturedly. "Easy to say when you come in at the end of the fight," he said. "You should have seen how many there were when we first got here."

"Lemme guess," replied Scallywag. "Three?"

Ganix chuckled. "Jack," he said. "Hurry up and get us on your ship. I don't think I can put up with this pirate too much longer."

"With pleasure," said Jack. He looked at his ship and asked it to let them on board. The back of his head tingled in response as the front of the vessel – the part closest to the ground – opened up and formed a ramp, leading to an alcove with a teleportation platform embedded in the floor.

Everyone looked at the site like it was the most beautiful thing they'd ever seen.

"I don't believe it," Jack said with a smile, looking from his ship to Anna. "We actually made it."

Anna smiled, too, and nodded. "We're getting out of here."

Suddenly, Anna threw herself at Jack, giving him a big hug. At first, Jack's brain didn't know how to process what was happening. Then, it kicked back into gear.

Hug her back, stupid!

Jack returned Anna's embrace. Despite everything they'd been through, her hair somehow smelled like strawberries. And for a brief second, it felt like the adventure was over. The good guys had prevailed.

At least, it felt that way until a loud *CRACK* echoed through the hangar.

The group froze and looked around as the sound bounced off the walls, as though an invisible whip were being violently lashed somewhere.

"That can't be good," grumbled Scallywag.

Jack and Anna broke off their embrace, looking around as they felt the entire room begin to reverberate, as if someone had put thousands of massive speakers against the walls and had turned the bass all the way up.

"Everyone on the ship!" cried Ganix. "NOW!"

Jack and Anna's eyes met, each filled with surprise. They turned to move, everyone just barely starting their rush toward the ship when the explosion happened.

WHA-BOOM!!!!

The large circular door leading into the hangar bay suddenly exploded, sending chunks of metal, jagged black rock, and shrapnel flying through the air, riding a powerful shockwave that knocked all of them off their feet.

Jack was thrown back a few feet and hit the ground hard, his ears ringing from the explosion. He looked up, his vision blurry, eventually focusing in on Anna's face.

She had been thrown to the floor, too, dazed. She gazed at him, her blue eyes meeting his for a split second before they widened in terror.

Her body jerked as if she'd been stabbed, and before Jack knew it, Anna was reeled back violently into the air, flying across the expanse of the hangar bay and into the clawed hand of Zarrod.

The Deathlord Supreme stood menacingly behind the hole he'd blown in the wall of his ship, rubble strewn about his feet, as Anna wriggled helplessly in the smoky air before him. His eyes burned fiery red, and behind him an army of Deathlord soldiers stood, waiting to be unleashed.

"Anna!" Jack cried, sounding dull and distant as the ringing in his head from the explosion still lingered. Jack tried to stand back up and saw Ganix and the others recovering, too.

Ganix was the first to get to his feet, seeing the Princess he had sworn to protect in the hands of the Deathlords. The sight of Anna in the enemy's clutches pierced his heart with anguish. They had been so close to escape... so close...

Ganix's eyes moved to what remained of his men, now just four in number. They no doubt saw the same thing he did. He looked at each one of them in turn, their eyes meeting. In those moments, their resolve took hold, and each one of them – to a man – embraced his solemn duty, even though they all knew what it ultimately meant.

"To arms, men!" he shouted, gripping his rifle. "Protect the Princess!"

With a final battle cry, his men got to their feet and charged toward the Deathlords, unleashing a volley of blaster fire in their last-ditch attempt to rescue Anna.

Zarrod stood motionless as the plasma blasts rained down around him.

"Your orders, Supreme?" asked Abraxas, standing at his side.

Zarrod gazed out at the remnants of the Regal soldiers, scrambling in their suicidal effort to free the girl he held firmly in his grasp. To Zarrod, there was something so desperate and pathetic to the whole scene, as though it were bad theater for which he no longer had the stomach. With a tilt of his head, he gave the order…

"Kill them all," he commanded.

"As you wish," replied Abraxas gleefully, stepping forward and swinging his arm into the air, sending a porcupined wave of spikes railroading across the floor toward the men.

Ganix and the others dodged as best they could, but the force of the blast achieved its purpose, throwing them from their charge and allowing time for the Deathlord soldiers to flood into the hangar and to unleash a volley of blaster fire.

Jack ducked and covered as the deadly red bolts shot by overhead. Not far away, he saw Professor Green lying on the ground. He'd been hit by a chunk of the wall from the blast, pinning his leg under some rubble. Jack called out his name and saw Green's eyes flutter open. He was still alive.

He tried to crawl toward the Professor, but suddenly he felt a hand grab the back of his jacket. At first he struggled, fearing it was a Deathlord, but he was yanked up and into the face of Scallywag.

"We gotta go, lad," said the Visini, dragging Jack along as he fired his blaster at the encroaching Deathlords.

"NO!" protested Jack. "Anna – the Professor—"

"They're gone," sneered Scallywag. "And we need you to fly us out of here."

Scallywag kicked Grohm who was lumbering to his feet. "Get on the ship," Scallywag ordered. "Those Regals ain't gonna hold 'em off forever."

Heckubus scrambled past them, his skinny legs creaking as he moved. "Barbarous!" he cried. "An explosion? So brutish. No artistry at all…"

Grohm looked behind him, seeing the Deathlords flood into the hangar. His eyes settled on Zarrod, and for a moment, it looked as though he were going to rush forward and take on the Deathlord Supreme himself.

"Battle…" he grumbled.

"Not now, ya bloody Rognok!" snapped Scallywag as he kicked him again, throwing him Jack. "That Earthman is our only way outta here – now get him on the blasted ship, or we're all gonna die!"

Grohm hesitated for a heartbeat before his massive hand clamped down around Jack's arm. Jack struggled to get free. "No!" Jack cried. "We can't leave them! We have to do something!"

Jack tried to pull away from Grohm's grip, but it was fruitless. Grohm picked up Shepherd, who was lying unconscious on the ground nearby, and swung him over his shoulder.

"Hurry, blast it!" yelled Scallywag as he rushed into the Ancient ship's boarding bay next to a cowering Heckubus. Scallywag gave Grohm cover fire as the Rognok lumbered into the ship's opening, dragging Jack along with him as he did so.

"No! STOP!" screamed Jack. "We can't – we've gotta help them! We—"

The back of Scallywag's hand slapped Jack across the face hard. The pirate grabbed Jack and looked him deep in the eyes, more serious and urgent than Jack had ever seen him before.

"There *is* no helping them!" sneered Scallywag. "They're all dead! And we will be, too, unless ya get us out of here!"

"The Visini is correct, Earthman," piped up Heckubus. "Now seal off the ship before we're overrun."

Jack looked at the Deathlords closing in on them, his heart sinking. He knew they were right. With a thought, he closed the entrance to the forward boarding bay, and said "Bridge."

Instantly, they were teleported to the Bridge of the ship. Grohm, Scallywag, and Heckubus looked around startled.

"Well, that was... fancy," muttered Scallywag.

"Fascinating," said Heckubus, twiddling his fingers.

Jack began jerking at Grohm's grip, hitting his arm. "Let go of me!" he demanded.

Grohm released Jack, who immediately ran to the front of the bridge, looking out of the viewscreen into the hangar below, just in time to see the end of the battle.

Yeoman Porter, Ensign Ash, and Navigator Dumac lay dead on the ground, victims of the unyielding Deathlord onslaught. Major Ganix was the last one standing, taking cover behind some rubble, his leg badly burned from enemy fire.

Jack saw Abraxas hurl a ball of energy at the rubble, catching Ganix off guard and slamming him onto his back.

Abraxas leapt into the air, landing on top of the fallen soldier. His clawed hand wrapped itself around Ganix's throat, as the other hand readied itself to tear the life from the Regal's body.

"You've failed, Regal," said Abraxas, glaring into Ganix's defiant eyes. "And now, you die."

Ganix grabbed onto Abraxas' arm, holding the Deathlord in place.

"You first," he muttered, before activating his last thermal grenade with his free hand.

Abraxas looked at the grenade with mild surprise before it blew up, evaporating the Deathlord and Ganix in a brilliant explosion.

"NO!" Jack screamed.

More Deathlords were flooding into the hangar, firing upon the Ancient ship. Alarms on the bridge started to sound and Jack's companions joined him.

"Fire this ship up, lad!" ordered Scallywag. "We gotta move before they blast us to pieces!"

Jack stood, immobile, looking down at Zarrod below him. The Deathlord Supreme, tall and ominous, gazed back up at the ship, Anna still hanging helplessly at his side. Jack looked at her, his heart tearing in two. He knew he had to escape, but the thought of leaving Anna behind was too terrible a choice for him to comprehend.

Jack could hear Heckubus running around the bridge trying to start up the ship himself, to no avail. He could hear Scallywag yelling at him to do something before it was too late. But all Jack could do was gaze down at Anna, helpless and afraid.

He saw her face, tears streaking down her cheeks as she looked up toward the ship, as though she could actually see him looking down at her. She moved her lips, and though Jack was too far away to hear her, the word was clear.

"Go."

Scallywag grabbed Jack and turned him face-to-face.

"WHAT ARE YA WAITING FOR?" the pirate screamed. "HURRY UP AND GET US—"

Suddenly, Jack's fist flew out and struck the Visini in the face. Scallywag jerked back, more surprised than hurt, and rubbed his mouth as Jack looked up at him angrily.

Without a word, Jack turned and hopped into the control chair. Instantly, the bridge of the starship came to life. Jack pulled up the Entanglement Engine screen. Outside he could hear the onslaught as the Deathlords fired upon the ship.

He called up Anna on the holoscreen in front of him and choked back tears as he took one last look at her.

"I'm sorry," he said quietly.

And with that, he jumped the ship.

CHAPTER  34

"**D**o something!" Jack cried over the alarms of the vital sign monitors.

"And what would you have me do?" muttered Heckubus. "I'm a doctor of evil, not medicine!" The robot was furiously tapping away at the main medical console as Jack, Grohm, and Scallywag tried their best to hold down Shepherd, who was convulsing violently on the table in the middle of the medical bay.

The problem had started almost immediately after they had jumped away from the Deathlord mothership. They had rematerialized somewhere in the relative safety of empty space, with no Deathlords in sight, much to the amazement of Jack's passengers, who'd never experienced a quantum space jump before.

"Blimee," breathed Scallywag, looking out at the viewscreens. "What just happened?"

"Fascinating," said Heckubus, tapping away at the ship's navigational console. "The entire ship has teleported! Instantaneous space travel from one point to another... why, imagine the possibilities!"

The robot twiddled his fingers.

"The *evil* possibilities! Mwuahaha!" he said.

No sooner had the robot's processors set about plotting numerous nefarious schemes using Entanglement Engine technology than a scream pierced the air. Jack turned, snapping out of the fog that had assaulted his head at leaving Anna behind in the grasp of the Deathlord Supreme. Up on the teleportation platform, still in the grip of Grohm, Shepherd was writhing and screaming in pain.

Jack leapt out of his chair and rushed to the Paragon's side.

"Shepherd?" Jack said. "Shepherd, what's wrong?"

Shepherd's eyes were rolling toward the back of his head and his jaw was clenched so tight Jack was afraid he might crack his teeth. Suddenly, the man began to convulse.

"What's wrong with him?" Jack cried out to no one in particular.

Scallywag knelt by Shepherd. "Hold him steady, Grohm," the pirate ordered. Grohm put his massive hands on Shepherd to keep him from flailing around. Scallywag turned to Jack. "He must've been injured worse than we thought in his fight with the Deathlord Supreme," Scallywag said. "Do ya have a medical bay on the ship?"

"I – I don't know…" replied Jack.

"Well, go find out," said Scallywag. "In the meantime, we'll just try and keep the bugger from hurting himself further."

Jack nodded and rushed out of the bridge and into the hallway of the ship. There were many doors lining the corridor, and Jack prayed one of them would be the medical bay.

Sure enough, the first door he tried seemed to be it. Jack had no idea what a medical bay looked like, but the room contained an observation table on which to lay a patient and lots of computers that looked like they belonged in some type of a hospital. He rushed back to the bridge and told Grohm to carry Shepherd there.

No sooner did they lay the Paragon on the table than the computers and monitors in the room sprang to life, showing various readouts and vital signs, none of which Jack understood. Heckubus quickly began pouring over the data.

"What's wrong with him?" Jack asked. "Can you fix him?"

"Curious…" said the robot. "There appears to be nothing which would indicate he's injured at all."

"Yer reading the bloody instruments cock-eyed," grumbled Scallywag. "There's clearly something wrong with the man."

"Far be it for me to argue with your vast medical knowledge, you dolt," replied Heckubus, "but according to these readouts, he's perfectly fine, barring a few minor electrical burns and bruises. Nothing that would explain the reaction we're seeing."

Shepherd screamed out in pain and his body jerked. Grohm leaned over him and tried to keep him from falling off the observation table. The monitors around the room began to beep in complaint.

"Are you sure?" asked Jack urgently. "He's obviously not fine."

"Of course, I am!" replied Heckubus, indignantly. "As if Regal physiology is too complicated for my massively brilliant mind to understand. Pah! All scans show that physically he is fine. No major wounds, viruses, cancers – not even a cavity. The computer shows he's perfectly healthy."

"*Then what's wrong with him?*" shouted Jack, his frustration with the whole situation building. Heckubus turned his oblong head toward Jack and focused his large round eyes on him.

"I don't know," replied the robot simply.

Then, Shepherd started to convulse uncontrollably, which brings us up to speed to where we were at the beginning, with Jack and the others trying to restrain the Paragon, while Heckubus frantically searched for a way to heal him.

"I say," muttered the robot. "There is some very impressive equipment in this medical bay. It's light-years beyond anything that's currently available in the known universe."

"Can any of it help Shepherd?" Jack asked.

"Hard to know what to do when we can't diagnose what's wrong with him," replied Heckubus.

"Well, do *something*, ya bloody tin can!" sneered Scallywag.

The robot sighed. "Fine. I suppose I can try this nervous system filter here. Perhaps that will get him to stop thrashing about so."

"Anything!" pleaded Jack. "Just do it!"

Heckubus tapped a few keys on the medical console and from the ceiling of the medical bay, a solid block of green light shone down, encapsulating Shepherd. Within the block of light, tiny blue webs of what looked like lightning began to appear, touching down all over Shepherd's body. Jack thought it almost looked like one of those weird science fair experiments where two charged metal balls shoot electricity between them.

All of a sudden, Jack could see Shepherd begin to calm down, and the Paragon stopped convulsing.

"It's working!" Jack breathed.

Heckubus looked around at the life-sign monitors at his station. "Heart rate dropping, pulse slowing, blood pressure returning to normal..." reported the robot.

Then, the webs of blue lightning stopped and the solid block of green light climbed back up into its original location in the ceiling. Jack leaned over Shepherd whose eyes were closed. It looked like he had passed out again.

"Took ya long enough," grumbled Scallywag.

"How often must I say it?" said Heckubus, exasperated. "You cannot rush genius."

"Looked more like guesswork to me," replied the pirate.

"Part of being a genius is guessing correctly," said Heckubus smugly. "But next time, you can be the one to decipher the

advanced medical technology while I deride your efforts, if that'll make you happy."

"Is he going to be okay?" asked Jack.

"Of course he'll be okay!" replied the robot. "The worst is obviously behind us."

Suddenly, Shepherd's body tensed, and his back arched in pain. Electrical tendrils began to erupt from the Paragon's armor. Jack, Scallywag, and Grohm all noticed them at the same time, just as they rapidly began to spark and snake around Shepherd.

"Uh-oh," said Jack.

Then, an eruption of electrical energy shot out from Shepherd's armor. The force of the blast knocked back Jack and the others, sending Grohm smashing into some of the equipment. Scallywag was thrown against the far wall, and Jack landed by Heckubus, who quickly retreated from the main console that began shorting out from electrical overload.

The medical bay went dead and all the monitors ceased to transmit. Jack's head was buzzing from the shock he had received. He looked up, his vision blurry, and he saw his companions strewn about the room. Scallywag was nursing the back of his head, while Grohm lay snorting in a pile of crushed computers.

"Hmmmmm. Perhaps I spoke too soon," said Heckubus meekly.

Shepherd was lying still on the table, groaning slightly.

"Jack…" he said weakly.

Jack struggled to his feet and made his way to Shepherd's side. Shepherd's hard, grey eyes were now cloudy and distant, and his skin was pale and cold. The Paragon wore a pained expression on his face as he wheezed, struggling to breathe.

Jack didn't know what to do. He reached out and grabbed the man's hand, though he wasn't sure if Shepherd could feel it through his armored gauntlet.

"I'm here, Mr. Shepherd..." said Jack.

Shepherd's eyes seemed to focus on Jack's face. "I'm... sorry..." Shepherd struggled. "It looks like... I won't get to train you after all..."

Jack felt a lump catch in his throat. "What's wrong with you?" he asked.

"I... don't know..." replied Shepherd. "It feels... like my very soul has been ripped apart... and it's getting worse..."

"But, the computers—" said Jack. "They say you're fine. They can't find anything wrong with you."

"The Deathlord Supreme..." continued Shepherd. "He was harvesting my life force... when you teleported me."

Jack thought back to the brief moment when the Deathlord Supreme had almost ripped his life from his body, and instantly, he knew what Shepherd was referring to. If indeed they had interrupted the process, could it be that half of Shepherd's soul had been left behind when they had rescued him? If that were the case, the shock might be the cause of what was happening.

"But, you'll be okay, right?" asked Jack. "We can fix you, can't we? Just tell me how, and we'll do it."

Shepherd shook his head sadly. "I... don't think you can fix this..."

Jack felt tears welling up in his eyes. He gritted his teeth and held onto Shepherd's hand tightly. "No," he said. "You're a Paragon. You're invincible! You can kick the butts of twenty guys single-handedly! You can't die."

"How I wish... that were true..." said Shepherd, his voice barely above a whisper.

"Just manifest something!" pleaded Jack. "Think of something that will save you, and we'll use it!"

"Jack, I–" suddenly Shepherd spasmed. Jack grabbed onto Shepherd's face and tried to keep the man focused on him.

"Stay with me, Shepherd!" Jack demanded. "I can't do this without you!"

Shepherd reached out, grabbing Jack's shoulder and looking him in the eyes. "You're going to have to..." he wheezed.

"No!" cried Jack. "Please!"

"Tell... Anna..." Shepherd struggled to speak, but before he could say any more, he began to convulse. Jack grabbed onto him and tried to steady him.

"Stay with me!" Jack pleaded. "Do you hear me, Shepherd? *Stay with me!*"

Shepherd looked at Jack, his eyes wide with pain, fear, and regret – a look that stabbed into Jack's very soul, and would weigh heavily on his heart for the rest of his days. With his final breath, Shepherd said simply...

"Be strong."

Jack looked on helplessly as Shepherd went limp, and his eyes stared vacantly into the distance as life left them.

Before he knew it, Jack had crumpled onto the floor, tears coming uncontrollably now. Feelings of fear and sadness crashed over him, wrapping around him like a constricting snake. His family and friends were gone. Anna was gone. And now, the one man he was relying on to save the day was gone, too.

Paragon Shepherd was dead...

...and all hope had just died with him.

EPISODE III:

EARTHMAN JACK

VS.

THE GHOST PLANET

CHAPTER ✦ 35

Jack sat in the corner of the medical bay, hugging his knees hard against his chest. He sniffed to keep his nose from running, and his red, puffy eyes stared across the room at the cold, hard table where Shepherd's body lay. For a moment, Jack wished things were like they were in the movies, where the wise old mentor's body would magically disappear and then his ghost would suddenly show up and tell him what to do.

But this wasn't a movie. Shepherd's body lay there, cold and still, a painful reminder that in reality, the dead didn't come back.

Jack didn't know how much time had passed since he watched the last bits of life fade from Shepherd's eyes. All he knew was that he had no more tears left. He remembered crawling into the corner and crying, losing himself in his own grief. He didn't notice when his companions had quietly left, leaving him to his sorrow in private. Jack didn't blame them. They didn't know Shepherd, and they barely knew him for that matter. What type of comfort would they have been able to provide?

As his grief subsided, thoughts raced through Jack's mind. He thought about everything he'd lost and all the people who'd died. His mother, his friends, Major Ganix and the Regal soldiers, Professor Green, and Anna. Now, with Shepherd gone, what was left? He had no home to go back to. No one was alive to take care of him. He had absolutely *nothing*.

His stomach felt as though it were filled with lead, and a blanket of hopelessness had wrapped itself around him. He wanted to cry some more, but he just wasn't able to. He gazed back at Shepherd, his once gleaming armor now seemed dull in the pale light of the medical bay.

This is all your fault, Jack thought. *You're supposed to be the hero. You're supposed to be the guy who saves the day. If you really believed all that bull-crap about taking responsibility for your actions, you wouldn't have allowed yourself to die!*

Jack got to his feet. He walked over to Shepherd and looked down at him. The numbness inside gave way to a small ember of anger as he gazed upon Shepherd's motionless face.

"What am I supposed to do now?" Jack asked.

Shepherd did not respond.

"You were going to teach me," said Jack, his fists clenching. "You said I'd get to learn to fight the Deathlords. That we'd find a way to defeat them, together!"

Shepherd did not respond.

"You said I didn't have to go through this alone! You said you'd be there for me!"

Shepherd did not respond.

"WHAT AM I SUPPOSED TO DO NOW???" Jack screamed.

Shepherd's lifeless body lay still. Jack turned away, sick of looking at it. He tried taking a deep breath, but the air tasted stuffy and stale to him. Suddenly, the room felt small, as if it were shrinking, closing in around him. He walked to the medical bay's exit, and the doors opened with a hiss.

Out in the hallway, he was greeted with better lighting, and he sucked in the air as though he'd just come up from underwater. His anger died inside him, and again he felt empty and helpless.

Jack turned and walked, shuffling down the hallway of his spaceship. Everything was gleaming and shiny, friendly and new looking. But none of it alleviated the heavy sadness that had taken root inside him. Jack just felt tired, so very, very tired.

Images of his room at home sprang into his mind. The small, cramped room with the closet overflowing with dirty clothes and the tiny window where sunshine would sneak in. All he wanted to do was crawl into his bed, pull the covers over his head, and sleep. Sleep, and make everything go away…

Home, Jack thought. *I want to go home.*

Jack heard a small "hiss" noise. He turned to his right where a door in the hallway had opened and stopped.

Jack's heart suddenly leapt, and it felt as though it were caught in his throat. His eyes went wide and his knees went wobbly. He didn't move – he *didn't want to* move, because he was afraid if he did, what he was seeing would disappear like some type of mirage.

But it didn't disappear. It was there; Jack was sure of it.

Jack slowly turned his body and tentatively stepped into the doorway that had just opened. It was a small room, no bigger than most people's bathrooms. Shoved into the corner, was Jack's bed – messy and unmade, as he had usually left it – with faded blankets adorned with starships and superheroes all in a tangle.

The walls were littered with posters of professional wrestlers and kung fu movies; dirty clothes erupted from the tiny closet and were strewn about the floor.

A small window above the bed looked out into the starry night of outer space, and there was even a banged-up digital clock duct-taped to the wall.

Jack stepped back into the hallway in disbelief, and the door hissed shut. He stared at the shiny, inviting hallway door dumbly. Was his mind playing tricks on him? Had he really seen what he thought he had just seen?

Jack stepped forward again, and the door hissed open in response.

Nothing had changed. Jack stepped inside and looked around. It was his room. It had all the same posters, all the same clothes, the same faded and stained wallpaper – it even *smelled* the same as he remembered it!

Jack collapsed on his bed and buried his face into his pillow. He wrapped the blankets around him, and a giddy laugh suddenly escaped from his throat. It felt exactly like his bed! It *was* his bed! He was home!

How? wondered Jack. *How is this possible?*

Jack rolled on his back and looked up at the water-damaged ceiling with a single lightbulb hanging precariously from its socket. That was his ceiling, all right. *This was his room.*

Jack sat upright in bed. His mind was racing. He knew what was happening was impossible. Every detail was exact – to a tee. How could an exact replica of his bedroom exist on a 50,000-year-old spaceship?

Jack thought about the ship. He remembered how, while he was piloting it, it seemed to change itself into what he was familiar with. He thought about finding the empty room where he could punch and kick and throw his tantrum. He thought about how he had found the medical bay the exact moment he needed it. And now, he had found his bedroom when all he had wanted more than anything in the world was to go home.

Jack got out of his bed and walked back into the hallway of the ship, the door closing behind him. Jack stared at the door, his brain buzzing. Could it be? Is it possible?

I'm hungry, thought Jack. *I want some food.*

Jack stepped forward, and the door, which moments earlier had led to his bedroom, opened. But this time, it was not his bedroom at all.

Instead, Jack was greeted with a large room, filled with scratched up wooden tables, its walls lined with faux wood paneling from the 1970's. Dirty green-red-and-white colored lamps hung from the ceiling. In the corner stood a scratched and rickety pool table and an on-the-fritz jukebox. The smell of bad pizza hung in the air, and Jack's heart thumped in his chest.

It was Big Jim's Pizza Palace.

Everything was exactly as Jack remembered it, down to the counter Fred would stand behind, serving up slices and yelling at annoying high schoolers. In the kitchen, Jack could see the aged and blackened pizza ovens fired up, and a fully cooked pepperoni pizza lay waiting on its conveyor belt.

Jack hopped over the counter and looked at the pizza with amazement. He picked a piece of pepperoni off the top and tasted it; its cheap, greasy goodness ran down his fingers.

This was what I wanted, thought Jack. *This is what I was hungry for!*

Jack looked around the room as if someone might be watching him.

"Is that what you do?" Jack asked the empty pizza parlor. "I think of something... and you give me what I want?"

Jack felt a small tingle in the back of his head, as though the ship were answering him.

"It's like... that stuff Professor Green was talking about? The quantum stuff — like Shepherd did? You can manifest things?"

Jack felt a tingle again. He smiled, a feeling of excitement washing over him. That's why the ship was so special! It wasn't just something that flew through space. It wasn't just a ship that was able to teleport anywhere it wanted. It wasn't even that it had some type of psychic link with its user... it was a machine that was able to manifest anything its crew needed! That's why it could change itself to make it easier to fly, and that's why it could keep the Deathlords from figuring it out. The ship could literally alter itself to suit any situation!

Suddenly, Jack found himself running out of the room and down the hallway to the medical bay. He stopped outside the door, his chest fluttering with nervous energy. He closed his eyes and thought really hard.

Alive, thought Jack. *Be alive!*

Jack opened his eyes and stepped toward the door. It hissed open, and Jack found the room inside to be brightly lit and fully repaired once again. The computers that were previously crushed and shorted out beeped and booped, all in full working order.

On the observation table lay Shepherd. Jack rushed up and began to shake him.

"Wake up!" said Jack. "Come back!"

Jack continued to shake Shepherd, but he remained unresponsive.

"I need you alive!" yelled Jack. "Be alive!"

But it was no use. Shepherd was dead, and he wasn't returning.

Jack stepped away from the body. He looked up at the ceiling, and around the walls of the room. "Can't you bring him back?" he asked. "You can manifest a freakin' pizza! Can you manifest a living Shepherd?"

Jack's head tingled again. But this wasn't like the other times. It was like a big, loud "No" in his brain. Jack's heart sank.

His ship could give him the warm, smelly blankets of home, the hot pizza with the cheap cheese and pepperoni of Big Jim's, but not a living, breathing Shepherd to save the day.

"That's your limit isn't it?" asked Jack. "You can't manifest life."

Jack's head tingled in response.

"What do you think I should do?" asked Jack. "What is there that's left for me?"

Jack waited for a response, but none came. The only sounds were the rhythmic beeps of the medical machines. Jack sighed. The ship that could give him anything couldn't give him an answer.

Jack looked down at Shepherd. It was hard for him to believe that at one point, he'd have given anything never to see the man again. And now, he'd give anything to have him back. Whether it was teaching class or fighting off an army of Deathlords, Shepherd always seemed to know what to do.

Jack thought back to his last detention with Shepherd. It was the very first time Jack had felt like the guy didn't have it out for him.

"There are people out there that believe life is just something that happens to them..." he heard Shepherd say in his memory, "that they have no control over the events and circumstances they find themselves in..."

Jack closed his eyes and remembered sitting in the classroom after school, Shepherd leaning against his desk looking down at him.

"But the truth is," continued Shepherd, "we are the ones who shape the lives we live. We are the ones who allow good things and bad things to happen to us. By taking responsibility for our actions, we are able to make our lives better. When we play the victim, we allow our lives to be miserable. If you can take responsibility for yourself, decide to make your life better – and take action to that effect – then you are the master of your own destiny. And when that happens, you are capable of great things."

"I'm just a kid," responded Jack. "I'm not capable of anything."

"You know that's not true," said Shepherd.

"It is," said Jack. "Nothing I do ever works out. I didn't want my planet to explode. I didn't want you to die. I didn't want to leave Anna behind. I didn't want any of this."

"What *do* you want?" asked Shepherd.

Jack sighed. His chest tightened again, as if he were preparing to cry. Jack fought against the feeling. He was tired of crying. He was tired of feeling sad and helpless.

"I want to rescue Anna," replied Jack. "I want to stop the Deathlords, and I want to make them pay for what they've done."

"And what's stopping you?" asked Shepherd.

"I'm scared," said Jack. "I'm alone, and I don't think I can do it."

Shepherd nodded.

"When we play the victim, we allow our lives to be miserable," he repeated.

"But if I take responsibility, then I am the master of my own destiny," said Jack, finishing the thought.

Shepherd nodded.

Images of Anna flashed into Jack's mind. The way the sunlight caught in her hair by the cornfield behind school. The cute and awkward way she looked when she showed up at his doorstep. Her smile when she tasted her first chocolate milkshake. In a way, she was the only thing from Earth that Jack had left, and now the Deathlords had her. They'd taken the last thing Jack had that reminded him of home, and in that moment, he knew he had to get her back – that it was his responsibility to save her. But in a way, that realization made him even more frightened.

"What if I fail?" asked Jack. "What if I die?"

"Then you die advancing," said Shepherd. "And you fail trying to succeed. But it's not the outcome that's important, Jack. It's the action that matters."

"It's my decision," said Jack.

"Yes," replied Shepherd.

"It's my responsibility."

"Yes."

"It's my destiny."

"You are the master of your own destiny, Jack," said Shepherd softly.

Jack opened his eyes and looked down at Shepherd, lying on the table before him.

"I finally understand," said Jack. "I get what you were trying to teach me."

Jack placed his hand on the breastplate of Shepherd's armor, as though it were a sacred book for him to swear upon.

"I'm going to save Anna. I'm going to take down the Deathlords. I'm going to get revenge for you, and everyone who has died. And I'm going to live through all of it."

Jack removed his hand, and with steely resolve, looked upon Shepherd one final time.

"That's the destiny I choose," he said.

CHAPTER ✺ 36

O n the bridge of the ship, Scallywag sat in the control chair, trying something – anything – to get the blasted thing moving. He'd been holed away in that dreadful Deathlord pit for far too long, and now the only thing he could think about was making his way to the nearest outpost's red light district and finding enough alcohol and female company to make the entire ordeal seem like some far-off nightmare. He didn't even care if the booze was watered down and the women were uglier than a beaten-up Skyrofish – he just desperately needed to relax someplace that wasn't constantly trying to kill him.

Of course, nothing he did seemed to have any effect. It appeared the Earthman wasn't kidding when he said he was the only one who could pilot this ship. Scallywag glanced up from his button pushing to see Grohm sitting quietly in a seat nearby. The massive Rognok looked to be asleep again, still as a rock – much as he was in the Pit when he wasn't fighting. For a brief moment, Scallywag wondered if it mattered to the blasted alien where he was – spaceship, Pleasure Planet, or endless Pit of death and despair – as long as he could sit around like a bump on a log and nap himself silly.

Scallywag looked away from Grohm, growing even more frustrated. He began to punch the buttons on the chair more forcefully, as if that would suddenly make them begin to respond to him.

"You're wasting your time," said Heckubus. The pirate turned and looked at the robot, who had stationed himself behind one of the ship's control panels with his feet leisurely kicked up upon it.

"Slag off," said Scallywag, before going back to hitting random buttons.

Heckubus sighed. "I've been through this ship's systems approximately a billion times. Everything about it is hard-wired to only respond to native inhabitants of the Earthman's planet."

"Ships are meant to be flown," said Scallywag. "They don't care by who."

"This one does," replied Heckubus. "Whoever made it wanted to be sure that only Earthmen could fly it, for some silly reason."

"So what's its deal, eh?" asked Scallywag. "Some type of DNA coding? Voice recognition? Brain scan tech?"

"Pah," muttered Heckubus. "If it were something as simple as that, do you think we'd still be here? I'd have hijacked this marvelous piece of machinery hours ago. No, this ship is far more advanced than anything I have ever come across. Even I am having difficulty understanding its inner-workings. And need I remind you... I am a genius."

Scallywag pounded his fist on the arm of the command chair. "I swear on Jerrimour the White and all his ancestors, if I hear ya proclaim yourself a genius one more time—"

"I *am* a genius," insisted Heckubus.

"Then figure out how to fly this bloody waste heap!" snapped Scallywag. "Teleport us again! Somewhere bright, and sunny, and decadent! Make yerself useful for once!"

"Shows how much you know," sniggled the robot. "This ship doesn't teleport."

"We were one place, now we're someplace else," said Scallywag. "What do you call that?"

"Entanglement."

"What the blazes are ya yammering about?"

"Have you any notion how teleportation works? And what it would take to teleport an entire spaceship across vast distances of space? I ask rhetorically because of course you have no idea, but let me just fill you in - the power requirements alone make the entire concept of a teleporting spaceship ridiculous. What this vessel appears to do is something far, far more sophisticated."

"Okay, I'll bite," said Scallywag, hopping out of the captain's chair and sauntering his way to Heckubus's console. "What does this ship do?"

"The quantum theory of Entanglement is that everything in the universe is connected," said Heckubus. "Everything we perceive in our universe – objects, spatial distance, even time itself – are all just things that are created by the minds of living beings, while the reality is that nothing actually exists. It's all just one big, entangled mess that you organics try to give order to with your feeble minds by creating these false constructs that come to define your reality."

"I'm already bored, robot," muttered Scallywag.

Heckubus rolled his large ocular orbs. "Think about it, you simpleton. Since everything is connected, then theoretically, we exist everywhere. Spatial distance has no meaning. If we wanted to, we could choose to stop existing here and exist someplace else instead."

Scallywag scratched his chin. "So... you're saying the ship didn't actually teleport... it just decided to exist someplace else?"

"Precisely!" said Heckubus. "And here's the really interesting part – only something with a living consciousness capable of defining its own reality can manipulate quantum entanglement. As far as anyone knows, only a select few

Paragons in history have been able to achieve this feat. And yet, here we have a ship that seems to be able to do it on command."

Scallywag raised an eyebrow. "Hold up," he said. "Are ya saying this ship is *alive?*"

"Of course not; don't be stupid," replied Heckubus. "I admit I am a bit stymied by how a machine is able to achieve something only organics are supposedly capable of, but one thing cannot be ignored – whatever this ship is, it is without a doubt the single, most powerful vessel the universe has ever seen."

"That's what I'm counting on," came a voice.

Heckubus and Scallywag turned to see Jack standing in the doorway of the bridge.

"Oy, there ya are," smiled Scallywag, relieved to see the boy had finished his crying. "Ya ready ta kick this ship o' yers into gear, lad?"

"I am," said Jack, walking down toward the others.

"Right-o!" cheered Scallywag. "We figured out where we are during yer downtime, and the good news is, there's a Pholon trading outpost not far from here…"

"We're not going there," said Jack as he walked up to a panel opposite Heckubus and began tapping some keys.

Scallywag shared a curious glance with Heckubus before responding. "All righty, lad. Ya got someplace else you wanna go?"

"I do," said Jack as he hit the final key on the console.

Behind Scallywag, a small circular platform raised up from the floor of the bridge. A holographic image of a barren, white planet popped into existence directly above it.

"There," said Jack.

"I say," said Scallywag as he regarded the image of the planet Jack had called up. "Is that what I think it is?"

"Terahades," said Jack. "The Deathlord's Ghost Planet."

Scallywag glared at Jack. "Funny," he said. "I was picturing someplace more tropical."

"The ship downloaded the entire Deathlord database while it was interfaced with the mothership," said Jack. "We know everything that the Deathlords do about this planet. Where it's located, what its defenses are – everything."

"Lad, we are not going to any bloody Ghost Planet," said Scallywag. "Having just barely escaped from the Deathlords' mothership, I can assure you, I have no plans on stepping foot anywhere near a Deathlord for the rest o' me life."

"For once, I'm in agreement with the pirate," chimed in Heckubus. "Really, Earthman, if you want to commit suicide, there are easier ways to do it than flying to that planet. Why, I know of approximately 237 ways we could assist you with common things we can find lying around this ship."

"They've got Anna," said Jack. "That's where they're taking her, so that's where we're gonna go."

"I don't give two swats about the Princess of the Regalus Empire," replied Scallywag.

"Nor I," intoned Heckubus. "Our best course of action is to travel to the nearest celestial hub and get as far away from any Deathlord incursion as possible."

"And after that?" snapped Jack. "What then? Wait for them to just show up again and keep running away?"

"The universe is a big place," said Scallywag. "Lots o' places to go."

"But for how long?" asked Jack. "How long can you run before they find you? You said yourself that you're one of the most wanted criminals in the galaxy, and yet even you were captured by them."

"A mistake I do not plan on repeating," replied Scallywag.

"And if you make a different mistake?" said Jack. "What's to prevent you from being on the next planet they blow up without warning?"

"You can spout what-ifs 'til yer jaw goes slack, lad," said Scallywag. "There is nothing in this universe that could possibly justify traipsing back into the midst of the Deathlord fleet."

"Are you forgetting everything we learned on that ship? Anna is the last surviving member of the royal family. She's the only one able to work Ancient technology! If the Deathlords bring her to the Ghost Planet and force her to unleash this invincible armada of the dudes who destroyed the Ancients – there is nothing that's going to be able to stop them! They'll just keep destroying the galaxy, one planet after another, unless we rescue her!"

"And what do ya propose we do, Earthman?" growled Scallywag. "Take on the entire Deathlord army ourselves?"

"No," said Jack. "We just go to the planet, bust Anna out, and then jump away."

"Just like that?" chuckled Scallywag.

"Yeah, why not?" replied Jack. "We got out of the mothership, didn't we? How hard can escaping an entire planet be?"

"This isn't just some run-of-the-mill planet, you fool," said Heckubus. "It is the barren wasteland of a long forgotten world, designed by the most advanced race in the history of civilization to keep anything from escaping it. It's a tomb, Earthman. According to the data I accessed while sneaking around... I mean, analyzing your ship's systems, the Ghost Planet is surrounded by a dense minefield hidden within a nebula that renders sensor readings useless. In addition to that, the Deathlords have recorded hidden platforms within the minefield that also fire anti-spacecraft missiles. Add to that a planet-wide repulsor shield and the firepower of an entire fleet of Deathlord Planetkillers, and anyone who gets even remotely close to that planet is dead – no matter how you look at it. And I, for one, happen to like not being dead."

"As do I," agreed Scallywag.

Jack looked at the holographic image of the Ghost Planet. Even through the digital blips and crackles of the holo-generator, it loomed as a cold, menacing, and dreadful object on the bridge of the ship, as though its mere presence would infect any who gazed upon it. For a brief moment, doubt took hold of him, and he realized he hadn't really thought through just how difficult something like this might be.

Seeing the uncertainty on Jack's face, Scallywag turned to Heckubus. "Put in the coordinates for the outpost," he said. "We're leaving."

In the back of his mind, Jack felt a twinge of anger brew, percolating up from Scallywag's sudden order, as though this were his ship. Jack pushed away any doubt he felt. He was going to do this. He *had* to do this.

"We're not going to the outpost," said Jack sternly.

"Yes, we are," replied Scallywag as he walked up to the control chair and gestured toward it. "Now hop in, and let's get a move on. I think I've suffered enough insanity for one lifetime."

Jack stepped forward, not willing to back down.

"We are going to the Ghost Planet, and we're going to rescue Anna," said Jack.

"No, we're not," insisted Scallywag. "Yer girlfriend is as good as dead, lad. Get over it."

"You're not the one in charge here," said Jack.

Scallywag scowled and unholstered one of his blasters, aiming it at Jack.

"This says I am," the pirate sneered.

"Ooooooo," twiddled Heckubus. "Things just got interesting."

Jack looked at the gun in Scallywag's hand, a little taken aback. "What are you doing?" he asked.

"I'm sick of arguing, lad," said Scallywag. "I feel for ya, I do. But I've been the captain of me own ship for many a cycle, and I don't take orders from anyone – especially some wet-behind-the-ears alien kid who happened to luck into a bloody mystery ship. Now get in the chair, fire up the engines, or I'll blast ya to shreds."

"If you kill me, you'll never be able to pilot this ship," said Jack.

"And what if I just maim you, hmmmm?" asked Scallywag. "You don't need both knees to fly, do ya lad?"

Jack regarded Scallywag for a moment, looking the pirate in his eyes. All the warnings he'd heard from Sergeant Rodham came flooding back to him. But in his heart, he still didn't believe them. This man had saved his life many times and shown incredible bravery since pretty much the moment they'd met. And for the life of him, Jack refused to believe Scallywag was as bad as everyone – maybe even the Visini himself – believed him to be.

"Need I remind you that Faruuz died on that ship? That he died because of the Deathlords?" said Jack.

"And what does that have ta do with anything?" asked Scallywag.

"Were you really trying to rescue Faruuz?" Jack asked. "Did you really want to make amends with him?"

"What's it matter?" replied the pirate. "The ol' brute is dead."

"It matters," said Jack. "Because despite everything I've heard about you and your kind, Scally, I believe in my heart that you really were there to try to help him."

Scallywag regarded Jack for a moment before finally lowering his pistol. "Ya don't know anything about me," he said.

"Maybe," replied Jack. "But I think you really are trying to be someone different. I think you're trying to be a better man than you believe you are. That's why you tried to help Faruuz. That's why you tried to help me."

"I was just surviving," replied Scallywag. "It's what I always do. I needed Faruuz on me side, and I needed *you* ta get off that bloody Deathlord ship. Simple as that, lad."

"So that's all you care about? Surviving?" Jack asked. "Because eventually, some day, the Deathlords are going to come to your homeworld. And when they do, you have to ask yourself if you're going to be okay to continue living after everything and everyone you've ever known have been destroyed."

"I don't care about me homeworld," said Scallywag. "I don't care about anybody except meself."

"You say that now," replied Jack. "But trust me. I watched when the Deathlords destroyed my planet. I saw it blow up right in front of me. Everyone I loved and cared about is gone, and that hurts. More than you can probably understand. But the funny thing is, even the things I hated about it, all the stuff I didn't care about or didn't like... I'd give anything to have any of it back now."

"Look, lad—"

"No, you look!" Jack persisted. "I don't care what color you are or how badly you say you want to save your own hide. When your world is gone, it's gone, and even the most selfish jerk in the universe is going to feel that kind of loss. You might be alive but if there's nowhere left for you to go, what's the point? What kind of life can you hope to live if you never get to see your own sun come up, or taste the food you grew up with? What happens when you never get to see any of your own people, anywhere, and don't have a single memento of what it means to have been born at all? What's worth living for, if everything you've ever known or loved has been erased from existence? You don't just lose a planet, Scally, you lose a part of yourself – a part that will never come back, no matter where you run to."

Scallywag sighed and looked away. If the alien had any heart at all, Jack hoped his words were having some kind of effect.

"I'm the last of my kind," said Jack. "Do you really want to be the last of yours?"

Scallywag's shoulders slumped. He turned to Jack, avoiding his gaze, his mouth turned in a sad frown. The pirate suddenly looked very tired.

"I'm no hero, boy," said Scallywag.

"No," said Jack. "But you're what I've got. I need you, Scally. I need all of you. I can't do this alone."

"Earthman not alone," said Grohm, standing up, now suddenly fully awake. Jack looked at the lumbering Rognok as the alien gazed down at him. "Grohm will go. Grohm will fight."

Jack smiled at Grohm. "Thanks, big guy," he said.

"Bloody Rognok," mumbled Scallywag. "He'll go anywhere there's a fight. He don't care if he dies."

Grohm looked at Scallywag, his red eyes narrowing. "Coward," he said.

Scallywag raised his eyebrow. "Beg yer pardon?" he replied, somewhat taken aback.

"Grohm help you in Pit," Grohm said. "Grohm fight for you. Grohm protect you."

"And now you want me to repay all that by going on a slagging suicide mission?" asked Scallywag.

"Visini can run," snorted Grohm. "Or Visini can fight. Live life in fear, running away – or live fighting for something greater than self."

Scallywag looked at Grohm uncomfortably. "Since when did you become a bloody philosopher?" he asked. "All that time in the Pit, I never heard you string more than two words together."

Grohm approached Scallywag, towering over the pirate, meeting his gaze with his hard red and black eyes. "Grohm sees more than Visini thinks," he said. "Grohm hears more than Visini knows. Grohm does not sleep. Grohm never sleeps."

"What the blazes are you going on about?"

Grohm reached out and put his massive hand on Scallywag's shoulder. "Grohm sees Visini pirate. Hears him when Visini pirate doesn't think Grohm is listening. Grohm knows why Visini fights. Grohm knows what Visini seeks."

"And what's that?" Scallywag demanded.

"Honor," rumbled Grohm. "Redemption. Justice." Grohm pointed at Jack. "Earthman gives you chance for all those things, and you want to run away?"

Grohm stepped back and stood side by side with Jack. "Grohm calls that a coward," he said flatly.

Scallywag stared at Grohm, eyes wide, unable to speak. It was obvious Grohm's words got to him, and Jack didn't want to let that go to waste.

"I know what I'm asking of all of you," said Jack. "But there's a reason why it was the four of us who made it out of that mothership. Heckubus has the brains. Grohm has the strength.

I have the tech. And you, Scally... you're the survivor. You know how to stay alive, no matter how bad things get. And among the four of us, I think we have a little bit of luck on our side, too."

Jack stepped toward Scallywag. "I may just be a kid, but I know what it takes to be a part of a team. And like it or not, the four of us *are* a team. A good one – a team that defied the odds and escaped something everyone thought was certain death. If we did it once, we can do it again. Because if we don't do this – if we don't act now to stop the Deathlords, they win! And if there's just one thing you need to know about me, Scally, it's this: I *hate* to lose."

Heckubus clapped his tiny metal hands together. "Oh, bravo!" the robot said. "If I had a heart, I'm sure it would be melting by now."

"Shut it, ya tin can," grumbled Scallywag.

Scallywag stared at Jack for a heartbeat before cradling his face with his hand. The Visini rubbed his forehead, and his expression curled up into the kind of look that told Jack the pirate knew he was about to do something he felt he'd regret.

"I shoulda let ol' Faruuz blast ya when he had the chance," smiled Scallywag.

Jack smiled back. "Does that mean you'll help?"

Scallywag looked from Jack to Grohm and sighed. "There's a lot that could go wrong with this insanity you've hatched, lad. This ain't some run o' the mill prison break, or ship raid for that matter. You know what we'd be up against. How do you propose the four o' us deal with *all* that?"

"Don't worry about it," said Jack as he glared at the image of the Ghost Planet. "I have a plan."

"Is that so?" replied Scallywag. "Yer saying ya have a plan that will allow us ta get past the planetary defenses, infiltrate the

Deathlord stronghold, and then escape the inescapable planet without getting killed?"

"I do."

Scallywag and Grohm exchanged a skeptical look.

"Very well," said Scallywag. "Let's hear it."

"Heckubus..." said Jack.

"Yes?" replied the robot.

"Think of a plan."

Scallywag laughed. "*That's* yer brilliant idea? Ask the robot?"

"Is he not the greatest evil genius criminal mastermind in seven star systems?" asked Jack.

"Eight, actually," corrected Heckubus.

"Well," said Jack. "Just imagine how many star systems you'd be known in if we can actually pull this off and rescue the heir to the largest empire in the entire galaxy."

Heckubus tilted his head thoughtfully. "Hmmm... interesting..."

"Forget it!" exclaimed Scallywag. "I am not putting my life in the hands of a bloody malfunctioning computer with legs. He can claim he's the most brilliant criminal mind in the entire universe, but I have yet to bloody see it."

"Well, now's his chance to prove it," said Jack. "What do you say, Heckubus? Can you come up with a plan?"

"Can it be an *evil* plan?" asked Heckubus.

"Yes," replied Jack.

Heckubus twiddled his fingers excitedly.

"Excellent..." the robot intoned.

CHAPTER ✺ 37

braxas stood on the bridge of the mothership, gazing up at the large viewscreen now filled with the thick blue and purple cloud of the nebula. He could feel the floor vibrate slightly as another explosion rocked the hull, echoing a dull thud throughout the room. The Supreme had been sending shards into the nebula for months to try to clear out the mines so the path to the Ghost Planet would be safe for the fleet, but it seemed like no matter how many they got rid of, more would somehow appear in their place.

After finally dropping out of hyperspace, Abraxas had sent the other Planetkillers into the cloud ahead of the *Inferno* so they might absorb the brunt of the damage during the journey through the nebula. Not that the *Inferno* couldn't take the damage the mines posed to it, but with what was about to happen, Abraxas did not want to take any unnecessary chances.

The Deathlord paced back and forth, gazing at the bridge's Acolytes as they silently manned their consoles. Acolytes were an efficient lot, but their inability to control the ship while the prisoners had made their escape was something that would need to be addressed. The higher in rank a Deathlord was, the more self-aware he became, and Abraxas worried the rank-and-file among the ship's crew were not sufficiently equipped for what had transpired. After the Earthman's ship had disappeared, full control had been restored, which led the Vicar General to conclude that the vessel had somehow infiltrated their systems when it was supposed to have been the other way around.

After admitting this mistake, the Deathlord Supreme had rightly culled the Vicar General for his failure. Abraxas hoped his replacement would be far more capable (and far less annoying). He had always known they should have simply destroyed the ship when they'd had the chance. Perhaps next time the Supreme would take his suggestions more seriously.

Abraxas flexed his hand as he paced. He always hated how stiff new bodies felt so soon after reincarnation. He'd have preferred to take the time to pull his former body back together after the Regal had suckered him with that cheap thermal grenade trick, but the Supreme did not want to afford him that luxury. By the time the Earthman and his friends had made their escape, the *Inferno* was almost to its destination, and Abraxas would be needed to look after the ship while the Supreme carried out his duties.

Another explosion echoed throughout the bridge as the ship hit yet another mine. Abraxas approached a console and called up more views from the outside. The nebula cloud was thick with dust and gas, making sensor readings impossible. All navigation had to be done by sight, and even that was a chore. Most of the navigation beacons they had seeded throughout the nebula during their time searching for the planet had been destroyed or had gone missing. New ones had to be constantly deployed and replaced.

On the port and starboard side of the ship, Abraxas could see the tiny beads of light mounted on the escort shards, which flew in formation around the vessel. Their job was to intercept any missiles that might be fired at the ship from the hidden weapon platforms strewn about the cloud – either by shooting them down or ramming them before they could reach the mothership. Missiles were always more troublesome than mines. The missiles could zero in on engines or shield generators or any number of places that could cause major headaches should they be damaged in some way. And with visibility so low and sensors not functioning, a missile could creep up on them before they knew it. The mothership's shields would, of course, protect them from such an attack, but they were under orders to preserve as much power as possible and, thus, to leave the shields to a bare minimum. Couple that with the constant mine strikes, and the journey to the Ghost Planet suddenly became quite problematic.

But then, it would all be worth it when they finally arrived. The Supreme had alluded to what would transpire once the fleet had reached its destination. It was not Abraxas's habit to doubt his superior, but even he harbored some skepticism about what was going to happen. However, if what he had heard were true, then all aboard the fleet would witness something beyond even their wildest imaginations.

"We are nearing the nebula oasis, Warlord," reported one of the Acolytes. "Estimated time to the Ghost Planet is five minutes."

"I shall inform the Supreme," replied Abraxas. No sooner had he completed his sentence than the main entrance to the bridge rolled open and Zarrod stepped through. Somehow, the Deathlord Supreme always seemed to know what was happening on his bridge.

Hanging in the air beside him was the Regal girl. Her body was rigid, her skin was pale, and her face was twisted in pain. Abraxas enjoyed seeing the suffering of such inferior life-forms. As he understood it, the Supreme had decided to spend the remainder of the journey torturing her to advance the assimilation process. The girl floated beside Zarrod as he walked and was thrown to the ground like a dying animal when Zarrod reached Abraxas's station.

The girl hit the ground heavily and Abraxas heard the sweet sound of a sob escape from her as she was suddenly able to breathe once again, free from the clutches of the Supreme's soul grasp. Abraxas glanced at her briefly. Tears stained her cheeks; her blonde hair, thick with sweat, clung to her skin. Her hands trembled, and her body shook as she coughed. But when she looked up at them, Abraxas could see in her eyes that she still remained defiant. Her will was strong, obviously, but in some way Abraxas was glad she was resisting. It just meant she'd suffer longer.

"Report," commanded Zarrod.

"Most of the fleet has reached the Ghost Planet and taken position around it as ordered, Supreme," replied Abraxas. "The first ones through the nebula report severe damage to their ships, though nothing that will impede the mission. Most others have only reported moderate damage to their hulls."

"And what of our ship?"

"We've had a few mine strikes, but nothing serious," said Abraxas. "The ship should be in almost perfect condition to make our descent."

"Excellent," said Zarrod. "Tell the Acolytes to prepare the shield generators. We will need them shortly."

Abraxas nodded and relayed the Supreme's orders. Zarrod stood gazing up at the viewscreen as the blue and purple of the nebula swirled before it, as if parting to allow them through. Abraxas stood by the Supreme's side patiently, awaiting further orders.

"It's beautiful, isn't it?" said Zarrod softly.

The comment caught Abraxas slightly off guard. His mind understood the concept of beauty, but Abraxas himself had never actually experienced it. He looked at the Supreme curiously.

"Beautiful, Supreme?" asked Abraxas.

"The moment," said Zarrod. "These quiet moments before the storm. There's a certain energy to them. Can't you feel it?"

Truth be told, Abraxas felt nothing.

"Of course, Supreme," he replied. "It is… quite exciting."

Zarrod looked at him as if he knew Abraxas had no concept of what he was talking about. But it didn't seem to matter. He turned his gaze back up to the viewscreen. "We stand on the precipice of our ultimate triumph," he said, "to achieve that which our Lords have set before us. The part we've played will be the first step in their plan. Soon, all life in this wretched universe will be extinguished... and we shall bear witness to its beginning right here. These moments leading up to that... what could they be called other than beautiful?"

"Futile," came a quiet voice.

Zarrod and Abraxas looked down toward the Regal girl as she gazed up at them, her sapphire eyes hard and cold.

"Enjoy these moments while you can, Deathlord," she said, "because your plan will not work. Whatever it is, I'll see it fail... so help me, I will."

Zarrod stepped forward and reached out his hand. The girl was jerked up into the air, her body twitching as his invisible hooks dug into her. She was raised to eye-level with the Deathlord Supreme, who gazed at her with his terrible, burning red eyes.

"Still trying to fight me, I see," said Zarrod.

"You might as well kill me..." said the girl through gritted teeth. "I'll never help you. Never!"

"You will," said Zarrod. "You're strong; I'll give you that. I was hoping to have control of you by now, but it matters not. Eventually you'll succumb to the slythru. But until then, I have other ways of controlling you."

"You have nothing," the girl replied.

"Don't I?" said Zarrod as he released the girl from his hold once more. She fell to the ground as the Deathlord moved to a nearby console. "Your will may be strong, Blood of the Ancients, but you do have one glaring weakness..."

The girl gazed at him defiantly as if daring him to reveal her shortcoming as Zarrod tapped a few keys on the console. The Deathlord looked at her, happy to oblige.

"You care far too much for your friends," Zarrod said.

With one more push of a button, a flash of purple light teleported two more Deathlords to the bridge right behind the girl. When she turned and looked at the new arrivals, she gasped. Between them was an ugly alien creature, with an oblong head, large eyes, and green skin. The Deathlords held him up limply between the two of them, and his large eyes drooped half-closed from either pain, exhaustion, or a bit of both.

"Professor!" squealed the girl.

The alien looked up, his eyes widening slightly at the sight of the Regal. "Your Majesty..." he started to say before one of the Deathlords reached up and began culling him.

The Professor's ghostly image seeped through his skin and the alien started screaming in agony as he was being torn between life and death. His cries of pain echoed throughout the bridge.

"NO!" cried the girl as she attempted to get to her feet and rush to her friend's aid. But before she could even regain her footing, Zarrod's clawed hand clamped down around the back of her neck and held her still, forcing her to look at her friend as he was tortured.

"Think back," Zarrod grumbled. "Think about what I was doing to you after you tried to escape me. And now, imagine it ten times worse. That's what he has been going through."

Fresh tears found their way down the girl's cheeks as the Deathlord guards released their hold on their alien captive, who crumpled to the ground in a heap, blubbering and sobbing pathetically.

"The type of pain we can inflict, Princess, is beyond anything you can comprehend," said Zarrod. "We can keep you alive indefinitely, never allowing you to escape it. We can hold off the madness, to prevent you from accepting it. We can give you unending agony for as long as we wish."

The Deathlords reached out toward the Professor again, and the alien started to spasm, crying out at the top of his lungs as his captors ripped at his soul.

"STOP!" cried out the girl. "PLEASE!"

The alien screamed louder.

"It will be never ending for him," said Zarrod. "Unless you cooperate."

The girl stared wide-eyed at her companion as he convulsed, thrashing about as though he were being ripped apart by the invisible knives of the Deathlord's magic. She hesitated, knowing what it would mean to give in, and yet, it was obvious what decision she would ultimately make. The Supreme was correct – she did have one glaring weakness, which she now had to accept she was unable to overcome.

"I will!" she said urgently. "I'll cooperate! Just, please, stop hurting him!"

Zarrod gave a nod to the guards, who released the alien from their death grips. The pathetic beast lay on the ground, whimpering, as Zarrod released his hold over the girl. She scrambled to her friend's side.

"Professor," she said quietly, cradling his head. "I'm sorry... I'm so, so sorry..."

The alien's large eyes focused upon her. "Your... Majesty..." he said weakly. "You mustn't... help them..."

"Shhhhhh..." said the girl, softly stroking the alien's forehead. "It'll be okay. I promise. Just... just stay with me."

"As always..." the alien responded. "I am... at your service..."

A sad smile grew on the girl's lips. Abraxas found their entire exchange pathetically annoying. So much so, he had to resist the urge to punch something.

"We are approaching the oasis, Supreme," reported an Acolyte, blissfully taking Abraxas's attention away from the lesser life-forms.

Zarrod turned and gazed up at the viewscreen as the last remnants of the nebula cloud cleared away, revealing the Ghost Planet of Terahades.

As though its mere presence were enough to scare away the dust and gas, the planet sat in the middle of a large empty oasis within the nebula. The planet glowed pale white, as if it were being illuminated by a sun that was not there. Its surface seemed to move and shift, so slightly one would think his eyes were playing tricks on him. And surrounding the planet was a large, slightly golden shell – the planet's shield – around which the Deathlord fleet had already taken position.

"Open a channel to the fleet," ordered Zarrod as he approached the holo-transmission platform on the bridge.

The Acolytes did as commanded, opening a fleet-wide holographic transmission, blasting the Deathlord Supreme's image to every Planetkiller ship. Zarrod stood, proud and imposing, gazing up at the Ghost Planet on the viewscreen as his ship began its approach.

"My followers," he said. "For years, we have worked. For years, we have waited. And now, the time has come for our efforts to be rewarded. Before you is the task handed down to us from our creators. They charged us with freeing their brethren from this prison, and on this day, we will have achieved that goal."

Abraxas and the other Deathlords on the bridge stomped their feet — a sign of excitement over the Supreme's words, which every Deathlord on the other ships would surely be doing as well.

"This is but the first step in the grand plan laid out by our masters," Zarrod continued. "Even now, Supreme Verrutus, Supreme Melegogg, and Supreme Ashtoroth work tirelessly to bring the other aspects of our Lords' commands to fruition. And once they do, we will sweep across every corner of the universe, wiping out everything that stands in our way!"

More stomping. Abraxas gazed at Zarrod, his chest swelling with the type of excitement he felt before charging into battle.

"We are Deathlords," said Zarrod, "granted ultimate power and control over the end of all things. That is the gift our creators gave to us. No fear. No uncertainty. Only order and mastery over that which all life cowers before and can never hope to understand. It is our charge to clear the way for our Lords' return by doing what we were created to do — spread death. Extinguish all life in the universe. Cleanse all abominations and aberrations that have spawned, and return purity to the Void!"

The stomping on the bridge increased, the rhythmic *thump-thump-thump* echoing off the walls. Zarrod's words washed over them like pure ecstasy, and Abraxas could feel the very core of his body blaze with the fire of the moment.

"Now is that moment — the moment that heralds the end of all things. The return of our Lords is at hand, and you shall all reap the rewards they will bestow upon you when they are resurrected. I hereby command all ships of the fleet to fire their primary weapons on the planet, and then to bear witness as I, Deathlord Supreme Zarrod, prove once and for all that the Ancient Heretics, with all their technology, are no match for the power and might of the *Deathlords!*"

An ecstatic scream erupted from Abraxas as he raised his fist into the air. All other Deathlords on the bridge erupted as well, celebrating their moment of victory. They had done all that was asked of them, and now, nothing could stop them.

On the viewscreen, the Planetkiller fleet fired their primary weapons one by one. Strong beams of swirling, ghostly light shot forth toward the planet. Each beam struck the shield surrounding the planet and spread across its surface until it met with the discharge of a beam from a sister ship, eventually enveloping the shield entirely with the chaotic death energy stored at the core temple of each vessel.

Abraxas glanced at the Regal girl and her alien companion and rejoiced as they stared at the viewscreen in abject fear of what they were witnessing.

Zarrod gazed at the scene that played out before him. As soon as the planet's shield was completely enveloped, he closed his eyes and reached out both his hands. The air around him seemed to shimmer and swirl. His long cape fluttered as the Deathlord Supreme took on a sickly white aura that seemed to emanate from his brilliant armor.

A small portion of the planetary shield began to twist and ripple as the death energy on top of it attacked, stabbing into it, bubbling on its surface, trying to force its way through.

The air in the bridge began to turn electric as lights dimmed on-and-off and an incessant howling sound whistled through the room. The Deathlord Supreme stood resolute, unmoving, as he concentrated all his energy on the planet before him. His armor started to shimmer and glow even brighter as his skin deepened into the purest black imaginable.

Slowly, the death energy began to open a breach in the planetary shield as the fleet continued to fire. More and more of the energy worked its way into the opening, and with Zarrod's urging, forced a bigger and bigger breach — until it was large enough to fly a Planetkiller through.

"Forward," ordered Abraxas. "Fly us into the breach!"

The Acolytes hopped to as the ship started its approach toward the planet. Abraxas gazed at the viewscreen. The planet looked different once it was unobstructed by the shield. Its surface was still, dry, and desolate, and pocked all over by massive craters. It was nothing like the haunting surface he'd come to know – yet another trick of the Ancient Heretics, no doubt.

Abraxas looked at Zarrod, who stood mightily on the holo-transmission platform, opening the impassible shield through the sheer force of his will. It was a feat unheard of by any within the Deathlords, and yet, here he was, revealing just how powerful a Deathlord could be.

"Shields up," commanded Abraxas as the ship neared the breach. "Full power. Prepare to brace them against the opening."

The Acolytes funneled the mothership's shields into the opening, using the power of the ship to take some of the strain off Zarrod and to keep the breach from fluctuating enough to damage their vessel. Abraxas kept a close eye on his console monitors as the ship passed through the Ghost Planet's shield. He watched the death energy strain and rage against the shield that fought with all its might to close the hole in its surface.

When the ship was clear, Abraxas ordered the shields lowered. Zarrod released his grip on the death energy and the rearview screen on Abraxas's monitor showed the planetary shield slam shut once more.

Zarrod fell to one knee as everything around him returned to normal. Abraxas gazed at the Deathlord Supreme, pride swelling within him. It was obvious the effort had taken a great deal out of his leader, but as Abraxas looked past him and saw on the viewscreen overhead the encroaching terrain of the Ghost Planet coming up to meet them, he couldn't help but remember the pure power he had just witnessed. And at that moment, he finally understood what the Supreme had been trying to tell him.

It was, indeed, beautiful.

CHAPTER ✺ 38

eanwhile, Jack and the others were barreling through hyperspace on the Earthship. After reviewing the ship's logs and accessing everything about the Planetkiller fleet and the Ghost Planet itself acquired from the ship's interface with the Deathlord mothership, Heckubus Moriarty had come up with an adequately evil enough strategy to rescue the Princess. His idea, while risky, has since been widely regarded by many military historians across the galaxy to be, all things considered, a rather good plan.

"I'd just like ta go on record and say this is the worst plan ever," grumbled Scallywag.

"Noted," replied Jack.

"Worst. Plan. Ever."

"Pah," muttered Heckubus. "I've had far worse plans…"

"I bet you have," replied the pirate.

"Not many, though…" whispered Heckubus.

"Wait, what?"

"Huh?" replied the robot. "I didn't say anything."

"Shut up, all of you," said Jack. "The plan's great. It's totally going to work."

"I wish I had yer confidence, lad," grumbled Scallywag.

"Don't worry. Totally awesome Ancient starship, remember?" reassured Jack. "We'll be fine."

"Ya put an awful lot of faith in this vessel o' yours, Earthman," said Scallywag. "For my sake, I hope yer right."

Me, too, Jack thought, as he flipped some switches on his chair's console, repositioning the ship's maneuvering thrusters in anticipation of what he was about to attempt. He and Heckubus had spent the better part of the last four hours formulating the rescue plan, and though the robot was confident his scheme would work, a lot of it depended on Jack to deliver.

I can do this, thought Jack. *I will do this! For Anna. For Shepherd. For everyone I've lost... I'll do this.*

Jack placed his hands on the control orbs of his chair and readied himself. He got the same feeling in his stomach that he always did right before he led his team into a game of *Arena Deathmatch*. He just hoped he was as good at the real thing as he had been at the simulation.

"Heckubus," said Jack. "Get ready to make those navigation calculations."

Heckubus checked his tethered connection to the ship's systems. "All set," he replied.

"Scally, prepare the weapons. Get ready to defend the ship."

Scallywag tapped a few buttons on his console. "Weapons ready," he murmured.

"Grohm..." said Jack, looking at the hulking Rognok beside him.

Grohm glared down at Jack and grunted.

"Um... just try not to break anything," said Jack.

Grohm snorted.

Jack took a deep breath and checked his holoscreen. Their destination was seconds away.

"Let's rock," he said.

Jack dropped the ship out of lightspeed and opened a hyperspace window, flying the ship through it and into the familiar darkness of space. He looked out the viewscreen and in the distance saw the same brilliant nebula as before, signaling the correct location.

"This is the place," said Jack.

"Sensors are picking up your massive wall of space bugs, Earthman," said Heckubus.

"Space bugs," said Scallywag shaking his head. "Now I've seen everything."

"You ain't seen nothing yet," said Jack, angling his ship toward the massive wall of black before him. "Get ready with those jump coordinates, I don't know how long I'll be able to keep them at bay."

"You worry about your part, Earthman," said Heckubus. "I have mine well in hand."

"Space bugs…" muttered Scallywag.

Jack kept an eye on his sensor readings as he maneuvered the ship toward the massive swarm of insects that had almost devoured them during his first escape from the Deathlord fleet. They were already beginning to stir as he approached, but he wanted to get the attention of as many of the insects as possible.

"Time to make 'em angry," said Jack. "Open fire!"

Jack turned the ship, strafing the insect wall while Scallywag let loose a few blaster bolts from the ship's weapon batteries. The blasts poked into the solid black of the massive swarm like angry red needles.

Alarms on the ship beeped as the sensors relayed their reactions. Immediately, thousands of the tiny insects began to separate from their swarm and chase after the ship.

"That got their panties ruffled," said Scallywag.

"You ready, Heckubus?" asked Jack.

"Yes, but you're going to need to get them closer…" replied the robot.

Jack glanced at Heckubus. "Um… closer?"

"I can only extend your ship's Quantum Entanglement field so far you know," snapped Heckubus. "I'm not a miracle worker."

"Did I just hear ya right?" asked Scallywag. "Ya want to bring the ship-eating space bugs closer to *our* ship?"

"Yes," replied the robot. "Oh, and if you could get them to surround us, too, that would be optimal. No sense in leaving any behind."

"Um… surround us?" asked Jack, suddenly wondering about how well this plan would actually work.

"The shields should hold them off long enough," replied Heckubus. "*Totally awesome Ancient starship, remember?* Whatever that means."

"Aren't we… like… going to need those shields for the fight?" asked Jack.

Heckubus sighed. "You get the bugs, or you get the shields. Not both. Did I really need to explain this to you? It's rather obvious, I'd say."

"Worst. Plan. EVER." repeated Scallywag.

Jack grimaced. "Transferring extra power to the shields," he said, making sure the ship's defenses were as reinforced as he could get them before pulling the ship into a tight turn. Alarms wailed as Jack watched the hefty swarm turn to match the ship, bearing down on it, ready to envelop it whole.

"Get ready!" yelled Jack, continuing his turn toward the swirling ball of impending death headed right for them.

"Yes, very good. A little closer…" said Heckubus.

The alarms grew louder and more insistent as Jack completed his turn, steering the ship directly toward the encroaching swarm.

"Closer…"

"Oh for the love of—" sneered Scallywag. "Jump the bloody ship already!"

Jack's stomach tightened nervously as he flew his ship right into the thousands of tiny bugs, which surrounded the vessel, ready to feast.

★★★★★

On the bridge of the Deathlord Planetkiller ship *Xenophon*, Commander Vermunt stood gazing at the Ghost Planet on the ship's massive viewscreen. Part of him wished he were on the planet with the Deathlord Supreme to witness their ultimate victory first hand. But another part of him was just glad to be in a position to witness any part of it at all. Even from his perch high above the planet, he'd be able to see the glorious return of their masters' invincible armada, and to be by its side as it tore through all remaining life in the universe.

"Status report," he growled toward his executive officer, a Deathlord named Himbalt.

"We sustained moderate damage from our journey through the minefield," Himbalt replied. "Our Acolytes estimate the repairs will take several hours; however, no systems will need to be taken off-line."

"And the Supreme?" asked Vermunt. "What of him?"

"Our sensors are indicating his ship has just landed on the planet's surface," replied Himbalt.

"Good," said Vermunt. "It won't be long now."

"Commander," said Himbalt. "We're getting communications from the other ships in the fleet. Most of their temple's power reserves were depleted maintaining the breach in the planetary shield. Since there were no life-forms to absorb during the attack, many ships are running dangerously low on energy. They are wondering when they'll be able to replenish their temples."

Vermunt grumbled. Peeling back the planet's shield had taken far too much of his ship's own power. He could only imagine how low on energy the others in the fleet might be. "We will wait until the Supreme has completed his task, and then he will let us know himself."

Himbalt nodded. "And if the Supreme should not return?"

Vermunt glared at his second in command. "What?" he growled.

"My apologies, Commander," said Himbalt. "But while the Supreme's ship is on the planet, we have no way of communicating with it. If something should go wrong, or the Supreme should fail in his task, how long should the fleet wait?"

Vermunt stalked up to Himbalt and glared directly into his eyes. "You think the Supreme will fail?"

"No, Commander," replied Himbalt. "I have every confidence in our Supreme. I am just asking a hypothetical."

"Let me make one thing clear," growled Vermunt. "There is no need for a hypothetical question such as yours. The Supreme is the ultimate Deathlord, destined to lead us to complete victory. He knows no such thing as failure. He has the power to overcome any adversity. And there is nothing – I repeat – *nothing* in this universe capable of stopping him."

"Commander!" called out an Acolyte over a tiny alert bell.

Vermunt turned toward the Acolyte sitting at a nearby command console. "What is it?" he barked.

"I have a sensor contact off our port side," the Acolyte replied. "It appears to be a ship."

"A ship?" muttered Vermunt. "Here? Where did it come from?"

"Unknown," said the Acolyte. "It just appeared out of nowhere."

"Put it on screen," Vermunt ordered.

On the large viewscreen, the image of the Earthship appeared, bucking and weaving directly toward the Deathlord's vessel, a trail of black smoke billowing behind it. Commander Vermunt and Himbalt regarded it curiously.

"What is it doing?" wondered Himbalt aloud.

"Perhaps they realize what they've stumbled into and they're panicking," laughed Vermunt. "Let's give them something to panic about. Launch a squad of fighters. Blow it out of the sky."

"Launching shards now, Commander," the Acolyte replied.

Vermunt crossed his arms and watched the viewscreen as five shards shot toward the Earthship, guns blazing. The Earthship continued heading toward the Planetkiller, though, expertly banking and weaving out of the way of the oncoming plasma blasts.

No sooner had the Earthship barreled by the squad of fighters than the Deathlord shards suddenly disintegrated into the trailing smoke of the ship.

Vermunt blinked, as if his eyes had just played a cruel joke on him.

"What? What just happened?" he demanded.

"Unknown, Commander," the Acolyte replied. "It would seem that all fighters have been destroyed."

"How?" Vermunt growled.

"Undetermined, Commander. We detected no weapons fire from the ship."

"Commander," said Himbalt urgently, "that vessel is closing in on us."

"Fire all port side cannons," Vermunt ordered. "Don't let it near the ship!"

On screen, the Earthship continued to bank, weave, and corkscrew its way toward them, even as needles of red blaster fire from the *Xenophon's* cannons lit up the blue and purple backdrop of the nebula.

"Such maneuvers!" said Himbalt. "I've never seen anything like it before!"

As the Earthship closed in, it turned and skimmed the exterior hull of the Deathlord Planetkiller, weaving back and forth along its surface.

Suddenly, the entire ship shook and alarms began to howl, echoing throughout the large command chamber.

"What's happening?" screamed Vermunt. "Report!"

Himbalt ran to a nearby console, checking readouts as they popped up. "Massive damage being reported on our port side," he replied. "It appears as though our outer hull is being stripped away!"

"How are they doing this?" growled Vermunt. "Stop them!"

"They are too close, Commander," said Himbalt. "They're inside the minimum range of our cannons. We cannot hit them."

"Reports from the outer decks, Commander," said the Acolyte at his station. "Whatever weapon they're using is penetrating multiple areas of the ship. At this rate, we may have critical breach in a matter of minutes."

"No, no, NOOOO!!!!" raged Vermunt. "Launch every fighter we have. Contact every Planetkiller in the fleet. Tell them to launch all shards from their hangars, to focus all their weapons on that vessel, and not to let it near their ships!"

As the Acolyte carried out the orders, Vermunt and Himbalt looked up at the viewscreen, watching the Earthship bank and weave across the surface of their vessel.

"Who are they, Commander?" asked Himbalt with a hint of awe. "A single ship, capable of destroying a Planetkiller?"

"I do not know," said Vermunt quietly, as alarms raged, signaling the impending death of his ship. "But whoever they are, they are the fiercest, bravest, and most skilled warriors we have ever faced."

★★★★★

Onboard the bridge of the Earthship, Jack, Scallywag, and Heckubus were all screaming in terror as alarms wailed and the ship banked and weaved uncontrollably.

Heckubus had been correct when he theorized that the ship's shields would offer them some protection from the space bugs. However, the shields had not lasted long after flying directly into the swarm. Though the quantum jump had worked as planned and had brought a sizable number of the voracious critters along to the coordinates of the Ghost Planet, they must have eaten something rather important before the Earthship had escaped from them because for the life of him, Jack could no longer fly the ship in a straight line.

Which, as one can imagine, made being charged by a squad of Deathlord shards while being chased by a swarm of ship-eating space bugs quite a harrowing experience. And now, it was all Jack could do to keep from crashing the ship right into the massive Deathlord Planetkiller that was right in front of them.

"This is the worst plan everrrrrr!!!!" cried Heckubus.

"Oh, now ya agree with me!" yelled Scallywag.

"Repair the steering!" screamed Jack as the ship narrowly avoided flying into a massive cannon jutting up from the Deathlord's hull. "Hurry up and fix it!"

"I'm trying, I'm trying!" responded the robot with a slight sense of annoyance as he frantically urged the ship's auto-repair systems to get their work done.

Jack focused as hard as he could on trying to pilot the ship, but it was responding sluggishly and erratically. Everything was upside down, control-wise. It was a miracle to him that they weren't dead already.

Suddenly, the ship began to become more responsive, and the minute he could, he peeled away from the Planetkiller. Nervous laughter erupted from Jack as relief washed over him like a splash of cold water.

"I got it!" exclaimed Jack. "Control is back!"

Scallywag and Heckubus slumped back in their seats, relieved, as Jack turned off the ship's alarms. Jack looked at Grohm who had been standing stoically beside him the entire time.

"Settle down, big guy. The worst is over," joked Jack.

Grohm simply glared at Jack in response.

"I think I just about browned meself," muttered Scallywag.

"Well, before you change your pants," said Heckubus, "you may want to feast your eyes on… this!"

On the ship's viewscreen, Heckubus put up the image of the Deathlord Planetkiller as the space bugs tore through it, causing it to break apart and disintegrate before their very eyes. Even the shards that tried to launch before the ship was completely consumed couldn't escape from the deadly, and now growing, swarm of space bugs.

"Blimey," said Scallywag. "Yer bloody horrible plan is actually working!"

"Was there ever any doubt?" snooted Heckubus, completely disregarding the last couple of chaotic minutes. "Bask! Bask in my genius! Mwuhahaha!"

"Wow, that was fast," said Jack as he checked his sensors. "It's like... the space bugs are multiplying..."

"Yes, it seems the more they consume, the more they are able to reproduce," said Heckubus. "That would explain their hibernated state near that nebula. They probably are quite active while there's material around to help them increase their numbers."

"Which means, hopefully, they'll be right busy with all the other Deathlords while we make it to the planet," said Scallywag.

An alarm beeped on Heckubus's console. "Uh-oh," the robot said.

"Uh-oh?" sneered Scallywag. "I don't like 'uh-ohs.' "

"Sensors say the other Planetkillers have launched their fighters to intercept us."

"How many?" asked Jack.

"From these readings," replied Heckubus, "I'd have to say... all of them."

"Perfect," frowned Scallywag.

"Battle," rumbled Grohm.

"No, no battle," said Jack as he turned the ship toward the planet. "We'll let the bugs deal with them. We need to get on that planet. Heckubus, are the hyperspace calculations ready?"

"Yes," said the robot. "I've estimated how far the shield is from the planet. We should be able to pull this off."

"Great," replied Jack. "Get ready to open the hyperspace windows."

"Not so fast," said Heckubus, as he pulled up a star chart on the holoscreen. "We need to be approximately right here if we're going to make this work."

A red dot appeared on the edge of the blue nebula's oasis. Scallywag scratched his head.

"Um… that's in the nebula cloud," he said.

"Yes, it would appear so," replied Heckubus.

"The one that's full of mines and booby-traps," Scallywag clarified.

"The very same."

"We don't have any *bloody shields*, ya twit!" sneered the pirate.

"Well, nobody said this plan was perfect," replied Heckubus.

"Yes, *you* did! Many times!"

"Look, you simpleton, we're too close to the planet to open a hyperspace window to bypass the planetary shield. If we do it any closer than that, we'll be flying right into its gravitational shadow, and if we do, we're dead."

"Yeah, and if we fly into that bloody minefield, we're dead!"

"And if we wait for those shards to reach us, we're dead," said Jack. "So we don't really have many other options, do we?"

"Yeah, we do," said Scallywag. "Let's hyperspace out of here and come back after the bugs have eaten all the Deathlords."

"I doubt the space bugs will be much friendlier than the Deathlords," said Jack. "Besides, we can't waste any more time. Who knows what they're doing to Anna down there."

Jack turned the ship and began heading for the cloud.

"This is suicide!" protested Scallywag.

"The Ancients put those mines out there, right?" said Jack. "Well, the Ancients also made this ship, so I'm willing to bet our sensors are going to be able to tell us where those mines are. So stop whining, get ready to shoot at anything that attacks us, and Heckubus…"

"Yes?" replied the robot.

"Shields," said Jack. "I don't care how you do it, just get me those shields back!"

Heckubus and Scallywag both slumped at their consoles and grumbled. Jack looked at his viewscreen as the overwhelming blue cloud of the surrounding nebula rushed up to greet him. *C'mon ship*, he thought. *Don't let me down now.*

Jack called up the long-range sensor readings on his holoscreen. A group of Deathlord shards was closing in behind him fast. He tried not to get distracted by that, however, focusing his attention instead on the readings in the nebula cloud. Sensor data was going to be limited, that much Heckubus had made clear to him before they had set out. But he was hoping that his ship's sensors were advanced enough to navigate the cloud without hitting any of the mines.

Can you see anything? Jack asked his ship. *Where are the mines?*

Tiny red blips began to appear intermittently on his sensor readout, indicating the positions of the mines hidden in the heavy blue cloud. The red indicators flickered in and out of existence, though, no doubt due to the interference of the nebula. But they were there, and that meant there was hope Jack wouldn't get the four of them blown up.

"Yes!" exclaimed Jack. "Sensors are picking up the mines!"

"Sensors are also picking up five shards closing in fast," said Scallywag as he opened fire using the Earthship's rear plasma cannon.

Jack pulled up another holoscreen right next to his sensor readings, giving him a rear view of the ship. Sure enough, five Deathlord shards were within firing distance and red needles of death were coming right toward them.

Jack banked the ship and weaved through the thick dust and gas of the nebula, hoping the Deathlords' sensors were useless enough to keep them from getting a good enough bead on the ship.

"Heckubus..." groaned Jack, trying not to take his attention off his screens.

"I know, I know," said the robot. "Ha! Shields at 15%! That should be enough to—"

Suddenly, a red blip appeared on Jack's screen directly in front of him. He jerked the ship as quickly as he could, but they still hit the mine, a loud boom bouncing off the hull and causing the entire ship to shake.

"Ugh. Never mind," muttered Heckubus.

"I don't care what you have to do, Heckubus," yelled Jack. "Get me more shields!"

"Well, try to stop flying into mines, you twit!" yelled Heckubus back.

Scallywag continued to fire as the Deathlord shards pursued them, but he was having a hard time locking-on with Jack maneuvering the ship all over the place. The pirate was just about to get annoyed when one of his blasts hit the mark and a shard exploded in a puff of sickly green fire.

"Got one!" Scallywag cheered.

Jack glanced at his screen and saw the other shards spread out as they continued their pursuit. One of them was trying to come up on his wing. Jack glanced at his sensor reading and adjusted his ship a little. The shard turned along with the Earthship, just as Jack hoped he would. Suddenly, there was another green-tinted explosion as the shard ran smack-dab into a mine.

"Got another," said Jack.

"Good flying, lad," said Scallywag, still focused intently on firing at their pursuers.

Jack looked at his readings. They'd flown far enough into the nebula to make the turn for their trajectory toward the Ghost Planet. Keeping a watchful eye on his read-outs, Jack began to bank the ship. If they could make the maneuver to bypass the planetary shield soon, it wouldn't matter if they still had a few Deathlords on their tail.

"Shields at 30%," reported Heckubus. "And don't ask for more, because unless you want to stop breathing for a while, there's no more power to redirect."

"That should be enough," said Jack. "Moving for approach to the Ghost Planet now."

Jack rolled the ship into a tight turn, allowing the three remaining shards to shoot past him further into the nebula. He glanced at his rear readout and saw a flash of green puff up in the deep blue mist, signaling another win for the mines.

We just might pull this off, Jack thought to himself with a smile… right before his ship's alerts started going crazy.

Scallywag and Heckubus looked up at the alarm and Jack glanced at his sensors. Two red blips were now moving across his screen and heading straight for him.

"Uh-oh," said Jack.

"I told ya I don't like 'uh-ohs,'" said Scallywag.

"Um… I think we have two missiles honing in on us," said Jack.

"Uh-oh," muttered Scallywag.

"You must have passed by one of those hidden weapon platforms," sighed Heckubus.

Jack gritted his teeth and poured on the engines, kicking the ship into high gear, hoping to outrun the new threat.

"Scally, try to shoot those things," said Jack.

"Shoot 'em?" frowned Scallywag. "I can't even see 'em!"

"Then just keep firing and hope you hit something!"

Scallywag began firing the ship's rear plasma cannon blindly, strafing it behind them as best he could.

Jack banked the ship, sharply turning to miss another mine in their path. Jack glanced at his sensor readout. One of the missiles was starting to get really close.

"Scally, one of them is closing in!" Jack said.

"I don't bloody see it!" the pirate yelled, continuing his pattern of firing. His eyes were glued to his targeting readout, but all he saw was blue and purple dust and gas.

Jack glanced at his sensors again. The missile was almost to them.

"Here it comes!" said Jack.

Scallywag focused intently on his screen and saw a small, slender shadow in the nebula, coming up at them fast. In the split second it took for his eyes to register the movement, Scallywag aimed the cannon and fired.

The ship's blasts streaked all around the shadow as it rocketed forward. Small enough to evade the cannon fire, the missile barreled directly toward them. Alarms blared incessantly throughout the bridge, signaling the impending approach of the weapon.

Scallywag had just enough time to recognize the thin, pointed warhead of the light blue missile as it closed in directly behind them before one of his blasts finally caught it, mere feet away from impact.

The missile exploded, causing the ship to shake violently as the instruments on the bridge flickered on and off in protest. Jack groaned trying to get back control and straighten out their course as the ship banked and weaved because of the explosion. He checked his readings and saw the shields had absorbed most of the blast, but it was clear they weren't going to survive a direct hit.

"Got it!" smiled Scallywag, quite pleased with himself.

"Don't celebrate yet, there's another one out there, and it's coming our way!" said Jack, checking the readouts again and seeing the second red dot heading right for them.

Scallywag's smile disappeared. "I swear, can't even have one bloody victory…" he mumbled as he went back to searching his screen for impending doom, part two.

Jack checked his trajectory. They were coming up on the coordinates Heckubus had laid out before entering the cloud. "We are all set for the hyperspace maneuver," said Jack. "You ready Heckubus?"

"Yes, yes," said Heckubus, sounding rather bored. "Prepare for jump to hyperspace in approximately 90 seconds…"

Jack looked at his viewscreen as the nebula cloud before them started to thin. In the breaks within the cloud, Jack saw a litany of red plasma fire lighting up the sky. Planetkillers surrounding the Ghost Planet were all firing wildly in every direction, some of them breaking apart while doing so.

Black tendrils swarmed through the air. Some followed tiny Deathlord shards while others focused on tearing through the larger vessels. From what little Jack could make out, the entire scene was one of pure chaos.

But the closer they got to the edge of the cloud, the more it became clear that something wasn't right.

Jack checked his sensor readings and sure enough, he saw a group of close to twenty Deathlord shards heading straight for them. And to make matters worse, right behind them was a large, angry cloud of space bugs.

"Oh, crap," said Jack. *The shards must be heading into the nebula cloud to try to escape the bugs,* he thought.

Then, the proximity alarm sounded, and Jack noticed the second missile was closing in fast.

"Oh, crap!" he said again.

"Sixty seconds," said the robot.

Jack was looking at his readings. He was heading right into a wall of Deathlord shards, and if he could somehow get past them, he'd be running right into the space bug swarm chasing the fighters. And if that weren't bad enough, any minute a deadly missile could hit them from behind.

"Heckubus, adjust your calculations!" screamed Jack.

"Huh?" perked up the robot. "For what?"

"For this!" yelled Jack as he corkscrewed the ship, punching up the acceleration and maneuvering through the tangle of fleeing shards as they entered the nebula cloud.

"Blast it!" Heckubus cursed as Jack sent the ship into a dive, narrowly missing the pursuing swarm of space bugs before pulling up in an attempt to get back to their original trajectory. "You're off course!"

"Deal with it!" said Jack, frantically trying to steer the ship as his missile alerts blared. The menacing red blip on his sensor screens was getting closer and closer.

"We're going to be too close to the planet!" said Heckubus.

"DEAL WITH IT!!!" screamed Jack and Scallywag.

By the time they had reached the edge of the nebula cloud, Jack had fixed the ship's trajectory. However, as soon as they exited, the ominous missile that was dogging them followed.

"I can't hit it!" screamed Scallywag, frantically trying to shoot down the encroaching projectile.

"DO IT!" cried Jack. "HYPERSPACE! NOW!!!"

After a quick re-calculation, Heckubus activated the Earthship's Brane Accelerator to open the hyperspace window.

Now, this was the tricky part – the plan was to enter hyperspace and then exit behind the shield surrounding the Ghost Planet, effectively bypassing it, since the shield itself had no gravitational presence in hyperspace.

However, in order to do so at this close of range to the planet, the exit window would have to be nearly on top of the entrance window, and as most hyperspace engineers know, a typical Brane Accelerator is not built to do that type of thing.

Of course, after some adjustments to the Earthship, Heckubus was able to account for its limitations and push the Brane Accelerator to pull off this rather admirable feat – even though Heckubus himself would have to handle the bulk of the navigational calculations and timing for the execution of the maneuver (a feat he boasted was mere child's play to one as brilliant as him).

No sooner had the hyperspace window opened than Heckubus immediately called up the exit, materializing it an impressive 20 micrometers away from the initial opening – about the diameter of the average human hair - just as Jack barreled the Earthship through.

But even though this maneuver was very impressive and successfully executed, there were a few things Heckubus did not count on occurring.

The first was that the strain from opening two hyperspace windows almost simultaneously so close to each other effectively shorted out the Brane Accelerator, causing it to stop functioning completely.

The second was that the missile from the minefield was close enough to the ship to successfully follow it though the hyperspace windows before they closed.

The third, and probably the most worrisome, was that because they had to make the jump outside the very edge of the nebula cloud, they exited from hyperspace far closer to the ground of the Ghost Planet than anyone had anticipated.

Thus, they found themselves speeding directly toward impending doom, followed closely behind by even more impending doom.

"PULL UP!" squeaked Scallywag. "PULL UP!!!!!"

Jack braced himself and frantically pulled on his ship to correct its flight path as warning alarms blared and the pale, unforgiving surface of the planet rushed up to meet him in the viewscreen.

The ship groaned and shook as Jack pulled it in a tight arc, the maneuver leaving his stomach behind him like the most intense roller-coaster ride he had ever experienced. He managed to level out the ship mere feet above the surface, the energy from the Earthship's engines flaying up a sharp cloud of dust and an angry bombardment of pebbles as the ship rocketed across the landscape.

No sooner had the Earthship narrowly missed crashing, than the missile following it through its hyperspace jump slammed into the ground behind it, helped along by the accelerated force of its hyperspace maneuver.

A raging cloud of fire and smoke erupted from the point of impact, the explosion rippling out a circular shockwave which was close enough to hit the rear of the Earthship, knocking it off-kilter and sending it skidding across the ground.

The ship rumbled as its belly met the surface below, causing the entire bridge to shake and vibrate as alarms blared and its occupants held on for dear life. Jack gripped the ship's control orbs, doing everything he could to keep the ship from spinning out of control.

In the viewscreen, a small outcropping of tall rock formations was rushing up to meet them. Jack threw his thrusters into reverse, slowing the ship and causing his stomach to lurch forward so intensely he thought he might throw up.

The ship skidded to a slow halt, stopping mere inches away from the sharp, cold rocks waiting patiently to impale it.

★ ★★★★

"Warlord Abraxas," called out the Acolyte from his control panel.

Abraxas approached the Acolyte, his heavy footsteps echoing throughout the cavernous control room of the Deathlord Mothership.

"What?" the Deathlord growled.

"Our scans have picked up an explosion, a few miles to the east of the ship," the Acolyte reported.

"An explosion?" mumbled Abraxas to himself. "On screen."

The bridge's viewscreen switched to an image of the planet's surface. In the distance, a plume of smoke billowed out from the ground, twisting up into the sky. Abraxas squinted at it, wondering if it were some type of unknown defense measure the Heretics had hidden on the planet.

"Should we report it to the Supreme, Warlord?" the Acolyte asked.

"No," replied Abraxas. "The Supreme is en route to the central chamber with the girl. His task is too important to be disturbed with something like this."

"Then what are your orders, Warlord?"

Abraxas glared at the smoke of the explosion for a moment, mulling over his options.

"Send a patrol to investigate," he said finally.

"Right away, Warlord," the Acolyte replied.

"And tell them after they send in their report… they're to destroy anything they find."

CHAPTER ✦ 39

Jack blinked his eyes open, his mind still hazy from the rough landing, and looked around the bridge. Nothing looked too terribly damaged from what he could tell... at least, not compared to what the ship had been through before. As his companions began to stir, Jack called up a systems report on his holoscreen in order to get a better sense of how damaged his spaceship might be.

"Great landing, lad," said Scallywag, picking himself out of his chair and giving his back a nice crack. "Very smooth. Couldn't a done it better meself. Oh, and in case you couldn't tell, I didn't mean any of that."

"Hey, we're alive aren't we?" grumbled Jack. "What more do you want?"

"Some bloody certainty for one thing," Scallywag replied. "The Ancients could create a sodding planet, you'd think they could invent shields that wouldn't die on ya every five minutes."

"Considering everything we just went though," said Jack after seeing the ship had sustained only minimal damage during the landing, "I think the shields we had held up just fine."

"Frankly, I think we're doing splendidly," piped up Heckubus as he picked himself up off the floor. "I fully expected at least one of you to have died by now. By my estimation, we're ahead of the game!"

The group all squinted at Heckubus.

"What?" asked the robot. "That was meant to be encouraging!"

Grohm lumbered up beside Jack. "Location?" the Rognok inquired.

"Good question," said Jack as he called up his sensor readings on the main viewscreen of the bridge so everyone could get a look. A 3D map grid appeared, marking the location of their ship and the location of the Deathlord Mothership some distance away. The group all looked at the readout and grumbled.

"Hmmmm…" said Heckubus. "It appears we're a couple miles away from our target."

"Can we still teleport down to where they have the Princess?" asked Scallywag.

"No, the sensors aren't picking up anything below the surface. We're too far out of range to see where she might be," said Jack.

"Well, could you fly us into range?"

Jack shook his head. "The ship's thrusters took a bit of a beating from the missile explosion. We can't go anywhere for now."

"Fan-tastic," muttered the pirate. "Anyone care to take a stroll on the life-sucking dirt?"

"Could be worse," said Grohm.

"Really?" said Scallywag. "We just crash landed on an inescapable planet, with an army of Deathlords all around, a swarm of omnivorous space bugs in the sky, and magical-mystical ground that's supposed to kill ya the moment ya touch it between us and our target. What, in the name of Jerrimour the White, could be worse than that?"

"Having a whining Visini around who doesn't stop complaining," grumbled Grohm.

Scallywag's eyes narrowed. "I liked ya better when ya didn't talk so much."

"Don't worry, Scally," said Jack as he tapped on a few of the buttons on his command chair. "Plan B is in full effect."

"Plan B? What's Plan B?"

"The plan where we use the ship's ability to make anything we want to help us get across the death-dirt and rescue the Princess," said Jack as he hopped out of the chair and turned to Heckubus. "Try to get as much repaired as you can while we're gone. When we come back with Anna, I expect we'll have to make a hasty getaway."

"But of course," drawled the robot.

"And no trying to reprogram the ship into an evil death machine," said Jack as he walked up to the teleportation platform. "Save the schemes for after we're out of danger, yeah?"

"Wouldn't dream of it," replied Heckubus, sounding only slightly disappointed.

"Oy, how come the rustbucket ain't coming?" grumbled Scallywag.

"What's he gonna do?" asked Jack. "Condescend the bad guys into submission? It's better to have him here repairing things and prepping for our getaway."

Scallywag scowled at Heckubus, who gave him a cheery wave good-bye. "Toodles!" sang the robot. "Have fun storming the Death Planet!"

★⟨★★⟨★

Jack, Scallywag, and Grohm appeared on the teleportation platform of a large room, facing an even larger door taking up the entire wall before them. A big diagonal crevice slashed across its face where the two ends of the door met.

"Where's this now?" asked Scallywag.

"The cargo bay," said Jack. "At least, I think that's what it is. What do you call the bay where you store a bunch of cargo?"

"Seriously, why am I following ya into battle again?" asked Scallywag.

"Don't be hating," smiled Jack. "Especially once you see what we've got behind door number one…"

Jack gave the command to the ship to open the door, the back of his head tingling in response. A dull *KLANK* heralded its unlocking as the two sides of it began to slide away, revealing a large room beyond.

The room was oval shaped, with catwalks and rafters with cranes attached for picking up cargo. In the center of the room was a selection of small vehicles that resembled motorcycles, only these had no wheels. Instead, they had small discs that faced the ground, two in the front, and one in the back, and heavy engines on their tails that looked like something that had been transplanted from a fighter jet.

Grohm grunted when he saw them and Scallywag gave a low whistle. "What be these funny lookin' things?" he asked.

"*Hoverbikes!*" said Jack with more than a hint of pride. They were based on one of the racing games Jack had for his *Gamerbox 3000*. He'd asked the ship if it could make something like that, and he was excited to see it could. "Fast, maneuverable, and best yet, they don't touch the ground! Totally sweet, huh?"

"Grohm can eat them?" asked the Rognok.

"Uh, no," said Jack. "I just meant they're really neat, right?"

"I guess they'll do," said Scallywag. "Woulda liked something with a bit more protection on it."

"I figured speed was more important for this stage of the rescue," said Jack. "Here's where protection comes in…"

He pointed at the wall beside them where metal panels flipped around, revealing racks of weapons and armor of all shapes and sizes. Plasma guns, plasma rifles, thermal grenades, and various other gadgets and doohickeys abounded.

"Now that's more like it!" said Scallywag, who immediately grabbed two new blaster pistols from the rack and gave them a twirl.

Grohm grunted in approval as well and went about collecting his arsenal. Each of them put on armored breastplates, along with shoulder pads, knee pads, and guards for their forearms and shins. The armor was lightweight but was made of what appeared to be metal. Jack could only assume it was totally awesome, though he hoped he didn't have to test it.

Grohm picked up a large club of smooth white steel, with three black rings circling around its head. When he gripped it, the rings sprung to life with a crackle of electricity. He grunted in approval and slung the club across his back before picking up a massive shotgun the size of his arm. He slung that across his back as well.

Jack grabbed a blaster pistol and several grenades, which he strapped to his belt. They were small cylinders, so he was able to fit a lot of them on his person. Finally, he grabbed a communications unit, with an accompanying earpiece, and strapped it to his forearm.

"Heckubus, can you hear me?" asked Jack into the headset.

"Yes, yes, loud and clear," replied the robot.

Scallywag and Grohm both activated their headsets as Jack hopped on his hoverbike and hit the ignition button. The bike came to life with a slight vibration and a low hum as it lifted a good three inches above the ground.

Scallywag slipped onto a thinner bike than Jack's, with a longer chassis. Grohm straddled a much bigger bike, more suitable to his size. It had a low seat and large handlebars that shot up from the front, which almost met Grohm at his chest. Jack mused that Grohm looked like a member of a biker gang whereas Scallywag looked like he was getting ready to go racing.

With a mental command to his ship, the wall to the cargo bay before them suddenly transformed into a door and opened, part of it breaking off into a ramp leading out onto the ground. Jack edged his hoverbike forward toward the ramp and stopped.

He looked down on the chalk-white terrain before him. It was dusty and rocky, like crushed bone. The sky shimmered a brilliant gold, almost like there was a sun, and the air tasted stale and lifeless.

Jack hesitated, his stomach a knot of apprehension, like the kind he got right before the first drop on a roller coaster. He stared at the ground, wondering what was going to happen the minute he embarked across it.

"What is it, lad?" asked Scallywag.

"The ground," replied Jack.

"What of it?"

"Well, it doesn't... I mean, it just looks like normal dirt," said Jack. "I was thinking it would look a bit more... I dunno... evil?"

"Take a look around, lad. It's light out, but there's no sun. We can breathe, but there's no atmosphere. You really gonna question whether the ground can kill ya or not?"

Jack chewed on his lip. "Good point," he said.

"When it comes to the Ancients and their creations, the greatest minds the universe has ta offer can't make heads nor tails o' 'em most the time," said Scallywag. "So regarding a race of beings who can get away with ignoring the laws of anything that makes a bloody lick of sense, I say we play it safe, savvy?"

"Savvy," replied Jack, making a mental note not to tempt fate by trying to touch the ground to find out if the whole death-dirt theory were true or not. "You two ready?"

"Aye," said Scallywag. Grohm grunted and nodded. Jack took a deep breath and looked out across the first alien planet he'd ever been on.

"Let's do this," he said, revving the engine of his bike and taking off, his two companions following him.

Jack's bike sped across the ground, the stale air of the planet turning into a pleasant breeze as he moved. The engine of his hoverbike purred as he pushed it to go faster, its hovertreads kicking up a small amount of dust as he did so.

Scallywag and Grohm fanned out beside him as they adjusted their course toward their destination. Scally's engine had a high whine to it, while Grohm's was low and rumbling, as if it were complaining about the weight of its passenger.

Before them the Deathlord Mothership loomed in the distance, menacing and magnificent. The dark claw contrasted against the stark dirt rock of the terrain as it dug its talons deep into the ground like an angry spider, its green and purple veins pulsing slightly as though it were a living thing.

Jack squinted at it as he sped along, the stagnant wind of the Ghost Planet rippling through his hair. The starship was slowly growing as he and his companions sped toward it. Its image was hazy, like a great mountain that looked small and scalable from a distance but grew bigger and more oppressive as one approached it.

The sight of the Planetkiller made Jack's stomach clench. Suddenly, he could feel his heart pounding against his chest, spurred by an injection of fear and doubt. Memories of recent events flooded into his head like a shoebox full of photographs being spilled onto the floor: the terrors of the Pit, the endless winding hallways with the Dark Soldiers who marched through them relentlessly, and the way the arms of the ship curled as they released their ghostly weapon to consume his planet. But most of all, he remembered the horrible red eyes of the Deathlord Supreme, burning through him with a hate and malice on a scale he had never known was possible.

And here he was, rushing back toward it, his hopes pinned on a crazy plan, two aliens, a snooty robot, and a spaceship in need of repairs.

It's just like a game of Arena Deathmatch, he thought. *Only here, you die for real.*

Jack glanced beside him at his companions. Grohm straddled his massive hoverbike, his hands, the size of hams, clenched tightly around its handles. His red and black eyes narrowed, his huge jaw set like stone. Scallywag leaned forward, hunched low on his bike, like a cat ready to pounce at the first sign of trouble. Pangs of guilt began to grip Jack's chest. If he were feeling this nervous, he could only imagine what they might be feeling… and they were there because of *him*.

When he led his team into battles on his Gamerbox, he knew just what to do. But there was never anything at stake there – nothing but a score on a stupid leaderboard. Not this time, though. This time, they either succeeded, or they died.

Jack glanced at the readout on the dashboard of his bike. They were making good time and had covered almost half the distance to their target already when Jack's communicator came to life.

"Come in, simpletons." Heckubus's voice squawked over Jack's headset. "Simpletons, come in. Do you hear me?"

Jack hit the response button on his communicator. "Simpletons? Really?" he said with a hint of annoyance.

"I am fully prepared to refer to you as dullards, inferiors, or ninny pickers, if you prefer," said Heckubus.

"How about just calling us Team One?" suggested Jack.

"Sorry, that is not one of the choices I recognize," responded the robot.

"Oy, Robot," chimed in Scallywag over the comms. "Ya got a reason for calling other than to annoy the lot o' us?"

"Of course, I do!" responded Heckubus. "You think I enjoy talking to you socially? Hardly the case. Hardly."

"Then what do you want?" said both Jack and Scallywag.

"Long-range sensors are picking up three contacts heading straight for you," Heckubus said. "Energy signatures are in-line with those of Deathlords, so just FYI."

Jack heard Scallywag curse and felt his throat tighten. The Deathlords were on the way, and they still had quite a bit of distance to cover. Jack tapped a few switches on the dash of his bike to bring up a sensor scan. Sure enough, the readout showed three contacts on the way right toward them.

Three against three, thought Jack. *At least we have a fair shot, for now.*

Jack looked up and squinted against the air that rushed by him. All he could see was the Deathlord Mothership before him. There was no sign of any approaching vehicles. He looked around, scanning the horizon. "See anything?" he shouted into his headset.

"Not yet," replied Scallywag.

Then, Jack saw something… a small movement against the black backdrop of the mothership. He tried to focus in on it. It was slight at first, almost like a mirage that was playing tricks on his eyes. But before long, he was able to separate out the movement as three tiny specks materialized, drawing closer and closer...

They were Deathlords, all right – three Dark Soldiers, armed with blasters, and they were flying right at them.

Jetpacks! thought Jack with a twinge of jealousy. *Why didn't I think of that?*

"We've got incoming!" cried Jack into his headset as he grabbed the blaster gun from the holster on his leg.

"I see 'em," grumbled Scallywag. "Hold tight until they get closer. Then get ready ta scramble."

Jack saw Grohm reach back and unholster the massive shotgun he carried, setting the barrel on the front of his bike to steady it. The weapon whined to life as it began to charge up.

Jack watched as the three Deathlords came closer, readying their weapons. He was suddenly aware of how every muscle in his body had tightened and how his heart was pounding...

"Wait for it..." he heard Scallywag's voice say over the coms.

Then, the Deathlords opened fire, sending streaks of red plasma light flashing through the air. Jack and Scallywag veered off, Jack firing his gun as he did so. Scally hugged his bike between his legs and let both his weapons answer in return.

Grohm stayed steady and unmoving as blaster fire streaked all around him. He calmly aimed his shotgun and unleashed a massive blast that tore across the sky in a chaotic ball of fury. The three Deathlords tried to maneuver, but it was too late – the blast caught the trooper in the middle dead on, causing him to blow up in a fireball of red and green flame followed by plumes of black smoke.

His comrades quickly scattered, and before they knew it, Jack and his team were past them and heading steadily toward their destination.

Jack let out a "whoop" of celebration. "Way to go big guy!" he cheered. "Nice shot!"

His jubilance was short-lived, however, as more plasma fire erupted from behind him. Jack turned and saw the two remaining Deathlords had quickly turned and were now on their tails, flying in the sky and raining hot death from above.

"Scramble!" ordered Scallywag over the comm.

Jack swerved his bike hard to the left, just as Grohm swerved to the right, their paths crossing. Scally veered in the opposite direction, and the Deathlords struggled to follow with their weapons' fire.

Jack watched as Scallywag rolled onto his back, balancing himself on the seat of his bike, and returned fire with both his blaster pistols. His shots sent the Deathlords scrambling, each one veering off to the side. Scallywag quickly rolled back to a more secure stance and gunned his engine.

Looking to his right, Jack saw one of the Deathlords coming back around. He aimed his gun at him and began to fire. The shots went wide until Jack adjusted his aim, and they started to get closer to their mark. The Deathlord, obviously not enjoying being shot at, returned fire, causing Jack to swerve and struggle to keep his bike steady as plasma blasts hit the ground around him.

One of Jack's blasts found its mark, striking the metal jetpack of the soldier, causing black smoke to billow forth from its wound. The Deathlord quickly began losing altitude and angled himself toward Jack as he was descending.

Jack swerved and kept firing, but the Deathlord matched his maneuvers. As he got closer, the blasts from Jack's pistol found their mark, tearing into the Deathlord and causing him to drop his gun, but he didn't disintegrate. Instead, the Deathlord managed to land on the back of Jack's bike and wrapped his claws around Jack's neck.

Jack struggled, trying to fight the Deathlord off while maintaining control of his bike at the breakneck speed at which he was travelling. "Help!" cried Jack into his headset. "A little help, please!!!"

Then, the whine of a powering-up weapon made its way to Jack's ears. He turned just in time to see Grohm speed up beside him, aiming his massive shotgun straight for the Deathlord's head. The Dark Soldier turned and looked at Grohm just as the barrel leveled right at him.

BOOM.

The shotgun fired, ripping into the Deathlord, causing him to disintegrate in a puff of black dust, his damaged jetpack flying off into the distance, tumbling to the ground, and exploding.

"Thanks, big guy!" said Jack. Grohm nodded. They both turned to see Scallywag had fallen behind them, dodging and weaving as the final Deathlord remained on his tail, doggedly trying to blast the Visini to pieces.

Jack sped up. Since his bike was much faster than Grohm's, he put a little bit of distance between them before skidding on the brakes and turning his bike around. He gunned the engine and started straight for Scallywag, who was too busy with out-maneuvering the Deathlord to see Jack barreling straight toward him.

Jack opened fire with his blaster pistol, firing directly over Scallywag's head at the Deathlord behind him. So focused was the Dark Soldier on his prey, he hadn't seen Jack until the blaster fire started to streak by. Jack's blasts hit their marks, and the Deathlord quickly lost control and plummeted toward the ground.

Jack passed within a foot of Scallywag as they crossed paths, but he was going too fast and was too close to the Deathlord when it hit the ground and exploded. Jack felt his hoverbike shudder as the shrapnel from the explosion caught its front-left hoverdisk, ripping it off. The bike dipped and skidded its nose across the ground. Jack fought to regain control, but it was no use. The bike slid out from under him as it slowed, and he hit the ground, rolling uncontrollably.

When he came to a stop, Jack was lying on his back looking up at the sky. He was dizzy, but otherwise unhurt. His body armor was scuffed and banged up, but luckily it seemed that other than a few bumps and bruises, he wasn't seriously injured. Jack could only guess that when the hoverbike lost one of its front discs, it slowed down enough before he fell off to keep Jack from breaking his neck.

Jack sat up and rubbed his aching shoulders, only faintly aware of a voice screaming his name. He looked down and saw his headset had fallen nearby. He picked it up and slung it back onto his ear.

"Chill out," said Jack. "I'm fine. I'm okay."

"The ground!" he heard Scallywag scream into his comm. "Get off the ground!!!"

Suddenly, Jack became aware that he was sitting smack dab on the life-sucking death dirt. Fear gripped his chest as he scrambled to his feet. He looked around, frantically, searching for someplace to run… but there was nowhere to escape to.

Then, he stopped. He looked up at his companions who had turned around and were speeding back toward him. If the ground was supposed to kill him, he figured he'd be dead by now. "I… I think it's okay," said Jack. "Nothing is happening. I'm not dying."

Then, a blood-curdling shriek pierced the air, echoing around Jack like a warning from a bird of prey. Jack glanced around him, suddenly alarmed, looking for the source of the noise.

"Behind ya!" yelled Scallywag into his comm. "Look behind ya!"

Jack turned. Behind him, in the distance, was a small shape. It was hazy at first but coming up fast. It looked like a queer miniature tornado, a small spout coming up from the bone white dust of the ground and swirling upward, its large apex eventually disappearing into nothing.

But it wasn't the swirling white tornado that suddenly frightened him. It was the sound... the sound of thousands of screaming people, moaning in pain, anger, and despair. It preceded the tornado, thumping against Jack's chest like the bass of a bad song, filling Jack with a feeling of impending doom.

Jack started to run. He ran away from the tornado as fast as his legs could carry him. He could see Scallywag racing toward him on his bike, but he could feel the impending doom of whatever was coming for him quickly rushing up from behind.

Grohm shot at the entity, hoping to draw its attention from Jack, but his blasts passed harmlessly through it as it continued to swirl angrily forward, its cry getting louder. Scallywag skidded to a stop right by Jack, swerving his bike to face the opposite direction for a quick getaway.

"Get on!" the pirate yelled. Jack didn't need to be told twice. He hopped on behind Scallywag and wrapped his arms around him as the bike shot forward. Grohm veered off and began heading in the opposite direction as the entity barreled forth, twisting and twirling and moaning.

"What the blazes is that thing???" cried Scallywag. Jack knew the pirate could feel the dread it was putting out, too.

"Whatever it is, I think it's what kills you when you touch the ground!" said Jack. "It must be some type of guard dog — touching the ground sets it off!"

Scallywag glanced behind them. "Whatever it is, lad, it ain't goin' away!"

Jack looked behind them as well. Sure enough, the entity was still there, and slowly gaining on them. "What do we do?" asked Jack, the cold grip of panic starting to tighten within him.

Scallywag cursed and activated his comms. "Robot!" he barked. "We need help!"

"With what?" Heckubus replied. "You obviously survived the Deathlords."

"Well, now we've got some type o' evil, angry tornado that's trying ta kill us!"

"Preposterous," said Heckubus. "I'm showing no weather patterns that would facilitate—"

"It's an Ancient security system," interrupted Jack. "It's activated when someone touches the ground, and then it comes after you! That's what they meant when they said the ground was deadly! It's not the dirt that kills you; it's this tornado thing!"

"Ah, interesting," responded the robot. "It would make sense that if this planet were designed as a prison there would be some kind of sentry designated to keep sentient beings from walking its surface and possibly escaping. I always thought the concept of dirt that kills you if you touched it was rather far-fetched..."

"And an evil tornado that kills ya instead is so much more believable???" screamed Scallywag.

The entity was growing closer and closer. Jack could see the tendrils of dust caught up in its wind swirling angrily. Shapes began to form as though the dust were brushing up against something invisible within the vortex.

"It's gaining on us, Heckubus!" said Jack. "How do we get rid of it?"

"How should I know?"

"Yer always saying how ya know everything, ya blasted tin can," yelled Scallywag into his headset. "For once, we need ya to prove it!"

"Have you tried shooting it?"

Scallywag gave a scream of frustration. "Shooting it? SHOOTING IT? That's yer brilliant idea? OF COURSE WE SHOT IT, YA IDIOT! It's a bloody tornado! Blasters have no effect on it!"

"Fine, fine, fine," said Heckubus. "Now, I assume it only appeared when one of you touched the ground, correct?"

"Yeah, that was my bad," said Jack.

"Tell me, is this 'evil' tornado thing making contact with the ground at all?"

Jack turned and looked. He could feel the entity closing in on him and Scallywag. It seemed much larger and more menacing now, and as it twirled Jack could see faces materialize within the chaos — stretched, and pained, and screaming in agony — hundreds of them forming and disappearing as the entity twisted and flailed about.

He glanced down and saw its skinny base, flittering to-and-fro over the ground as it trailed behind them, its large, swirling top gyrating around it.

"Yes!" said Jack. "It's making contact with the ground!"

"Hmmm. Then it might be safe to assume that it has some type of connection with the natural terrain of the planet."

"What the bloody difference does that make?" growled Scallywag.

"Well, perhaps if you weren't over the ground, it wouldn't be able to get you," replied Heckubus. "I'm sending you coordinates of a nearby crater. I recommend you turn your hover stabilizers up to maximum and try to make it over there before you die."

The hoverbike beeped as it received Heckubus's new coordinates. Scallywag cursed under his breath as he turned his bike in the new direction. "I hope this bloody works!" he said.

Jack felt the bike shiver as Scally punched the accelerator. Jack turned and saw the swirling chaos of the entity grow closer. It pursued them relentlessly, the faces within its funnel growing more and more rabid, as if they could smell a fresh kill in front of them. The moaning grew louder, and Jack could feel the malevolence oozing from it.

"Faster! Faster! FASTER!" screamed Jack. "Can't you go any faster???"

"Maybe if one o' us weren't here to weigh us down," grumbled Scallywag.

Jack could see a metallic glint in the distance, the large metal ringed opening signaled that it was one of the mysterious craters that led deep within the planet. They were heading right toward it, but would it really save them?

Jack glanced behind him again. The entity was practically on top of them. Swirling and moaning ferociously, it had almost reached their engine. Jack could see the tiny grains of bone white sand as it swirled around and melded into faces, open mouths screaming, eyes deep pits of sadness and pain. Little things that looked like fingers began to form, as if the entity contained hands that were eager to reach out and grab him.

Suddenly, red blasts of plasma shot through the entity. Jack turned and saw Grohm beside them, a few feet away, blasting at the thing with his large gun. It didn't seem to faze the entity at all. It loomed over Jack, so he could feel the wind from it biting at the back of his neck. Jack closed his eyes, hugging Scallywag tight, trying desperately to inch up, away from the thing that was behind him…

And then, it was gone.

Jack opened his eyes. They had crossed over the crater, and the entity stood at its edge skidding restlessly back and forth along the precipice of the metal ring that encircled the crater, unable to cross it. It moaned in protest, crying out for its prey.

Scallywag brought the bike to a stop, as did Grohm beside them. They hovered over a pit that descended deep into the planet, disappearing into utter darkness far below. The group stopped and took a breath for a moment as they looked at the entity, the Doom that roamed the surface of the Ghost Planet.

"Well now, this is peachy," said Scallywag.

Jack looked at him, surprised by his tone. "What's the matter?" he asked. "Heckubus was right, as long as we're not over the ground, it can't hurt us."

"Aye," said Scallywag. "But in case ya haven't noticed, we're not exactly at our destination either."

Scallywag pointed toward the Deathlord Mothership, which was still a few good miles away. Jack's heart sank. If they left the crater, the entity would surely try to kill them again. As long as it was there, they couldn't get to Anna.

"Still alive?" sang Heckubus's voice over the comm.

"Alive, but trapped," replied Scallywag. "We're stuck over this crater until that blasted tornado thing gets bored."

"Pah, ye of little faith," replied Heckubus. "What you're over is part of a complicated network of tunnels that crisscross the planet, all of which eventually lead to its core."

"So?"

"SO… all you need to do is descend into the tunnels and make your way to the Princess underground. I am sending you maps I was able to construct using our own sensor readings and the data the Earthship stole from the Deathlord Mothership. They will get you to where the Deathlords are most likely taking her. I postulate they should be accurate enough to get you there safely."

The hoverbikes both beeped as they received the maps. Jack couldn't help but smile. "Way to go, robot," said Jack. "Guess we're not as stuck as we thought."

Scallywag grumbled, looking down into the abyss beneath them as it tapered off into complete darkness. "Let's just hope that whatever's down there ain't nearly as bad as what's up here."

Jack looked across the chasm toward the entity as it whirled about, howling at them. Jack gritted his teeth and gazed down into the darkness below. "No sense in waiting to find out," he said.

Grohm and Scallywag nodded in agreement, flipping the switches on their bikes and descending deep into the shadowy heart of the Ghost Planet.

CHAPTER ✷ 40

t felt like they had been travelling for hours before the craft came to a stop. Professor Green didn't know how long they had been working their way down the long, dark tunnel. The aches and pains that ran throughout his body made everything seem like it took longer than it probably did.

His eyes fluttered open, and he looked around. It was dark, but small lights from the rails of the vehicle gave off enough illumination for him to see. They were on a circular platform – some type of hovervehicle he guessed – big enough for 12 men. Its sides rose up waist high, with a control panel at the front for the pilot to operate.

He could sense the Princess beside him. She was holding onto his hand, a bit too tightly for comfort, but he understood why. Three armed Dark Soldiers surrounded them. Two more were with the Deathlord Supreme at the front. It was a pilot at the controls who was the first to speak.

"Contact, Supreme," he said simply. "We've found the energy signature."

"Show me," came the reply.

Lights on the front of the vehicle came to life, shining a spotlight on the wall before them. The side of the tunnel was made of metal – not solid metal, but ringed panels which seemed to snake down its sides like armor, each one overlapping the one beneath it. Green glanced upward; far off in the distance above him, he could see faint signs of light from the surface, where they'd exited the Deathlord Mothership and made their descent. As far as he could tell, this tunnel did not bend or twist; it was a straight drop down from where they had been.

The craft turned slowly until it came to a half-moon shaped opening in the tunnel to their right. The light from the craft shone as far into the darkness as it could before being swallowed up by the void that lay beyond. The pilot steered forward into the tunnel and landed the circular shaped hovervehicle right inside the opening.

"The activation terminal should be ten meters ahead, according to our readings, Supreme."

"Acknowledged," Zarrod replied, before turning to the Dark Troopers guarding Anna and Green. "Bring them."

Green felt the clawed hands of his captors tighten around his shoulders and yank him to his feet. His legs felt wobbly, but he was able to stay standing. The Princess had to let go of her grip so he could steady himself with his hands bound in front of him by a painful cord of ghostly energy.

The Deathlord Supreme exited the craft where the side paneling opened up for disembarking. The Princess and Green were both ushered out behind him, followed by the rest of their deadly company.

Though it was dark, the Deathlord Supreme moved as though he could see everything. His footsteps echoed through the shrouded void like the heartbeat of some terrible animal that was stirring from slumber. Finally, he stopped before what looked like a waist-high pillar of stone jutting up from the ground. He looked down at it and motioned with his hand – a casual gesture to his troops, signaling for them to bring the prisoner to his location.

A Dark Soldier grabbed Anna and brought her forward. She didn't protest at her handling; she didn't make a sound. Even in the dark, Green could imagine the look of defiance on her face.

"Activate it," the Deathlord ordered when she was beside him.

"I don't know how," said Anna.

The Deathlord reached out behind her head, without touching her, and closed his fist. Green saw Anna's body stiffen and she gasped as though he'd dug his claws directly into her skull. He could see the faint outline of her body in the darkness, shivering and twitching, helpless against whatever hold the Deathlord Supreme wielded over her.

"Activate it," he repeated.

Green watched as Anna raised her hand, her arm shaking as if it were being forced to act against her will. She placed her hand on the flat part of the top of the pillar, and upon contact, the area she touched lit up with a brilliant white light.

"Now," said the Deathlord, "bring this planet back to life."

"I... I..." said Anna through clenched teeth, as though she were struggling with her own body.

"Do it," commanded Zarrod.

Anna had no choice but to obey. She closed her eyes, and after a moment, the floor shook as a tremor snaked through their surroundings. A low rumble echoed all around them, as if the planet itself were some giant being awakened from a long slumber. Behind him, light shone suddenly as though someone had turned on a light switch. Green saw the metal rings of the tunnel were now illuminated, each overlapping ring its own source of soft, white light, dispelling any hint of darkness.

Before him, the passageway they were in slowly came to life. They were in what appeared to be a long, high-ceilinged hallway, the sides of which were lined by majestic pillars marked with brilliantly glowing symbols at their top. The floor was made of smooth yellow stone, and the ceiling was arched and adorned with intricate carvings.

The hallway seemed to stretch on forever, with various sister tunnels branching off at random intersections. Strange murals with more glowing symbols adorned the walls. Green gazed at the architecture in awe. It was of Ancient design, no doubt about it, beautiful and perfectly preserved. Under any other circumstance he would have let out a gleeful cry and fought back tears of amazement and joy. Scientists could spend their entire lives looking for such a thing, and his natural instinct was to want to study every nook and cranny of it.

"What is this place?" asked Anna, giving voice to the question that had been running through Green's mind.

"It never ceases to amaze me how little your kind knows of its past," growled the Deathlord Supreme.

"Then perhaps you'd care to enlighten me, since you seem to know so much," said the Princess. Zarrod looked down at her, his eyes burning with a hint of amusement at the girl's challenge.

"It's a prison," he replied. "A place where your Heretic Ancestors tried in vain to stop the unstoppable. Where they trapped the invincible armada of the Void Lords in a state of quantum flux, at the core of this planet."

"Quantum flux?" asked Anna.

Zarrod laughed, a terrible sound, thick with condescension. "The only way to contain the greatest weapons the universe has ever seen," he said. "The invincible armada cannot be destroyed. They are great ships of incredible power that put our motherships to shame. Our masters designed them to sweep through galaxies, like some terrible force of nature, destroying everything in their path, and with each victory, the ships grew stronger and more powerful. So how does one stop that which cannot be defeated? You trap it, of course. Your ancestors were quite clever in that sense. This planet is in a state of quantum flux, you see. It exists everywhere, yet at the same time, nowhere, randomly choosing to exist in different dimensions, different realities, different streams of space and time. Should we try to leave, there is no telling what reality we may end up in, if any at all. But that is only part of the prison, a last desperate attempt to safeguard your universe from the terrors here. The core of this planet, where the armada lies, is in an even more concentrated state of flux. The planet itself is meant to keep it that way, so intense and chaotic, that the armada could never break free."

"And that's why we're here, to free this armada of yours from its prison?"

"Obviously," growled Zarrod. "Down this corridor is the source of the planet's power: a vault where your ancestors sealed away their collective knowledge – an energy source designed to power this planet and all its safeguards. When you shut it off, the quantum flux will stop, the planet will return to its proper reality, and the invincible armada will be unleashed, ready to complete its mission."

Green felt his breath catch in this throat upon hearing the Deathlord's words. The back of his mind tingled with excitement. *Could it be?* he thought. *Is it possible?*

"For what purpose?" asked Anna. "What happens when you destroy every living thing in the universe? What could you possibly gain from such destruction?"

"It is part of a plan. One that is far beyond your understanding or mine. It is not our place to question the Lords of the Void. Only to obey them."

"So that's all you are, is it?" said Anna bitterly. "The mighty Deathlords, nothing but servants, slaves to the whims of some long dead group of genocidal maniacs."

Zarrod's hand lashed out, almost lazily, and struck Anna across the face, yet the force was so strong she stumbled and fell. Green watched her in despair as she sat up on her elbows, her lip bleeding from the slap.

"Best hold your tongue, lest I rip it from your mouth," said Zarrod. "We hold the honor of our service in high esteem. Our

Lords created us for a single purpose, and to serve them faithfully is the greatest reward we can hope for. I will not have you insult us or them by denigrating it."

"We used to think there was something more to your kind," said Anna, getting to her feet, unfazed by the Deathlord's threats. "We thought you were something beyond just simple machines. But now I can see it clearly. You're just robots – mindless robots designed to carry out your programming no matter what. You claim to have power over life, yet you have no soul of your own. You have no concept of what it means to be a living, breathing, *thinking* being. It's something you could never understand, because if you did, you'd see how pointless your true purpose is."

"I think you over-estimate the importance of being a living, breathing, thinking being," scoffed Zarrod. "In case you haven't noticed, we 'mindless robots' are winning."

Zarrod leaned down, bringing his burning red eyes at a level with Anna's.

"Look me in the eyes and tell me that little fact is *pointless*," he said, his voice dripping with triumph.

Anna met his gaze but said nothing. There was nothing she could say, and her silence was all the answer the Deathlord needed. Standing up straight, he gave the order: "Bring them."

With a flourish of his cape, he turned and started walking down the hallway. The Dark Soldiers ushered Anna and Green along behind him. Anna marched ahead, quietly, her face hard and resolute. Green, however, couldn't stop thinking about what the Deathlord had said: *"A vault where your ancestors sealed away their collective knowledge."*

He looked around as he walked, glancing at the symbols that shimmered at the top of the columns, at the murals on the walls filled with even more strange symbols and archaic writing. His mind was racing as he tried to remember all his studies – his lessons in Old Solar, in Ancient semiotics, quantum theory, and anything else related to Ancient technology.

"A vault where your ancestors sealed away their collective knowledge."

That had to be the answer; he knew it. But what was the knowledge? What was sealed away? He had to figure it out, and he didn't have a lot of time in which to do it.

He continued looking at the writing on the walls as they walked down the corridor. They seemed to repeat every few meters, the same symbols, the same writing.

Green looked at each in turn, his mind turning them over, trying to fit them together like pieces of a puzzle. He had some knowledge about the planet they were on, and he had gleaned a bit more insight from the Deathlord Supreme himself. He knew the writings had to relate to it all somehow...

Then, he started to make sense of the symbols and the writings, bit by bit, until certain revelations began to fall into place. And finally, when it all clicked together for him, his eyes lit up with the kind of excitement only an academic could experience when solving a very important riddle.

"Great Scott!" said Green upon his realization.

He'd involuntarily opened his mouth, unable to control his sudden outburst like one is unable to control a sneeze or a cough. But he realized immediately what a mistake he had made. The Deathlord Supreme stopped and turned toward Green, who immediately looked away, hoping he would go back to being ignored.

He could feel the Deathlord glaring at him with those horrible eyes of his. Green squirmed under his gaze and felt a rising sense of dread as the Deathlord turned and approached him.

"What did you say?" grumbled the Deathlord.

Green's mind raced. His first instinct was to deny he said anything, but he knew the Deathlord would know it was a lie. For the life of him, he didn't want to go through another agonizing torture session. "I... uh... said Great Scott."

"Why did you say that?"

"It's... just something I say..."

"But the way you said it..."

Green was quiet, silently kicking himself for being so careless. Of course, anyone listening would have known from the way he had spoken that he'd had some kind of revelation. He tried to keep avoiding the Deathlord's gaze but couldn't help glancing at him, meeting his eyes, if only briefly.

"I... uh..."

The Deathlord looked away, glancing at the walls and the symbols, then back at Green. "You can understand this."

Green knew it wasn't a question.

"You know what it all means," said the Deathlord, his voice low and menacing.

Green swallowed hard, a lump of anxiety forming in his throat. "I... wouldn't presume to tell you my deductions, Supreme," said Green. "Surely one such as yourself, who's as great and powerful as you are, already has a firm grasp of the symbology of the Ancients, and you probably already know everything that is written on these walls. Please forgive my outburst; it takes some time for a lowly life-form such as myself to figure things out."

A low groan came from Zarrod as he stared intently at Green, as though he wanted to give into the flattery but was still smart enough not to. Green knew the Deathlord probably could not understand the Ancient symbols, most likely because he had no real interest to, but it was also probably not a good idea to try to lie to him either. The Deathlord was unlikely to admit to any sign that an alien such as Green was smarter than him in any respect.

After a long moment, Zarrod turned to the three guards around Green. "Take him back to the ship," said Zarrod. "Have him interrogated. I want to know everything he does."

"No!" cried Anna.

A feeling of despair filled Green's stomach. He knew he was on borrowed time with this journey he was on, but the prospect of the pain he'd have to endure before it was over frightened him to no end.

"If you hurt him, I won't help you, I swear to the Great Observer I won't!" protested Anna.

"You're far enough along where we don't need your willing cooperation," said Zarrod flatly as he reached behind Anna's head and clenched his fist again. She stood straight and ridged, unable to move or talk, even though it was clear she wanted to. Whatever power the Deathlord had over her, it was growing with each passing moment. Zarrod turned back to the guards. "Take him to Warlord Abraxas. I wish for him to handle the interrogation personally."

The guards nodded and grabbed Green, turning him around and prodding him with their weapons to walk. Green glanced back at Anna one last time, seeing the tears streaking down her cheeks as the Deathlord Supreme and his remaining entourage continued marching her down the corridor.

Green sighed sadly as he walked along with his captors, his feet shuffling with the weight of a man condemned to die. In his mind, he started to think of all the things he'd never get to accomplish in his life: all the papers he'd yet to write, all the planets he'd yet to explore, and the family he'd never get to have. Suddenly, his decision not to take on a mate for so many years while pursuing his work seemed like a foolish one. After all, who would there be to mourn his passing? No one but Anna, and Green felt even sadder knowing that her time was likely limited, as well.

He continued to walk silently with the Dark Soldiers, a blanket of depression and sadness wrapped around him. He took some small solace in knowing that the Ancients, in their wisdom, had set up some type of protection should the Deathlord succeed. But it seemed a rather shallow kind of victory when put in context with everything he was about to lose.

Eventually, in the distance before him, he saw the hovervehicle they had taken down to the entrance. The white light of the tunnel shone through the half moon opening, as though some happy paradise awaited him down there. He wondered if it would be wiser to try and slow down the pace of his walk to stretch out what little time he had left, or if it was better to quicken his fate? Perhaps the smart thing to do would be to rush ahead and throw himself down the tunnel, robbing the Deathlords of the chance to torture him and learn what he had figured out. Then again, his guards probably had the power to use their magic to lift him into the air before his feet could carry him very far. He shuddered at the thought of the invisible hooks digging into his skin.

Before he knew it, they were almost to the hovervehicle. It sat there, mocking him, as though it knew it would be the thing that carried him to death's door. In fact, he could almost hear it laughing…

Oddly enough, that laugh sounded rather like the high-pitch whine of some type of battery powering up.

BOOM!

A hot orange blast suddenly tore through the guard to his left, disintegrating him in a puff of dust.

Green gave out a cry of surprise and fell to the floor, covering his head. He heard blaster fire ring out all around him, and within a few more seconds, more black dust showered down upon him signaling the end of his remaining two captors.

Green looked up, almost in shell-shock, glancing around him. His bindings had disappeared with the death of his captors, his wrists now blissfully free of their painful restraints. His vision was blurred, possibly from tears of sudden and inexplicable relief. A hazy image made its way toward him, coming into focus on a smiling face he thought he'd never see again.

"Jack?" he said, his voice thick with emotion. "Jack! My boy! I don't believe it…"

Jack rushed up beside the Professor and knelt next to him. "Hey Professor," he said, glad to see the old green alien still alive.

"I thought… I thought you'd gone," Green said, his wide lips quivering. Jack suddenly felt his stomach tighten with guilt, the image of the Professor lying on the cold floor of the hangar as Jack and the others left him behind playing out in his head. He reached out and put his hand on Green's shoulder, flashing the bravest smile he could.

"And let you have all the fun?" said Jack. "C'mon, you know me better than that."

Green smiled and looked at Grohm and Scallywag, who came walking up from behind, both of them sporting rather impressive looking weapons. "Well, it would appear I've stumbled across a good old fashioned rescue. And not a moment too soon, I might add," he said. His voice was thick with the cheeriness he'd been known for. As the first sliver of hope since he'd been captured worked its way into him, relief seeped into his muscles and filled him with warmth.

"Well, not so sure ya'd call it *good*," said Scallywag, scratching his head with the muzzle of his pistol. "Or old fashioned, for that matter."

"Don't mind him," said Jack, helping Green up to his feet. "He gets kinda cranky when storming the Deathlords almost single handedly."

"Right," replied Green. "Where is Paragon Shepherd?"

The smile on Jack's face immediately disappeared at the mention of Shepherd's name. He glanced at his two companions, who remained silent. "He… uh… he didn't make it," said Jack meekly.

Green's large eyes blinked, as if his brain hadn't quite registered what Jack had just said. After a few moments, Jack's words seeped in. "I see…" he said, frowning. He felt his heart break a little at hearing of the loss of his friend. Then, the reality of the situation hit him. "Wait, you mean, you came here on your own? Just – just the three of you?"

"Well, we have a fourth back on the ship," said Jack, as though that evened the odds they were facing.

"Oh, dear," mumbled Green.

"Yeah, welcome to my world, Greenskin," muttered Scallywag.

"Hey, we've made it this far, haven't we?" said Jack defensively.

"No, no, don't get me wrong," replied Green. "Kudos for bravery my boy, kudos. It's just that the situation is, uh, complicated."

"Ain't that an understatement if I ever heard one," said Scallywag.

"What do you mean, Professor?" asked Jack.

"Do any of you know what this place is?" Green asked.

"Yeah, we all saw the slideshow, remember?" said Jack. "Big scary Ghost Planet."

"Yes, you told me about Terahades and that it was created to imprison a fleet of powerful enemy ships," replied Green. "But this place is more – much more – than just a simple prison."

Jack, Scallywag, and Grohm all exchanged glances. None of them liked where this might be going.

"Professor," said Jack. "We don't really have a whole lot of time here. Can you just cut to the chase?"

"Jack, I've spent my life studying the Ancients," said Green. "Much of their history, their story, is still unknown to us, even after thousands of years of the greatest minds in the galaxy studying them. But one thing every Ancient scholar knows about is what's called The Great Prototypes."

"Oy, I hearda those," said Scallywag. "They're those Ancient inventions – the ones nobody can figure out what makes 'em tick?"

"Indeed," said Green. "The portgate system, the very thing that ties the Regalus Empire together, was the first Great Prototype ever discovered. It's been used for millennia, and we have yet to scratch the surface of how it's able to operate. But there are other Great Prototypes... things the Ancients created that are so powerful, so wondrous, they could change the very foundation of the universe."

"Don't tell me," said Jack.

"Yes," said Green, smiling. "I believe this planet is one of them."

"This place?" said Scallywag. "A bloody rock in the middle of nowhere? This is a Great Prototype?"

"This is far from just a rock, my friend. Look..." Green pointed to the pillars, which were engraved with glowing symbols.

"From what I can gather," said Green as he gazed up at the pillars, "the Ancients were experimenting with the genesis of life. They were trying to figure out how to create *worlds*."

"They wanted to create planets?" asked Jack.

"Not just any planets," said Green. "Habitable planets! The universe is vast, and finding planets capable of supporting life can be difficult. But if you could simply create a habitable planet anywhere you wanted – one with light, atmosphere, water… why, you could colonize the universe! You'd never have to worry about destroying another planet's ecosystem, or misplacing indigenous life-forms, or settling someplace that's potentially dangerous to your species. You could literally create life!"

"Wow, that's cool," said Jack, not really caring. "So, anyway Professor, which way did the Deathlords take Anna?"

Green's smile disappeared, as though he suddenly remembered everything that was happening. "They took her to the Great Seal," he replied.

"The what?"

"That's what I was about to get to," said Green. "Every Great Prototype is a type of experiment, a work in progress. Often times, it will defy the laws of physics, nature – pretty much anything we accept as scientific fact. It is able to do this through the use of something called a Great Seal – the very thing I was searching for when I stumbled across your planet."

"You mean, this Great Seal is the reason why this planet has breathable atmosphere, a world-wide shield, and a big angry tornado?" asked Jack.

"An angry what?" asked Green.

"Long story," said Jack, dismissing the question.

"There's a living tornado on the surface of the planet that kills ya," mumbled Scallywag.

"Yeah," sighed Jack. "I really gotta learn how to summarize stuff…"

"Well, yes. Everything about this planet is tied to its Great Seal. Scientists have tried to figure out what is behind the Portgate network's Great Seal since it was discovered, but it was always considered too risky to investigate since disrupting the Portgate system would be disastrous for the Empire. But whatever is behind it, we theorize, is some type of quantum energy source capable of stabilizing whatever science the Ancients invented to create the Great Prototype. If what the Deathlord said is true, then that energy source is actually the knowledge of the science behind these prototypes, converted into the very energy needed to create it!"

"Professor…" said Jack impatiently.

"The Deathlords plan to use the Princess to release that energy," said Green. "She is the blood of the Ancients. The only one capable of accessing the energy that's contained behind the Great Seal."

"All the more reason to hurry up and get her," said Jack, turning to hurry down the corridor.

"You have to let them!" called out Green urgently.

Jack stopped in mid-step along with the rest of his group and turned to Green.

"What?" said Jack, uncertain whether he had correctly heard the Professor.

"You have to let the Princess unleash the quantum energy that's trapped behind the Great Seal," said Green.

"Hold up now," said Scallywag. "I thought doing that would free a fleet of unstoppable evil spaceships?"

"It will," said Green.

Jack slapped his palm to his face. "Then why—"

"Because the only way to save what the Ancients created here is to release that energy back into the universe," said Green. "As long as it is trapped here, behind that seal, the knowledge of this science is not accessible to anyone. As long as that knowledge is being used for such energy, it's trapped, shielded from even the most free mind, inaccessible to the universe at large."

"Who cares?" said Jack.

"You should!" said Green. "We all should! Don't you see? The Deathlords don't understand what they have here! With this knowledge, we could rebuild what they've taken from us! Create new planets to replace the ones they've destroyed. Fight death... with new life."

Grohm grunted. Jack couldn't tell if the Rognok was getting bored, or if he was impressed with what Green had just shared.

"Lemme get this straight," said Jack. "We have to let the Deathlords force Anna to unleash whatever's behind this Great Seal, because otherwise no one will be able to figure out what the Ancients did?"

"Yes," said Green. "This place was not meant to be a prison, Jack. I believe the Ancients modified it out of necessity. Whatever is behind that Seal was not meant to be trapped there forever. Once it is released, the knowledge of the Ancients will be freed upon this universe. The science behind this is so vast, so new, that the only hope we have of harvesting it lies with tapping into that energy. And somewhere, someone will tune into it. When that happens... we may finally have an advantage over the Deathlords."

"Yeah, that's nice and all... but I'm still not hearing anything about the invincible evil spaceships," said Scallywag.

"Oh, well there's a relatively simple way to handle that," said Green. "We'll just need to blow up the planet."

This time, both Jack and Scallywag hit their faces with their palms.

"I think the Deathlords tortured yer friend a tad too much," mumbled Scallywag.

"I know how it sounds," said Green. "But there is a Deathlord Planetkiller docked right above this silo leading directly to the unstable quantum core of this planet where those ships are imprisoned. If the state of quantum flux is as intense as I believe, I am willing to bet the mothership's main weapon will start a chain reaction that will detonate the core and cause the 'invincible armada' to cease to exist."

"Blowing up the planet in the process?" said Scallywag.

"Yes," said Green. "And most likely the better part of this sector of space."

"Charming," replied the pirate.

"Well, it's just a nebula," said Green. "There are no life-forms here the explosion would hurt."

"Yer forgetting about us," said Scallywag. "I'm pretty sure *we'd* be hurt."

"Well, how were you planning to escape the planet to begin with?"

"Uh..." said Jack. "We were just gonna use the ship's Entanglement Engine to jump out of here."

"Ah!" said Green. "Brilliant. Chances are its coordinates would take you back to your own space/time, so you'd be able to get off the planet without a worry. Good thinking, my boy."

"Thanks," said Jack, even though the idea had been Heckubus's, and none of them was even sure it would really work. But bottom line, being anywhere away from the Deathlords was preferable, even if it meant hopping into another reality.

"That should work just fine," continued Green. "It will take some time for the chain reaction to trigger and destroy the planet. If we can make the jump before it happens, we should be okay."

"Yeah, this plan was bad enough before adding a massive explosion into the mix," said Scallywag.

"It's really the only way to ensure the Deathlord's invincible armada is never unleashed," said Green. "The Ancients meant for the seal to be a failsafe. As long as the knowledge is contained behind the seal, it would keep the invincible armada captive. If the seal were broken and the armada were released, the knowledge to defeat them would once again be available to the universe. If we can destroy the armada AND release the knowledge, then we just may be able to have a significant advantage over the Deathlords for the first time."

"So now, we're not just supposed to rescue the Princess," said Scallywag, "we've gotta free the Ancient forbidden knowledge, infiltrate a Deathlord Mothership, and blow up a planet?"

"Precisely!" smiled Green.

Scallywag stared at the Professor dumbly for a moment.

"I think I was better off in the bloody Pit," hissed the pirate.

Jack sighed and looked at Green. The alien stared back at him, his large lips curling around his face the way his human version used to smile when he was leading Jack to the correct answer during class.

"Shepherd would've gone for this plan, wouldn't he?" asked Jack.

"Without a doubt," replied Green.

Jack nodded and looked at his companions. Scallywag rolled his eyes. Grohm just stared stoically.

Jack reached up to his earpiece and activated his comm unit.

"Heckubus," said Jack. "We have a change of plans…"

"You have what???" squawked the robot in reply. "How dare you alter my brilliantly plotted scheme! As if any of you nitwits have the wherewithal to account for all the various details and nuances of—"

"We're gonna have to blow up the planet," interrupted Jack.

After a moment of silence, the robot answered.

"Oh, well that's okay then."

"Good. Now listen up because there's a lot you need to know, and we don't have much time…"

After Jack explained the situation to Heckubus, it took the robot a few minutes to come up with a strategy for the group that seemed somewhat viable to everyone involved. After the plan had been formulated, Scallywag looked at Jack and frowned.

"Remember before when I told ya storming this planet was the worst plan I'd ever heard?" he asked.

"Yeah," said Jack.

"I take it back," replied Scallywag. "*This* is the worst plan I've ever heard."

"And yet, the plans keep working," said Jack, smiling as he gave Scallywag a chummy slap on the arm.

"Now buck up," said Jack. "It's time to save the day."

CHAPTER ✺ 41

nna was beginning to have trouble feeling her legs as she marched down the hallway beside the Deathlord Supreme. It was almost as if they were asleep – she knew she was walking, that her feet were touching the ground and swinging back and forth, carrying her along with them – but she did not feel it. She did not will it. She did not want it. She was no longer in control of her own body.

If she were, she'd be running away, struggling against her captors, doing everything in her power to resist their will. Instead she walked, and kept on walking dutifully by the side of the creature that planned to use her and discard her after it had taken all it could from her.

She looked around, her mind racing, as it seemed to be the only thing left that she had any control over. Even that, she felt, was slowly slipping away as she found her concentration waning, making it hard for her to organize her thoughts.

She didn't know how long they had been walking. It seemed as if the hallway they were marching down were growing bigger. The footsteps of her and her captors echoed as they walked, bouncing off the walls like the beat of a drum. Finally, they came to a place where many different hallways merged into a semi-circle, and before them was a long, narrow passageway, its entrance buttressed with ornate designs, as if to signal that they had reached some important destination.

Zarrod entered first, and she followed behind him, with the three remaining Dark Soldiers bringing up the rear. The passageway they walked down was simple and free of any of the ornate symbols and decoration of the hallways leading up to it.

The walls were made of old, crumbling yellow brick and pressed in on them narrowly, making the hallway just wide enough for two men to walk down it side by side. The ceiling had no arch; it was just a flat, oppressive plane that lorded above them. It glowed slightly, giving a warm yellow hue to the hallway as soft as though it were torchlight.

At the end of the hall was a simple door made of the same stone that comprised the walls. It was wide and rectangular, stretching up to the ceiling, engraved with the Ancient writings of Old Solar.

Anna tried to read what was there, but the figure of the Deathlord Supreme blocked her vision. He stood before the door, as though he were standing before some ominous foe that was challenging him to battle. With the flick of his arm, he sent a screaming blast of ghostly white fury at it, and the door cracked, spiderwebbing from corner to corner like a pane of glass that had been impacted by a rock. Dust seeped from the door like blood from a wound, and a loud "crunching" sound echoed down the corridor as sorrowful as the cry of a dying beast.

Zarrod raised his hand again, a ball of death energy swirling between his claws, growing louder and more violent with each passing second. Finally, he released his hold on it, and it shot forth like a cannonball, tearing through the door and setting off an avalanche of rock and dust. They hit the ground in bits and pieces, thick dust spewing into the air and crawling along the ground like snakes seeking to escape a cage.

Anna's eyes watered, but she was unable to lift her hands to rub them. Her body stood still, not able to move no matter how hard she tried to make it obey. Zarrod turned and looked at her, as though he knew of her struggle and found it amusing. She could almost imagine the hideous smile his horrible helmet hid behind it.

"You three," he said, referring to his guards. "Stay here. What lies beyond is for me and my captive only."

The three Dark Soldiers nodded in submission. Zarrod stepped aside and extended his arm toward the opening, as if inviting Anna to enter first.

Anna moved forward, her legs obeying in the same manner a marionette obeys the puppet master who holds its strings. She wanted to scream, a flurry of anger, frustration, and helplessness swirling within her. But she held her tongue as she approached the doorway. There was nothing but darkness beyond its frame, but as she got closer she could see a series of stone steps leading downward – to what, she did not know.

She descended, and the Deathlord Supreme followed close behind her.

Scallywag stood at the controls of the Deathlord hovervehicle with Green beside him as they made their way up the tunnel. The Professor scratched at his wrists. The bindings around them had disappeared, but he kept them crossed to try and make it appear as though he were still a prisoner.

Scally looked up at the ever-encroaching Deathlord Mothership as the craft continued to climb toward it. "This is insane," he mumbled aloud. "Bloody insane. There must be somethin' wrong with me brain to agree to go along with this."

"Courage, dear friend," said Green, a bit too cheerily for Scallywag's liking. "I am confident we can succeed in our task."

"Confidence don't shield ya from plasma blasts, Greenskin," grumbled Scallywag.

"Neither does complaining," replied the Professor.

Scallywag glanced down at his hands. The sight of the black talons being there as opposed to his normal five red fingers still freaked him out a bit. When the Professor had handed over his hologuise emitter turning Scallywag into the very image of a Dark Soldier, his pirate instincts told him that at the very least, he had some type of cover should things go wrong. But looking like a Deathlord still put his teeth on edge. After all he'd been through, it just felt wrong.

The controls on the hovervehicle beeped, signaling that the Mothership had noticed their approach. Scallywag transmitted a signal that the Professor had set up for him, requesting permission to board. Within seconds, a panel to a docking bay opened high above them, like a terrible mouth ready to swallow them whole.

"Well, here goes nothing," said Scallywag.

"Remember," said Green, "try not to talk if you can help it."

"I'll be quiet as a tunnel rat," replied Scally.

"No sudden movements, we don't want to give them reason to be suspicious."

"Slow and robotic, gotcha."

"And don't let any of them get too close," said Green. "We haven't exactly tested the effectiveness of the hologuises at close range."

"They won't even notice I'm there."

Green nodded and cleared his throat nervously, gazing up at the opening as they approached. It grew bigger and bigger until their craft passed its threshold and entered the hanger. Though it seemed small from the outside, above them hung numerous shards, docked in individual hangars high above the opening, ready to drop and spring into action at a moment's notice.

Scallywag looked around. The bay was long and rectangular, possibly a hundred yards, more likely a little longer. Catwalks high above them stretched out, crisscrossing the area, leading to the various shards that were docked there. As far as Deathlords went, he didn't see any, and that made him breathe a sigh of relief. Far to the left, he spotted an area containing similar circular hovervehicles and started to make his way toward it, assuming that was where he'd have to park.

He landed in an empty alcove designed to house the vehicles. Both he and the Professor looked around nervously. The hangar was quiet. There was no sign of movement at all. For a moment, Scallywag dared to hope that it was as simple as that. There was to be no greeting party, and the Deathlords were not expecting any trouble on the planet, so security was not to be an issue.

"Well," said Green. "That wasn't so bad."

As if on cue, a door to the bay slid open, revealing two Dark Soldiers marching toward them.

"Ya had ta say something, didn't ya?" mumbled Scallywag. Green kept his mouth shut. Scallywag wasn't sure if the look of fear and misery on the Professor's face was part of an act or just an honest expression of how he was feeling.

The two Deathlords stopped before the vehicle, looking up at Scallywag on the landing platform. The pirate stared at the new arrivals, a tad too long, as though some unpleasant odor hung in the air between them. Green's large eyes shot nervously from the soldiers to Scallywag and back again. The Visini stood still, unsure of what to do next, but his brain was screaming at him that he had to do something.

"Greetings!" he said, holding up his clawed hand. "I am here under the orders of the Supreme."

The soldiers looked at him, unmoving.

"He wanted me to bring the prisoner back to the ship," he said.

The soldiers glanced at the Professor, who smiled at them weakly. The Deathlords betrayed no sense of any type of expression from behind their helmets.

"So, uh… that's what I did. Brought him back. As ordered. By the… uh, Supreme."

Scally's voice trailed off awkwardly. The two Deathlords slowly turned their heads to look at each other, and then back to Scallywag.

"Ah, blast it," Scallywag mumbled, before making a sudden move to the rail of the vessel. He leapt out, tucking and rolling toward the Dark Soldiers, who instinctively took a step back.

"An impostor!" one of the Dark Soldiers called out, seeing through his hologuise.

They made a move for their weapons, but Scallywag already had his pistols out. Rolling up to one knee, he leveled his weapons and fired at point blank range before the Deathlords had time to react, dispatching them both in a puff of dust.

Scallywag got to his feet and glanced around, weapons at the ready, but there was no sign of any other danger.

"Boring conversation anyway," the pirate muttered.

"I say," said Green as he got out of the hovervehicle. "You did exactly everything I told you not to do."

Scallywag holstered his weapons and deactivated his hologuise, looking at the Professor with just a hint of insolence. "Yeah," he said. "I've never been good at following directions."

Green nodded. "Well, my guess is they were sent to greet us, assuming we were coming back from the Deathlord Supreme's party. I do not know how long we have before they will be missed."

"Then we'd better get a move on," said Scallywag.

"Agreed," replied Green, smiling. "Now, let's go find us a terminal to hack."

Jack ran down the hallway as fast as he dared, sticking as close to the wall as possible. He felt his heart thumping in his chest and looked around nervously, as though expecting the Deathlord Supreme to pop out of one of the adjoining hallways at any second.

Jack had spent half his youth playing video games where the object was to run through corridors and shoot bad guys, and now he was practically living one. Unfortunately, the reality of "running and gunning" was far different than it had ever been on his *Gamerbox 3000*. Time was of the essence, but he couldn't just haphazardly rush ahead, guns blazing. This was real, and his life – as well as the lives of his friends – was on the line.

As he made his way down the Ancient corridor, Jack could feel the hulking presence of Grohm close behind him. Though the Rognok smelled like a cross between a wet dog and a sweaty gym shoe, his behemoth presence was the only thing that was giving Jack some sense of safety. After all they'd been through, Jack knew if there were one person he could rely on to watch his back, it was the massive alien by his side right now.

"Hey, just in case I don't get a chance to say it later," said Jack. "Thanks. For coming here and backing me up. I appreciate your help."

Grohm grunted. Jack wasn't sure if that was his way of saying "You're welcome" or not. He still had yet to learn how to read the Rognok. "I mean, I know this is crazy. By all rights, we probably shoulda done what Scally suggested and run away the

first chance we got. But I think we can actually do this! We've made it this far, right?"

The Rognok was silent. Jack figured he should probably be quiet as well, but talking helped keep his mind off how nervous he was. He was about to say something else when suddenly he saw something further down the corridor.

"Whoa, whoa, hold up," said Jack as he quickly crept up behind a large pillar to the side of the main walkway, motioning Grohm to follow him.

Once they were safely tucked away from view, Jack peeked around the side of the pillar. From there, he could see that the corridor down which they had been running ended in a half-circle area. Two Deathlords stood guard on either side of a small entrance on the far wall, with a third one pacing back and forth around the area, glancing down each hallway in turn.

"Crap," muttered Jack. He turned to Grohm. "There are three Deathlords down there – two guarding some entrance, and one patrolling around. My guess is Anna was taken in there."

Grohm leaned out and took a look, snorting at what he saw. Jack's mind raced. If this were a video game, there would be cover to hide behind as they made their way down the hall, allowing them to hop to-and-fro while picking off the Deathlords who were out in the open. However, the pillars ended too far from the opening, and the area between the end of the corridor and where the Deathlords had taken up position was too far. If either he or Grohm tried to take them on, chances were the Deathlords would cut them down.

"We need a plan. There's gotta be a way past them," mumbled Jack. "Think, think... maybe there's a ventilation shaft we could crawl through?" Jack looked around briefly. "Who am I kidding? There aren't any vents in this place. Not that you'd be able to fit in one if there were." He looked down at his side and saw the grenade belt. "I guess we could toss a grenade down there, but that would make too much noise. If the Deathlord Supreme came out here, we'd be toast. Maybe we could double back and head down another hallway and flank them? One of us would need to distract them while the other opened fire. Can you make any bird noises?"

Grohm's gaze said it all.

"Look, I'm just trying to figure out the situation," said Jack testily. "Do you have any ideas?"

"Battle," grumbled the Rognok.

"No!" whispered Jack as loudly as he dared. "They're too far away, and there are too many of them. We can't just rush in there head on. They'll kill us for sure."

Grohm sneered at Jack. "There is nothing more glorious than to die in battle."

"Oh, no, I'm totally with you on that, dude," said Jack. "I mean, I wake up every day hoping to die in battle. We are so on the same wavelength there. It's just... I don't want to die in *this* battle!"

"Then leave it to Grohm," the Rognok said before taking his mammoth fist and pounding it against the pillar three times.

BOOM, BOOM, BOOM.

The sound echoed down the hallway in all directions. Down near the door they were guarding, the Dark Troopers snapped to attention, drawing their plasma rifles in alarm.

Jack looked at Grohm in shock. "What are you doing!" he cried in the loudest whisper he could muster.

Grohm banged on the pillar again.

BOOM, BOOM, BOOM.

"Stop doing that!" whispered Jack again, panic slowly gripping his stomach. Grohm looked at Jack and held a finger to his lips, indicating the necessity for quiet. Jack didn't need to be told twice.

What followed was silence. Then, a steady — *pat, pat, pat* — sound echoed toward them.

It was the sound of footsteps. One of the Deathlords was coming to investigate the noise. Jack raised his plasma pistol, ready to blast the Dark Soldier as soon as he showed his face. Was this Grohm's plan? Take out one of the guards so they had a better shot with the other two? *Doesn't seem like a very good plan,* he thought fatalistically.

That notion went out of Jack's mind as soon as Grohm's giant hand wrapped around him and pushed him flat against the pillar beside the Rognok and held him there, destroying his vantage point for any blaster fire against the Dark Trooper.

Pat, pat, pat…

The footsteps were getting closer. Jack wanted to ask Grohm what the heck he was doing, but he was afraid to open his mouth. His heart was racing, and the sound of blood pounding in his ears was quickly giving him a headache.

Pat, pat, pat…

Jack could tell the footsteps were almost to them when suddenly they stopped. Grohm released his arm from Jack and slowly crouched, like a cat getting ready to pounce on a bird.

Then, the Dark Soldier swung out from behind the corner of the pillar, rifle trained right for Grohm's head.

With speed betraying his size, Grohm's arm shot out, his massive reach allowing him to close the distance between him and the Deathlord and quickly slap the nozzle of the Dark Soldier's rifle aside, causing its shot to go wide and miss.

He fired the arm that had been holding Jack back straight at the Deathlord like a piston, cracking the facemask of the Trooper with a powerful blow, causing the Deathlord to drop his rifle.

Before the Dark Soldier could stumble back, Grohm dug his fingers into its armored breastplate. The Rognok swung out from behind the cover of the pillar, holding the dazed Deathlord in one hand, and unslinging his massive plasma shotgun off his back with the other.

The two Dark Soldiers by the entrance began to fire immediately. Grohm raised the Deathlord in front of him like a shield, letting his hostage absorb the blaster fire as the massive Rognok sprinted down the hallway, firing his shotgun at the two soldiers as his long legs quickly closed the distance.

Some of his shots went wide, but one hit a Dark Soldier head on, causing it to disintegrate in a puff of black dust.

Jack swung around the corner of the pillar and took aim at the remaining Deathlord at the end of the corridor, hoping to give Grohm some cover fire. He opened up on the Dark Soldier just as the one Grohm was using as a shield took its last blast and disintegrated. However, Jack was too far away, and his shots weren't even close to their mark.

Before Grohm could reach the final guard, one of the Trooper's blasts caught him in the shoulder. Grohm grunted in pain, dropping his weapon in the process. The Dark Soldier dropped to one knee and leveled his rifle at the oncoming alien.

As soon as Jack saw this, he ran out from behind his cover and began firing at the Deathlord, causing the Dark Soldier to dodge his plasma blasts and giving Grohm the time he needed.

With a burst of speed, Grohm lunged toward the final Deathlord. With a powerful shoulder thrust, he slammed into the Dark Trooper with the force of a mack truck, sending him flying back into the wall like roadkill.

As the Dark Trooper struggled to his feet, Grohm descended upon him. With one sweep of his arms, he knocked the weapon from the soldier's hand. A massive fist landed squarely in the Deathlord's gut, and a swift kick to the back of the Deathlord's legs brought the soldier to its knees. Grohm then grabbed the Deathlord's head between his two massive hands and squeezed until the Dark Soldier's helmet crushed together like an aluminum can. The soldier's body erupted into black grains of dust as it disintegrated between Grohm's fingers.

Jack ran down the hallway just in time to see the Deathlord's body waft away. "Dude!" cried Jack. "That was the coolest thing I think I've ever seen in my life! I mean, a head's up would have been nice, but... WOW! You totally crushed that guy's head!"

Grohm sneered and inspected his shoulder. Jack saw that the blast had torn through his armor and there was blackened and scorched skin underneath.

"Are you okay?" asked Jack.

"Fine," grumbled Grohm as he picked up his fallen plasma shotgun. Grohm quickly checked the weapon and then moved toward the entrance the Deathlords had been guarding. Jack followed behind as they made their way into the narrow hallway. Grohm walked quickly, with Jack rushing to keep up.

"Grohm! Big guy!" cried Jack, trying to get his companion's attention. "Hold up! Wait!"

The Rognok didn't slow down. Finally, Jack ran past him and stood in his way, a few feet from the final entrance.

Grohm stopped and looked down at Jack, a deep grunt escaping from him.

"Look, all your awesomeness aside, before we head down there, we need to get on the same page. We're a team, we need to communicate if we're gonna make it out of here, okay?"

Grohm glared at Jack in a way that made him a bit uncomfortable. But Jack soldiered on.

"Okay, so remember the plan we came up with earlier," said Jack, unstrapping the grenade belt from his waist and holding it out to Grohm. "We wait for Anna to open the seal, then sneak up on the Deathlord. You strap these grenades to him and toss him as far away as possible before he gets a chance to react. We grab Anna, and run for it, and hope to God the blast is enough to destroy him or at least to slow him down."

Grohm's eyes narrowed as he looked at the grenade belt. "No," he replied.

Jack hesitated a moment at Grohm's response. "Look, I know it's not the best plan, but at least it gives us a chance to get out of there."

"Earthman take the Regal Princess," Grohm said. "Grohm will stay behind."

Jack gazed at Grohm, taken aback. "But... but he'll kill you."

Grohm snorted. Somehow, Jack knew that's what the massive alien seemed to be expecting. "No," Jack replied. "You don't have to. We can still make it out, all of us."

"Grohm doesn't want to make it out," the Rognok replied. "Grohm wants to fight. Grohm wants to face Deathlord Supreme."

"But... but why?"

"Revenge," said the Rognok, simply.

Jack gazed into Grohm's narrow red and black eyes, and suddenly it all made sense. His time with the alien in the Pit, why he had agreed to Jack's crazy, suicidal plan... it became clear that Grohm hadn't backed Jack because he thought he would succeed, but rather because Jack was the best chance he had at getting to the Deathlord Supreme.

"The Deathlords," said Jack. "They destroyed your planet. So you're trying to get revenge on the ones responsible?"

Grohm nodded.

"That's why you were in the Pit," continued Jack. "You tracked them down…"

"Grohm was in exile," the Rognok said. "Far from Rognok planet when destroyed. Searched for the Deathlord fleet. Was captured when Grohm found them."

"And you came with me… why? So they could kill you, too?"

"Rognoks do not fear death, Earthman," grumbled the alien. "Grohm will face Deathlord Supreme, and Grohm will make him suffer."

"But you saw how powerful he is!" pleaded Jack. "He can't be killed!"

"Everything can be killed."

"Listen to me," said Jack. "Pounding on him for a little while and letting him kill you is not the way for you to get revenge for your planet. You really want revenge? Let's get Anna out of here safely and all of us get away to fight another day. That'll drive the Supreme bonkers!"

Jack held up the grenade belt to Grohm again. Grohm reached out and gently pushed it back toward Jack. "Earthman saves Regal Princess. Earthman part of Grohm's revenge. Cannot blow up Deathlord Supreme. Deathlord is too powerful. Grohm will face him while Earthman flees. It is only way."

"You're going to sacrifice yourself, so we can escape?"

"It is the way Grohm chooses to die."

"In battle," said Jack, sadly. "Against a worthy foe."

"A glorious death. One every Rognok lives for."

"But it's still death," said Jack. "Can't you—"

"No."

Jack looked at Grohm helplessly. He thought he could see a hint of sadness in the alien's eyes, but Grohm had made up his mind, and Jack knew there was nothing he could say to get him to change it. Jack could feel tears pooling in the corners of his eyes. He did not want to see his friend die, but deep down, he knew their plan was risky. If Grohm could hold off the Deathlord Supreme long enough, it was his best chance to get Anna to safety. Jack choked back his emotion and quickly rubbed away the tears.

"You've wanted this showdown for a long time, huh?"

Grohm nodded.

"Okay," he said. "We'll do it your way, big guy."

Jack strapped the grenade belt back around his waist and gazed toward the opening before them. "But I want you to do me one favor," said Jack.

Grohm looked at Jack questioningly. Jack turned to him and smiled.

"There's something I want to say to this jerk before you kick his butt. Can you give me that chance?"

Grohm's lips curled into a hint of a smile.

"Grohm can do that," he replied.

Scallywag paced back and forth nervously, his fingers brushing the handles of the pistols at his sides. He kept looking toward every possible door into the room, as if at any moment one could open to unleash a flood of Deathlord soldiers upon them.

Green stood at the nearby console, a cheery smile on his face as he happily typed away at it, doing whatever it was he was doing. Scallywag wasn't an expert at computers, but he wished that whatever it was the Professor was up to, he'd hurry up and get it done.

"Care to speed it up any?" the pirate muttered.

"I am going as fast as I can," replied Green.

"Figure out how to go faster," grumbled Scallywag. "More Deathlords could be here any moment."

"I know we're not that familiar with each other, dear fellow," said Green. "But I think I should point out I do not work better under pressure."

Scallywag rolled his eyes. It hadn't taken the two long to find what looked like a control room attached to the hangar bay they had entered. It had an overview of the entire hangar, but in addition to a doorway that led up to it from below, it also had a second entrance in the back of the room, and the hangar itself had three or four doorways that appeared to lead back into the ship. That was far too many entrance points for Scallywag's liking. He'd narrowly escaped the Deathlord mothership before, and being back on it didn't make him feel comfortable in the slightest. The sooner the Professor was able to do what he needed to get done, the sooner they could be on their way.

Unfortunately, it didn't seem like the Professor was making much progress.

"Listen, mate," said Scallywag. "I don't know how the Deathlords do things, but if they sent an escort ta this hangar, that means they're gonna start wondering what happened to 'em eventually, and we've already been here far too long. What is the hold up?"

Green let his smile turn upside down with frustration. "This task might be a bit more difficult than I'd anticipated."

Scallywag raised an eyebrow. "Ya saying ya can't do it?"

"No, no, I can do it," replied the Professor. "It's just..."

"Just what?"

Green sighed. "Anything I do here can be undone by the Deathlord's on the ship's bridge. As soon as I start fiddling with anything, they'll know where we are, shut us down, and come for us."

"Can't ya lock 'em out?"

"Not from here. The bridge controls can override any other system. I'm afraid we won't be able to activate the main weapon before they have the chance to stop anything we set in motion."

"There must be something ya can do," growled the pirate. "Yer supposed ta be smart! Ya said you knew the system. Can't ya hack in, or do something to freeze their controls, or anything computer-savvy like that?"

"I wish I could. I did not anticipate the Deathlord's central control of their systems," said Green. "My guess is they may have changed protocol after our escape."

"Ya telling me we're completely browned here? That we broke into a Deathlord mothership for no reason?"

Green shrugged his shoulders. "I don't know. I mean, I can think of a few possibilities that might work..."

"Such as?"

"I could probably try overriding the Deathlord's central control, but it would require a complex algorithm to attack and take over the system, and I'm afraid I don't have the time to build one from scratch."

Scallywag stopped. "Wait," he said. "What did ya say?"

"I'm afraid I don't have the time—"

"No, no, the other thing."

"Um... that it would require a complex algorithm to attack and take over the system—"

"A complex algorithm," mumbled Scallywag. As his mind raced to where he'd heard that before, his eyes rolled. "Crikey," he grumbled.

"What? What is it?" asked Green.

"I think I know how ta get us control of the ship," said Scallywag.

"Well then, make haste dear fellow!" replied Green. "Time is short!"

"I can't believe I'm about ta do this," muttered Scallywag, gritting his teeth and activating his comm unit.

Back inside the Earthship, Heckubus was busy at an open terminal panel in the wall of the bridge, systematically poking through the technology that was fascinating, even for him. Just as he began contemplating how to use the new application of trans-plasmatic genesis he'd garnered from the ship to take over the sub-species of Hablaxus IV and rule them as their lord and master, a voice piped up from the intercom.

"Robot," said Scallywag. "Do ya read me?"

"Since you are neither a data pad, nor a sequence of alpha-numeric symbols, I can only assume you're asking me if I can hear you. In which case, the answer should be obvious."

"That algorithm o' yours, the one you used on the Zeroastrian fleet," said Scallywag. "Assuming it actually works - could it be used to take over the Deathlord mothership's systems?"

"Pah! Of course it works!" snapped Heckubus as he took his attention away from the Earthship's systems for a moment to consider Scallywag's request. "With a few modifications, I don't see why it shouldn't be able to take complete and utter control of the mothership. The Deathlord programming language isn't that complicated once you break it down. Assuming one has a grasp of inter-species transcodes. Which I do."

"So can ya do it?" asked Scallywag.

"Well, modifying the algorithm is not a problem. However, we'd need a way to upload it to the mothership's central computer in order for it to work—"

Suddenly, the Earthship's systems beeped in reply. Heckubus quickly interfaced with them and began to chuckle. "Ah ha! It would seem the Earth vessel still has an active link with the mothership's central computer. That should do nicely."

"Good," said Scallywag. "Upload it, lock out every system but ours, and seal off all access around the ship. When the Deathlords find out what we're up to, they'll come at us hard. We don't want any Dark Soldiers breaking down our door before we get a chance to escape."

"I will do so immediately," replied the robot. "As soon as you admit I am the greatest evil genius in eight star systems."

Scallywag could feel an involuntary spasm in his brow. "What?" he grumbled.

"Admit that I, Heckubus Moriarty, am the greatest evil genius in eight star systems, and I will unleash my diabolical algorithm to help you accomplish your mission."

"Ya gotta be kidding."

"You scoffed at my algorithm before, yet you need it now," replied Heckubus. "This is what we advanced sentients like to call *irony*. Now, should you wish to use it, you must first admit that I am, indeed, everything I told you I was."

Scallywag gritted his teeth.

"I'm waiting..." sang Heckubus.

Scallywag tried to force the words out of his mouth, all the while wondering exactly how vital his mission actually was. Eventually, he was able to mumble...

"Yer an evil genius."

"I'm sorry? I didn't quite hear you…"

"Yer an evil genius," repeated Scallywag.

"The greatest in eight star systems?"

"Yes."

"Say iiiiiit…"

"Yer the greatest evil genius in eight star systems," sneered Scallywag.

"Mwuahaha!" laughed Heckubus. "Now admit you're a dimwitted primeval jackanape!"

"Robot," growled Scallywag into his comm. "Upload the bloody algorithm right now, or I swear to the Great White Umber, I will rip out yer gizzards and have ya converted into a toaster."

Heckubus immediately set one of his subprocessors on a master plan to unleash a dastardly plot for revenge, should Scallywag somehow manage to survive this mission and try to make good on his threat. After all, no one messes with Heckubus Moriarty, intergalactic evil genius. No doubt, should things work out in the pirate's favor, he'd probably try and take sole credit for the use of the algorithm. Heckubus would have to set one of his subprocessors to begin planning sweet, sweet revenge for that, as well. But for now, he'd give the Visini what he wanted.

"Very well," sighed the robot as he established the data link to the Deathlord mothership and began sending his reprogrammed computer virus. "Uploading now."

"Thank you," sneered Scallywag.

"You are a dimwitted primeval jackanape, though," replied the robot before signing off the comm. Scallywag clenched his fists as he felt another involuntary brow spasm come upon him.

After a long descent, the steps finally ended. By this point, they were enshrouded by darkness, and Anna could not see a thing. If it were not for the skin-crawling presence of the Deathlord beside her, she'd have felt like she were floating in an empty void. Then, she felt his cold, taloned hand wrap itself around her shoulder, and when he spoke, his voice echoed all around her as if there were a hundred of him.

"Bring in the light," he commanded.

Before she had a chance to react, she felt that part of her mind attuned to Ancient technology seek out a connection to her surroundings. She tried to will it to stop, but she felt like she had no control, as though a part of her body, such as an arm or a leg, suddenly had a mind of its own and was operating without her guidance.

She felt herself make connection to a strong presence somewhere in the darkness – a familiar presence that was common with all forms of Ancient technology. Once plugged in, she felt herself give the command for illumination.

Slowly, light began to break through the darkness far above them. It started as a single dot high above and grew, spreading out to reveal a majestic domed ceiling. As the light from the dome above spread, it grew stronger and brighter. The darkness around Anna and the Deathlord fled to reveal a huge room, the size of a stadium, in the shape of a perfect circle. In its center was a large empty area, surrounded by ascending amphitheater-style stone benches, which circled the room all the way up to the dome.

There were no fancy decorations or architectural indulgences. Everything was made from what looked like simple sandstone. Everything except what stood before them in the center of the arena.

Against the far wall, facing them, was a triangular outcropping that extended forward from the dome. The stone benches ended far enough away from the triangular wall so that it seemed no matter where a person sat, he would always have a view of it.

On the face of the triangle was a large circular stone emblem – one that must have been two stories high and two stories wide. It was one solid, smooth slab of rock, its brilliant white color a sharp contrast to the dull yellow of the structures surrounding it. At its center was an ornate carving of an eye.

Anna could feel her heart quicken as she looked at the symbol, as though the eye were alive, aware, and gazing right at her.

"You know what this is," said the Deathlord. It was not a question.

"A Great Seal of the Ancients," replied Anna.

Zarrod began to walk down the stairs toward the central area before the seal. Anna followed.

"A long time ago, your ancestors filled this room and channeled their collective heresies into one of their infernal creations, sealing it off with this abomination after constructing the prison we find ourselves on." Zarrod approached the seal and gazed up at it; then he turned away as if the carving on its face disturbed him. "Once the seal is broken, the quantum energy that powers this planet will escape, and the defenses that the Heretics created will wither and die."

Zarrod stood before Anna, looking down at her with his blazing red eyes. "Break the seal," he commanded.

No, thought Anna desperately. She struggled with all her might as her body responded immediately to the Deathlord's command. She walked to the middle of the open area before the seal and called forth a kiosk, which rose from the floor. A white orb of energy sprang to life above the small pillar, and Anna reached out and placed her hands upon it.

Immediately, she was tuned into the room around her, her consciousness whisked away into the Ancient construct within the orb. She found herself floating in a dark void before a circle of light, a single eye at its center. She looked into it, and it met her gaze, unmoving. In the eye, she caught a glimpse of something — something fantastic, and wonderful, and peaceful. Her heart thumped the way it did when she witnessed a thing of such amazing beauty that it affirmed everything it meant to be alive.

She reached out to it, wanting to grab it — to possess it. The eye came closer, as though responding to her desire. Anna could feel the eagerness growing inside her as the eye approached. *Yes,* she thought. *Yes, I must have it... I must!*

The eye stopped before her, big, and bright, and beautiful. She reached out and touched it, the thing she wanted danced in its iris, far behind it.

"Give it to me," she heard herself say.

She laid her hands on it, and veins of gold began to ripple from the spot she touched, spider webbing throughout the eye.

"GIVE IT TO ME!" she screamed, her heart pounding. She'd never felt emotions like those she was experiencing that very moment. Pure and utter desire coursed through her, along with a burning jealousy, and the need to completely possess the thing that lay behind that eye.

No, called out a tiny voice in the back of her mind.

Anna's breath caught in her throat. What was that? Who had spoken? She turned her attention back to the glimpse of beauty within the eye. She pushed on it harder, the veins growing brighter, slowly turning into cracks in its visage, spreading and growing as she pushed harder and harder.

No, came the voice again. This time, it was clearer, and she could not ignore it.

It was her own voice.

"But I want it," she said. "I must have it!"

You can't.

She pushed harder. The golden cracks in the eye began to splinter deeper around her hands.

"It's so beautiful…"

You must not release it.

"Why? Why shouldn't I?"

Because of him.

Anna turned away from the eye and looked behind her, and for the first time noticed the grotesque visage of a Deathlord there. His skin was black and wrinkled, his muscles tightly wound and sinewy. His face was that of a twisted skull, no nose, no lips, just red eyes gazing at the eye before her greedily. Its hands were dug deep into her back, and she could feel them trying to control her, to move her body and her thoughts to suit its own purpose.

Anna felt a shiver of revulsion run up her spine. Was this what was controlling her? What was it? How did it get there?

It wants you to destroy the seal, her voice said. *If you do, all will be lost.*

Anna looked up at the eye as it splintered and cracked, ready to shatter into pieces any moment. Deep inside her, she knew she was right. Unleashing what was behind that seal, no matter how amazing, would give the Deathlords what they needed to destroy everything she held dear.

Suddenly, images flashed into her mind. Images of her father, and how he held court upon his throne, making decisions that affected an entire galaxy. Images of the digital paintings of the great Emperors of old that lined the palace hallways where she had played when she was young – these men, who reigned with strength and wisdom, who fought to protect those who had placed trust in their leadership.

Anna gazed into the eye before her, looking beyond that thing of beauty - into a deeper universe, one filled with things she could not understand or comprehend. But there, within the chaos of the visions present within the eye, she saw her family...

Not just her parents and her brothers, but the very line of men and women who had forged her birthright: rulers of strength and wisdom, warriors of ruthlessness and cunning, devotees of purity and moral fortitude. Tens of thousands of generations – they all stood before her, arrayed in a bloodline filled with a pulsing power - a power that belonged to her, a power that had eluded her for so long, and one of which she was not sure she was worthy. A power that burned so brightly and brilliantly, the thought of possessing it sent shivers of fear coursing through her body.

You are the Blood of the Ancients, she could hear herself whisper in her mind. *You are the light that shines in the darkness. You are the beacon within the storm. You are the protector of all life. This is your duty. This is your destiny. It is time for you to claim it!*

She felt the Deathlord's claws moving inside her. They tried to make her press harder, to break the seal, to ignore the last remnants of her own consciousness.

Anna gritted her teeth. With all her might, she pressed back against the Deathlord. She pulled her hands back, away from the eye, straining with every fiber of her being. She felt like she were fighting against a massive weight, something attempting to crush her as she tried to hold it back. She could feel the tightness in her chest and the blood pumping behind her ears as she fought to control her movements.

She heard the Deathlord behind her cry out, a dry rasp of agony, as though her struggle against it brought it pain. *Yes,* she thought. *Fight it. Hurt it!*

Anna reached back behind her, her hands groping around, settling on either side of the Deathlord's head. She could feel it struggle, its claws buried deep inside her trying desperately to control her. She fought against it harder, her hands gripping its head as strongly as she could.

"I am Glorianna of Legacy Prime, heir to the bloodline of the Ancients. I will no longer be your slave! By my command, you WILL let me go!" she screamed, and with every last bit of strength left in her, she pulled on the Deathlord's head. She heard the gasp of a mouth with no tongue, as the Deathlord tried to cry out. She pulled more forcefully, and could feel the creature's neck giving way as she tugged, harder and harder...

"I said... LET... *GO!*"

With a final burst of energy, she yanked the Deathlord's head forward, ripping it off. She felt a shiver run through her as the void around her disappeared.

Suddenly, she was back in the arena. Her body completely numb, she fell to the floor. The orb she had been interfacing with disappeared and the kiosk sank back into the ground.

Her head buzzed and her vision circled around in a dizzy stupor. She focused on the great seal before her. It stood, its smooth white stone now marred and spiderwebbed with large, gaping cracks, each one pulsing with a brilliant white light as though whatever was behind it was fighting to break through.

She pushed herself up to a sitting position as the Deathlord Supreme looked down at her. She met his gaze defiantly.

"The seal stands," she said. "Kill me now. I will not do your bidding."

Zarrod chuckled. "Impressive," he said. "But futile. Look before you, Princess…" the Deathlord swept his hand toward the seal. "The seal is all but broken. Whatever protection your ancestors had fortified it with is now gone, thanks to your efforts. I can merely flick my wrist and destroy what is left. You have served your purpose well."

Anna's shoulders slumped. She felt so tired, so very tired. All the fight had gone out of her. She'd failed. She'd failed her family, her bloodline, and all who had placed their faith in her - now the entire universe would suffer because of it. Tears welled in her eyes. She hadn't been worthy after all.

"And now, I'm going to do what I've wanted since the moment I laid eyes on you," said Zarrod. "I'm going to kill you, Princess. I'm going to rip the life out of you and swallow it whole. But before I do, I'm going to teach you a lesson in agony…"

Zarrod reached out his clawed hand. Anna jerked as she felt thousands of razor sharp invisible hooks dig into her. She gasped as she was lifted into the air before the Deathlord Supreme, his horrible eyes burning into her as she stared back at him helplessly.

"No one defies me," sneered Zarrod. "Especially not a weak, heretical abomination such as *you!*"

Anna screamed. Excruciating pain coursed through her body as the Deathlord used his evil magic to tear at the inner core of her being.

"I'm going to make this slow, and I'm going to make this last," said Zarrod over her screams. "I'm going to open your eyes to a new meaning of pain and anguish never before witnessed by any living thing. And by the time I'm through, you will be begging me to snuff out your pitiful existence, and to give you the sweet release only death can provide."

Anna stopped screaming as Zarrod briefly stopped his torture. Anna looked at him, her eyes wide with terror, darkness beginning to creep into the edges of her vision.

"Any last words, while you're still able to speak?" asked the Deathlord.

Anna's mind was clouded with pain. Images flashed before her: hazy ones of her family – her brothers, her mother, her father. And finally, the image of Shepherd, the man who'd been her protector. The man she had loved above all others. If she had to die, she wanted to do so with his image in her head and his name on her lips.

She opened her mouth, but before she could speak, another voice rang out.

"Hey, jerk-face."

Zarrod turned away from Anna and looked down to his side where Jack stood, hands on his hips, glaring at the Deathlord with the same intensity he'd direct at something foul caked on the bottom of his shoe. Zarrod tilted his head, momentarily surprised at the sudden reappearance of the little alien boy.

"Pick on someone your own size," said Jack.

Zarrod heard the sound of an electric ping humming to life behind him. He turned to see Grohm there, a massive club in his hand, ringed with conduits crackling with blue electricity.

Before the Deathlord could react, Grohm swung the club, slamming into Zarrod's chest.

WHAM!

With an explosion of electric current, Zarrod went flying into the air, twisting and turning as the force of the impact sent him plummeting far back into the benches surrounding the arena, crashing to the ground in a most undignified manner.

"So glad I got to say that," smiled Jack to himself.

Anna fell to the ground, now fully released from Zarrod's grasp, and Jack moved to her side. He looked up at Grohm who gazed down at him.

"He destroyed our planets," said Jack, jerking his head toward Zarrod. "Go destroy him."

Grohm smiled. "Good luck, Earthman."

"Same to you, big guy."

CHAPTER  42

With precision movement, Grohm began to run toward Zarrod. With a powerful leap he hurled himself into the air, his electrified club raised high over his head, humming with fury waiting to be unleashed.

Zarrod glanced up just in time to see the massive Rognok heading straight for him. Quickly collecting himself, he sprung up off one hand, twisting away just as Grohm landed, his club smashing into the stone where the Deathlord had been not a moment before, sending rubble and debris flying in all directions.

Grohm turned, swinging his club in a backhanded arc aimed right for Zarrod's head. Zarrod ducked, only to find himself looking down the barrel of the plasma shotgun which Grohm had unslung from his back in a swift movement during his swing. Zarrod pulled back instinctively just as Grohm pulled the trigger.

WHOOM!

The blast from the shotgun hit Zarrod squarely in the chest, sending him flying back with violent speed, the breastplate of his dark armor smoldering and smoking from the force of the plasma projectile. He hit the ground hard, tumbling head over heels, crashing through the stone seating in the theater.

No sooner had the Deathlord come to a stop than he pushed himself to his feet, standing straight and taut with anger, as though the point-blank blast hadn't fazed him at all.

"Enough of this," he grumbled as he saw the Rognok begin to run at him, the plasma shotgun in his hands, firing as quickly as he could recharge the weapon.

Zarrod hurriedly manifested death energy around his hands, using it to swat at the plasma blasts, ricocheting them away.

In between the blasts, Zarrod hurled a ball of ghostly death energy toward Grohm, who spun just as it flew by him. Grohm flung his weapon at the Deathlord, who knocked it away, but not before Grohm had the chance to leap toward him.

Zarrod narrowly dodged Grohm's fist as it landed on the ground, the impact cracking the stone. Grohm pressed the attack, swinging his massive fists, trying to land a blow on the Deathlord who danced between his punches before finally catching Grohm's fist — aimed directly at Zarrod's head — in one of his clawed hands.

"Blasted Rognoks," sneered Zarrod as he let loose a blast of death energy with his free hand. It hit Grohm squarely in the chest and sent him flying into the air, landing hard a good ten feet away.

Meanwhile, Jack was at Anna's side, desperately trying to get her to wake up. She had passed out after Grohm had freed her from Zarrod's hold, and Jack was doing his best to rouse her by shaking her shoulders and patting her on the cheek.

"C'mon, c'mon, c'mon," Jack muttered. "You gotta wake up!"

Anna's eyes fluttered open briefly. "Jack…" she said.

"Anna!" said Jack urgently. "Please, you need to finish breaking the seal!"

"No… no…" she said weakly.

"It's okay, we have a plan!" replied Jack. "It might not be the best plan, but it kinda requires the seal to be broken. We were going to rescue you after you finished doing it, but for some reason, you stopped… which was totally cool, by the way! Just, a little inconvenient. Now, I don't know how long Grohm can keep Zarrod busy, so I really need you to—"

Anna's eyes fluttered again as Jack was talking, and she passed out.

"Oh, crap," muttered Jack.

Up in the stands, Zarrod stalked toward Grohm as the massive alien got back to his feet. He held a hand to his chest where the Deathlord's blast had impacted him and glared at Zarrod as he approached.

"That blast would have killed any other being," growled Zarrod. "But you Rognoks have some strange immunity to our powers. That was why we eliminated your planet so early on."

Zarrod hurled another death blast at Grohm. Grohm moved to dodge, but Zarrod's initial blast had weakened him and he was sluggish. The blast caught Grohm in the shoulder, sending him stumbling back.

"I can only assume you're here for some type of revenge," said Zarrod, "which I respect, but it isn't me you should be angry with."

He sent another blast toward Grohm who raised his hands in defense, but the blast hit him straight on, knocking him to the ground. Zarrod stood over him, his hands alive with raging death energy.

"You should be angry with your creators, The Ancients. They made your kind, you see, in answer to us. You were made big, strong, durable, and dumb. But most of all, you were made without souls. The perfect soldiers to fight against the army of their enemy."

Grohm tried to rise, but Zarrod delivered a powerful punch to his face, knocking him back down.

"They gave you life, but they denied you so much more. Without the souls all other beings in this universe possess, your kind could never be more than what you are. You could never be culled by us, true. But you could also never evolve. You could never understand things like love, or beauty, or anything else the pathetic life-forms you were created to protect seem to hold in such high regard. You would forever be slaves, doomed to this life and this life alone, never able to experience anything more."

Again, Grohm tried to rise, and again, Zarrod knocked him down with a fist clad with deadly death energy.

"So I ask you, Rognok," said Zarrod as he put a foot on Grohm's chest. "Who has done you more harm? Me? The one who finally freed your people from their bondage? Or your creators? The ones who denied you any shred of happiness?"

Grohm met the Deathlord's stare with his red and black eyes. "You," Grohm replied.

Zarrod couldn't help but laugh. "Is that so?"

"Yes," sneered Grohm. "Happiness is for the *weak*."

With surprising quickness, Grohm grabbed Zarrod's leg and twisted it. Zarrod cried out and fell to his knees in the direction of the twisting, bringing him within striking distance of Grohm's free hand, which shot out like a piston directly at Zarrod's face, knocking him back.

Grohm sat up and quickly made his way on top of the Deathlord, straddling him under his massive weight and pounding on him with one punch after another, wordlessly trying to pummel him into the ground.

Down below the seating where the Rognok and the Deathlord were fighting, Jack had Anna slung over his shoulder and was trying to make his way to the stairs.

She's heavier than she looks, thought Jack, whose shoulder was already starting to ache after just a few feet. He looked up the long stair climb to the exit in dismay. *They invent a planet with a shield and a spaceship that can travel anywhere in an instant, but they refuse to install escalators anywhere. I am never going to understand these guys...*

Jack began making his way up toward the exit when a voice rang out over the comm unit in his ear.

"Jack? Jack, my boy, do you read?"

"Professor?" responded Jack as he shifted Anna's weight on his shoulder.

"We are almost ready to fire the weapon on our end," said Green. "Has the Princess destroyed the seal yet?"

"Yeah, about that..." said Jack as he took a few more steps. "Anna's been knocked out. She cracked the seal pretty good, but it's still up, and I don't think we're gonna have time to get her to finish it."

"Oh, dear... but, we can't destroy the planet without first breaking the seal!"

"You're gonna have to."

"But all that knowledge will be lost! It won't survive the quantum explosion!"

"I'm sorry, Professor. Better it than us."

"You said she cracked the seal?" asked Green. "If she did enough to break the Ancient protection, you might be able to destroy what is left yourself."

"With what?"

"Do you still have any explosive devices on you?"

Jack looked down at his grenade belt.

"Kinda," said Jack, not really liking where this was going.

"If you can plant the explosives before you leave, you can trigger them remotely from a safe distance as you make your way to the rendezvous point."

Jack glanced over to where Grohm was fighting with Zarrod. "I don't know, Professor..."

"Please, Jack! The knowledge contained behind that seal could be vital to the survival of the universe! It could save countless lives! You cannot simply abandon it!"

Jack turned back to glance at the Great Seal, its massive eye gazing at him amid the luminous cracks all throughout it. Something about it called to him. The eye, as fractured as it was, felt like it had made contact with his stare. Jack remembered that moment in the temple at the center of Earth when an eye had appeared in his mind, and had spoken to him, the words ringing through his head at that very moment:

Eldil Meldilorn.

And then for some reason Jack couldn't explain or comprehend, despite all his instincts telling him otherwise, Jack knew the Professor was right.

That seal had to be broken.

Jack sighed. He set Anna down gently behind one of the stone benches by the stairway and started to run back toward the seal.

"Okay, Professor, you win," said Jack. "But if you don't hear from me in ten minutes, fire that weapon anyway and get the heck out of here!"

"May the Great Observer watch over you, my boy," said Green.

"Uh, you, too," said Jack, not really knowing how to respond.

As he ran toward the seal, Jack glanced over and saw Grohm and Zarrod engaged in some kind of hand-to-hand wrestling. It was hard to make out what was happening; he just hoped that whatever was going down, Grohm was winning (or at least was buying him some time).

Once Jack reached the seal, he found the largest crack he could and unbuckled his grenade belt. He looked at the grenades, remembering what Major Ganix had shown him when they were in the Pit.

Jack popped the cap off one of the grenades and twisted the button until it clicked. He slid out the narrow remote cylinder from the center, its detonator on the top, and hooked it to his gun belt. All he'd need to do is press the button and the grenade would go off instantly, its explosion causing the others on the belt to blow in a chain reaction. Hopefully, the range on it would be far enough that Jack would have Anna well on the way to the hoverbikes by the time he was ready to detonate it.

Suddenly, a deafening *BOOM* echoed throughout the dome as a flash of light momentarily blinded Jack. When he looked back up, he saw Grohm high in the air, falling back down with a thunderous *THUD*.

Zarrod stood fifteen feet before Grohm, ghostly energy seeping from every nook and cranny of his dinted and beaten armor, giving him a horrific aura Jack could feel even from where he was standing.

"Enough of this!" raged the Deathlord.

Grohm unsteadily got to his feet. No sooner had he regained his footing than Zarrod unleashed another powerful death energy attack. It plowed into the Rognok, blasting him backwards through the stone seating, all the way back to the dome itself where Grohm impacted the wall with such force that he formed a small crater.

Then, a shrill screeching sound filled the air as Zarrod harnessed a ball of chaotic, swirling energy in his hands. It quickly grew to the size of a basketball. Jack watched in horror as Grohm got to his feet, stumbling slightly, unaware of what awaited him.

"GROHM!" yelled Jack. "LOOK OUT!"

But the warning came too late. Zarrod unleashed the ball of death energy that shot forth, screaming right at the Rognok. It hit Grohm dead-on, hurling him back into the crater he'd just made. The energy swirled around him, and when it disappeared, the Rognok slumped to the ground and lay still.

Jack felt frozen for a moment, his eyes fixed on his friend. His heart felt like it had stopped and his breath was stuck in his throat. Then, something within him made him look away, and his gaze landed on the Deathlord Supreme.

And the Deathlord Supreme was looking right back at him.

He pointed a crooked claw directly at Jack, his voice booming with anger.

"You," he said, simply.

"Ohhhhhhh, crap," muttered Jack, panic starting to grip his belly. In this situation, there was little Jack could think of to do other than to fall back to his patented strategy number one for avoiding a beat down - which was to run away. Fast.

Without another moment's hesitation, Jack took off running as quickly as he could for the stairs. He heard something whizzing in the air, and turned in time to see a ghostly ball of white barreling toward him. He turned just as the death energy impacted the ground where he was going to be. The blast exploded on impact, its force sending Jack flying into the air.

The room turned topsy-turvy as Jack spun head-over-heels. He landed on his back hard, his head ringing from the impact. Spots of color assaulted his vision as he opened his eyes. His hearing was dulled, and he felt fingers of pain running up and down his spine.

He tried to sit up, but his back wasn't having it. Slowly, Jack rolled over onto his belly. The ringing in his ears subsided, and he blinked his eyes to clear his head. When he did, he saw Zarrod.

The Deathlord stood before him, the massive Great Seal behind the alien, its cracked visage dancing with brilliant light. Zarrod looked down at Jack, his terrible red eyes practically burning with hate and malice. Ghostly white energy seemed to fall off him like smoke, and the Deathlord's hands shimmered with furious power.

Jack gritted his teeth, the image of what the Deathlord had done to Grohm fresh in his mind. His memory jumped to Shepherd's last pained breath and to Anna hanging helplessly at the Deathlord's side – both in the hangar of the mothership and in this very room.

Then, the words of the Regal Soldiers rang in his mind. *If you're going to die, die advancing.*

Jack pushed himself up.

Jack got to his feet.

And Jack gazed at what was to be certain death with a courage he had never known he had until that very moment.

"I destroyed your planet, I've killed everything you've ever cared about, and now, I'm going to kill you," rumbled Zarrod.

Jack looked at Zarrod, and for some strange reason, his mind flashed back to his first fight ever... the one in the school cafeteria with J.C. Rowdey, the bully he had suddenly punched to the surprise of everyone, including himself.

And Jack just couldn't help it. He had to laugh.

Zarrod hesitated a moment, taken aback by Jack's reaction. The Deathlord's eyes grew wide with indignation, anger and fury building inside him.

"You... dare... laugh at me?" the Deathlord growled.

"Sorry, dude," said Jack as a strange feeling of peace came upon him. "I just realized that there's a point where bullies stop being scary."

"You say you're no longer afraid?"

"Oh, no, I'm afraid," said Jack. "Just not of you."

"Is that so?" the Deathlord growled.

Zarrod reached out his hand, and Jack felt the sharp pain of razor-like hooks digging into him all over his skin. Jack writhed and gritted his teeth as he felt himself lifted into the air, trying desperately not to scream.

Zarrod brought Jack, hovering helplessly in the air, to him The two of them stood in the middle of the open arena, face to face, eye to eye.

Jack felt Zarrod pull at his soul, pain shooting through every fiber of his being, but he kept his gaze on Zarrod, and bit down so hard to keep from screaming it felt like he might break his teeth.

Zarrod looked at Jack with a hint of amusement in his horrible red eyes. "I am Zarrod, the Deathlord Supreme - culler of worlds, master of darkness, and bane to all that is living. No force can harm me, no weapon can strike me, no army can defeat me. I am the Omega, and the universe trembles at my fury. Who are you not to fear me?"

Jack's body trembled as pain shot through every nerve like a fire ravaging unchecked through a defenseless forest. He could feel the cold hand of despair tighten around his gut and gnaw like a rabid animal. Flashes of light shot off in sparks in the periphery of his vision, and it was almost as if he could feel the frigid embrace of darkness begin to wrap itself around his very soul.

Then, in the far reaches of his mind, for some reason, he remembered an afternoon sitting in a classroom with a man he thought he hated. He remembered the talk they'd had, and the strange sense of pride he had felt when he had suddenly earned that man's respect.

He remembered the courage that man had shown, fighting a foe he knew he could not defeat.

He remembered the trust that man had placed in him, even though he wasn't sure he deserved it.

But most of all, he remembered how much he *hated* to lose.

With every ounce of strength he could muster, he clenched his teeth, grabbed the detonator on his belt, raised it right in front of the Deathlord's face, and said...

"I'm... *Jack!*"

And with that, he pushed the trigger.

The explosion erupted, smoke and fire racing up the face of Great Seal. Shrapnel and debris shot forth, and Jack could feel them whizzing by, though if they had any impact on Zarrod, he did not show it.

There was the sound of a massive CRACK and the Great Seal broke in half, giving into its wounds and crumbling to the ground in a cloud of dust and smoke. Behind it was nothing but a brilliant white light.

Jack gazed at the light as the Deathlord stood before him, not moving, not taking his venomous gaze off Jack for one instant. Jack heard Zarrod laughing.

"Foolish boy," the Deathlord growled. "You did exactly what I had wanted."

Deep in the light, Jack could see blue sparks start to dance around, and lightning start to cascade, swirling into a maelstrom in the shape of one great, all-seeing eye.

"Trust me," said Jack. "I don't think you wanted this..."

Zarrod turned, shifting his attention from Jack to the opening behind him. Whether the Deathlord was frightened, confused, angry, or just plain indifferent, he couldn't tell. All Jack did know was that in his final moments, he had succeeded.

Just as Jack was about to succumb to the darkness of the Deathlord's culling, an ear-shattering *BOOM* exploded from the opening.

For an instant, time seemed to stand still, activity from the opening ceased, and all was quiet.

Then, with the might of a star going supernova, the energy the Great Seal had been protecting mere moments before shot forth with the strength of a thousand furies, crashing through Zarrod, and funneling directly into Jack.

Both Jack and Zarrod screamed as the energy from the opening coursed through both of their bodies. It was almost as if Jack could feel the very atoms that made up his being dance, as they threatened to rip apart and never come back together.

As more and more of the energy channeled into him, he was bombarded with flashes of images - people, places, things — an avalanche of information, as though they were being etched onto the very fiber of his being.

It was just like the feeling he had experienced in the temple leading to the Earthship, only a billion times stronger. More images danced before his eyes, all of them strange, familiar, and fantastic. It was as though the entire universe was laid out before him, and he was only able to perceive a tiny glimmer of its majesty and wonder.

But there was a darkness there, too. It was small but noticeable. It writhed, drenched in fear, and pain, and sorrow - scared of what was happening to it. It was seeing what Jack was seeing, but unable to understand the overwhelming light that was at the center of the message that was being shared.

It was a message of hope, of peace, of wonder... of life itself.

It was a message looking for a home, a place to take root and grow and flourish. Instantly, Jack knew he could be that home. But the darkness wrapped itself around the message, like a scared snake coiling around its enemy, and Jack realized that if he were to let in the light, he'd be forced to let in the darkness, as well.

Jack considered himself to be many things, but he never considered himself to be a very good student. However, this was one lesson he was willing to learn - no matter what the cost.

He opened his mind and invited the message in.

Jack awoke, floating. Light was all around him. It was bright, but it did not hurt his eyes. It was warm but comfortable. It was as though he were lying on a cloud, drifting in a still, clear lake on the most beautiful day he could ever have possibly imagined.

Then came the voice.

"Hello, Jack."

Jack turned. Before him stood a man. He was tall and slender, with wavy light-brown hair that was just starting to grey at the temples. He had kind hazel eyes, a warm smile, and a glimmer of familiarity that Jack couldn't quite place.

"Am I dead?" Jack asked.

"No," replied the man.

"Then where am I?"

"Same place you were before."

"This doesn't look like the same place."

"Well, I guess it depends on how you're looking at it."

"Are you sure I'm not dead?"

The man laughed. "Quite. Don't you trust me?"

"I guess. Who are you?"

The man's smile turned slightly sad.

"Someone who wants to help," he answered.

"Well, you could start by being a bit more clear with your answers," said Jack. "I'm not big on reading between the lines."

The man chuckled. "Fair enough. But I'm afraid there's only so much I'm allowed to tell you."

"Okay," said Jack, more than a little bit confused. "Are you allowed to tell me what the heck just happened?"

"You freed the quantum energy that was behind the Great Seal, and you opened your mind to it."

"All that stuff I saw," said Jack, "that was the knowledge the seal was protecting?"

"Yes. And now you're its vessel."

"Wicked," said Jack. "Does that make me the smartest guy in the universe or something?"

"Not exactly," the man chuckled. "With your current level of development, if you had access to all that information at once, it's very likely you'd go insane."

"That's... not cool," said Jack.

"Try to understand something, Jack... all knowledge exists in the universe. Everything anyone could ever think or discover is already out there. It just has to be found by a mind that's open to it. The Great Seals were designed to harness some of that knowledge, which in effect hides it even from minds open to discovering it. You were at ground zero when this knowledge was unleashed from its prison. And somehow, without any training whatsoever, you opened your mind to its entirety. Where it might take some a lifetime to discover even a fraction of what was contained in there, some part of you will know where to look for all of it. So its not that you can't access the knowledge, it's just that you'll have to figure out what you want to access, and do so when the time is right."

"Is that why you're here?" asked Jack. "To teach me how to access it?"

"No. I'm here to deliver a message."

"What kind of message?"

"A message of hope."

"There you go," said Jack, "being all cryptic again."

"Well, get used to it kiddo, because before all this is over, you're going to run into a lot of stuff that won't make any sense."

"How do you know?"

"I'd tell you, but then I'd just have to be all cryptic again."

Jack nodded. "Okay, fine. Can you at least tell me what your message is, straight up?"

"Okay," said the man. "The message is: You can save Earth. Is that straight up enough?"

Jack's heart skipped a beat.

"What?" he asked.

"You can save Earth, and every other planet the Deathlords have destroyed."

"But... how is that possible?" Jack asked. "They blew up Earth!"

"Anything is possible," said the man. "If you find the final creation of the Ancients."

"The final creation? You mean that thing Anna's looking for!" exclaimed Jack. "The Ancient weapon? It really exists?"

"It does," said the man. "And now, you know how to find it."

"I do?" asked Jack. "Was it one of the things that just got downloaded to my brain? How do I access it? What is the weapon? How does it save Earth?"

Jack stopped talking when he realized the man was grinning at him strangely.

"Let me guess," said Jack. "You're not allowed to tell me."

"No, no..." said the man. "It's just... well, it's just that I see a lot of potential in you."

For the first time, Jack tried to clear his mind of confusion and really look at the man standing before him. Deep in his gut, Jack felt like he somehow knew this man, like in the back of his mind, he could remember someone saying the exact same thing to him, long ago.

"Who are you?" asked Jack again. "Are you an Ancient?"

The man shook his head. "No, unfortunately, I'm not."

"Then who? Please, tell me."

For a moment, it looked like the man was going to answer, then suddenly, a piercing *SHRIEK* cut through the air. The light around them began to dull, as streaks of darkness soaked its way in and swirled around with the light.

The man looked around, startled.

"No," he said. "We're supposed to have more time!"

"What is it?" asked Jack, as he began to feel a cold wind swirl around him. "What's happening?"

The man turned to him, looking at Jack intently, a sudden urgency in his voice. "Jack, you need to listen to me very carefully..."

Jack could feel himself slowly start to be pulled away from the man. He struggled, trying to stay with him, but the more he tried, the more he seemed to slip backwards.

"What's going on?" yelled Jack over the increasing wind that was swirling around him. "Help me!" he screamed.

"Jack - your ship—" yelled the man. Jack tried to focus on what he was saying, but the wind was screeching in his ears so loudly he could barely make out the words. "...the key to <*whoosh*> final creation... You must <*whooooooooosh*> Shadow Zone... There, you'll <*whoosh whooooosh*> but be careful! <*Whoosh*> not what it seems! You must first <*whoosh*> travel back in <*whoosh whooooooooosh*> the Void Lords..."

"I can't hear you!" cried Jack. He could feel himself slipping away faster and faster.

"Only way <*whoosh*> to save Earth and <*whoooooosh*>..." screamed the man.

"But how!" yelled Jack. "Where do I start!?!?"

"Go to <*whoosh*> Khoruhar..."

Jack was barely able to make out the last word. As the darkness and the light around him mixed together and the wind engulfed him, he took one last look at the man as he began to fade away in the distance.

"I love you... son..." the man cried.

Jack's eyes grew wide. What was nagging him in the back of his memory quickly flooded to the forefront. He had indeed met that man before, when he was very young. How could he have not seen it?

Dad!

"NO!" Jack cried. "Come back! Come BACK!"

He reached out toward the fading image of his father just as a brilliant blue lightning bolt shot out from where he had been, streaking through Jack's body. Suddenly, Jack was in pain and his muscles twisted and writhed from the fury of the electricity that was shooting through him.

The lightning stopped, and Jack fell to the floor. His chest burned, and his eyes were blinded by tears. *Had it been a dream?* he wondered. *Was any of it real?*

He looked up to see a black figure crumpled on the floor before him. It was Zarrod, his armor charred and smoldering from the blast unleashed by the breaking of the seal. The Deathlord stirred and started struggling to get back to his feet.

Jack tried to get up, but his legs didn't seem to want to work. Every muscle in his body ached, and his head felt like it was about to be split open from the inside. He couldn't think, he could barely see, and he was in no condition to face the Deathlord again. So he did the only thing he could, which was to try to put as much distance as possible between himself and his foe by crawling away.

Zarrod had made it to his feet, only to fall down again weakly. Jack could hear his guttural growl of frustration, which only made Jack try harder to escape, working his elbows back and forth as he crawled along the floor, his legs dragging behind him.

Finally, Jack was able to get a knee under him and pushed himself up to his feet. The room seemed to sway as he stumbled to and fro, but he was off the ground at last.

Each step was a battle. Jack felt sensation creeping back into his limbs, but he still was not able to walk straight. He shook his head, trying to clear his vision and to make his way to the stairs. In the periphery of his eyesight, he knew Zarrod was still there, and each moment he stayed within reach of the Deathlord, he was in danger.

Then, Jack felt a tingle in the back of his head - a slight buzzing sensation, as though an alarm was going off. Suddenly, he knew he was in deep trouble.

With every ounce of strength he could muster, he dove aside, just as a ball of death energy whizzed by, impacting the stairs before him and blowing a crater into the stone.

Jack rolled to his side. The tingling in his head returned and he looked over to see Zarrod limping toward him, his soulless red eyes blazing with fury.

"What did you do?" cried Zarrod. "What did you do... to me!!!"

Zarrod stumbled and fell to one knee. As he struggled to get up, Jack realized, with a glimmer of hope - the Deathlord was actually hurt.

Jack mustered what strength he could and climbed to his feet. The Deathlord followed suit, and within moments, the two were staring each other down.

"It's called pain, Zarrod," said Jack. "Not so fun when you're on the receiving end, is it?"

"I underestimated you, Earthman," growled Zarrod. "But I learn from my mistakes..."

Zarrod straightened and reached his clawed hand out toward Jack.

Suddenly, time seemed to slow...

Jack's mind instantly became clear. It was an odd sensation, as though he were acutely aware of everything around him. All his senses were heightened, and as his eyes focused on the Deathlord before him, it was as if he could see everything there was to observe – his skin, his muscles, his armor, the molecules that made them, the electrical impulses that sparked within him – everything.

Jack was able to see inside the Deathlord, and saw a spark of energy emanate from the center of Zarrod's chest. It wound its way through his body, snaking around his outstretched arm, sprouting from his clawed fingers, and writhing toward Jack as tiny blades of energy formed like barbs around it.

Jack's mind flashed to a mental image of Zarrod's body, looking past his armor and into his very being. He saw the flow of the Deathlord's energy and how he was able to channel it. Suddenly, it all made sense. Energy is what animated the Deathlord's body, and energy could not be destroyed. That is why the Deathlords could not be killed, because despite their outer shell, inside, they were just energy that could be manipulated, controlled, and rechanneled as they saw fit.

In his mind's cye, Jack saw an image of the human body, in much the same way he saw Zarrod's. Though humans were made up of flesh and blood, they too had an energy flow. It was this energy the Deathlords fed on and ripped from their victims.

And that's when Jack realized... there was no difference between the two types of energies.

Instinctually, Jack raised his hand as the Deathlord's soul culling shot toward him, and rather than allow it to burrow into him and withdraw back to Zarrod, Jack allowed it to flow into his body, and grabbed onto it with his own, not letting it leave.

Jack could feel the Deathlord try and tug his energy tendril back, but Jack wasn't about to let go. Instead, he pulled, taking in more of Zarrod's energy.

Zarrod cried out in surprise, and tried to pull back again, but Jack refused to release his hold.

"What – what's happening?" cried Zarrod. For the first time, Jack heard fear in the Deathlord's voice. "What are you doing?!?!"

Jack grinned.

"Where I'm from," said Jack, "it's called *kicking your ass!*"

With that, Jack let go of his hold on Zarrod's energy. The sudden release caused the Deathlord's energy tendril to sling shot back toward Zarrod violently, crashing into him.

Zarrod screamed as his body disintegrated in a puff of black dust and smoke, lingering sparks of his ghost energy wriggled in the air like a fish out of water and slowly vanished.

Jack lowered his hand, absolutely amazed. He had done it! He'd actually defeated a Deathlord! Not just a Deathlord, but a Supreme one at that! Then, he realized that he wasn't hurting any more. In fact, he felt incredibly energized. It was as though he had somehow absorbed some of what Zarrod had thrown at him, and it had invigorated him.

Jack looked around. The massive room seemed quiet and peaceful, and for the first time since setting foot on the planet, Jack felt safe. He smiled, allowing himself a moment to feel victorious.

Then he remembered Grohm.

Jack looked up where Zarrod had thrown Grohm and saw the giant Rognok lying hunched against the crater he'd made in the dome.

"Grohm!" yelled Jack as he ran up to him, leaping from bench to bench, making his way to his friend.

Jack approached. The gargantuan alien lay still, and for a moment, Jack was afraid he was dead. He had seen Grohm take some punishment before, but what the Deathlord had dished out might have been too much, even for him.

Grohm wasn't moving. Jack tried shaking him, to no avail. He put his ear to Grohm's chest, but heard nothing – he wasn't even sure if Rognok's had hearts, let alone where they'd be.

"Please, don't be dead…" he muttered aloud.

Jack tried to access whatever it was that had shown him how to take on Zarrod, but whatever switch was flipped mere moments ago didn't seem to want to work again. When it came to Rognok anatomy, Jack was drawing a blank.

Jack then remembered how Zarrod's energy flowed through his hand, and how Jack's was able to do the same. Grohm had two arms, sure enough, so maybe they could act like conduits, too?

Jack grabbed one of Grohm's massive mitts and tried to remember what he did that shot his energy back into Zarrod. If he were able to transfer some of what he'd stolen from the Deathlord, maybe he could save Grohm?

It's worth a try, he thought.

Jack held tight to Grohm's hand and concentrated.

And concentrated…

And concentrated.

But nothing seemed to be happening. Jack couldn't feel the flow like he had with Zarrod. He didn't feel any differently. He had no idea if what he was doing was even working.

"C'mon," Jack muttered, squeezing Grohm's hand tighter. "I was flinging awesomeness not two seconds ago! Why isn't this working?"

Jack closed his eyes and tried to imagine his life energy flowing into Grohm. He concentrated so hard, every muscle in his body tensed and felt like it was going to rip.

Finally, he relented, and his head slumped in defeat.

He'd failed.

"I'm sorry, big guy," he said.

"Earthman…" came a familiar, gravelly voice.

Jack looked up. Grohm's eyes were open, looking directly at him.

"No way!" exclaimed Jack. "You're alive? YOU'RE ALIVE!"

Grohm snorted. "Why is Earthman holding Grohm's hand?"

Jack looked down and realized he was still grasping Grohm's palm. He let go abruptly.

"I was... uh... just trying to save you with my sweet new superpowers. Did it work?"

Grohm furrowed his brow. "Is Earthman suffering from head wound?"

"I don't think so," said Jack. "But... I guess it is a possibility, considering what I've just been through."

Grohm gently shoved Jack away and struggled back to his feet. Jack could see the Rognok was still wobbly in the knees and visibly weakened.

"Dude, I wish you could have been conscious. Zarrod was about to kill me, but I broke the Great Seal, and absorbed some Ancient knowledge, and then blew that jerk up!"

Grohm sniffed the air and looked down at Jack, his brow raised slightly in surprise. "Earthman killed Deathlord Supreme?"

"What? Oh yeah, totally. You should have seen it, dude. I had this great line about kicking his ass. It was so awesome..."

Grohm started to lumber away.

"Hey," said Jack, "Where are you going?"

"Back to ship," said Grohm. "Battle is over."

So much had been happening, Jack had almost forgotten about the fact they were still on the Ghost Planet.

"Wait up," said Jack. "I need you to carry Anna. She's unconscious and heavier than she looks."

Grohm stopped and looked at Jack wearily. Jack could tell that the Rognok was hurting. Suddenly, he was worried Grohm might not be able to help, but the giant alien simply nodded. Anna was right where Jack had left her, and Grohm knelt down and gently picked her up, swung her over his shoulder, and began making his way up the stairs, with Jack not far behind.

"So… you believe me about killing the Deathlord, right?" asked Jack as they walked.

Grohm snorted. He kept walking.

"Uh, right?" asked Jack again.

CHAPTER  43

"**W**hat is happening?" growled Abraxas as chaos reigned down around him.

Too much time had passed since he'd last heard from the scout team he had sent out to investigate the mysterious explosion they had detected earlier. He had been about to join a group of Dark Soldiers he'd summoned at one of the disembarkment hatches to investigate the matter himself when every computer on the bridge had suddenly gone haywire.

Acolytes immediately went into crisis mode, opening panels to check for hardware malfunctions while others frantically tried to get responses from their assigned consoles. Even the lights on the bridge began to flicker, as if fighting to stay alive.

"Report!" he barked, to no one in particular.

"Warlord," replied a nearby Acolyte. "We have been locked out of all systems. Computers are unresponsive."

"How is this possible?"

"Unknown, Warlord. I have never seen anything like it."

Abraxas reached out and dug his claws into the Acolyte's shoulder, pulling him close and gazing fiercely into his eyes. "Don't just stand there – FIX IT!"

Annoyed, Abraxas threw the Acolyte across the room into two of his companions, sending them crumpling to the ground. The others began to try to diagnose the problem even more frantically in response. All Abraxas could think about was how fortunate it was that he did not have the authority to cull his own people, otherwise half the Acolytes in the room would be gone by now.

Then, a familiar alarm rang out – one which normally filled Abraxas with anticipation and joy but now just served to confuse him.

"Why is the main weapon powering up?" he yelled.

"Unknown, Warlord," responded an Acolyte.

"If we've lost control of the computers, then who's firing up the weapon?"

"Unknown, Warlord," responded another Acolyte.

"Don't any of you know ANYTHING?" the Deathlord raged.

"Funny," came a voice. "I wonder the same thing constantly."

Abraxas turned to the source of the voice that had responded, looking up at the bridge's large viewscreen, which was now dominated by the image of a rather odd looking robot.

"Who are you?" growled the Deathlord.

"Me?" said the robot innocently. "Why isn't it obvious? I am the one who has unlocked the secret to your technology. I am the one who has taken over your ship. I am the one powering up your weapon to blast the unstable core of this planet and destroy you and every last one of your minions with it. I am your Superior. I am your DOOM. I am Heckubus Moriarty, the greatest evil genius in eight star systems! And I am the one who has beaten you! Mwuahahahahaha!"

As the robot laughed, Abraxas squinted at the image before him. In the back of his mind, he seemed to recall he'd seen this robot somewhere before.

"Remember my name, fools!" said the robot triumphantly. "It is I who have brought the greatest threat the galaxy has ever known to its knees! I, and I alone have—"

"Wait a minute," said Abraxas. "I know you…"

The robot stopped suddenly and looked at Abraxas curiously. "You… you've heard of me?"

"No," responded the Deathlord. "You were with the Earthman!"

"Hmph. I don't really see how that's relev—"

"He's here!" cried Abraxas. "He's the one behind this!"

"Now wait just one minute—"

"ACOLYTES!" Abraxas screamed. "Destroy all current systems. Use your node stones to grow new ones and wipe out whatever pathetic virus this robot uploaded before our weapon has a chance to fire."

"Yes, Warlord!" all the Acolytes responded in unison.

"Pah!" sneered Heckubus. "You won't have time to—"

"Are our emergency communications still on a separate system from the mainframe?" asked Abraxas.

"They are, Warlord," replied a nearby Acolyte.

Abraxas punched an emergency switch at a console, causing a circular podium to rise from the floor. Holographic representations of his Lieutenants from around the ship sprang to life before him.

"Quickly, have we had any disturbances on the ship?" he inquired.

"None," replied one of the holographic Deathlords. "Except, the escort from the Supreme's return party has not checked back in, Warlord."

"Then that must be where they infiltrated our systems," growled Abraxas. "Send security squads two and three to that hangar. Kill anyone you find. Air Squad six and seven…"

"Yes, Warlord?" replied two of the holographic Deathlords.

"Prepare to launch and cut them off if they try to escape. I'll be joining you shortly. After the intruders have been dispatched, we'll head to where their ship crashed and finish the job."

"Yes, Warlord!" replied all the Lieutenants at once before their images disintegrated.

"Well, uh…" twittered Heckubus nervously. "It doesn't matter. You're entire ship is locked down. You'll never be able to get to—"

Before Heckubus could finish his sentence, Abraxas hurled a few balls of death energy against the blast door to the bridge, blowing it off its frame.

"Oh. Oh, dear," said the robot.

Abraxas turned and looked at the robot's image on the viewscreen, his eyes burning red. "Thank you for alerting us to what was going on," he growled. "And don't worry. I'll make sure every Deathlord in every corner of the galaxy knows the exact name of whom to hunt down and destroy, should you somehow manage to survive what I am about to do to you and your friends."

And with that, the Deathlord rushed into the hallway.

"What do you mean we're going to have company?" asked Scallywag.

"'Tis a mystery to me how they figured out what we were up to," said Heckubus over the comm unit, "but regardless, they are sending two security squads to your location, and will be there any minute. I recommend firing the weapon and making a hasty retreat."

"But the bloody weapon ain't even fully charged yet!"

"Oh, dear. Oh, dear. Oh, dear," muttered Green as he frantically typed away at the console in front of him.

"All that means is that it will take a little longer for the planet to blow up after we fire it," said Heckubus. "Which, all things considered, might not be a bad thing."

"Not a bad thing at all," came another voice over the comms. Green and Scallywag immediately perked up.

"Earthman?" said Scallywag with just a hint of amazement. "Is that you?"

"The one and only," said Jack. "Mission accomplished, fellas. Anna is safe, the Great Seal is broken, and the Deathlord Supreme's butt has officially been kicked. So fire that baby off, and let's blow this popsicle stand."

Green and Scallywag shared a look communicating that the mention of a so-called "popsicle stand" was the least confusing thing about what Jack had just said.

"Jack, my boy… that's amazing!" said Green. "How did you—"

"It's a long story Professor – and I mean that this time. I'll fill you in once we've made our escape. Right now Grohm and I are on our way back to where we stashed the hoverbikes. Just do what you need to and meet us back at the ship."

"Smartest blasted thing I've heard all day," said Scallywag, turning to the Professor. "You heard the lad, Trundle. Engage that weapon and let's skirt out o' here before this pop-cycle thing explodes, whatever that means."

Green continued to type furiously at the control panel. "I'm engaging the sequence now. We'll have a few minutes before the weapon is charged up enough to fire. I just hope your robot friend's algorithm can keep the Deathlords locked out of their systems long enough to keep them from shutting it down."

"Pah! Ye of little faith," squawked the robot over the comms. "It would take more than a few mindless Deathlords to unravel my brilliant—"

Scallywag shut off his comms. "Guess we'll just haveta hope our luck holds out. Ya all done?"

Green tapped a few final keys triumphantly. "Indeed," he replied. "Firing sequence initiated."

"Good," said Scallywag as he backed Green away from the Deathlord console and unholstered one of his blasters, promptly firing at it to ensure it couldn't be accessed again. "Now get a move on."

The Professor didn't wait to be told again. He immediately followed Scallywag out of the control room, bounding down the stairs two and three at a time on the trek to the hangar bay floor.

No sooner had they touched down at their destination than an explosion rocked a nearby door.

"Blast!" swore Scallywag as he grabbed Green by the arm urgently. "RUN!"

The two sprinted off, making directly for the hovervehicle on which they had arrived, still parked in its alcove awaiting their return.

Two more loud explosions echoed throughout the massive hangar bay. The last one was followed by the whine of bending metal as the entrance door flew off its hinges and blew apart.

Scallywag glanced up briefly from the controls of the hovervehicle just long enough to see eight Dark Soldiers rush in, led by a particularly nasty looking Deathlord whose elongated head was wrapped in dark cloth, shrouding his face.

Scallywag grabbed the control stick to their vessel with one hand and a blaster pistol with his other, firing at the group as he clumsily backed the hovercraft out of its alcove. The Deathlords responded in kind, with their leader creating a glowing white orb of death energy in his hand.

Anticipating the attack, Scallywag banked the craft sharply to the side as the Deathlord unleashed his orb, which rocketed right toward them, narrowly missing. Green stumbled from the abrupt maneuver and hit the rail of the craft, nearly toppling over it. Scallywag was sure if the Deathlord's attack had made contact, the hovercraft would have been rendered useless. He quickly holstered his weapon and focused on getting the heck out of there.

"KILL THEM!" raged the head Deathlord. "Do not let them escape!"

Obediently, the Dark Soldiers all opened fire, sending a barrage of plasma blasts toward the hovercraft. Green and Scallywag ducked as the pirate continued to maneuver the hovercraft toward the exit. Some plasma blasts sparked off the craft's sides as they hit their mark.

"Oh, dear," cried Green. "I do so hate being shot at!"

"Shoulda thought about that before hatching this bloody brilliant scheme of yours," muttered the Visini.

"No plan is perfect, my dear fellow," the Professor replied.

"Well, buck up," said the pirate. "'Cause I've got a feeling things are gonna get a lot less perfect real soon."

Scallywag punched up the hovercraft's engine and dropped out of the hangar bay into the tunnel below. No sooner had they exited than Abraxas rushed up to the ledge of the hangar, watching his prey make their escape.

"Jetpacks!" he ordered. "Strap up! NOW!"

The second Scallywag was clear of the hangar bay, he banked the hovercraft hard to the right and started to make for open ground, away from the mothership and toward the Earth vessel. Sure, the Deathlords would more than likely follow them, but the hovercraft they were on seemed plenty speedy for their purposes, and they would more than likely be able to make it back to their ship before any of the Dark Soldiers could catch up with them.

Of course, if Jack and Grohm weren't back before them, that would be *their* problem, not his.

However, what *was* his problem were the two full squads of jetpacked Deathlords that suddenly appeared from the lip of the mothership, effectively cutting off his escape route and charging toward him, guns blazing.

"Blast it!" Scallywag growled as he turned the hovercraft sharply, avoiding the angry red plasma fire that streaked toward them. As he made his maneuver, he glanced around, looking for another way to escape. The mothership loomed over them ominously, a sickly white glow pulsing from its center, giving Scallywag flashbacks to the pillar at the core of the Pit. Twelve Deathlords were on their tail, and the hovercraft didn't offer much in the way of cover from those blasters. If it came down to a straight up chase, he and the Professor were dangerously exposed. All in all, Scallywag did not like his options.

In fact, he liked them even less when he saw more Dark Soldiers drop from the hangar bay he'd just exited, their jetpacks roaring to life the second they saw their prey. One of them, with the bandaged head, threw a ball of energy at them almost immediately.

Scallywag turned the hovercraft and barely missed getting hit by the ball of death that screamed by. Green stumbled from the sharp maneuver and collapsed, grabbing onto the rail of the hovercraft and holding on tightly.

"Oh dear, oh dear," he muttered like a scared little mouse.

Scallywag gritted his teeth as he punched up the acceleration of the hovercraft and turned away from their new arrivals. The original squads of Dark Soldiers kept firing behind them, and there was no sign they were going to let up anytime soon. Finally, Scallywag had an idea, though he didn't like it anymore than he was sure the Professor would.

"Hold on tight, Trundle," said Scallywag. He glanced down at the scaly, flat-headed alien whose large eyes stared up at him, wide and fearful. "This ain't gonna be pleasant."

No sooner had Green wrapped his arms as tightly as he could around the hovercraft's railings than Scallywag pointed the ship downward, hitting the acceleration as much as he was able. Even bracing against the control panel of the craft as tightly as he could, it was all Scallywag could do to keep from floating away as the hovercraft shot down into the massive tunnel below them.

Scallywag could feel the sickening sensation of his stomach being left behind as they rocketed downward. Somewhere in the distance, he heard one of the Deathlords scream something along the lines of, "Follow them!"

He looked up as he saw the army of Deathlords above him engage their jetpacks, charging down in pursuit. Further back, he saw the central eye of the mothership, swirling chaotically with ghostly white energy, growing brighter and brighter by the second.

"Oy, Greenskin," shouted Scally over the blasting of air as they continued their descent. "Keep an eye on that mothership weapon, let me know the second it's about ta fire."

Green glanced up at the seemingly shrinking mothership, the energy rumbling about its center swirling even more chaotically as he and Scallywag continued to plummet down the tunnel, the Deathlords in hot pursuit directly behind them.

"I say," cried out the Professor. "How am I to know that?"

"Yer supposed to be smart, ain't ya?" replied Scallywag.

"Being smart doesn't make one an expert on knowing when a massive death ray is about to engage."

"If ya don't keep an eye out, we're gonna be caught in that blast," barked Scallywag. "And I, for one, wouldn't care for that at all."

"Then should you not simply stay away from the blast radius? Perhaps stick to the edges of the tunnel?"

"If I did that, me plan wouldn't work."

"You have a plan?" the Professor blinked, confused.

Scallywag looked over at the Professor and smirked. "What? Ya think you and the Earthman are the only ones who can come up with terrible ideas?"

Scallywag's moment of levity was short-lived; plasma blasts started raining down around them as the Deathlords above opened fire. Scallywag adjusted their descent, spiraling away from their attackers as he continued to corkscrew down the massive planetary tunnel.

Professor Green squeaked at the maneuver and hugged the rail tightly, burying his head into his shoulders.

"Oy!" yelled Scallywag. "Eyes topside, remember?"

Green looked up at the twenty Deathlords looming over them. A small group was following closely behind, while others fanned out trying to get a drop on their position. Green squinted his eyes as some of the Deathlords became tiny black specs against the ever growing light from the mothership's central weapon.

"Um... dear fellow... Mr. Pirate?"

"Name's Scallywag."

"Indeed. You know how you told me to tell you when the weapon was about to fire?"

"Yeah."

Green gazed up as tendrils of energy started to snake out from the glowing chaos of the mothership's center, like worms bursting forth from a rotten apple.

"I think it's about to happen…" Green said.

Without a word, Scallywag abruptly turned the hovercraft, shooting toward the wall of the tunnel. The adjustment was so abrupt, Green was afraid he'd spill his stomach contents (but considering he couldn't remember the last time he'd eaten, there probably wasn't much danger of that happening).

High above them, the Deathlords scrambled to adjust to their prey's new course, just as the mothership unleashed its fury.

A solid pillar of sickly white light rocketed downward, enveloping fourteen unlucky Deathlords in its path.

Scallywag reached the edge of the tunnel just as the death beam shot by. The pirate recoiled slightly as the energy blasted past them, with only a few feet between it and their vessel. No heat came off the beam, but an emotional wave of fear and despair hit Scallywag like a truck. He glanced over and saw the swirling beam of light, churning chaotically, its sound like the screams of a million beings crying out in agony.

Within the beam, it was almost as if he could see images. Faces of people he wanted to forget. Memories of deeds he wished he could take back. Emotions he never wanted to experience – they all flooded over him like a cresting tidal wave.

"*And here… I thought you loved me…*" came the voice he never wanted to hear again, from the memory he so desperately wanted to forget.

For a moment, time seemed to stand still as events from so long ago flashed into his mind. The memory came back so vividly, that for an instant, it felt to Scallywag as though he were there, actually reliving the incident that changed his life forever.

"I'm sorry," he whispered, salty tears blurring the edge of his vision.

Then, he heard Professor Green scream, snapping him out of his trance and back into the urgency of their current situation.

"Look out!" cried the Professor, mere seconds before blaster fire rained down around them.

Scallywag moved the hovercraft, but they were boxed in between the death beam and the edge of the tunnel, with almost no room to maneuver. Scally glanced behind them and saw six Dark Soldiers, including the one with his head wrapped in rags. He held a ball of death energy in his hands, waiting to unleash it.

The pirate looked back down at the control panel. The readout on the display showed they were getting close to their destination. Scallywag just hoped they could survive that long.

"Hold on tight, Trundle," said Scallywag.

"I'm already holding on tight!"

"Hold on tighter..." said the pirate.

Scallywag could see the half-moon opening coming up before them quickly. One last glance behind him revealed the lead Deathlord unleashing his ball of death energy. Scallywag hit the reverse on the hovercraft's engine and angled the circular vehicle toward the wall, bringing its side up at a forty-five degree angle.

He punched the acceleration just as they came to the opening to the Great Seal's tunnel, shooting the hovercraft toward it. Their momentum brought them crashing up hard against the side of the hallway's wall, but the angle at which Scallywag had brought the vehicle in had allowed the brunt of the impact to be distributed evenly across the bottom of the craft. It scraped against the wall with a screech of metal on stone, and the entire hovercraft shook in protest.

The death energy blast from the Deathlord hit the side of the entrance, knocking off a chunk of the wall before the Deathlords followed the craft into the tunnel. One Dark Soldier, however, couldn't adjust to the angle in time and evaporated in a puff of dust as he slammed into the wall of the entrance, his jetpack exploding, shooting a fireball of ignited rocket fuel down the tunnel.

Scallywag straightened out the hovercraft as he looked at the explosion behind him. Much to his dismay, he saw the five remaining Deathlords emerge from the ball of fire, angry smoke trails billowing off of them as they raced after their prey.

He glanced down at the Professor, who was looking even more green than usual.

"Cheer up, Trundle," smiled Scallywag. "At least we ain't dead!"

Scally increased their acceleration as blaster fire erupted behind them, rocketing faster down the hallway.

"Not yet, anyway…" muttered the pirate.

CHAPTER  44

"**A**nna? Anna, wake up…"

Anna's eyes fluttered open. Jack's face slowly came into focus as it hovered above her. She gazed at him a moment, the numbness in her mind morphing into a tingling feeling of disbelief. Was this a dream? How was this even real?

"Jack?" she said hoarsely.

"Hey," he responded with a smile. "How you feeling?"

Anna reached out with a shaky hand and cupped Jack's face, as if to reassure herself he was truly there. She gazed into his deep green eyes and felt her heart race, beating with a sense of joy, excitement, and relief all balled up in an explosion of emotion that coursed through her body. She sat up with a start, wrapping her arms around Jack's neck and hugging him like a drowning person would a life preserver.

"You're real," she gasped, choking back a sob of pure happiness. "I can't believe it!"

Jack held her gently in his arms while patting her back reassuringly. "Not that this isn't awesome," he said, "but could you relax the kung fu grip? I kinda like being able to breathe…"

Anna pulled back, a nervous giggle escaping from her lips, which she quickly covered shyly with her palm. Her brain was still buzzing with disbelief. She had been on death's doorstep, at the mercy of a foe she was sure would kill her. One moment, she had been facing her own mortality, defeated by her enemy, shrouded in the shame of failure – and now, from what she could tell, she was safe! The feeling threatened to completely overwhelm her.

"Wow," said Jack rubbing his neck. "You know, if the whole Princess thing doesn't work out, you could totally have a career as a professional wrestler."

Anna couldn't keep herself from grinning; she was smiling so hard her cheeks were hurting. Tears blurred the edge of her vision as she grabbed Jack's hands tightly in her own, as though he could siphon away some of the emotion that was causing her to feel as though she were making a complete fool of herself.

"What happened?" she asked.

"Despite what *some people* might think," said Jack, casting a wry stare in Grohm's direction, "I totally saved the day."

Grohm grunted. Anna looked over at the hulking alien as he went back to unstrapping a large weapon from the back of a massive hoverbike and holstering it across his back.

"Don't mind him," said Jack. "He gets kinda grumpy when there's nothing around to smash."

Anna looked back at Jack, noticing for the first time that he was wearing body armor and had a blaster gun strapped to his side.

"You… you came back for me…" she said.

"Of course," Jack replied. "I'd never leave you behind."

Anna bit her lower lip. She still couldn't believe it. Jack had always been an interesting boy. She'd never met someone who could make her laugh or have a good time quite like him. He'd shown astounding bravery and resourcefulness during their time on the Deathlord ship, which was amazing in-and-of itself. But now, as she looked at him, Anna saw him as something more. Something she never would have suspected from the boy she'd always catch shyly staring at her in homeroom.

He was a hero.

"Thank you," Anna said, meaning it with every fiber of her being.

"No problem," replied Jack, completely missing the weight with which Anna had said the words. "But now we really need to get out of here before the planet blows up."

Anna blinked at Jack, as though she didn't comprehend what he'd just said. "Wait... what?" she asked.

"Long story short," explained Jack, "we have to blow up the planet to save the universe, and we don't have a lot of time left before it happens. So I need you to get on the bike so we can get back to the ship and jump out of here before everything goes boom. Cool?"

While Anna was still trying to process what Jack was saying, he hopped up and helped her to her feet.

"Oh, and uh... there may be an evil tornado thing on the surface that'll try to eat us once we're up there, so try not to touch the ground. Or it. In fact, try not to even look at the thing, 'cause it's pretty creepy."

"Huh?" said Anna, her previous jubilation now suddenly replaced with growing concern.

"Relax," smiled Jack, patting Anna on the shoulder reassuringly. "Short of an army of Deathlords showing up, I can't think of anything that could possibly mess up our escape."

"Oy! Earthman!" Scallywag's voice rang out from the comm unit in Jack's ear. "I got an army of bloody Deathlords on me tail, and we're headed yer way!"

Jack sighed. "I really gotta be more careful about what I say."

"I can't shake 'em!" said Scallywag urgently. "If I don't get some help soon, the Trundle and I are gonna be wet spots on the walls!"

Grohm growled and straddled his hoverbike, the massive machine humming to life. "Battle," he said.

"Looks like it," said Jack, more than a little annoyed. Jack hopped on his hoverbike and motioned for Anna to join him as he started it up. She climbed on behind him and wrapped her arms around his waist.

"Hold on tight, Princess," said Jack. "Looks like we're not out of the woods yet."

The walls of the Ancient hallway raced by in one direction as plasma fire streaked in from the other. Scallywag gritted his teeth as he crouched low over the control panel of the hovercraft, trying to maneuver in the confined space of the hallway. *We ain't gonna last too much longer like this*, the pirate thought. Indeed, though the hallway was large, it did not give him enough room to maneuver. The Deathlords had been relentless, and it had taken all of Scallywag's skill as a pilot to keep from getting hit by the lead Deathlord's cannonballs of death energy.

"Scally, you there?" came Jack's voice over the comm.

"Where else would I bloody be?" replied Scallywag testily.

"Pretty soon you're going to be coming up to an area where a lot of hallways meet," said Jack. "You'll want to take the exit to the far right. The far right, understand?"

"Aye, and where's that lead?"

"To a tunnel that will take you to the surface."

"Fat lotta good that'll do me if I'm blown ta pieces in the meantime!"

"Relax, Grohm and I got your back," replied Jack. "Just remember – the far right tunnel, 'kay?"

Scallywag grumbled in response and looked down at the sensor readout on his control panel. The area Jack had mentioned was coming up fast. The moment they entered the half-moon area where all the hallways seemed to converge, Scallywag banked the hovercraft sharply, angling for the exit farthest to the right. The Deathlords behind him did not miss a beat, staying stubbornly on his tail.

"I'm here," said Scallywag into his comm. "Now what?"

"Now, DUCK!" replied Jack.

Red plasma fire streaked by Scallywag. He watched as one of the Deathlords following him was hit by the blasts, lost control and crashed into the wall, causing its jetpack to explode. The hum of hoverbikes echoed through the hallway as Jack and Grohm rocketed forward, blasting their weapons directly at the Deathlords who scrambled to avoid being shot.

Scallywag couldn't help but cheer as his allies raced by him on either side of the hovercraft, a blast from Grohm's massive shotgun taking out another Deathlord. Abraxas twisted around as the duo shot by, his fiery red eyes meeting Jack's for the briefest of moments. The smug smile on the boy's face sent shivers of unadulterated rage up the Deathlord's back.

"EARTHMAN!!!!" he screamed.

Jack and Grohm hit the brakes, their hoverbikes skidding forward as they turned, crisscrossing each other's position before gunning their engines and racing ahead, now behind the three remaining Deathlords, their weapons blazing.

"Oy, Greenskin," said Scallywag, grabbing the Professor by the collar of his shirt and pulling him toward the controls. "Take over."

"What? Me?" replied Green. "But-but-but... I'm no pilot!"

"How are ya with a gun?"

"Horrible."

"Then yer now a pilot."

Scallywag left the nervous Trundle alone to steer the hovercraft as he turned and unholstered his guns, smiling to himself as he took aim. "Time for a bit o' payback," he said to himself as he opened fire.

His blasts narrowly missed Abraxas, who quickly spun out of the way. The remaining Deathlords were now caught between Scallywag's fire from the front, and Jack and Grohm's fire from behind – a situation that did not please Abraxas one bit.

Green looked down as the control panel on the hovercraft beeped at him. The sensor readout showed the exit tunnel to the surface rapidly approaching.

"Um... Mr. Scallywag..." he said nervously. "The tunnel to the surface is approaching..."

"So?"

"So it... ah... it doesn't seem to go there right away."

Scallywag turned and raised an eyebrow. "What? Where's it go?"

Green looked up as the hallway's exit rushed toward them. The illuminated metal rings of the greater tunnel into which it emptied lay in the distance.

"Um... down!"

Green braced himself against the control panel. Scallywag quickly wrapped his arm around the side railing of the hovercraft, and not a moment too soon as they emerged from the hallway and Green angled the vehicle downward sharply. Scallywag briefly lost his footing, his legs kicking up into the air as the floor of the vehicle fell out from under him. Gravity soon caught up, and he crashed back down.

"Bloody hell!" spat Scallywag. "What was that???"

"The tunnel angled in such a way so that we could only follow it downward at our current velocity," Green said.

Scallywag quickly holstered his weapons and pushed Green aside. "Look at the size o' this tunnel," he said. "Ya don't need to make sharp turns like that."

"I told you - I'm a scientist, not a pilot," whined Green.

Scallywag glanced at the sensors. The tunnel they were in seemed to straighten out horizontally for a few miles before curving upward for the surface. He looked behind them to see the Deathlords were down to three, but Abraxas and his two remaining minions were better able to dodge the blaster fire in the larger tunnel than they had managed back in the Ancient hallway. Jack and Grohm found themselves having to adjust course constantly to try to stay on the Deathlords' tails.

Abraxas saw Grohm veer to the side, taking aim at one of his Dark Soldiers. He summoned another ball of death energy into his hand and seized the opportunity.

"FALL BACK!" he ordered.

Immediately, he and his two remaining followers cut propulsion to their jetpacks, slowing their momentum and allowing Jack and Grohm to overshoot the Deathlords before they re-engaged their forward thrust. No sooner had Jack and Grohm passed than Abraxas hurled his death energy right toward Grohm.

Grohm saw the attack heading directly for him and tried to adjust his course, but it was too late. The death energy hit his hoverbike's rear stabilizer just enough to take a rather significant chunk out of it, causing its engine to whine loudly in protest.

"Grohm!" yelled Jack as he watched the Rognok's hoverbike spin out of control, sparks flying and smoke billowing from the damaged vehicle.

Scallywag glanced behind him to see Grohm's bike flip over, the massive alien falling from its seat before it veered off wildly and smashed into pieces against the side wall of the tunnel. Immediately, Scallywag cut the acceleration of the hovercraft, allowing it to slow enough to meet Grohm's velocity as the Rognok plummeted toward the ground.

Grohm landed flat on his back in the center of the hovercraft's passenger platform, impacting its floor with a loud THUMP. The weight of the alien's landing forced the hovercraft down, its bottom skimming the surface of the tunnel. The entire vehicle rattled violently before Scallywag could correct its motion and compensate for their new passenger.

"If we somehow manage ta live through this," Scallywag yelled at Grohm. "Yer going on a bloody diet!"

Grohm only had a chance to growl in response before blaster fire erupted around them. Scallywag swerved the hovercraft to and fro as he tried to avoid the blasts while gaining altitude once again.

Jack banked to the side just as Abraxas let loose another ball of death energy that rocketed by him. He glanced down and saw that Grohm, Scallywag, and Green were all in the hovercraft, but they were having a hard time avoiding the relentless blaster fire from the Deathlords who now enjoyed the advantageous position of being on the craft's tail.

"Jack," he heard Anna say in his ear. "Try and hold it steady for a little bit."

"What?" replied Jack. "Why?"

"You can't dodge these attacks and fight back at the same time," said Anna. "I just need you to keep the bike steady long enough for me to do something."

"What are you gonna do?"

"This," said Anna as she angled her left leg across Jack's lap and reached across his chest with her hand to grab the handlebar of the bike. In a quick motion, Anna spun herself around Jack and into his lap, so they were now face-to-face. Jack locked eyes with her, wide-eyed at the maneuver. Anna smiled as she grabbed Jack's pistol from his hand.

"You keep us alive," she said. "I'll keep them off our backs."

"Yes, ma'am," replied Jack, smiling.

Anna hugged Jack close, bringing his chin up to her shoulder so he could see past her. She raised her arm over his other shoulder and opened fire, hitting the first Deathlord before he had time to react, striking his jetpack and sending him spiraling out of control. He crashed into the wall of the tunnel in a fiery explosion. Anna smiled to herself as her heart pounded in excitement. It felt good to be fighting back for a change.

Abraxas and his remaining soldier began evasive maneuvers. As long as the Deathlords were focused on not getting shot by Anna, it made things easier for Jack and Scallywag.

"Kill her!" screamed Abraxas.

The Dark Soldier fired directly at Jack and Anna as Abraxas hurled yet another death energy attack at them. Jack swerved left and right, trying his best to avoid the incoming fire, but one of the plasma blasts hit his left forward stabilizer. Before he had a chance to react, the hoverbike rotated violently to the left, almost turning upside down. Anna shrieked as she fell out of Jack's lap, losing her pistol in the process.

"ANNA!" screamed Jack as he reached out and grabbed her by the wrist, his thighs tightening around the seat of the hoverbike and his right hand gripping it's handle as he held on for dear life. Anna dangled in mid-air, looking up at Jack as her hair whipped around her face. Jack's hand burned and his arm ached as she swung in his grasp. He gritted his teeth, trying desperately to hold on, even as his hand refused to obey – his grip slowly slipping.

Below them, Jack could see Scallywag bringing the hovercraft in line; Grohm was there waiting to catch her. *God, I hope this works*, Jack thought as his grip finally gave out. Anna fell, squealing slightly before she landed in Grohm's arms. Jack breathed a sigh of relief and looked behind him just in time to see Abraxas hurl another ball of death energy.

"*Oh, crap!*"

The blast rocketed toward Jack. He let go of his grip on his bike and fell just as the death energy impacted it. What was left of the hoverbike twisted away, disintegrating as it hit the side wall of the tunnel.

Jack screamed as he fell – the fall from his bike wasn't on target for the hovercraft below him, and it became frighteningly clear that he was going to miss it. Suddenly, Grohm reached out, his massive hand wrapping around Jack's forearm as he fell. The hulking alien was leaning halfway out of the hovercraft, his other hand holding firmly to its railing as Jack flapped about like a rag doll in his grip.

More blaster fire and balls of death energy shot toward them, with Scallywag frantically moving the hovercraft to and fro, its engine whining with the weight it now carried. Jack flailed about helplessly outside the hovercraft as it banked and juked, the Deathlords not letting up on their assault even for a moment.

"Somebody – do – *something!*" Jack yelled.

Professor Green reached over and grabbed one of Scallywag's pistols from its holster and with a scream rushed toward the back of the hovercraft, firing the weapon wildly at their pursuers. Abraxas wheeled away from the sudden blaster fire but his sole remaining Dark Soldier was not so lucky. He was hit directly by the Professor and tumbled to the ground, his jetpack erupting in an explosion.

Taking advantage of the sudden respite, Anna helped Grohm pull Jack onto the hovercraft's platform. Scallywag looked at Professor Green, who was grinning proudly.

"Horrible with a blaster, eh?" said Scallywag.

"Easier than flying, my good fellow," responded Green.

The control console beeped at Scallywag. He looked down to see that the tunnel was about to change directions, curving vertically toward the surface.

"Everyone, hold onto something!" Scallywag ordered as they raced toward the incline of the tunnel.

All who could, wrapped their arms around the side railing of the hovercraft bracing themselves as Scallywag angled it into a climb and gained altitude. Above them, the golden hue of the Ghost Planet's sky revealed itself in the distant opening. Jack glanced beneath them and saw Abraxas below.

"Professor!" Jack said urgently. "Your gun!"

Green glanced at the pistol in his hand like he'd forgotten it was there. He slid it across the floor of the hovercraft to Jack, who snatched it up and immediately started firing at Abraxas. The Deathlord avoided the blasts easily, trying to angle himself into the ship's blind spot directly beneath it. Jack could see he was charging up another attack.

"Scally! INCOMING!" Jack yelled as Abraxas unleashed his projectile.

Scallywag jerked the hovercraft to the left, but the death energy grazed their side, taking a small part of the ship with it as it flew by. The hovercraft jolted, and alarms on the control console beeped in protest. Scallywag cursed as he tried to regain control. The hovercraft swayed unstably as they continued their ascent, the opening to the surface growing bigger and bigger as they got closer to it.

Jack glanced down again just in time to see Abraxas fire another attack. "RIGHT!" he screamed. "To the right! The right!"

The group slid to the right as Scallywag banked in the direction Jack had ordered. The death energy blast sailed by, just inches from the ship.

"Somebody kill that sodding browner!" Scallywag snarled.

Jack, happy to try to oblige Scallywag's request, looked over the side of the hovercraft, blaster pistol at the ready — but there was no Abraxas to be seen. He glanced around frantically, trying to see where the Deathlord had gone, when suddenly the hovercraft jolted, as if something had hit it from the bottom. Alarms on Scallywag's console blared angrily as it happened again. This time a ball of death energy shot right through the center of the hovercraft's floor.

"Blast it!" yelled Scallywag . "We're losing engines!"

"Get us to the surface!" yelled Jack as he climbed to the hole in the floor. "Whatever it takes!" Jack shoved his arm through the hole the death energy blast had formed and fired blindly, hoping to flush Abraxas off their tail. Meanwhile, Scallywag tried to level off the hovercraft, redistributing the strain of their ascent to the outer areas of its stabilizers. They continued to climb, but their speed was steadily slowing.

"C'mon ya bloody piece of..." grumbled Scallywag as he angled the vehicle to the side, the tunnel's exit steadily coming toward them.

No sooner had they passed the edge of the opening to the surface of the planet than Abraxas appeared by their side, having come up from under them, a ball of furious death energy swirling in his hand.

"DIE!" he screamed as he raised the attack over his head, ready to unleash it.

A collective scream emanated from the group at the Deathlord's sudden appearance. Scallywag banked the hovercraft to the side, away from the Deathlord and his attack, but without much luck. The blast impacted the side of the hovercraft, sending them spinning like a top. The hovercraft hit the ground like a frisbee, its metal undercarriage shrieking as rock and dirt tore at it.

The vehicle's rotational frenzy came to an abrupt end as it impacted a large rock, sending those inside of it flying out as it flipped over. Jack and the others flew a few feet into the air before hitting the ground, rolling as they did so.

Jack shook his head, dizzy from the impact, his joints protesting as he tried to sit up. He looked around him, the hovercraft's carcass smoking and sparking a few feet away and his companions all coming to, nursing injuries from the landing. Then, Jack's eyes looked down and focused on his hand as it lay flat against the dirt of the Ghost Planet.

Oh no, he thought.

A blood-curdling shriek pierced the air, echoing out from far away. Jack got to his feet, his heart racing with panic. "Off the ground!" he shouted. "We gotta get off the ground!"

"Jack – LOOK OUT!" he heard Anna cry.

Before he had time to react, Anna had hurled herself into him, tackling him to the ground as a death energy blast impacted right where he had been standing. Jack glanced in the sky as Abraxas hovered there, lording over them.

"Behind," bellowed Grohm as the massive alien grabbed what was left of the hovercraft and wielded it like a shield in front of him. The group scrambled to its shelter as Abraxas lazily tossed another ball of death energy their way, laughing as he did so.

"We are so bloody kittened," grumbled Scallywag.

"We gotta get off the ground," said Jack. "That thing will be here any minute!"

"Great idea," the pirate responded. "In case you haven't noticed, the flying DEATHLORD has us pinned down!"

Another death energy blast shook the hovercraft. Grohm grunted under its impact.

Jack's mind raced. They couldn't allow Abraxas to keep them on the ground while the Ghost Planet's security system came rushing up to eat them. He needed a plan, and he needed one fast.

Almost as though it were responding to his desperate request, the back of Jack's head started to tingle as he felt his connection with the Ancient Earthship. He smiled as a new strategy popped into his mind. It certainly wasn't the best plan in the world, but it was better than nothing.

"Scally," said Jack urgently. "Distract him!"

"What?" growled the pirate. "How am I supposed ta do that?"

"Shoot at him, keep him busy, I don't care!" said Jack. "I just need Grohm to be free for a few seconds. As soon as I draw him away, get off the ground! Then, come and get me."

Anna, Scallywag, and the Professor all looked at each other skeptically.

"Trust me," smiled Jack. He turned to Scallywag. "Now, Scally! Shoot that jerk-wad!"

Scallywag grumbled but proceeded to pop out from behind the cover of the hovership, unleashing his remaining blaster at Abraxas. The Deathlord saw the blasts coming and dodged them, momentarily taking his attention off the group and hurling a blast of his ghost energy toward Scallywag.

"Quick, Grohm, throw me at that Deathlord!" ordered Jack.

Grohm raised his massive brow inquisitively.

"Remember how you did it in the Pit?" Jack asked.

Grohm's lips curled into a smile. "Yes."

"Do it exactly like that! Just, uh... don't miss!"

With that, the Rognok dropped the hovercraft and grabbed Jack, flinging him high into the air directly at Abraxas, who was still hurling his death energy blasts at Scallywag.

Abraxas didn't seem to notice Jack until the Earthman was almost upon him, and if the Deathlord did have time to react, the sight of a flying boy heading right toward him no doubt caught him a tad off guard. Jack slammed into the Deathlord in mid-air, quickly wrapping his arms around the alien's neck. The momentum of the impact caused Abraxas to lose control of his jetpack, sending the two flying off away from the crash site.

"Blimey," muttered Scallywag. "The lad's got some stones, I'll give 'em that."

The screeching sound was getting louder. The group turned to see the Ghost Planet's swirling mass of doom heading right toward them, the angry tornado speeding across the surface directly for their location.

"Quickly," said the pirate. "Get onto the ship!"

Grohm flipped the carcass of the hovercraft over and the group all climbed onboard. The Professor looked up at the encroaching ghostly entity that was rapidly approaching.

"Oh, dear," he muttered.

"Everyone stay together!" ordered Scallywag.

The group huddled together on the flimsy remains of the hovercraft as the tornado of doom rushed up to them. The vicious cloud began to swirl around the hovercraft's location, unable to reach its targets because of the cover the metal body of the vehicle provided. The group watched in fear as the doom cloud almost enveloped them. Ghostly figures within its winds writhed and moaned, their pained faces appearing and disappearing as it twirled around their location. Occasionally, it looked like hands reached out to grab at the group, wanting to pull them into the tornado's ghastly vortex.

"Son of a—" growled Scallywag, holding tightly onto the Professor as the ghostly wind bit into his eyes and a hand narrowly missed reaching out for him.

"Stay close!" screamed Anna. "Don't let it touch you!"

"Brilliant idea!" Scallywag yelled in response.

Beneath their feet, the hovercraft shifted, its metal frame groaning in complaint as the doom cloud swirled around it. Had it not been for the hulking weight of Grohm, there was a good chance the craft might have flipped over.

"We can't last much longer like this!" said the Professor over the screeching howl of the death cloud's wind.

"If ya got any sodding ideas," replied Scallywag, "Now would be the time ta share 'em!"

"Grohm have idea," grunted Grohm.

"Great," said Scallywag. "And what, pray tell, is the Rognok's bloody brilliant plan?"

"Get on ship," Grohm replied. He looked up, and the group followed suit. There, above them, hovered the Ancient Earthship.

"But how—" Scallywag started to say, when suddenly, in a flash of blue light, the group found themselves huddled together on its bridge.

"Welcome back," said Heckubus, who was standing by one of the consoles. "I see my plan worked brilliantly. As usual."

"Ya bloody tin can..." said Scallywag as he approached the robot and wrapped his arms around Heckubus, lifting him into the air with a big bear hug. "I never thought I'd be happy to see yer rusty mug! Ha, ha!"

"Un... hand... me... you... jackanape!" mumbled Heckubus in between joyful shakes of the hug.

Scallywag set the robot down. "So ya figured out how to take control of the ship?" the pirate said. "And ya still came back for us? I say, I underestimated ya, robot."

"Yes, well..." said Heckubus. "Not from lack of trying, but this wasn't me."

"What?" replied Scallywag.

"I'm not in control of the ship," said Heckubus. "It flew here on its own."

Scallywag scowled at the robot. "Shoulda known. I take back everything I just said about ya."

"Good," replied Heckubus. "Because things were starting to get awkward."

"So if you're not controlling the ship," asked Anna, "who is?"

"Your guess is as good as mine," replied Heckubus.

"Look!" said Professor Green, pointing to the viewscreen. "The tornado – it's leaving."

The group turned to see the Ghost Planet's doom cloud tearing off away from the ship.

"Good riddance," muttered Scallywag.

"Curious," said Heckubus. "I wonder where it's going."

Anna's heart almost skipped a beat as the answer to the robot's question became clear to her.

"Jack…" she said.

★★★★★

In the skies above the surface of the Ghost Planet, Jack was still struggling with the Deathlord – though it was actually more of a combination of trying to keep the Deathlord from killing him and hanging on for dear life.

Jack had managed to climb behind Abraxas, wrapping his arms around the Deathlord's neck. Abraxas continued to try to reach back and grab Jack, but he was having a hard time controlling the jetpack and fending off the Earthman all at once.

"Fight!" cried the Deathlord. "Fight like a warrior!"

Jack knew he wouldn't be able to last much longer, especially if Abraxas were able to regain some control over the jetpack and manage to shake him off. He decided to risk letting go with one of his hands to make a grab for his blaster pistol.

"Sorry, dude," said Jack as he quickly pulled out his pistol and shoved it into the back of the jetpack. "I fight to win!"

Jack pulled the trigger and instantly the jetpack sparked as the plasma blast tore through its casing.

Jack turned his face just in time to avoid an eruption of flame as the jetpack fuel escaped from the breach he'd created. Almost immediately, the two began to twist uncontrollably in the

air as the jetpack lost altitude; they began plummeting straight toward the ground.

Jack let go of his pistol and held on as long as he could as Abraxas frantically tried to regain some measure of control over their descent. But it was no use.

The ground came rushing up to meet them.

At the last minute, Abraxas was able to pull up out of the dive, but not soon enough to keep from crashing.

Jack jumped off before the two hit the ground. He tucked and rolled as he landed, though not as gracefully as he would have liked, since his momentum still caused him to hit the ground hard, knocking the wind out of him.

Jack looked up to see that Abraxas had been able to land better than Jack had. The Deathlord climbed back up to his feet, completely unscathed. He shrugged off the broken jetpack and turned to face his enemy. Jack got back up, not taking his eyes off the Deathlord.

"Earthman," growled Abraxas.

"Sorry," said Jack. "Were you expecting someone a little less *petulant?*"

"We should have killed you the moment we teleported you aboard our ship."

"Well, now's your chance, jerk-face," said Jack. "Bring it."

Abraxas hurled a blast of death energy toward Jack. The chaotic ball screamed toward him, but again, Jack could suddenly see the energy for what it was — something he could control. As it neared him, Jack reached out with his own energy and redirected the projectile, sending it veering away from him and impacting the ground harmlessly.

Jack wasn't sure if the Deathlords had expressions behind their masks, but if they did, he took a little bit of pleasure in thinking that Abraxas was completely, and utterly, surprised.

"Uh, huh – that's right," said Jack, smugly. "I've learned a few new tricks since we last met. How ya like me now?"

Abraxas tilted his head, regarding Jack for a moment, before hurling another death blast at him. Jack swatted it away. Abraxas hurled two more. Again, Jack deflected them both with ease.

"I can do this all day, Abby," chided Jack.

"So, you've learned the ancient art of Servuchur," said Abraxas. "How did this come to be?"

Jack raised an eyebrow. Since this whole adventure had started, he'd figured out how to do a lot of things because of the Ancient brain-dump he'd been privy to. Speaking different languages, flying spaceships, and opening doors to temples at the center of planets – but he'd never heard of "Servuchur" before.

"I'm just... that awesome..." said Jack, not really knowing how to respond.

"Only the Void Lords have the knowledge of Servuchur," said Abraxas. "It was their gift to us when we were created. Our ultimate weapon handed down from our masters. How did one such as you come by it?"

"The Void Lords?" asked Jack. "They *created* you?"

Abraxas's eyes narrowed. "Are you... *him?*" the Deathlord asked.

Jack was starting to get pretty sick of never knowing what anyone was talking about. *"Him" who?* he wondered. Why was it nothing about the Deathlords ever made any sense?

"I'm Jack," he responded. "I'm the guy who's gonna beat you. And if these Void Lords are the ones calling the shots, then I'm pretty sure I'm gonna beat them, too."

In the distance, an ear-piercing screech rang out. Abraxas and Jack turned to see the haze of the Ghost Planet's doom thundering toward them. Suddenly, Abraxas leapt into the air, flying directly at Jack.

Before Jack had a chance to react, Abraxas landed on him, pinning him down with a knee to the chest, his clawed hand wrapping tightly around Jack's neck.

"Then I will ensure you die here, with me, Earthman," growled the Deathlord.

The screeching of the impending doom grew louder.

"Sorry, Abby…" said Jack as a large shadow grew over him.

Abraxas looked up to see the Ancient Earthship hovering overhead. He looked back down at Jack, the Deathlord's eyes wide with surprise.

"This time, you die alone."

And with that, Jack teleported onto the ship, disappearing in a flash of light.

The Deathlord looked up as the Earthship sped away, releasing one last defiant scream of anger as the Ghost Planet's doom swept over him. His body disintegrated, and his very essence was absorbed into the swirling chaos that was the Ghost Planet's final security measure.

Though it is impossible to know what was going through Warlord Abraxas's mind right before his ultimate defeat, one thing is for certain…

Earthman Jack had finally proven, once and for all, that you could indeed kill a Deathlord.

Chapter ✦ 45

Jack rematerialized onto the bridge of his ship in a spark of blue light, his friends all turning to him as soon as he appeared.

Man, thought Jack. *No one's ever around to hear my best lines.*

"Jack!" Anna cried as she rushed to his side. "Are you hurt?"

"Please. After taking out a Deathlord Supreme, that guy was a joke," replied Jack.

"Lad, next time I head to Vasgalas to hit the casinos, yer definitely comin' along," said Scallywag as he helped Jack to his feet. "Ya have enough luck to make even Osirus the White jealous."

"Thanks, I think," said Jack. "So no one got eaten by the angry evil tornado?"

"No, everyone's fine," responded Anna. She hugged Jack's arm and whispered in his ear. "You were right. It was soooooo creepy!"

"It would appear we were rather fortunate that your ship seems to have gained the ability to operate itself," replied Green. "Its timing was impeccable."

"Fly itself?" said Jack. "I made it to do that."

"You did what?" asked Heckubus.

"Psychic link to the spaceship, remember?" said Jack tapping his head. "I had it come get you guys. Think I'd run off and let you all get eaten by the dust storm of doom?"

"Well played, lad," smiled Scallywag.

"So, you're able to communicate with this ship and operate it mentally?" said Green his eyes wide with wonder. "Even from a distance?"

"Pretty much," replied Jack.

"Fascinating," responded Green and Heckubus at the same time, their minds buzzing with completely different ideas on how such a thing would be useful.

"Yeah, it's cool, I'm cool, the spaceship is totally awesome," said Jack offhandedly. "Now I don't know about the rest of you, but I am ready to get the heck out of here."

"Amen to that," said Scallywag as Jack hopped into the captain's chair. "Jump us away, lad. Preferably someplace tropical with cheap drinks."

"Um… yes, about that…" said Heckubus.

The group turned and looked at the robot in unison, a chill running through them collectively at the implication of his words.

"I'm afraid the ship's Entanglement Engine is not ready yet," Heckubus finished.

"What?" replied Jack. "That doesn't make any sense! It's had plenty of time to charge back up!"

"Robot," Scallywag sneered. "What did you do?"

"Don't act like this is my fault," retorted Heckubus. "Remember how you asked me to bolster the shields during our rather harrowing entrance here?"

"Don't tell me," said Jack, exasperation growing on his face.

"Yes, I had to divert energy from the Entanglement Engine," replied Heckubus. "I'm afraid that set us back a bit in its recharge cycle."

"The bloody planet is about to explode ya twit!" growled Scallywag.

"If you remember, at the time, that was not part of our plan," Heckubus shot back. "How was I to know we'd be rushing against the clock to escape a planetary explosion?"

Scallywag looked like he was about to pounce on the robot before Anna placed her hand on his arm to calm him.

"How much time before the Entanglement Engine is ready?" she asked.

Jack called up the information on the holoscreen. "Ten more minutes," he said.

"Well, that's not all that long," said Green cheerily. "How much time before the planet explodes?"

"Approximately nine minutes, by my calculations," said Heckubus.

Scallywag smacked his palm to his forehead.

"You gotta be kidding me," muttered Jack. The thought of them dying at this stage of the game, after all they'd just been through, did not sit well with him.

"Luckily for all of you, I was smart enough to anticipate this situation," Heckubus continued. "If we can get far enough from the planet before the explosion occurs, we'll be able to make up those sixty seconds and initiate the jump just before the shockwave reaches us."

"Get far enough away?" growled Scallywag. "We're surrounded by a bloody minefield!"

"Don't forget the space bugs," chimed in Jack.

"How could I? Or the fact that we're trapped inside a *bloody planetary shield!*"

"Oh, ye of little faith," twittered Heckubus. "While you all were off gallivanting around with the Deathlords, I was not here twiddling my thumbs idly. First of all, the chain reaction currently occurring in the planet's core will cause the planetary shield to dissipate in approximately 90 seconds. Once that happens, we use the enhanced shields I've been able to configure to simply punch through the mess of space insects that will surely swarm toward the planet, and then we make our way through the nebula with the enhanced engine speed I've engineered for you, avoiding the mines and the missiles with your newly upgraded sensors, and engaging the Entanglement Engine the moment it's ready, effectively jumping away to safety approximately 0.25 seconds before we're utterly destroyed by the explosion. It's quite simple really."

The group stared at Heckubus blankly. The robot squinted at them in response.

"What?" he asked.

"Well, better than nothing," sighed Jack. He turned the command chair to face the main viewscreen of the ship, commanding it to raise the shields and rev up the engines. "Buckle up, everyone. It's gonna be a bumpy ride."

Heckubus settled himself in front of an engineering console while Scallywag took his seat in front of the weapons station, grumbling as he did so. Anna joined Professor Green in front of the navigation console, while Grohm stood nearby, his massive hand wrapped around one of the bridge's railings.

Jack brought the Earthship around and began climbing into the sky toward the Ghost Planet's shield. What was once a solid golden shell was now discolored and chaotic, like oil trying to mix with water. It seemed to pulse like a lightbulb on the fritz. Behind its shell, Jack could make out a huge swarm of activity as the space bugs they'd brought with them surrounded the shield, trying to chew away at it.

"That's a lot of space bugs," muttered Jack, doubt and worry starting to take root in his gut.

"Fear not, Earthman," said Heckubus. "After extensive review of our last encounter, I'll assure you that our shields will now adequately protect the ship from them. The shields will not survive their onslaught; however, they shouldn't be able to damage us in any significant way before we break through their swarm."

"Great," said Scallywag. "Round two with mines and missiles and no bloody shields."

"After analyzing the Earthman's reflexes, I have no doubt we can avoid anything that might harm us in the nebula," replied the robot. "I've had the opportunity to apply one of my more experimental programs to the ship's sensors which should compensate for our previous lack of signal strength. It's never been tested in the field before. However, considering that I am, in fact, a genius, there is little doubt that—"

"Heckubus," interrupted Jack.

"Yes?"

"Shut up," he said.

"Hmph," muttered Heckubus as he went back to monitoring the ship's systems. "The slightest bit of insurmountable danger and you organics get so testy."

Jack checked the sensors. The planetary shield was about to go at any second. He took a deep breath and steeled himself. *Nothing more than level 19 on Nova Commander IV*, he thought to himself. *Time to finally break my top score.*

"Here we go," said Jack as he punched the ship's engines, accelerating fully toward the planet's shield. All across the viewscreen of the Earthship, holes began to form in the shield, like paper burned over a flame. The holes grew slowly as the energy of the shield died. Black tendrils made up of hundreds of trillions of insects shot through, greedily rushing toward the planet to consume anything they could find.

As he angled the ship toward a newly opening hole in the shield, Jack could almost feel his companions on the bridge tense their bodies, much as people brace themselves right before the apex of a rollercoaster ride. A swarm of black death rushed up to meet them as Jack pushed the engines as hard as he could.

An alarm sounded as the Earthship met the swarm, its shields rapidly depleting. Jack gritted his teeth as he felt his vessel shake from the impact of pushing through the swarm. In reality, it had happened in half a second, but it felt like it had been an eternity. After he broke through and saw the brilliant blue and purple of the surrounding nebula before him, he was finally able to breathe again.

"Ha, HA!" exclaimed Heckubus. "What did I tell you? Made it through without a scratch, and with 2% shield strength left to spare. Sometimes my brilliance even amazes me."

"Heckubus," said Jack.

"Yes?"

"Shut up," the group said in unison.

"So ungrateful," muttered the robot as he sullenly went back to monitoring his console.

"Oy, we got company," said Scallywag as his station beeped at him urgently. Jack called up a rear view on his holoscreen. The Ghost Planet was now covered with a swirling black mess, peppered with pale white oases where bits of its surface were still visible. But more disconcerting than the image of an entire planet in the process of being eaten, a large cloud of darkness trailed behind the Earthship as a swarm of the insects had broken off to pursue them.

And it was gaining.

"Those things are faster than I thought," said Jack.

"Bloody insects," growled Scallywag. "Ya got a whole sodding planet ya could eat! Why chase us?"

"It's quite simple really," chimed in Green. "They're predatory insects. They see prey; they pursue it. It's simply their nature to—"

"Professor," said Heckubus.

"Yes?"

"Shut up," the robot said.

Green blinked at Heckubus. "Not so nice when someone says it to you, hmmmm?" chided the robot smugly.

"Guys, get me everything you can to the engines and get our shields back up!" ordered Jack. They were racing toward the lip of the nebula, but even at their current speed Jack could tell the swarm would eventually overtake them. "Scally, shoot at them — see if that will at least slow them down."

"Aye-aye, capt'n," the pirate muttered, having already opened fire on the pursuing insects.

The red plasma blasts from the ship's rear battery tore through the swarm that was following them. Where they hit, the swarm briefly hollowed out but quickly reformed. If the blasts were indeed slowing them down, it was not by much.

The Earthship raced into the blue and purple of the nebula, the front viewscreen now just displaying an ocean of gorgeously colored gas. Jack called up the new enhanced sensors Heckubus had configured. On the viewscreen the ship quickly added wire-frame outlines in the shape of diamonds and orbs in various places on the readout, giving the whole thing the odd feel of a 1980's video game.

Jack's link with the ship instantly let him know that the diamonds seemed to be mines, and the orbs seemed to be missile platforms. He made a mental note to stay as far away from the orbs on the screen as possible.

All in all, there didn't seem to be that many around. As long as Jack had some idea where they were located, he felt confident their escape was all but guaranteed.

We may just get out of this yet, thought Jack, allowing a small smile of relief to form on his face.

Suddenly, out of nowhere, a mess of diamonds appeared on the viewscreen in front of them. Jack's heart leapt into his throat as he frantically jerked the ship into a corkscrew, narrowly missing the closest new mine that had magically appeared out of nowhere. A proximity alarm blared as they rushed deeper into a suddenly dense minefield. Jack did everything he could to bank and weave to avoid hitting them.

"Heckubus!" he screamed. "Fix your stupid sensors! They almost flew us right into a butt-ton of mines!"

"My sensors are working perfectly," the robot replied. "Those mines were not there a second ago."

"Mines just don't appear outta thin air," said Scallywag.

"Seriously?" said Heckubus as he stared down Scallywag. "After being on that planet, you're going to question instantly appearing minefields?"

Scallywag looked like he was about to say something, but then he acknowledged his defeat to logic. Grohm chuckled.

"Quiet, you," retorted Scallywag.

"Jack," said Anna. "Those circles... the missile platforms in the nebula... they're moving."

Jack checked his sensors. Sure enough, the circles seemed to be repositioning themselves toward the path of their ship.

"Son of a..." mumbled Jack.

"I say," said Green. "I don't suppose it's possible that those platforms aren't just for shooting missiles but perhaps for laying the mines, as well?"

"That would make sense," replied Heckubus. "My guess is they have some type of replication technology allowing them to create missiles and mines as needed. It could be as simple as them tracking ship movements and teleporting mines into their path."

"Great!" sneered Scallywag. "How the bloody hell do we avoid a minefield that can appear right in front of us?"

"Easy," said Jack. "We don't fly in a straight line."

With that, Jack began to bank and weave the ship, pulling it into wide arcs and corkscrews. The wireframe diamonds on the viewscreen started popping up, but quickly moved out of the way as Jack tried his best to keep the ship's path random – all the while keeping an eye on the rearview as the space bugs struggled to keep up with them.

"It's working!" said Anna. "The platforms aren't able to pinpoint our trajectory, and the insects are having a hard time following your movements."

"I say, nice flying my boy!" cheered Green. "Top notch!"

"Yes, yes, yes - if you enjoy *dying*," chimed in Heckubus. "At this rate we will not reach our minimum distance in time to outrun the explosion!"

With a few taps at his console, Heckubus brought up a glowing blue ring on Jack's sensor readout, indicating the mark he'd have to meet in order to be far enough away from the explosion to make the jump safely. And, at the top of his holoscreen, was a clock rapidly counting down the time they had left to do it.

"If we don't reach that mark in four minutes, we're all dead," said the robot ominously.

Jack clenched his jaw and looked at the goal line Heckubus had drawn for him. The robot was right; avoiding the minefield and the insects was just slowing them down. Whether they were blown up by a mine, eaten by space bugs, or evaporated in a ginormous explosion, the outcome was all the same.

Jack thought about all the harrowing situations he'd been in recently – the escape from the Pit, the fight through the Deathlord mothership, the showdown with Zarrod and Abraxas. They had all been as bad as this, if not worse. In each of those situations, death and defeat had stared him right in the face. Yet he'd survived them all. How?

Then, he remembered Major Ganix in the Pit, and the mantra that had carried them out of an impossible situation. When faced with a dire outcome, where you're doomed no matter what you do, there's only one preferable choice.

If you gotta die, die advancing, Jack thought.

"Everyone listen up," he said, his voice so sure and steady it hit the group on the bridge like a blast from a speaker cranked to the max. "Divert power from all non-essential systems to the engines – shields, weapons, everything that's not needed to keep us breathing. Give me all the speed you can squeak out of this ship. Heckubus, do what you can to overclock the engines. If we're gonna die, it's not gonna be because we couldn't outrun this explosion."

"But what about—" Scallywag started to say.

"Let me worry about it," cut off Jack. The mines, the bugs, anything else that could conceivably pop up – it didn't matter. This was Jack's ship, these were Jack's friends, and no matter what was going to get in his way, he was determined not to lose any of them.

After all, if there's one thing everyone should know about Earthman Jack by now...

He hated to lose.

Jack straightened out their trajectory and gunned the engines. The increase in speed from the power diversion his group had initiated wasn't a lot, but it was noticeable. The lights on the bridge dimmed and the cabin started to grow colder as the energy was diverted from life support and electrical. What was left of the ship's shields on Jack's readout quickly disappeared, and the only things running were the main thrusters and the Entanglement Engine.

More mines popped up on the screen, their wire-frame outlines quickly rushing up to greet them. Jack didn't break course. He flew into the minefield, only minutely adjusting his trajectory to avoid running into any head-on. Mines exploded and rocked the ship as it flew by too closely.

Jack glanced at the rearview, and the dark cloud of space bugs was still there, shying away from the exploding mines while still slowly creeping up behind the ship, relentless and hungry.

The clock continued to tick away, its numbers racing by as a constant reminder of the impending danger, even as the ship got closer and closer to the goal line.

Three minutes.

More mines appeared. This time Jack had to bank away and corkscrew back into position to avoid running into them. He cursed under his breath. What had that cost them? Ten seconds? Would that be the difference between life and death?

The swarm grew larger in his viewscreen, gaining on the ship's tail.

The finish line loomed on his sensor screen, so close, yet still so far away.

Two minutes.

"Heckubus, get me more speed!" said Jack urgently. "I need more power!"

"I'm giving her all we've got," replied the robot. "If I push it any harder, the whole thing will blow."

Red lights bleeped on his sensor array as the back of Jack's head tingled. The ship was warning him of a new danger as a nearby platform launched two missiles directly toward them.

"Incoming!" yelled Scallywag to no one in particular.

The missiles gained on the ship, the sensor array in front of Jack showing him their steadily encroaching position.

He glanced back at the countdown: 60 seconds.

More mines materialized. Jack didn't bother to change course, choosing to rush right into the minefield, again making only minor adjustments to avoid getting hit. The ship rattled as it was rocked by explosion after explosion from the narrowly missed mine strikes.

Jack could feel those in the cabin with him collectively holding their breaths. Then he realized he, too, had stopped breathing as his focus on the task in front of him consumed all effort of his mind and body. In his rearview, the swarm had almost caught up with them, nipping at their tail like a chained rabid dog about to break loose.

More alerts popped up on his sensor reading. More missiles had been launched from another platform. The previous two were closing in fast.

He kept the ship on course and steadily rocketed toward the finish line.

Jack could feel his heart racing as he glanced back at the clock, blood pounding in his ears and behind his eyes.

10 – 9 – 8 – 7...

The line on the sensor reading grew closer...

6 – 5 – 4...

Closer. Closer...

3 – 2...

The Earthship crossed the line.

Then, a flash of light so bright and massive occurred that the blue and purple of the nebula lit up like a neon sign. Jack looked at his rear display and saw a hazy glow far in the distance where the Ghost Planet had been, its dying image so bright he could even see it through the nebula's cloud.

Remember, back when the Earth had been destroyed, it was established that when a planet blows up, there isn't simply some sort of massive explosion and suddenly the entire thing has vanished in a violent ball of fire. Normally, this would be correct. However, since this explosion was caused by the collapse of a massive quantum energy flux upon itself thanks to the Deathlord mothership's main weapon, it is an entirely different situation all together.

Forget about exploding with the power of a hundred quadrillion nuclear weapons. This type of explosion was, for lack of a better word, biblical.

The explosion that occurred after the collapse of the Ghost Planet's unstable core evaporated everything it touched – stone, metal, dirt, the space bugs, and whatever was left of the Deathlord mothership and every one of its inhabitants.

It spread out in all directions from its epicenter, soundlessly raging forth with a might and fury of such epic proportions, there are simply no words that can be used to adequately describe it.

The force of the blast was so great, in fact, that any dust, particles, and debris that weren't instantly consumed were pushed away from it on a shockwave that rocketed forth in every direction, growing in power as it moved, the herald of the quantum destruction that was following in its wake.

"Great Observer…" Green said breathlessly.

"Holy kitten," said Scallywag.

"Oh… crap," said Grohm.

The buzzing in the back of Jack's head grew loud and urgent as the ship screamed at him about the oncoming destruction. Jack's first instinct was to toss some power to the shields, but a glance at his readout told him that if he slowed down, even for a bit, the space bugs or the missiles would reach them before the explosion did.

Jack called up the Entanglement Engine. It was almost ready, just a little bit longer.

The ship started to shake, every chair and console rattling violently as the shockwave raced up behind them.

The swarm that was pursuing them started to nip at their tail, the ship complaining as parts of its aft section began to be stripped off.

Jack could see the missiles on the sensors, racing forward, almost right on their location.

C'mon c'mon c'mon... thought Jack urgently, every muscle in his body tensed, his jaw clenched so tight his teeth were starting to hurt.

The nebula behind them rolled back upon itself, like storm clouds assaulted by a violent wind, forming a tidal wave of destruction that was about to come crashing into the Earthship without mercy. The light from the explosion that followed it grew exponentially.

Almost there, thought Jack as he watched the charging screen for the Entanglement Engine. *Almost there...*

The red bar on his readout indicating the recharge cycle on the Entanglement Engine continued to fill, bit by bit, little by little, almost to full.

"COME ON!!!!!" Jack screamed at his ship, as though willing it to complete the charging as the missiles came within striking range and the remaining swarm of insects threatened to envelop it.

Then, with a friendly "ding," the ship signaled that the Entanglement Engine was finally ready.

Jack engaged the engine just as the shockwave rushed up, catching the missiles and the swarm of space bugs in its violent fury. The Earthship flipped to the side, turning chaotically as the crest of the shockwave caught up with it, the light of an Entanglement jump filling its metal hull with a brilliant glow.

And just like that, with milliseconds to spare, the Earthship jumped away to safety as the Ghost Planet's final fury continued its rampage, consuming everything in its path.

CHAPTER ✵ 46

Anna rubbed her eyes. After crying for so long, they were red and itchy, and completely emptied. No matter how much she felt like it, she just couldn't shed any more tears.

She gazed at Shepherd's face, his expression peaceful, as though he were merely sleeping. He was still clad in his armor, laid out on the bed of the medical bay with his hands folded across his chest. Her heart heavy with sorrow, she gazed at him and wiped her nose with the back of her hand. After all she had been through with the torture the Deathlords had inflicted, nothing they had done hurt as much as seeing her protector like this.

Cold. Still. Lifeless.

She had hazy memories of her mother and father. Being from the royal bloodline, their likenesses would never be forgotten to history. But after so long, Anna could barely remember a thing about them. Since the day they had died, Shepherd had been the one who had taken care of her. He was the closest thing she had to family.

And now he was gone.

In the chaos of their escape from the Ghost Planet, she hadn't even noticed he was missing. Everything had happened so fast, she hadn't had time to think about her beloved guardian's absence. It wasn't until after they had jumped to safety and the celebratory high of succeeding in making it out alive had wound down that Jack had broken the news to her.

He had taken her into the medical bay, her brain still numb from the tragic revelation, and she had seen Shepherd's body. It had been a surreal experience for her, as though the whole world dropped away the moment she had seen him lying there, and a cold feeling of emptiness had taken root in her stomach. Jack told her Shepherd had a message for her – his last words before he died.

Be strong.

It was at that moment she had broken down. The tears had flowed out uncontrollably. She had cried out, hugging Shepherd's body as she collapsed on top of it, as though she were not able to bear the weight of the situation. Jack had tried to comfort her, but he might as well have not even been there; she had been so lost in her grief. Eventually, he had left her alone to mourn.

Anna didn't know how long she'd been in the medical bay or how long she'd cried. But it had been long enough for the feelings of sadness and grief to subside and for her to be left feeling exhausted and empty.

She reached out and stroked Shepherd's head, her hand brushing over his short, buzzed hair, feeling both prickly and soft at the same time. She bent over and kissed Shepherd on the forehead gently.

Be strong.

She could almost hear him saying the words. Even as he was dying, Shepherd's thoughts were of protecting her: one last order, one last piece of advice, one last mantra to live by.

How she now wished she'd taken more time to appreciate him. The things he did that annoyed her so much... how she'd give anything to experience those moments again. His overprotective ways, his tendency to order her around as if he knew what was best for her, his stubbornness – she wished she hadn't spent so much time resenting those things.

Be strong.

"I will," Anna whispered, her voice cracking. "If I can be half as strong as you, I'll be able to survive anything."

Anna breathed deeply and sighed, letting the last bit of sorrow flow out of her with the breath. She was still sad, and most likely would be for some time, but her grief had passed, and the world around her was returning into focus – the friendly metal of the walls, the soft, warm lighting of the room, the beeps and blips of the medical equipment. And suddenly she realized where she was – safe and sound on the Earthship, rescued from certain doom by an Earthboy, without any help or guidance in the least.

And at that moment she realized that though her losses had been great, she also had a lot to be thankful for.

When Anna entered the bridge of the ship, the image of the Ghost Planet's destruction played over and over again on a holoscreen. Heckubus Moriarty, the greatest criminal mind in eight star systems – and now self-proclaimed "destroyer of worlds" – watched the recording with glee.

"Mwuahahahaha!" the robot laughed. "Mwuahaha... MWUAHAHAHAHA... MWU-hahahahahaha!!!!"

Anna gave him a curious look as she approached Scallywag, who was lazily sitting at the navigation terminal with his feet kicked up, examining the back of his hand as though he were looking for some type of change in it.

"Is that robot malfunctioning?" asked Anna.

"Mwuahahahahahahahahaaaa!" Heckubus laughed.

"Bloody tin can's been laughing like that fer the last hour," mumbled Scallywag. "Thinks he's all hot stuff because he hatched a plan that blew up a blasted planet. Now we'll never hear the end o' it."

Anna smiled. She hadn't known this odd band of rogues long, but if anything, they certainly were colorful.

"Have you seen Jack?" she asked.

"I think he's somewhere to the aft," he said. As Anna began to walk away, Scallywag piped up again. "Oy, by the way, Your Majesty…"

Anna stopped and turned to face the pirate.

"I hope when we return ya safe and sound back ta civilization, you'll remember all I did ta risk my rather pretty neck to save yers."

Anna nodded. "Don't worry," she said. "I promise your good deeds will not be forgotten."

Scallywag smiled smugly and sat back in his chair.

"Nor will all the bad ones you commit from here on out, either." finished Anna.

The quickness with which Scallywag's smile disappeared was enough to let her know she'd made herself clear, and she abruptly headed toward the back of the ship in search of Jack.

"Mwuahahahahahahahahahahahaha!!!!!" laughed Heckubus as the Ghost Planet blew up, yet again.

"Oh, shut up!" said Scallywag sullenly.

On her way out, she saw Grohm standing in the corner, the Rognok gazing out the viewport at the swirling fractals of lightspeed as they sped by. Anna approached him and gently touched his arm. The large alien looked down at her.

"Grohm," she said. "Thank you so much for bringing Shepherd to the ship and for coming to rescue me. When we get back to Imperial space, if there is ever anything I can do for you – anything at all – please, just let me know. I was in your debt before, but now I shall be forever grateful."

Grohm grunted and turned back to the view. For some reason, Anna thought he looked sad, but then again, it was always hard to tell what, if anything, Rognoks were feeling.

After exiting the bridge, Anna made her way down the hallway toward the aft of the ship. She'd just started to explore the rooms when Professor Green came walking out of one and looked at her with a big toothy grin.

"Ah, Princess," he said, bowing slightly. "How are you feeling?"

"Better, thank you," replied Anna. Green had been close to Shepherd, as well. She knew he'd be dealing with his own grief of the loss, but one of the things she had always admired about the Professor was his tendency to put the well-being of others before himself. "I see you're exploring as well."

"Indeed!" he said excitedly. "Out of everything I've seen these last few days, this ship still manages to amaze me. To think, a machine that can perform quantum manifestation! Can you imagine the possibilities?"

Anna smiled. "Any I don't think of, I'm sure you will."

"Yes, yes, yes. Why, not long ago, I was thinking how wonderful it would be to get back to my lab and start collecting my findings from our rather harrowing adventure. And lo-and-behold…"

The Professor stepped to the door he had just come out of, and it opened with a hiss. Anna glanced inside to see a room so cluttered it was a wonder anyone could navigate through it at all. Bookshelves, file cabinets, and computers of various ages and states of disrepair lining the lime green walls were overflowing with books, charts, graphs, doohickeys, and artifacts from around the galaxy. Monitors, mounted in odd places, were displaying various bits of scientific data, and the lushly maroon-carpeted floor was pimpled with piles of books, papers, and data pads. Somewhere at the center of the mess was a large elderwood desk, practically overflowing with papers marred with various scribblings, which Anna could only assume were the Professor's notes.

"This is your lab?" Anna asked.

"Exactly how I remember it," replied the Professor with a happy sigh. "Everything is perfect, to a tee. Even the half-eaten ugonabutter sandwich on my desk."

Anna raised an eyebrow. "Um... you didn't..."

"It was still delicious," said the Professor, licking his lips.

Anna giggled. "We'll have to see about manifesting you a maid to go along with your new quarters."

"Your Majesty, don't be ridiculous!" said Green. "I know exactly where everything is. Someone cleaning up after me will only serve to ensure I'll never be able to find a thing. Besides, in my opinion, a clean desk is the sign of an inactive mind."

Anna nodded and smiled. "Far be it from me to ruin your system of organization, Professor. You haven't seen Jack around, have you?"

"But of course!" Green responded. "After he explained to me about the ship's quantum manifestation ability, he led me here and helped me to recreate my lab."

"And where is he now?"

"Oh!" exclaimed Green, as though the idea that Anna actually wanted to see Jack had just occurred to him. "I believe he retired three doors down, on the right if I'm not mistaken."

"Thank you, Professor. I'll leave you to get back to recording your notes."

"Yes, yes, yes. Best to do it while the memories are fresh. Wouldn't want to forget anything important. But where to begin? Where to begin? Why, there's the Deathlord language, their apparent religious fundamentalism, their propensity to espouse megalomaniacal monologues..."

Anna left the Professor mumbling to himself about all the things he needed to write down and headed to the door he'd indicated. She hesitated a second in front of it, not sure if she should just enter unannounced. For a moment, she had the same feeling in her stomach that she'd had the first time she'd sought Jack out, walking from her house up to his on Eagle Hill and knocking on his door, unsure of what was going to happen. It was a nervous kind of excitement, something she was surprised she could still feel after all they'd just been through.

She knocked on the door. After a moment, it hissed open, revealing a room with which Anna was already familiar.

The discolored ceiling tiles scarred with water damage, broken up occasionally by dirty plastic panels that housed the unflattering fluorescent lights she had always disliked. Rows of abused single-seat desks were arranged from the back of the room to the front, atop the scuffed light beige tiles of the floor. The large chalkboard at the head of the room was in bad need of a cleaning, and Shepherd's desk was off to the side, neat and empty, with a stack of pink demerit slips on it ready to be issued.

Against the far wall were three windows, recessed slightly into it. Normally, they would have had a view of the school's parking lot with the edge of the football field and an ocean of corn stalks in the distance, but now they had the beautiful and chaotic swirl of blue and white lightspeed rushing by.

Jack sat on the sill of the window by Shepherd's desk. His legs kicked up casually ran the length of it. His head leaned up against the glass as he stared out into the haze of lightspeed. He'd changed back into his jeans and t-shirt, and his hair looked rumpled and uncombed in a way Anna couldn't help but feel suited him perfectly. If it weren't for the view, Anna would have sworn she was back on Earth. When she entered, he looked at her and smiled.

"Hey," he said.

Anna put her hands on her hips and looked around. "Really?" she smiled. "A ship that can manifest any location you desire, and you choose homeroom?"

"Don't be hating," Jack replied. "Believe it or not, I learned some important stuff here."

"Oh, yeah? Such as?"

"Meh. It's kinda hard to explain. Let's just say that this place helps me think."

Anna walked up to the window and leaned against the sill. "And here I thought out of all the things that've been blown up lately, this would be the place you'd miss the least..."

Anna caught herself just as she finished talking, embarrassment flushing her face. "I'm so sorry," she said. "I... that was me trying to be funny."

Jack laughed. "It's cool," he said.

"No, no, it isn't. I lost somebody, but you... your family, your friends... everything – it's not something to be joking about."

"It wouldn't be..." responded Jack, "if I'd really lost them."

Anna looked at Jack quizzically. "What?" she asked.

Jack grinned at her as if he knew a secret she didn't. "Something happened when I busted open that Great Seal on the Ghost Planet. Something that makes me think they can be saved."

"Who?"

"My mom," said Jack. "My friends. Shepherd. Everyone."

Anna furrowed her brow as if Jack's words were too difficult to comprehend.

"Jack," she said. "You're not making any sense."

"Hey, I gave up on sense the minute aliens shot up the Burger Shack."

Anna couldn't keep herself from chuckling at that. She caught Jack's eyes and felt her heart flutter slightly. She may be a galactic princess, but to him, she was still that somewhat socially awkward girl from West Virginia, trying her first milkshake on a date that felt like it happened decades ago. And for some reason, that made her feel good. She reached over and placed her hand on top of Jack's.

"Tell me what happened to you," she said.

Jack shifted on the windowsill a tad uncomfortably. He licked his lips as if to get them ready to form words he didn't quite know how to speak.

"I saw my dad," he said softly.

"Your dad?" asked Anna.

"I know, right?" said Jack. "I don't know if it was a figment of my imagination... like some strange electrically induced hallucination that just showed me the thing I wanted to see the most... but if that were the case, why wouldn't it have been my mom? I hadn't seen my dad in forever – didn't even remember what he looked like anymore. Except it felt real. HE felt real. As real as you and I are right now."

"What did he say?" asked Anna.

"A bunch of stupid stuff," muttered Jack. "He was being all cryptic and not making any sense. Didn't even bother to mention he was my dad until I was being sucked away by a weird vortex thingy."

Anna looked at Jack quizzically.

"Yeah," Jack responded. "I don't know how else to explain it."

"I've navigated a lot of Ancient technology, Jack," said Anna. "But I've never encountered another person while doing so. Or a weird vortex thingy for that matter. Of course, I've never broken open a Great Seal either. But my guess is whatever you were exposed to, on some level, you know how to access it."

"That's kinda what he said," replied Jack. "Like, my brain downloaded everything that was in the Great Seal and is hiding it all somewhere 'cause if I remembered it, my head would explode or something."

Anna laughed.

"What? What'd I say?" asked Jack. "Does my head blowing up amuse you?"

"No, not at all, it's just... the brain's not a computer, Jack," said Anna. "It can't *download* stuff."

Jack blinked, confused. "But then... how do I know all these weird things? Like, how can I understand these alien languages and speak them?"

"I actually have a theory about that," said Anna. "For whatever reason, I think the Ancients wanted your people to find this ship. And when they did, they wanted your people to be ready to meet with the other races of the galaxy. So the access orb was meant to prepare whatever Earthman touched it for venturing out into the universe."

"So you're saying that access orb thing taught me every language in the universe?"

"It didn't teach you, it opened your mind to them."

"What's the difference?"

"The Ancients had a different way of sharing knowledge than most of us do, Jack," explained Anna. "They believed that all knowledge already exists, and that our minds don't learn things, so much as we open them to what's already there. Do you remember the words you spoke that opened the temple that housed this ship?"

"Kinda hard to forget them," said Jack. "Eldil Meldilorn."

Anna nodded. "That's the Ancient language of Old Solar. It was the mantra of the Ancients and the code by which Paragons live. It's also the philosophy around which the entire Regalus Empire is based. It means 'free your mind.' When you free your mind and allow yourself to shed its constraints, you can tap into any knowledge in the universe. Anything you want to know, you realize you already know. You just needed to open your mind to it."

"So, the access orb helped to open my mind to all the languages of the universe?"

"Probably to all the languages that ever existed and ever will exist, which is highly unusual, since freeing one's mind typically can't be assisted by machines. I'm guessing that because your species evolved under the influence of Ancient technology at the core of your planet, you have some type of pre-disposition to be affected by it. That would allow your mind to be opened more easily than the minds of other species. Couple that with the fact that you're young and your brain is still forming... that would make you the perfect test subject."

"Whoa. So I'm like... special, right? Ancient technology can give my brain super powers?"

"I'm saying your entire race was special," smiled Anna. "There's no telling what the people of Earth would have been capable of, if this is true."

Jack was quiet for a moment. "But, why does it only work sometimes and not others?" Jack asked. "After I broke open the Great Seal, I could do some kick-butt stuff. But now, it doesn't seem to be working."

"Freeing one's mind is a complicated thing," said Anna. "I've been in training to do it almost all my life, and I still don't fully understand it. Shepherd was one of the most talented Paragons I'd ever met, and even he would struggle with it. We all put limitations on our minds without even knowing it. We can spend all our efforts to open our minds, and then fall back into bad habits that close them off again. Maybe in your case, you were able to open your mind when you needed to, and after the need passed, your brain allowed it's former limitations to settle in."

Jack frowned. "So no superpowers anymore, huh?"

Anna shrugged. "Well, you did it once. Maybe you can do it again?"

"Yeah, if I figure out how to open my stupid mind."

"Well, from what I know, the first step is always the hardest," said Anna. "But after you've been exposed to knowledge once, it's easier to access it. Whatever you were exposed to when the Great Seal fell, that's knowledge you are now aware of, even if you're not conscious of it. Which means that with the right training and discipline, maybe you can access it again."

"Training and discipline, eh?" smiled Jack. "You realize this is me we're talking about, right?"

Anna giggled. "I wouldn't sell yourself short, Earthman. I think you've proven beyond any doubt that you are, in fact, pretty awesome."

Jack's chest puffed up slightly at Anna's compliment, and he flashed a smug smile. "You forgot incredibly good looking, brave, smart, and most of all – modest."

Anna couldn't help but laugh and nod good-naturedly in agreement. "You are all that and more, yes," she said. "When we get back to Omnicron Prime, you will be a fine addition to my service."

At that, Anna noticed Jack's smile fade slightly. "That is," she quickly added, "if you still plan on entering into it."

Jack was quiet for a moment before speaking. "After Earth was destroyed, Shepherd told me that if I were going to survive, I'd have to find a cause to devote my life to. He told me it would give my existence meaning, because a cause can't be destroyed, it can't be corrupted, and it will live on far beyond me, even if I were to die. A cause could be a testament to my people, my planct, and myself. Something that will carry on in their honor, forever."

"That sounds like Shepherd," said Anna sadly.

Jack looked at her and smiled. "I had decided to make my cause the same as his. It was going to be you, Anna."

"Going to be?" asked Anna. "Not any more?"

Jack shook his head. "Don't get me wrong. I'll be there for you no matter what. But..."

Anna raised an eyebrow. "What?" she asked.

Jack looked at Anna dead on, more confidently than he ever had before.

"I'm going to save Earth," said Jack, "And every other planet the Deathlords have destroyed. And bring back everyone they've ever killed."

Anna looked at Jack, the conviction in his voice ringing in her ears. He sounded so sure, but as much as she wanted to believe him, as desperately as she wanted his words to be true, she just couldn't bring herself to accept them.

"Is... is that even possible?" she asked.

"Anything's possible," responded Jack. "Right?"

"But to bring back the dead? To restore all that's been destroyed? How do you do it?"

"No idea," said Jack. "But I know it *can* be done."

"Are you sure?"

"I've never been so sure of anything in my life."

Anna nodded. *Shepherd*, she thought. If what Jack was saying were true, he could be brought back. Her mother and father could be brought back. Her brothers, too. Everyone who had lost their lives, both on Earth and Regalus Prime. It was almost too good to be true. Never in history had there been any record of bringing back the dead. But then again, she'd seen a lot of things lately that had no precedence in history. Could this be true? And if so, how?

"The Great Seal," said Anna, the wheels in her brain turning. "Professor Green said... it contained the knowledge of how to manifest life."

Jack nodded. "Knowledge we freed. Knowledge that can now be discovered."

"Knowledge that could allow us to somehow... recreate what's been lost?"

Jack shrugged. "Recreation, time travel, quantum manifestation, cloning, mad science, mad libs, a partridge in a pear tree – you're asking the wrong guy. I have no idea how it's possible. But I know what we need to do it."

"You do?"

Jack nodded. He leaned toward her, and Anna inched closer to him, her growing excitement visible.

"You know that Ancient weapon you were searching for? The one that could defeat the Deathlords once and for all?"

Anna's eyes sparkled as a glimmer of hope shot into them. She nodded.

"That's what we'll need."

"Do you know where to find it?" Anna asked.

"Not yet," said Jack. "But I know where to start looking."

"Where?"

Jack leaned back and put his arms casually behind his head.

"Ever hear of a place called Khoruhar?"

Anna's mind raced to find an answer. "No," she said.

"That's where it is," said Jack. "And when we get back to your planet, that's what I'm going to start searching for. We're going to find this weapon of the Ancients, and when we do, we're going to save our planets, our friends, our families, and kick the Deathlords' sorry butts back to hell where they belong."

"This is your new cause?"

"Yep."

"And you really think you can do it?"

Jack leaned in and looked Anna in the eyes. His gaze was confident and steady, and somewhere in the back of her mind, he reminded her of Shepherd. When he spoke, deep inside Anna's heart, all doubt disappeared.

"Count on it," he said.

EPILOGUE

heavy blue light, with nothing but pitch black outside its harsh circle, shone down from above and encircled Zarrod like a noose ready to constrict.

Stripped of his armor, his body seemed long and gangly. It was a new body, not nearly as strong and opulent as his former one. No doubt this, too, would be part of his punishment, relegated to a weaker form... should he survive his current circumstance.

In the darkness, high above him on ornate thrones, sat three robed and hooded figures. The avatars of his masters — each with a face of smooth stone with three holes, two for eyes, one for a mouth — were illuminated by a light signaling that the avatars were being used by his Lords. They gazed down upon him in harsh judgment. The one on the left was possessed by a sickly green light. The one to the right, a deep blood red. And the one in the middle glimmered with a harsh purple.

Zarrod's entire body ached under their gaze. He had one knee on the ground, the other up to his chest with his hands rested atop it. His head was bowed low. He dared not look upon the face of his masters, or even their avatars, at a moment like this.

He had been summoned almost immediately upon his resurrection, where he then learned the extent of his defeat. Zarrod's first reaction was disbelief, for the sheer scale of the failure was unlike anything he could have possibly imagined. To think that it was not only he who had been destroyed, but also all who followed him — by a single, solitary Earthman.

His Lords spoke, their voices booming, washing over Zarrod like a foul wind that caused him to cringe under its might. Their words stung his ears like they were filled with vicious insects, and he felt shame assault every fiber of his being as they talked.

"Zarrod," they said. "You have disappointed us."

Zarrod felt a stinging sensation in his chest. To fail his Lords was the greatest horror any Deathlord could comprehend.

"Our entire Planetkiller fleet destroyed. The Invincible Armada lost. All our plans are now in disarray."

"Your failure is unforgivable."

"Yes, my Lords," said Zarrod. "You have every right to destroy me for my failure, and I will accept your ultimate judgment. I simply ask you grant me one final plea."

The three robed figures sitting above gazed down on him for a moment, weighing his words.

"Proceed," they responded.

"You have a new enemy, my Lords. One none could have foreseen. He is the reason our fleet was destroyed. He is the reason we lost our armada. He is the one who defeated me."

"You speak of this... *Earthman?*"

"Yes," said Zarrod. "Somehow he was able to gain knowledge of Servuchur."

"Impossible."

"It is true, my Lords. He used it on me himself."

"How can this be?"

"I do not know, my Lords. But I know this Earthman. I made the mistake of underestimating him and paid for it dearly. Should you choose to have another of your servants deal with him, they may suffer the same fate."

"What are you suggesting?"

"Grant me your permission to pursue him. I will be patient, methodical. I will learn of our enemy, discover how he came to possess your sacred knowledge, and when the time is right, I will strike him down."

"And why should we let one such as you, who has already failed us, have such an important task?"

"Because I am familiar with him. I have spoken to him. Gotten insight into how he acts and thinks. But most of all, I have the motivation to succeed – more motivation than any other to whom you could grant such a task. Not only for your glory, my Lords. Not just for the sake of my life. But for the thing which you, above all, hold most holy and righteous – revenge."

Silence greeted Zarrod's plea. For a moment, he was afraid his Lords would reject his request. But then, they spoke.

"You shall be stripped of all rank and position. You are no longer a Deathlord Supreme, and you will not be granted full mastery of Servuchur as you were before."

"Your new task shall be to hunt down this Earthman and to kill him once you learn how he came to possess our sacred knowledge."

"And after you have achieved your revenge and eliminated this threat, you shall be culled for your failure."

Zarrod felt an odd sensation run up his back. It was a cold, tingling chill. He knew he was to be punished, and the thought of getting his revenge should have been enough to satiate him. The punishment his masters were handing down was deserved – he had indeed failed them. It had always been enough for him to do as they wished, and he had experienced no greater satisfaction than carrying out their will, even if that will was that he should ultimately be destroyed.

But something was different now. Ever since his experience with the Great Seal, something had changed. He didn't know what it was, or even how to describe it, but it was there, like a gnat buzzing around his head too small to see or to catch.

Memories of his time on the Ghost Planet flashed into his mind. He remembered the feeling of the energy from the Great Seal tearing through him. The visions he experienced had been overwhelming and terrifying, even to him – so much so that he had felt relegated to a single essence of darkness. It was as though his mind and soul were so lacking compared to the majesty of what was before him, that he existed in a state of complete emptiness.

The memories were hazy and jumbled, but the feelings were not. He could remember the sheer terror he had felt – an emotion he had never experienced before at such a level. In his panic he had done something... wrapped himself around something... it was a message of some type, a message the Ancient heretics had meant to be discovered.

Zarrod could not remember what it was, though. It had gone somewhere, and taken him with it. During that time, he had almost lost himself, and only after he had begun to strike out and fight it, had he returned to his body. But he had taken something back with him, something that was not meant for a Deathlord to possess.

Whatever had changed him raged within him now. It coursed through his body, growing more acute with each passing second. It tingled in the back of his very essence, refusing to go away – violating every thought and feeling he'd ever had.

In that moment, when his sentence was handed down, he... *felt* something. Something he had never experienced when it came to his masters...

Resentment.

Zarrod knew what it meant to be culled. To have his essence ripped from him. To have his consciousness obliterated.

It should not have scared him. He was their faithful servant, with the only goal of his existence being to serve them. In his mind, he knew that he should be grateful they were allowing him one final task before receiving his punishment. But at his core, he felt completely different.

In his gut, he did not want to be culled. And that meant something unprecedented – that meant he actually wanted to defy his masters.

At that moment, Zarrod, the culler of worlds, master of darkness, and bane to all that was living, finally understood what it was like to *want* to live.

"I thank you for your wise judgment, my Lords," said Zarrod, careful to conceal his true feelings. "I swear to you, your will shall be done."

"See that it is," his masters said. "You will not be given another chance."

"Now go forth, and serve your masters," they said in unison. "Serve the Lords of the Void."

With that, the glow left his masters' avatars, their smooth stone heads slumping down now that they had been released. The light from above faded, and Zarrod found himself back in the Central Temple of Akkadia, the most holy location for Deathlords, for this was where they communed with their Lords. His ship had had its own temple where his masters had left their orders infused into an avatar, which then had instructed him when he was a Supreme. But that paled in comparison to where he was now.

Zarrod got to his feet, his body stiff and awkward. His mind raced as he tried to understand the emotions he was feeling. They were new, yet familiar, as though he'd experienced them before, a lifetime ago. Did he really want to defy his masters? Could he?

Yes, he thought. *Yes, I do. And yes, I can.*

It was then he realized that he had indeed been a slave. All that time serving his Lords, he had never truly had a choice. His actions had never actually been his own. He had been an extension of their will, programmed to behave in a way his masters had dictated - never questioning, always serving. He had no real sense of self, just like every other Deathlord. His species had been designed to feel joy at death and destruction; to take satisfaction in nothing but serving their masters; to blindly follow orders and to do what they were told, without exception. They were nothing more than mere robots.

But all that had changed. The Great Seal had done something to him. It had given him something he'd never known he was lacking – free will – the ability to think for himself and to do what he wanted, not just what he was commanded.

Zarrod realized that had been what he'd felt since he was resurrected. Independence. The feeling of freedom was strange and foreign to him, yet liberating at the same time. It was like he'd taken his first step into a new world, unshackled from the chains of servitude that had kept him imprisoned for so long.

In that instant, Zarrod couldn't help but laugh. He was no longer a Deathlord Supreme; this was true. But he had been transformed into something far more powerful. Something not even his masters could anticipate – a Deathlord who could think for himself and could do as he wished beyond the influence of his Lords – a Deathlord with his own consciousness.

A Deathlord with the potential to free his mind.

And what could a Deathlord with a free mind accomplish? Could he get his revenge? Could he kill every one of his enemies? Could he rise up and even overthrow his own gods?

All that and more, thought Zarrod as the genesis of a plan began to form in his mind. And at its center was the Earthman.

For some reason, he was the key to what had transformed Zarrod. Yes, he would kill him, and yes, he'd make the child suffer before he did. But not right away. Zarrod would need to take his time, to play along with his "masters" so that they would not notice what he was up to.

In the meantime, though, he'd have to focus on something else... something that had been rattling around in his brain like a caged animal desperate to break free... something that had been in his mind ever since the Great Seal had shattered. He did not know what it meant, what it was, or why it was so important. But he knew he had to find it, and quickly, because it was the key to his ultimate revenge. And all he had to go on was a single, solitary word...

Khoruhar.

Earthman Jack will return in…

EARTHMAN JACK

VS.

THE SECRET ARMY

SPECIAL THANKS TO:

Jon Nunan

Stephen Ladd

Jamie Brown

Paul Kadish

Brian Kadish

Melissa Kadish

Ron Kadish

Cindy Kadish

Your Feedback & Support Made This Book Possible.

If you enjoyed this book and would like to support the series, please follow the author on Facebook & Twitter, and visit:

www.MatthewKadish.com

www.Facebook.com/MatthewJKadish

www.Twitter.com/MatthewKadish